HILARY MANTEL

THE MIRROR & THE LIGHT

4th ESTATE • *London*

First published in Great Britain in 2020 by
Fourth Estate
An imprint of HarperCollins*Publishers*
1 London Bridge Street
London SE1 9GF

www.4thestate.co.uk

A catalogue record for this book is
available from the British Library

HB ISBN 978-0-00-748099-9
TPB ISBN 978-0-00-758083-5

Typeset in Stempel Garamond
Printed and bound in Great Britain by
CPI Group (UK) Ltd, Croydon

MIX
Paper from
responsible sources
FSC™ C007454

This book is produced from independently certified FSC™ paper
to ensure responsible forest management.

For more information visit: www.harpercollins.co.uk/green

THE MIRROR
& THE LIGHT

To Mary Robertson,
in honour of enduring friendship

CONTENTS

CAST OF CHARACTERS

The recently dead

Anne Boleyn, Queen of England.

Her supposed lovers:

George Boleyn, Viscount Rochford, her brother.

Henry Norris, chief of the king's privy chamber.

Francis Weston and William Brereton, gentlemen in the king's circle.

Mark Smeaton, musician.

The Cromwell household

Thomas Cromwell, later Lord Cromwell, Secretary to the king, Lord Privy Seal, and Vicegerent in Spirituals: that is, the king's deputy in the English church.

Gregory, his son, only surviving child of his marriage to Elizabeth Wyks.

Mercy Prior, his mother-in-law.

Rafe Sadler, his chief clerk, brought up within the family: later in the king's household.

Helen, Rafe's wife.

Richard Cromwell, his nephew, married to Frances Murfyn.

Thomas Avery, household accountant.

Thurston, chief cook.

Dick Purser, keeper of the guard dogs.

Jenneke, Cromwell's daughter. (Invented character)
Christophe, a servant. (Invented character)
Mathew, a servant, formerly of Wolf Hall. (Invented character)
Bastings, the bargemaster. (Invented character)

The king's family and household
Henry VIII.
Jane Seymour, his third wife.
Edward, her infant son, born 1537: heir to the throne.
Henry Fitzroy, Duke of Richmond: Henry's illegitimate son by
    Elizabeth Blount; married to Mary Howard, daughter of the
    Duke of Norfolk.
Mary, Henry's daughter by Katherine of Aragon: excluded from the
    succession after her parents' marriage is declared invalid.
Elizabeth, Henry's infant daughter by Anne Boleyn: excluded from
    the succession after his second marriage is declared invalid.
Anna, sister of Duke Wilhelm of Cleves: Henry's fourth wife.
Katherine Howard, maid of honour to Anna: Henry's fifth wife.
Margaret Douglas, Henry's niece: daughter of the king's sister
    Margaret by her second husband, Archibald Douglas, Earl of
    Angus; brought up at Henry's court.
William Butts, physician.
Walter Cromer, physician.
John Chambers, physician.
Hans Holbein, artist.
Sexton, known as 'Patch': a jester, formerly in Wolsey's household.

The Seymour family
Edward Seymour, eldest son, married to Anne (Nan) Stanhope.
Lady Margery Seymour, his mother.
Thomas Seymour, his younger brother.
Elizabeth, his sister, widow of Sir Anthony Oughtred, later married
    to Gregory Cromwell.

Politicians and clergy

Thomas Wriothesley, known as Call-Me-Risley, Clerk of the Signet: former protégé of Gardiner, later attached to Cromwell.

Stephen Gardiner, Bishop of Winchester, ambassador to France: formerly Cardinal Wolsey's Secretary, later the Secretary to the king, displaced by Cromwell.

Richard Riche, Speaker of the House of Commons, Chancellor of the Court of Augmentations.

Thomas Audley, Lord Chancellor.

Thomas Cranmer, Archbishop of Canterbury.

Robert Barnes, a Lutheran cleric.

Hugh Latimer, reformist Bishop of Worcester.

Richard Sampson, Bishop of Chichester, a canon lawyer and conservative.

Cuthbert Tunstall, Bishop of Durham, formerly Bishop of London.

John Stokesley, conservative Bishop of London, associate of the executed Thomas More.

Edmund Bonner, ambassador to France after Gardiner, Bishop of London after Stokesley.

John Lambert, reformist priest, convicted of heresy and burned 1538.

Courtiers and aristocrats

Thomas Howard, Duke of Norfolk.

Henry Howard, his son, Earl of Surrey.

Mary Howard, his daughter, married to Fitzroy, the king's illegitimate son.

Thomas Howard, his half-brother, known as Tom Truth.

Charles Brandon, Duke of Suffolk, old friend of Henry, widower of Henry's sister Mary.

Thomas Wyatt, friend of Cromwell: poet, diplomat, supposed lover of Anne Boleyn.

Henry Wyatt, his aged father, an early supporter of the Tudor regime.

Bess Darrell, Wyatt's mistress, formerly a lady-in-waiting to
    Katherine of Aragon.
William Fitzwilliam, later Lord Admiral and Earl of Southampton:
    initially an ally of Cromwell.
Nicholas Carew, prominent courtier and supporter of Mary, the
    king's daughter.
Eliza Carew, his wife, sister of Francis Bryan.
Francis Bryan, known as 'the Vicar of Hell', an inveterate gambler
    and undiplomatic diplomat: brother-in-law to Nicholas Carew.
Thomas Culpeper, gentleman attending the king.
Philip Hoby, gentleman attending the king.
Jane Rochford, lady-in-waiting, widow of the executed George
    Boleyn.
Thomas Boleyn, Earl of Wiltshire, father of Anne Boleyn and
    George Boleyn.
Mary Shelton, cousin of Anne Boleyn and former lady-in-waiting.
Mary Mounteagle, lady-in-waiting.
Nan Zouche, lady-in-waiting.
Katherine, Lady Latimer, born Katherine Parr.
Henry Bouchier, Earl of Essex.

The household of the king's children
John Shelton, governor of the household of the king's two
    daughters.
Anne Shelton, his wife, aunt of Anne Boleyn.
Lady Bryan, mother of Francis Bryan and Eliza Carew: brings up
    the king's daughters, Mary and Elizabeth, and later the child
    Edward.

At the convent in Shaftesbury
Elizabeth Zouche, the abbess.
Dorothea Wolsey, known as Dorothea Clancey, illegitimate
    daughter of the cardinal.

Henry's dynastic rivals

Henry Courtenay, Marquis of Exeter, descended from a daughter of Edward IV.

Gertrude, his wife.

Margaret Pole, Countess of Salisbury, niece of Edward IV.

Henry Lord Montague, her eldest son.

Reginald Pole, her son, abroad: proposed leader of a crusade to bring England back to papal control.

Geoffrey Pole, her son.

Constance, Geoffrey's wife.

Diplomats

Eustache Chapuys, London ambassador of Emperor Charles V: a French-speaker from Savoy.

Diego Hurtado de Mendoza, an envoy from the Emperor.

Jean de Dinteville, a French envoy.

Louis de Perreau, Sieur de Castillon, French ambassador.

Antoine de Castelnau, Bishop of Tarbes, French ambassador.

Charles de Marillac, French ambassador.

Hochsteden, envoy from Cleves.

Olisleger, envoy from Cleves.

Harst, envoy from Cleves.

In Calais

Lord Lisle, Lord Deputy, the governor, the king's uncle.

Honor, his wife.

Anne Bassett, one of Honor's daughters by her first marriage.

John Husee, member of the Calais garrison, the Lisles' man of business.

At the Tower of London

Sir William Kingston, councillor to the king, Constable of the Tower.

Edmund Walsingham, Lieutenant of the Tower, Kingston's deputy.

Martin, a gaoler. (Invented character)

Cromwell's friends

Humphrey Monmouth, London merchant: formerly imprisoned for sheltering William Tyndale, the translator of the Bible into English.

Robert Packington, merchant and member of Parliament.

Stephen Vaughan, Antwerp-based merchant.

Margaret Vernon, an abbess, formerly Gregory's tutor.

John Bale, a renegade monk and playwright.

The Tudors (simplified)

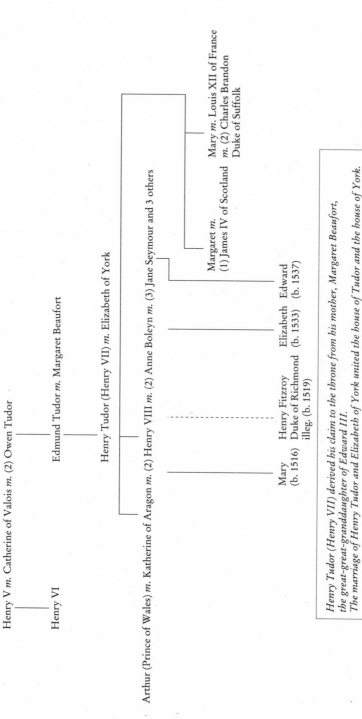

Henry V *m.* Catherine of Valois *m.* (2) Owen Tudor

Henry VI

Edmund Tudor *m.* Margaret Beaufort

Henry Tudor (Henry VII) *m.* Elizabeth of York

Arthur (Prince of Wales) *m.* Katherine of Aragon *m.* (2) Henry VIII *m.* (2) Anne Boleyn *m.* (3) Jane Seymour and 3 others

Margaret *m.*
(1) James IV of Scotland

Mary *m.* Louis XII of France
m. (2) Charles Brandon
Duke of Suffolk

Mary
(b. 1516)

Henry Fitzroy
Duke of Richmond
illeg. (b. 1519)

Elizabeth
(b. 1533)

Edward
(b. 1537)

Henry Tudor (Henry VII) derived his claim to the throne from his mother, Margaret Beaufort,
the great-great-granddaughter of Edward III.
The marriage of Henry Tudor and Elizabeth of York united the house of Tudor and the house of York.

Henry VIII's rivals from the House of York (simplified)

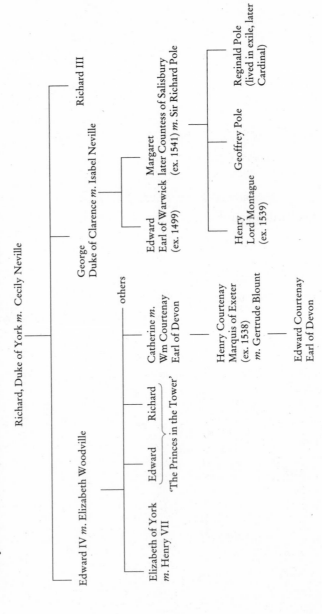

Richard, Duke of York *m.* Cecily Neville

Edward IV *m.* Elizabeth Woodville

Elizabeth of York
m. Henry VII

Edward   Richard
'The Princes in the Tower'

others

Catherine *m.*
Wm Courtenay
Earl of Devon

Henry Courtenay
Marquis of Exeter
(ex. 1538)
m. Gertrude Blount

Edward Courtenay
Earl of Devon

George
Duke of Clarence *m.* Isabel Neville

Richard III

Edward
Earl of Warwick
(ex. 1499)

Margaret
later Countess of Salisbury
(ex. 1541) *m.* Sir Richard Pole

Henry
Lord Montague
(ex. 1539)

Geoffrey Pole

Reginald Pole
(lived in exile, later
Cardinal)

Frères humains qui après nous vivez
N'ayez les cuers contre nous endurciz.

Brother men, you who live after us,
Do not harden your hearts against us.

FRANÇOIS VILLON

Look up and see the wind,
For we be ready to sail.

Noah's Flood, A MIRACLE PLAY

PART ONE

I
Wreckage (I)
London, May 1536

Once the queen's head is severed, he walks away. A sharp pang of appetite reminds him that it is time for a second breakfast, or perhaps an early dinner. The morning's circumstances are new and there are no rules to guide us. The witnesses, who have knelt for the passing of the soul, stand up and put on their hats. Under the hats, their faces are stunned.

But then he turns back, to say a word of thanks to the executioner. The man has performed his office with style; and though the king is paying him well, it is important to reward good service with encouragement, as well as a purse. Having once been a poor man, he knows this from experience.

The small body lies on the scaffold where it has fallen: belly down, hands outstretched, it swims in a pool of crimson, the blood seeping between the planks. The Frenchman – they had sent for the Calais executioner – had picked up the head, swaddled it in linen, then handed it to one of the veiled women who had attended Anne in her last moments. He saw how, as she received the bundle, the woman shuddered from the nape of her neck to her feet. She held it fast though, and a head is heavier than you expect. Having been on a battlefield, he knows this from experience too.

The women have done well. Anne would have been proud of them. They will not let any man touch her; palms out, they force back those who try to help them. They slide in the gore and stoop over the narrow carcass. He hears their indrawn breath as they lift what is left of her, holding her by her clothes; they are afraid the cloth will rip and their fingers touch her cooling flesh. Each of them sidesteps the cushion on which she knelt, now sodden with her blood. From the corner of his eye he sees a presence flit away, a fugitive lean man in a leather jerkin. It is Francis Bryan, a nimble courtier, gone to tell Henry he is a free man. Trust Francis, he thinks: he is a cousin of the dead queen, but he has remembered he is also a cousin of the queen to come.

The officers of the Tower have found, in lieu of a coffin, an arrow chest. The narrow body fits it. The woman who holds the head genuflects with her soaking parcel. As there is no other space, she fits it by the corpse's feet. She stands up, crossing herself. The hands of the bystanders move in imitation, and his own hand moves; but then he checks himself, and draws it into a loose fist.

The women take their last look. Then they step back, their hands held away from them so as not to soil their garments. One of Constable Kingston's men proffers linen towels – too late to be of use. These people are incredible, he says to the Frenchman. No coffin, when they had days to prepare? They knew she was going to die. They were not in any doubt.

'But perhaps they were, Maître Cremuel.' (No Frenchman can ever pronounce his name.) 'Perhaps they were, for I believe the lady herself thought the king would send a messenger to stop it. Even as she mounted the steps she was looking over her shoulder, did you see?'

'He was not thinking of her. His mind is entirely on his new bride.'

'*Alors*, perhaps better luck this time,' the Frenchman says. 'You must hope so. If I have to come back, I shall increase my fee.'

The man turns away and begins cleaning his sword. He does it lovingly, as if the weapon were his friend. 'Toledo steel.' He proffers it for admiration. 'We still have to go to the Spaniards to get a blade like this.'

He, Cromwell, touches a finger to the metal. You would not guess it to look at him now, but his father was a blacksmith; he has affinity with iron, steel, with everything that is mined from the earth or

4

forged, everything that is made molten, or wrought, or given a cutting edge. The executioner's blade is incised with Christ's crown of thorns, and with the words of a prayer.

Now the spectators are moving away, courtiers and aldermen and city officials, knots of men in silk and gold chains, in the livery of the Tudors and in the insignia of the London guilds. Scores of witnesses, none of them sure of what they have seen; they understand that the queen is dead, but it was too quick to comprehend. 'She didn't suffer, Cromwell,' Charles Brandon says.

'My lord Suffolk, you may be satisfied she did.'

Brandon disgusts him. When the other witnesses knelt, the duke stayed rigid on his feet; he so hated the queen that he would not do her that much courtesy. He remembers her faltering progress to the scaffold: her glance, as the Frenchman says, was directed over her shoulder. Even when she said her last words, asking the people to pray for the king, she was looking over the head of the crowd. Still, she did not let hope weaken her. Few women are so resolute at the last, and not many men. He had seen her start to tremble, but only after her final prayer. There was no block, the man from Calais did not use one. She had been required to kneel upright, with no support. One of her women bound a cloth across her eyes. She did not see the sword, not even its shadow, and the blade went through her neck with a sigh, easier than scissors through silk. We all – well, most of us, not Brandon – regret that it had to come to this.

Now the elm chest is carried towards the chapel, where the flags have been lifted so she can go in by the corpse of her brother, George Boleyn. 'They shared a bed when they were alive,' Brandon says, 'so it's fitting they share a tomb. Let's see how they like each other now.'

'Come, Master Secretary,' says the Constable of the Tower. 'I have arranged a collation, if you will do me the honour. We were all up early today.'

'You can eat, sir?' His son Gregory has never seen anyone die.

'We must work to eat and eat to work,' Kingston says. 'What use to the king is a servant who is distracted, merely for want of a piece of bread?'

'Distracted,' Gregory repeats. Recently his son was sent off to learn the art of public speaking, and the result is that, though he still lacks the command that makes for rhetorical sweep, he has become more interested in words if you take them one by one. Sometimes he seems to be holding them up for scrutiny. Sometimes he seems to be poking them with a stick. Sometimes, and the comparison is unavoidable, he seems to approach them with the tail-wagging interest a dog takes in another dog's turds. He asks the constable, 'Sir William, has a queen of England ever been executed before?'

'Not to my knowledge,' the constable says. 'Or at least, young man, not on my watch.'

'I see,' he says: he, Cromwell. 'So the errors of the last few days are just because you lack practice? You can't do a thing just once and get it right?'

Kingston laughs heartily. Presumably because he thinks he's making a joke. 'Here, my lord Suffolk,' he says to Charles Brandon. 'Cromwell says I need more practice in lopping heads.'

I didn't say that, he thinks. 'The arrow chest was a lucky find.'

'I'd have put her on a dunghill,' Brandon says. 'And the brother underneath her. And I'd have made their father witness it. I don't know what you are about, Cromwell. Why did you leave him alive to work mischief?'

He turns on him, angry; often, anger is what he fakes. 'My lord Suffolk, you have often offended the king yourself, and begged his pardon on your knees. And being what you are, I have no doubt you will offend again. What then? Do you want a king to whom the notion of mercy is foreign? If you love the king, and you say you do, pay some heed to his soul. One day he will stand before God and answer for every subject. If I say Thomas Boleyn is no danger to the realm, he is no danger. If I say he will live quiet, that is what he will do.'

The courtiers tramping across the green eye them: Suffolk with his big beard, his flashing eye, his big chest, and Master Secretary subfusc, low-slung, square. Warily, they separate and flow around the quarrel, reuniting in chattering parties at the other side.

'By God,' Brandon says. 'You read me a lesson? I? A peer of the realm? And you, from the place where you come from?'

'I stand just where the king has put me. I will read you any lesson you should learn.'

He thinks, Cromwell, what are you doing? Usually he is the soul of courtesy. But if you cannot speak truth at a beheading, when can you speak it?

He glances sideways at his son. We are three years older, less a month, than at Anne's coronation. Some of us are wiser; some of us are taller. Gregory had said he could not do it, when told he should witness her death: 'I cannot. A woman, I cannot.' But his boy has kept his face arranged and his tongue governed. Each time you are in public, he has told Gregory, know that people are observing you, to see if you are fit to follow me in the king's service.

They step aside to bow to the Duke of Richmond: Henry Fitzroy, the king's bastard son. He is a handsome boy with his father's fine flushed skin and red-blond hair: a tender plant, willowy, a boy who has not yet grown into his great height. He sways above them both. 'Master Secretary? England is a better place this morning.'

Gregory says, 'My lord, you also did not kneel. How is that?'

Richmond blushes. He knows he is in the wrong, and shows it as his father always does; but like his father, he will defend himself with a stout self-righteousness. 'I would not be a hypocrite, Gregory. My lord father has declared to me how Boleyn would have poisoned me. He says she boasted she would do it. Well, now her monstrous adulteries are all found out, and she is properly punished.'

'You are not ill, my lord?' He is thinking, too much wine last night: toasting his future, no doubt.

'I am only tired. I will go and sleep. Put this spectacle behind me.'

Gregory's eyes follow Richmond. 'Do you think he can ever be king?'

'If he is, he'll remember you,' he says cheerfully.

'Oh, he knows me already,' Gregory says. 'Did I do wrong?'

'It is not wrong to speak your mind. On selected occasions. They make it painful for you. But you must do it.'

'I don't think I shall ever be a councillor,' Gregory says. 'I don't think I could ever learn it – when to speak and when to keep silence, when I should look and when I should not. You told me, the moment you see the blade in the air, then she is dying – at that moment, you said, bow your head and close your eyes. But I saw you – you were looking.'

'Of course I was.' He takes his son's arm. 'It would be like the late queen to pin her head back on, pick up the sword and chase me to Whitehall.' She may be dead, he thinks, but she can still ruin me.

Breakfast. Fine white loaves, wine of head-spinning strength. The Duke of Norfolk, the dead woman's uncle, gives him a nod. 'Most corpses wouldn't fit in an arrow chest, eh? You'd have to hack the arms off. Do you think Kingston's getting past it?'

Gregory is surprised. 'Sir William is no older than yourself, my lord.'

A bark of laughter: 'You think men of sixty should be put out to grass?'

'He thinks they should be boiled for glue.' He puts an arm around his son's shoulders. 'He'll soon be boiling his father, won't you?'

'But you are far younger than my lord Norfolk.' Gregory turns to the duke, the better to inform him. 'My father is in sound health, if you except his special fever, which he got when he was in Italy. It is true he works long hours, but he believes long hours never killed anybody, he often says so. His doctor says you couldn't fell him with a cannonball.'

By now the witnesses have seen the late queen nailed down and are packing in at the open doors. The city officers jostle, keen for a word with him. One question in their mouths: Master Secretary, when shall we see the new queen? When will Jane do us the honour? Will she ride through the streets, or sail in the royal barge? What arms and emblems will she take as queen, and what motto? When may we notify the painters and artificers and set them to work? Will there be a coronation soon? What present can we make her, that will find favour in her eyes?

'A bag of money is always acceptable,' he says. 'I do not think we will see her in public till she and the king are married, but that will not be long. She is pious in the old style and any banners or painted cloths depicting the angels and saints, and the Holy Virgin, will be well-accepted by her.'

'So,' says the Lord Mayor, 'we can look out what we have had in store since Queen Katherine's time?'

'That would be prudent, Sir John, and save the city's funds.'

'We have the life of St Veronica in panels,' an elderly guildsman says. 'On the first, she stands weeping by the route to Calvary, as Christ bears his cross. On the second –'

'Of course,' he murmurs.

'– on the second, the saint wipes the face of our Saviour. On the third, she holds up the bloody cloth, and there we may see the image of Christ, printed clearly in his precious blood.'

'My wife observed,' says Constable Kingston, 'that this morning the lady left aside her usual head-dress, and chose the style the late Katherine favoured. She wonders what she meant by it.'

Perhaps it was a courtesy, he thinks, from a dying queen to a dead one. They will be meeting this morning in another country, where no doubt they will have much to tell.

'Would that my niece had imitated Katherine in other particulars,' Norfolk says. 'Had she been obedient, chaste and meek, her head might still be on her shoulders.'

Gregory is so amazed that he takes a step back, into the Lord Mayor. 'But my lord, Katherine was not obedient! Did she not defy the king's will year after year, when he told her to go away and be divorced? Did you yourself not go down to the country to enforce her, and she slammed into her chamber and turned the key, so you were obliged to spend the twelve days of Christmas shouting through a door?'

'You'll find that was my lord Suffolk,' the duke says shortly. 'Another useless dotard, eh, Gregory? That's Charles Brandon over there – the mighty fellow with the big beard. I am the stringy fellow with the bad temper. See the difference?'

'Ah,' Gregory says, 'I remember now. My father enjoyed the tale so much, we performed it as a play at Twelfth Night. My cousin Richard played my lord Suffolk, wearing a woolly beard to his waist. And Mr Rafe Sadler put on a skirt and played the queen, insulting the duke in the Spanish tongue. And my father took the part of the door.'

'I wish I had seen it.' Norfolk rubs the tip of his nose. 'No, I tell you, Gregory, I honestly do.' He and Charles Brandon are old rivals, and enjoy each other's embarrassments. 'I wonder what you'll play this Christmas?'

Gregory opens his mouth and closes it again. The future is a curious blank. He, Cromwell, intervenes, before his son attempts to fill it. 'Gentlemen, I can tell you what the new queen will take as her motto. It is *Bound to Obey and Serve.*'

There is a murmur of approbation that runs right around the room. Brandon's big laugh booms out: 'Better safe than sorry, eh?'

'So say we all.' Norfolk tips back his canary wine. 'Whoever crosses the king in the years ahead, gentlemen, it will not be Thomas Howard here.' He stabs a finger into his own breastbone, as if otherwise they might not know who he is. Then he slaps Master Secretary on the shoulder, with every appearance of comradeship. 'So what now, Cromwell?'

Don't be deceived. Uncle Norfolk is not our comrade or our ally or our friend. He is slapping us to appraise how solid we are. He is eyeing the Cromwell bull-neck. He is wondering what sort of blade you'd need, to slice through that.

It is ten when they break away from the company. Outside, sunlight is dappling the grass. He walks into shadow, his nephew Richard Cromwell by his side. 'Better see Wyatt.'

'You are well, sir?'

'Never better,' he says flatly.

It was Richard himself who, a few days back, had walked Thomas Wyatt to the Tower, without display of force, without armed men: taking him into custody as easily as if they were taking a riverside stroll. He had requested the prisoner be shown every courtesy, and be kept in a pleasant gatehouse chamber: to which the gaoler Martin now leads the way.

'How is this prisoner?' he asks.

As if this prisoner were just anyone, instead of what Wyatt is – as dear to him as any person now living.

Martin says, 'It seems to me, sir, he is in much disquiet of mind about those five gentlemen who lost their heads the other day.'

The gaoler makes it sound incidental, like losing a hat. 'I dare say Master Wyatt wonders why he was not among them. And so he paces, sir. Then he sits, a paper before him. He looks as if he will write, but not a word goes down. He doesn't sleep. Up in the dead hour, calling for lights. Pulls up his stool to the table, sharpens his pen; six o'clock, broad day, you fetch in his bread and ale and there's his paper blank and the candle still burning. Wasteful, that.'

'Let him have lights. I will pay for what he needs.'

'Though I say this – he is a very gentleman. Not proud like those we had over the other side. Henry Norris – "Gentle Norris", they called him, but he spoke to us as if we were dogs. That's how you can tell a true gentleman – when he is in peril of his life, he still speaks you fair.'

'I'll remember, Martin,' he says gravely. 'How's my god-daughter?'

'Rising two – can you believe it?'

The week Martin's daughter was born he had been at the Tower to visit Thomas More. It was early days in their contest; he still hoped More would concede a point to the king and save his life. 'You'll stand godfather?' Martin had asked him. He chose the name Grace: after his youngest daughter, dead some years now.

Martin says, 'We cannot watch a prisoner every minute. I am afraid Mr Wyatt might destroy himself.'

Richard laughs merrily. 'What, Martin, have you never had a poet in your prison? One who sighs heavy and sleeps short hours, and when he prays he prays in verse? A poet may be melancholy but I tell you, he will look after himself as well as the next man. He must have food and drink to tempt his appetite, and if he has an ache or a twinge you will hear about it.'

'He writes a sonnet if he stubs a toe,' he says.

'Poets prosper,' Richard says. 'It is their friends who sustain the hurt.'

Martin announces them with a discreet tap, as if they were in a lord's private suite. 'Visitors, Mr Wyatt?'

The room is full of dancing light, and the young man sits at a table in full sun. 'Move, Wyatt,' Richard says. 'The rays illuminate your scalp.'

He forgets how ruthless the young are. When the king says, 'Am I going bald, Crumb?' he says, 'The shape of your Majesty's head would please any artist.'

Wyatt runs his palm across his fine fair hair. 'It's going fast, Rich. By the time I am forty no woman will look at me except to try to crack my skull with an egg spoon.'

Wyatt could as easily laugh as cry this morning, and it would mean nothing either way. Still alive when five other men are dead, still alive and astonished to be so, he is poised on the edge of devastating pain – like a man who is teetering on a spike, a toehold his only support. It is a sort of interrogation method he has heard of, though never had need to perform. You rope the prisoner to a beam, his arms crossed behind his back: his body hangs in space, supported by this one exquisite inch. If he moves, or you jerk his foot away, his whole weight drops onto his arms and his shoulders are dislocated. That part of the procedure should be unnecessary. You don't want to disable him; you just want to keep him there, balanced, till he has satisfied you with answers.

'We have had our breakfast, anyway,' he says. 'Constable Kingston is such a blunderer that we expected mouldy bread.'

'It is a novelty for him,' Wyatt says. 'A queen of England to behead, and five of her lovers. A man does not do it every week.'

He is swaying, he is swaying, on the spike: soon he will slip and cry out. 'So it's done, I suppose? Or you would not be here with me.'

Richard crosses the room. He stands over Wyatt and looks down at the nape of his bent neck; he rubs his shoulder, friendly and firm like a man with his favourite dog. Wyatt is unmoving, his face in his hands. Richard glances up: are you going to tell it, sir?

He inclines his head to his nephew: you tell it.

'She made a brave end,' Richard says. 'She spoke short and to the point, asking forgiveness, praising the king's mercy, and offering no extenuation.'

Wyatt looks up. His face is dazed. 'She accused no one?'

'It was not for her to accuse,' Richard says gently.

'But you know Anne's spirit. And she was kept here long enough, she had time to think and plan. She must have thought,' his blue eyes flick sideways, 'here I lie a prisoner, and where is the evidence against me? She must have prayed for the five men who went out to die, and she must have wondered, why is Wyatt not one of them?'

'Surely,' he says, 'she would not have wanted to see your head in the street? I know all love was lost between you, and I know she was a creature of supreme malice, but surely she would not have wished to add to the number of men she has ruined?'

'I did not assume that,' Wyatt says. 'She might have thought it was justice.'

He wants Richard to lean forward, and place his hand firmly over Wyatt's mouth.

'Tom Wyatt,' he says, 'let us have an end of this. You may think confession would ease your mind, and if that is what you think, send for a priest, say what you must, get your absolution and pay him for silence. But do not for God's sake confess to me.' He adds, softly, 'You have come so far. You have done the difficult thing. You spoke when you should speak. Now speak no more.'

'You must not indulge yourself,' Richard says. 'It would be at our expense. My uncle has walked a knife-edge for you. The king's suspicion of you was such that no one but my uncle could have dispelled it, for the king would not have listened, but killed you with the rest. Besides ...' He looks up. 'Sir, may I tell him? The court did not need the evidence you gave us. Your name did not arise. The lady's brother

13

convicted himself out of his own mouth, sniggering at the king in the very face of the court, and saying that despite the valour he claims, Henry lacks all skill and *vertu* to do the deed with a woman.'

'Yes,' he says, to Wyatt's incredulous face, 'this is the fool George Boleyn was, and I had to deal with him for years.'

'And George's wife,' Richard says, 'made a written deposition against him, testifying she had seen him kiss his sister with his tongue in her mouth. Describing the hours they were alone together, behind a closed door.'

Wyatt has edged his stool back from the table. He raises his face to the sun and the light washes away all expression.

'And Anne's women,' Richard says, 'gave statements against her. All the comings and goings in the dark. So it was enough, without your help. They have witnessed her tricks these two years and more.'

Oh, Jesus, he thinks, let's stop this now. He takes a wad of folded papers out of his jacket and drops them on the table. 'Here is your testimony. Do you want to destroy it yourself, or shall I do it?'

'I will,' Wyatt says.

He thinks, Wyatt doesn't trust me: still, even now. God knows, I have not played him false. This last week, hour by hour, he has traded for Wyatt's life. What he has offered Henry is Wyatt's knowledge of the accused queen. Whether the knowledge was carnal – he has never asked Wyatt that, and never will. He assured the king it was not – though not in so many words. If he has misled Henry, better not to know. He says to Wyatt, 'I told your father I'd look after you. I have.'

'Indebted,' Wyatt says.

Outside, the red kites are skimming over the Tower walls. The king did not choose to display the heads of Anne's lovers on London Bridge; in case he decides to ride through with his new wife, he wants to keep his capital tidy. The kites, therefore, are cheated of their prey; no doubt, he says to Richard, that's why they're yearning for Tom Wyatt.

14

Richard says, 'You see how it is. A very proper man, Wyatt. Even his gaolers are in love with him. His pisspot admires him, for deigning to use it.'

'Martin was angling to know what will happen to him.'

'Aye,' Richard says, 'before he becomes too attached. And what will?'

'He is safe where he is for now.'

'Are the arrests finished? Was he the last?'

'Yes, I think so.'

'Is it over, then?'

'Over? Oh, no.'

Thomas Cromwell is now fifty years old. The same small quick eyes, the same thickset imperturbable body; the same schedules. He is at home wherever he wakes: the Rolls House on Chancery Lane, or his city house at Austin Friars, or at Whitehall with the king, or in some other place where Henry happens to be. He rises at five, says his prayers, attends to his ablutions and breaks his fast. By six o'clock he is receiving petitioners, his nephew Richard Cromwell at his elbow. Master Secretary's barge takes him up and down to Greenwich, to Hampton Court, to the mint and armouries at the Tower of London. Though he is a commoner still, most would agree that he is the second man in England. He is the king's deputy in the affairs of the church. He takes licence to enquire into any department of government or the royal household. He carries in his head the statutes of England, the psalms and the words of the Prophets, the columns of the king's account books and the lineage, acreage and income of every person of substance in England. He is famous for his memory, and the king likes to test it, by asking him for details of obscure disputes from twenty years back. He sometimes carries a sprig of dried rosemary or rue, and crumbles it in his palm as if inhaling the scent would help him. But everyone knows it is only a performance. The only things he cannot remember are the things he never knew.

His chief duty (it seems just now) is to get the king new wives and dispose of the old. His days are long and arduous, packed with laws to be drafted and ambassadors to beguile. He goes on working by candlelight through summer dusks, through winter sunsets when it is dark by half past three. Even his nights are not his to waste. Often he sleeps in a chamber near the king and Henry wakes him in the small hours and asks him questions about treasury receipts, or tells him his dreams and asks what they mean.

Sometimes he thinks he would like to marry again, as it is seven years since he lost Elizabeth and his daughters. But no woman would tolerate this kind of life.

When he gets home, young Rafe Sadler is waiting for him. He pulls off his cap at the sight of his master. 'Sir?'

'Done,' he says.

Rafe waits, eyes on his face.

'Nothing to tell. A prayerful end. The king?'

'We hardly saw him. Went between bedchamber and oratory and spoke with his chaplain.' Rafe is in the king's privy chamber now, his liaison man. 'I thought I should come in case you have any message for him.'

Verbal message, he means. Something better not committed to ink. He thinks about it. What do you say to a man who has just killed his wife? 'No message. Get home to your wife.'

'Helen will be glad to know the lady is beyond her misfortunes now.'

He is surprised. 'She does not pity her, does she?'

Rafe looks uneasy. 'She thinks that Anne was a protector of the gospel, and that cause is, as you know, near my wife's heart.'

'Oh, well, yes,' he says. 'But I can protect it better.'

'And besides, I think, with women, when something happens to one of them, all of them feel it. They are more pitiful than us, and it would be a harsh world if they were not.'

'Anne was not pitiful,' he says. 'Have you not told Helen how she threatened me with beheading? And she was planning, as we now know, to cut short the life of the king himself.'

'Yes, sir,' Rafe says, as if he is humouring him. 'That was stated in court, was it not? But Helen will ask – forgive me, from a woman it is a natural question – what will happen to Anne Boleyn's little daughter? Will the king disown her? He can't be sure he is her father, but he can't be sure he is not.'

'It hardly matters,' he says. 'Even if Eliza is Henry's child, she is still a bastard. As we now learn, his marriage to Anne was never valid.'

Rafe rubs the crown of his head so that his red hair stands up in a tuft. 'So as his union with Katherine was not valid either, he has never been married in his life. Twice a bridegroom yet never a husband – has it ever happened to a king before? Even in the Old Testament? Please God Mistress Seymour will go to work and give him a son. We cannot seem to keep an heir. The king's daughter by Katherine, she is a bastard. His daughter by Anne, she is a bastard. Which leaves his son Richmond, who of course has always been a bastard.' He squashes on his hat. 'I'm going.'

He skitters out, leaving the door open. From the stairs he calls, 'I'll see you tomorrow, sir.'

He gets up, shuts the door; but he lingers, his hand on the wood. Rafe grew up in his house, and he misses his constant presence; these days he has his own house, his own young family in it, new duties at court. It is his pleasure, to make Rafe's career. He is as dear to him as a son could be, dutiful, dogged, attentive and – the vital point – liked and trusted by the king.

He resumes his desk. It is only May, he thinks, and already two queens of England are dead. Before him is a letter from Eustache Chapuys, the Imperial ambassador; though it is not a letter Eustache intended for his desk, and its news must be already out of date. The ambassador is using a new cipher, but it should be possible to see what he is saying. He must be rejoicing, telling the Emperor Charles that the king's concubine is living her last hours.

He works at the letter till he can pick out the proper names, including his own, then turns to other business. Leave it for Mr Wriothesley, the prince of decipherers.

* * *

When bells are ringing for evening prayer across the city, he hears Mr Wriothesley down below, laughing with Gregory. 'Come up, Call Me,' he shouts; and the young man takes the stairs two at a time and strides in, a letter in his hand. 'From France, sir, from Bishop Gardiner.' To be helpful, he has opened it already.

Call-Me-Risley? It is a joke that dates from the time when Tom Wyatt had a full head of hair; from when Katherine was queen, and Thomas Wolsey ruled England, and he, Thomas Cromwell, used to sleep at nights. Call-Me skipped in one day to Austin Friars – a fine-drawn young man, lively and nervous as a hare. We took a look at his slashed doublet, feathered cap, gilt dagger at his waist; how we laughed. He was handsome, able, argumentative and prepared to be admired. At Cambridge Stephen Gardiner had been his tutor, and Stephen has much to teach; but the bishop has no patience, and something in Call-Me craves it. He wants to be listened to, he wants to talk; like a hare, he seems alert to what's happening behind him, half-knowing, half-guessing, always on edge.

'Gardiner says the French court is buzzing, sir. The gossip is that the late queen had a hundred lovers. King François is amused.'

'I'm sure.'

'So Gardiner asks – as England's ambassador, what am I to tell them?'

'You can write to him. Tell him what he needs to know.' He considers. 'Or perhaps a little less.'

The French imagination will soon supply any detail Stephen lacks: what the late queen did, and with whom, and how many times and in what positions. He says, 'It is not good for a celibate to be excited by such matter. It is up to us, Mr Wriothesley, to save the bishop from sin.'

Wriothesley meets his eye and laughs. Now he is out of the realm, Gardiner depends on Call-Me for information. The master must await the pleasure of his pupil. Wriothesley has a position, Clerk of the Signet. He has an income, and a pretty wife, and basks in the king's good graces; at this moment, he has Master Secretary's attention. 'Gregory seems happy,' he says.

18

'Gregory is glad to have got through the day. He has never witnessed such an event. Not that any of us have, of course.'

'Our poor monarch,' Call Me says. 'His good nature has been much abused. Two such women no man ever suffered, as the Princess of Aragon and Anne Boleyn. Such bitter tongues. Such cankered hearts.' He sits down, but on the edge of his stool. 'The court is anxious, sir. People wonder if it is over. They wonder what Wyatt has said to you, that is not placed on record.'

'They may well wonder.'

'They ask if there will be more arrests.'

'It is a question.'

Wriothesley smiles. 'You are a master at this.'

'Oh, I don't know.' He feels tired. Seven years for the king to get Anne. Three years to reign. Three weeks to bring her to trial. Three heartbeats to finish it. But still, they are his heartbeats as well as hers. The effort of them must be added to all the rest.

'Sir,' Call-Me leans forward. 'You should move against the Duke of Norfolk. Work his discredit with the king. Do it now, while you have him at a disadvantage. The chance may not come again.'

'I thought the duke was very pleasant to me this morning. Considering we were killing his niece.'

'Thomas Howard will speak as pleasant to his foe as to his friend.'

'True.' The Duchess of Norfolk, from whom the duke is estranged, has often used the same words: or worse.

'You would think,' Call-Me says, 'that with both Anne and his nephew George disgraced, he would creep away to his own country and be ashamed.'

'Shame and Uncle Norfolk are not acquainted.'

'Now I hear he is pressing for Richmond to be made heir. He reasons, if my son-in-law becomes king, and my daughter sits on the throne beside him, all England will be under my Howard thumb. He says, "Since all Henry's three children are now bastards, we may as well prefer the male – at least Richmond can sit a horse and draw a sword, which is better than the Lady Mary, who is dwarfish and sick, and Eliza, who is still of an age to soil herself in public."'

He says, 'No doubt Richmond would be a fine king. But I don't like the thought of this Howard thumb.'

Mr Wriothesley's eyes rest on him. 'The Lady Mary's friends are ready to bring her back to court. When Parliament is called they expect her to be named heir. They are waiting for you to keep your promise. They expect you to turn the king her way.'

'Do they?' he says. 'You astonish me. If I made any promise, it was not that.'

Call-Me looks rattled. 'Sir, the old families united with you, they helped you bring the Boleyns down. They did not do it for nothing. They did not do it so Richmond could be king and Norfolk rule all.'

'So I must choose between them?' he says. 'It seems from what you say that they will fight each other, and one party will be left standing, either Mary's friends or Norfolk. And whoever has the victory, they will come after me, don't you think?'

The door opens. Call-Me starts. It is Richard Cromwell. 'Who were you expecting, Call-Me? The Bishop of Winchester?'

Imagine Gardiner, rising through the floor with a sulphur whiff; lashing out with his cloven hooves, sending the ink flying. Imagine drool running from his chin, as he upturns the strongboxes, and snouts through the contents with a rolling, fiery eye. 'Letter from Nicholas Carew,' Richard says.

'I told you,' Call-Me says. 'Mary's people. Already.'

'And by the way,' Richard says, 'the cat's out again.'

He hurries to the window, letter in hand. 'Where is she?'

Call-Me beside him: 'What am I looking for?'

He breaks the seal. 'There! She's running up the tree.'

He glances down at the letter. Sir Nicholas seeks a meeting.

'Is that a cat?' Wriothesley is amazed. 'That striped beast?'

'She has come all the way from Damascus in a box. I bought her from an Italian merchant for a price you would not believe. She is supposed to stay indoors, or she will breed with the London cats. I must look out for a striped husband for her.' He opens the window. 'Christophe! She's up the tree!'

What Carew proposes is a gathering of the dynasts: the Courtenay family, with the Marquis of Exeter leading them, and the Pole family, where Lord Montague will represent his kin. These are the families nearest the throne, descendants of old King Edward and his brothers. They claim to speak for the king's daughter Mary, to represent her interests. If they cannot rule England themselves, as Plantagenets once did, they mean to rule through the king's daughter. It is her bloodline they admire, the inheritance from her Spanish mother Katherine. For the sad little girl herself, they care much less; and when I see Mary, he thinks, I will tell her so. Her safety does not lie that way, with men who live on fantasies of the past.

Carew, the Courtenays, the Poles, they are papists every one. Carew was the king's old comrade-in-arms, and Queen Katherine's friend too, in the days when those positions were compatible. He sees himself as the mirror of chivalry, and a favourite of fortune. To Carew, to the Poles, to the Courtenays and their supporters, the Boleyns were a crass blunder, an error now cancelled by the headsman. No doubt they assume Thomas Cromwell can be cancelled too, reduced to the clerk he used to be: a useful man for getting money in, but dispensable, a slave that you trample as you stride up the stairway to glory.

'Call-Me is right,' he says to Richard. 'Sir Nicholas is taking a lofty tone with me.' He holds the letter up. 'These people, they expect me to come to their whistle.'

Wriothesley says, 'They expect your service. Or they will break you.'

Below the window, all the young persons at Austin Friars are milling, cooks and clerks and boys of every sort. He says, 'I think my son has taken leave of his senses. Gregory,' he calls down, 'you cannot catch a cat in a net. She has seen you now – back away.'

'Look at Christophe shaking the tree,' Richard says. 'Stupid little fucker.'

'Take heed of this, sir,' Call-Me begs. 'Because this last week ...'

'It is natural she keeps escaping,' he says to Richard. 'She is tired of her celibate life. She wants to find a prince. Yes, Call-Me? This last week, what?'

'People have been talking of the cardinal. They say, look at what Cromwell has wreaked, in two years, on Wolsey's enemies. Thomas More is dead. Anne the queen is dead. They look at those who slighted him, in his lifetime – Brereton, Norris – though Norris was not the worst ...'

Norris, he thinks, was good to my lord – to his face. A taker and a user, was Gentle Norris: a hypocrite. He says, 'If I wanted revenge on Wolsey's enemies, I would have to strike down half the nation.'

'I only report what people are saying.'

'Young Dick Purser's here,' Richard says. He leans out of the window. 'Get hold of her, boy, before we lose her in the dark.'

'They ask,' Wriothesley says, 'who was the greatest of the cardinal's enemies? They answer, the king. So, they ask – when chance serves, what revenge will Thomas Cromwell seek on his sovereign, his prince?'

Below in the darkening garden, the cat-hunters raise their arms as if imploring the moon. High in the tree, the cat is a soft shape visible only to the educated eye: limbs dangling, she is perfectly at one with the branch on which she lies. He thinks of Marlinspike, the cardinal's cat. He had brought him to Austin Friars when he was still small enough to carry in a pocket. But when Marlinspike came of age, he ran away to make his fortune.

I have risen above this, he thinks: this day, this waning light, these snares. I am the Damascene cat. I have travelled so far to get here, and nothing they do disturbs me now, nor disquiets me, high on my branch.

And yet Wriothesley's question seeps into him, and leaves in his mind a chilly trickle of dismay, like water creeping into a cellar. He is shocked: first, that the question can be asked. Second, because of who asks it. Third, that he does not know the answer.

Richard turns back into the room: 'Sir, what's Christophe saying below?'

He translates: the boy's argot is not easy. 'Christophe swears that in France they always catch cats in a net, any child can do it, he will be pleased to demonstrate if we give him full attention.' He says to Wriothesley, 'This question of yours –'

'Do not take it ill –'

'– does it come from Gardiner?'

'Because,' Richard says, 'who but the bloody buggering Bishop of Winchester would come up with a question like that?'

Call-Me says, 'If I report Winchester's words, that is all I do. I do not speak for him, or on his behalf.'

'Good,' Richard says, 'because otherwise, I'd have to pull your head off, and cast it up the tree with the cat.'

'Richard, believe me,' Wriothesley says, 'if I were the bishop's partisan, I would be with him on his embassy, not here with you.' Tears well into his eyes. 'I am trying to make some sense of what Master Secretary intends. But all you care about is the cat, and trying to frighten me. You are making me pick my way through thorns.'

'I see the wounds,' he says gently. 'When you write to Stephen Gardiner, tell him I will see what I can get him by way of spoils. George Boleyn had a grant of two hundred pounds a year out of the revenues of Winchester. For a start, he can have that back.'

He thinks, that will not mollify the bishop. It's just a token of goodwill for a disappointed man. Stephen hoped that when Anne Boleyn fell she would take me with her.

'You talk of the cardinal's enemies,' Richard says. 'Now I would put Bishop Gardiner among them. Yet he is not harmed, is he?'

'He thinks he is harmed,' Wriothesley says. 'After all, he was the cardinal's confidant, till Master Cromwell shouldered him aside. He was Secretary to the king, till Master Cromwell whipped his office from under his feet. The king sent him out of the realm, and he knows Master Cromwell contrived it.'

True. All true. Gardiner knows how to do damage, even from France. He knows how to scratch the skin and poison the body poli-tic. He says, 'Any notion that I hold a grudge against my sovereign – it is some fantasy out of the bishop's sick brain. What have I, but what my king gives me? Who am I, but who he has made me? All my trust is in him.'

Wriothesley says, 'But shall I carry a message to Nicholas Carew? Will you meet him? I think you ought.'

'Placate him?' Richard says. 'No.' He draws the window shut. 'My money is on Purser to catch her.'

'Mine is on the cat.' He imagines the world below her: through the prism of her great eye, the limbs of agitated men unfurl like ribbons, yearning through the darkness. Perhaps she thinks they are praying to her. Perhaps she thinks she has climbed up to the stars. Perhaps the darkness falls away from her in flecks and sparks of light, the roofs and gables like shadows in water; and when she studies the net there is no net, only the spaces between.

'I think we should have a drink,' he tells Wriothesley. 'We will have lights. And a fire, by and by. Send Christophe in, when he comes from the garden. He will show us how the French start a blaze. Perhaps we will burn Carew's letter, Mr Wriothesley, what do you think?'

'What do I think?' It is almost a snarl worthy of Gardiner himself. 'I think, Norfolk is against you, the bishop is against you, and now you are going to take on the old families as well. God help you, sir. You are my master. You have my service, and you have my prayers. But by the holy bones! Do you think these people brought the Boleyns down so you could be cock of the walk?'

'Yes,' Richard says. 'That's exactly what we think. It may not have been their intention. But we aim to make that the result.'

How steady Richard's arm, stretching to hand him the glass. How steady his own, accepting it. 'Lord Lisle sends this wine from Calais,' he says.

'Confusion to our enemies,' Richard says. 'Good luck to our friends.'

Wriothesley says, 'I hope you can tell them apart.'

'Call-Me, warm your poor shaking heart.' He casts a glance at the window, sees a faint fogged outline of himself. 'You can write to Gardiner and tell him he has money coming. Then we have ciphers to break.'

Someone has brought a torch into the garden below. A dusky flicker fills the panes. His shadow in the window raises a hand; he inclines his head to it. 'Drink my health.'

That night he dreams the death of Anne Boleyn, in panels. In the first he stands watching as she walks to the scaffold, wearing her clumsy gable hood. In the second she kneels in a white cap while the Frenchman raises his sword. In the last, her severed head, smothered in linen, bleeds its image into the weave.

He wakes as the cloth is shaken out. If her face is imprinted, he is too dazed to see it. It is 20 May 1536.

II
Salvage
London, Summer 1536

'Where's my orange coat?' he says. 'I used to have an orange coat.'

'I have not seen it,' says the boy Christophe. He says it sceptically, as if he were talking about a comet.

'I put it away. Before I brought you here. While you were still across the sea, blessing a Calais dunghill with your presence.'

'You scorn me.' Christophe is offended. 'Yet it was I who caught the cat.'

'You did not!' Gregory says. 'It was Dick Purser caught the cat. All Christophe did, he stood by making hunting cries. Now he looks to get the credit!'

His nephew Richard says, 'You put that coat away when the cardinal came down. You had no heart for it.'

'Yes, but now I am feeling cheerful. I am not going to appear before the bridegroom as a mourner.'

'No?' Christophe says. 'With this king one needs a reversible garment. One never knows, is it dying or dancing?'

'Your English is improving, Christophe.'

'Your French is where it was.'

'What do you expect, of an old soldier? I am not likely to write verse.'

'But you curse well,' Christophe says, encouragingly. 'Perhaps the best I have heard. Better than my father, who as you know was a great robber and feared through his province.'

'Would your father recognise you?' Richard Cromwell asks. 'I mean, if he saw you now? Half an Englishman, and in my uncle's livery?'

Christophe turns down his mouth. 'By now he is probably hanged.'

'Don't you care?'

'I spit on him.'

'No need for that,' he says soothingly. 'Coat, Christophe? Go and seek?'

Gregory says, 'The last time we all went out together ...'

Richard says, 'Do not. Do not say it. Do not even think of the other one.'

'I know,' Gregory says amiably. 'My tutors have imbued me with it, from my earliest days. Do not talk about severed heads at a wedding.'

The king's wedding was in fact yesterday, a small and private ceremony; today they are a loyal deputation, ready to congratulate the new queen. The colours of his working wardrobe are those sombre and expensive shades the Italians call *berettino*: the grey-brown of leaves around the feast of St Cecilia, the grey-blue of Advent light. But today an effort is called for, and Christophe is helping him into his festival garment, marvelling at it, when Call-Me-Risley hurries in. 'Not late, am I?' He stands back. 'Sir, are you wearing that?'

'Of course he is!' Christophe is offended. 'Your opinion not wanted.'

'It's only that the cardinal's people wore orange tawny, and so if it reminds the king ... he may not like to be reminded ...' Call-Me falters. Last night's conversation is like a stain on his own garment, something he can't brush out. He says meekly, 'Of course, the king may admire it.'

'If he doesn't, he can tell me to take it off. Mind he does not do the same with your head.'

Call-Me flinches. He is sensitive even for a redhead. He shrinks a little as they go out into the sun. 'Call-Me,' Gregory says, 'did you see, Dick Purser ran up the tree and caught the cat. Father, can he have some addition to his wages?'

Christophe mutters something. It sounds like, *heretic.*

'What?' he says.

'Deek Purser, heretic,' Christophe says. 'Believes the host is but bread.'

'But so do we!' Gregory says. 'Surely, or ... wait ...' Doubt crosses his face.

'Gregory,' Richard says, 'what we want from you is less theology and more swagger. Prepare for the king's new brothers – the Seymours will be in glory today. If Jane gives the king a son, they will be great men, Ned and Tom. But mind. So will we.'

For this is England, a happy country, a land of miracles, where stones underfoot are nuggets of gold and the brooks flow with claret. The Boleyns' white falcon hangs like a sorry sparrow on a fence, while the Seymour phoenix is rising. Gentlefolk of an ancient breed, foresters, masters of Wolf Hall, the king's new family now rank with the Howards, the Talbots, the Percys and the Courtenays. The Cromwells – father, son and nephew – are of an ancient breed too. Were we not all conceived in Eden? *When Adam delved and Eve span/Who was then the gentleman?* When the Cromwells stroll out this week, the gentlemen of England get out of their way.

The king wears green velvet: he is a verdant lawn, starred with diamonds. Parting from his old friend William Fitzwilliam, his treasurer, he takes Master Secretary's arm, draws him into a window embrasure, and stands blinking in the sunlight. It is the last day of May.

So, the wedding night: how does one ask? The new bride is of such virginal aspect that it would not surprise him if she had slipped beneath the bed and spent the night rigid on her back, praying. And Henry, as several women have told him, needs a lot of encouragement.

The king whispers, 'Such freshness. Such delicacy. Such maidenly *pudeur.*'

'I am happy for your Majesty.' He thinks, yes, yes: but did you manage it?

'I have come out of Hell into Heaven, and all in one night.'

That is the answer he needed.

The king says, 'The whole matter has been, as we all know, a difficult and delicate ... and you have shown, Thomas, both expedition and firmness.' He glances around the room. 'Gentlemen – and ladies too, I may say – have prompted me: Majesty, it is not time Master Cromwell received his deserts? You know I have hesitated to promote you, only because your grip is wanted in the House of Commons. But,' he smiles, 'the House of Lords is equally unruly, and wants a master. So, to the Lords you shall go.'

He bows. Small rainbows flit and dance across the stonework.

'The queen is with her women,' Henry says. 'She is getting her courage up. I have asked her to show herself to the court. Go to her, and speak a few comfortable words. Lead her out, if you can.'

He turns, and there at once is Ambassador Chapuys. He is one of the Emperor's French-speaking subjects, not a Spaniard but a Savoyard. Though he has been in England some years now, he does not venture conversation in our language; his skills are not sharp enough for the kind of conversation an ambassador needs to hold. His keen ears have picked out the word '*pudeur*' and smiling he asks, 'Well, Master Secretary, whose is the shame?'

'Not shame. Modesty. A proper modesty, on the bride's part.'

'Ah. I thought it might be your king who is shamed. Considering the events of recent days. And what came out in the courtroom, about his lack of skill and vigour with the other one.'

'We have only George Boleyn's word for that.'

'Well, if the lady slept with George, as you allege – with her own brother – you would imagine there would be pillow-talk, and what more natural than that she should complain of her husband's incapacity? But I can see that Lord Rochford cannot defend his version, now his head is off.' The ambassador is afflicted by a brightness in the eye, a twitch of the lips: which he controls. 'So the royal bridegroom has hit the mark. And he thinks that till last night Madame Jane was a virgin? But of course he can't tell. He thought Anne Boleyn was a virgin, and that, believe me, strained the credulity of all Europe.'

The ambassador is right. When it comes to maidenheads, Henry is easier to play than a penny whistle.

'I suppose he will be content with Madame Jane a month or two,' Chapuys says, 'till his eye lights on some other lady. Then it will be found that Jane has misled him – she was not free to marry after all, as she had some pre-contract with another gentleman. Yes?'

Eustache is fishing. He knows Anne Boleyn's head is off, but he wants to know on what grounds her marriage was dissolved. For it had to be dissolved: death was not enough to take her child Eliza out of the succession, it had to be shown the marriage was no marriage, defective from the start. And how did the king's clergy achieve this for him? He, Thomas Cromwell, is not about to say. He simply inclines his head and makes his way through the crush, changing his language as he goes. The new queen speaks only her mother tongue: and even that, not very often. Her brother Edward speaks French well. The younger brother, Tom Seymour – he doesn't know what he speaks. He knows he never listens.

The women around Jane are in their finery, and in the heat of mid-morning the scent of lavender ripples into air like bubbles of laughter. It is a pity that preservative herbs can do nothing for the dowagers of England's old families, who now stand about their prize like sentinels in brocade. The Boleyn women have melted from view: poor Mary Shelton, who thought that Henry Norris was going to marry her, and the vigilant Jane Rochford, George's widow. The room is crowded with faces not seen at court since Queen Katherine's day: and Jane, regrettably pale and as usual silent, is a little dough-figure in their midst. Henry has endowed her generously with the pick of the dead woman's jewels, and her gown has been hastily sewn over with goldsmiths' work, hearts and love-knots. As she stirs to greet him, a knot detaches itself; she stoops, but one of her attendants is quicker. Jane whispers, 'Thank you, madam, for your courtesy.'

Her face is dismayed. She cannot believe that Margaret Douglas – the king's niece, the Queen of Scotland's daughter – is here to pick up after her. Meg Douglas is a pretty lass, nineteen or twenty now. She stands up with a flash of red hair, and steps back to her place. Her hood is the French style that Boleyn favoured, but most of the ladies have reverted to the older sort, concealing the hair. By Meg's side is her best friend Mary Fitzroy, young Richmond's wife; her husband has been and gone, one assumes, after congratulating his father on the new marriage. She is a very little wife, not seventeen; the clumsy gable gives her a scalped, wary look, and her eyes are travelling around. She sees him; nudges Meg; drops her eyes, breathes, 'Cromwell.'

At once, both young women look away, as if to disappear him. Anne's ladies don't like to admit how they deluged him with gossip, once they knew the queen's day was done. They don't like to admit how fast they talked, what evidence they gave against her. Cromwell tricks you, they say. He puts words into your mouth. With his manner so suave, he makes you say things you don't mean.

Before he can come at the new queen, her family sweep in: her mother Lady Margery, two brothers. Edward Seymour looks discreetly joyous. Tom Seymour looks rumbustious, and is dressed with a lavishness that even George Boleyn might have thought *de trop*. Lady Margery's glance stabs the old dames. None of them have kept their looks as she has, nor have their girls become queen. She makes a deep, straight-backed curtsey to her daughter, then rises with an audible snap of knee-joints. The poet Skelton once compared her to a primrose. But now she is sixty.

Jane's pale glance washes over her family. Then she turns her head, and lets it wash over him. 'Master Secretary,' she says. There is a long pause, while the queen masters her diffidence. At last she whispers, 'Would you like to … kiss my hand? Or … or anything at all … like that?'

He finds himself on one knee, lips touching an emerald he had kissed on the narrow hand of the late Anne. With her other hand, with her stubby little fingers, Jane brushes his shoulder; as if to say, ah dear, it's hard for both of us, but somehow we'll stumble through the morning.

'Your lady sister is not with us?' he asks Jane.

'Bess is on her way,' Lady Margery says.

'Only,' Jane says, 'it's all been so sudden. Bess never thought I would be getting married. She is still in mourning for her husband.'

'I think she should come out of black. Let me help dress her. I know the Italian clothiers.'

Lady Margery subjects him to a sharp scrutiny. Then she turns, and flicks a dismissive hand at the dowagers. For a moment, these great ladies lock their eyes with hers. They inhale, as if in pain. They lift their hems, and drop back a few paces. They see they must allow the bride's immediate family to surround her, and pose the indelicate questions that must be asked the day after a wedding.

'So, sister?' Tom Seymour says.

'Voice down, Tom,' says brother Edward. He glances over his shoulder; he, Cromwell, is standing as an impassable barrier between the family and the court.

'So,' the new queen says.

'We only require,' her mother says, 'the merest word of reassurance. As to how you find yourself this morning.'

Jane considers. For a long time she looks at her shoes. Tom Seymour is fidgeting. You almost think he's going to pinch his sister, as if they were in the nursery still. Jane takes in a breath. 'Yes?' Tom demands.

Jane whispers, 'Brothers, my lady mother … Master Cromwell … I can only say I find myself wholly unprepared for what the king asks of me.'

The brothers stare at Lady Margery. Surely the girl knows how a man and woman couple? And besides, she is not a girl, isn't that the point?

'Surely,' Lady Margery says. 'You are twenty-seven years old, Jane. I mean, your Grace.'

'Yes, I am,' Jane agrees.

'The king should not have to coddle you like a thirteen-year-old,' her mother says. 'If he showed himself impatient, well, that is how men are.'

'You'll get used to it,' Tom encourages her. 'There's a price to be paid for everything, you know.'

Jane nods miserably.

'I am sure the king was not unkind,' Lady Margery says firmly.

'No, not unkind.' Jane glances up. 'But my difficulty is, he wants me to do some very strange things. Things I never imagined a wife had to do.'

They look at each other. Jane's lips move: as if she were trying out her words, before daring to expose them to the air. 'But I suppose … well, I hardly know … I suppose there are things men like.'

Edward looks desperate. Tom begs, 'Master Secretary?'

How is he to intervene? Is he responsible for the king's tastes?

Lady Margery's face is taut. 'Unpleasant things, Jane?'

'I think so,' the queen says. 'Though I have no experience of them, of course.'

Tom looks wild. 'My advice,' he says. 'Accommodate him, sister.'

'The point is,' Edward says, 'this … whatever, his desire, his command … does it conduce to getting a child?'

'I wouldn't have thought so,' Jane says.

'You'll have to talk to him,' Edward says. 'Cromwell, you'll have to recall to him how a Christian man behaves.'

He takes Jane's hands between his. It is a bold move but he can see no alternative. 'Your Grace, put aside modesty, and tell me what it is the king requires of you.'

Jane slides her hands away. She slides her pale little person away, and nudges aside her brothers: she falters in the direction of her king, her court, her future. She whispers as she goes, 'He wants me to ride down to Dover with him, and see the fortifications.'

Unsmiling, Jane walks the length of the great chamber. Every eye is on her; she looks proud, someone whispers. And if you knew nothing of her, you might think that. Henry stretches out his arms, as one does for a child learning to walk, and when he has her, he kisses her, full on the mouth. His lips form a question; she whispers an answer; he bends his head to catch it, his face full of solicitude and pride. Chapuys is in a huddle with the old dames and their menfolk.

As if he were their envoy – as if he were their envoy to Cromwell – the ambassador peels himself away and says, 'She appears to be wearing all her jewels at once, like a Florentine bride. Still, she looks well enough, for a woman who is so plain. Whereas the other one, the more she dressed up, the worse she looked.'

'Latterly. Perhaps.'

He remembers the days, when the cardinal was still alive, when Anne needed no ornament but her eyes. She had dwindled away in those last months, her face pinched. When she landed at the Tower, and slipped from his grasp and fell at his feet on the cobbles, he had lifted her and she weighed nothing; it was like holding air.

'So,' Chapuys says. 'While your king is in this merry mood, press him to name the Princess Mary as his heir.'

'Pending, of course, his son by his new wife.'

Chapuys bows.

'Press your master to speak to the Pope,' he tells the ambassador. 'There is a bull of excommunication hovering over my master. No king can live like that, threatened in his own realm.'

'All Europe is keen to heal the breach. Let the king approach Rome in a spirit of penitence, and undo the legislation that has separated your country from the universal church. As soon as that is done, His Holiness will be pleased to welcome his lost sheep, and accept the restitution of his revenues from England.'

'With interest paid, I suppose, on the missing years?'

'I imagine the normal banking rules will apply. And also –'

'There is more?'

'King Henry should withdraw his delegates to the Lutheran princes. We know you are holding talks. We want you to break them off.'

He nods. In sum, Chapuys is asking him to destroy the work of four years. To take England back to Rome. To recognise Henry's first marriage as valid, and the daughter of that marriage as his heir. To break off diplomacy with the German states. To forswear the gospel, embrace the Pope, and bow the knee to idols.

'So what shall I do,' he asks, 'in these brave new days? I mean, me personally? Thomas Cromwell?'

'Back to the smithy?'

'I think I've lost the blacksmith's art. I'll have to take to the road as I did as a boy. Cross the sea and offer myself as a footsoldier to the King of France. Do you think he'd be pleased to see me?'

'That is one course,' Chapuys says. 'On the other hand, you could stay in post, and accept a generous retainer from the Emperor. He understands the labour involved in returning your country to the *status quo ante*.' The ambassador smiles at him; then swivels on his heel, his arms held out in greeting. 'Cara-vey!'

That plush frontage, that deep chest emblazoned with gold: who can it be, but Sir Nicholas Carew? The grandee, in a lilting tone, corrects the ambassador's pronunciation: 'Car-ew.' He waits for it to be repeated.

Chapuys signals regret. 'It is beyond me, sir.'

Carew will let it pass. He fixes his attention on Master Secretary. 'We should meet.'

'That would honour me, Sir Nicholas.'

'We must arrange an escort to bring the Princess Mary back to court. Come out to my house at Beddington.'

'Come to me. I'm busy.'

Sir Nicholas is annoyed. 'My friends expect –'

'You can bring your friends.'

Now Sir Nicholas heaves closer. 'We made a bargain with you, Cromwell. We expect it to be honoured.'

He doesn't answer Carew, merely adjusts him so that his path is clear. Passing him, he touches his hand to his heart. It looks like the gesture of a man suddenly anxious. But that's not what it is, and that's not what he's doing.

At once his boys are beside him.

Richard asks, 'What did Carew want?'

'His bargain honoured.'

It is true what Wriothesley says: there was a bargain. In Carew's version: we, friends of the Princess Mary, will help you remove Anne

Boleyn, and afterwards, if you grovel to us and serve us, we will refrain from ruining you. Master Secretary's version is different. You help me remove Anne, and … and nothing.

Richard says, 'Do you know that the king had Carew's wife in his bed? Before Carew married her, and after?'

'No!' Gregory says. 'Am I old enough to know? Does everybody know? Does Carew know they know?'

Richard grins. 'He knows we know.'

It's better than gossip. It's power: it's news from the court's inner economy, from the counting house where the units of obligation are fixed and the coins of shame are weighed. Richard says, 'I could like her myself, Eliza Carew. If a man were not a married man …'

'Out of our sphere,' he says.

'When has that stopped you? It's only a fortnight since you and the Earl of Worcester's wife were shut in a room together.'

Getting evidence.

'And she came out smiling,' Richard says.

Because I paid her debts.

Gregory says, 'And she's big with child. Which people do talk about.'

'Let's go,' Richard says, 'before Carve-Away comes back. We might laugh at him.'

But their names are called: Rafe, whisking around a corner. He has come from the king, and his expression – if you could parse it – is a compound of reverence, wariness and incredulity. 'He wants you, sir.'

He nods. 'You boys go home.' Then a thought strikes him. 'But Richard –'

His nephew turns. He whispers. 'Do you attend Sir William Fitzwilliam. See if he will stand my ally in the king's council. He knows Henry's mind. He knows him as well as any man.'

It was Fitzwilliam who came to him, last March, to spell out to him how the Boleyns were detested, and how this detestation might unite natural foes, give them a common interest. It was Fitzwilliam who hinted at the king's own need for a change: who did it with the calm authority of a man who had known Henry since his youth.

Richard says, 'I think he will follow your star, sir.'

'Find out his hopes,' he says. 'And raise them.'

'Sir –' Rafe prompts.

He takes Rafe's arm. A knot of gentlemen turn their faces, and watch them pass. Rafe looks over his shoulder as the gentlemen fall behind, arranged as if waiting for Hans to paint them: silken hose, silken beards, their daggers in scabbards of black velvet, crimson velvet books in their hands. They are all Howards, or Howard kin, and one is the Duke of Norfolk's young half-brother, who shares his name: Thomas Howard the Lesser. No danger of confusing the two. The Lesser is the worst poet at court. The Greater never rhymed in his life.

Rafe says, 'The king is not as sanguine as he appears. He is not sure now of what he believed yesterday. He says, is justice served? He does not doubt Anne's guilt, but he says, what about the gentlemen? You remember, sir, what ado we had to get him to sign the warrants? How we stood over him? Now he has fallen into doubts again. "Harry Norris was my old friend," he says. "How is it possible he betrayed me with my wife? And Mark – a lute player, a boy like that – is it likely she would sin with him?"'

Time was a king lived under the eye of his court. He ate in the great hall, spoke out all his thoughts, shat behind a scant curtain and copulated behind one too. Now rulers enjoy solitude: soft-slippered servants guard them, and in their recessed apartments noise is hushed. As the minister heads for the inner rooms, hat in hand, he institutes an inner process whereby he becomes pliable, infinitely patient. Usually, in cases of disturbance to the king's peace of mind, he would call on the archbishop. But not in this matter. Since the former queen was indicted, Cranmer has had no peace of mind to spare.

At the door of the privy chamber he is ushered through. In the old days – that's to say, a month ago – the king's gentlemen would be vigilant to intercept him. You would expect Harry Norris, sliding out: *I regret, Master Secretary, his Majesty is at prayer.* And how long will he be praying, Harry? *Oh, the whole morning, I don't doubt …* Norris fading away, with a charming smile of apology; while from behind a closing door he would hear a giggle from that little ape Francis Weston.

The courtiers ask, is it possible, really, that the queen was bedding such a grinning pup as Weston?

What can you do but shrug?

The king is seated, slumped, elbows on knees. In the hour since he left the public gaze his verdant sheen has greyed. Charles Brandon is with him, standing over him like a sentinel.

He makes his reverence: 'Majesty.' And a polite murmur, as he rises: 'My lord Suffolk.'

The duke gives him a wary nod. Henry says, 'Crumb, have you heard this story about Katherine's tomb?'

Suffolk says, 'It's in every tavern and marketplace. At the very instant Anne's head leapt from her body, the candles on Katherine's tomb ignited – without touch of living hand.' The duke looks anxious to have it right. 'You need not believe it, Cromwell. I don't.'

Henry is irritable. 'Of course not. It is a story. Where did it start, Crumb?'

'Dover.'

'Oh.' Henry had not expected an answer. 'She is buried in Peterborough. What do they know of it in Dover?'

'Nothing, Majesty.'

He's going to plod like this, till Henry sends Brandon out.

'Well, then,' Brandon says. 'If the tale began in Dover, you may be sure it came from France.'

'You defame the French,' Henry says, 'and yet you take their money, Charles.'

The duke looks mortified. 'But you know I do.'

'Of course, Majesty,' he says, 'my lord Suffolk takes certain sums from the Emperor too. So it all balances out.'

'I know the arrangements,' Henry says. 'God knows, Charles, if my councillors did not take retainers and pensions, I would have to pay them myself, and Crumb here would have to find the money.'

'Sir,' he says, 'what is to happen to Thomas Boleyn? I see no need to disturb him in his earldom.'

'Boleyn was not a rich man, before I raised him,' Henry says. 'But he did some service to the state.'

'And he is heartily ashamed, sir, of the crimes of his daughter and son.'

Henry nods. 'Very well. But as long as he does not employ that stupid title, *Monseigneur*. And as long as he stays away from me. He should go to his own country, where I don't have to look at him. So should the Duke of Norfolk. I don't want to see Boleyn faces or Howard faces or any of their kin.'

He means, not unless the French or the Emperor take it in their heads to invade; or if the Scots come over the border. If war breaks out, Howards are the people you send for.

'Then Boleyn remains Earl of Wiltshire,' he says. 'But his office as Keeper of the Privy Seal –'

'You can do that, Crumb.'

He bows. 'And if it pleases your Majesty, I shall continue as Secretary.'

Stephen Gardiner was Master Secretary, until – as Mr Wriothesley points out – he was displaced. He doesn't want Stephen erupting into the king's mind, spilling his putrid flatteries in the hope of recall. The way to prevent that is to offer to do all the jobs himself.

But Henry is not listening. On the table before him is a stack of three small books bound in scarlet leather and tied with green ribbons. Beside them, lying open, his walnut writing box: a relic from Katherine's day, it is ornamented with her initial, and with the emblem of the pomegranate. Henry says, 'My daughter Mary has sent a letter. I do not recall I gave her permission to write to me. Did you?'

'I would not presume.' He wishes he could get the letter out of the box.

'She seems to entertain expectations about her future as my heir. As if she believes Jane will fail in giving me a son.'

'She won't fail, sir.'

'That is easy to say, but the other one made promises she could not keep. Our marriage is clean, she said: God will reward you. But last night in a dream –'

Ah, he thinks, you see her too: Ana Bolena with her collar of blood.

Henry says: 'Did I do right?'

Right? The magnitude of the question checks him, like a hand on his arm. Was I just? No. Was I prudent? No. Did I do the best thing for my country? Yes.

'It's done,' he says.

'But how can you say, "It's done"? As if there were no sin? As if there were no repentance?'

'Go forward, sir. It's the one direction God permits. The queen will give you a son. Your treasury is filling. Your laws are observed. All Europe sees and admires the stand you have taken against the pretended authority of Rome.'

'They see it,' Henry says. 'They don't admire it.'

True. They think England is low-hanging fruit. Exhausted game. A trophy for princes and their huntsmen. 'Our walls are building,' he says. 'Forts. They will not dare.'

'If the Pope excommunicates me, France and the Emperor will get a blessing for invading us. Or so the Pope will tell them.'

'They will not go to war for a blessing, sir. Think how often they say, "We will crusade against the Turk." But they never do it.'

'Those who conquer England will get their sins remitted. Which amount to a great heap.'

'They will be adding new sins all the time.' He stands over Henry: time to remind him what the bloodletting has been for. 'I am talking to the Emperor's man every day. You know his master is ready to make an alliance. While Anne Boleyn was alive he felt obliged to keep up a quarrel with you. But now you have removed the cause of that quarrel. With the Emperor at our side, we need not fear King François.' (Though, he thinks, I am talking to him, too: I am talking hard.) 'And should the Emperor fail us, there are friends to be had among the princes of Germany.'

'Heretics,' Charles Brandon says. 'What next, Crumb? A pact with the devil?'

He is impatient. 'My lord, the German princes are not heretics – they are like our prince – they give a lead to the people of their territories, and refuse to hand them body and soul to Rome.'

Henry says, 'My lord Suffolk, will you leave us?'

Charles looks mutinous. 'As it pleases you. But remember what I say, and lift your chin, Harry. I got a fine son on my wife last year, and I am older than you.'

He strides out. The king looks after him: wistful, as if the duke were going on a journey. '*Harry,*' he repeats. His own name is tender in his mouth. 'Suffolk forgets himself. But I will always be a boy to him. I cannot persuade him that neither of us is young any more.' His hand steals out, furtive, and caresses the books, their soft scarlet covers. 'Do you know that Jane has no books of her own? None except a girdle book with a jewel, and that is of little worth. I am giving her these.'

'That will give her much pleasure, sir.'

'They were Katherine's. They are devotional in nature. Jane prays a great deal.' The king is restless; he looks as if prayers are his best hope. 'Crumb, what if some accident befalls? I could die tomorrow. I cannot leave my kingdom to my daughters, the one truculent and half-Spanish, the other an infant – and neither of them born in wedlock. My next heir would be the Queen of Scotland's daughter, but my sister being what she is,' he sighs, 'we cannot be wholly sure Meg was born in wedlock either. And I ask you – a woman, weak in body, weak in will – can she rule, with all the frailty of her sex? No matter if she is blest with firmness, with nimble wit – still the day comes when she must marry, and bring in a foreigner to share her throne – or else exalt a subject, and who can she trust? A woman ruler, it is only storing up trouble – you may stave it off for ten years, twenty, but trouble will come. There is only one way. We will have to bring young Richmond forward as my heir. So I put it to you – how will Parliament take it?'

Very ill, he thinks. 'I believe they will urge your Majesty to trust in God and use your best endeavours to get a son of your marriage.

42

In the interim, we can make an instrument that allows your Majesty to name a successor at your pleasure. And you need not reveal your choice. Any such person might be too much emboldened.'

Henry appears to be only half-listening; which means he is listening hard. 'I had her library inventoried.' The late Anne, he means. 'There was seditious matter, and much that bordered on heresy. And in her brother's books, too.'

Those fine French volumes: the names of George and Anne set side by side, with the Rochfords' sable lion and the falcon crowned: his traces darkly inked, *This book is mine, George Rochford.* He waits. The king is quieting his conscience: he is assuring himself that the Boleyns and their friends were enemies of God. He doubts any book of theirs would be objectionable to him; or to Henry either, if his mind were more resolute. The king picks up one of the scarlet volumes. He glances into it, while he broaches his real concern: 'The Commons will say to me, the crown is not yours to dispose of.' A small hiccupping laugh: 'They will put me in my place, Crumb.'

'True.' He smiles. 'They may even call you Harry. But I have ways around them, sir.'

'Who is Mr Speaker this session?'

'Richard Riche.'

'I see,' Henry says. 'Do you sleep at nights, Crumb?'

The question is not barbed: the king means no more than he says. 'Only,' Henry adds, 'the Privy Seal is a great office of state, and as you are my deputy in church affairs, and the bishops meet soon in Convocation – and if you remain Master Secretary, as I am pleased you should – it is a burden of work no man has carried before. But then, you are like the cardinal, you can do the work of ten. I often wonder where you come from.'

'Putney, Majesty.'

'I know that. I mean, I don't know what makes you as you are. God's mystery, I suppose,' Henry says, and leaves it at that.

* * *

In the guard chamber, Charles Brandon is waiting for him. 'Look here, Crumb, I know you're angry with me. It's because I didn't kneel when that whore's head was smitten off.'

He holds up a hand, but you can no more stop Charles than you can stop a charging bull. 'Bear in mind how she persecuted me!' the duke roars. 'She accused me of swiving my own daughter!'

Every head in the crowded hall turns. His mind ranges over Charles's offspring, born in and out of wedlock.

'As if it were Wolf Hall!' Charles shouts. 'Not,' he adds in haste, 'that I believe those slanders about Old Sir John. It was Anne Boleyn said he was tupping his own daughter-in-law. She only said it to draw attention from her own sin with her brother.'

'Possibly, my lord, but do you wonder that she had a grievance against you? You told the king she had to do with Tom Wyatt.'

'Aye, I said so – and I admit it! Can you stand by, and watch your friend made a cuckold? Not that Harry liked the news – he kicked me out like a dog. Well, he's the king, he kills the messenger.' He drops his voice. 'But I would always, because I am his friend, I would always tell him what he should know, even if he ruins me for it. I propped him in his saddle, Crumb, when he was a green boy in the lists. I held him steady when he couched his first lance, to run against a knight and not a foe of painted wood – I saw his wrist tremble in its glove, and I said naught but, "*Courage, mon brave!*" – which I learned of the French, you know. No bolder man at the tournament than Harry, after his first course or two. I could help him, for I was a seasoned fighter – I was older, you see, and still am.' The duke's face clears. 'Your little lad Gregory, he shapes in the tilt yard. Very fine turnout, cuts a good figure, nothing wanting by way of harness, weaponry, very sound, very gallant. Your nephew Richard, there's a stout fellow – perhaps a touch rustic – came late to it as we all know, but he has some weight behind him – no, I tell you, he and Gregory, they are of that breed, always Forward, Forward! – they show no fear. It must be in the blood.' The duke looks down, from his towering height. 'You must *have* blood, must you not? I reckon a man could do worse than be born of a blacksmith. Better than some quill-nibbling clerk who is half-goose. Iron in the blood, not ink.'

Charles's father died at Bosworth, close to the person of Henry Tudor. Some say he was bearing the Tudor banner, though truth is hard to pluck from a battlefield. If he fell beneath that banner, a living hand picked it up; the Tudors ascended, and the Brandons with them.

He says, 'My father was a brewer as well as a blacksmith. He brewed very bad ale.'

'I'm sorry to hear it,' Charles says sincerely. 'Now look – what I wish to impart is this. Harry knows that he did wrong. First he married his brother's wife, then he had the misfortune to marry a witch. He says, how long must I be punished? He knows very well what witches do – they take your manhood away. They shrivel your member and then you die. Now I've told him – Majesty, don't brood on it. Fetch the archbishop in, discharge your conscience, and start again. I don't want this in his mind – following him, like a curse. You tell him to press on and never look back. He will take it from you, you see. Whereas me – he thinks I'm a fool.' The duke thrusts out his vast hand. 'So – friends?'

Allies, he thinks. What will the Duke of Norfolk say?

At Austin Friars there are always crowds about his gate, shouting his name and thrusting papers at him. 'Make way, make way!' Christophe gathers up an armful of petitions: 'Get down, rats! Do not harass Master Secretary!'

'Oy, Cromwell!' a man shouts. 'Why do you keep this French clown, are there no Englishmen to serve you?'

That sets up a cry: half of London wants to get inside these gates and get a position with him, and now they shout out their names, or those of their nephews and sons. 'Patience, friends.' His voice carries over the crowd. 'The king may make me a great man, and then you can all come in and warm yourselves by my fire.'

They laugh. He is already a great man, and London knows it. His property is walled and guarded, his gatehouse manned day and night. The keepers salute him; he passes into the courtyard, and through a door beside which, left and right, are two gaps through which one could slide a blade, or slot the muzzle of a gun; they are aligned so any malefactor can be pierced or blasted from both sides at once. His chief cook, Thurston, had said to him, 'Sir, I am no military man, but it seems excessive to me: having killed your foe at the gate, would you slaughter him again at the door?'

'I neglect no precaution,' he had said. 'The times being what they are, a man may enter the gate as your friend and change sides while he crosses the courtyard.'

Austin Friars was a small place once: twelve rooms, when he first took the lease for himself and his clerks, for Lizzie and the girls, for Lizzie's mother Mercy Prior. Mercy has now entered into her old age. She is the lady of the house, but she mostly keeps to her own part, a book open on her knees. She reminds him of an image of St Barbara he saw once in Antwerp, a saint reading against the noise of a construction site, backed by scaffolding and raw brick. Everybody complains about builders, the time they take, the mounting expense, the noise and the dust, but he likes their banging and thudding, their songs and their chat, their shortcuts and secret lore. As a boy he was always climbing about on somebody's roof, often without their knowledge. Show him a ladder and he was up it, seeking a longer view. But when he got up there, what could he see? Only Putney.

In the great hall, his nephew Richard is waiting for him. Standing under the tapestry the king gave him, he opens a letter from the king's daughter, written in her own hand.

Richard says, 'I suppose Lady Mary thinks she's coming home.'

He is heading for his own rooms, shaking off the clerks who sway after him, weighed down by files of paper, by bulging books of statute and precedent, by parchments and scrolls. 'Later, boys …'

In his chamber the air is sharply scented: juniper, cinnamon. He takes off his orange coat. In the dimness of the room, shuttered against the afternoon, it blazes as if he handled fire. There were certain miserable divines, in darker days than these, who said that if God had meant us to wear coloured clothes He would have made coloured sheep.

Instead, His providence has given us dyers, and the materials for their craft. Here in the city, amid dun and slate, donkey's back and mouse, gold quickens the heart; on those days of grey swilling rain that afflict London in every season, we are reminded of Heaven by a flash of celestial blue. Just as the soldier looks up to the flutter of bright banners, so the workman on his daily trudge rejoices to see his betters shimmer above him imperial purple, in silver and flame and halcyon against the wash of the English sky.

Richard has followed him. He closes the door behind them. The sounds of the house recede. He puts a hand to his chest – that habitual motion – and from a pocket inside his jacket, he takes out a knife.

'Still?' Richard says. 'Even now?'

'Especially now.' Without the weight next to his heart, he would hardly know himself.

'Carry it on the street, yes,' Richard says. 'But at court, sir? I cannot imagine the circumstance in which you could use it.'

Nor can I, he thinks. It is because I cannot imagine the circumstance, that I need it. He tests the blade against his thumb. He made his first knife for himself, when he was a boy. That was a good blade, and he misses it every day.

'Go and get Chapuys,' he says to Richard. 'My compliments to him, and may I give him supper? If he says no, tell him I feel a lust for diplomacy – say I must have a treaty before sunset, and if he won't come I'll fetch in the French ambassador instead.'

'Right you are.' Richard goes out. And he, lighter by the orange coat, lighter by the knife, runs downstairs into the fresh air of an inner courtyard, and crosses to the kitchens to see Thurston.

He can hear Thurston before he sees him: some underling wishes he had never been born. 'Told you once,' Thurston roars, 'told you twice, and next time, boy, that you use that mortar for garlic, I will personally knock out your brain, place it in the said mortar, pestle it to a fine paste and give it to Dick Purser for feeding the dogs.'

He passes the cold room where two peacocks hang on a rack, their throats cut, weights on their heels. He rounds the corner, meets the face of the chastened boy: 'Mathew? Mathew, from Wolf Hall?'

Thurston snorts. 'Comes from Wolf Hall! He comes from the pit!'

He is astonished to see the boy. 'I brought you here to clerk for me, not for kitchen work.'

'Yes, sir, I told them so.' A pale, modest young man, Mathew had brought his letters courteously each morning, last year when the king had visited the Seymours. He had thought him too personable and deft to be left in the country; the boy's face lit up when he'd asked, would you like to come away and see the world?

'This boy is out of his right place,' he says to Thurston. 'There has been a mistake.'

'Good. Take him. Take him away before I do him some mischief.'

'Off with this.' He indicates the boy's spattered smock.

'In truth, sir?'

'Your day has come.' He helps the boy free himself and emerge thinner, in shirt and hose. 'How's your friend Rob? Do you hear from him?'

'Yes, sir. And he does as you bade him, he keeps an eye out, who visits Wolf Hall, and he faithfully writes down their names. Only I could not come at you, to give his news.'

'I am sorry for your rough treatment. Cross the court and ask for Thomas Avery – say I have sent you to learn the household accounts. Perhaps when you have mastered that, you might go into some other family for a while.'

The boy is hurt. 'I like it here.'

'Despite this churl?' He indicates Thurston. 'If I sent you away, you would still be in my service.'

'Would I go under another name?' The boy hitches an imaginary coat on his shoulders. 'I understand you, sir.'

Thurston says, 'I'm glad somebody does.'

Around them, two dozen boys are dragging panniers across a stone floor, sharpening their paring knives, counting eggs, pricking off an inventory and plucking fowl. The house goes on without him, its arrangements complete. In here the blood puddings are stirred, the fish gutted; across the court, the bright-eyed clerks perch on their stools, hungry to incise. Here the chafing dish and the latten pan, there the penknife and the sealing wax, the ribbon and silk tags, the black words that creep across the parchment, the quills. He remembers the day in Florence, when the call came for him in his turn. 'Englishman, they want you in the counting house.' And how, leisurely, he had untied his apron, and hung it on a peg, and left behind him the copper pans and basins, and the row of lipped jars for oil and wine that stood together in an alcove, each as high as a child of seven. He had run up the stairs two at a time, and as he passed the *sala* he heard the drops of water falling from the wall fountain into its marble basin, a tiny erratic drum-beat, *pit-pat … pit … pat-pit*. The boy scrubbing the steps got out of his way. He sang: *Scaramella's off to war …*

He says to Thurston, 'Chapuys to supper. It will be just the two of us.'

'Of course it will,' Thurston says. He sieves his flour, allowing little puffs and billows to rise between them. 'Somebody said to me, that Spanish fellow, that one who is always at your house – he and your master plotted it all between them to kill the queen, for she was in the way of their friendship.'

'Chapuys is not a Spaniard. You know that.'

Thurston gives him a look that says, it is demeaning and futile to differentiate between foreigners. 'I know that the Emperor is the King of Spain and lord of half the world. No wonder you want to be in bed with him.'

'I have to be,' he says. 'I clasp him to my bosom.'

'When's the king coming again to dine?' Thurston asks. 'Mind, I expect he's lost his appetite. Wouldn't you, if your bollocks were insulted in open court?'

'Would I? I don't know. It's never happened to me.'

'The whole of London listening,' Thurston says with relish. 'Of course, we don't know for sure what George said, it being in French. We speculate it was along the lines of, the king can get it up, he can get it in, but he doesn't last long enough to please a lady.'

49

'See,' he says, 'now you wish you'd learned French.'

'But that was the gist of it,' Thurston says comfortably. 'If you can't please a lady, she don't get a child, or if she does, it's some puny object that never lives to be christened. You remember the Spanish queen. When she was young she dropped them by the dozen. But they none of them lived, except for that little lass Mary, and she's the size of a mouse.'

At his feet, eels are swimming in a pail, twisting and gliding; interlacing in their futile efforts, as they wait to be killed and sauced. He asks Thurston, 'What are they saying on the street? About Anne?'

Thurston scowls. 'She never had friends. Not even among the women. They say, if she went to it with her brother, that would explain why no child she got would stick in there. A brother's child, or a child got on a Friday, or one got when you shove it in from the back – it's against nature. They shed themselves, poor sinful creatures. For what's the point of them being born only to die?'

Thurston believes it. Incest is a sin, we all acknowledge; but then so is congress in any position other than the one approved by priests. So is congress on a Friday, the day of Christ's crucifixion; or on Sundays, Saturdays and Wednesdays. If you listen to churchmen, it's a sin to penetrate a woman during Lent and Advent – or on saints' days, though the calendar is bright with festivals. More than half the year is accursed, one way and another. It's a wonder anyone is ever born.

'Some women like to go on top,' Thurston says. 'That's not godly, is it? You can imagine the sort of runt that would result from that carry-on. It doesn't last the week.'

He speaks as if a child were a stale cake, a fading flower: doesn't last the week. He and Lizzie had lost a child once. Thurston made a chicken broth to strengthen her and prayed for her while he diced the vegetables. That had been at Fenchurch Street. He was just a jobbing lawyer in those days, and Gregory was still in skirts, and his daughter Anne not weaned, and his little daughter Grace not even thought of; and Thurston himself was just a family cook and not the master chef he is now, with a brigade at his command. He remembers how, when the broth was put before her, Lizzie had cried into it, and they took it out untouched.

'Are you just going to stand talking,' Thurston says, 'or are you killing those eels for me?'

He looks down into the pail. When he was a cook, he kept his eels in their watery world till the pans were hot. Still, it's not worthwhile to argue. He turns back his sleeves. 'Skin them while you're about it,' Thurston says.

'In my days in Italy, as a student,' Ambassador Chapuys says, 'I never took more than bread and olives for supper.'

'Nothing more healthful,' he says. 'Sadly, our English climate does not permit it.'

'Perhaps a handful of tender broad beans, still in their pod. A small glass of *vin santo*.'

It is Gregory who, to honour their guest, brings in the linen towels and the basin. The ambassador's fingers ripple through sprigs of dried lavender. 'You will be hunting this summer, Master Gregory?'

'I hope so,' Gregory says. He dips his head; the ambassador blesses himself and offers up a grace. One forgets Chapuys is in holy orders. How does he manage about women? Either he is celibate or, like his host, discreet.

The eels come in, presented in two fashions: salted in an almond sauce, and baked with the juice of an orange. There is a spinach tart, green as the summer evening, flavoured with nutmeg and a splash of rosewater. The silver gleams; the napkins are folded into the shapes of Tudor roses; the coverpanes at each place are worked with silver garlands. '*Bon appetit*,' he says to the ambassador. 'I've had a letter.'

'Ah yes, from the Princess Mary. And she says?'

'You know what she says. Now listen to what I say.' He hunches forward. 'The princess, as you call her – the Lady Mary – believes her father will welcome her back to court. She thinks that with the change of wife her troubles are over. You must disillusion her, or I will.'

Chapuys takes a portion of eel between finger and thumb. 'She blamed Anne Boleyn for all her afflictions these last years. She is convinced it was the concubine who had her separated from her mother and shut up in the country. She reveres her father and believes him at all times wise. As a daughter should, of course.'

'So she must take the oath. She has evaded it, but now I see no help. All subjects must take it, when the king requires.'

'Let me be exact about what you ask of her. She must recognise that her mother's marriage was of no effect, and that she, though the king's eldest child, is not his heir. She must swear to uphold, as the king's successor, the little daughter of Boleyn, whom he has just killed.'

'The oath will be revised. Eliza will be excluded.'

'Good. Because she is Henry Norris's bastard, as I understand it. Or is she the lute player's? This is excellent,' he says, addressing the eel. 'So what does Henry intend now? My master will not accept young Richmond in Mary's place. Nor, I think, will the King of France.'

'Parliament will settle up the succession.'

'Not Henry's whim, then?' The ambassador chuckles. 'Have you told Henry?'

'Mary claims she has no desire to be queen. She says she will support whatever successor her father chooses. But she cannot accept her father as head of the church.'

'That is also a difficulty,' the ambassador admits.

Old Bishop Fisher refused the oath, and last year Henry executed him. Thomas More refused it, and he too is shorter by a head. He says, 'Mary is living in a fool's paradise. Does she think we are headed back to Rome, because Anne Boleyn is dead?'

Chapuys sighs. 'It grieves me, Thomas, that in the old days we were in Rome at the same time and did not know each another. How congenial, if we had been able to take supper together! Did you ever try those little ravioli, stuffed with cheese and herbs? They were light as air, if the cook knew his job.' The ambassador adjusts his napkin over his shoulder. 'The Emperor wishes the king success, of course, in his new marriage. He is sorry that your master did not pause to consider a bride of the Emperor's choosing. With not much trouble, he could have had the Duchess of Milan, a tender little widow of sixteen. But it is done now, and we must make the best of it – the Emperor believes that if Madame Jane has a son, it will conduce to peace and stability. And from your point of view, *mon cher*, make Henry more ...' his eyes move sideways, 'tractable. So despite what the lady's brother said of his impotence, we must wish the king – how does Boccaccio put it? – "a resurrection of the flesh".'

A boy brings the veal; he himself, Cromwell, takes up the carving knife.

'I believe ...' Chapuys pauses, to let the servant go, '... I believe there is a general bewilderment in Germany. Your heretic friends know that Madame Jane was lady-in-waiting to Queen Katherine. They ask, has Cremuel lost his senses? Why would he destroy the concubine, who was a heretic like himself, and replace her with a good daughter of Rome?' He dabs his mouth. 'Unless Cremuel has a plot. But then, I say to the Emperor, Cremuel always has a plot. And as the evidence of the last fortnight shows us, his plots succeed.'

'I was not responsible for Anne's death,' he says. 'She herself brought it about, she and her gentlemen.'

'But at a time of your choosing.'

He puts down the knife. The handle gleams, mother of pearl. 'I could hardly dictate the timing of their quarrels.'

'You told me that you did not know how to put an end to her, but you must do it, or she would kill you. You said you would go to your house and imagine it, how it might be. It seems your imagination is the most powerful in England. I dare say Henry was appalled at what emerged, once the investigation began.' Chapuys wipes his fingers. 'What a picture you have put in the mind of all Christian men! The Queen of England on her back with her skirts hauled up, "Come one, come all!"'

'You must toss and turn at night, dwelling on it.'

'Henry Norris, the king's great friend. Francis Weston, some vain youth who was wandering past when she chanced to be naked. That north country ruffian Will Brereton. The boy Smeaton ... she was not too proud to go to it with the poor child hired to play the lute.

But why would she be? She was pleased to rut with her own brother.'
Chapuys puts down his napkin. 'I understand how it was – Henry is
tired of her, he wants the little Jane, he says, "Cremuel, find me a
reason to be rid of her." But he cannot have been prepared for what
you would uncover. Perhaps he will not forgive you, *mon cher*, for
exposing him to ridicule.'

'On the contrary. He is promoting me.'

'Yet the business must rankle. He may think about it later. But
come now – I should congratulate you. You are to become a milord.
Baron Cromwell of –'

'Wimbledon.'

'No,' Chapuys says. 'Choose some other place. One I can
pronounce.'

'And I am to be Lord Keeper of the Privy Seal.'

'Ah. Privy Seal is greater?'

'Privy Seal is all I could desire.'

The ambassador takes a sliver of veal. 'You know, this is very
good.'

'I warn you,' he says. 'If Mary enrages her father, it will come
home to your door.'

'If your cook ever wants a new post, send him to my door also.'
Chapuys picks up the carving fork, and admires its tines. 'We know
that the princess will not take an oath which declares her father head
of the church. She could not swear to what she regards as an impossibility. Perhaps, rather than persecute her, Henry would let her enter
a nunnery? She could not then be suspected of wanting the throne. It
would be an honourable retreat from the world. She could go into
one of the great houses, where in time she might become abbess.'

'Yes. Shaftesbury perhaps? Wilton?' He puts his glass down. 'Oh,
spare me, ambassador! She will no more enter a convent than you will.
If she cares so little for the world and all in it, why does she not take
the oath and have done? No one will trouble her then.'

'Mary may agree to give up her claims on the future, but not on
the past. She will not believe that her mother and father were not
married. She does not agree to have her mother called a whore.'

'She was not called a whore. She was called Princess Dowager. And you know that after they separated Henry maintained her honourably and at some expense.'

'Look, Katherine is dead.' The ambassador speaks with passion. 'Let her rest, yes?'

She doesn't, though. Katherine pulls and drags at her daughter. She walks by night, at her side her lean and ancient counsellor Bishop Fisher, and in her hands a parchment pleading her cause. When the news of Katherine's death came, there was dancing at court. But on the day of her funeral, Anne Boleyn miscarried a child. The corpse had risen from her bier, and bounced her supplanter till her teeth rattled: shaken her, till the king's son came loose.

'Ambassador,' he puts his fingertips together, 'let me assure you, Henry loves his daughter. But he expects obedience, as a father and a king.'

'Mary gives first place to her Heavenly Father.'

'But what if she were to die, with the sin of disobedience staining her soul?'

'You are a ruffian, Cremuel,' Chapuys says. 'You cannot help yourself. Threaten, when you ought to conciliate. Henry will not kill his daughter.'

'Who knows what Henry will do? Not I.'

'This is what I tell the Emperor. Henry's subjects live in fear. I exhort my master: it is your Christian duty to free England. Even the usurper Richard, the Scorpion, was not abhorred as is this present king.'

'I discourage that phrase, "the present king". It comes near treason. Anyone who uses it must have another king in view.'

'Treason is only a crime in those who owe loyalty. I owe Henry nothing, except perhaps a formal thanks for his hospitality – which is no better than perfunctory, and far inferior' – the ambassador bows – 'to your own. All Europe knows how frail is his grip on the future. Only last January –'

Put the fork down, he thinks; stop stabbing me. The memory is sharp: a day of dazing cold and confusion, and he dragged from his desk to witness a catastrophe. The king's horse had come down in the tilt yard. Henry took a blow to the head and was carried to a tent. He looked dead; we thought he was dead, as he lay like a bloodless effigy, no breath, no pulse. He remembers laying his hand on Henry's chest, and feeling for the frailest thread of life – but what the bystanders told him, after, was that he called on God and then struck the king with enough force to break his ribs. What had he to lose? Shuddering, wheezing, retching, the king sat up – back in the land of the living. 'Cromwell?' he said. 'I thought I should see angels.'

'Very well,' Chapuys says. 'We will not mention his accident if it puts you off your supper. But it must be acknowledged that there are men in England, the best blood of your nation, who remain loyal sons of Rome.'

'Do they?' he says. 'How can that be? Because they have all taken their oath to Henry. The Courtenays have taken it. The Poles. They have recognised him not only as their king to whom they owe their duty, but as head of the church.'

'Of course,' Chapuys says. 'What else could they do? What choice did you give them?'

'You think oaths mean nothing to them, perhaps. You expect them to break their word.'

'Not at all,' the ambassador says soothingly. 'I feel sure they would not move against their anointed king. My anxiety is that, inflamed by the justice of their ancient cause, some renegade supporter of theirs might give the king his death blow. A dagger thrust, it is easily done. It may be, even, it needs no human hand to strike. There is plague that kills in a day. There is the sweating sickness that kills in an hour. You know it is true, and if I were to shout it out to the populace at Paul's Cross, you could not hang me for it.'

'No.' He smiles. 'But ambassadors have been murdered in the street before now. I only mention it.'

The ambassador bows his head. He picks at his salad. A leaf of sweet lettuce, a spear of bitter endive. The boy Mathew comes in with fruit.

'I am afraid once again we have failed with our apricots,' he says. 'It seems years since I ate them. Perhaps Bishop Gardiner will bring me some, if he comes over.'

Chapuys laughs. 'I think they would be dipped in acid. You know he is assuring the French courtiers that Henry has plans to take your country back to Rome?'

He did not know, but he suspected. 'In default of the apricots I have preserved peaches.'

Chapuys approves. 'You do them in the Venetian fashion.' He takes a spoonful and looks up, slyly. 'What will happen to Guiett?'

'What? Oh, Wyatt. He is in the Tower.'

'I know well where he is. He is where you can watch him, while he writes his baffling verses and riddles. Why do you protect him? He should be dead.'

'His father was a friend of my old master, the cardinal.'

'And he asked you to cover for his son's delinquencies?' Chapuys laughs.

'I gave my word,' he says stiffly.

'I perceive such a promise is sacred to you. Why? When nothing else is sacred? I do not understand you, Cremuel. You are not afraid, when you should be afraid. You are like someone who has loaded the dice.'

'Loaded the dice?' he says. 'Is that what people do?'

'You are playing with the greatest men in the land.'

'What, Carve-Away and those folk?'

'They know you need them. You cannot stand alone. Because if the new marriage does not last, what have you? You have Henry's favour. But if he withdraws it? You know the cardinal's fate. All his dignities as churchman could not save him. If he had not died on the road to London, Henry would have struck off his head, cardinal's hat and all. And you have no one to protect you. You have certain friends, no doubt. The Seymours are grateful to you. The councillor Fitzwilliam has been a go-between, helping rid the concubine. But you have no affinity of your own, no great family at your back. For when all is said, you are a blacksmith's son. Your whole life depends on the next beat of Henry's heart, and your future on his smile or frown.'

In January when I thought the king was dead, he thinks, when they burst in shouting, I leapt up and said, 'I'm coming, I'm right behind you' – but before I quit the room I sanded the paper and dried the ink, and I picked up from the desk the Turkish dagger with the sunflower handle, which lay there as an ornament: so I had one knife in the coat, and one knife extra; then I went and found Henry, and I raised him from the dead.

'I remember those little ravioli,' he says. 'At the Frescobaldi house, once Lent was over, we used to stuff them with minced pork. At the family table they liked them sprinkled with sugar.'

'How typical of bankers,' Chapuys says, sniffing. 'More money than taste.'

Wriothesley sails into Austin Friars as they come from evening prayers. Richard says, 'Call-Me is here, but you've had enough today – shall I sneck him off?'

'No. I want him to go and see Mary.'

'You trust him with that?'

'I will send Rafe too, if the king will spare him. But Mary is tender of her status and she may think Rafe is too much associated with ...'

'With us,' Richard says.

Mr Wriothesley, on the other hand, descends from a family of heralds. Heralds have a status all of their own, and they are keen on according to others what is due to them and no more. Call-Me comes in with parchments in hand: 'When shall we begin addressing you as Lord Cromwell, sir?'

'Soon as you like.'

'I wonder ... now that you are elevated, would you like a fresh look at your provenance?' He unrolls coloured devices. 'Here we see the arms of Ralph Cromwell, of Tattershall Castle, who was Lord Treasurer to the great Harry who conquered France.'

We have been here before. 'I am nothing to Lord Ralph's folk, nor they to me. You know my father and where I come from. If you don't, you can ask Stephen Gardiner. He sent a man down to Putney to dig out my secrets.'

Call-Me longs to ask, and did he? But he holds to his point. 'You should revisit the matter. The king would feel more at ease with you.'

Richard says, 'He could hardly be more at ease than he is.'

'But you would be the more esteemed if you had an ancient name. Not just by your peers, but by all the common people, and in foreign courts too. They slight you, abroad – they are saying that Henry has dismissed you and appointed two bishops to govern.'

'I would lay a wager one of them is Bishop Stephen.' He admires these speculative worlds, that grow up in the crevices between truths. 'What else are they saying?'

'That the lovers of the concubine have been quartered, she forced to watch before she was burned. They take us for barbarians like themselves. They say her whole family is locked up. I can see the lady's father will have trouble convincing people he is not dead too. I suppose you spared him because …' Call-Me hesitates. 'I suppose he fell in with your wishes, and you need to show people that you can reward them for doing that.'

If you call it a reward, the life Thomas Boleyn will lead now. He says, 'I believe in economy of means. The headsman has to be paid, you know, Wriothesley. Do you think he practises his trade *gratis*?'

Call-Me checks, and blinks, and takes a breath: earnest, he sticks to his task. 'They are saying that the Lady Mary is back at court already, and wearing the jewels of the late queen. They say that the king has in mind to marry her to the French king's son, the Duke of Angoulême, and that the prince will come and live in England, to be trained up as king.'

'I hear she is disinclined to matrimony.'

'You have broached it then?'

'One must keep French hopes alive.'

Call-Me is not sure whether he is being teased. He – Lord Cromwell – examines the other Lord Cromwell's coat of arms. 'I prefer the Cornish choughs I got from the cardinal. Anything today from Calais?'

In Calais, the spites and feuds of the leading families are enclosed by the town walls: those crumbling walls, England's defence, are a sink of expenditure, and riddled by rumour, undermined by intrigue. Calais is a sort of purgatory; pained, one waits and waits, not for forgiveness but for a favourable wind. What is said in the citadel is carried across the sea, hissing, rustling, amplified by the waves; it breaks against the king's attention in Whitehall. Calais is our last foothold on the mainland. Its pale is our last territory. It should be ruled by the strongest and steadiest man the king has. Instead it is ruled by Lord Lisle. Lisle is the king's uncle – one of old King Edward's bastards – and Henry is fond of him, having found him a genial playmate when he was a child. Already he is pestering for some advantage from recent events. Mindful of the need to be constantly in the king's thoughts, he had Harry Norris in his pocket, pushing his name forward for sinecures and promotions. That's all gone now, Norris being worm-food.

Call-Me says, 'It's Lisle's wife who causes the trouble. She is a shrew and I hear she is a papist. You know she has daughters from her first marriage? She was always trying to get one of them placed with Anne. She will want to try again with our new queen.'

'I think Jane is supplied,' he says. 'Call-Me, I want you and Rafe to go up to Hunsdon and try and talk Mary into sense. But be gentle with her. She's not well.'

Mary's letter is in his pocket. Even in his own house he dare not leave it down. Mary says she has a rheum in her head. She cannot sleep. Her teeth ache. It would comfort her to see her father. False friends keep them apart. When the false friends are cast aside or smitten by the sword of justice, when the false counsellors are elbowed into the Thames, her father the king will turn to her, she says – the scales falling from his eyes – and see her for what she is, his true heir and daughter.

But first the king must send for her. Bring her to the light of his presence. Till then she is the maiden embowered. She sits in the closed garden, ready to be discovered. She lies under an enchantment, in a thicket of thorns, and waits for someone who has the commitment to hack through.

'Go yourself, sir,' Wriothesley says.

He shakes his head.

'Perhaps you do not want to be the one to bring her bad news.'

'She loves her father,' he says. 'She cannot believe – well – but she must be brought to believe. He will not tolerate defiance. Not from a child to whom he gave life.'

The sun is declining: a last ray of warmth flits across the books on his table: the Decretals of Pope Gregory, a copy heavily annotated, and marked with the monogram 'TC' – *Thomas Cardinalis*. In the shifting twilight, shadowed like water, he can see a figure of the king's daughter: huddled into herself, her face pale and set. It entrances him, the stealthy movement of the light where she forms herself, a living ghost. She does not look at him; he looks at her. 'You must tell her, Wriothesley, "Obedience, madam, is the virtue that will save you. Obedience is not servility, either of your person or your conscience. Rather, it is loyalty."'

'Well,' Call-Me says, 'yes … if you think I should address her as you might address the House of Commons. I might suggest, I suppose, that with obedience comes some diminution of responsibility.'

'That might ease her mind. But Call-Me, don't speak to her as if she were a little girl. And don't try to frighten her. She is brave like her mother and will strike out, she is stubborn like her mother and will dig in. If she angers you, step back and let Rafe speak. Appeal to her womanly nature. To her daughter's love. Tell her how much it hurts her father,' he puts a hand to his heart, 'tell her it hurts him, here, that she should put the dead before the living.'

The outlines of Master Wriothesley have blurred; he sinks into indistinction, as if the night were lapping at him. He would like the princess to linger, till she melts in the heat of his will: till she dissolves into acquiescence – which she will, if only he can find the right phrases to unresolve her.

'Sir,' Wriothesley says, 'I think you know something no one else does.'

'Me? I don't know anything. Nobody tells me a thing.'

'Is it something to do with Wyatt?'

Rafe has told him that verses are written against Wyatt, coded accusations and bitter jokes, circulated by the courtiers within breath of the king's own person. A paper is inserted into a prayer book, or tucked into a glove, or played instead of the king of spades. 'They are all afraid,' Call-Me says. 'They are looking over their shoulders. They don't know if more charges will be laid. I was deep in talk with Francis Bryan, and when Wyatt's name came up, he lost the thread of what he was saying, and he looked at me as if he had never seen me before.'

'Francis?' He laughs. 'He was probably drunk.'

'The women are afraid too, it seems to me. When I carried a message to Jane the queen, there were glances – hushing, and shuffling, and signs between them –'

'My poor boy! You come in and women make signs at each other? Has this happened before? Tell me what the signs were and I will try to interpret them.'

Call-Me flushes. 'Sir, it is not a joke. The queen – I mean, the other one – she is paid out for her evil dealings, but there is more. There is something else. You go into a room, you hear a door bang, you feel someone has run from your approach. But at the same time, you feel that someone is watching you.'

Someone is, he thinks.

'Everyone believes,' Call-Me says, 'that it was Wyatt's testimony that condemned Anne – but they do not know why he would give it, because they think him brave and reckless and ...'

'Witless?'

'Not that, but he is very gallant – and they think, what did Anne do to him, to turn the honey to gall? They imagined he would be buried in her tomb with her, rather than –'

No wonder you break off. Sometimes our fantasies make a leap, sudden and precise, like dancers in a line. We see the arrow chest, barely wide enough for one. 'They think Wyatt should have died for love? When they would not cross the street for it?'

He thinks of Wyatt in his prison, as dusk slips through the runnels and estuaries of the Thames, where the last light slides like silk, floating, sinking; it is the light that moves, when the stream is still. Wyatt seems distant to him, as if held in a mirror; or as if he had lived a long time ago. He says, 'Safe journey tomorrow. Remember everything Mary says. As soon as you leave her, write it down.'

He goes to his room, Christophe thumping along behind him. 'The ridiculous Mathew,' Christophe says. 'I hear he is promoted. You should send him back to Wolf Hall. He is more fit for a pig-keeper than for a servant to a lord.'

'I could go up and see Mary myself,' he says. 'There and back before anyone knew I was gone.'

He closes the door of his chamber, shutting the day out. Christophe says, 'Like when we went up to Kimbolton, in secret to see the old queen. When we stopped at the inn, and the bold wife of the innkeeper –'

'Yes. Enough.'

'– jumped into your bed. And next morning you said to me, "Christophe, pay the reckoning," and gave me your purse. And then when we got to Kimbolton we went to the church. You remember I whistled, and the priest appeared?'

He remembers the stone devil, his serpentine coils; the archangel Michael, his wings with teal-coloured feathers, his sword raised to hack.

'We all thought you would make confession. We hoped to hear it. But you did not. Besides, even if we are sorry for a thing, we cannot be forgiven if we fully mean to do it again.'

He sees himself in the glass, stripped to his shirt, a startling flash of white. Out of his brocade and velvet, his person is broad, a graceless slab of muscle and bone. His greying hair is cropped, so nothing softens the features with which God has punished him – small mouth, small eyes, large nose. He wears linen shirts so fine you can read the laws of England through them. He has a green velvet coat that was made for him last year and sent down to Wolf Hall; he has a riding coat of deep purple; he has his robe from the last coronation, a darkish crimson in which, said one of Anne's ladies, he looked like a travelling bruise. If clothes make the man, he is made; but no one ever said, even when he was young, 'Tommaso looks handsome today.' They only said, 'You've got to be up early to get ahead of that squat English bastard.' You can't even say he looks well on a horse. He just looks useful on a horse. He gets in the saddle and he goes somewhere. He sets an ambling pace, but he is there before anyone else.

The night is warm, but Christophe has lit a small, crackling fire, and set the perfume pan to burn. Sweet herbs, frankincense: these drive off contagion in any season. A bank of beeswax candles, ready for the touch of a taper; ink at his hand, his day-book ready on the table, turned to a blank leaf in case he wakes and remembers something for tomorrow's list. I think I shall rest tonight, he says to Christophe, and Christophe says, the ambassador has long departed, even Call-Me is turned out, Master Richard is at home with his wife, the king is saying his prayers, or perchance he labours with the queen to please her; birds have tucked their heads beneath their wings, the prisoners of London are snoring in the Tower and the Marshalsea, the Clink and the Fleet. In the precincts of Austin Friars, Dick Purser has loosed the watchdogs. God is in His Heaven. The bolts are on the gates.

'And I,' he says, 'am at home in my own chamber for once.' Seven years back, when Florence was besieged by the Emperor and begging for French aid, the burgesses went to the merchant Borgherini's house: 'We want to buy your bedroom.' There were fine painted panels, rich hangings and other furnishings they thought might make a bribe for King François. But Margherita, the merchant's wife, stood her ground and threw their offer back in their faces. Not everything in life is for sale, she said. This room is my family's heart. Away with you! If you want to take away my bedroom, you will have to carry your loot over my corpse.

He would not die for his furniture. But he understands Margherita – always supposing the story to be true. Our possessions outlast us, surviving shocks that we cannot; we have to live up to them, as they will be our witnesses when we are gone. In this room are the goods of people who can no longer use them. There are books his master

Wolsey gave him. On the bed, the quilt of yellow turkey satin under which he slept with Elizabeth, his wife. In a chest, her carved image of the Virgin is cradled in a quilted cap. Her jet rosary beads are curled inside her old velvet purse. There is a cushion cover on which she was working a design, a deer running through foliage. Whether death interrupted her or just dislike of the work, she had left her needle in the cloth. Later some other hand – her mother's, or one of her daughters' – drew out the needle; but around the twin holes it left, the cloth had stiffened into brittle peaks, so if you pass your finger over the path of her stitches – the path they would have taken – you can feel the bumps, like snags in the weave. He has had the small Flanders chest moved in here from next door, and her furred russet gown is laid up in spices, along with her sleeves, her gold coif, her kirtles and bonnets, her amethyst ring, and a ring set with a diamond rose. She could stroll in and get dressed. But you cannot make a wife out of bonnets and sleeves; hold all her rings together, and you are not holding her hand.

Christophe says, 'You are not sad, sir?'

'No. I am not sad. I am not allowed to be. I am too useful to be sad.'

My first thought was right, he says: I should not go to Mary, or not yet. Let it run … see what Rafe and Call-Me bring back. He thinks, the cardinal would have known how best to manage this. Wolsey always said, work out what people want, and you might be able to offer it; it is not always what you think, and may be cheap to supply. It didn't work with Thomas More. He was a drowning man who struck away the hands stretched to save him. Offer after offer was made, and More took none. The age of persuasion has ended, as far as Henry is concerned; it ended the day More dripped to the scaffold, to drown in blood and rainwater. Now we live in an age of coercion, where the king's will is an instrument reshaped each morning, as if by a master-forger: sharp-pointed, biting, it spirals deep into our crooked age. You will see Henry, profound in deception, take an ambassador's arm and charm him. Lying gives him a deep and subtle pleasure, so deep and subtle he does not know he is lying; he thinks he is the most truthful of princes. Henry says that he, Cromwell, is too humble a man to deal with foreign grandees, so he stands against the wall and keeps his eyes on Henry's face. Afterwards he will have his own hurried conversation with the ambassador: *Cremuel, am I to believe him this time?* And he will say earnestly, You should, ambassador, you must. *Do you think I am new-hatched? He tells me this now, but what will he say next week?* Trust me, ambassador, I swear I will keep him to his word. *Yes, but by what do you swear, now you have thrown out the holy relics?*

Then he puts his hand on his heart. By my faith, he says. 'Ah, Master Secretary,' the ambassador will say, 'your hand is on your heart too often. And your faith I think is a very light matter and changeable from day to day.'

And then the ambassador will glance over his shoulder, and edge towards him. 'Meet me, Cremuel. Let us dine.'

Then the dice is shaken in the bone cup – and never mind who is humble. He will deal and deal again and, brimming to confide, the ambassador will unfold his grievances. *My master, my master the Emperor, my master the king ... he is very like your master in some ways ... and I should hazard, my dear Cremuel, that day by day your anxieties are not unlike mine.* The envoy will then proffer little bluffs and double-bluffs, looking keenly to see how they are taken; and when Cremuel nods and says, 'I see,' then they are gaining firmer ground; with the lift of an eyebrow, the flicker of a smile, they proceed, negotiating the necessary falsities with the ease of men skipping over puddles. His new friend will understand that princes are not as other men. They have to hide from themselves, or they would be dazzled by their own light. Once you know this, you can begin to erect those face-saving barriers, screens behind which adjustments can take place, corners for withdrawal, open spaces in which to turn and reverse. There is a smooth pleasure in the process, a gratifying expertise, but there is a price too: a bilious aftertaste, a jaundiced fatigue. Jean de Dinteville had said to him once, have you ever considered, Cremuel, why do we lie and lie? And when we make our deathbed confession, will force of habit carry us to Hell?

But that again was a ploy; just something the Frenchman was trying out on him. In Henry's own council chamber, with or without the king's presence, there is a conspiracy of gestures, of sighs, a counter-point to what can be spoken aloud; but when a messenger from the privy chamber comes in to say, 'His Majesty is delayed,' there is a shuffle and covert relief. The councillors may speculate as to why: gone riding, perhaps, or bowels recalcitrant, or just feeling lazy – or tired, who knows, of the sight of our faces? Someone will say, 'Master Secretary, will you?' And led by him through the agenda, they will begin their round of scrapping and cavilling, but with a furtive cama-raderie they would not like Henry to witness, for he prefers his coun-cillors divided. If councillors frown at the foe, the king can smile – ever-gracious prince. If they bully, he can reward. If they insist, he lulls, he coaxes, charms. It is his councillors, as mean a crew as ever walked, who carry his sins for him: who agree to be worse people, so Henry can be better.

It is June and the nights are short; but when the city gates are closed, the fires covered, then he, Cremuel, draws the bedcurtains and is shut in with the business of England. Outside this room, this bed, a long darkness stretches away, to the seashore and across the waves: to the walls of Calais, through the sleeping fields of France, across the dark snow peaks and through Italy to the sultanates. Night covers London like a blanket, as if we were gone already and under our pall, black velvet and a cold silver cross. How many lives have we, where we sleep and dream, and lost languages flow back into our mouths? All knew Cromwell, when he was a child. Put an Edge on It, they called him – because his father sharpened knives. Before he was twelve, he was his father's little debt collector: amiable, smiling, tenacious. At fifteen he was on the road with his bundle, bruised and fleeing, heading for another bruising and another war; but at least, as a soldier of King Louis, he was paid to receive blows. He spoke French then, the argot of the camp. He spoke whatever language you need for trading and bartering – anything from a canvas sack to a saint's image, tell me what you want, I'll get it. At eighteen, two of his lives were behind him. His third life began in Florence, in the courtyard of the Frescobaldi house, when he crawled smashed from the battlefield; propping himself against the wall, he saw with glazed eyes his new field of endeavour. In time the master called him upstairs: the young Englishman, able to disentangle the affairs of his compatriots, and then to become perfect in the business of his new masters, trusted, discreet, reverent to his elders, never fatigate, nor despondent, nor overthrown by any demand. He is not as other Englishmen, his masters said, when they sent him to their friends: does not brawl in the street, does not spit like a devil, carries a knife but keeps it in his coat. In Antwerp he began afresh, clerk to the English merchants. He is Italian, they cried, full of sleight and guile – whisking up a profit out of air. That was his fourth life: *pays bas*. He spoke useful Spanish, and the Antwerp tongue. He left it – left the widow Anselma in her waterside house full of shadows; you must go home, she said, and meet a young Englishwoman of good fortune, and I hope she will make you happy at bed and at board. In the end she said, Thomas, if you do not leave now I shall pack your bundle and throw it in the Scheldt – *take this boat*, she had said, as if she thought there might never be another.

His next life was with his wife, his children, with his master the great cardinal. This is my real life, he thought, I have arrived at it now: but the moment you think that, you are due to take up your bundle again. His heart and mind travelled north, with the cardinal into exile; it ended on the road, and they buried him at Leicester, dug in with Wolsey. His sixth life was as Master Secretary, the king's servant. His seventh, Lord Cromwell, now begins.

First we must, he thinks, have a ceremony: crown Queen Jane. For Anne Boleyn I filled the streets with speaking saints, with falcons the height of men. I unspooled a mile of blue, like a path to Heaven, from the abbey door to the coronation chair: I costed it by the yard and, lady, you walked it. Now I must begin again: new banners, painted cloths with the emblem of the phoenix; with the day star, the gates of Heaven, the cedar tree and the lily among thorns.

He stirs in his sleep. He is walking the blue, the waves. In Ireland they want longbows, and good bows come in at five marks for twenty. In Dover they want money for wages for the king's works on the walls. They want spades, scoops and forty dozen shovels, and they want them yesterday. I must make a note, he thinks, indent for them, and I must find out what ails the women at court. Call-Me has seen it, I have seen it. There is a story beneath the story. They have secrets not yielded yet.

George Boleyn's widow, Jane, is down in Kent, trying to pick up her affairs and face her future; she has written to him about her want of money. The Earl of Worcester's wife, Beth, has gone off to the country carrying her big belly. Not his child, despite what the gossips say. If it is a boy, the earl may fuss about its provenance. If a girl, he may shrug and agree to own her. Women can be out in their reckoning. Their midwives can mislead them.

Once in Venice, he thinks, I saw a woman painted on a wall high above the canal, stars and moon at her back. 'Hold up that torch,' his friend Karl Heinz had said. 'Tommaso, do you see her?' And for an instant he did; from the wall of the German House, she looked down at Cremuello, come all the way from Putney. He was her pilgrim, she his shrine; naked, garlanded, she touched her burning heart.

When Anne died, four women attended her. They waded in her blood. Their faces were veiled and he does not believe they were the same women who had watched and waited with her through the final week, women he had planted around her to record all she said. He believes that the king, beseeched by God knows who, had allowed her to choose her own companions for her last walk over the rough ground, the wind pulling at her clothes, and her head turning, turning, for news that never came.

Lady Kingston, he thinks, would tell me who those women were. But must I know? They will have memories of the day. They might try to share them.

Leave me, he says to them, I need to sleep. Stay at the corners of the bed, under your draperies. Swaddle that gasping head in cloth and wrap it round and round. You know what Medusa does. You cannot look in her face. You must trap her image in polished steel. Gaze into the mirror of the future: the unspotted glass, *specula sine macula*. We will dress the city for Jane. At every corner a paradise, with a maiden seated in a rose arbour, the roses being striped, argent, vermilion; a serpent coiled about the apple tree, and singing birds, trapped by Adam, hanging in cages from the bough.

Tomorrow he will answer the letter from George Boleyn's widow. Jane wants to get hold of her late husband's plate and goods. She has nothing but a hundred marks a year, and it's not enough for a gentle-woman who will never marry again: for who will take on a woman who trotted in to Thomas Cromwell and accused her own husband of sleeping with his sister and planning to murder the king?

We shall not escape these weeks. They recapitulate, always varied and always fresh, always doing and never done. When Anne was arrested, every hour had brought him letters from Kingston, the Constable of the Tower. Rafe scrutinised them, marking some, filing others. 'Sir William says the queen still talks of how the king will send her to a nunnery. Then in the next breath, of how she will go to Heaven, because of the good deeds she has done. He says she keeps laughing. She makes jokes. Says she will be known hereafter as Anne the Headless.'

'Poor woman,' Wriothesley said. 'I doubt she will be known at all.'

Rafe looked down at the letter. 'I will give you Kingston's phrase. "This lady has much joy and pleasure in death."'

'It sounds to me as if she is in terror,' Richard Cromwell said.

'If that is so,' said Call-Me-Risley, 'her chaplains should attend to it.'

'And also,' Rafe read, 'she wishes Master Secretary to know that seven years after her death a great punishment – the nature of which she does not specify – will fall on the land.'

'Good of her to hold back,' he said.

'Anne may find,' Rafe said, 'that God will not jump to her bidding, as men did.' He had opened another letter, run his eyes over it: 'George Boleyn wants to see you, sir. A matter that touches his conscience.'

'He wants to confess?' Wriothesley raised an eyebrow. 'Why would he do it now, when the sentence is already passed, his proven offences so rank that the most merciful prince who ever reigned would not remit his punishment? For I should think that if he were to be excused the penalty, the common people would stone him in the street; or failing that, God would strike him down.'

'And we should spare God the trouble,' Richard said. 'He has much to do.'

He had noted Wriothesley's darting look. The boys are beginning to scrap over him, who controls access. 'Lord Rochford leaves debts,' he said, holding up the letter. 'He wants me to put his affairs in order.'

'I should not have thought George would care,' Rafe said. 'It seems I fail in charity. I'll go for you, sir, shall I?'

He had shaken his head. What is he, George Boleyn, but a man who got up to glory because his two sisters worked for him, on their backs: first Mary in the king's bed, then Anne. But when the dying ask for you, you must appear in person.

Later, leading him into the Martin Tower, Kingston said, 'It seems only you will do, Master Secretary. You'd think he'd have a friend. But then,' he glanced about him, 'his friends are in like case, I suppose.'

George was reading a book of devotion. 'Sir, I knew you would help me.' Scrambling to his feet, his words tumbling out: 'There are debts I owe, and sums owed to me –'

'Wait, my lord.' He held up a hand. 'Should I send for a clerk?'

'No, everything is here.' A heap of papers on the table; George pawed through. 'Also, I have a company of players. Can you give them employment? I would not like to see them put out on the road.'

He can. He means to divert the Londoners with certain spectacles. 'Monks and their impostures,' he says. 'Farnese in his court at Rome, among his sycophants.'

George was eager. 'We have everything needful. We have a pope's hat, and croziers and stoles, we have bells, scrolls, and asses' ears for the monks to sport. One of my company, he plays at Robin Goodfellow, he comes with broom and sweeps before the actors. Then comes again with candle, to signify the play is done. Here, sir.'

He thrust papers at him. 'The king gets everything, my debts too –
but these small people who owe me, I don't want them harassed.'

He took the papers. 'Never too late to consider your fellow man.'

George flushed. 'I know you think me a great sinner. And so I am.'

George, he saw, was not well. The skin beneath his eyes was
bruised, and he was ill-shaven, as if he could not sit still for the barber.
He sank down into his chair; his hand gripped the chair arm, to
control its shaking, and he looked down at it as if it were strange to
him, and it was true it appeared shockingly naked. 'I have given my
rings into safekeeping.' He held up his other hand. 'But my wedding
ring, I can't …'

It will come off later, when your hands are cold. Who will wear
George's jewels? His wife will sell them. 'Do you want anything, my
lord? Kingston does all he should?'

'I wish I could see my sister, but I suppose you would not permit
it. Better she should settle her mind and frame herself to meet God.
The truth is, Master Secretary' – he gave a little laugh – 'I cannot
imagine meeting God. I am already dead by the law, but I do not
seem to know it. I wonder how I am still breathing. I need to write
myself a letter, perhaps, to explain it, or … can you explain it to me,
Master Cromwell? How I am alive and dead at the same time?'

'Read your gospel,' he said. He thought, I should have sent Rafe
after all. He would have been too proud to break down in front of
Rafe.

'I have read the gospel, but not followed it,' George said. 'I think
I have hardly understood it. If I had done so, I would be a living man
as you are. I should have lived quiet, away from the court. And
disdained the world, its flatteries. I should have eschewed all vanities,
and laid aside ambition.'

'Yes,' he said, 'but we never do it. None of us. We have all read the
sermons. We could write them ourselves. But we are vain and ambitious all the same, and we never do live quiet, because we rise in the
morning and we feel the blood coursing in our veins and we think,
by the Holy Trinity, whose head can I stamp on today? What worlds
are at hand, for me to conquer? Or at the least we think, if God made

me a crewman on his ship of fools, how can I murder the drunken captain, and steer it to port and not be wrecked?'

He was not sure if he had spoken aloud. George did not seem to think so. He had put a question, and was waiting for an answer, leaning forward, hands joined on the table. 'Did Tom Wyatt claim he had tupped my sister?'

'His evidence was private. It was not given in court.'

'But it reached the king. I don't know how Wyatt can make such claims, and live. Why Henry does not strike him dead on the spot.'

'After a certain point, the king was not concerned with her chastity.'

'You mean, what's one man more?' George flushed. 'Master Secretary, I do not know what you call this, but you cannot call it justice.'

'I don't call it anything, George. Or if I must, I call it *necessità*.'

He was aware of George's pisspot in the corner. As if noting his delicate attention to it – as if his nostrils had twitched – George said, 'I would empty it myself, but they will not let me out.' He opened his hands. 'Master Secretary, I will not dispute with you. Neither verdict nor sentence. I know why we are dying. I am not the fool you have always thought me.'

To that, he had said nothing. But George pushed back his chair and followed him to the door: 'Master, pray to God to strengthen me on the scaffold. I must give an example if, as I think, we observe order of rank –'

'Yes, my lord, you will be first.'

Viscount Rochford. Then the gentlemen. Then the lute player. 'It would have been better to send Mark before us,' George said. 'Being a common man, he is the most likely to give way. But I suppose the king would not have the order broken.'

And at this, he burst into tears. He threw out his arms, a swordsman's arms, young, strong, springing with life, and locked them around Thomas Cromwell as if grappling with Death. His body trembled, his lower limbs shook, he sagged and staggered as he rehearsed what he would never let the world see, his fear, his incredulity, his hope that this was a dream from which he might wake: his eyes slitted by tears, his teeth chattering, his hands blindly grasping, his head seeking a shoulder where it might rest.

'God bless you,' he had said. And he had kissed Lord Rochford, as one gentleman might, leaving another. 'You will soon be past your pain.' Going out, he had said to the guards, 'Empty his pisspot, for God's sake.'

And now he is awake, in his own house. George recedes, and the taste of his tears. There are footsteps in the room. He pulls aside the bedcurtains: heavy brocade, embroidered with acanthus leaves. It is half-light. I have hardly slept, he thinks. Sometimes, if you think of money as it flows in, flows out, you can drowse; the river brings it, you comb it from the shore. But then persons step into his dream: *Sir, if you require clerks for the king's new enterprise, my nephew is exact with numbers* … It is no easy matter, to break up the monasteries. It is only the small houses, and even so. Some of them have land in ten counties. Real property and movables add themselves, assets for the king's treasury … but then out of those sums subtract the monks' debts and liabilities, the pensions, settlements, annuities. He has had to start up a new department to handle the work of survey and audit, collection and disbursement. *Sir, my son is learning Hebrew and seeks a post where he can also employ his Greek* … He has thirty-four boxes stuffed with papers, left over from when he did such work for Wolsey. He must arrange their carriage. *Can your son shift heavy weights?* Perhaps Richard Riche should keep the boxes at his house. Freshly appointed, he is Chancellor of Augmentations, and there are no premises yet for the new court, just some space in the Palace of Westminster he must contest with mice. It won't do, he thinks. I shall build us a house.

On the sword of the Calais headsman, a prayer was written. 'Show me,' he said. He remembered the incised words, their feel under his fingers. Anne's lovers died by the axe, and when they were dead they were stripped. Five linen shrouds. Five bodies in them. Five severed heads. On the day the dead rise, they hope to recognise themselves. What kind of blasphemy would it be, to mismatch heads and bodies?

The sheer ineptitude of these people at the Tower, you would not believe it. When the sodden load was tumbled from a cart, bare of any badge of rank, they found they had no note of who was who. He was not there – he was at Lambeth, with the archbishop – so they turned to his nephew Richard: 'What do we do now, sir?'

He thinks, I would have opened the shrouds and looked at their hands. Norris had a scar in his palm. Mark's fingers were calloused from the lute-strings. Weston had torn nails, like the child he was. George Rochford … George still wore his wedding ring. And the one remaining, that must be Brereton – unless, in error, they had severed the head of some passer-by?

What I need, he thinks, are men who can count. Keep track of five heads and five bodies, thirty-four boxes of papers. *Can your son count? Does he mind being out in all weathers? Will he ride the winter roads?* Officers have been appointed for Augmentations, honest and able men: Danaster and Freeman, Jobson and Gifford, Richard Paulet, Scudamore, Arundell, Green. Did he appoint Waters, so he could introduce him to Spillman? Then his friend Robert Southwell, and Bolles and Morice and – who? Who's missing?

When Anne was cut in two pieces the man from Calais showed him the sword and he passed his fingers over the prayer. The steel is cold and his fingers numb; when I am cold, I shall slide off this wedding ring. He walks towards, always towards the king, his naked hands held out, no weapon. Three silken gentlemen, in his dream, turn to watch him pass, Howard faces stamped with Howard sneers. Thomas Howard the Greater, Thomas Howard the Lesser. Half-waking he asks himself, what is the Lesser *for*? What does he do with his time? It is he who is the bad poet. His lines go thump and flop. *Me/see. Too/do. Thing/bring. Flip-flap*, they go, *pit-pat*.

Don't count Howards, he thinks. Count clerks. Beckwith, I did forget Beckwith. Southwell and Green. Gifford and Freeman, Jobson and Stump – William Stump. Who could forget Stump?

Me. Evidently.

You need to write everything down, he tells his people. Distrust yourself. Human memory is fallible. You are Augmentations men.

Twenty pounds per annum plus generous expenses. You will never be at home, always quartering the kingdom, slicing it; you will kill horses under you, when the business of revenue is urgent. Each house of monks has different obligations, and different customs, personnel. Certain abbots say 'Spare us'; he says, perhaps. Pay in two years' income to the Treasury and we may give you a stay. He must steady the pace of closures, because the monks – those who wish – must be found places in larger houses. Auditors must be appointed. Several are in place already, and three are called William. And there is Mildmay and Wiseman, Rokeby and Burgoyne. But not Stump. Get out of my dream, Stump. In Christ's time there were no monks, no Stump either. The court must have messengers, it must have an usher; there must be someone to keep back the tide of petitioners, yet open the door. Put the usher on a *per diem*, he will make enough from gratuities; wouldn't you want the door opened to you, if you stood to make your way in the world? Fortune, your gate is unlatched: Thomas Lord Cromwell, stroll through.

Now Austin Friars begins to shape like the house of a great man, its front lit by oriel windows, its small town garden expanding into orchards. He has bought up the parcels of land that adjoin it, some from the friars, and some from the Italian merchants who are his friends and live in this quarter. He owns the neighbourhood, and in his chests – in a walnut chest carved with laurel wreaths, in an armoire that's higher than Charles Brandon – he keeps the deeds that have divided, valued and named it. Here are his freedoms and titles, the ancient seals and signatures of the dead, witnessed by city wardens and sergeants, by aldermen and sheriffs whose chains of office are melted for coin, whose corpses rest under stone. Citizen tailors, citizen skinners have plied their trades here, Broad Street and Swan Alley and London Wall. Two sisters have inherited a garden; before their husbands sell it to the friars, they stroll under the fruit trees together, skins fresh in the apple-scented evening, fingers of Isabella resting on Margaret's arm: through the braided pattern of branches they look into the sky, and their feet in pattens leave bruises on the grass. A vintner sells a warehouse, a chandler conveys a shop:

the warehouse and the shop come to the prior, a century rolls by and then – his finger tracks them – they come to me. Careful, do not smudge them, their names are not yet dry, Salomon le Cotiller and Fulke St Edmund. Here are their seals, showing rabbits, lions, flowers and saints, a bird with fledglings in her nest; the city's arms, a horseshoe, a porcupine and the Sacred Heart. History inks the skin: it writes on the hide of sheep long slaughtered, or calves who never breathed; the dead cut away the ground beneath us, so that when he descends a stair at Austin Friars, the tread falls away under his foot, and below him there is another stair, no longer visible except in the mind's eye; and down it goes, to the city where the legions of Rome left their ashes beneath the earth, their glass in the soil, their bones in the river. And down it plunges and down, into the subsoil of himself, through France and Italy and the *pays bas*, through the lowlands and the quicksands, by the marshes and meadows estuarine, through the floodplains of his dreams to where he wakes, shocked into a new day: the clang of the anvil from the smithy shakes the sunlight in a room where, a helpless child, he lies swaddled, startled from sleep, feeling as if for the first time the beat of his own heart.

In his room at the Tower, Thomas Wyatt is sitting at the table where he left him, in the same bright light, as if he has not moved since the day of Anne's death. He has a book before him, and he does not lift his gaze from it, much less rise or greet them: simply says, 'You would like this, Master Secretary. It is new.'

He picks up the book. Verses of Petrarch; he leafs through. Wyatt says, 'In this edition the verses are arranged in an order that corresponds to the poet's life. They tell a story. Or they seem to. I always want a story, don't you?' When he looks up, his blue eyes are dazzling. 'Let me out. I cannot sit here a day longer.'

'Just now the king has decided that it was in the court of France that Anne was seduced into losing her maidenhead. I want him to be fixed in that opinion, and not reminded of any Englishmen who may have been near her. You are safer here.'

'I will go down to Kent. I won't hover in his sight. I will go anywhere you bid me.'

'You like to be on the road,' he says. 'Never mind the destination.'

Wyatt says, 'I have been adding my life up – it is ten years this year since I first went to France, with Cheney on his embassy. They said my legs were young and my stomach strong, so I was the go-between, tossed on the waves. I would turn up sweating and desperate with a killed horse under me, and Wolsey would say, "Where in God's name have you been, boy – picking flowers?" The Lord Cardinal was a great man for speed.'

'He was a great man for everything.'

'Now the Boleyns and their friends are gone, you have made space for yourself. You can put your own people close to the king. Harry Norris, I see why you would want him gone. Brereton, George Boleyn – I see the benefit to you. But Weston was a boy. And Mark may have had a jewel in his bonnet, but I warrant he had not twenty pence to buy his shroud.'

'Poor Mark,' he says. 'He knelt at Anne's feet and she laughed at him.'

He imagines the cart, the pile of corpses, a canvas over them smeared and stippled with blood; the boy's hand tumbling out, as if wanting to be held. He says, 'I only wanted Mark as a witness. But he accused himself. I did not hurt him.'

'I believe you. Though no one else does.'

'Give me a few days. A week, at the outside. When you get out you will have a hundred pounds from the Treasury.'

'I don't want it.'

'Believe me, you do.'

'They will say it is a reward for betraying my friends.'

'Jesus Christ!' He slaps Petrarch down on the table. 'Your friends? What friendship did they ever show you? What was Weston – a grinning puppet who couldn't keep his prick in his breeches. Or Brereton, that braggart – I tell you, his folk in the north are well-warned. They think they write the law. But those days are done. There are no private kingdoms now. There is one law, and that is the king's.'

'Be careful,' Wyatt says. 'You are on the brink of explaining yourself.'

Or I am just on the brink, he thinks. 'I sweated blood to save you, Tom. Your life hung by a hair.'

Wyatt looks up. 'I will tell you why I am still alive. It is not because I fear death or am content to live in shame. It is because a woman is having my child. If it were not for that, then if you wanted Anne dead you would have had to contrive it some other way.'

He stares at him. 'Who is she?' He sits down on a three-legged stool. 'You know you will tell me sooner or later.' A thought strikes him. 'Tell me it is not Edward Darrell's daughter. She who followed Katherine, when the king banished her?'

Wyatt inclines his head.

'Can you not love a woman, except she is poised to do you harm?'

'I am as I am. It is a poor excuse.'

He says, 'I remember Bess Darrell as a child when she was in the Dorset household. I used to do business for them. I know her father was bound in loyalty – he was Katherine's chamberlain. But he is dead now, and the girl was never bound.'

'You think she would have been better off with Anne Boleyn?'

Fair point. 'Better in a nunnery. But I suppose you have your ways.'

'I suppose I have,' Wyatt says sadly. 'I love her, and I have loved her a long time. It is only because she was away from the court we could keep it secret.'

When I rode up to Kimbolton, he thinks, to Katherine – was Bess there in the shadows? He remembers the old Spanish ladies; they did not trust the kitchen so they were cooking for Katherine in their own chamber, and the smell of smoke and vegetable water was trapped in their clothes. They insulted him in their own tongue, wondering aloud if he had a hairy body like Satan. He sees himself walk into Katherine's presence, sees her huddled in her furs; the invalid smell envelops him, and from the corner of his eye he sees a slight form sliding away with a bowl. He had thought at the time, her maid carries the queen's vomit covered, as if it were the sacred host. That must have been Edward Darrell's daughter, golden hair under a servant's cap.

'I begged her,' Wyatt says, 'if she would not leave Katherine, then at least to take the oath when it was put to her. What is it to you, Bess, I said, if the king wants to call himself head of his church? I cited the precedents. I argued my best. Bishop Gardiner had not more force. But she would not let Henry win the argument. She was with Katherine when she died.'

'Money?' he says.

'She had none. What Katherine left her was never paid. She has no protector if I fail. She knows I am married and nothing to be done there. She cannot go back to her family, carrying my child. I cannot send her home to Allington, my father will not receive her. I do not know who will take her in, because my wife's family have turned everyone against me. This will give them occasion to rejoice. Nothing they love more, than to see me clawing my way through thorns.'

Wyatt won't speak his wife's name, not if he can help it. He has a child with her, a boy, but God knows how he got it.

'Allington is your best hope. Shall I talk to your father?'

'He is ill. I want to spare him. I dread his contempt. And I know I have earned it.'

He wants to say, it is not contempt, it is the opposite, he loves and admires you, but fortune has made him harsh. When Henry Wyatt lay in this fortress, it was not in an airy chamber but fettered in a cell, his ears straining, waiting for the footsteps of his torturers and the rattle of their keys. Torturers do not need extraordinary means, or special instruments. Opportunities for pain lie all around, in items of common use. His gaolers pulled Wyatt's head back and wedged a horse's bit into his mouth. They poured mustard and vinegar into his nostrils, so he was half-drowned in the acrid brew, spewing out what he could, inhaling the rest. Richard the usurper came to watch him suffer, and he urged him to give up his allegiance to the Tudor, who then lay out of the realm, a man without hope or resource. 'Wyatt, why art thou such a fool? Thou servest for moonshine in the water a beggarly fugitive. Forsake him and become mine, who can reward thee.'

He would not forsake. They dropped him bleeding on the straw, in the dark. His teeth were broken and he heaved up his guts on the filthy floor. His belly was empty, the corrosive at work in his throat; he had neither clean water nor, when he could eat, did they bring him bread. Wyatt says, 'It is a pretty story, how a cat brought my father food. I never believed it, even when I was a child. I thought, it is a tale for children who are simpler than me. But now I see what it is to be locked away. Prisoners believe all sorts of things. A cat will come and save us. Thomas Cromwell will come with the key.'

'I wonder, would Bess take the oath now? Katherine is dead and it cannot offend her.'

'I have not asked her,' Wyatt says. 'Nor I would not. Surely Henry will not pursue her? He has enough people to tell him he is head of the church and stands next to God. And we hope that once the Lady Mary is back at court, she will help us. She must have a care for Bess – for a young woman alone in the world, who held her mother's hand when she was dying.'

'No doubt,' he says. 'But while you have been here with Petrarch, the world moves on. The king will require Mary to take the oath herself. If she says no, she will be in here with you.'

Wyatt looks away. 'Then you must help us. It is my honour that is at stake.'

He thinks, where was honour when you lifted Bess Darrell's skirts? He stands up from the stool and gives it a nudge with his foot. It's a miserable seat for a king's councillor. 'I'll talk to Bess. There must be a place for her somewhere. Take the king's money, Tom. You need it.'

'I will obey you,' Wyatt says, 'as my father said I should. I suppose you can err like other men, and God he knows, you may be heading for disaster. But for me all roads lead there. I reach the crossroads and I throw the dice, and whichever comes up, it is the same – it is the swamp, or the abyss, or the ice. So I shall follow you as the gosling its mother. Or as Dante followed Virgil. Even to the underworld.'

'I doubt I'll be going further than the south coast this summer. Perhaps down to the Isle of Wight.' He picks up the book of verses.

It is unbruised, though the binding is soft as a woman's skin: a Venetian printing, the title set within a woodcut of tumbling putti, the printer's mark a sea-monster. Suppose someone saved the scraps of Wyatt's verse – the pastoral scratched on the back of an armourer's bill, the lyric a woman lays to her naked breast? If an editor applied himself to this writer's life, he would find a story to ruin many. Wyatt says, 'She never leaves me, Anne Boleyn. I see her as I saw her last, here in this place.'

He thinks, I see her too, in her little hat with the feather. With her tired eyes.

He goes out: 'Martin! Who gave Wyatt such beggarly furnishings?'

'He's not complained, sir. Mind you, a gentleman – he doesn't.'

'But I'm a lord,' he says. 'And I'm complaining.'

He thinks, I didn't notice that whoreson stool when I visited the prisoner before. But I can be forgiven, as I had just come from watching the Calais executioner perform his trick.

At Austin Friars, Gregory is waiting: 'You are sent for by Fitzroy.'

'I saw Wyatt,' he says.

'And?' Gregory is anxious.

'I'll tell you later.' We shouldn't keep the king's son waiting.

'Rafe supposes Fitzroy will ask you if you are going to make him king.'

'Hush.'

'I mean, one of these days,' Gregory says. 'It's no treason to say all men are mortal.'

'No, but it's not your best idea either.' He thinks, that was Anne Boleyn's mistake. She took Henry for a man like other men. Instead of what he is, and what all princes are: half god, half beast.

Gregory says, 'Richard Riche is here. He is writing a loyal address. Shall we go and look on? I love to watch him work.'

Sir Richard goes through paperwork like a raven through a rubbish heap. Stab, stab, stab – with his pen, not a beak – till everything before him is minced or crushed or shattered, like a snail-shell burst on a stone.

'Hello, Mr Speaker,' Gregory says.

'Hello, Little Crumb,' Riche says absently.

Handsome and leisured, his boy gazes down at Sir Richard as he toils. 'Riche considers his name his destiny,' Gregory says. 'He can turn ink into cash. You have a fine mind, don't you, Ricardo?'

'Ingenious,' Riche says. 'Retentive. I would not lay a claim beyond that.'

Riche's duty is to welcome the king, when he opens Parliament. 'May I read to you, sir? I have got some way with it.'

He sits. 'Pretend I am the king.'

'Let me get you a better hat,' Gregory suggests.

Riche says, 'By your leave, I am ready to begin.'

He reads. Gregory fidgets: 'You remember the hat Ambassador Chapuys had? We wanted to borrow it for our snowman?'

'Hush,' he says. 'Give heed to Mr Speaker.'

'I wonder what happened to it.'

Riche breaks off, frowning. 'You do not like my beginning?'

'I think the king will like it.'

'I next compare him to Solomon for wisdom –'

'You can't go wrong with Solomon.'

'– then Samson for strength, and Absalom for beauty.'

'Wait,' Gregory says, 'Absalom had luxuriant hair, or else he could not have been caught by it in the boughs of a tree. The king's hair is … well … it is less profuse. He may think you are mocking him.'

'No one will suspect Mr Speaker of mockery,' he says firmly.

'Still,' Gregory says. 'The conduct of Absalom was often deplorable.'

'Put your speech aside,' he says to Riche. 'Come and see Fitzroy with me.'

Riche is more than ready. Christophe runs up as they are leaving. 'Do not go without me, sir. What if some ruffian accosts you? Now you are a lord, you must be attended with force at all times.'

'And you are force, are you?' Riche is amused.

'Let him come with us, he likes to be useful.'

Increasingly, he thinks Christophe's dull appearance an advantage. No one would be cautious in front of such a churl. As they go out, he takes him by the front of his livery coat, straightens him, dusts him. 'You're supposed to do this for me,' he says. 'Were you walking about in my room in the night?'

'In the night I was asleep,' Christophe says. 'It was some old ghost, I suppose.'

'Surely not,' Riche says. 'I never heard of ghosts that walk in June.'

There's something in that. It was the veiled ladies – living women, as far as one knows – who attended him, till dawn came and they faded into the wall. He remembers the dappling of their garments, the streaks of darkness where they had wiped the queen's blood on their robes.

The king has gone hunting; but because of some anxiety of his doctors, his son has stayed in London, at St James's, the palace they have been carving out of the site of the old hospital. They have cleared and drained the ground, which was flooded by the Tyburn, and now a pleasant park stands all about. It is a retreat for the king and his family, away from the crowds that surge around Whitehall.

Inside the gateway, the courtyard is piled with scaffolding, and as they step inside workmen's shouts greet them, and the noise of chipping and hammering. At the sight of lords, the clamour falls silent, but the space still echoes with the sounds of metal against stone. A labourer slides down a ladder and pulls off his cap. 'We're knocking down the HA-HAs, sir.'

The initials, he means, of Henry and the late queen: so fondly intertwined, like snakes breeding.

'I want you to leave off for an hour, while I talk to my lord Richmond.'

The man knocks dust off his cap. 'We dursn't, sir.'

'Obey this man,' Christophe says.

'You'll be paid for the time,' he urges.

'The master of works will need it in writing.'

He drops his hand flat on the man's head, draws him nose to nose. 'Why don't I write your gaffer a love letter? Tell me his name and I'll put his initials in a heart.' He can smell the man's sweat. 'Christophe, go out to the kitchen and ask for bread, ale and cheese for these fellows. Tell them Cromwell said so.'

The man rams his cap back on. 'It's dinner time anyway. When you see King Harry, tell him we're raising a beaker to the new bride.'

Behind the presence chamber, in a small panelled cabinet, the young Duke of Richmond receives them as an invalid, wearing a long gown and a nightcap. 'I ran a fever last night. So once again my physicians will not let me stir.'

A few spots of rain spatter the window. 'It's no sort of day, sir. Better indoors.'

'It's not the sweating sickness,' Riche says reassuringly.

'No,' the boy says. 'Or I would not have summoned you here, masters, lest you be infected.'

They bow, thankful that their lives are considered: common men, such as they be.

'Nor the plague,' Riche adds. 'There is none in fifty miles. At least, not yet.'

He laughs out loud. 'Remind me to keep you from my bedside, if ever I take sick. Is that the way to lift my lord's spirits?'

Stiffly, Riche begs the duke's pardon. But he is puzzled: what was the joke?

The boy says, 'Riche, I thank you for your gentle attendance, but now I wish to confer with Master Secretary.'

Riche is inclined to stand his ground. 'With respect, my lord, Master Secretary has no secrets from me.'

He thinks, how profoundly wrong you are. Riche falters, lingers, bows himself out. Fitzroy says, 'The hammering has stopped.'

'I bribed them with bread and cheese.'

'They cannot work quick enough for me. I want her gone, that woman. All traces. At least, everything visible.' The boy casts a glance at the window, as if someone were signalling him from outside. 'Cromwell, are there such things as slow poisons?'

He is startled. 'God save your lordship.'

'I thought perhaps, having been in Italy –'

'You suspect the late queen has poisoned you?'

'My father said she would have done it if she could.'

'But your lord father was in a state of ...' Of what? 'He was shocked by the discovery of the late queen's crimes.'

'And those crimes are greater, are they not, than common report? My lord Surrey tells me he was made privy to evidence that was never given in court. Worse was done, than was ever admitted. I would have punished her more straitly.'

How? he wonders. What would you have done, sir? Hacked her head off with a rusty kitchen knife? Burned her with green wood?

'And,' Richmond says, 'she was a witch.' His fingers, restless, tug at the string of his cap. 'Some people do not believe in witches. Though St Thomas Aquinas makes mention of them. I have heard they can sour milk, and cause cattle to abort. They can cause a horse to shy in his path – always at the same place, to the injury of the rider.'

He thinks, if it's always at the same place, the rider should keep a grip.

'They can wither a man's arm. Did not the usurper Richard suffer that fate?'

'So he maintained, and yet it was as good an arm after the curse as before.'

'Sometimes they harm children. They can do it with prayers, which they say backward. Or with poison. Do you not think it was Anne Boleyn who poisoned my lord cardinal?'

He had not expected that. Truthfully he answers, 'No.'

'Yet his end was not natural. I have been told it by wise and discreet gentlemen.'

'It may be someone bribed his physicians.' He thinks of Dr Agostino, taken from Cawood a prisoner, his feet bound under his horse. Where did he vanish to? Straight into Norfolk's custody. He cannot tell the boy that, if there is a poisoner in the case, it is likely to be his own father-in-law.

Fitzroy says, 'When I was a little child – I believe I told you once – the cardinal brought me a doll. It was an image of myself, in a robe all broidered over with the arms of England and France. I do not know where it is now.'

'I can make a search, sir. You do not think your lady mother has it?'

The boy had not thought of that. 'I do not think so. It was after we parted. She has other children now, and I suppose never thinks of me.'

'On the contrary, sir. You are the origin of her fortune, of her present honourable marriage and rank. I am sure you she remembers you every day in her prayers.'

For six or seven years, male children live with the women. Then without choice or discussion, one day they are plucked away, their hair cropped so their ears are always cold, and thrust into the sullen world where everyone finds fault and visits punishment, and until you are married there is no kindness unless you pay for it. It was not how he had been reared, of course. When he was five he was foraging for items for the smithy's scrap pile. At six he was with his father's apprentices, under their feet, accustoming himself to the white-hot sparks that leap and arc, to the ringing pitch of the anvil and the thud, thud that goes on in your brain when the day's work is done. At seven, able to curse but barely read, he was running wild like a tinker's son.

Richmond says, 'I did not know when I was a child that Wolsey was of low birth. He seemed to me a very splendid man. Well, his end was miserable. He was fortunate not to die by the axe. They tell me that his heart broke on the road, and that is what killed him.'

There is that possibility. Those who think a heart cannot break have led blessed and sheltered lives. The boy shifts in his chair. 'Do you think Jane the queen will bear a son?'

'All England knows, my lord, she comes from fertile stock.'

'Yes, but if it is true what was claimed in court, that the king cannot please a woman or serve her as he ought –'

'I recommend, sir – I earnestly recommend – drop this matter.'

But Richmond is a king's son, and he sails on. 'My brother Surrey tells me –' he means his brother-in-law – 'my brother Surrey says the Parliament has done ill, in framing the new bill of succession. They have left the king to choose his own heir, when they should have named me foremost.'

Thank God the boy had the sense to send Riche out of the room. If Riche heard that, he would be straight to Henry with the tale.

'I want to be king,' Richmond says. 'I am fitted for it. Surrey says my father should recognise that. If he should die now, I am not afraid of the whelp Eliza, for she is only the concubine's child – unless, as they say, she was a foundling picked up in the street. There is not a man in the nation who will lift a finger for her claim.'

He nods; this much is true.

'As for the Lady Mary, if I am a bastard, so is she, and I am true English and she is half-Spanish, and I am a man. Besides, they say she will not swear to my father's titles as head of the church. And if she will not, she is a plain traitor.'

'Mary will swear,' he says.

'She may say the words. She may sign a paper, if you force her. But my lord father will see through her. Mary should not thrive, nor she will not.'

When he last spoke to Richmond, the boy was content with his situation. So who can be behind this surge of unholy ambition? His father-in-law Norfolk? Norfolk might scheme, but he does it silently. No, this is Norfolk's son, that foolish, headstrong boy, pushing his friend towards a throne that is not empty. He says, 'Did my lord Surrey suggest to you –'

'I am my own man.' The boy cuts him off. 'Surrey is my friend and he gives me good counsel, but no man will dictate my actions when I am king, nor cozen me in the way my father is cozened. I will not have women lead me.'

He inclines his head. 'My lord, I cannot remake the succession. The new arrangement reflects the king's will. I do not see what I can do for you.'

'You will find a way. Every man says you are master of the Parliament. When I am king I shall reward you.'

When you are king? 'I shall hardly live so long.'

'I think you will,' Richmond says. 'My father's leg is sore, since he took his fall in January. I am advised an old wound has reopened and there is a channel in his flesh that lies open to the bone.'

'If that is true, then he bears the pain with great fortitude.'

'If that is true, it cannot remain clean. It will putrefy and he will die.'

With every breath he commits treason, and does not hear it. He sees the will stirring, inside the body becoming a man's. The strand of hair that escapes from his cap is red, the Plantagenet colour. His great-grandfather Edward would own him; the house of York would claim him; King Edward's disappeared sons, if they had lived, would have looked like this, the gleam in the eye like light on the blade of a sword; the fine skin, where the colour comes and goes, betraying every passion. Richmond says, 'If my lord cardinal were still alive, he would have made me king. He advised that I should be King of Ireland, did he not? In this pass, he would have wanted me to be King of England too.'

He turns away. 'You should rest, my lord, and let your indisposition pass.'

He thinks, lions sometimes eat their cubs. Is it any wonder?

The boy calls after him, 'Do it, Cromwell.'

He is in a state of dull astonishment, like a man dealt a blow from out of the air. God help me, what are princes? They think on murder all day long. A patricide, now: as if the season does not hold enough surprises.

Riche is leaning against the wall, gossiping with Francis Bryan. They straighten up when they see him. Bryan's jewelled eye-patch gives a knowing wink. 'Greetings from France. Bishop Gardiner sends you his special love, kiss-kiss. I'm only back till the turn of the tide. Collect dispatches. Whisper in the king's ear. Check up on you. Gardiner doesn't believe it, that you're to be a baron. He says your luck can't last.'

'Does he? Kiss him back for me.'

'Oh, I will,' Francis says. 'He wonders why you are so fond of Katherine's whelp. He claims you are protecting Mary, and it will undo you. He says – mark this – "For Henry's daughter to deny he is head of the church is as great a treason as to deny he is king." He says, "Believe me, Francis, Cromwell will go too far, this affair will bring him down."'

'Thank you,' he says. 'You are a great aid to me, Francis.'

Riche looks uneasy. Is Master Secretary ironical? Riche can't tell. He asks, 'What did Fitzroy want, sir? I suppose he is in debt?'

'How much?' A veteran spendthrift, Bryan takes an interest in a promising youngster.

'He spoke of the cardinal. He is in a fit of melancholy, I believe.'

Riche says, 'If you are uneasy about his health, should we tell the king?'

'He has the best advice. And the king will not go near him, you know how he is about any illness.'

'But the king came to see you, sir, when you had a fever.'

'Only when I was over it. And besides, it was a special Italian fever.'

A true, bone-shaking tertian: not like the little bouts of sweating and shivering that afflict those who've never been south of the Kent marshes.

'It was a signal favour.' Riche sounds envious.

The fever will come back, he thinks. And very likely, Henry will come back too. He does not believe the king is going to die soon – though a man may as well be dead, if his only son turns against him. The father loves the son, but not the son the father. The son wishes him gone. He wants to take his place. That is the way it is. Of course. It must be that way.

He thinks of the cardinal on the day of his arrest, Harry Percy's men thundering in to where he lodged: the hand he laid to his ribs. 'I have a pain,' he said. 'A pain as cold as a whetstone.' If his heart broke, who broke it? No one but the king himself.

'Shall I order the men back to work?' Riche asks.

Francis says, 'I'm told that one of Katherine's carved pomegranates is still dangling in the roof timbers at Hampton Court. I can't see it myself. The surgeons say that when you lose an eye, the sight of the other starts to fail. I shall be a blind man begging alms on the high road, and kind Bishop Gardiner will lead me.'

Rafe Sadler and Thomas Wriothesley return from Mary at Hunsdon, without a paper in hand, without her oath. Wriothesley says, 'Why did you send us, sir? You must have known we could not succeed.'

'How did she look?'

'Ill,' Rafe says.

'The king is incensed against her advisers,' he says.

'In all honesty,' Rafe says, 'I don't think it's her advisers. It's her own stubborn pride.'

'Whichever.' He is indifferent.

Wriothesley says, 'Sir, never send me there again.' Vehement, he flushes. 'If Master Sadler will not tell you how it was, then I will tell you. The house was full of Nicholas Carew's people, and servants of the Courtenay family, and others in Lord Montague's livery. They did not have your licence to be there, and they boasted, it doesn't matter now, Cromwell is naught – Mary is returning to court, and the Pope will be restored, and the world put to rights again.'

'They gave her the title of "Princess", Rafe says, 'and they did not mind who heard.'

'We greeted her as Lady Mary,' Call-Me says. 'She looked enraged. She expected the title of Princess, and she expected us to kneel to her. Then as we delivered your compliments she broke out, "Tell me how she died." All she wanted was to curse Anne Boleyn. We said, she died calmly, and Rafe said –'

'"An example of Christian resignation."' Rafe looks away, astonished by his own phrase: he was not even there.

'But she did not want to hear that. She called Anne "the creature" and said she should have been burned alive. She asked what prayers she said, was she pale, did she tremble … I did not think a young girl could be so cruel, or one person of the female sex so hate another. I could have spewed, so help me. She has a black heart, and she showed it.'

Rafe is watching Call-Me. 'Hush,' he says. 'It is hard, but it is done now. And besides, sir, Mary is not as strong in her resolve as her people think. She asked us, "What, Master Secretary does not come himself?" It's almost as if she is waiting for you. So she can take the oath and it be no blame to her. She will tell the world you have threatened her, enforced her. Rome and all Europe will believe it.'

'I had rather she obeys from free choice. Whatever the world says.'

'Obeys?' Wriothesley says. 'I never saw any person less likely to yield or obey. What does she think about, abed at night? Does she lie awake devising torments? Sir, you know I do not flinch. I know what manner of things are done. I was at the Tower, when you hung the friar up by his hands –'

'I didn't –' he says.

'– and I did not demur. I understood his cries were those of a treacherous knave who could still see his duty and save himself –'

'I didn't,' he says. 'Rafe? Tell him.'

'You misremember,' Rafe says gently. 'There was talk of hanging him up. But it only happened in your imagination.'

'It happened in the friar's imagination,' he says. 'That was the point. I set his fantasy to work.'

'Then set Mary's to work,' Call-Me says. 'See if her fantasy will sicken her, as she sickened me. She thinks her cousin the Emperor will crest the sea on a white horse and sweep her away across his saddle. Tell her that no one will rescue her, and that no one will speak for her, but her father will hurt her and bend her to his will.'

June: the Duke of Richmond walks in procession with the House of Lords. How like his father he is, onlookers say: heavy muscle already under the hot drag of the Parliament robes. His handsome face is flushed with portent, as if he feels his future in a warm breeze.

The king seems to enjoy Richard Riche's speech of welcome. He is not averse to the comparisons: King Solomon, King David. And he has forgotten that Absalom said, 'I have no son to keep my name in remembrance.'

It's not only the folk at Hunsdon who believe that with the change of queen, the tide will turn, and England go back to Rome. As sufficient answer, he – Lord Cromwell – brings in a measure: An Act Extinguishing the Authority of the Bishop of Rome. The title is a guide to its content.

As Parliament meets, so too bishops meet in Convocation. They rustle and grumble, censure and debate – old bishops, new bishops – *my* bishops, as Anne used to call them. They wrangle dawn till dusk about the sacraments of the church, their nature and number; which ceremonies are laudable, which idolatrous; who should be allowed to read the gospel, and in what language. He, Lord Cromwell, is enthroned among them as Henry's deputy, Vicegerent of the church under God and the king; where once, in Archbishop Morton's day, he was the littlest and the lowest of the boys who scrubbed vegetables in the kitchen at Lambeth Palace. Gregory exclaims, 'To think my father is over all the bishops!'

'I am not over them, I am only –' He stops. 'True. I am over them.'

Since the week of the lady's death, his archbishop has been elusive. Now, trapped in a side room, Cranmer makes himself busy, pulls out a bundle of writing. The papers are inked with amendments. 'Look,' he says, 'where Bishop Tunstall has written all over me. So now,' he picks up a quill, 'I am going to write all over Bishop Tunstall.'

'You do that,' Hugh Latimer pats his archbishop's shoulder. 'Cromwell, how is it that Richard Sampson has been made a bishop? He has so papist a flavour I think I am chewing the Bishop of Rome himself.'

Cranmer says, 'He made speed with the king's annulment, that is why, it is his reward. Though I wish the king … I wish he had elected a period of reflection, between the two …' his voice fades, '… before the new …' He puts the papers down. He rubs the corners of his eyes. 'I cannot bear it,' he says.

'Anne was our good lady,' Hugh says. 'So we thought. We were much misled.'

'I heard her last confession,' Cranmer says.

'Yes,' he says. 'And?'

'Cromwell, you do not expect me to tell you what she said?'

'No. But I thought your face might tell me.'

Cranmer turns away.

Latimer says, 'Confession is not a sacrament. Show me where Christ ordained it.'

Cranmer says, 'You will not get the king to agree.'

Henry likes to utter his sin and be forgiven. He is sincerely sorry, he will not do it again. And in this case perhaps he will not. The temptation to cut off your wife's head does not arise every year.

'Thomas ...' the archbishop says. He pauses. His face mirrors an inner struggle. 'Thomas ... about the manor at Wimbledon ...'

Hugh stares at him. Whatever he thought Cranmer was going to say, it wasn't that.

'Since it pertains to your new title,' Cranmer says, 'you will want it, I suppose. At present it belongs to me – to the archdiocese, I should say.'

'And the house at Mortlake,' he says. 'If you would. The king will compensate you.'

Hugh Latimer says, 'You can hardly demur, Cranmer. You owe Cromwell money.'

The bishops mean to beat out some statement of common faith, which will stand against the malice of ill-wishers and the misconstructions of fools; which will please the German divines, with whom they wish to come into concord, but will also assuage the fears of the king, who distrusts novelty, and German novelty above all. They mean to issue a statement, if it takes them till next Easter to do it. Considering the differences they have to reconcile, and the parties they wish to please, you would be surprised if they could contrive it before the sun goes out and the earth grows cold.

We need the counsel of dead men, Hugh Latimer says. Father Thomas Bilney should be here with us. He taught us the way and the truth. He opened our insensate hearts. But Little Bilney was burned in a ditch in Norwich, and his bones thrown to dogs: and whenever you think about it, you can hear Thomas More, chuckling.

It is Latimer, as Bishop of Worcester, whose sermon opens the session. 'Define me first these three things: what prudence is; what is the world; what light; and who be the children of the world, who of the light.'

Latimer smells of burning too. The air sparks around him as he walks.

The king, bearing in mind his daughter's care for her status, orders the Duke of Norfolk to visit her at Hunsdon and get her compliance; Norfolk, after young Richmond, ranks highest in the land.

Norfolk calls him in, to complain of a fool's errand. But the duke is, he points out, lucky to have any errand at all. In the days after his niece's death, as Norfolk admits, he did not know which way to run; except that he did good service at her trial, he thinks that Henry would have banished him and taken his title away. Now, fuming with impatience, he rattles as he paces. About his neck is a heavy gold chain, where the emblems of the Howards alternate with the Tudor rose. Under his shirt, in a filigree case, he wears the relics of saints, faded hairs and splinters of bone; on his sword hand, a stout gold band, set with a greyish diamond like a chipped tooth. 'I told Henry,' he says, 'look here, I have no parlour manners, I am no man for sweet-talk with some little coquette. If Mary were mine – but no use to think of it.' As if restraining an impulse, the duke folds one fist into the other.

The Duchess of Norfolk had once told him that when Thomas Howard wanted to marry her – she having a sweetheart already – he had stormed into her father's house and threatened to break the place up; and so she had given way to him, to her rapid regret. Perhaps Mary will do the same? The duke's voice runs on, anticipating knock-backs: '… so the girl will say … then I say … I declare the whole realm considers her obstinate, disobedient, worthy of exemplary punishment – but the king, out of his gracious and divine nature – is that right, Cromwell, do I say divine?'

'Try "fatherly". It gives the same idea, without hyperbole.'

'Right,' the duke says, uncertainly. 'Gracious and fatherly, et cetera and so forth – the king considers that as a woman, frail and inconstant, she is easily led – but she must name them, those who are feeding her obstinacy – and she must say if she will or will not recognise his full authority and submit to his laws – which frankly, it seems to me, Cromwell, is the least a king should require of a subject. Then she, et cetera and so forth, must forswear all attempts to seek remedy from Rome – is that correct?'

He nods: all quarrels are to be pursued in English and here at home.

A young man is at his elbow, bowing. It is Thomas Howard the Lesser. Ah, he thinks, I dreamed of your verses: *flip/snip, lip/pip, love/dove.*

The Greater is not pleased to see his half-brother. 'What brings you out, boy, crawling from under some trull's skirt?'

'Sir – my lord –'

'An idle generation.' Norfolk sucks his lip. 'Naught but riddles and games.'

'What would your lordship like instead?' the young man says. 'A war?'

He suppresses a smile. 'Tom Truth,' he says.

'What?' The young man jumps.

'Is that not how you style yourself? In your verses. *Your man, Tom Truth.*' He shrugs. 'The ladies share these things.'

The duke laughs – though perhaps it's more of a snarl. 'Master Cromwell here, he knows what the ladies are up to. Naught is secret from him.'

'No harm sharing verses,' he says. 'Even poor ones are not a crime.'

Tom Truth reddens. 'The king wants you, sir.'

'Me too, of course,' Norfolk says.

'No, your Grace. He only wants my lord Cromwell.' The boy turns his shoulder to the duke. 'If you please, the king has hit Sexton the jester. The fellow made a – well, a jest. Now he has got a bleeding pate. God help him, he chose the wrong moment. His Majesty has received a letter from a cousin of his, and he is screaming as if it came hot from the pit and signed by the devil. And I do not know – we do not know – which cousin writ it. He has so many.'

So many cousins. So few of them what they ought to be, loyal or true. 'Let me through,' he says. 'All will be well. Give you good day, my lord Norfolk.' He says to Tom Truth over his shoulder, 'Pole is the name of his cousin. Reginald Pole. Lady Salisbury's son.'

As he walks towards the king's apartments, there is a bounce in the soles of his boots. He is aware that in his wake, the Howards are agitated – the Lesser Thomas has grabbed the Greater's arm, and is whispering urgently. Whatever it is, it must keep.

In the guard chamber Sexton is sitting on the floor, his legs spread out before him as if he has just been felled. The injury is hardly worth rubbing, but he is holding his head and bleating, 'My brain doth leak.'

He stands over him. 'Why are you here, Patch?'

The man looks up. 'Why are you? Unless you want my job.'

'I thought you were fled. I heard the king turned you out last year.'

'Aye, he did, and beat me too, because I called his woman a ribald. And Nicholas Carew took me in, out of his charity, till my jokes were in season again. Which they are, aren't they? Now the whole world knows what Nan Bullen was. She was as common as a cart-way. She would go to it with a leper in a hedge.'

He says, 'The king has got Will Somer now. He doesn't need you.'

'Aye, Somer, Somer, that's all I hear. Sexton? Kick him out, his day's done. "Thomas Cromwell," all say, "he is good to masterless men – he took in the cardinal's folk when they were turned out." But not Patch – no, kick Patch in the ditch.'

'I'd kick you in the midden if I had my way. You mocked the cardinal, that was nothing but good to you.'

'So how am I still alive?' Sexton says. 'The four masquers are dead, who dragged the cardinal to Hell; and Smeaton too, only for making a pig's bladder of old Tom Wolsey's head, and kicking a doll up and down, and singing a ditty while winding sausages from its gut. They are dead as you could require, and I hear you buried them with their wrong heads, so when they rise on the last day, Smeaton will be George Boleyn, and the addled pate of Weston joined to Gentle Norris.'

He thinks, much occurred to shame us, but that did not occur.

'It is heavy work, executing. I suppose you were too busy to think of Patch.' Sexton hauls up his checkered robe and scratches himself. 'Lord Tom from Putney. You put the jesters out of occupation and make them beg a living. Let Somer watch himself. Who needs make a joke, when the jokes are walking and talking and calling themselves by the title of baron?'

He has to step over the man's legs. 'Pull down your clothes, and get away, Sexton. Never let me see you here again.'

When he enters the royal presence, Henry says quite pleasantly to the buzzing swarm, 'Will you allow me to have conference now with my lord Privy Seal?'

There is a stir – Henry is, for the first time, speaking his new title aloud. After the stir, a shuffle – then a scuttle backwards, bowing. They cannot go fast enough, swept by the king's stare.

Henry has a thick folio in front of him. His hand lies on it, as if forbidding it to open. 'Before you were my councillor ...' He stops, and looks into empty air. 'Pole,' he says. 'His book has come, out of Italy. My subject, my liegeman, Reginald Pole. My cousin, my trusted kin. How can he sleep at night? The one thing I cannot endure,' Henry says, 'is ingratitude, disloyalty.'

While the king goes on to enumerate the things he cannot endure, his councillor's eyes rest on the book. It is not, to him, a closed book. He had warning. He is only surprised at the extent of it. There must be three hundred leaves, each leaf veined with treason. He knows the story, but that will not stop the king's need to rehearse it – the history of the Pole family, their grievance and grudge: the long butchery before the Tudors, when the great families of England hacked each other apart on the battlefield; when they murdered each other with the headsman's axe in the kingdom's market squares, and hung body parts on town gates. The process that has put the manuscript on the table, this summer's day, began before any of us were born: before Henry Tudor landed in Milford Haven and marched through Wales under the emblem of the red dragon on a banner of white and green. That banner kept on marching, till it was laid by the victor on the altar at Paul's. He came with a ragged army, with a prayer on his lips: he came for the salvation of England, with a broom to sweep the charred bones out, and a rag to mop up the gore.

And what was left of the old regime, after the battle was won, after Richard Plantagenet was dropped naked into his grave? Old King Edward's sons vanished into the Tower and never came out. His bastards and daughters remained, and a nephew, a child not ten. After showing him to the people, the Tudor locked the child away. He never denied his title, Earl of Warwick: just denied him the right to threaten the new regime.

Henry Tudor was blessed with many children, but then they themselves must breed. A bride for Prince Arthur, the first son, must be secured among the princesses of Europe. The King and Queen of Spain offered one of their daughters, but made a stipulation. They hesitated to part with Catalina to a country so easy to destabilise. His whole reign, Henry Tudor had been plagued by dead men rising and claiming the crown; and though young Warwick was locked up, what would stop some pretender raising troops under his name? So the claimant must die: not in some hole-and-corner scuffle, some stabbing or smothering, but in daylight, on Tower Hill, by the axe.

Treason was alleged: an escape plot. Who believed it? The young man, a prisoner since childhood, was a stranger to ambition; he knew no knightly exercises, he had never taken sword in hand. It was like killing a cripple; but Henry Tudor did it, so as not to lose the Spanish bride. With Warwick dead, his sister Margaret was in the hands of the king; he made her safe with marriage to a loyalist. 'My grandmother wed her to Richard Pole,' the king says. 'It was a modest match, but honourable. It was I who reinstated her in her former fortunes. I revered her family for their ancient blood. I pitied their fall. I made her Countess of Salisbury. What more could I do? I could not give her brother back. I could not raise the dead.'

Catalina, the Spanish princess, knew what lay behind her marriage. In her whole life after, she tried to atone to Margaret Pole. She placed trust in her, making her Lady Governor to Mary, her only child. 'But,' Henry says, 'I have been told there is a curse.'

Don't repeat it, he thinks. Repetition is the only force it has.

'The marriage with Katherine was made, and in weeks Arthur was dead. Thereafter, as you know ...'

He thinks of Katherine's miscarried children, their blind faces and their vestigial hands joined in prayer. 'It was not I caused Warwick's death,' Henry says. 'It was not even my father, it was Katherine's people. I do not know why my father allowed the Spaniards to put a bloody hand into this realm's affairs. How long must I suffer, to ease the conscience of Castile? And what more can I give Warwick's family? I have promoted them. I have enriched them. Other kings would have kept them low.'

So much is true. They have worked on your shame, he thinks. 'Who can read Margaret Pole, sir? Not I.'

Henry says, 'Her son Montague has never liked me. To speak truthfully, I have never liked him. His brother Geoffrey is not a man to trust. But Reginald, I had hopes there – a gentle soul, one worthy to be cherished – or so I was told. I paid for his studies. I funded him to travel in Italy. I trusted him to go to the Sorbonne for me, to put my case in the matter of my annulment.'

His first annulment, he means. 'I heard he put it very well.'

'I would have rewarded him. I would have made him Archbishop of York. You know he is in minor orders, he is not yet a priest, but my thought was, he might quickly be ordained, and as the see was vacant after Wolsey – but he would none of it. Said he was too young. Not worthy. I should have known then, he meant to turn.' The king thumps the folio. 'All I asked of him was one word out of Italy – a statement, a scholar's opinion, something I could set before the world, to show his family's support. I told him, I do not need a book, I have books enough, I need just a word, to justify how and why I am head of my own church. And I waited. In great patience. And I was promised and promised, but nothing forthcame. Always some reason for delay. The heat, the cold, an outbreak of disease, the poor state of the roads, the untrustworthy nature of messengers, and his need to remove, to travel, consult some rare volume or some learned divine. Well, now it has come at last. It is a book after all.' The king looks exhausted, as if he had written it himself. 'And worth the waiting, because now the scales fall from my eyes.'

He moves to pick up the manuscript, but the king drops his hand on it. 'I will save you the trouble. First there is a note to me, cold and insolent in tone. After that, each page more bitter than the last. I am a greater danger to Christians than the infidel Turk. He calls me a Nero, and a wild beast. He advises the Emperor Charles to invade. He claims that for the whole of my reign I have plundered my subjects and dishonoured the nobility. They are now ready to revolt, he claims, lords and commons both, and he exhorts them to do so, to rise up and murder me.'

'It must appear to your Majesty –'

'And I am damned,' Henry says. 'Hell gapes for me. Or so he says.'

'– it must strike your Majesty that a rising, such as he advocates, cannot only be against somebody. It must also be for somebody.'

'Of course. You see how it all works together? Pole exhorts Europe to take arms against me, and at the very same hour, my own daughter defies me. Tell me this – why is Reginald not a priest yet? When he is so fond of his prayers? I will tell you why. Because his family schemes to marry him to my daughter.'

Neat, if they could do it. Mary Tudor carries the best blood of Spain. Unite it with Plantagenet blood: that's the thinking. The Pole family and their allies dream of a new England: which is to say, an old one, where they rule again.

'I believe,' he says, 'that the Lady Mary regards your Majesty's favour more than that of any bridegroom. Even if Heaven sent him.'

'So you say. But then you always defend her.'

'She is a woman, she is young. Trust me, your Majesty, she will see her duty, she will comply. These people who call themselves her supporters, they take advantage of her. I don't believe she can penetrate their schemes.'

101

The king says, 'I lived with her mother for twenty years, and I tell you, she could penetrate any scheme. You said yourself, if Katherine had been a man, she would have been a hero like Alexander.'

He had once said to Cranmer, the dreams of kings are not the dreams of other men. They are susceptible to visions, in which the figures of their ancestors come to speak to them of war, vengeance, law and power. Dead kings visit them; they say, 'Do you know us, Henry? We know you.' There are places in the realm where battles have been fought, places where, the wind in a certain direction, the moon waning, the night obscure, you can hear the thunder of hooves and the creak of harness and the screams of the slain; and if you creep close – if you were thin air, suppose you were a spirit who could slide between blades of grass – then you would hear the aspirations of the dying, you would hear them cry to God for mercy. And all these, the souls of England, cry to *me*, the king tells him, to me and every king: each king carries the crimes of other kings, and the need for restitution rolls forward down the years.

'You think me superstitious,' Henry says. 'You do not understand me. However Pole's family offends me, I am fastened to them, by the history that binds us together.'

The bonds of history can be loosened, he thinks. 'If there was a crime, it is an old crime. If there was a sin, it is stale.'

'You cannot enter into my difficulty. How can you?'

You're right, he thinks, how can I? Ghosts don't oppress the Cromwells. Walter does not rise by night, ale pot in hand, chisel in his belt, roistering by the wharves and showing his bruised knuckles to Putney. I don't have a history, only a past. 'Given my poor understanding, what shall I do for you, sir?'

'Go and see Margaret Pole. She is here in London. See if she knew about her wretched son's book. See if his brothers knew.'

'They will disclaim it, I am sure.'

'I ask myself, what did *you* know?' The king's eyes rest on him. 'You do not seem amazed by it, as I was amazed.'

'Your Majesty will remember why my lord cardinal employed me, in times past. It was not for my knowledge of the law. There are lawyers enough. It was for my connections in Italy. I am good to my friends there. I write them letters. They write to me.'

'If you knew, you could have stopped it.'

'I could have stopped Reginald sending the book to your Majesty. But he was determined to speak his mind. I could not, for example, stop him sending it to the Pope.'

Henry pushes the book across the table. 'He swears there is only one copy, and this is it. But why should I believe him? In two months it could be printed and read everywhere. Likely the Pope is reading it now. And the Emperor too.'

'I suppose Charles needs to be alerted. If he is to lead this invasion force that Pole seeks.'

'They will never make landfall,' Henry says. 'I will eat them alive.'

Now everything falls away, the pain, the doubt and the jaundiced fear that has shadowed Henry this last hour. Now he slaps his hand down on the book, and a cannibal glint in his eye reminds you: dog eat dog, but no man eats England. He rises from his chair. You think he is going to say, Fetch me Excalibur.

But these are not the days of heroes and giants. He tells the king, 'I believe men in the Pole livery have been seen at Hunsdon, with messages for Lady Mary – though of course, we do not know that she has read them. The Courtenays are there too, though she is forbidden visitors –'

'The Courtenays? Lord Exeter himself?' The king is shocked.

'No. His lady wife. I think Lady Mary could not prevent her. You know what she is, Gertrude Courtenay.'

'She will thrust herself in, by God. She tries my patience. Tell Exeter he is expelled from the council. A man who cannot control his wife is not fit to serve his country.' Henry frowns. His mind runs over sundry faces. 'What about Riche, shall we have Riche on?'

He would just as soon the council were smaller. But it would help to have another man with a head for figures.

'Good. You can tell him,' Henry says.

Richard Riche on the council! He can see Thomas More, turning in his grave like a chicken on a spit. As if he can see it too, Henry points to the folio. 'Pole says I murdered More and Fisher. He says that he hesitated to write against me, loyalty constrained him. But when he got the news of their deaths, he took it as a message from God.'

'He should have taken it as a message from me.'

Henry walks to the window. 'Get Reginald back here.' His form shows faintly in the leaded panes. His clothes seem to weigh heavy on him, and he can hardly raise his voice above a murmur. 'Promise what you like. Assure him what you like. Tell him to come back to England. I want to look him in the eye.'

In the watching chamber, a knot of councillors, whispering. He walks into their midst. They fall silent. He looks around the circle. 'Did you hope he would beat me about the head, like Patch?'

Word has leaked out. Pole's book has come, Henry mislikes it, it calls him Nero. William Fitzwilliam says, 'Pole could not have timed it worse if he had tried. It will go hard with Mary, if Henry thinks her complicit.'

'This looks black for Pole's family,' says Lord Chancellor Audley. 'It looks black for all the ancient blood. The Courtenay family too.'

'Exeter is off the council. You're on, Riche.'

'What, me?'

'Hold him up, Fitzwilliam.'

'Jesus! Thank you!' Riche says. 'Thank you, Lord Cromwell.'

'It was the king's idea. I think he liked what you said, about Absalom.'

'What?' the Lord Chancellor says. 'King David's son? He that hangs in the tree by his hair? What did Riche say about him? When did he say it?'

Someone takes Lord Audley aside, and explains it all to him.

Riche looks dazed. Fitzwilliam says, 'Crumb, you had warning of this book.'

'I have entered into the mind of Reginald like a worm into an apple.'

'When? When did you know?' Fitzwilliam's mind is busy.

Riche says, 'No wonder you dealt so boldly these last weeks. With that card in your hand. No danger now the king will revert to Rome.'

'The lad is getting an education,' he says to Fitz.

I have been watching Pole for a year, he admits – as in Italy the young man procrastinates. Tortured by his own prose Reginald scribbles, then erases. He amends, and then he writes more and does worse. But the day must come, the letter be signed at last – the ink blotted, the papers rolled and tied, and the messenger summoned to carry it to England. Anne Boleyn's death would speed the matter: for Pole would think, 'Now Henry's resolve is weakened, now he is ready to repent, now I will threaten him with damnation and scare him back to Rome.' So he might, if he had modulated his argument. But Reginald does not understand Henry, not as a man: still less does he comprehend the mind and will of a prince.

'I have met him,' he says. 'Pole.' He remembers a fledgling scholar, body neither tall nor short nor stout nor lean; fairish hair, broad pleasant countenance. Reginald's plain exterior gives no idea of the elaborate, useless nature of his mind, with its little shelves and niches for scruples and doubts. 'One time I believe I laughed at him,' he says. The boy had prated about how virtue should rule nations. I do not disagree, he had said; but read some books to bolster your scant practical experience. The Italians understand these matters.

Since then Reginald has been frightened of him. He speaks ill of him: says he is a devil, and you can't speak worse than that. And yet, when a travelling scholar calls on him, or a noble young Italian wishing to improve his English, Pole never thinks to ask, 'Could this be an emissary of Satan, alias Cromwell?' Time was, Reginald was tempted by Luther's teachings; we know how he wobbled onto that course, and wobbled off again. Time was, he doubted the Pope's authority; his doubts were recorded. Pole's folly is, that he thinks aloud. Some apprentice phrase, modelled on Cicero, trembles in the air; he believes no one hears. He writes, and he thinks no one reads; but friends of Lucifer look into his book. At dusk he locks his manuscript in a chest, but the devil has a key. Demons know every crossing-out and every blot. His ink betrays him. The fibres in his paper are spies. When he lies down at night, the horsehair in his mattress and the feathers in his bolster are eavesdropping on England's behalf, as he supplicates, in hedging, quibbling terms, whatever form of God he believes in that day.

Fitz says, 'You could bring the Poles down now. The whole family.'

'Except for Reginald,' Riche chips in. 'He is out of the jurisdiction.'

Lord Audley says, 'A good point, Mr Speaker. But you leave one singing bird in the cage, to lure another home.'

Riche says, 'How is that on the point, Lord Chancellor? It is rather the opposite, do you not think? Pole being free, his song lures out the others. We see treason on the wing.'

'Oh,' Audley says. 'Yes, I suppose you are right.'

He says, 'I could have brought them down two years ago.'

'The prophetess,' Fitz says, 'Eliza Barton, there was a great traitor. That was like them, to shelter behind the skirts of some deluded little nun who thought God talked to her. Only – tell me if I am wrong – did not Barton favour the Courtenay claim over the Poles?'

'The difference between the families kept eluding her,' Riche says. 'That was my view. I believe Master Secretary is right. Let their designs play out. We should stay our hand. They will hang themselves.'

'By God, a councillor already,' Fitz says. He snatches Riche's hat off and lopes the length of the chamber, throwing it up to the Tudor roses in the ceiling. Is that a stray HA-HA lurking up there? The Lord Chancellor, loyal soul, is squinting up and craning his neck.

L'Erber, the Pole house: Margaret, the countess, looks up at his entrance, but does not speak.

What's she doing? Needlework, like any beldame. Her hawk's profile is lowered over her work, as if she is pecking it.

Margaret's son, Henry Lord Montague, winces visibly at the sight of him. 'Master Secretary. Please sit.'

He would rather stand. 'I take it you know what's in the book, more or less? The king keeps it close. He will treat you to some extracts, but he would like you to write to your brother in Italy, to tell him he is not offended.'

Montague stares at him. 'Not offended?'

'Your brother is welcome to return to England to put his case.'

'I ask you,' Montague says, 'would you come, if you were Reynold?'

Reynold: that's what his family call him. A name with a liquid, subtle nature.

'The king would offer him a safe-conduct. And you have always found the king a man of his word.'

Montague says, 'We, his family – I tell you, Cromwell, we are amazed by my brother's proceedings. I think you knew more of this than we did.'

'Shall I tell the king that you repudiate him?'

Montague hesitates. 'That is strong ...'

'Deprecate.' Margaret Pole speaks. 'You may say we deprecate his writings and are dismayed.'

'Astonished,' he suggests. 'Struck by sorrow and frozen with horror, to find he sets up his judgement against the king's. That he belies his prince, slanders him, threatens him with invasion, and tells him he is damned.'

'I am not my brother's keeper,' Montague says.

'Someone must be. If not you, then me. Reginald needs to be locked away for his own protection. At present, I stand between you and the king's displeasure.'

'Good of you,' Montague says.

'I stand also between the king and his daughter. You must see that, before this book arrived, the Lady Mary was in jeopardy through her own foolish pride. But now, because the king suspects she is complicit in this, her position is graver still. And it is your family who has put her in danger.'

Montague is a languid man, hard to arouse, hard to bait. It is Margaret Pole who puts down her work and speaks. 'We helped you pull down the Boleyns, when they were threatening your life.'

'I took the risks of that enterprise. Not you.'

'You owe us a debt,' she says, 'and now you do not have to pay it. You knew the book was in preparation. You knew all that would occur.'

'Can you explain that to Nicholas Carew? He doesn't seem to take it in. I owe him nothing. I owe you nothing, madam. The obligation is on the other side. And whether Mary lives or dies – I will not say it is in my hands, but it may be in yours. I look for your aid to keep her in the land of the living. Where I think she can do most good.'

'Her mother, God rest her soul, made me her Lady Governor,' Margaret Pole says. 'How would I repay Katherine's trust, if I advised the princess to act against her own conscience?'

Montague says, 'I do not see, Cromwell, what is your interest in this. You appear to want to save Mary from herself, and save her from her friends too. But you cannot imagine she will favour you thereafter?'

'Should she become queen,' Margaret Pole says, 'and I hope and pray she never has that misfortune, then she will at once, surely –'

What? Put me in the Tower? Strike off my head? Make me Lord Chancellor?

'My lady mother …' Montague warns.

'Ah, I see the Treason Act,' Margaret says gaily. 'I see its trip-wire. It is a crime to envisage the future. We are trapped in the hour we occupy.'

'In past months,' he says to Montague, 'you have spoken with the Emperor's man Chapuys, and assured him that England is ready to rise against the king.' He holds up a hand: do not interrupt me. 'Only two, three weeks ago, in the West Country, we saw simple people in arms.'

'That is Courtenay land,' Montague says. 'So tax them with it.'

No loyalty among thieves, he thinks. 'It is lucky for you no great harm is done, and the country now quiet. But any repetition – any further breach of the king's peace, in any part of the realm – it will be hard for you to show you are not the instigator.'

'But could you show that he is?' Margaret puts in. 'Because in my poor understanding, it is for the accuser to demonstrate guilt.'

'That should not be a matter of great difficulty. Besides, the common law provides ways to protect the realm from traitors. I mean an attainder, by which no trial is needed.'

Margaret is still. She glides her needle into her cloth. Her father died this way.

'Madam,' he says, 'do not by your resistances and your evasions and your plots corrupt a good king who has done everything in his power to recompense your family for what it has suffered. Pray for concord, as all good Christians ought. And write the Lady Mary a letter.'

'You will carry it?' Montague says.

'Give it to your friend Chapuys. That way, the young lady will not say it is forged.'

Margaret says, 'You are a snake, Cromwell.'

'Oh no, no, no.' A dog, madam, and on your scent. He interposes his reassuring bulk between her person and the light. Margaret is sewing a border of flowers. It is the emblem of her family, the viola: known also as the pansy, or heart's-ease. 'I compliment you. I am surprised your sight is still sharp enough for that work.'

She reaches for her scissors. 'I have seen other days, and better.'

He sends nephew Richard to the Tower with an order to free Thomas Wyatt. The arrival of Pole's book, as news of its content seeps and leaks through the court, has caused such a stir that no one is looking Wyatt's way. No one has seen the text, but when they guess at what is in it, their guesses are not bad enough; they cannot imagine its bitter prolixity, its heedless squandering of the favour of the living, its praise of dead men. Rumours of new arrests are flying. Lady Hussey, who once served in Mary's household, is whisked into the Tower. He sends Wriothesley to talk to her. She admits that when, by the king's grace, she had licence to visit Hunsdon at Whitsuntide, she addressed the Lady Mary as Princess.

'She claims it was old habit,' Wriothesley says. 'She swears she did not mean, God strike her, to claim that Mary was Henry's lawful successor. She spoke unthinkingly. She says.'

Richard Cromwell, banging in. 'I told Wyatt, go down to Kent and never dwell on the dead. Stay there till he's told. Constable Kingston wants to know, will he need lodgings for any other noble prisoners, and if so, can you say how many and specify their rank and sex and age, and tell him when they will be arriving? He wants to be ready.'

'Is Kingston not always ready? You astonish me.'

'Sir,' Wriothesley says, 'I know you pity the Lady Mary. But let her go now.' He says to Richard, 'She looks modest as any maid, she speaks low, she shrinks from men, but when Sadler and I went to Hunsdon – if she had a dagger I swear she would have stuck it in me, when I told her how neat a job the man from Calais made.'

She's hard to like, he says. That's all he will say.

As Henry takes his place at the council board, he rests a fist on the table to steady himself; he moves cautiously, steering himself so as not to knock or jolt. Courteous, he murmurs his thanks to his new councillor, as Riche eases back a chair to give clear passage to his bandaged leg. 'Sworn in, Riche? Good.' He falls into his seat with a little grunt, and grips the council board to drag himself towards it.

'A cushion, Majesty?' Lord Audley suggests.

Henry closes his eyes. 'Thank you, no. Today there is only one matter –'

'A more capacious chair perhaps?'

The king's voice shakes, '– one salient matter … Thank you, Lord Audley, I am comfortable.'

He catches the Lord Chancellor's eye, and presses a palm across his own mouth. But Richard Riche is not so easily suppressed. At the sight of Edward Seymour: 'You here, sir? I did not think you were sworn?'

'Well, it appears –' Edward says.

'It appears that I want his opinion,' the king says. 'In this instance at least. These are matters that come very near me. You understand, Riche?'

Edward is the king's brother now; of course he wants his advice. But Edward sits awkwardly on a stool at the end of the table. He looks like a man who is on trial, to see if he gives satisfaction; perhaps his sister is in the same case.

Richard Riche cannot settle. He leans over to whisper: sir, is this truly a meeting of the council, or some other form of conference? He, Cromwell, whispers back: just sit still and listen. Fitzwilliam looks around. 'Where is my lord of Norfolk?'

'I have directed him,' Henry says, 'to avoid my sight.'

Good news for Fitz. His quarrels with the Howards go back a decade and more. 'You should never have sent him to Mary, sir. You know what he is. He talks to a woman as if she were a town wall and he has to breach her.'

'I do not think,' the Lord Chancellor says, 'that you should speak of the king's daughter as "a woman".'

'Well, what else is she?' Fitzwilliam says. 'If I call her a lady, it does not alter the case. Norfolk was the last man to do anything with her.'

Henry says, 'I admit, I chose ill. It is not likely she will yield to force.' Is there a hint, in his tone, of perverse pride? 'We must choose another messenger. Perhaps my lord archbishop, with his gentle persuasions …'

Fitz stares at him. 'She hates Cranmer. How would she not? Cranmer divorced you from her mother. He called her the product of incest.'

'And so she is.' The king bows his head. 'It was a great sin – committed, as you know, in ignorance.'

'Majesty,' Edward Seymour says, 'we are all cognisant – there is no need – spare yourself –'

'Forgive me if it appears the weight of twenty years is on my shoulders.' The king seems calm, resigned: but I know, he thinks, that dangerous twitch of his mouth. 'Since in Christendom for a clear generation it has been debated in every students' hall, bawled out in every pulpit, and jangled in every alehouse, I have no objection if the matter be stated again. Though the scripture is clear that such a marriage is not licit, I believed, in those days, that the Pope had power to dispense. I know better now. My daughter Mary is the product of a union illegitimate. If Katherine would not acknowledge the sin in this life, as she would not, then I fear she will suffer for it in the place where she is now.'

Peterborough, he thinks.

'For my part,' the king says, 'my eyes being opened to the abusions and pretences of Rome, I have wrought for seven years to rid myself of that accursed jurisdiction and to lead my country on a true path to Christ. If I have not atoned by this time – then, gentlemen, I know not how, and I know not when. To be defied by my daughter, to know that my own kin and cousins urge her on, to be reviled in my own house by that monster of ingratitude, Pole – to be called heretic and schismatic and Judas –'

'No, sir,' Riche interrupts. 'It was not your Majesty that Pole called a Judas. It was Bishop Sampson, for acting as proctor in your divorce.'

'Our new councillor is an exact man.' Henry turns to Riche. 'Then what *does* he call me? Antichrist, is it? Lucifer?'

Day star, he thinks, bringer of light.

'So I warn you,' Henry says. 'If I hear one voice raised in support of that errant creature my daughter, I shall know I am hearing treason. I am taking advice. I have called in the judges to consider what is the best way to bring her to trial.'

Fitzwilliam slaps his palm on the board. 'Trial? Jesus save us! Your flesh and blood? I implore you, think before you do this. You will make yourself a monster in the sight of all.'

He cuts in, 'Majesty, Mary is ill.'

'The king will be ill!' Riche says. 'Look at him!'

Edward Seymour whispers, 'Riche, forbear.'

Henry turns to him. 'Tell me, Crumb, when is she not ill? I wonder if so weakly a creature can be mine. Her brothers and sisters all died. I wonder how she lived. I wonder what God meant by it.'

Fitzwilliam says, 'Well, if you don't know, Harry, who does? You are His deputy, are you not? You know all our fates.'

'I know yours,' Henry says.

Henry glances up to the doors. A nod, and the guards would march in. Richard Riche sits frozen on his bench, jaw dropped, fingers poised as if to make a note. Edward Seymour half-rises: 'Pardon, Majesty. Pardon Master Treasurer's plain speaking. We are all ... we are all over-wrought ...'

Henry sighs. 'Over-wrought, abused, exhausted. True, Ned, we are. Go on, Fitzwilliam, take yourself out of the council chamber before I have you taken, my patience is not infinite, neither with you nor my daughter. So, Crumb, tell us about her illness. What is it this time? I heard it was cramps, then fever, then headache, then toothache.'

'I am afraid it is all of them. She writes –'

'Let me see her letter.'

The letter is in his pocket.

'I shall send for it, sir.'

'Some of you councillors know more of my daughter's mind than I do myself.' Again, that tight smile: Henry is in pain. 'Master Secretary promised me he could get her compliance – that he would make her swear the oath without stirring himself from Whitehall. But he too has failed me.'

Fitzwilliam is almost out of the room; but he turns to face the councillors, his papers held across his chest. 'Some of us are trying to save you from yourself, Majesty. You are flailing and injuring all about, because Pole has insulted you. Reckon with your enemies, not your friends. As for Mary – lock her up, yes, keep her close where she can do no harm – but that you should go so far as to consult the judges, that you should consider bringing your own daughter before a court – because what then? I tell you, she is guilty. What needs a judge? What needs a jury? She will not swear the oath and she will give you her reasons, as Thomas More would not. She will say she is not a bastard, but a princess of England, and that you are no more head of the church than I am. Then what will you do? Cut off her head?'

Audley turns down his mouth. 'Brave man.'

'Dead man,' Seymour murmurs.

He, Lord Cromwell, rises from his place. He strides across the room, grasps Master Treasurer by his coat, trips him off-balance, tumbles him backwards and bundles him towards the doors. They open smoothly, like the gates of Hell. He seizes the treasurer's chain of office, trying to loop it over Fitz's head. The councillor bellows, the chain twists; Fitz threads his fingers into it; they tussle. 'Hands off me, Cromwell,' Fitz bawls, and swipes at him with his other fist. But he has a grip on the chain and he hauls Fitz nose to nose, spitting into his face, 'Give it over, you dolt.'

Fitz comprehends. He yields his grip. He yelps, a finger still caught, as the chain flies free. A shove in the chest: Fitz staggers backwards. The doors slam.

He, Lord Cromwell, crosses the room and drops the chain on the table before the king. Clank.

'No, that won't do,' Henry says. 'Getting up a fight for my benefit, when I know you agree with him.' His fingers reach out for the chain, the gold still warm from where it lay against a velvet chest. 'Still, I applaud your effort, my lord. Fitz is no mean weight.' He won't look at his councillors. 'Bring Lord Montague to see me. I wish to read him extracts from his brother's letter. Fetch Bishop Judas – strangely enough, I find Sampson is one man on whom I can rely. Perhaps we should bring Gardiner back from France. He usually has ideas about what to do, and none of you seem to know. Remind Sir Nicholas Carew I forbid him to communicate with my daughter. Tell the Courtenay family I know their practices. Warn them of my extreme displeasure. Commit Francis Bryan to the Tower. I hear he has been hawking his opinions about the town, saying that Mary is ill-used and I am an unnatural father.'

'Oh, you know Francis,' Edward Seymour says. 'He doesn't mean it. He loves your Majesty.'

'And Fitzwilliam?' Audley is frowning. 'Must we appoint a new Master Treasurer?'

'Fitzwilliam,' the king says gently, 'is not greatly to be blamed. He is my old friend, and I think you commonly say, you councillors, that he understands me better than any man alive.' Henry looks around the table, fearfully leisured; all their hours are his. 'You see,' he says, 'I do know what you councillors say, and how you scheme to govern me, and talk of who I love and who not. If there is one being in this world a man should trust, it is his maiden daughter. She should have no will but his, and no thought but what comforts him; in return, he protects her, and works her advancement. But Master Treasurer has no children. God has so disposed it. Not being a father, he cannot feel what I feel, and he does not know what I have suffered these last weeks. For I have never varied: Mary knows what declaration I require of her, and has known since the oath was first framed. If she chose to believe my title and right was some whim of that woman lately dead, then she was much mistook, and much misled, and if she has entertained some notion that I will creep back to Rome, she is a greater fool than I thought her. But what you do not see, what none of you seems to understand, is that I love my daughter. I think of all my children dead in the cradle, or dead before they saw the light. If I lose Mary, what have I? Ask yourselves … what comfort have I in this breathing world but her?'

The room is silent. I felt, Audley will say later, that I should cross and say '*Amen.*' Not even the new councillor is crude enough to say, 'In fact, Majesty, you have young Richmond,' or remind him of the ginger pig Eliza, squalling somewhere up-country. But Edward Seymour is frowning: if the king has nothing, where does that leave sister Jane, where does that leave the family at Wolf Hall?

'So, good Master Secretary,' the king says. 'Lord Cromwell – as you love me and love my service, you will bring this matter to a conclusion. We shall not come here to debate it again.'

The king puts his palms on the table and levers himself to his feet. The councillors tumble from bench and stool, and kneel. They kneel till he is out of the room. Even when the doors are closed after him they do not speak. Till the Lord Chancellor says, 'Conclusion? What does that mean?'

'God knows,' he says.

Riche says, vehement, 'I wish I were never a councillor! I wish I were in China.'

Seymour mutters, 'I wish you were in Utopia.'

Mary's letter, which is still in his pocket, tells him: Cromwell, I can go no further, I can concede no more. I will sign no articles that slander my mother the queen. I will never agree my father is or ought to be head of the church. Do not let them push me, do not let them entreat me, I have moved as far as my conscience will let me move. You are my chief friend and sustainer. My very trust is in you.

'I think he wants you to kill her,' Edward Seymour says.

The cardinal, in his day, used to laugh about the time when the young Henry thrust a leg forth from his gown and invited the French ambassador to admire his calf. 'Has your king a leg like that?' he asked. 'Tell me, has he? King Francis is a tall man, I know, but is he broad in the shoulder like me?'

Now the same prince, dragging away from the council chamber, wraps his gown about himself, the fine calf visibly bandaged, his face puffy and pale. Henry is the site, his body the locus, the blood and bile and phlegm; his burdened and oppressed flesh the place where all arguments come to rest.

At the Tower, Francis Bryan says, 'Was this where you kept Tom Wyatt?'

'Airy,' he says, 'isn't it? I always get good lodgings for my friends.'

'One in, one out.' Francis slides low in his chair, and looks around him; one eye patched, the other bleared. 'I take it house arrest would not have been enough?'

'You're safer here. That's what I told Wyatt.'

'I hear you are Privy Seal. You climb so fast, my lord, the kingdom has not ladders enough.'

'Ladders? I have wings.'

'Then flit into the dusk,' Francis says, 'before they melt.'

'The king thinks Mary would not defy him unless a man were behind her. In chief he suspects your brother-in-law Carew.'

'Old Carve-Away.' Francis laughs. 'He paints a picture of himself, the loyal chevalier in black armour. He gives Mary to understand he will make her queen.'

There is no note-taker. Only Lord Cromwell's own folder of papers, on the table where the book of Petrarch's verse lay: the putti, the sea monster, the binding soft as skin. His hand does not move. Time enough to write. 'Carew, then. Who else?'

'Lord Exeter's tribe. And snivelling little Montague.'

'If the king fetches them in, will you give testimony?'

'Yes. If it's me or them. Why should I be better than Tom Wyatt?'

'No one ever thought you were.'

'But you don't want to bring them in, do you? You'd rather cut deals.'

'It is my merciful nature prevents me –'

Francis snorts. 'Nothing prevents you. But you cannot destroy Mary's people unless you destroy her, and you don't want to lose her, and you don't think you can control Henry, if he keeps killing close to home.'

He remembers Francis standing beside the scaffold, sweating in his leather jerkin, waiting to sprint to the Seymours with the news that Anne's head was off. If you want speed, choose Francis Bryan. Your impulses ripple beneath his skin, ready for action. If you want someone bribed, if you want someone charmed, if you want some secret and dirty dealing, you know where to go. If you want the unspeakable thing spoken, then give Francis the nod. 'I know you, Cromwell,' he says. 'You think yourself a cautious politic man. But you are a gambler, like me.'

'Not like you. You would crawl to the card table if you were poisoned. When you go blind you will sniff out the cups and wands. Your fingertips will feel out the spots on the dice.'

Francis says, 'Another man, from the place where you come from, would get himself to a quiet spot and count his takings. Not Cromwell. He will have all to rule. If Seymour's girl makes the king a son, who will oversee his princely education, but Cromwell? If Fitzroy is named heir, Cromwell is in his graces. If Mary survives to reign, she will always know that Cromwell saved her life.'

'Believe me, Francis,' he says, smiling, 'I have no expectations. All I want is to get through the week.'

'You won't stop till you're a duke. Or king.' Francis pushes up his eye-patch. He rubs the scar tissue beneath. 'Not that you would be a bad king, by the way.'

His glance flicks away from the wreckage of Bryan's face. Its owner laughs. 'You've seen worse.'

He goes to the door. 'Martin? Fetch me a proper chair. How is this miserable stool still here? Didn't I kick it out?'

Martin appears. 'It must have trundled back by itself. I'll toss the little bugger downstairs.'

'Chop it up for firewood,' Francis says. 'Show it who's master.'

'And fetch claret,' he says to Martin. 'Put it on my tally.'

'You keep an account?' Francis says. 'St Agnes bless me.'

'I think of setting up my own cook, with a few spit boys and a cold room for pastry. I keep spare shirts here, and my lambskin coat. I keep clerks.'

'No clerks,' Francis says. 'Or I fall silent.'

'If you will give me the testimony you promise, I will put it away till such time as I can use it. I will write down what you say myself, and no one need ever know it comes from you. But if any of us are to live to see next week, Carve-Away must write to Mary, and admit she can look for no practical help from him or his friends, and that if she does not do exactly as I tell her, she will be lost. And I will speak to Henry for you and' – he rubs his own eyes – 'as soon as we are to the other side of this, you will be free. It will not be long. Mary must choose now: her father or the Pope.'

'Her father or her mother,' Francis says. 'You cannot fight the dead. You may have to cede her to them. God knows why you think she is your future. Even if you save her now, she will die on you; she is always ailing. And if the king turns on you, it will not be like when old Henry Guildford quit and went off to the country to prune his fruit trees and enjoy the birdsong. Remember how Wolsey fell. Bungle this, and Henry will put you where I am now. Or in a worse place, where you would be glad of the three-legged stool.'

'You sound as if you care,' he says. 'Giving me good advice.'

Francis says, 'What is this commonwealth without you? I would like to see you thrive. After all, I may have to borrow money from you.'

Martin comes in, bumping a chair before him. He thinks, this will need patience: even if I get sure proofs of treason, can I afford to use them? Bryan is right. It is no small matter to bring down two great families and their affinities, when you have scarcely buried the Boleyns; and to do it without damage to the young woman whose cause they claim they promote. Henry cannot be ready before I am ready: I must restrain my cannibal king.

'One more thing, Francis. When Carew has written his letter, your sister Eliza must take it to Hunsdon herself, and confer with your lady mother. Lady Bryan has brought up Mary from her infancy. I trust her to have her interests at heart.'

'And,' Francis says, 'my lady mother is not the dottypoll she seems.'

'They must go to Mary, mother and daughter, and be earnest with her, and use any persuasion. I am trusting your whole family to serve me in this.'

'Well,' Francis says with distaste, 'if you must pull the women into it.'

'The women are already in it. It's all about women. What else is it about?'

Francis looks into his cup. He swills the contents about, as if he were divining and trying to change the fate in the lees. 'People say, Henry will not make away with his daughter. Others say, we did not think he would make away with his wife. But I – I always knew he would kill Anne Boleyn. Or if not, then some other man would do it for him.'

The warm weather is here. The long days in which, if rumour is true, the Lady Mary does not eat: the short, light nights, in which she paces sleepless, her face swollen, her eyes red-rimmed; in which she swims in her salt tears as in a drowning pool. Tears are good for young women, especially those in whom the menstrual flow is stopped, or those who want a man in their bed but are obliged to do without. If Mary stopped crying, she might be even sicker than she is now. So when she sobs and retches, no one stirs to comfort her. When she cries, 'Jesus pity me,' it appears He does not.

The jurists whom the king consults suggest that the oath should be put to Mary again, so there can be no doubt that she knows what is required. Of course she knows, the king says. She is in no doubt. But he adds, as he did last month in the matter of Anne Boleyn, 'Cromwell, I wish to stand right with the law in every particular.'

'Send for Chapuys,' he tells Richard: he, Lord Cromwell. 'He must take supper with me. He will plead he has no appetite. But he can watch me eat.'

Richard says, 'You could have resolved this two weeks ago. You have put us in peril day after day. Why do you not go to Mary yourself?'

'Because I can only do this at a distance,' he says.

He remembers the castle at Windsor, a day of baking heat; the year of our salvation, 1531. In the great courts, the king's baggage wagons stood ready, the household departing for a summer of hunting, dancing and other sport. He himself, compelled to melt into shadow, up staircases and through shuttered rooms empty of contents; through the queen's suite of rooms to find Katherine sitting alone, abandoned, obdurate, knowing but not consenting to know that Henry had gone without a word of goodbye; the child Mary, fragile as straw, leaning on the back of her chair. Madam, he said, your daughter is ill, she should sit. A spasm of pain shook the girl and caused her to droop, and clench her hand on the gilding. Katherine spoke to her in Castilian: 'You are a daughter of Spain. Stand up.'

He battled that day for the sick, narrow body, and he won. At his feet, a stool: on the stool, a cushion embroidered with a mermaid. He picked up the stool in one hand, the mermaid in the other. He held the gaze of the Spanish queen, and slammed the stool down on the flags. The sun streamed through coloured glass; squares of light, pale green and vermilion, fluttered like standards against pale stone.

Katherine had closed her eyes. As if she herself were suffering, she made the barest concession to a nod. Then she opened her eyes and shifted her gaze to the middle distance. He saw the princess sway; he moved and caught her, arm outstretched. He steadied her: he remembers her tiny bones, her weightless body quivering, her forehead sheened with sweat. She sank to the stool. He passed her the cushion, studying her face. She hugged the mermaid against her belly, wrapping her arms across herself, bending double to ease her pain. After a moment, she let out her breath with a grunt. Then her head jerked up, and she took him in, astonished and grateful. In an instant she had wiped the expression away. It was a transaction so swift that you could barely say it occurred. But until the interview was concluded and he bowed himself out of the room, her eyes followed him everywhere he moved.

After supper, as a hush falls and the long midsummer day folds itself and disposes to dusk, he and the ambassador climb one of the garden towers. London lurks below them in the blue haze. Before them is a dish of strawberries they must finish before the moon rises. The ambassador has left his papers at the foot of the tower. His folio of white leather, stamped with the Emperor's double eagle, rests on a bank of turf starred with daisies.

'What irks me,' he tells Chapuys, 'is that no prince in Europe has a place to stand and look down at Henry. They have broken their parliaments, such as they were, racked their people with taxes, raided the church coffers, killed their councillors – but if they crook their knee to the Vatican, all is well, they are moral fellows and the Pope sends them a blessing and tells them what glorious monarchs they are. Which of them would have endured a barren wife, year after year? They would have poisoned her. Which of them would bear with a disobedient child? If Mary were the daughter of some other prince, she would be walled up and forgotten, or she would meet with an accident.'

'Yes,' Chapuys says. 'But that is not what you are going to recommend.'

'It doesn't matter what I recommend. This affair has broken me. I am a dead man.'

'You said that before. When the concubine was plaguing you.'

'I said it and I meant it. I have gone so far in this matter there is no way back – I assured the king that Mary would comply. He hates a promise-breaker.'

Chapuys is pensive, tracing with a finger the faint, feathery pattern on the marble tabletop. 'How did you get this up here?'

'Winched it through the window. Did you think I prayed to the holy bones of Bishop Fisher, and he made it fly?'

He has leased this house from the canons at Smithfield, at St Bartholomew's. Their prior Will Bolton was the king's builder, a man with a good head for planning big works and seeing them through; bless me, Bolton, he sometimes says, when he arrives here and takes a breath, his horse walked to the stable, his bags hauled in by Christophe. The prior used to come out here to hunt in summer and recreate himself, and his rebus – a barrel or tun shot through with a crossbow bolt – is set into the garden walls. It is a small house with one good square chamber on each floor, and fruit trees and arbours all around, and garden towers so placed that they catch the summer breezes, and look down over the treetops to the city.

'Prior Bolton was lame the last five years of his life,' he says. 'He can never have made it up here to get the view. Though one could not expect it, he was eighty-two at his decease.'

'You are going to live for ever, of course,' Chapuys says. 'Always climbing.'

'When we go in I will show you the enamelled tiles in the parlour. They are a pure lapis blue. He must have got them from Italy.'

The low murmur of their voices, the settling, preening doves in their cote: like a flake of summer snow, a stray feather floats past, and his eyes follow it into the dusk. Chapuys says, 'Of course, I do not wonder everyone in this country has contempt for the Vatican. Rome let Katherine down, vacillating year after year.'

'Everybody let her down. Her advisers were a set of old women. Fisher may have been a very holy man, but he was useless. As far as I can see, he told her to keep cheerful and hope for the best. And as for her friends abroad – what did your Emperor do? He made warlike noises.'

Chapuys says, 'My master has the Turks to fight. He has more to do than quarrel with a wilful prince in a small island.'

'So why should my king hold back now? He is at ease in his own kingdom. He can deal with his daughter as he pleases.'

'You will forgive me for saying this,' Chapuys says, 'and I hope the dead will forgive me too – if the Emperor did not make shift to rescue his noble aunt, perhaps it was because he did not know what he would do with her thereafter. She would only have been a charge on him. She was used to spending money, as a queen does. And she might have lived to a great age.'

You must respect a man who cuts through the pieties as the ambassador does. He always tells people, don't underestimate Chapuys. Behind his politesse there is a passionate little man, a cunning man too, and one prepared to take risks.

'With Mary it is otherwise,' the ambassador says. 'Even if she does not achieve the throne, her children may, and they may turn the world in a way that is very much to the Emperor's mind. You say Henry is at ease. But though the Emperor will overlook much, he will not suffer Mary to be mistreated. He will send ships.'

'He will never make landfall.'

'Have you studied a map of these islands? My prince is master of the seas. While you are guarding the coast of Kent, his ships will be bobbing in from Ireland. While you are watching the south-west, he will invade from the north-east.'

'His captains will die on these shores. The king has said he will eat them.'

'I am to carry that message?'

'If you like. You know, and I know, the Emperor in arms has no power to save Mary. Her case is urgent.'

A head emerges, coming up the winding stair. It is Christophe. 'Lords, will you have comfits?' He clatters down a silver tray. 'Master Call-Me is here.' He casts an evil glance at Chapuys. 'He is here for breaking ciphers. None may stand against his wit.'

Chapuys clasps his hands together. He fears for his papers, left below. His knee joints are sore, and a small groan escapes him, at the thought of lurching down three flights then climbing up again.

'Ask Call-Me to sit beneath the vine and listen for the nightingales. Then fetch up the ambassador's papers. Do not look into them.'

Christophe's head sinks out of sight. 'What a donkey that boy is!' Chapuys selects a strawberry and frowns at it. 'Thomas, I see it is not an easy thing to do, to show an innocent girl that the world is not as she thinks. The late Katherine never let the child hear a word in dispraise of her father. Everything was the fault of the cardinal, or his council, or his concubine. Nothing was the fault of Henry. Naturally she expected to be embraced, without question, once Anne Boleyn was dead.' He takes a chary nibble. 'Naturally, you must disabuse her.'

He nods. 'She does not know her father.'

'How could she? She has hardly seen him in five years. She has been in prison.'

'Prison? She has been kept in great comfort.'

'But we must not tell her that, Thomas. Better to tell her she has suffered grievously, in case she feels she has not done enough. She boasts to me she is not afraid of the axe.'

'Is she not? When her last night on earth falls, and she must wait it out sleepless, and all that is before her is a sorry breakfast with the headsman, it will be no good crying for me to save her then.'

In the silence that ensues he wonders, where has Christophe got to? Is he reading the ambassador's papers after all? What a breach of decorum that would be. But profitable, if the papers were in French. Christophe has sound recall.

'It is her mother …' Chapuys says. He is afraid, as shadows gather, at having spoken ill of the dead. 'I believe she vowed to Katherine she would never give way. Vows to the living may be set aside, with their permission. But the dead do not negotiate.'

'She does not want to live?'

'Not at any price.'

'Then how will history regard her – the grandchild of the kings of Spain, with not the wit or policy to save herself?'

Christophe whoops from below: the ambassador, who has selected an aniseed sweet, almost swallows it. The boy erupts among them, slaps down the Imperial folio: the black eagle flies against white marble. 'What kept you, Christophe?'

'One came up from Islington and says they fear thunder, the cows are lying down in the fields. I pray you, come down at the first spot of rain. If lightning strikes you are undone. Only a fool would stay at the top of a tower.'

'I shall watch the sky,' he says. 'It will break over London first.'

Christophe's head declines from view, a greasy planet in a crooked cap. He waits till he is sure the boy is out of earshot, then says, 'If her father were to die now, then Mary might find herself queen, despite any disposition her father has made, despite any act of Parliament. Then as queen, she could put all to rights. Reunite us with Rome. Rivet on our shackles. She would have the pleasure of striking off my head. I do not trust her fair words.'

'And what words are they?'

He takes out Mary's letter and skims it across the table. 'Shall I have Christophe fetch lights?'

'I will puzzle it out,' the ambassador says. 'It is her hand,' he allows. He squints at the paper. The arch behind him fills with the evening's lustre, a pale opaline glow. 'She is adamant she will resist the oath. But she calls you her friend – next to her father, God save her innocence, she calls you her chief friend in this world.'

'But why should I trust her? I think she is full of guile.'

He is enjoying himself. The ambassador, he thinks, must woo me. I shall pretend I am a flighty heiress, and he must soothe my fears and caress me with his promises.

'Mary has led me into a place of great peril,' he says. 'I have lost my reputation with the king. And what had I, but my reputation? Even if he does not kill me, nobody wants a used councillor.'

The ambassador knows the game but he will not play. Grimly he says, 'Why does she think you are her friend? Something her mother told her. It can only be that. To think that after all this toil –' He breaks off. He looks both angry and ashamed. 'It seems to me that, if she trusts you, so must I. Which is an unfortunate situation to be in.'

'You must advise her to give in, and you must make it right with the Emperor. Get his permission. His blessing.'

'Unfortunately I do not keep the Emperor in my closet, where I can consult him at will.'

'No? You should hang up his portrait. Perhaps in time you could teach it to speak.'

He thinks he hears a footstep below. 'Hush.' He is on his feet. He calls into the stairwell: 'Who is that?' The ambassador tenses and gathers himself, as if at any peril he would launch himself from the tower. The window is unglazed; the fading light softens the brickwork to a faint, flushed rose.

No answer. Prior Bolton did not build his garden walls high, or secure his fences. An ill-wisher can bend wattle or willow; through a fence of pliant hazel, a felon insinuate. He touches his heart and feels the knife, nestled between silk and linen.

'Defence of a tower is easy,' he says. 'Even a garden tower. Anyone coming up, you just push them down again.'

'You would relish that,' Chapuys says. 'They tell me you greatly enjoyed your tussle with the councillor Fitzguillaume. Really, Thomas, you are such a boy.'

'Christophe?' he calls. His voice curves in the stone spiral. 'You are there?'

An answer echoes: 'Where else?' Christophe is surprised. He is always on guard, it is his early training as a thief. In his unoccupied moments, he sinks on his heels, his back against the wall, his head dropped as if he were dozing; but his ears are open, his eyes scanning for movement at the edge of his vision.

'No one is there,' he reassures the ambassador. 'It is only Christophe.' Chapuys settles back in his chair. 'Eat up the strawberries,' he tells him. 'Write to Rome.'

'But should one trust this fruit? To eat it raw?' Chapuys frowns. '*Chez-moi*, we bake it in tarts.'

'The Pope will forgive her, if she submits to save her life. Tell her you have asked for absolution for her. If you're worried about the cost, I'll cover it with Rome myself.'

'I am more worried about my digestion. And I doubt she will credit this specious reasoning.'

'Go to her first thing tomorrow, I'll write you a pass.' He leans towards the ambassador. 'Tell her this. While Anne Boleyn was alive, there was no chance that Henry would restore her to the succession. But now, if she obeys him in every particular, her fortunes may look up.'

'You are making her this offer?' Chapuys raises an eyebrow. 'Will Henry not prefer his bastard boy? I thought you favoured Richmond yourself. What has happened?'

'Richmond cannot be put in place without great quarrel and grudge. Whichever lady the king has been married to – if he was ever married to anybody – the whole world agrees it was not to Richmond's mother. As for any new heir he may get – the life of a young child, you cannot count on it from hour to hour. Tell Mary: if ever she is to compromise her conscience, now is the time, when she can do herself some good.' He leans back in his chair. 'Yes, of course she will despise herself afterwards. But that is the price. Tell her time will ease the sting of it.'

'It seems to me,' the ambassador says, 'you are saying, you can live, but only as Cromwell permits. You can reign even – but only through Cromwell's grace.'

'If you wish to explain it like that.' He has lost patience. 'Explain it how you like. I will send her a document to sign. A deed of submission. She need not read it. In fact, she must not, as she may need to repudiate it later. But she must have a clerk copy it, because it cannot go to the king in my hand.'

'No, that would wreck everything,' Chapuys smiles. 'She is not simple, you know.'

'Tell her that from now on I will make sure she is protected. She will live at her ease, as a king's daughter, and no one will trouble her to make the same prayers as I do, or to give up her saints, or her ceremonies. But then tell her – if she does not give way now, she is lost. I will regard her as the most obdurate and ungrateful woman who ever lived. I will not block the king's will. And even if by some miracle she survives, she is dead to me. I take my leave of her for ever. I shall never come into her presence. I will never see her or speak to her again.'

A pause. 'I see.' The ambassador looks sardonic. 'You had better write that yourself. I will carry your letter faithfully.'

'Shall we go down?'

Chapuys winces as he stands, and rubs his back. 'You first, my lord. I am so slow.'

He scoops the papers from the marble. 'I'll carry these.' He is ahead of the ambassador. At the first landing he calls up, 'I am not looking into them, I promise!'

Christophe is squatting, vigilant, in the posture he had imagined. Standing by him, another shape in the dimness. 'Good evening, sir,' the shape says softly. It is Mr Wriothesley, a sheaf of peonies in his hand.

In the parlour with the lapis tiles, the flame of a single wax candle shimmering in the blue, he makes his first draft; it is hard for him, to become the king's daughter. At dawn he takes the draft back to the city, and in the morning light sits before it again: humble, trembling, obedient. Perhaps he should do this in a room alone; but he does not want to think about it too much.

He picks up a quill. Examines its tip. 'This will require self-abasement.'

Richard Cromwell says, 'Shall I go out and find somebody who's better at it than you are?'

'Richard Riche knows the art of creeping,' Gregory offers. 'And Wriothesley can crawl when required.'

He begins: '*Most humbly prostrate before your Majesty …*'

'Try, *prostrate at the feet of your Majesty*,' Gregory says.

'Redundant,' Richard says.

'Yes, but it makes her sound … flatter.'

He amends the phrase. 'Don't let our efforts be mentioned outside this room. The king must think she composed it herself. *I write to …* why do I write?'

... To open my heart to your grace ... as I have and will put my soul under your direction ... so I wholly commit my body ... desiring no state, no condition, nor no manner or degree of living but such as your grace shall appoint ...

'It sounds straight out of a law book,' Richard says. 'Not this, not that, not the other.'

'True. She is not a Gray's Inn man.' He is exasperated. He knows no way to draft, but to cover every circumstance; no way to write that leaves a gap, a hairsbreadth, a crack, that would allow meaning to slide or leak away. *Forgive my offences ... I do recognise, accept, take, repute and acknowledge ...*

'The king must expect her to take a lawyer's advice,' Gregory says. 'He will expect it to show.'

... repute and acknowledge the king's highness to be supreme head, under Christ, of the church of England ...

I do freely, frankly ... recognise and acknowledge that the marriage formerly had between his majesty and my mother ... was by God's law and man's law incestuous and unlawful ...

'Incestuous and unlawful,' Gregory repeats. 'It covers everything. Nothing is left to want.'

'Except,' Richard says, 'that she has not actually taken the oath.'

He dries the ink. 'As long as no one makes Henry face that fact.'

Let this be her own form of oath, crushing and comprehensive. When she writes of Katherine, she says, *the late princess dowager*, as any subject might; but she also writes *my mother*, my dead mother: whose hand now falls incapacitate, and flinches into its shroud. Catalina, today you are put down; the living beat the dead, England conquers Spain. I have written letters for Mary before, he thinks, more pitiful than this and more yielding: *I am but a woman, and your child.* They met with small success. They did not touch the king's heart. What touches his heart is giving him everything he wants: and in such a form that, until he had it, he did not know what he lacked. *I put my soul under your direction. I commit my body to your mercy.*

'I want Rafe to take this to Hunsdon,' he says. 'Get it signed tonight.'

* * *

129

We are now in the third week of June. A gusty wet spring when Anne died; a month passes, and we are in high summer. On a hot morning you close your eyes and on your lids is stamped a blazing pattern of cloth of gold. You raise your arm to cover your face and the glare shifts to purple, as if bishops were hatching through flames. With the dukes of Norfolk and Suffolk, he rides up to Hunsdon to honour the young lady who – penitent, chastened, abased – is once again fit to be called the king's daughter.

Hertfordshire is a moneyed and populous country, well wooded and well furnished with the residences of gentlemen and courtiers. The house itself, brick-built on high ground, is fit for the accommodation of a king's family. The manor itself is ancient, but this present house is perhaps eighty years old; they show as antiquities their charters with painted shields bearing the emblems of long-dead lords: the bend sable of a Despencer heiress, the Mowbrays' lion argent, and the royal arms of Edmund Beaufort, with their broken border of silver and blue. Two years back the king laid out near three thousand on new tiles and timbers, and sent up people from Galyon Hone's workshop to glaze the principal chambers with striped roses, lovers' knots, shivering white falcons and fleur-de-lys. At the same time – providentially, as it turns out – the whole house was made more tight and secure, with new hinges, clasps, hooks, bolts and locks.

On the journey the trains of the three lords keep separate, for fear of quarrels between servants. Norfolk says, cackling, 'It is well-known what Cromwell does when he strays north of London, he will stop at some low hostelry to drag out a pot-washer and have his pleasure of her.' Except that the duke uses a coarser expression, accompanying it with a driving elbow and a pumping fist.

Charles Brandon roars. It's Brandon's sort of joke.

He notices the Lesser Thomas is riding with Norfolk. Whatever the half-brothers were whispering about when he left them together, they are whispering still. 'You see that?' he says to Suffolk.

'I do,' Suffolk says. 'Your man, Tom Truth. *Walking/talking. Dipping/snipping. Wishing/fishing.*'

Poor boy, he thinks. Even Suffolk knows how evil he rhymes. He recalls the young Howard's stricken face, when he broke it to him that the ladies shared their verses. As if he never thought that could happen. As if he thought they read the poem then ate the paper.

In the great hall, Lady Shelton meets them; she has been Mary's custodian these last three years, not a post anyone envies. Brandon strides in: she makes her reverence: 'My lord Suffolk. And Thomas Cromwell, at last.' She kisses him heartily, as if he were her cousin; whereas to Thomas Howard, who really is her cousin, she says, 'May we hope your lordship will not abuse the furnishings? Inventory is kept, and the tapestry that was rent by your lordship, the other week, was worth a hundred pounds.'

'Was it so?' Norfolk says. 'I wouldn't use it to wipe my arse. Where's John Shelton? Never mind, I'll find him myself. Charles, come with me.'

The dukes exit, hallooing for their host. He says, 'He attacked the arras? What else did he do?'

'He threatened Lady Mary with a beating, and drove his fist into the wall, injuring himself.' Lady Shelton raises a hand to hide her smile. 'He was like a drunken bear. I thought Mary would faint from fright. I thought I would. Anyway, you are here now, thank God.'

'Uglier than ever,' he says. 'While you, my lady, the more cares are heaped on you, the more gracefully you wear them.'

It is clear Lady Shelton bears him no ill will: which she might have, as the late queen was her niece. With a whisk of her hand she brushes his compliment away, but, 'By Our Lady,' she says, 'we have wanted you here a long season. Lady Bryan, as you know, is solely in charge of the nursery and what appertains to the little child, but having nursed Mary herself when she was scarcely weaned, she thrusts her advice in at every turn, and she presumes to tell Shelton how to run the wider household, as if the whole world must revolve about my lady Eliza. We have no instructions about the baby, except that she is no longer to be called "the Princess Elizabeth". What do you think, will the king disown her?'

He shrugs. 'We dare not ask. His leg has been paining him and he is out of temper because he cannot ride three hours in the morning and play tennis all afternoon. It is never sweet dealing, when he wants exercise. But who knows – now he has Mary's conformity, we may be able to approach him. What do you think? You see the child daily.'

'I think she's Henry's. You should hear her bawl. Had any of Anne's gentlemen red hair?'

'None of the dead gentlemen,' he says.

She hesitates. Then, 'Ah, I see … there may have been others? Who were not brought to trial?' He can see her mind ranging. 'Wyatt you would call blond …'

'Wyatt I would call bald.'

'You men are cruel to each other.'

'The king said Anne slept with a hundred men.'

'Did he? Well, I suppose he could not be any ordinary cuckold.' She glances over her shoulder. 'Is it true Wyatt is released?'

He wants to say, the ground is closing over your niece, we are moving on. 'No one is detained now – not in connection with that affair. You have heard of this letter come from Italy?'

'Reynold. Yes. The great fool. I thought he had ruined Mary, I tell you. And what about John Seymour's daughter? How does she do, now she is mistress of all?'

'She is good for Henry. She soothes his temper.'

'A wet cloth can do that. Still, good luck to her. She must have more about her than first appears, if she was able to displace my niece.'

Lady Shelton takes his hand and draws him into the house and calls for wine. 'I will tell you how it was, when Sadler brought your letter. We may as well sit. Shelton will be an hour with the dukes, pouring out his complaints about Lady Bryan.'

He likes to be told a story by Lady Shelton. He feels it will be one he can keep a grip on. 'You can go, Rob,' she says to the waiting boy. The boy – it is Mathew, from Wolf Hall – turns at the door and catches his eye. He looks away. I shall say to him, he thinks, lonely though you be – in a strange house, serving under a strange name

– you must make no signal, and certainly never in a woman's presence: they see plenty that men miss.

'We hourly expected your letter,' Lady Shelton says, 'and the paper for Mary to sign – because the Emperor's man Chapuys came two days past, and was shut up with her three or four hours. When he arrived here he would not eat, but drank off a great draught of ale before he went in, and Shelton said, "I hope the poor fellow does not regret that last swill" – for when a young woman insists she is a princess, how can you say, "Pardon me, Highness," and leave her to call for a pisspot? We could hear her all the while, talking, talking, talking. And the ambassador putting in a word, as he could. When he came out, he looked as if he had been on trial for his life. Shelton walked him out to his horse and waved him off, and as he came back in and was pulling off his boots, Mary ran to her chamber and slammed her bolt and shoved a chest against the door. It is not the first time. We have a burly fellow who cuts wood for us, and Shelton sent for him to set his shoulder at it. And when the woodsman fell in at the door, Mary ignored him, and went on saying her prayers.'

But then, he thinks, she had all next day to dwell on what she must do.

'So when Sadler rode up, it was long after dark, I believe it was eleven o'clock. Mary was still awake, stretched on her bed in her shift – lying on the counterpane, we could not get her to go between the sheets. She said, "If it is a gentleman, I will get dressed. But if it is only a letter, I declare I will not read it till morning." We said, "It is Sadler," and then we did not know what she would do, because she held before that he was not a gentleman, and yet she knows he serves in the king's privy chamber.'

I wonder how I would stand with her, he thinks.

'But then she exclaimed, "Sadler is Lord Cromwell's servant!" She ran down the stairs, no shoes on her feet, and snatched the package from his hands. "Give it to me, and let us have it over with," she said. And she crushed it to her, and made away with it, back up the stairs. She shouted out, "I will sign. I must. Ambassador Chapuys counsels it, and my cousin the Emperor commands it, and the Pope will forgive it, for I am enforced, and so it is no sin." And,' Lady Shelton says, 'I was never so surprised. A little later she came out of her chamber seething with spite, and called to me, "Shelton! You will soon be put out of your place. My good father will bring me to his side now. You will never have my keeping again."'

She cradles her cup in her hands. 'By midnight she had signed. She said she wanted the paper out of the house. She commanded Master Sadler to set out in the dark. "Either the letter leaves the house," she said, "or I do. I will not be under roof with it." Which was foolish talk, for the gate to the park was guarded, she would not have got fifty paces. And all this while, you must picture, Lady Bryan was scuttling in her wake bearing a beaker of camomile, the steam rising from it, and she wailing, "My darling, you will fall into a fever!" And in the nursery that demon child was howling – for her great teeth are not through yet – and Shelton, who is mannerly on ordinary occasions, roared out, "Get you away, Lady Bryan, and you, Princess, drain that beaker, or I will hold your nose and enforce you thereto!" You will forgive him for using that title, but it is the quickest way to get her to do anything. Then Master Sadler very civilly and properly spoke up, and said, "I would not disdain a pallet in your summer-house, and would take the letter out with me; it seems to me a solution that would unite all parties."'

Good boy. He smiles. Rafe had told him, I swear to you, sir – so that I got out of that house, I would have slung a hammock. I would have lain in a manger, or slumbered on the sward. As it was, I passed a pleasant night, and dreamt of my wife Helen. And I woke with the birdsong, with Helen in my arms. They brought me bread and ale, water to wash; unshaven and with curt farewells I mounted up, and rode to you. And it is worth a night under the stars, sir, to put this paper in your hand, and see your face clear.

He puts down his cup. 'My lady, we should join the others. I shall stand between you and Norfolk. If he rends the arras, he shall not rend me.'

He thinks, Mary Boleyn once leaned against me, mistaking me for a wall. Norfolk will drive his fist into me, but it will bounce.

Lady Shelton says, 'John and I wonder – is this household to be broke up?'

'Not yet.' He hesitates. 'The king will not receive Mary himself till news of her submission has gone abroad, and he knows from Rome and the Emperor that they have understood.'

'Of course. Or it would look as if he had just changed his mind, and let her off. Or as if the Emperor had frightened him.'

'You are a woman of sense. Come here.' He holds out his hand to her. He thinks, all the Boleyns are politicians. 'You might ease her conditions. No visitors unless I say so, but let her take the air in the park. She may have letters.'

She takes his hand. 'I think she only simulates her obedience.'

'Lady Shelton,' he says, 'I don't care.'

When they come into Mary's presence they kneel. It is for Norfolk, as their senior, to greet her on behalf of her father, that puissant and merciful prince, long may he reign: begging her pardon for any offence given, by their rude solicitations, on a previous occasion. Their severity occasioned only, he says, by their fear for her.

'Thomas Howard,' Mary says, 'I wonder you dare.'

Norfolk's head rears back; he glares.

'My lord Suffolk,' Mary turns to Brandon, 'you have given no offence.'

'Oh, in that case ...' Brandon begins to scramble to his feet; but one look, and he subsides again.

'You must think a woman a very feeble creature,' Mary tells Norfolk, 'if you think her memory does not reach back a week. Mine is good for that, and more. I know very well how you persecuted my mother.'

'Me?' Norfolk says. 'What about –'

'I know how you promoted the ambitions of Anne your niece, and afterwards disowned her, and condemned her to death. Do you think I have no pity for that misguided woman?' She checks herself, drops her voice. 'I have compunction. I am no stranger to it.'

From his kneeling position, he appraises the king's daughter. She is twenty, so it is not to be expected she will grow. Her person is as meagre as when he saw her at Windsor five years back: her face wan, her eyes dull, puzzled and full of pain. She wears a bodice and gown of tansy colour, which nothing becomes her, and her hair is scooped into a net of braided silk; she has left off her hood, no doubt because her head aches too much to bear the weight.

'My sweet lady,' Charles says. His voice unexpectedly lulling, he repeats the phrase: but then, it appears, he has nothing to add. 'Well,' he says, 'here's Cromwell. All will be right.'

'It will be right,' she snaps, 'when my lord Norfolk makes it right. Would you use me as you do your wife?'

'What?' The duke's eyebrows shoot up, and an unwilling grin creeps over his face.

She blushes. 'I mean, would you beat me?'

'Who told you I beat my wife? Cromwell, was it you? What has that blasted woman been telling you?' He wheels around, arms spread to the company. 'That scar she shows folk, on her temple – she had that before ever I knew her. She says I dragged her up from child-bed and knocked her across the room. By John the Baptist, I did no such thing.'

Mary says, 'If I did not know this tale before, I know it now. You have no respect for any woman, though she be set above you by God. Go out of here. I want to speak with Lord Cromwell alone.'

'Oh, do you?' Norfolk is chastened, but not chastened enough. 'And why can you say things to him that you cannot say to us?'

Mary says, 'To explain that to you, my lord, eternity is not long enough.'

Brandon is on his feet. His dearest wish is to be out of the room. For Norfolk, getting up is less easy. A leg shoots out – he treads down hard on the rushes, trying for leverage – he grunts, and an arm thrashes the air. Charles grips him under the elbow, ready to hoist. 'Hold hard, I've got you, Howard.'

Norfolk beats off assistance. 'Unhand me. It's cramp.' He will not admit it's age. But he swerves around both dukes – allow me, my lord

Suffolk – grips Thomas Howard, double-handed, by the back of his coat, and sets him on his feet with one contemptuous twitch. His heart is singing.

'So,' she says. 'I hear you are Lord Privy Seal. What will happen to Thomas Boleyn?'

'The king has permitted him to go down to Sussex, and live quietly.'

She sniffs. She rubs her forehead; even the net seems to fret her. 'I will say that Boleyn was civil in his dealings with my mother, unlike Thomas Howard. He never gave her harsh words – not in her hearing, at least. Still, he was a cold and selfish man, and he consorted with heretics. The king is merciful.'

'Some say, too much so.'

It is a warning. She does not hear it.

'You are grown very grand, Lord Cromwell. I suspect you were always very grand, only we did not see it. Who knows God's plan?'

Not I, he thinks. 'I directed Carew to write to you. I trust he did?'

'Yes. Sir Nicholas gave me certain advice.'

'Which disappointed you.'

'Which surprised me. You see, my lord, I know that he has taken the oath, even though he loved my mother and stood up in her cause. I think all have taken it, who are alive today.'

Not all, he thinks. Not Bess Darrell, Tom Wyatt's lady.

'My lady Salisbury signed it,' Mary says. 'And Lord Montague her son, and Lord Exeter and all the Courtenays. When Anne Boleyn was alive, they would have suffered if they had not bent to that lady's will. But when I knew she was cut down, I thought, what needs this concealment now? Will they not say plain what I know they believe, that my father should reconcile with the Pope? And will they not aid me, to be restored to my father's favour, and to have my rights and title? I did not know he meant to persist in error, I did not know –'

That you had so many faint hearts about you? Time-servers and placemen and cowards? 'They left you to bear the risk,' he says. 'They have practice in scuttling for cover.'

'Since then – since I received this advice from my friends, so much contrary to what preceded it – you must understand me, my lord, I have felt so alone.'

She moves towards him – he's forgotten her clumsiness, the way she blunders like a blind woman. A low table is set with wine, in a jug of silver and crystal; she sees it, sidesteps, clips it; it sways, the wine slops, a tide of crimson washes over the white linen. 'Oh,' she cries, and her hand dives out – the jug leaps from her fingertips –

'Leave it,' he says.

She stares at her shoes, appalled. Picks her feet out of the shards. 'It is John Shelton's. He had it of the Venetians.'

'I will send him another.'

'Yes, you have friends in those parts. So Ambassador Chapuys tells me.'

'I am glad he succeeded in bringing home to you the peril in which you stood. This last week has been –' He shakes his head.

'Chapuys said, "Cromwell has used all the grace that is in him. Risked all." He said, "He feels the axe's edge."' The hem of her skirt has soaked up the claret. She shakes it, ineffectually. 'No other lord has spoken for me. Not Norfolk, he would not. Not Suffolk, he durst not. This goes far with us to mitigate –'

She breaks off. He thinks, she is using the royal plural. Already.

'The ambassador says, "Cromwell is a heretic. But we may hope God will guide him to the truth."'

'We may all hope that,' he says piously.

'I often think, why did I not die in the cradle or the womb, like my brothers and sisters? It must be that God has a design for me. Soon I too may be elevated, beyond what seems possible now.'

The peril in the room is as quick and rank as a flare of sulphur. The tansy bodice casts an aura as she moves, a wash of jaundiced light. She is like Richmond; she thinks Henry is dying. 'What design could there be,' he asks, 'but that you should live content, and be a good daughter to your father?'

'The king will find me always obedient. But I have another Father, and a higher.'

'The will of the heavenly Father is often obscure. The will of your earthly father is plain. It is not for you to make reservations now, Mary. You have signed.'

She lifts her eyes, and her glance is rinsed with rage. And the next second, once again a mild passionless blue, like Henry's. 'Yes. I set my hand to it.'

'Chapuys is right. I could have done no more for you. I doubted my powers to do so much. Your resistance has injured your father. It has made him ill.'

'I believe it,' she says. 'It has made me ill too. So when shall I come back to court? I will come with you today, if you will take me. Let them find me a mount. We could be at Greenwich before dark.'

'The king is at Whitehall. And there are matters to settle.'

'Of course, but I do not mind about my lodging. I will share a truckle bed with a laundrymaid, if it means I am nearer my father.' She stumbles across the room again, trampling the shattered glass. 'I know you think me weak. Lady Shelton says a corpse has more colour and she is right. But I have always been a good horsewoman. I can keep pace with you, I swear it.'

'Lady Mary, you must have patience. The king must make sure news of your reformation travels to all parts, here and abroad.'

'So everyone will know,' she says. 'I see.'

'And few will doubt you have done right.'

'Chapuys told me about Reynold's letter. It is nothing to do with me. I had no foreknowledge.'

He thinks, I can pity you, without entirely believing you. He says, 'These supporters you think you have – the Courtenays, the Poles – forget them. They say they revere your ancient blood, but they think more of their own. Oh, they may spare one of their boys to marry you, but then they will exact your obedience, for a wife must obey her husband, no matter what her degree. And if your father, God forbid, should die before he gets a son, they will bid for the crown, and they may march behind your banner, but by their grace you will never rule.'

She has turned her back. In the sunlight that filters through the royal arms, through the tawny hide of glass lions, she raises her arms, and fumbles with her cap, and then lifts it free. Head dropping, she rubs her temples and forehead, then reaches up and pulls her hair from its pins.

He stares at her, dumbstruck. He cannot remember watching a woman do this, except in one circumstance. Even then, he has known a woman of business signal the start of proceedings by knotting her hair more firmly, and pinning it on top of her head.

She says, 'I suffer so much, Master Cromwell, that I think God must love me. Forgive me, I could not bear the confinement one minute more. My scalp throbs and my teeth ache. John Shelton says, perhaps you should have them pulled out, at least then the pain would be over. I have had a rheum in my head and here' – she puts her hand to her cheek – 'a swelling the size of a tennis ball.'

She is innocent, he thinks. Surely. Look how she said to Norfolk, 'You would use me as your wife,' and did not know why he was grinning. 'My lady,' he says, 'let me help you. Your eyes, your head, your understanding, all parts of you have been rebellion; you could not digest what you ate, if you slept it did not restore you. But now you have chosen a wise course, you have done as others have – men and women who love God, just as you do – all of whom have embraced conformity, and seen their duty to this realm. You have put all your strength into saying no. Now you have said yes. You have chosen to live and you must find a way to thrive. Do you think only weak people obey the law, because it terrifies them? Do you imagine only weak people do their duty, because they dare not do other? The truth is far different. In obedience, there is strength and tranquillity. And you will feel them. Believe me, I am earnest when I tell you this. It will be like the sun after a long winter.'

She says, 'I would give anything to ride again. But I have no saddle horse. They would not let me have one.'

'As soon as I get back to London, I will find you a mount, it will be the first thing I think of. And I will tell John Shelton you are to ride out with an escort, whenever you choose.'

'He was afraid the country people would see me, and would kneel to me, and acclaim me as princess.'

If that happens, he thinks, Shelton will know how to quell it. And I hardly think Chapuys will rise out of a ditch and carry you away. He says, 'I have a pretty dapple grey in my stables, a very gentle beast. She can be here with you in no time.'

'What is her name?'

Her hair, hanging limp, is a thin russet streak. She drags at it, anxious. At this moment she looks half her age.

'She is called Douceur. But you can change it if you like.'

'No. It is a good name.'

She drops her silk net on the table, and he watches it soak up the spilled wine. He wants to pick it out of the liquid, but he knows it is spoiled. She says, 'I can get another.' Her eyes pass over him; she looks covetous. 'Your jacket is a good blue. I like that figured stuff.'

He thinks of Mary Boleyn: *I like your grey velvet.* It seems so long ago, it could be another life. I was a different man then, he thinks, inside my jacket. A little thinner, perhaps. More tentative, certainly. He says, 'When you come back to court, you can have all the silk and damask your heart desires. The king has spoken to me of what he will give you.'

Mary puts her hand over her mouth. She gives a little moan, and her forehead tents in a deep frown, and the next moment, her nose is running and tears are rolling down her cheeks – cold weighty tears, like stones before a tomb.

He crosses the room to her. On a thin note, from between her fingers, she keens as if she had stumbled over a corpse. She sways and bleats, and he grips her to keep her on her feet, mouse bones jumping and trembling in his grasp. The door opens. Lady Shelton sweeps a glance over the smashed crystal, the crimson spill, the girl with her terrible naked face, and she speaks as directly as a mother to her daughter: 'Mary, stop that noise. Let go of the Lord Privy Seal. Put on your cap.'

Mary's wail cuts off. Her face is streaked; she shakes like someone in the grip of fever. 'I cannot. My cap is spoiled. I walked into the table and smashed Sir John's jug, for which I am sorry, and then I –'

'Never mind,' Lady Shelton says. 'I have never made any sense of what you say, and I suppose I shall not begin now.' She gathers up the girl's hair and stands holding it in her fist, as if to lead her from the room; then with a sound of exasperation, lets her go. 'I shall take you to Lady Bryan to put you to rights. Blow your nose.'

He can hear Mary's thoughts, as loud as if they were slapping the walls: I am a princess of England, you have made promises to me. 'Mary,' he says, 'mark this. My promises are kept now. You have my duty and regard. Count on that. No more.'

Mary's eyes flicker with dismay. 'But you said I should be – that if anything befell the king – that you would help me to – did you not promise the ambassador?'

'I promised what I had to,' he says. 'It was an extremity.'

With a tug to her scalp, Anne Shelton stops any further questions. She speaks to him over the girl's head. 'You cannot leave without you see Eliza. Lady Bryan insists.'

What Lady Bryan has to exhibit is a convulsing mass of linen, red flailing fists, a maw emitting shrieks. 'Now, my lady!' She sweeps up the little girl. 'Show your goodness to these gentlemen. They have ridden to see you to tell your lord father how you do.'

He is dismayed. 'She screams as if she had seen Bishop Gardiner.'

A chortle from Brandon. A tight smile from Thomas Howard.

'Will you tell their lordships you are glad to see them?' Lady Bryan asks her charge. 'Will you sing them a song?'

'I take leave to doubt it,' Norfolk says.

'*Fol-de-dee, fol-de-dee, fol-de-dee-do*,' trills Lady Bryan. '*When sparrows build churches upon a green hill* … No? Never mind, darling. Bite on this.' She produces a circle of ivory, garlanded with green ribbons; the child seizes it and falls to. 'Her teeth come very slowly forth.'

Suffolk stares down from his vast height. 'Thank God they are no faster. I should be afraid she would nip me.'

'Perhaps we could come back at a better time,' he says.

'Aye,' Suffolk mutters, 'when she is thirty.' But he likes children, and he cannot help leaning down and making faces at her. The little girl breaks off grizzling, touches his beard; she rubs it, and looks at her fingers, dubious.

'It doesn't come off,' Charles tells her. The child's black eyes snap at him; she thrusts her ivory ring back into her mouth, but she does not cry again.

'I never saw a child suffer so,' Lady Bryan says. 'It makes me give way to her when perhaps I should not. Sir John lets her sit at table, and she is too young to be refrained from what she has a fancy for.' She turns to him. 'Master Cromwell, how does your little Gregory these days?'

'A head taller than me, and in want of a wife.'

'How the years fly! It seems no time since you brought him to … wherever we were …'

'Hatfield.'

'Mary was wasting away.' She turns to the dukes. 'Till Thomas Cromwell came, we could do nothing with her. We could not make her come to the common board, because she would have had to sit lower than her sister – Eliza was a princess then. And Sir John said, mark my words, give way to one, and they will all be wanting to dine in private, and the cooks will be put about, and the expense will run beyond my means – no, he said, Mary dines and sups in the hall with us, or she must go without. But Master Cromwell got the physicians to state, on their honour, that Mary could not thrive without a trencher of red meat at her first rising in the morning. Sir John could hardly refuse her a breakfast, for that meal we all take apart. So she had her fill of venison while the larder lasted, and salt beef when needs must.'

Suffolk smiles. 'She breakfasted like Robin Hood and his men, feasting in the green wood. I trust it did her good.'

'So is Mary now a princess again?' Lady Bryan asks.

He says, 'She remains as she was, Lady Mary the king's daughter.'

'And this lass,' Norfolk says, 'is to be known as My Lady Bastard, till you hear different.'

'For shame!' Lady Bryan is distraught. 'Whoever she may be, she is a gentleman's daughter, and I know not how to keep her in that degree. All children do grow, sir, and this last month she has outgrown every stitch she owns, and Sir John says he has no budget and no instructions. We have patched and mended till we can do no more. She needs nightgowns, she needs caps –'

'Madam, am I a nursemaid?' Norfolk says. 'Tell Cromwell about it – I dare say he can understand the child's requirements. No trade is beyond him – give him some cambric and a needle and you will find your little dame clad before supper time.'

The duke turns on his heel and stalks out of the room. They can hear him on the stairs, calling for John Shelton to fetch the horses.

'Write to me,' he says to Lady Bryan. He wants to get after Norfolk. He doesn't want him alone with Mary.

But Lady Bryan follows him, a buzz at his elbow. On the stairs, 'Cromwell, I spoke to her. As you demanded. So did my daughter, Lady Carew.' Her voice is low. 'We did what you asked.'

'Good.'

'You have broken her pride. It is ill-done.'

'It saved her life.'

'To what purpose?'

He strides ahead. 'Send me a list of what the little maid needs.'

Shelton is outside, with the horseboys. Lady Shelton says, laughing, 'No need to haste away. Mary has run upstairs. Did you think she would be rushing to confer with your enemies? You take her for a fickle mistress.'

He checks his pace. 'The dukes are not my enemies. We are all the king's servants.'

'You appear to have Suffolk in awe.'

True, he thinks. Brandon gives no trouble these days.

He turns and takes her hand; but there is a yell from below, like a hunting call. 'Cromwell!'

It is Charles, stopped on the threshold, head thrown back, pointing upwards. 'Cromwell, see that?'

He has to clatter downstairs, to look from another angle. Far above them, in a haze of blood-coloured light, the initials of the late Anne rest on a glazed cushion.

'Shelton!' the duke yells. 'You've got a HA-HA. Knock it out, man. Do it while the weather's fine.' Charles bellows with laughter. 'Get the Lady Mary to heave a brick at it.'

The boy Mathew is outside, holding his horse's bridle. 'Keep steady,' he says. He doesn't mean the horse.

He mounts, and below the creak of saddle and harness the boy murmurs, 'Get me home when you can, sir.'

'I'll tell Thurston you miss him.'

Mathew backs away. 'God be with you, sir.'

He gathers his reins. John Shelton is standing in their path, apologising for the HA-HA. 'I thought I had got them. Every last one.'

He says, 'It's scarcely a month since Galyon Hone sent in his bill from Dover Castle, for setting the queen's badges in the private lodgings.'

'What?' Norfolk says. 'The queen that is now, or the other one?'

'Wasted,' he says. 'Two hundred pounds.'

Brandon whistles. 'It's the devil. Stone, you can chisel it off; wood, you can rip it out or reshape it; whitewash and repaint your plaster-work, and stitching you can unpick – but when it's blazing down at you, the sun behind it, what can you do?'

They get on the road. The early-summer day will allow them home by dusk. 'Which is sad for you, Cromwell,' Norfolk says. 'You'd rather make a stop, I suppose. Still, keep looking in the ditch, you might spot some drab with her legs apart.'

Norfolk rides ahead with his people; but he and Brandon ride companionably, knee to knee. In Southwark, Brandon says, where his family has a great house and the glassmakers have their shops, they are at constant peril from the fires that blaze away when their kilns are opened. 'Catch a wisp of straw,' Brandon says, 'and *whoosh* – the whole district goes up.'

Well, at those temperatures, he thinks. A blacksmith's forge is dangerous, and smiths are always blackened and burned, but you don't find them pierced to the heart with their own product, or hurtling to their deaths from church towers, as glaziers do every day of the week.

As they meet the road to Ware, Thomas Howard stops and turns in his saddle, watching them. His half-brother Tom Truth stops too, and twists to look back.

'Look at the Howards, twitching,' he says. 'They want to know what we are talking about.'

Glazing still, as it happens. 'Do you know, Cromwell,' the duke says, 'I was a rare hand at smashing glass in my youth? I expect you were. Though perhaps you didn't have the chance?'

'Yes, my lord, we had glass in Putney.'

'My lord Norfolk?' Charles calls out. 'Just telling Cromwell here – I've not broken a window in years.'

In the first week of July, the king indicates that he is ready to meet his daughter. Not, yet, to bring her to court: 'But the queen is urging me,' he says. 'And I thought you might manage it so as ... just to allow me to see her. Allow me to judge her feelings towards me. And Crumb,' he says, 'I don't want to ride far.'

The physicians are in daily consultation. The king's good humour is soured by the nagging pain of his injured leg. I have feared for some time, Butts says, there is residual foulness in the bone. What is in the flesh, we can wash out – cut out, if we have to. But the bone must mend itself. Or not. Young Richmond was right. Decay runs deep. Next year the king might not be here.

At Austin Friars, he goes to Mercy Prior's chamber. 'Mother, the king would like to see his daughter. I thought we might use our new house at Hackney.'

Mercy's lodging gives out onto the garden, so she can sit in the sun when there is any. She keeps up letter-writing with her friends, many younger than herself, some of them learned, some of them Lutherans.

Sometimes Mistress Sadler comes to read to her; Helen can read now as well as if she had learned as a child, and can write a fair hand too. But today Mercy is alone with her New Testament, the book of Tyndale's making. If she cannot always make out the words, she likes to have the text to hand. She sets it down and watches it for a moment, as you might watch a child to see if it will settle. 'I suppose there is no news?'

The Bible scholar has been in the Emperor's prison at Vilvoorde for a year now, ever since he was taken up in Antwerp. Now his time is short. Tyndale will recant, or he will burn. Perhaps he will recant *and* burn. The Emperor wishes to make an example, and keep the town of Antwerp in fear. The King of England will not stir for this subject of his, as Tyndale stood against him in the matter of his divorce. Because you are against the Pope, it doesn't mean you are for Henry; Tyndale has always said, as Martin Luther does, we do not love Rome or its authority, but we cannot fault your marriage to Katherine, it is good and it must stick.

'You cannot move the king to speak for him?' Mercy asks. 'Now he has his new queen and is at ease … you say he will reconcile with his daughter, and the other party in the quarrel is dead and gone.'

Katherine is dead and not dead. Her cause flourishes, its taproot deep in acid soil. Mercy says, 'I think of Tyndale in his cell. Could you fetch him out of there, before winter comes? Would it be possible?'

'You mean, would it be possible for me? You think it is a thing I might attempt?'

'You might attempt anything.' She does not mean it as a compliment.

He has a ground plan of the fortress of Vilvoorde. He knows where Tyndale is kept. But if he got him to the coast, where would he go? 'I think we will see the Testament in English soon. I think Henry will allow it. The work will be Tyndale's. But it cannot have his name on it.'

'I hope I live so long,' Mercy says. 'I blame Thomas More for Tyndale, his nest of spies that lived on after he was dead, and if I thought the dead in their graves felt pain I would grub him from the ground and kick him up and down Cheap, for what he inflicted on men and women who are nearer to God than he will ever be.'

'Blessed are the meek,' he says.

'Yes, so they claim. I notice where it gets you.'

He has often thought, these last weeks, that if you matched the king's daughter with Tyndale – to see which was the more stubborn, the more set on self-destruction – it would be a close contest. 'But you see,' he says, 'she has yielded. If we bring her to Hackney, then if it goes ill, the king can quickly be away.'

For the last year, he has been rebuilding a place made over to the king by the Earl of Northumberland. Young Harry Percy is sick, and deep in debt to the crown. He offered in part-payment the house with all its contents; Henry had said, why don't you move in, Crumb, during the renovations, then you can keep a hand on the workmen? With young Sadler building his house just across the meadow, you can redirect the labour as needed ... The king had sent seasoned oak from the royal forests, and he and Rafe had set up a brickfield, the water from the brook supplying it. Mercy had said, 'You'll see, Thomas, as soon as all the hard work is done, Henry will turn you out.'

Of course – but it's the king's house, after all. He is laying out a new garden and he has ambassadors alert for cuttings and seeds, of plants not grown in England. Light will flood the old rooms. There will be no HA-HAs, nor need he bear the arrogance of Hone's glaziers – James Nicholson is just as skilled at a lower rate. He has walked the ground with the builders, deep in talk about pipes and culverts, the capacity of cisterns, hidden springs that can be tapped. Even in his early days at Austin Friars, he had made a bathroom, but it is hard to get piped water to more than a trickle; you need a healthy supply for a kitchen, if it has to feed a king.

'Will you come out there?' he asks Mercy. 'Everything must be ready for royal ladies to lodge one night.'

'Helen Sadler will do it. I am too old to go jolting out to the country. And as neither of us have ever been near the court, she can guess as well as I what is wanted. Mary is only human, I suppose, and a girl like other young girls.'

Yes, he thinks, and Jane a queen like other queens. Henry has been showing her off to the ambassadors, allowing her to converse. He is surprised – everyone is surprised – by her calm and poise. But afterwards she seems to withdraw into herself. During her first week on show, her eyes had sought out her brothers, or his, for a signal what to do. The women around her are still set fluttering by any disturbance. Francis Bryan says, what do you expect, Thomas? It is only weeks since you were questioning them one by one and tying their poor little stories in knots. They need time to recover from the fright.

The day is upon us. Helen has a list in hand. Harry Percy's furnishings have been under covers to protect them from plaster dust and the smell of fresh paint. In the chief bedchamber, the earl's arms have been unpicked from bed hangings of blue and cloth of gold. The counterpane of gold damask and blue velvet came with the house; beneath it, layers of new blankets of dense white wool. He woke, this morning, thinking of Tyndale, lying in the running damp. If the executioner does not kill him, another winter will. In Antwerp they slide the printed sheets of the gospels between the folds of bales of cloth, where they hide, white against white. Warm, nestled, God whispers within each bundle; His word sails the sea, is unloaded in eastern ports, travels to London in a cart. He makes a note to himself: Tyndale, talk to Henry, try again.

For the Lady Mary's use, he has advised choosing the warmest room in the house. A great bed of down is ready, hangings of tawny velvet, cushions of russet velvet and figured green satin. 'It could be a bridal bed,' Helen says. He can see the pleasure it gives her – a poor girl, brought up hard – to handle the fine stuff and have a brigade of cushions at her command. She says, 'I have moved the great purple chair to the gallery for the king. I must find a lower one for the queen. There is a little gold brocade chair for the Lady Mary. They say she is spare of habit and small.' She hesitates. 'Shall I see her?'

Helen is the wife of a man in the king's privy chamber, close to his person; why should she not make her curtsey? But there are customs, and she will not break them. 'When you show them in to their supper, I shall stand with the servants. You must not bring me forward, I should not like that.'

They are in the gallery as they speak; Helen looks up at the arras, at the white thread limbs of running figures, a maid with streaming hair. 'I have no idea who these folk are.'

It is the story of Atalanta and her unfortunate start in life. 'She was a king's daughter too,' he says.

'And?'

A king's daughter cannot just live quiet. There is always an *and* or a *but*. 'But the king wanted a son. So when a daughter was born, he left her to die on the mountainside.'

'A blameless infant?' Helen is shocked.

'It was a long time ago,' he says, 'and in Arcadia. But she was saved, because by good fortune a she-bear was passing, and gave her milk.'

'Ah, I understand. It is a fairy tale. And then what?'

'She grew up to be a huntress. She lived in the wilderness. She vowed herself to virginity.'

'What did she do that for?'

'I think it was an offering to the gods. It was before popes. Before Christ. They had small gods of their own in those days.'

Noise from the courtyard brings them to the window. Thurston is here. The kitchen staff are braced for him. In an English summer you must make your own sunshine. Downstairs, Thurston will attend to fine detail: rosewater jelly, quaking puddings, curd tarts.

The king wears white and gold, the queen white and silver. 'Better today,' the king says: meaning himself. In no haste to see his daughter – or wishing to seem in no haste – he strolls in the garden, Rafe Sadler at his side, examining the new planting. 'I shall spend a week here. Perhaps towards the end of the summer.'

That's you out on the road, he thinks. Rafe catches his eye. 'I shall visit you, Sadler,' the king promises. 'Master Sadler lives down the lane,' he tells Jane. 'Did you know that he married a beggar woman?'

'No,' Jane says: adding nothing.

'She came to the gate of Lord Cromwell's house, two little children at her skirts. And no resource in the world – but Cromwell here, perceiving her to be of an honest demeanour, he took her in.' Henry warms to his own story; his colour is high, his manner easy and gracious, his eye brighter than for weeks. 'Master Sadler, seeing her flourish day by day, his heart was won – and despite her want of fortune, he married her.'

There is something lacking in Jane's response – or at least the king thinks so. 'Was that not great charity?' Henry urges. 'A man who might have married to his advantage, to match with a lowly woman, only for the virtue he perceived in her?' Jane murmurs; the king leans down to catch it. 'Oh yes, I expect they were marvellously put about. Cromwell, were Sadler's family not angry? But Cromwell here pleaded their cause. He said nothing must stand in the way of true love. And,' the king lifts Jane's hand, and kisses it, 'Cromwell was right.'

The signal is given, the moment arrived. The king beams around the room. 'This day has been long in coming. You may conduct her to us, Cromwell.' He turns to Rafe: 'Lord Cromwell has behaved to my lady daughter with such tenderness and care that he could not have done more if he were my kinsman. Which of course,' the king seems surprised at his own words, 'he could not be. But I mean to reward him, and all his house. Lady Shelton, will you go with him?'

Lady Shelton has ridden from Hertfordshire in Mary's train, along with her chest of new clothes. As they walk upstairs together, she says, 'The king looks lighter in himself. You would almost think Jane has given him good news, though I suppose it is too soon for that.'

'Some women seem to know it the very moment they conceive.'

'When there is a king in the case, you would not risk a mistake.'

At the head of the stair he stops. 'How shall I find her?'

'Silent.'

'The tansy bodice ...?'

'Extirpated as thoroughly as the name of the Pope.'

'Never to return?'

'It is made into a cushion, and sent to the nursery. We can expect the Lady Eliza to deal with it, as soon as her teeth appear. I must confess it was my fault in the first place. The king supplied her well with mourning clothes for her mother, he did not stint. But I thought your lordship might not like her to appear in black.'

Thirty-two yards of black velvet at thirty pounds and eight shillings. Forty-two shillings and eightpence to the new Master of the Merchant Tailors, for making up. Fourteen yards of black satin at six pounds and six shillings. Thirteen yards of black velvet for a nightgown and taffeta lining. Ninety black squirrels' skins. Plus kirtles, partlets, bodices, sleeves, sundries: one hundred and seventy-two pounds, sixteen shillings and sixpence in total, on the king's account. Now she will wear brighter hues. Every day since his visit – or rather, since the king signalled he was content – bounty by the cartload has been bumping over the roads out of Bishopsgate. He has spoken to the Italian cloth merchants, and to Hans about a design for a fine emerald, to be set as a pendant with pearls. Katherine's furs will be inspected, and, if the king sees fit, given to Mary this winter ahead.

Tyndale, he thinks. Remember the winter ahead.

Mary looks up at his arrival. She meets his eye. The beauteous Eliza Carew is with her; Eliza does not look at him at all. Another lady is kneeling, making some adjustment to Mary's hem. It is Margaret Douglas, the king's red-headed niece. 'Lady Meg is here,' Mary says: as if he might not notice her. 'The king thought ... as it was a family occasion ...'

Every time I see you, Meg, you are on your knees. He offers a hand. She ignores it, flounces up, crosses to the window and stares out over the garden. Carew's wife is left to fuss about Mary's train. 'My lady?' he says. 'Are you ready?'

Meg is train-bearer. As they sweep out, Mary stiff and precarious in her new gown of crimson and black, he holds back Lady Carew with a gesture: 'Thank you.'

'For what?'

'For your part in saving her.'

'I had no choice. I was *told*.'

Women, staircases, words behind the hand: are the Emperor's servants, he wonders, forced to work like this? You have to hold your breath, as Mary negotiates every tread on the stair. The King of England's daughter, the Queen of Scotland's child: such moments seem like the work of some artificer, who designs to weave them in wool or flowers. Mary glances around, as if to check he is following. Meg gives her train a shake. She seems to steer her from behind, with clucks and murmurs, like a woman driving a cart. When Mary stops, Lady Meg stops. What if Mary panics? What if she thinks at this last moment, I cannot do it? But, he murmurs to Lady Shelton, my anxiety is not so much, will she change her mind – it's will she trip over her feet and land before her father in a heap.

'We have done our best with her,' Lady Shelton sighs. 'In my opinion, a gentler hue would have flattered her complexion, but she wished to be as regal as possible. What's the matter with the Scots girl? Doesn't she like you?'

'It happens,' he says.

They had received no notice that there would be three royal ladies – Mary, the queen, Meg Douglas too. They had expected the queen to bring her familiar chamber women. But the party had not dismounted before he had called out to Helen, and she had sped away. In short order she was back: got the red tinsel cushions, she said, and laid a foot carpet down. Hung up the story of Aeneas; at least, that's what Rafe said it is. He had thought, I hope Dido is not in flames.

At the foot of the stairs, Mary stops abruptly. 'My lord Cromwell?'

Meg releases one long outraged breath: 'Madam, the king is waiting.'

'I forgot to thank you for the dapple grey. She is a gentle creature, as you promised.' She says to Meg, 'Lord Cromwell sent me a pretty mount from his own stable. Nothing has pleased me more – I have not ridden in five years, and it is much comfort to my health.'

'She does look better,' Lady Shelton says. 'A little colour in her cheeks.'

'Her name was Douceur,' Mary says. 'It is a good name, but I have renamed her. I have called her Pomegranate. It was my mother's emblem.'

Lady Shelton closes her eyes, as if in pain. Mary gains the threshold. She disposes her skirts. The doors are flung open. The king and queen are still against the light: golden sun and silver moon. Mary takes in a deep, ragged breath. And he stands behind her: because, what else can he do?

That evening, the king releases him, so he can be alone with his family. They will retire early, and there will be no policy discussed, or papers signed. Helen says, 'You are exhausted. Will you not stroll down the lane and sit in our summerhouse for an hour? Gregory and Mr Richard are there already.'

The evening, dove-like, is settling itself to rest. When the chronicles of the reign are composed, by our grandchildren or by those in another country, distant from these fading fields and glow-worm light, they will reimagine the meeting between the king and his daughter – the orations they made each other, the mutual courtesies, the promises, the blessings. They will not have witnessed, they could not record, the Lady Mary's wobbling curtsey, or how the king's face flushes as he crosses the room and sweeps her up; her sniffling and whimpering as she grips the white-gold tissue of his jacket; his gasp, his sob, his broken endearments and the hot tears that spring from his eyes. Jane the queen stands, dry-eyed, shy, until a thought strikes her and she removes a jewel from her finger. 'Here, wear this.' Mary's mewling cuts off. He is reminded of Lady Bryan, holding out a teething ring to the Lady Bastard.

'Oh!' Mary juggles with the ring, almost drops it. It is a vast diamond, and it holds the light of the afternoon in an ice-white grasp. Margaret Douglas grips Mary's wrist and hoops the jewel on a finger. 'Too big!' She is desolate.

'It can be reset.' The king holds out his flat palm. The gem vanishes into some pocket. 'You are generous, sweetheart,' he says to Jane. He, Cromwell, has seen the flicker in the king's eye, as he calculates the worth of the stone.

'You are gracious, madam,' Mary says to the queen. 'I wish you nothing but what is for your comfort. I hope you will have a child soon. I shall pray for it daily. I take you now as my own lady mother. As if God had ordained the same.'

'But,' the queen says. Perturbed, she motions her husband to bend his head: whispers to him. He says, smiling, 'The queen says, it would be hard even for God to ordain, as she is but seven years your senior.'

Mary stares at the queen. 'Tell her it is an expression of my regard. It is an established form of well-wishing. Her Grace should not –'

'She understands, don't you, sweetheart?' Henry smiles down at Jane. 'Shall we go in?'

The servants wait, kneeling, for the royal party to pass. But Helen wafts in with halved lemons on a silver tray – seeing she has come at the wrong moment, she draws back and curtseys deeply. The scent of the lemons cuts the air. Jane smiles absently at Helen. Mary does not seem to see her, but she does not trip over her either. The king checks his stride and seems about to speak; then turns to his wife and daughter, who face each other in the doorway.

'I will not go before you,' Jane says.

'Madam, you are the queen, you must.'

Jane holds out her hand, naked without its diamond. That star, pocketed, beams its rays at the king's belly. 'Let us go in like sisters,' Jane says. 'Neither one before the other.'

Henry glows with pleasure. 'Is she not a jewel in herself? Is she not, Cromwell? Come, my angels. Let us ask God to bless our repast and our new amity, and I pray it may never falter.'

But later, when their grace is made, and the king has washed his hands in a marble basin, and the dishes are served, and he has eaten artichokes and said they are his favourite thing in this world, he falls silent and seems to brood; at last bursts out, 'Sadler, is that your wife? She who made her curtsey as we came in?' He chuckles. 'I think if she had come a beggar to my gate, I would have married her too. I see it was no charity. Such eyes! Such lips!' He glances at Jane. 'And she has already given Sadler a son.'

Jane neither sees nor hears. She just goes on steadily eating her way through her trout pasty, slices of cucumber scattered around her like green half-moons. It is as if the blessed Katherine is inspiring her. If it had been the other one sitting here, she would have laughed, and set up some peevish revenge.

Down the lane, '*Pomegranate?*' Rafe says. He groans. 'I should have known it was going too well.'

Strawberries and raspberries arrive. Wriothesley arrives, arm in arm with Richard Riche. They take their seats in the arbour. Pitchers of white wine rest in a bowl of cold water on the ground. He thinks, if Mary were here she would tread in that.

Rafe's goblets are decorated with pictures of Christ's disciples. 'I hope it is not the Last Supper,' Rafe says. 'Here, sir. This one for you.'

He recognises St Matthew, the tax-gatherer. He raises the saint, and offers them the Tuscan merchants' toast: '*In the name of God and of profit.*'

The weight of the day has fallen on him. He listens to the rise and fall of their voices, and allows his mind to drift. He thinks of the wings he wears; or so he boasted to Francis Bryan. When the wings of Icarus melted, he fell soundless through the air and into the water; he went in with a whisper, and feathers floated on the surface, on the flat and oily sea. Why do we blame Daedalus for the fall, and only remember his failures? He invented the saw, the hatchet and the plumbline. He built the Cretan labyrinth.

He comes back to himself; from the house, a baby's cry. Helen jumps up. 'Small Thomas. His window is open. To the night air!'

They look up; a nurse's face appears, the shutter is drawn close, the wail cuts off. Rafe stretches out his hand. 'Sweetheart, take your ease. He has attendance enough.'

They want her to stay in the garden with them, her beauty like a blessing. She sits down, but she says, 'My breasts ache sometimes when he cries, even though he is weaned now. My girls I fed myself – the children I had before. But now I am a lady. So.'

They smile: they are fathers, except only Gregory. And he is already thinking how with advantage Gregory could be wed.

Riche raises St Luke. He will never stray long from the business in hand. 'To your success, sir.' He drinks. 'Though you ran it to the danger point.'

Gregory says, 'By the time my father let our friend Wyatt go free, Wyatt had pulled out what was left of his hair. He delays to show his power.'

'Nothing amiss there,' Riche says. 'Since he has it. My lord – Christopher Hales is sworn in as Master of the Rolls today. He asks, do you mean to vacate the Rolls House?'

He has no plans for moving. Chancery Lane is easy for Whitehall. 'Tell Kit we'll lodge him elsewhere.'

'You should have heard the king,' Rafe says, 'when he spoke of what he owes our master. He said, Lord Cromwell could not be more to me if he were my own kin.'

'Then he remembered I was of mean parentage,' he says, smiling. 'If it were not for that, he would very much like to be related to me.' He looks around at them. They are waiting. He remembers how Wyatt had said, you are in danger of explaining yourself. 'God knows,' he says, 'I would have moved sooner, but I had to let Mary fetch herself to where we needed her to be. You were there, Riche, that day the king threw Fitzwilliam out of the council chamber –'

'It was you who threw him out, I think.'

'Believe me, it was better so.' It was hard for me to walk back, he thinks, with his chain of office in my hand. I felt a breeze on my neck, as if my head were lifting away. I could have kept walking. Like Jesus, walked on the water. Or deployed my wings.

Master Wriothesley touches his arm. 'Sir, your friends wish me to say – they have authorised me to say – that they hope you do not lose by the amity you have shown the king's daughter. For while, on the one hand, it must be a blessed work to reconcile father and daughter, and bring an unruly child to proper obedience –'

'Call Me, have a strawberry,' Rafe says.

'– yet on the other hand, we have no reason to believe proper gratitude will follow. Let us hope you have no reason to regret your goodness towards her.'

'Gardiner will be in a rage,' he says. 'He will think I have stolen a mean advantage.'

'You have,' Helen says. 'Mary cannot take her eyes off you.'

'But not like that,' he says. She watches me, he thinks, as one watches some rare beast – what might it do, if it would? 'I promised Katherine I would look after her.'

'What?' Rafe is shocked. 'When? When did you?'

'When I went up to Kimbolton. When Katherine was ill.'

'And you bedded that woman at –' Gregory breaks off. 'Sorry.'

'At the inn. Yes. But I did not have her husband poisoned. Or invent a new crime and have him hanged for it.'

'No one thinks you did,' Riche says soothingly.

'Bishop Gardiner does.' He laughs. 'I never saw the woman after.'

But I remember her, he thinks: at dawn, singing on the stairs. I remember the sickroom at the castle, and Katherine shrunken into her cape of ermines: her face marked with what she had already endured, and what she knew she would endure in the weeks to come. No wonder she was not afraid of the axe. 'Contemptible,' Katherine had called him that day. He remembers the young woman – whom he knows, now, was Bess Darrell – gliding away with a basin. Master Cromwell, Katherine had asked him, do you take the sacraments still? In what language do you confess? Or perhaps you do not confess at all?

What had he said? He can't recall. Perhaps he said he would confess if ever he was sorry, which mostly he wasn't. He was leaving, but – 'Master Secretary? A moment.'

He had thought, it is always the case: it is just as you are heading out of the door – as if to show you no longer care – that your prisoner concedes guilt, or offers you a bargain, or yields up the name you have been waiting for. Katherine had said, 'You recall when we met at Windsor?' She had added, unflinching, 'The day the king left me?'

The very swans on the river stunned with heat, the trees drooping, the hounds from the courtyard making their hound music, till their bell-like voices withdrew into the distance, and the train of gallant horsemen moved away over the meadows, and the queen knelt praying in the afternoon light, and the king who went hunting never came back.

'I remember,' he said. 'Your daughter was ill. I made her sit. I did not intend she should faint and crack her head.'

'You think I am a bad mother.'

'Yes.'

'But still I believe you are my friend.'

He had looked at her, astonished. Painfully, clasping her hands on the arms of her chair, the dowager got to her feet. The ermines slid to the floor, nosing each other, curling at her feet in a soft feral heap. 'I am dying, as you see, Cromwell. When the time comes that I can no longer protect her, do not let them harm the Princess Mary. I commend her to your care.'

She did not wait for his answer. She nodded to him: you go now. He could smell the leather binding of her books, the stale sweat from her linen. He made his reverence to her: Madam. Ten minutes later he was on the road: and ridden here, to the conclusion of the enterprise, to the place where promises are kept.

Gregory says, 'Why did you do it?'

'I pitied her.' A dying woman in a strange country.

You know what I am, he thinks. You should by now. Henry Wyatt told me, look after my son, don't let him destroy himself. I have kept the promise though I had to lock him up to do it. In the cardinal's day they used to call me the butcher's dog. A butcher's dog is strong and fills its skin; I am that, and I am a good dog too. Set me to guard something, I will do it.

Richard Cromwell says, 'You could not know, sir, what Katherine was asking.'

That's the point of a promise, he thinks. It wouldn't have any value, if you could see what it would cost you when you made it.

'Well,' Rafe says. 'You kept this close.'

'Since when was I an open book?'

'I don't think it was a good idea,' Gregory says.

'What, you don't think it was a good idea to stop the king killing his daughter?'

Richard Riche says, 'Tell me, sir, I am curious – how far does your care of her extend? Were she openly to rebel against the king, what would you do then?'

Richard Cromwell says, 'My uncle is the king's sworn councillor. The promise he made to Katherine was – I will not say a word lightly given, but it was no solemn oath. It could not bind him, if there were any conflict with the king's interest.'

He is silent. Chapuys had said, you may renegotiate with the living, but you cannot vary your terms with the dead. He thinks, I bound myself: why did I? Why did I bow my head?

Riche says, 'Does Mary know of this … what shall we term it … this undertaking?'

'No one knows, except myself and the dowager Katherine. I have never spoken about it till now.'

Riche says, 'Best if it goes no further. We will consign it to the shadows.' He smiles. Perhaps nothing is quite clear, that is spoken in a garden on an evening like this. In Arcadia.

Richard Cromwell looks up. 'Don't try and make it a dirty little secret, Riche. It was an act of kindness. No more.'

'But here comes Christophe,' Rafe says. *'Et in Arcadia ego.'*

Christophe's bulk occludes the last rays of sunlight. 'Chapuys is here. I told him, stay in the house, till I see if my lord desires your company.'

'I hope you put it more courteously,' Rafe says. He gets up.

'I'll fetch him,' Gregory says.

His son has seen that Rafe needs to arrange his face. Rafe takes off his cap and flattens down his hair.

'You look tidier now,' he tells him, 'but no happier.'

Rafe says, 'Truly, Mary shocked me, when I went up to Hunsdon with the papers for her to sign. Running downstairs like that – I never saw a gentlewoman go unshod – at least, not unless a fire broke out.

When she snatched the letter from my hand, I thought she meant to rip it up. Then she went shrieking away with it as if it were a map for buried treasure.'

'That treasure,' he says, 'is her life.'

'I could not answer for the worth of that lady,' Riche says. 'I fear she may be counterfeit coin.'

Helen looks up. 'Hush. Our visitor.'

Gregory says, 'He doesn't understand English.'

'Doesn't he?' Helen says.

They watch the ambassador pick his way across the lawn, flickering like a firefly in his black and gold. 'I took a chance on my welcome,' he says. 'Master Sadler, how happy I am to see you in the midst of your family. How well your garden flourishes! You ought to set a vine here, and train it over a trellis, like the one Cremuel has at Canonbury.' He takes Helen's hand. 'Madame, you have no French, and I no English. Yet could I command your tongue, words are needless, for at so sweet a flower, it is enough to gaze.' He swivels on his heel. 'So, Cremuel, we survive the *dies irae*. And all your boys are here. I think we may congratulate ourselves. Echoes have reached me. I hear the king has given his daughter a thousand crowns, not to mention a diamond worth as much again, and made her great guarantees as to her future. And I tell you, gentlemen, if Cremuel can pacify the Lady Mary, I expect soon to see him descend to Hell and fetch up Satan to shake hands with Gabriel. Not that I compare the young lady to a devil, you understand. But he is quite justified in reproaching her with being the most stubborn woman alive.'

Ah, he thinks. She showed you the *billet doux* I sent her. They embrace. He is careful not to crush the ambassador's bones. Chapuys looks around him, smiling. 'My friends, let this be a new era of concord. No one wants another dead lady, or a war. Your prince cannot afford it, and mine is a lover of peace. What I always say is, wars begin in man's time, but they end in God's time. What a pretty summerhouse.' He shivers. 'Forgive me. The damp. We could go inside, perhaps?'

'What a deficient climate,' Rafe says.

'Alas,' says the ambassador. He follows Rafe towards the house. 'When once you have been in Italy ...'

Helen collects the disciples. 'Christophe, you can take these, but mind St Luke, I think he is chipped. Richard Riche must have gnawed him. I shall have to use him for flowers.'

'Chapuys looks upon you with lust,' Christophe tells her. 'He says, when I gaze on Mistress Sadler, I burn with desire, I wish command of her tongue. I shall fight King Henry for her.'

'He does not!' Helen is laughing. 'Get inside, Christophe.' She takes his arm. 'You did not finish the story, sir. About Atalanta. In the tapestry.'

He thinks, I wish it were some other story.

'She was a virgin,' Helen prompts. 'But her father, you said. Then you stopped.'

'He wished to find her a husband. But she was averse to matrimony.'

'She challenged her suitors to a race,' Gregory says. 'She was the fastest person in the world.'

'If the man outpaced her, she must wed him,' he says, 'but if she won, then –'

'Then she was allowed to cut off his head,' Gregory says. 'Which she greatly enjoyed. There were heads bouncing everywhere, you could not go a pace without one rolling out of an olive grove and eyeing you. In the end she married a man who outran her, but he only did it with the help of the goddess of love.'

Later, back at his own house, in the gallery's waning light. 'You see the golden apples?' Gently, Gregory aligns her, points them out. 'Venus gave them to the suitor, and when they began to race, he threw them at Atalanta's feet.'

'Those are apples?' Helen is staring at the arras. She sucks her finger, laughs. 'I did not know they were running, I thought they were having a bowling match. Look at her hand – I thought she had just sped the ball away.'

He sees how it scoops the air. He grasps her error. 'So, what happened,' someone says, 'did she trip on the apples?' Their voices are a murmur. They recede. The light falters. Nesting birds rustle under the eaves. Vespers are sung and Compline, the offices of night. The dew is cold in the grass. Shutters are closed against the exhalations from meres and ponds. Atalanta snapped up the gold, she sold the race. You cannot say she lost on purpose, but she knew the consequence if she swerved. 'Perhaps she was tired of running,' Helen says.

'She was not insensible to the value of money,' he says. '*Et in Arcadia.*'

'Did she like being married?' Helen appraises her – a wild-haired woman, a bare arm flung before her. 'I suppose her husband stopped her running around like that, with her duckies on view. Or perhaps a husband didn't mind in those days.'

He thinks, I have seen her in Rome, carved in marble: her slim running legs, her pleated tunic, her torso straight as a boy's. She got a taste, some versions claim, for the carnal life. She bedded her spouse in the temple of a heathen god, after which she was changed into a lioness.

At least, he thinks, that's one worry I don't have. Daughter into beast, it won't happen to Henry's child. One day she will have to marry, but for now she is safe from adventurers who have special arrangements with the goddess of love. She is to go back to Hertfordshire tomorrow morning. The king and queen are planning their first summer together. They will make their visit to Dover. When Parliament rises, they will go hunting. The ring, impulsively offered, will be reduced to fit. In recompense, the emerald pendant will be worn not by Mary, the branch and flower of Aragon and Castile, but by Jane, the daughter of John Seymour of Wolf Hall.

Perhaps you have seen, in Italy, a painting of a house with one wall removed? The painter does this to show you the deep interior of a room, where at a prie-dieu a virgin kneels, surrounded by bowls of ripening fruit. Her expression is private and reserved; she has kicked off her shoes and she is waiting to be filled with grace. Already you can see the angel hovering above the rooftops, a blur of gold on the skyline, while below in the street the people go about their business, and some of them glance upward, as if attracted by a quickening in the air. In the next street, through an archway, down a flight of steps, a housewife is hanging out washing, and someone is rising from the dead. White pelicans sit on rooftops, waiting for Christ's imminence to be pronounced. A mitred bishop strolls through the piazza, a peacock perches on a balcony among potted plants, and striated clouds like bales of silk roll above the city: that city which itself, in miniature form, is presented on a plat for the viewer, its inverse form dimly glowing in the silver surface: its spires and battlements, its gardens and bell towers.

Imagine England then, its principal city, where swans sail among the river-craft, and its wise children go in velvet; the broad Thames a creeping road on which the royal barge, from palace to palace, carries the king and his bride. Draw back the curtain that protects them from the vulgar gaze, and see her feet in their little brocade slippers set side by side modestly, and her face downturned as she listens to a verse the king is whispering in her ear: '*Alas, madam, for stealing of a kiss* ...' See his great hand creep across her person, fingertips resting on her belly, enquiringly. His hands are alive with fire, rubies on every finger. Within the stones their lights flicker, and clouds move, white and dark. This stone gladdens the heart and protects against the plague. The speculative physicians speak of its heated nature: notice the heated nature of the king. The emerald too is a stone of potent virtue, but if worn during the sexual act is liable to shatter. Yet it has a greenness to which no earthly green can compare, it is an Arabian stone and found in the nests of griffins; its verdant depths restore the weary mind and, if gazed on constantly, it sharpens the sight. So look ... see a street opened to you, a house with its walls folded back: in which the king's councillor sits, wrapped in thought, on his finger a turquoise, at his hand a pen.

At midsummer, the walls of the Tower are splashed with banners and streamers in the colours of the sun and the sea. Mock battles are staged mid-current, and the rumble of celebratory cannon fire shakes the creeping channels of the estuaries and disturbs the fish in the deep. In sundry and several ceremonies, Queen Jane is shown to the Londoners. She rides with Henry to Mercers' Hall for the ceremony of setting the city watch. A parade of two thousand men, escorted by torchbearers, walks from Paul's down West Cheap and Aldgate, and by Fenchurch Street back to Cornhill. The city constables wear scarlet cloaks and gold chains, and there is a show of weaponry, and the lord mayor and sheriff ride in their armour with surcoats of crimson. And there are dancers and morris men and giants, wine and cakes and ale, and bonfires glowing as the light fades. 'London, thou art the flower of cities all.'

III
Wreckage (II)
London, Summer 1536

Do you know why they say, 'There's no smoke without fire?' It's not just to give encouragement to people who like fires. It's a statement about the danger of chimneys, but also about the courts of kings – or any space where trapped air circulates, choking on itself. A spark catches a particle of falling soot: with a crackle, the matter ignites: with a roar, the flames fly skywards, and within minutes the palace is ablaze.

Early July, the *grandi* hold a triple wedding, combining their fortunes and ancient names. Margaret Neville weds Henry Manners. Anne Manners weds Henry Neville. Dorothy Neville weds John de Vere.

My lord cardinal had these things at his fingertips: the titles and styles of these families, their tables of ancestry and grants of arms, their links by second and third marriages; who is godparent and godsib, guardian and ward; the particulars of their landed estates, their income, their outgoings, their law suits, ancient grudges and unpaid debts.

The celebrations are graced by Norfolk's son and heir, Henry Howard Earl of Surrey. The young earl intends to pass the summer in hunting, with the king and Fitzroy. Since childhood he has been a companion to the king's son, and Richmond looks up to him. Surrey is conspicuous in all he does: laying down the cards and throwing dice, playing at tennis and betting on it, cantering in the tilt yard, dancing, singing his own verses and inscribing them in the manuscript books kept by the ladies, where they decorate them with drawings of ribbons, hearts, flowers and Cupid's darts. His marriage to the Earl of Oxford's daughter is no bar to gallantry. We give poets latitude – we need not think Surrey performs all he promises. He is a long youth: long thighs, long shins, long parti-coloured hose; he picks his way on stilts among common men. His disdain for Lord Cromwell is complete: 'I note your title, my lord. It does not change what you are.'

The triple wedding makes the king project other weddings. His niece the Scottish princess is a great prize, as she is now very near the throne. If Jane the queen should fail and if Fitzroy cannot command the support of Parliament, Margaret Douglas will some day rule England. No one wants a woman; but at least Meg is bonny and has shown herself governable. She has been under the king's guardianship since she was twelve or so, and he is as fond of her as if she were his own daughter. Cromwell, he says, make a note: we will find her a prince.

But the king hesitates, the king delays. The difficulty is repeating, it is intractable, it is the same he faced when his daughter Mary was his heir, when (briefly) the child Eliza was his heir. Choose a husband for a future queen, and you are also choosing a king for England. As a wife she must obey him: women must obey, even queens. But what foreigner can we trust? England may become a mere province in some empire, and be governed from Lisbon, from Paris, from the east. Better she should marry an Englishman. But once he is named, think of the pretension it will breed in his family. Then think of the envy and malice of those great houses whose sons are passed over.

You watch at Jane the queen and you say *if*, and *when she*. The women prick off, on papers they keep, the days when they expect their monthly courses. Probably they keep papers for each other, casting a practised eye, ready to spread good or evil tidings. It is not yet two months since the king's wedding, and already you sense he is impatient for news.

With Fitzwilliam and young Wriothesley, he melts away from the wedding party to shuffle papers in a side room. Fitzwilliam has regained his chain of office as Master Treasurer. The king has pardoned him for his outburst in the council chamber; it was done, Henry has said, out of love for us. The treasurer fingers his chain now; he speculates on what maggots of ambition might be burrowing into the mind of the Duke of Norfolk. 'I tell you, Crumb, if young Surrey were not married already, his father would be coveting the Scottish princess for him – or the Lady Mary at the least, in case ever she is restored in blood. Because when his niece Anne was alive, Norfolk could boast that a Howard sat on the throne – and that is not a boast he likes to give up.'

Not that she ever took any notice of Uncle Norfolk, he says. The late queen chose her own path, she heeded to no one. Not me, not you, and not the king, in the end. Anyway, he says, the long youth is fast married, so Uncle Norfolk is out of hope there. 'And even if Surrey were free,' Mr Wriothesley says, 'I doubt Lady Mary will favour that family again. Not after Norfolk threatened to beat her head to mash.'

The king himself goes to Shoreditch for the marriage celebrations. He and his suite are dressed as Turks, in velvet turbans, breeches of striped silk and scarlet boots with tassels. At the end of the evening the king unmasks, to general astonishment and applause.

The young Duke of Richmond leaves early, heated and flushed from dancing and wine. So does Mr Wriothesley, though his exit is more sudden. 'Sir, I am going to Whitehall, and as soon as I ...'

Fitz looks after him. 'Do you trust him? Gardiner's pupil?' He rubs his chin. 'You don't trust anybody, do you?'

'We all need second chances, Fitz.' He flips the treasurer's chain of office. This last week or so, whenever Cromwell comes near, Lord Audley clutches his own chain in mock-panic.

Just Audley's little joke. He knows well enough by now that he, Lord Cromwell, has no ambition to be chancellor. Master Secretary's post gives him warrant for anything he needs to do, and keeps him close to Henry day by day, privy to his every sign.

By mid-July, arrangements are under way to set up the Lady Mary in a household of her own. Following her visit to Hackney – to the house that will now be known as King's Place – she has returned to Hertfordshire. After the tears, the promises, after her father's vows that he will never let his daughter out of his sight, a period of reflection has set in: he should, the king feels, keep her at arm's length to quash any rumour he means to make her his heir again. Lady Hussey, the wife of her former chamberlain, remains in the Tower after her rash mistake at Whitsuntide. The king will not have his daughter disrespected, but he doesn't want people calling her 'princess' either. And he wants the situation to be clear to Europe: his daughter needs him, he doesn't need her.

At Hackney she had said, in a low voice meant only for him: 'Lord Cromwell, I am bound to you: I am bound to pray for you during my life.' But it may be that fortune turns and he needs more than prayers. He has called in Hans, to design a present for her. She is a young woman who needs presents, he feels. He wants to give her something that will outlast the pretty saddle horse, something to remind her of these last perilous weeks: the brink, and who pulled her back from it. He is thinking of a ring, engraved with proverbs in praise of obedience. Obedience binds us together; all practise it, under God. It is the condition of our living as humans, in cities and dwelling houses, not in hides and holes in the fields. Even beasts defer to the lion: beasts show wisdom and policy thereby.

The engravers are cunning. They can write a prayer or verse very small. But, Hans warns, such a ring must be of a certain weight, and perhaps more than a woman with small hands can conveniently wear. But she can hang it on a chain at her girdle, just as she can hang an image of her father, in miniature – where formerly she carried two or three pious tokens, emblems of those saints to whom maidens pray: St Ursula and the eleven thousand virgins, or Felicity and Perpetua, eaten alive in the arena.

Hans has a round face, practical and innocent. He would not say things against you, with a covert meaning: surely not.

'Or why should you not,' Hans says, 'have it made into a pendant? A medal? You could get more good advice on it, that way.'

'But a ring is more –'

'More of a promise,' Hans says. 'Thomas, I wonder that you can be so –'

But then a message comes in, to tell him to attend the Duke of Richmond. He never manages to finish a conversation these days, in his own household or in the king's, in stable yard or chapel or council chamber. 'Yes, I'm on my way,' he says. And to Hans, 'Give it some thought.'

He leaves the table strewn with sketches – his offers, Holbein's emendations. There is something he needs to repeat to Mary, because he hasn't said it strongly enough. These last few years you have carried a great burden, and carried it alone – and look at the result. You are stooped, you are worn, you are bowed under the weight of your past, and you are only twenty years old. Now let go. Let others bear the burden, who are stronger, and appointed by God to carry the cares of state. Look up at the world, instead of down at your prayer book. Try smiling. You'll be surprised how much better you feel.

Not that you can put it like that to a woman. Stooped, worn – she might take it badly. Sometimes Mary looks twice her age. Sometimes she looks like an unformed child.

At St James's, Richmond's people usher him to the sickroom, shuttered against the midsummer heat. 'Dr Butts,' he says, nodding, and makes his bow to a miserable heap under the bedclothes.

At the sound of his voice the young duke stirs. He pushes the covers back. 'Cromwell! You did not do what I said. I told you Parliament must name me heir.' He punches a pillow away, as if it were interfering with his rights. 'Why is my name not in the bill?'

'Your lord father is still advising on the matter,' he says easily. 'The bill permits him liberty to decide who follows him. And you know you stand high in his favour.'

Attendants cluster around the bed, and under the doctor's eye they ease the boy back against the bolsters, shake the quilts, swaddle him.

A great bowl of water stands atop a brazier, bubbling away to moisten the air. Richmond leans forward, coughing. His face is burning, his nightshirt patched with sweat. When he masters the fit he subsides, white as the linen. He touches his breast. 'Sore,' he tells Butts.

Dr Butts says, 'Turn on your afflicted side, my lord.'

The boy slaps out at his attendants. He wants to view Cromwell and he means to do it. He begins to talk, but there is little sense in what he says, and presently his eyelids flutter and close; at a signal from the doctor they ease away the cushions and settle him.

Butts makes a gesture: creep over here, my lord. 'Usually I would keep him upright to ease his breathing, but he needs to sleep – I have prescribed a tincture. Otherwise I fear he would be up and fomenting trouble. He was fretting about poison. He mentioned you.' The doctor pauses. 'I do not mean to say he accused you.'

'Some men always think they're poisoned. In Italy one hears it.'

'Well,' Butts says, 'in Italy they are probably right. But I said to him, my lord, poison most usually shows in gripes and chills, vomiting and confusion, a burning in the throat and entrails. But then he talked about Wolsey, the pain in his chest before he died –'

He takes Butts by his coat, unobtrusively. He doesn't want this conversation public. The outer chamber is seething with people – retainers, well-wishers, probably creditors, too. Safe in a window embrasure, he murmurs: 'About Wolsey – I do not know how young Fitzroy heard it, but what is your opinion? Could he be right?'

'That he was poisoned?' Butts looks him over. 'I really have no idea. More likely his heart gave out. Consult your memory, if you will. I admired your old master. I did all I could to reconcile him with the king.' Butts seems anxious: as if he fears he, Cromwell, is nourishing a grudge. 'Dr Agostino was with him at the end, not I. But they say he starved and purged himself, which is never advisable while travelling in winter … and think what he was travelling towards. A trial or an act of attainder, and the Tower. The fear would act upon a man.'

He says, 'The cardinal was not afraid of the living or the dead.'

'And he told you so, I am sure.' It's clear the doctor thinks, why fret about it now? 'Do not think I heed young Richmond's talk.

When the king is ill he believes the whole world is against him. The boy is the same, a bad patient. When the fever was high he said, "I blame the Howards for this – Norfolk has no father's heart towards me, he only loves me because I am the king's son – and if I am not to be king, I am no use to him. Besides," he said, "Norfolk does not need me now – he has thought of another way towards the throne, he will get it by fair means or foul.'"

'They could not be fair means,' he says. 'If you think about it.'

'I would rather not,' Dr Butts says.

'Any witnesses to my lord's words?'

'Dr Cromer was standing by. But with God's help and with our science, we have suppressed the fever and with it all talk of treason.'

'So if not poison, what does ail him?' Apart from pique, he thinks.

The doctor shrugs. 'It is July. We should be elsewhere. You are bringing in too many laws, my lord. Let Parliament rise, and we can all quit London. They say that Cain invented cities. And if it was not he, it was someone else fond of murder.' The doctor is turning away, but then he hesitates. 'My lord, about the king's daughter … Dr Cromer would wish me to speak for both of us. We consider you have done a blessed work. You have done better than we healers could. Her spirit was so taxed by papish practices that her health and judgement failed. But they say your lordship's presence at Hackney worked on her like a potion from Asclepius.'

Asclepius, the doctors' god, learned his art from a snake. He could bring his patients back from the edge, or beyond it; Hades grew jealous, fearing lack of custom. 'I take no credit,' he says. 'It was more that she warmed to the company, and ate her dinner. She is given to fasting. As if she is not meagre already in her person.'

'If the king should ask our opinion,' Butts says, 'we are inclined to give it heartily in favour of her marriage. My fellow physicians have shown me where, in the writings of the ancients, such cases are described – young girls who are fervent, studious, given to fantasies, and prone to starving themselves if forced into any course that does not suit. They are virgins, and there lies their disease – if their single state is prolonged, they will see ghosts, and attempt to hang and drown themselves.'

'Oh, I should say we are clear from that.' He wonders, can you help seeing ghosts? Don't they just turn up and make you see them? When people raise the cardinal's name, he asks himself: if I had been with him in the north, would he have succumbed – to poison, to fear, to whatever? Some said it was self-slaughter. He thinks of the cold dark weather, the back end of 1529: Thomas Howard and Charles Brandon kicking their way into York Place as only dukes can kick, tossing Wolsey's treasures into packing cases; clerks humming under their breath as they listed plate and gems; the chilly scramble to the water gate, the dripping canopy of the barge, the phantom jeering on the riverbank from voices in wet mist. At Putney horses met them, and they rode over the heath: there came Harry Norris in a lather, flinging himself from the saddle with an incomprehensible message from the king. He saw the spark in Wolsey's eyes, his face light up; he thought the horror was over, that Norris was coming to lead him home, and he knelt to him – the cardinal, kneeling in the mud.

But Norris shook his head, and spoke in the cardinal's ear, and pretended to be sorry. When hope drained away the cardinal's strength went with it – as if by operation of a spell he was changed, suddenly elderly, fumbling, heavy. They dusted off their hands and hoisted him into his saddle, put the reins in his hand as if he were a child. No dignity, no time for it – and that knave Sexton, his jester, giggling and capering till he stopped him with a threat. They rode to the cardinal's house at Esher: to the fireless grate, the unprovisioned kitchen: to truckle beds, lighting their way with tallow candles on pewter prickets. The cellar was full, at least: he sat up, drinking through the night with George Cavendish, one of the cardinal's men – too scared, if he was honest, to sleep.

If I had known how it would end, he thinks, what would I have done different? Ahead was a harsh winter: half-drowned in puddles, unfed, unkempt, daily and desperate he forged across the Surrey bridleways in half-light, bringing his master news from Parliament – what was said against him and what was done, Thomas More's twisted sneers and Norfolk's common slanders: never in time for meat or sleep or prayer, always leaving and arriving in the dark, heaving himself onto a steaming horse: a winter of fog and wet wool and rain cascading from slick leather. And Rafe Sadler at his side, drenched, frozen, and shivering like a greyhound whelp, nothing but ribs and eyes: bewildered, bereft, never complaining once.

Yet here he is at St James's: six years on, Baron Cromwell, the sun shining. Over the heads of Richmond's retainers, Mr Wriothesley calls his name. Shouldering through, he swats the air with his feathered cap, his face glowing, his shirt neck unlaced.

'Don't go in there,' he says, barring the way to the sickroom. 'Fitzroy will accuse you of poisoning him.'

Dr Butts chuckles. 'I see you are agog with news, young man. Well, I leave you to tell it. But whatever the urgency, do not hurry in the heat. Let your hat be on your head and not in your hand – the rays are too burning for one of your fair complexion. Be advised, tepid liquids are more refreshing than cold, which may cause colics. And do not be tempted to jump into rivers.'

'No.' Wriothesley stares at him. 'I wouldn't.'

The doctor touches his cap in farewell. Wriothesley asks his retreating back, 'Will Fitzroy mend?'

Butts is tranquil. 'I have seen off worse trouble.'

Wriothesley talks at him; they walk into a blaze of sunshine, feel the heat on their backs. 'Sir, I have made pressing enquiries, among the Scottish princess's folk.'

'To what end? Put your cap on, by the way. Butts talks sense.'

The young man places his cap carefully, though he lacks a mirror to admire its angle; he looks closely at his master, as if trying to see a little Call-Me reflected in his eyes. 'I have been sure this long while that something is amiss with her – I had been turning it over in my mind for weeks – her furtive manner whenever you were by, as if she was afraid some mischief would be found out – and also –'

'You thought the ladies were making secret signs to each other.'

'You laughed at me,' Wriothesley says.

'I did. So what have you found? Not a lover?'

'You will excuse me, sir, for running ahead of you – it came to me at the wedding, but I could not speak till I had proof. I questioned her chaplain, and her men Harvey and Peter, and the boys who see to her horses, in case she had ridden out to some tryst. And they were not shy to speak – all except the chaplain, who was afraid.'

He begins to get the drift. 'I wonder that I could be so simple. So who is he? And who knew? Which of the women, I mean?'

Mr Wriothesley says, 'Sir, I leave the women to you.'

The scuffling and haste, the sudden vanishing of papers, the shushing, the whisk of skirts and the slammed doors; the indrawn breath, the glance, the sigh, the sideways look, and the pit-pat of slippered feet; the rapid scribble with the ink still wet; a trail of sealing wax, of scent. All spring, we scrutinised Anne the queen, her person, her practices; her guards and gates, her doors, her secret chambers. We glimpsed the privy chamber gentlemen, sleek in black velvet, invisible except where moonlight plays on a beaded cuff. We picked out, with the inner eye, the shape of someone where no one should be – a man creeping along the quays to a skiff where a patient oarsman with bowed head is paid for silence, and nothing to tell the tale but the small wash and ripple of the Thames; the river has seen so much, with its grey blink. A rocking boat, a splash, a stride, and the boots of Incognito gain the slithery quay: he is at Whitehall or Hampton Court, wherever the queen goes, with her women following after. The same trick suffices on land: a small coin to the stables, an unbarred door or gate, a swift progress up staircases and through flickering candlelit rooms to – to what? To kisses and illicit embraces, to promises and sighs, and so to feather bed, where Meg Douglas, the king's niece, disposes herself against the pillows and waits for her pleasure.

Call-Me says, 'It is Thomas Howard. The younger, I mean. Norfolk's half-brother.'

'Thomas the Lesser,' he says.

'Your man, Tom Truth. Wooed her with his verses, sir. Undressed her with his wit.'

Wreckage, he thinks. Winter and spring we watched Anne, but should we have watched another lady? Truth was on the river, Truth was in the dark; Truth stripped to his shirt and his member jutted beneath the linen, while the Princess of Scotland lay back and parted her plump white thighs. For a Howard.

He says to Call-Me, how did Meg contrive to be alone with him? There are some sharp old dames at court. My lady Salisbury for one, Margaret Pole – still in post about the new queen because, though the king is enraged with her son, he would rather have the countess where he can see her. And of course, to save face, we are still pretending to the world that Reynold's poisoned letter has never been received: that the wretched document is still in Italy, where Pole plays with his phrasing.

Many things have occurred, that we pretend have not occurred. This must be another. 'We'll talk to Meg first,' he says. He pictures her running towards him, hair loose and streaking behind her, like Atalanta in the footrace: her mouth open, emitting a steady wail.

First comes her shock, indignation, denial: how dare he enquire into her life? I am informed ... he says, and she says, 'How? How are you informed?'

'By your own people,' he says. He sees how hard she takes that, bursting into hot angry tears the size of apple pips.

Her friend Mary Fitzroy, Norfolk's daughter, stands behind her chair. 'And what have the servants told your lordship?' She makes their words contaminated, even before they are aired.

'I am informed that Lady Margaret has resorted to the company of a gentleman.'

Mary Fitzroy presses a hand on Meg's shoulder: say nothing. But Meg flashes out: 'Whatever you think, you are wrong. So don't look at me like that!'

'Like how, my lady?'

'As if I were a harlot.'

'God strike me if I ever thought so.'

'Because I tell you, Thomas Howard and I are married. We have given our promise and it holds good. You cannot part us now. We are every way married. So you are too late, it is all done.'

'It may not be too late, at that,' he says. 'Let us hope not. But when you say "every way married", I cannot guess at what you mean. Look at Mr Wriothesley here – he cannot guess either.'

On the table before them are the sketches for the Lady Mary's ring. Mr Wriothesley fingertips the sheets together, solemn, like an altarboy. His glance rests on the papers, where lines lace and intersect: 'Excuse me, sir,' he murmurs, and plants a book on the sheets to secure them.

Good. We don't want Meg picking one up and blowing her nose on it. He asks Mary Fitzroy, 'Will you not sit?'

'I do well on my feet, Lord Cromwell.'

'Let's set the facts down.' Mr Wriothesley pulls up a stool, expectant eyes on Meg. When her handkerchief is sodden she balls it up and drops it on the floor, and Mary Fitzroy passes her another: it is sewn over with Howard devices, so Meg dabs her cheeks with the blue-tongued lion of the Fitzalans. 'Cromwell, you have no right to cast doubt on my word. Take me to see my uncle the king.'

'Better off with me, my lady, in the first instance. Certainly I can broach it with the king, but first we must think how to present your case. Naturally you wish to keep your good name. We understand that. But it is of no help to you or to me to insist you are married, since you and Lord Thomas have pledged yourself without the king's permission or knowledge.'

'And,' Wriothesley says, 'we will not lie for you.' He picks up a pen. 'The date of your pledge was …?'

A fresh flood of tears, another handkerchief. He thinks, what is Mary Fitzroy to do? She cannot own many more. She will have to pick up her skirts and start ripping up her underlinen. Meg says, 'What does the date matter? I have loved Lord Thomas a year and more. So you cannot say, and my uncle cannot say, that we do not know our minds. You cannot part us, when we are joined by God. My lady Richmond here beside me will bear out what I say. She knows all, and if it were not for her help, we should never have enjoyed our bliss.'

He raises his eyes. 'You kept watch for them, my lady?'

Mary Fitzroy shrinks into herself. She is very young, and to be dragged into this debacle … 'You gave the signal,' Wriothesley suggests to her, 'when your seniors were gone? You encouraged them to meet? And you witnessed their pledge?'

'No,' she says.

He turns to Meg: 'So no one was present when these words were spoken – I say "words", I will not dignify them as "pledge" or "promise" –'

Deny it, he tells Meg under his breath: deny the whole and deny every part, then persist in denial. No words. No witnesses. No marriage.

Meg flushes. 'But I have a witness. Mary Shelton stood outside the door.'

'Outside?' He shakes his head. 'You can't call that a witness, can you, Mr Wriothesley?'

Wriothesley looks at him fiercely. It is he who has found out the plot, and he doesn't want it talked away. 'Lady Margaret, have you and your lover exchanged gifts?'

'I have given Lord Thomas my portrait, set with a diamond.' Proudly, she adds, 'And he has given me a ring.'

'A ring is not a pledge,' he says reassuringly. His eye falls on the drawings. 'For example, look at these – I am having a ring made for the Lady Mary. A pleasant token that indicates friendship, nothing more.'

Mary Fitzroy interrupts. 'It was only a cramp ring, such as acquaintances exchange. It was of little worth.'

Wriothesley says, 'And next you will tell me it was a very small diamond.'

'So small,' Mary Fitzroy says, 'that I for one never noticed it.'

He wants to applaud. She is not afraid of Call-Me; though sometimes, he thinks, I am.

'There's nothing on paper, is there?' he says to Meg. 'I mean, other than …?'

The rhymes, he thinks.

The girl says, 'I will not give you my letters. I will not part with them.'

He looks at Mary Fitzroy. 'Did the late queen know of these dealings?'

'Of course.' She sounds contemptuous; but whether of him, or the question, or of Anne Boleyn, he cannot say.

'And your father Norfolk? Did he know?'

But Meg cuts in: 'My husband –' she relishes the word – 'my husband said, let us be secret. He said, if my brother Norfolk hears of this, he will shake me till my teeth fall out, so let us not tell him till we must. But then –' Meg closes her eyes. 'I don't know. Perhaps he did tell him.'

He remembers the day at Whitehall – he in conversation with Norfolk, Tom Truth trotting up with a message – when he had said, 'The ladies show your verses around,' the poet had panicked. He grabbed his kinsman's arm and as he, Cromwell, walked away, the two Thomas Howards fell into furious whispering. When he thinks back, he reads an irate, confused expression on the duke's face: *what*, you've done *what*, boy? It all fits. It would not be like Norfolk to make a plot *ab origine*, with so many fissile elements, but he can believe Tom Truth has appealed to him for protection and that the duke, after blasting and damning him, has worked out how he can turn this folly to his family's advantage.

He leans across the table towards Meg. If she were not a royal lady – and she is at pains to point out she is – he might pat her hand. 'Dry your tears. Let us think afresh. You say that Lord Thomas has visited you in the queen's chambers. All come there, I do suppose, for purposes of pastime. They come to sing and make merry. There need be no sinister intent. So over the months – in that very busy place – you have been drawn into some conversation, and Lord Thomas admires you, as is natural, and he has said, "My lady, if you were not far above me –"'

'He is a Howard,' Wriothesley says. 'He does not think anybody above him.'

He holds up a hand. His scene is too gorgeous to be interrupted. '"If you were not far above me, and intended by the king for some great prince, I swear I would beg your hand in marriage."'

'Yes,' Mary Fitzroy says, 'that is exactly how it was, Lord Cromwell.'

'And you of course said, "Lord Thomas, I am forbidden to you. I see your pain, but I cannot assuage it."'

'No,' Meg says. She begins to shake. 'No. You are wrong. We are pledged. You will not part us.'

'And being a man and ardent, and you so lovely and a great prize, he did not desist – he presented you with verses – he – well, and so on. But you stood firm and permitted him not so much as a nibble of your nether lip.'

He thinks, I shouldn't have said that. I should have made do with 'kiss'.

Meg stands up. Her handkerchief is bunched in her fist – this one is scattered with the Howards' silver crosslets, light as summer snow. 'I will unfold this matter to the king alone. Even despite this dignity to which you are raised, he will not permit you to hold me and question me and make such imputations, that I am not married when I say I am.'

Mr Wriothesley says, 'My lady, can you not grasp the point? It would be better for you to be seduced and slandered, and to have ballads sung in the streets, than to promise yourself in marriage without the king's knowledge.'

Mary Fitzroy says, 'For the love of Christ, sit down, Meg, and try to comprehend what my lord is telling you. He is trying his best.'

'He cannot part what God has joined!'

Mary Fitzroy raises her eyes to his. 'I am sure Lord Cromwell has been told that before.'

He smiles. 'We must ask ourselves, Lady Margaret, what marriage is. It is not just vows, it is bedwork. If there were promises, and witnesses, and then bed, you are fast married, your contract is good. You would be Mistress Truth, and you would have to live with the king's extreme displeasure. And I cannot say what form that would take.'

'My uncle will not punish me. He loves me as he loves his own daughter.'

She falters there. From her own mouth, she hears it, and now she understands: *how* does the king love his daughter? Two weeks past, Mary stood on thin ice. It was cracking under her feet. Only Thomas Cromwell would walk on it to retrieve her.

Call-Me rises, as if Meg might faint. But the princess sits down neatly enough. 'The king will say I have been foolish.'

'Or treacherous.' Mr Wriothesley stands over her: he looks almost tender now.

Meg says, 'My marriage is not a crime, is it?'

'Not yet,' he says. 'But I am sure it will be. We can get a bill through before Parliament rises.'

Mary Fitzroy says, 'You are making a law against Meg Douglas?'

'You can see the sense of it, my lady Richmond. Ladies do not always know their own interests. Sometimes they do not know how to protect themselves. So the law must do it. Otherwise, any poet can try to carry them off as a prize, and if he succeeds he makes his fortune, and if he fails he suffers nothing but a blow to his pride. That cannot be right.'

'You do not write verse yourself?' Mary Fitzroy asks.

'Why enter a crowded field?' he says. 'Mr Wriothesley, would you take a note for me?'

Call-Me resumes his seat and dips a quill. He dictates: 'An Act against those who, without the king's permission, marry, or attempt to marry, the king's niece, sister, daughter –'

'Better throw in aunt,' Call-Me says.

He laughs. 'Throw in aunt. The offence will be treason.'

Mary Fitzroy is incredulous. 'Marrying will be treason, even though the woman consents?'

'Especially if she consents.'

'*Tra-la*,' Call-Me says, scribbling. '*Trolley lolly ... hey ho ... hey derry down*, penalties the usual. I'll get Riche on the wording.'

'Luckily,' he says, 'in this case there is no issue of consent. It is doubtful Lady Meg really made a marriage, because it lacks consummation, as Master Wriothesley says.'

'I do?' Call-Me raises his sandy eyebrows, and blots the paper.

Mary Fitzroy says, 'Meg, nothing of an unchaste nature occurred between you and Lord Thomas. You will say that and you will stick to it.'

'Lady Margaret, you have a good counsellor in your friend.' He turns to Mary Fitzroy. 'You should be with your husband. I will give you an escort to St James's.'

Mary says, 'Fitzroy doesn't need me. He doesn't even like me. He doesn't count me as his wife. My brother Surrey takes him whoring.'

Blunt as her father. 'My lady,' he says, 'you bear much blame for this intrigue. As we have not yet defined the scope of the new law, we do not know what penalties you might face. But I doubt the king will pursue you, if you are watching at his son's sickbed. Do not fret over Lady Margaret, she will be well-attended at the Tower. But unless you want to go with her, I advise you to get to St James's and stay there.'

Meg is on her feet, bursting into tears again; she clings to the back of her chair. Mr Wriothesley rises and takes charge. He is firm and cool. 'Lady Margaret, you will not be put in a dungeon. No doubt Lord Cromwell will arrange for you to have the late queen's apartments.'

He gathers his papers. 'Come, my lady,' Mary Fitzroy pleads, 'do this as befits your royal dignity. Do not make these men have to carry you. And thank Lord Cromwell – my trust is in him, he will divert the king's anger if any man can.'

He thinks, it will be diverted to Tom Truth: Henry will hate his proceedings. He stands by the wall till the women are gone, sweeping by him without a word. But the Princess of Scotland is still protesting: 'What harm can I take by telling the truth?'

Her voice rings in the stairwell, then she is gone. Call-Me says, 'I thought she would never grasp your saving hand.'

'She's not by nature stupid. She's in love.'

'It's lucky it doesn't make men stupid. I mean, look at Sadler.'

Yes, look at Sadler. Besotted with his wife, and no blunting of his wits at all.

Mr Wriothesley's mood has softened. With Meg in the Tower, he knows he will have another chance to bring her down. 'Were you ever in love, sir?'

'It's eluded me.' He remembers asking Rafe, *what is it like?* Although Wyatt has alerted him to the signs. The burning sighs, the frozen heart. Or is it the other way around?

He thinks, I must make shift to help Bess Darrell. I am caught up in this fresh Howard knavery, while Wyatt's child is growing inside her. 'I want Francis Bryan. Is he at home or abroad?'

'Favours to call in?' But Call-Me is restless, excited; he does not pursue it. 'Who's going to break it to the king that Meg is married?'

He sighs. 'I am.'

'I would not like to be in Norfolk's shoes. His niece disgraces him in spring, and his half-brother in summer. You can easy pull him down now.' Call-Me flits a glance at him. 'If you want to.'

He thinks, I don't know that I do. Whether the duke planned this misalliance, or just concealed it, it is a grave matter. But no graver than crimes in the past, for which I appear to have forgiven him. 'Suppose the Scots come over the border? If not Norfolk, who would go up against them?'

'Suffolk,' Wriothesley says.

'And if the French come in by the other door?'

'You were a soldier, sir.'

'A long time ago.' I carried a pike. Or I was the boy to the man who did; one fights as a unit. I was a child. Now I am fifty. I could perhaps win a brawl in the street, though I would rather stop one. 'I have aged into accommodation, Call-Me. As you have noticed, this hour past. It would be a meagre triumph to have saved the king's daughter, if he now turns and executes his niece.'

'But why,' Call-Me says, 'would they let a year pass – in love, as she says – and only then take a vow? I think he was not so passionate, till the date Eliza was declared a bastard, and Meg stepped nearer the throne.'

'Unless he was weary of making rhymes without result. Surely they took the vow so he could bed her?'

'Surely. And what if inconvenience should ensue?'

He shrugs. Meg must trust to luck. And sometimes a woman gets a child, but loses it before anyone knows it but herself. It's only afterwards they tell you about such things: twenty years on, sometimes. Call-Me says, 'The king will want her pressed on the date and the witnesses.'

'Then we'll press Tom Truth. He already thinks I know more than I do.'

'Most people think that,' Mr Wriothesley says.

'He fears everybody knows where his cock has been just by reading his rhymes. But Norfolk's daughter has a stout heart. She should be on the king's council. You recall how she tried to bar the door to me, on the day Anne was crowned?'

Wriothesley doesn't know, why would he? What Call-Me witnessed was the public show, the seething crowds, trumpet blasts, banners, snorting horses, trampling hooves. Anne, fragile, heavy with child in the humid heat, must sustain three days of ceremony under the hostile eyes of the people. The flower of England's nobility, under protest, carried her train. At the altar, the weight of the crown bent her neck. If her face shone, that was not sweat – it was a sense of destiny. Her hand, itching for so long, took a sure grip on the sceptre. Archbishop Cranmer smudged her forehead with holy oil.

Then after the ceremony she withdrew, away from the gaze of the city and its gods, to a chamber where she could lay aside her robes. He followed. He had seen the look of glazed fatigue on her face. But now he must get her up and out, to the feast in Westminster Hall; if he could not, short of carrying her, then he must speak urgently to the king, because rumour spreads like a blaze in thatch; if Anne was too exhausted to be propped up in public view, they would say she was taken ill, they would say she was losing the child.

At the chamber door he met Norfolk's daughter, an obdurate fourteen-year-old shocked to her marrow: 'The queen is undressed!' Anne's voice, fractious, called out to him, and setting the little girl aside, he stepped in. On a high bed the queen lay on her back like a corpse, her thin shift draping the mound of her belly. Her narrow hand rested on her person, as if she were calming the prince within; her hair was loose and fell around her like black feathers. He had looked at her in pity and in wonder and a kind of appetite, imagining that he himself had a woman heavy with child. She turned her head. A ripple of hair slid away, spilled over the side of the bed. In an impulse of – what, of tidiness? – he had lifted the strand, held it for a moment between finger and thumb, then smoothed it with the rest.

Mary Norfolk had yelped, 'No! Don't touch the queen.'

The dead woman spoke: 'Let him. He has earned it.'

Her eyes snapped open. They moved over him. She gave him her strange, slow smile. I knew then (he would say later) that Anne would not stop at the king, but consume many men, young or old, rich or poor, noble or common. But at the last, she did not consume me.

He remembers her swollen feet, blue-veined, bare. How helpless they seemed, as if on that hot June day they might be cold.

At the king's command, a lodging is prepared for Tom Truth. Constable Kingston comes in person, and suggests the upper floor of the Bell Tower, which has a good fireplace. Let's put a hopeful face on it, Kingston says, and assume the king will show mercy, and the young man will still be alive this winter.

He says to Kingston, 'You know the turnkey Martin?'

'I know him. One of your gospellers.'

'Martin ought to attend Lord Thomas,' he says. 'He respects those who write verse.'

Kingston stares at him as if he were ignorant. 'They all did it. All those late gentlemen.'

'George Boleyn, certainly,' Mr Wriothesley says. 'And Mark, I concede. But can you see Will Brereton juggling with *terza rima*? As for Norris, he was more interested in listing his emoluments and tabulating his assets.'

Kingston says, 'They tried their hand. I am no judge. But the queen said there was only Wyatt who could do it.'

'Sir William,' he says, 'ask your wife to sit with Lady Margaret, as she sat with the late queen. Let me know what she says.' He adds, 'I do not say it will end the same way. Let Lady Kingston encourage her to think she can live and thrive, if she sees her duty.'

'I hear you will bring in a law,' Kingston says. 'It seems harsh, to make them commit a crime in retrospect.'

They try to explain it to the constable. A prince cannot be impeded by temporal distinctions: past, present, future. Nor can he excuse the past, just for being over and done. He can't say, 'all water under the bridges'; the past is always trickling under the soil, a slow leak you can't trace. Often, meaning is only revealed retrospectively. The will of God, for instance, is brought to light these days by more skilful translators. As for the future, the king's desires move swiftly and the law must run to keep up. 'Bear in mind his Majesty's remarkable foresight, at the trial of the late queen. He knew the sentence before the verdict was in.'

'True,' Kingston says. 'The executioner was already on the sea.'

Kingston has been a councillor long enough. He should know how the king's mind works. Once Henry says, 'This is my wish,' it becomes so dear and familiar a wish that he thinks he has always had it. He names his need, and he wants it supplied.

'But surely he won't kill her?' Kingston says. 'The Princess of Scotland! What would her countrymen say?'

'I don't think the Scots have a use for Meg. They think she is an Englishwoman now. Still,' he says, 'I always pray for a good outcome. As for Lord Thomas – I'm sure the Duke of Norfolk will make his plea.'

'Norfolk?' the constable says. 'Henry will throw him downstairs.'

No doubt, he thinks. I hope I am there to witness. 'Be ready, Sir William. That's all I advise. I wouldn't like you to be caught out.'

After all, it's nearly two months since the death of the queen. Quite possible that Kingston's inner machinery will have rusted. The constable says, 'Whatever occurs, I suppose we wouldn't be having that fellow back?'

'The Frenchman? No. Good God. I can't afford him.' Back to old-fashioned hacking. Of course, the Howards are stout for tradition. They wouldn't want to die with any refinements.

'He did a fine job,' Kingston says. 'I admit that. Beautiful weapon. He let me see it.'

He thinks, we all killed Anne Boleyn. We all imagined it, anyway. Soon I'll hear that the king himself came down and said, 'Master Executioner, can I try the swing of your blade?' It's as Francis Bryan said: Henry would have killed her one day, but in the event some other man saved him the trouble.

He remembers the weight of the weapon, when the Frenchman put it in his hand. He saw the light flash on the steel and he saw that there were words written on the blade; he drew his finger over them. Mirror of Justice. *Speculum justitiae.* Pray for us.

At Austin Friars, they admire Mr Wriothesley: his tenacity, his willingness to back his belief that there's no smoke without fire. And lucky for Meg Douglas that he did not hesitate, once he grasped the facts. 'Because imagine,' Richard says, 'if someone had walked in and found her naked in the arms of Truth.'

Richard Riche says, 'I would not offend the king in such a way and expect long continuance in my life.'

Riche is busy drafting. The new clauses won't necessarily stop royal persons doing stupid things. But they will create a formal process for dealing with them, when they do. The question is, who is complicit in Meg's crime? He had asked for the rotas, to see which ladies were attending the queen – the dead one – during March, April and what she saw of the month of May. But the haughty dames who arrange such matters – Lady Rutland, Lady Sussex – had simply raised their eyebrows at him, and hinted that the whole thing was a mystery. Whereas with the king's privy chamber, as

Rafe Sadler says, you have a list, you know who should be where, and when.

Not that it necessarily works. Vagrant habits took hold this spring.

Approaching the king with the bad news, he had found him in a huddle with his architects, plotting to spend some money. 'My lord Cromwell? Which of these?' He had flourished a baton patterned with egg-and-dart moulding, which he was narrowly preferring to laurel wreaths.

'Wreaths,' he had said. 'I have something to tell you.' The draughtsmen rolled up their plans. His eyes followed them to the door.

Once the king had grasped what he was being told, he had shouted at the top of his voice that the business should be kept quiet. The baton was still in his royal hand: if Meg Douglas had been standing there, he would have broken the eggs over her head and stuck her with the darts. 'I want no repeat of what happened in May, a royal lady before a public court. Europe will be scandalised.'

'Then what shall I do?'

Henry dropped his voice. 'Choose some neater way.' As for Truth: 'Draw up a charge of treason – I want it recorded in the indictment that the devil inspired him. Unless it was my lord of Norfolk?'

He had offered no comment. Meanwhile – as one of Truth's own rhymes states, *'False report as grass doth groweth.'* Word has got around that Lord Thomas is arrested, and so it is assumed that he has been revealed as one more lover of the late Anne.

At the Bell Tower he and Wriothesley approach Truth by the turret stair, passing the lower chamber where Thomas More's shadow squats in the dark with the shutters closed. He puts his palm against the wall, as if feeling for a minute tremor in the stonework that would tell him More was talking in there: chattering to himself, jokes and stories and proverbs, scripture verses, mottoes, tags.

Christophe comes behind with the evidence. It is not stained bed sheets, but something nastier. The poems – Tom Truth's and Meg's mixed with others – have come to him in sheaves – some found, some left, some handed over by third parties. The papers are curled at the edges, and some are folded many times; they are written in divers hands, annotated in others; scribbled, blotted and smudged, they vary in skill of construction, but not in content. I love her, she loves not me. O she is cruel! Ah me, I shall die! He wonders if any of Henry's poems have got mixed in. It was alleged, against the recently dead gentlemen, that they had laughed at the royal verses. But the king's handwriting, fortunately, is unlike any other hand. He would know it in the dark.

In his upper room, Tom Truth is staring at the wall. 'I wondered when you would get here.'

He – Lord Cromwell – takes off his coat. 'Christophe?'

The boy produces papers. They look more crumpled than he remembers. 'Have you been chewing them?'

Christophe grins. 'I eat anything,' he tells Tom Truth. As he, Lord Cromwell shuffles through the papers and prepares to read aloud, Truth becomes irate and tense, like any author whose work is under scrutiny.

> 'She knoweth my love of long time meant,
> She knoweth my truth, nothing is hid,
> She knoweth I love in good intent,
> As ever man and woman did.'

He looks at Tom Truth over the paper. 'Nothing is hid?'

'Have you tupped her?' Mr Wriothesley asks.

'Oh, for God's sake,' Tom Truth says. 'What opportunity? With your eyes on us?'

Many-eyed Argus. He holds the paper at arm's length. 'Can you go on, Mr Wriothesley? I cannot. It's not the handwriting,' he assures Truth. 'It's that my tongue refuses to do it.'

Mr Wriothesley takes the paper by one corner.

> 'What helpeth hope of happy hap
> When hap will hap unhappily?'

'Perhaps it sounds better if you sing it,' Mr Wriothesley says. 'Shall we have Martin fetch a lute?

> 'And thus my hap my hope has turned
> Clear out of hope into despair.'

'Pause there,' he tells Wriothesley. He accepts the paper back, between finger and thumb. 'It seems you declared yourself, even at the risk of a rebuff. *She knoweth my truth, nothing is hid.* At this date she does not seem amenable. Though it is usual, is it not, to say that you love the lady more than she loves you?'

'It is considered polite,' Wriothesley assures him.

'And yet she loved you well enough to give you a diamond.'

Tom Truth says, 'I do not know if I wrote this verse.'

'You have forgot it,' he says. 'As would any man of sense. Yet in the fifth stanza you write, *Pardon me, your man, Tom Truth.* Which you rhyme, unfortunately, with *growth*.'

Christophe sniggers. 'Even I know better, and I am French.'

'There is many a Thomas at court,' the accused man says, 'and not all of them tell the truth, though I am sure they all claim to.'

'He's looking at us,' he says to Thomas Wriothesley. 'I hope you aren't saying one of us wrote it?'

Call-Me says, 'All the world knows you go by that name, so you may as well stand to it. You have married her, her servants say.'

Tom Truth opens his mouth, but leafing through the pages he cuts in: 'You ask her to ease you of your pain.'

'Would that be the pain in your bollocks?' Christophe says.

He quells him with a look; but he cannot help laughing. 'You have been in love for a certain space – *Although I burn and long have burned* – and then you make some pledge – why would you do that, unless to make her think it is lawful to go to bed?'

Wriothesley says, 'The lady tells us there are witnésses to the pledge.'

When the pause prolongs, he says, 'You need not reply in verse.'

Tom Truth says, 'I know what you do, Cromwell.'

He raises an eyebrow. 'I do nothing, unless with the king's permission. Without that, I don't swat a fly.'

'The king will not permit you to ill-use a gentleman.'

'Agreed,' Wriothesley advises, 'but don't try Lord Cromwell's patience. He once broke a man's jaw with a single blow.'

Did I? He is astonished. He says, 'We are tenacious. In time you will confess you meant to do ill, even if you did not achieve your purpose. You will acknowledge your error to the king, and beg his pardon.' Though I doubt it will forthcome, he thinks. 'We understand your situation. You come of a great family, but all you younger Howards are poor. And being of such exalted blood, you cannot soil your hands with any occupation. If you want to make your fortune you must wait for a war, or you must marry well. And you say to yourself, here I am, a man of great qualities – yet I have no money, and no one regards me, except to confuse me with my elder brother. So I know what I'll do – I'll marry the king's niece. Odds-on I'll be King of England one day.'

'And till then I can borrow against my expectations,' Wriothesley adds.

A line of Wyatt's comes to him: *For I am weak, and clean without defence.* In Wyatt's verse there is a tussle in every line. In the verse of Lord Thomas, there is no contest at all, just a smooth surrender to idiocy. Though he is staunch under questioning – you must concede that. He does not weep or beseech. He just says, 'What have you done with Lady Margaret?'

'She is here in the queen's rooms,' Mr Wriothesley says. 'Though probably not for long.'

They leave him with that ambiguous thought. The harmless truth is that Meg may have to be lodged elsewhere if the king decides to go ahead with a coronation, because by tradition Jane will spend the night there before her procession to Westminster. The king had talked of a ceremony at midsummer. But now there are rumours of plague and sweating sickness. It is not wise to allow crowds in the street, or pack bodies into indoor spaces. The Seymours, of course, urge the king to take the risk.

He and Call-Me go downstairs. One fights as a unit, he thinks. He misses Rafe, always at his right hand. But if the king wants Rafe's presence he must have it. He says, 'Did I? Broke a jaw? Whose?'

'The cardinal used to tell about it,' Wriothesley says happily. He passes into the sunshine. 'Sometimes it was an abbot, sometimes a petty lord. In the north somewhere.'

When this is over – however it ends – he will try to return the poems to their owners, though they don't put their names to them. He pictures himself on a windy day, throwing them into the air so that they flap down Whitehall, sailing across the river and landing in Southwark: where they will be giggled at by whores, and used to wipe their arses. When he gets home he says to Gregory, 'Never write verse.'

Bess Darrell had sent him a message: come to me at L'Erber. It is not surprising the Pole family should offer her shelter; she is a legacy from the late Katherine. But she must have kept it from them that she is carrying a child. The old countess would not want Wyatt's bastard under her roof.

He finds Bess and Lady Salisbury sitting together, peaceful as St Ann and the Virgin in a book of hours. A strip of fine linen lies across their laps, and on it a needlework paradise, a garden of summer flowers. He greets the countess with elaborate courtesy – as perhaps he did not at their last meeting. He notes that Bess has not unlaced her bodices yet. She is a delicate woman; how long can she keep her secret?

The countess indicates her sewing: 'I know that of your gentleness you interest yourself in the work we women do. You see I have found young eyes to help mine.'

'I compliment you. I wish my flowers would bloom as fast.'

'Your gardens are all new-planted,' Lady Salisbury says sweetly. 'God takes His time.'

'And yet,' Bess says, 'He made the whole world in a week.'

He nods to her gravely; says to the countess, 'I hear your son Reynold has been summoned by the Pope.'

'Has he? It is more than I know.'

He has only just heard himself, and it may not be true. 'I wonder what Farnese intends. He would not whistle him to Rome for a hand of Laugh and Lie Down.'

The countess looks enquiring. 'It is a card game,' Bess says. 'For children.'

The countess says, 'We do not know my son's plans, any more than you do.'

'Less.' Bess merely breathes it, stirring the petals beneath her fingers.

'You know the king wants him to come home?'

'That is a matter that lies between Reynold and his Majesty. As I have explained – and his Majesty well accepts it, if you do not – neither I, nor my son Montague, knew in advance of his writings against the king. And we do not know where he is now.'

'But he has written to you?'

'He has. It is a letter that goes straight to a mother's heart. He says that whoever observes the laws of this realm and this king is shut out of Heaven – even if they are tricked or coerced into obedience.'

'But you are not tricked or coerced, are you? Your loyalty comes from gratitude.'

'There is more,' Margaret Pole says. 'My son bids me cease dabbling in his affairs. He says I cast him off as a boy – that I had no use for him. It is true I sent him away from home to his studies. But my understanding was, I gave him to God.' She lifts her chin. 'Reynold severs his ties to us. He says we are damned by our obedience to Henry Tudor.'

He thinks, it is very sad he should write you such a letter. It is also convenient. The countess takes a neat loop of her thread and slips her needle into the cloth. 'But you want to speak with Mistress Darrell.' Rising, she slides the work into Bess's lap, and murmurs a question not meant for his ears.

Bess says, 'No, I trust my lord Privy Seal.'

'Then so do I,' the countess says.

He smiles. 'Encouraging for me.'

Lady Salisbury draws together her skirts. Ah, she is cold to my charms, he thinks. Bess Darrell sits with bent head, and does not look up even when they are left alone, the door ajar. Her hood hides what Wyatt has seen, her hair of crisped gold. He had imagined Wyatt would only chase what flies; that the pursuit would interest him, but not the capture. Yet Bess looks not simply captured but tamed, a woman trapped by her own ill-luck. He looks after Lady Salisbury: 'You may judge how far she trusts me. Not enough to close the door on us.'

Bess says, 'She does not think you will throw me to the floor and ravish me. Perhaps she fears you will sit and whisper bad verses, and coax me into marriage.'

So she has heard about the Douglas affair. No doubt the gossip is everywhere. He says, 'I have found a refuge for you. As I promised Wyatt. The Courtenay family will ask you to be companion to my lady marquise.'

'Gertrude?' She folds the linen on her lap; folds and folds it again, so it becomes a square, the needle inside. 'But she doesn't like you.'

'She is in my debt.'

'True. You could have brought her family down two years ago. What a forbearing man you are. I suppose you hold back, in the hope of a greater destruction. Queen Katherine always said, "Cromwell keeps his promises, for good or ill."' She looks away. 'I know you kept your promise about Mary. I was in the room at Kimbolton when you made it. All I will say, my lord – beware of gratitude.'

I do not wonder, he thinks, that Wyatt cleaves to you. A jaundiced riddle sits as well on your lips as on his. 'As for your condition, I leave to you what explanation you make. The Courtenays know what is owed to you. You helped Katherine in her last hour. It was you who wiped her death sweat. Now they boast of what they did for her, but they did nothing really. They will not press you for the man's name. And if they do, and they don't like it – they are still bound to you.'

'They ought to like it,' she says. 'They are indebted to Wyatt and his testimony. Because it wrought this.' She gestures around. 'This land we live in now. England without Boleyn.'

'Wyatt wrought nothing. His evidence was not needed.'

'So you say. But then, you like to offer comfort, my lord. You pick your way over the battlefield with prayers for the wounded and water for the dying.'

'It is true,' he says simply. 'I gave him the papers back so he could tear them up. He told me of the understanding between you, and I said I would find you a place of safety ... I would offer you my own poor house, or any of my houses, but my counsellors – I mean those in my household who advise me, and have my interests at heart – have suggested to me –'

She laughs. 'No, Lord Cromwell, I cannot lodge with you. An unmarried female, estranged from her family – your enemies would suggest such knavery – and you being the king's Vicegerent, you would look no better than any lustful bishop, or Roman cardinal.'

He says, 'The Courtenays do not know my part in this. Let us keep it so. Francis Bryan spoke to them for you. He has worked your salvation. He loves Tom Wyatt and admires him.'

'I expect Francis is used to ridding himself of women,' she says. 'No, do not doubt me – I will take the chance, since you offer it. You have my gratitude during my life. You saved Tom Wyatt when he would not save himself.'

'I unlocked the door,' he says, 'but it was you who made him walk out of his prison. If it were not for the child you carry, he did not care to live. Man or maid, this is a child of great power. It has already preserved its father from the axe.'

'The child?' she says. 'It seems I was wrong about that.'

'There is no child?'

'No.'

'Never was?'

'I cannot be sure.'

'Does Wyatt know you have deceived him?'

Fiercely she says, 'He knows he's still breathing.'

A silence. She unfolds her sewing, its whiteness flowering out across her skirts. She finds the needle, and examines it between finger and thumb, as if daring it to draw blood. She says, 'Considering the result, you will understand my deceit.'

'I like your deceit,' he says. 'It makes me think highly of you.'

'You are right I need a refuge. No one wants me except Wyatt and he cannot have me. I have made him promises in my heart's blood, and I count myself as well married as any woman in England, except he has a wife living.'

Amor mi mosse, he thinks: love moves me, love makes me speak.

'Perhaps you want to stay here with Lady Salisbury.'

'She can get another pair of eyes. And I think you are already provided with spies here. When I go to the Courtenays, what shall I do?'

'You will live.'

'But for you, Lord Cromwell – what shall I do for you?'

'Write to me. Someone within the household will approach you. A servant. I will even send you the paper.'

'And what shall I say?'

'You will tell me who visits. If any of them plan to travel. Whether any of their ladies are breeding.'

She says, 'I have no money.'

He has settled her gambling debts a time or two. The pious Katherine, even in her days of exile, played for high stakes, and she expected her household to pay out. 'I will take care of that, if Wyatt cannot.'

She says, 'I will be the judge of what passes among the Courtenays, and I will protect what is private. I shall tell you what touches the public weal. I shall tell you whatever it is in your interest to know.'

'Thank you.' He gets to his feet. 'Bear in mind my field of interest is very wide.'

'Before you go, let me show you my sewing.'

'That would be pleasant,' he says.

She holds up the work; she shows him how the Pole emblem, the pansy or viola, is worked in a border with the marigold. 'They do it to encourage each other, and they give such work as tokens to their supporters. They are sewn into altar cloths, or made into cap badges. They gave one this last week to Ambassador Chapuys. The marigold stands for – well, I see you have arrived already – it stands for the Lady Mary, that exemplar of shining virtue. Look here,' she indicates with the needle tip, 'at how the flowers entwine. So may Reynold entwine himself about her body and heart.'

'So was Lady Salisbury lying to me *in toto* this last hour or only in part?'

She glances at the door. 'It is true Reynold has written her a letter.'

'But surely the family have concocted it between them. It is a device, to shift blame away from them.'

'It appears she is struck to the heart.'

'That is how the king feels. Stung, dismayed, betrayed. They are prodigious efforts, these letters of Reynold's. I marvel he does not write to me.' He touches her hand. 'Thank you,' he says.

He can't see Richard Riche framing a law against embroidery, but then he doesn't need to. The laws are already capable of stretching to cover anything the Pole family have in mind – especially when you add in the new penalties against plotting to marry the king's daughter. Nothing he has learned about the hopes of Lady Salisbury surprises him, but it's useful to have the evidence stitched together. 'I hope when that cloth is finished,' he says, 'the family will protect it from the light.'

Like the treasures of Heaven, he thinks, where no moth nor rust consumes.

She says, 'I wonder where Anne Boleyn is now?'

It is not a question for which he came prepared. He imagines her whipping down some draughty hall of the hereafter, where the walls are made of splintered glass.

When he goes to see Jane the queen, he takes Mr Wriothesley with him. 'Just in case there is another plot among the women. I shall trust only you from now on. If you see that anyone is married who should not be, point out the offender. Don't try to be subtle. We've had enough of that.'

It is mid-morning, a broad summer light. The ladies have come from their devotions. Bess Oughtred, the queen's widowed sister, is at her side. On her other hand sits Edward Seymour's wife, Nan: Nan Stanhope, as she was before her marriage. She is not, of course, the wife who sinned with Old Sir John. That one is dead, and never mentioned at Wolf Hall. No gap is visible, where the Scottish princess should be. The ladies are settling to the task which has absorbed them for weeks – erasing the initial 'A' from satins and damasks, and replacing it with Jane's initial, so she can wear the clothes of the late queen. A sympathetic murmur from Mr Wriothesley: 'Will that false lady never be gone?'

'She had a lot of clothes,' Bess Oughtred says. 'I remember sewing this one *in*.' Her tone is low and absorbed; seed pearls shower from her scissors, and Nan is catching them in a silk box.

'Praise God for generous seams,' Nan murmurs. 'Her present Majesty is broader than the other one.' She flips Jane's sleeve. 'And broader still soon – God willing.' Jane dips her head. Nan glances up, scissors poised: 'We are glad to see handsome Mr Wriothesley.'

Call-Me blushes. Jane says to her sister, 'Mr Wriothesley is the … thing of the Signet. Clerk of the Signet, I should say. And of course you know Master Secretary. Though he is now Lord Privy Seal.'

'Instead?' Bess Oughtred says.

He bows. 'As well, my lady.'

Jane explains, 'It is he who does everything in England. I did not understand that, till one of the ambassadors told me. He marvelled that one man could have so many posts and titles. It is a thing never seen before. Lord Cromwell is the government, and the church as well. The ambassador said the king will flog him on to work till one day his legs go from under him, and he rolls in a ditch and dies.'

Call-Me tries a change of tack. 'My lady Oughtred, may we hope you will live at court now?'

Bess shakes her head. 'My husband's family want me back in the north. They want to keep hold of little Henry, and bring him up a Yorkshireman. And much as I wish to see my sister in her pomp, I don't want the little ones to forget me.'

Jane is working on a private piece of sewing. The women have rules about these matters that men do not understand; perhaps it is unbecoming in a queen, to snip away her predecessor. She holds it up – a border of honeysuckles and acorns. 'Nice for a country girl,' she says.

He thinks, it is as Norfolk says, I will soon be so expert I will be able to ply the needle myself. 'Majesty, I have a request, and perhaps you will not like it. I must meet with those ladies who served the late queen. We must invite them back to court.' He feels, suddenly, very tired. 'I need to ask them questions. It may be that misunderstandings have occurred. We must revisit certain matters that I wish were forgot.'

'I pity Meg Douglas,' Bess Oughtred says. 'The king should have found a husband for her long ago. Leave any sweet thing unattended, and the Howards settle on it like flies.'

'Who do you need?' Nan asks him.

'Who do you suggest?'

'Mistress Mary Shelton.'

Shelton was clerk of the poetry book; it was she who decided which rhymes were saved and which suppressed, and knew how they were encoded.

'And,' Nan says, 'George Boleyn's wife.'

'Lady Rochford is a very busy active lady,' Mr Wriothesley says. 'She remembers everything she sees.'

An image swims into his mind, clouded, as if from distance: Jane Seymour, padding softly through the apartments of the late Anne, her arms laden with folded sheets. Anne was not queen then; but she lived in expectation, and she was served like a queen. He remembers the white folds. He remembers the soft perfume of lavender. He remembers Jane, whose name he hardly knew, her dipped glance casting a lavender shade against the white.

Nan says, 'I think it was Rochford who was witness to Meg's marriage. She is not averse to seeing another woman ruined.'

Bess Oughtred is puzzled. 'But she did not ruin her. She did not speak out.'

That is true. But as the other Bess – Bess Darrell – has recently pointed out, a proper, comprehensive wreckage takes work and deliberation. Meg's disgrace, if it had come out earlier, would have been a mere coda to that of the late queen: wasted.

Nan says, 'Meg and Shelton and Mary Fitzroy, they were always scurrying and hushing and spying. Of course we thought it was all …' She bites her lip.

Bess says, 'We thought it was Boleyn's secrets they were keeping.' She looks sobered. *'De mortuis nil nisi bonum.'*

He is astonished. 'You know Latin, my lady?'

'My sister didn't listen in the schoolroom, but I did. Much good it brought me. Jane is raised high, and I am a poor widow.'

The queen only smiles. She says, 'I don't mind if Mary Shelton comes back to court. She is not envious or mean.'

And, he thinks, the king's already had her, so that's one less thing for you to worry about.

'But Jane,' Bess says, 'you do not want Lady Rochford near you, surely? She joined with the Boleyns in mocking you. And she is a traitor's wife.'

'She cannot help that,' Mr Wriothesley says.

'But still.' Bess is indignant. 'I wonder the king asks such a thing of Jane.'

'He doesn't,' the queen says. 'The king never does an unpleasant thing. Lord Cromwell does it for him.' Jane turns her head: her pale gaze, like a splash of cold water. 'I am sure Rochford would like to have her place back. Lord Cromwell is in debt to her for certain advice, which she gave freely when he needed it.'

Nan says, 'If Rochford comes back to court, she will never go again. We will never be rid.'

'But never mind,' Jane says. 'You will be a match for her.'

Is it a compliment? Nan does not know. Bess says sharply, 'Sister, do not be so humble. You forget you are Queen of England.'

'I assure you, no,' Jane murmurs. 'But I am not crowned yet, so no one notices.'

'All the realm notices,' he says. 'All the world.'

'They know you even in Constantinople, madam,' Mr Wriothesley says. 'The Venetians have sent their envoys with the news.'

'Why would they care?' Jane says.

'Princes like to hear of the household affairs of other princes.'

'But Turkish princes have a dozen of wives each,' Jane says. 'If the king had been of their sect, he could have been married to the late queen, God rest her, and Katherine, God rest her, and at the same time to me, if he liked. For that matter, he could have been married to Mary Boleyn, and to Mary Shelton, and to Fitzroy's mother. And the Pope could not have troubled him about it.'

Mr Wriothesley says feebly, 'I do not think the king will turn Turk.'

'That's all you know,' Jane says. 'If you are going to him now, you will see he is wearing his special costume. He does not feel he wore it enough at the wedding. Try to be surprised.'

Nan says, 'Surely Lord Cromwell cannot be surprised.'

Jane turns to her. 'One time or other, before he had so much to do, Lord Cromwell used to bring us cakes. Orange tarts in baskets. When she was displeased with him, the queen threw them on the floor.'

'Yes,' he says. 'And there were worse things she did. But *nil nisi …*' He meets Bess Oughtred's eye, and smiles.

As they leave the queen's rooms he says, 'Nan is wrong. I am not beyond astonishment. At Oughtred's widow and her Latin, for one thing.'

He calls her 'Oughtred's widow', in a distant way, as if he never thought of her. He pictures Sir Anthony, that veteran of the wars; he pictures his own dead wife. He thinks, the dead are crowding us out. Rather than not speak ill of them, how if we don't speak of them at all? We don't speak of them, we don't think of them, we give their clothes to beggars and we burn their letters and their books? After they had left Tom Truth and descended the stair at the Bell Tower, Christophe had slapped the wall, *thwack, thwack* with his palm, as if to roust out any shades who were attempting to rest in peace. It's two years since Bishop Fisher tottered down that stair, led to his execution. He was old, spent, frail; his body lay on the scaffold like a piece of dried seaweed.

A crush of petitioners, waiting outside the queen's rooms, surges after him. 'Lord Cromwell, a word!' 'Over here, sir!' 'My lord Privy Seal, something you should see.' Papers are thrust at him, and the Thing of the Signet gathers them into his arms. He sees a man in young Richmond's livery, and hails him. 'How is my lord today?'

'He is worse. We do not want to tell the king.'

'I'll tell him.'

'The king should go,' the man says. 'He should go and see his son.'

The king is very tall in his turban. Since the triple wedding he has embellished it with a jewel and extra plumes. At his side is a curved dagger, its sheath inlaid not with the crescent moon, but with the Tudor rose.

He, Lord Cromwell, kneels before the king, with Call-Me beside him. They do not remark on his costume. There is a limit to how much awe a man can feign. 'I was hoping to astonish you,' Henry says, petulant. 'But I hear the queen has prepared you.'

How fast a word travels, in a palace. 'She did not mean to spoil it,' he says.

Irritated, the king motions them to their feet. 'You don't think I have married a fool? She seems not to comprehend even ordinary things.'

He hesitates. 'She is of that chastened spirit, sir, that never presumes to understand her betters. Your Majesty has ruled for many years, for which we thank God daily: whereas the queen lacks experience in worldly affairs.'

The king eases his silver belt. 'I believe the ambassadors think she is plain.'

'But why are they looking?' He is impatient. 'Chapuys is no judge of women.'

'And the French envoys,' Wriothesley says, 'they are mostly in holy orders – they should be ashamed to state an opinion.'

Henry seems mollified. A mirror is half-hidden by a curtain; he takes a sidelong glance at himself and likes what he sees. 'So,' he says, 'why have I sent for you?'

He takes a silk bag out of his pocket. 'I wanted to ask your Majesty's permission to give this to the Lady Mary.'

Henry empties the present from the bag. He turns it over and over and squints at the workmanship. In case the engraving is too delicate to decipher, Mr Wriothesley quotes the inscription.

'In praise of obedience,' Henry says. 'Very apt. And you think my daughter will take the point?' Without waiting for an answer, he says, 'Am I working you too hard, Thomas? You should hunt with me this summer. And I shall keep my son by my side. I hope by the time I am ready to leave London he will be strong enough to ride.'

The king likes saying that: my son. He says, 'Majesty, the duke's household suggest you might go to St James's.'

'Is that what you advise?'

He feels enquiry ripple through the body of the Thing of the Signet; every fibre of Mr Wriothesley is alert. Such advice could breed consequences. For as Henry now says, 'The nature of his illness may not have shown itself. If it should prove contagious –'

'God forbid,' Mr Wriothesley says.

Henry is looking down at the gift, cupped in his palm. 'I like this so well, I think I shall give it to my daughter myself. You can find something else, can't you?'

He bows. What choice has he? The king nods as they leave, his blue eyes mild. The emerald in his turban gleams, the eye of a false god, and his big pink feet in their velvet slippers look like pigs walking to market.

The ladies exiled from court must have been waiting with their clothes packed, because they are back in no time, and he is calling on them to welcome them. Mary Shelton reminds him of one of those virgins of Nikolaus Gerhaert's carving: pink and white and dimpled, but with shrewd eyes. Though she is not a virgin, of course.

When Shelton had charge of the manuscripts that circulated among the dead queen's slaves and admirers, she collated the riddles, jests and profane prayers, copying them and sometimes annotating them and deciding who could respond, with a verse or another riddle. Her editor's hand was light, or she would have crossed out Tom Truth and all his work. He agrees with the dead queen: only Wyatt can do it.

He tells her, 'I am sure your cousin the queen knew all about Meg and Tom Truth. So was she pleased, when she knew another of her Howard kin was rising in the world?'

'No. But she was entertained.'

'She didn't think to give Lady Meg a warning?'

'Why would she?'

He concedes that. Why would one woman help another? Mary Shelton says, 'It is all my cousin Anne's fault, I agree. It was she who taught us to be selfish, and to reach for our desires. *Amor omnia vincit*, she said.'

'Perhaps for a season it did.'

'Love conquers all?' Poor gentle creature, she bends her head. 'With respect, my lord, love couldn't conquer a gosling. It couldn't knock a cripple down. It couldn't beat an egg.'

Shelton was going to be married to Harry Norris; at least, she thought so, until Anne told her, 'If the king dies, Norris will marry *me*.' She had built a little house for love, and it was flattened by one remark: now she lives in the wreckage. He asks, 'What about Norfolk's daughter? I know she was the lookout for Meg. She does not live with Richmond as his wife, does she? She has never been permitted. So does she not have a lover of her own?'

Shelton shakes her head. 'Too frightened of her father. Wouldn't you be?'

'Insofar as I can think myself into her place,' he says, laughing, 'yes, I would. Where was Jane Rochford in all this?'

'She's on her way, isn't she? Ask her yourself.'

'I'm asking you.'

'I will not say she was in the room on Meg's wedding night. But I will say that she brought fresh linen.'

He holds up a hand. 'No talk of linen. Meg Douglas is a maid. Intact, like Norfolk's daughter. Clean as from her mother's womb.'

'I see,' Mary Shelton says. 'Be sure to apprise Jane Rochford. Tell her to rinse her memory clean.'

He thinks, why must you bed on white linen? God gives you a whole realm for your pleasures: you would be safer in the park against a tree.

Ahead of her return to court, the relict of George Boleyn has stated her demands. She specifies which rooms she would like, asks for stabling for two horses, and bed and board for herself, two maids, and a manservant. He sends a message to the royal household: give Lady Rochford what she wants. But as soon as she arrives, send her to me.

'What do you hear from Beth Worcester?' she says, settling herself to conversation as if the last weeks had never been. There is a gleam in her eye. 'Beth must be in her seventh month now. I wonder if the earl has decided whose child it is?'

'The king wants to know about Meg Douglas,' he says.

'No, he doesn't. Why would he want to know his niece is ruined? What he wants is to show that all her friends have been questioned, so he can claim he has pursued every road to the truth. One must pity him. He will think he is held of little account these days – his friends cuckolding him, his daughter defying him, his niece contracting herself in marriage. And you yourself, using him so roughly.'

'How, roughly?'

'"Set me free," Henry said. And so you did. He meant, free like a prince – not free like a beggar. You knocked down his palace of dreams and left him stark in the ruins. You showed him his wife was false, that his friendships were feigned. Of course, the treachery of a wife, it is only what you men expect; it is the sin of Eve, you say, betrayal is her nature. But the treachery of Norris – of Weston, whom he nursed in his bosom –'

'I gave the king what he asked for.' He thinks, she agrees with Chapuys: she believes Henry will never forgive me for it.

'But did he know how he would be laughed at?' Lady Rochford asks. 'His clothes, his verses, his manhood? He must live with his shame now, and you must live with him. You will have to build him up again, as you can. You and the Seymours.'

'Build him up? He is King of England.'

'But is he a man?' She laughs. 'I suppose he can do the deed with pasty Jane. She will not expect too much of him. I do not envy her, these nights. Anne said it was like being slobbered over by a mastiff pup.'

He closes his eyes.

'I hear the coronation is postponed,' she says.

'Get the hot weather over. Michaelmas, perhaps.'

He thinks, I hope for notice: time to paint out the dark-eyed goddesses I ordered for Anne, and replace them with Englishwomen dancing in a bower, with rounded bellies and rosy uplifted arms. Lady Rochford says, 'I think he will not crown Jane till she can satisfy him she has an heir inside her.'

'Satisfy him? You think she might lie about it?'

'It has been known.'

We'll let that pass, he thinks; she wants to draw him where he will not go, into the thickets of the past.

'Seymour will know how to play her hand,' she says. 'Because Seymour has watched and waited. And God knows she has no conscience. I have been in the country and had to endure the prating of my neighbours – "Our lord king will be happy now, England is happy, this is a blessed marriage." But how can it be blessed? A wedding dress made from a shroud?'

'Who sewed it, my lady?'

'Well, there is a question. You, or me, or Master Wyatt – who took the greater share in the work? I think it was you. We pricked out our little pattern, but you cut the cloth.'

'In May, I counselled you, think before you speak. I warned you, if you give evidence against your husband, you will be shunned. You will be held in odium. You will be alone.'

'How little you know of our lives,' she says. 'The lives of women, I mean. I have been alone for years.'

'You must forget those days. No one speaks of Anne Boleyn. No one thinks of her. You must be jocund and pleasant and adapt yourself to the new queen, or you will be sent away again, and I shall not speak for you.'

'Jane Seymour will not send me away. I know what she is. I know a thing about her.'

Inside his chest, a horrible slither and flip of the heart: Chapuys had asked, how could she be at your court so long, and still a virgin? He thinks, some wretch has dishonoured her. A wash of rage, like a current in the sea, almost knocks him off his feet.

Jane Rochford smirks. 'It is not what you think. No one wanted Jane in their bed, she was too cold a fish. It is another thing, that I know – I know her method. I witnessed everything that she worked against Anne, maid against mistress. You will remember a day when Anne took fright because she found a paper in her bed? A drawing of a man crowned, and beside him a woman without a head?'

Dr Cranmer was there, and had reached across him to snatch it from Anne's hand and tear it up. But Anne pulled away and read aloud: *Anne Sans Tête.* Anne had said, it is Katherine's people, they did this, they watch me. *Cremuel,* she had clutched his arm, *I am not safe. How can they come at me, in my own chamber?*

He says, 'Jane did not do it, she does not speak the French tongue.'

'Everybody speaks that much.' She laughs at him. 'Do you know, I believe all these years you have been thinking it was me?'

'It would have been a natural thought. There was no love lost between you and Anne.'

She says, 'I have suffered since I was a girl from these people – the Howards, the Boleyns. George Boleyn talked to me as if I were a girl who carries coals for a living, or scrubs shirts. My family was as good as his. Why should Anne Boleyn be uplifted, and not me?'

She is like a starved child, he thinks. Offer her a morsel of attention and she feeds till she is sickened. He had seen Anne Boleyn in fear that day, but he had also heard her scorn. *Let them do their worst. I will be queen, though hereafter I burn.*

'At least that was spared,' he says. 'Burning.'

Jane raises an eyebrow. 'In this world, perhaps. I am sure the devil knows his business.'

He picks up his papers: though they have not completed their own business, indeed they have not begun it.

'So, I am dismissed?' Lady Rochford stands. 'I thank you for my return to court. With what I have from my settlement from the Boleyns, and with my allowance for waiting on Jane, I shall be able to keep myself as a gentlewoman, if I am careful. And I dare say you will help me out if I am not.'

'My obligations are not unlimited.'

'At least you do not say, "My coffers are not bottomless." Now that would make me laugh.' She turns at the door. 'About Meg Douglas,' she says. 'You will be asking yourself, could I have mistaken the meaning of what I saw last spring – the coming and going by night, the hasty flitting, those swift glances, those burning sighs ...'

'My lady, if you knew of this intrigue, why did you not come to me? It would have prevented much mischief. It would have helped me –'

'How would it have helped you? You never supposed for one moment those men to be guilty of all you charged them with. You said, let us throw mud, and see what will stick. But for all that, you may be easy in your mind. Do not think a mistake has been made, nor an injustice done. You were not wrong about Anne Boleyn.'

'I trust your word,' he says, lying.

'She was false to the core. False in her heart. Whatever our deeds, it is the heart that God sees. Is that not so, Master Secretary?'

He says, 'You must learn to use my new title, madam.'

As he walks into Austin Friars he meets Richard Cromwell. 'My doorkeeper,' he says. 'Never let a woman in here. I never want to see or speak to one.'

'What, never?' Gregory says. 'Will you join a monastery? But then I hear they are full of women, and women of the worst sort too. What if the queen sends for you – what excuse shall we make?'

'Tell her she can write me a letter. I'll write her one back. But I will never read another verse in praise of love. I will read stanzas in praise of military victories. Metrical translations of the psalms. But women's matters – no.'

Gregory says, 'It is only the other week you were speaking warmly of the Lady Mary, and saying she ought to have presents.'

His nephew says, 'Richard Riche is here. And Call-Me.'

'And Rafe,' Gregory says. 'They look grave. We sent them into the garden.'

'Rafe is here? Why did you not say so?'

He hurries out. It has rained within the hour, and the air is warm and grass-scented. Even the stocks that support his young trees seem to quiver with their own green life. The young men stand on a path of damp beaten earth, their sleeves brushing tangled roses, their hems stuck with briars. They are speaking in low voices, and as he approaches they break off and look at him, shifty, almost guilty.

Rafe says, 'I cannot think how this has happened. It seems someone has taken letters of yours, or memoranda. It would not have occurred when I oversaw your desk.'

'I assure you, Sadler,' Richard Cromwell says, 'there is nothing leaves this house that should not. Nor word, nor paper.'

'Every household has traitors,' Call-Me says.

Richard Riche says, 'We would not for the world any baseless rumour traduce your reputation. Or set up a misunderstanding between you and our royal master.'

Mr Wriothesley says, 'Your friends have often begged you to remarry.'

'For God's sake!' he says. 'What has happened?'

'Chapuys seems to have some information, or has drawn some inference. He says that the king has promised the Lady Mary in marriage. To you.'

He is silent. 'By the bones,' he says. 'I gave that lady a jewel to wear. Or at least, I attempted it.'

'The rumour is everywhere by now,' Call-Me says. 'It swam to Flanders, rolled through France, scaled the mountains and flew back to us from Portugal.'

'And does the king know?'

'If he does not, he is the strange exception,' Riche says.

Wriothesley says, 'Sundry letters between you and his daughter were warm in tone. Someone has stolen them.'

'Not necessarily,' he says. Freely he had shown the ambassador letters from Mary; she in turn had shown the ambassador letters from him. 'We cannot say they were stolen. We may say that they have been misread, on purpose to make a ruffle in the world.'

'Your friends warned you,' Call-Me says. 'We warned you in the garden at Sadler's house. You gave her mother a promise, you said. Now it comes home to you.'

He sees Henry's face, as it broods over the gift in the palm of his hand. I'll give it her, he said, you find her something else. Has the king saved him from himself? He says, 'The king has not, he could not make any such proposition, as to marry his daughter to his councillor. And if he did, then I would refuse. He cannot believe I would seek such a match.'

'Not for now,' Gregory looks shocked. 'But if he chose to believe it …'

Riche says, 'It is a potent weapon, sir, for your enemies to turn against you. For many believe that the husband of the Lady Mary, whoever he be, will be king one day. And any man who offers himself to wed her, stands in treasonable light.'

'Yes,' Richard Cromwell says. 'You need not go on spelling it out and spelling it out, Riche. This is my uncle's reward for his goodness. He saved her, and now they say he did it to serve himself.'

He thinks, when fire breaks out you run to the rescue with a bucket. But it's not the smoke and flames that kill you, it's the bricks and timbers that fly out when the chimney blows up.

Gregory says, 'Here is what to do, sir. Nothing will counter the rumour unless you can say, "I am married already." Go out into the street and offer yourself to the first woman you see.'

'I concur,' his nephew says. 'Old or young. Whatever her condition or degree.'

'If she is already wed?'

'Leave that to us,' Richard says. 'I am sure we can see off a husband. What do you think, Riche?'

The ghost of a smile: 'We will dispose of him. Most of us do wrong, if we know it or not. Enquire into any man's conduct, and I am sure some charge will lie.'

'Or we can just knife the fellow and toss him on a dungheap,' Richard says. 'It's what they think we do, anyway.'

'I'll knife the ambassador,' he says, 'when I see him.'

He finds Chapuys in his garden, sitting beneath a tree, a book on his knees. He proffers it: *A Dialogue between Law and Conscience.*

He takes the book and turns it over in his hands. John Rastell's printing. 'I can lend you the second part. But it's in English.'

'It continues?' The ambassador is surprised. 'I thought all was said. Matters of conscience do not fall outside the law. Therefore, what need of special laws made by churchmen?' He takes the book back. 'Soon, some Englishman will ask, what need of churchmen? Why not every man his own minister? The Germans are saying it already.'

He says, 'I believe I am to be married.'

At least Chapuys has the grace not to lie. He does not deny knowledge of the rumour; he simply waves a hand and denies he is its source. 'My dear Thomas, do you believe I would say such a thing of you? It would lead to your murder by the noble lords of England, and then I should have to deal with the Duke of Norferk as chief minister. And – I swear by the Mass – the mere thought of it and I am withered by ennui.'

'I think you are trying to ruin me,' he says.

'Please,' the ambassador signals to his people, 'a glass of this excellent Rhenish?'

'Put it on a sponge,' he says. 'I'll have it when I'm nailed above London.'

'You blaspheme,' Chapuys says pleasantly. He hands a goblet. 'I have only reported what I have heard from honourable and good men – that the king means to bestow his daughter on an Englishman, and has chosen you. But I have said to the Emperor, I believe

Cromwell will decline the honour. He admits he is a blacksmith's son, and is not lost to all sense.'

'I could hardly deny my father.' He thinks of Walter plunging his head in a water butt at the end of the day: coming up spitting, and spluttering for air. Why did he do it? He was no less filthy afterwards.

'Of course, if the king did make the offer, face to face,' Chapuys says, 'how could you refuse him?'

'He has not. He will not. He could not. He would rather see Mary dead. His pride would not allow such a match.'

'Ah yes,' the ambassador says, 'his pride. I know from my own observation that the Lady Mary blushes when your name is mentioned.'

'She blushes with rage,' he says. 'She is thinking how she will kill me when she has the power. Crucifixion would be a mercy.' He downs the Rhenish. 'She will hate me worse now. By the way, I like your cap badge. That is ingenious work.'

He could swear Chapuys pales. His hand goes to it: a marigold, a petal tipped with a pearl. But he is not a seasoned diplomat for nothing. He removes his cap, and begins to unpin the jewel. '*Mon cher*, it's yours.'

He almost laughs. 'You are gracious.' The traitorous emblem rolls into his palm. He puts it in his pocket. 'I shall fix it on later,' he says. 'Before a mirror.'

At home Rafe is waiting for him. 'It is a sorry tale against Chapuys. After our amity in my garden.'

'Oh, Chapuys is not our friend.' He thinks, should I show him the cap badge? But does not.

'And now?' Rafe says.

'Now let us visit the French ambassador and see what he knows.'

'Monseigneur is from home,' says the usher. Then, as if he might not understand, he says in English, 'He is out.'

'Really?' He removes his hat. 'Not just playing at being out? He didn't spy me from the window? If I were to lift the lid of that chest, I would not find him crouching there with his knees under his chin?'

The ambassador in residence is Antoine de Castelnau, Bishop of Tarbes; and at the thought of a bishop crammed into this ridiculous posture, the usher cannot help but smile. Or perhaps it is because Cremuel rewards well, that he is so affable? 'But milord, another friend of yours is within. Come …'

Jean de Dinteville is sitting by a good fire. Outside the birds hang listless on the bough, and lawns are baking to straw. 'You!' he says.

'Alas, Thomas: your manners. "Welcome back, ambassador," is the usual greeting.'

'We shall have the pleasure of a long visit?'

'Not if I can help it.'

'But what brings you?' You are on the scent of disaster, he thinks. Nothing else would fetch you. 'Have you heard of my forthcoming nuptials?'

The ambassador does not smile. 'My king said, get over there, Jeannot, bring Cremuel our felicitations in person. It will mean all the more, he said, coming from an old friend.'

He snorts. 'He wants me dead, not wed.'

'He lives in hope.'

'If these ludicrous rumours take hold in France, I trust our own ambassador to pour scorn on them.'

'Well, certainly, Bishop Gardineur does not see you as a fit spouse for a princess. He sees you more as – how does he put it? – fit to shoe horses.' Dinteville turns his sad dark eyes on him. 'You seem disconcerted, Thomas? You were not prepared for treachery? What do you expect, of Chapuys?'

He, Cromwell, edges away from the hearth. 'Are you really cold? You can't be cold,' he says. 'I don't know what I expected. Not this.'

The ambassador stirs crossly inside his furs. 'You think the Emperor and his people will be grateful to you, because you kept a promise to Catalina. I assure you, Cremuel, they think it is some trick you worked, at the bedside of a dying queen. They hold you a man of no honour nor compunction. But then, they think the same of Henry, so they would not be surprised at anything he did. Nor are we surprised.'

'I don't know what else I can do,' he says. 'I dealt fairly with the girl. Henry would have killed her. I saved him from a great crime.'

'I don't doubt. And now you must save him from another. I mean the Queen of Scotland's daughter. What will you do there? If they say you preserved Mary for your own usage, they will say the same again. I have seen the Scottish princess. She is a sweeter morsel than the king's daughter, is she not?'

He sees himself, coughing, labouring through the smoke. *I've got you, girl!* Carrying the maiden from the inferno. *Bang!* The house has gone up. He sprawls beneath the debris.

'You know,' he says, 'if you walked about, ever? Get some air? Stir your blood? When Parliament rises, come out to the country with me.'

'I assure you,' the Frenchman says, 'diplomacy excites me enough.' He waves his hand at a blowfly that has taken his furs for some carcass; in the heat of midsummer a smell of must creeps through the room. 'Take heart. I think my master King François may make you offers. I have told him, you should have regard to Cremuel and put greater sums in his pocket. My king understands that you do nothing except for money. And he sees that although you may be a heretic, you keep Henry from war. If it were not for you, he might be still indulging his belief that he is ruler of France.'

'What does your king want?'

'Calais.'

'Never.'

'Give it on your terms, or one day soon we will take it on ours. As you will concede, Henry has enough to do, to keep his own little kingdom. His foot should shrink from French soil. If he keeps within his own walls, perhaps we will not molest him. But then again, perhaps we will.'

At the envoy's door, Christophe is entertaining a crowd of his compatriots. He breaks away from them, shouting, waving a fist in farewell. 'I have been telling them,' he says cheerfully, 'that you have the vigour of a bull, and very fit to get offspring on the Lady Mary. But they say, that is why the king chooses Cremuel – on purpose to dishonour the granddaughter of Spain. They say that if you have children, Henry will make them scrub his floors. They will scour out privies for a living and haul shit in carts by the light of the moon.'

18 July, Parliament rises. Tom Truth is attainted. All he has – not much – is forfeit to the king, and he is entitled to nothing but a traitor's death. Each dawn he will wake listening for footsteps. First comes Kingston or his deputy, always before nine. After him the priests.

'Is his date to be deferred?' he asks the king.

Henry says, 'Yes. He can wait.'

'And Lady Margaret? You know, sir, she was much misled. An innocent maid, sick at heart, and hopeful of your Majesty's forgiveness.'

'I shall allow her – I shall allow them both – an interval to think on their follies and crimes, before they receive their deserts.'

As the king and queen begin their progress to Dover, French ships are seen haunting the coast. In London, after their months of argument, the bishops make a statement of faith, which comprises ten articles. Rumour comes from Basle that Erasmus is dead. Hans, who has people there, says it is true.

In one of his last acts before departing Whitehall, the king has confirmed and augmented his state as Vicegerent of the church, and knighted him, so he is Sir Thomas as well as Lord Cromwell. If the king believes he has tried to entice, lure or seduce his daughter Mary, he gives no sign: amiably, he lays plans to see him, when business should spare him from the capital. Richmond is still confined to the sickroom, but the king says, if we linger the whole court may fall ill. 'Be sure and send me Gregory,' he says, waving a farewell.

His son is in demand. From Somerset to Kent, from the midlands to the northern fells, castles and manors compete to entertain him: a pleasant youth of competent good looks, never over-familiar but at ease with great men, discreet with servants and gentle with the poorer sort; able to play upon the virginals and lute, to sing his part, converse in French, and to take his hand at any game of skill or chance, indoors or out. On the hunting field he is tireless and without fear. He practises daily in the butts, giving example thereby – only modesty prevents his being as sharp as his father with the longbow. He, Lord Cromwell, thanks God daily for his accurate view of the middle distance. For close work now he needs spectacles. They are clumsy things, but Stephen Vaughan sends him good lenses from Antwerp. Sometimes his clerks read out letters to him. They mean to save him strain. He says, 'Every word, mind. Not the gist of it. Not your version. Every word.' If they cough or hesitate he makes them start again.

At Austin Friars, he asks Mathew to bring him The Book Called Henry. He hopes, though he lacks time, to record everything he has learned since Anne Boleyn was taken to the Tower. He means to set down the sum of advice he gives to the king's councillors, especially those recently sworn. Their part is to animate and quicken virtue in their prince. If Henry can think himself good, he will do good. But if you cast a shadow on his soul, comparing him to princes who are morally perfect and lucky as well, do not be surprised if he furnishes you with reason for complaint.

Sometimes he reads a little in the book, to restore his faith in himself. He has hopes for the volume. It need not be long, but it must be very wise.

The day after the king's departure he is at the Rolls House on Chancery Lane. Richard Cromwell comes in and lays papers before him. 'Verses come up from Kent.'

He holds the papers to his face, imagining they smell of apples. It is Wyatt's hand but as he reads he asks, 'Is this his verse?'

'It came from his desk, sir.'

'So we are spying on Wyatt, are we?' He is amused.

What he sees written are the names of dead men. Rochford. Norris. Weston. *In mourning wise since daily I increase* ... 'He increases,' he says. 'Why does he?' He reads. *Brereton, farewell.* 'Brereton, good riddance,' he says.

He slaps the paper flat on the desk and runs his finger down the page. 'Mark is not forgot.' He pictures the boy's whey-face. *A time thou had'st, above thy poor degree ...* Addled, desperate, banging on a door in the middle of the night; shut in the dark he believed a phantom had caressed him, with feathers for fingers and holes for eyes.

He thinks, these lines lack form and force. Some of them are more Tom Truth than Tom Wyatt. And yet they present to him those corpses, promiscuous, heaped upon a cart: their pale English limbs intermingled, their heads in sodden bags. *And thus farewell each one in heartiwise. The axe is home ...* He says to Richard, 'You see that the writer does not plead their case. He says they are dead, he does not say they should be otherwise. He calls George Boleyn to account for pride ... and here he says he scarce knows Brereton. So why mourn?'

'Because grief spreads as a contagion, sir. It grows day by day.'

'Up to a point.' He knows about grief. He reads out loud. '*Ah, Norris, Norris, my tears begin to run, to think what hap did thee so lead or guile, whereby thou hast both thee and thine undone ...*' He breaks off. Is that 'guile'? Or 'guide'? 'You note, he does not say anyone else has undone Norris. He does not say someone led him. He says chance led him, or circumstance.'

Richard says, 'He believes Norris was guilty. It is plain enough.'

'Well, well,' he says. 'And I thought I arranged his fate. But perhaps he did it all himself.' He holds the paper up to the light. There are no scores or corrections. The watermark is a unicorn.

Richard says, 'I do not know if these are Wyatt's own verses, but whoever made them, he knows what passed. You see there is no mention of the lady.'

None is needed, he thinks. Anne is always in the room.

Richard says, 'Perhaps Wyatt wrote it after all. With his left hand.'

Or his double heart. 'It changes nothing,' he says. *The axe is home, your heads be in the street.* It is only one man's opinion. But it is one more blow to our faith in our judgement. We did thus, and thus: we might have done less, and let guilty tongues speak for themselves.

He watches as Richard draws the papers together. *Pray for the souls of those be dead and gone.* 'I'm going to Mortlake,' he says. 'To my new house.'

On his first night he cannot sleep. He walks in the garden till dusk, deciding what needs to be done first: some old rotten stumps to haul out, and fresh planting. He walks the rooms of the house, replanning them, extending them: hall, great chamber and gallery, chapel and library, and the kitchens, sculleries, pantries; the wood store and coal store, wet larder, dry larder, bakehouse. This chamber could be for Call-Me, he thinks, when he stays, and Richard could have this corner room next door – new windows, perhaps? There is still material left over from the king's rebuilding of Hampton Court, he can order it sent by barge. The principal chambers are served by a privy stair; he will need to set a guard there.

He knew this place in the time of his sister Kat and her husband Morgan Williams. The Williams family had a house on the river, almost under the manor's wall. They were substantial people, good at laying plans: Thomas, they would say, you've not a bad head on your shoulders and if you got away from Walter you could make something of yourself. They imagined he might go as clerk to some cronies of theirs, or be kitchen steward for some dotard, work his way up to book-keeper for a great man. He pictured himself going to Morgan Williams's tailor and getting a good town coat like his: wearing that coat when, at thirty or thirty-five, he dipped his children in old Bouchier's font in the parish church. The manor house had always belonged to the archbishops. His uncle had worked in the kitchen one time, and half the lads he knew had picked up pennies for carting wood, for unloading at the wharf, cleaning the fishponds. It did not seem possible he would enter those gates as anything other than a labourer: that he would walk in one day with building plans in his hands, with a new owner's appraising eye. After all, he never aimed to be an archbishop.

If you marvel at your good fortune, you should marvel in secret: never let people see you. When you are Lord Privy Seal you must walk abroad with solemn countenance, looking chosen by Jesus, like More did when he was chancellor. Once he had shrugged off his early life – the Williamses and their plans, as well as Walter, his slaps and kicks – he did not think he would ever come back to those streets. But we yearn for our origins; we yearn for an innocent terrain. Ship Lane has always been there, running downhill to the wharves. The town he knew had been a territory of back alleys and rat-runs, robbers' dens with broken doors, keel-up boats rotting, frayed rope dissolved into vegetable matter, riverine mud and riverine gravel. His birthplace squatted there, around the bend in the river.

On his journey today from London, he felt he brought guests: Norris and George Boleyn, young Weston, Mark, and William Brereton. As he stepped out of his barge they stepped out too; they stood on the banks of the Styx, waiting to cross. They died within minutes of each other, but that does not mean they are together now. The dead wander the lanes of the next life like strangers lost in Venice. Even if they met, what would they have to talk about? When they stood before their judges they edged away from each other, as if fearing contamination. Each man had made a case against the other, hoping he might save his own life.

Get out, he tells them. Don't think you can move in here. Pay the ferryman, and away you go. His spaniel turns in his arms as they walk in the twilight, her muzzle raised, her tasselled ears pricked; though she is small of her kind, her nose is as sharp as a hunter's. There is always a current of disturbance, till a house settles about you: till your dog finds its way to the hearth and the sheets to the beds, the beef to the table. There is a scent in the air that reminds him of something from the past – it is yeast, perhaps, hops – though when he was a boy, they had no hops but what came in on the boat; the hometown brewers still used burdock root or marigold. Hops poison dogs, they said, when foreigners boasted about why their ale kept better.

He remembers standing behind the king, at his shoulder, as he signed the death warrants in May: Rafe Sadler, silent, at the king's other hand: the windows open to admit soft air, and the king an unwilling scholar, truculent as some infant set down for the first time with a slate. It is hard labour for Henry, it is irksome toil, signing lives away. And the king's hand rests, it seems, for long moments together, to allow him to view the half-made strokes – as if they might form by themselves and relieve him of the task.

Henry Norris, yes. He wills the royal arm to move. William Brereton, yes: he can feel, as if he himself were the king, the concentrated power of Rafe Sadler's gaze on the nape of his neck. The lutenist Smeaton, yes, that is easily done, ink slips like oil onto the paper, into the vital space: resolving easily, a day or so from now, into the boy's liquid death. As a man of no birth or breeding, Smeaton should have been strangled in a noose and, before he died, his guts pulled out before the crowd. But he had said to Henry, 'Be merciful because ...'

The king had said, 'Why would I? Why would I show mercy, to a man who has debauched a queen of England?'

'Mark is very young and fearful. No creature in terror can make a good death. And he must be sensible of his sins at the last, and able to frame a prayer.'

'Do you think that a man meeting the headsman is composed?'

'I have seen examples.'

Henry had closed his eyes. 'Very well.'

And there Henry had paused. One saw again a child, bowed under the heavy grief of infancy: the schoolmaster's *mauvais sujet* twisting in his seat, kicking his stool, watching out of the window as a blithe day draws to its close. I could be out there, the child thinks, in the last of the sun. Wherefore must I engrave these letters, does my tutor hate me that he keeps me to this task? And from the table before him, with a sigh, the king had picked up his little knife (smooth ivory handle) to mend his pen. 'Weston,' he said. 'You know ... he's very young.'

Over the king's head, his eyes had met Rafe's. It must be all of them: no doubts, no exceptions. All are guilty.

Rafe reaches out, takes the knife and the quill, sharpens it for the king. Henry receives it with a murmur of thanks: always gracious. He takes a breath and, neck bent, patient as an ox yoked to his future, he reapplies himself to his task: Francis Weston, *yes*. He, Cromwell, thinks, I have done this before, surely? Some other time, some similar form of coercion?

Henry's arm, his jewelled and heavy sleeve, trails across the table; an ink blot forms by Weston's name, and blooms there; it unfolds, a solitary black flower, and forty years glide into ink-dark. His face does not change, he can trust it for that, but he is a child now, and standing, arms folded, feet planted apart in the posture of a man. He stands in a diffuse glow; it is afternoon sun, and it kindles in a curve of burnished copper. He sees the low rippling gleam of pewter plates, the sharp mirror flash from the blades of kitchen tools, from paring knife, boning blade, cleaver. It is Lambeth Palace, the cook's domain: the echo of raised voices, among them his Uncle John's.

What has occurred here? Someone is to be whipped. The kitchen steward's hand slaps the table. The misdeed stated: who and what and why. (Well, not why, no one is interested in why.) The theft, the infraction, the breach – of manners or protocol, piecrust or bowl: the kitchen sin, the pantry crime: whatever it is, Uncle John's senior means to skin somebody for it, he is bellowing his intentions so loud that his voice bounces around the cold vaulting above and reverberates in the chambers of the skull. And it is the eel boy who sits weeping, neck bent, knuckles pressed into his eyes, while the kitchen steward pummels him for information: the red-headed eel boy who he, Thomas Cromwell, had half-drowned in a water butt only yesterday. 'It was me!' The eel boy is streaked with angry tears, nose bubbling with snot, eyes screwed tight. 'Leave me. Get off me. Enough. It was me.'

He hides his smile: a bad week for the eel boy.

It is only as the boy is hauled away to his punishment, and the knot of gawping menials disperses, that his uncle says to him, his voice low: 'You demon, it was you, wasn't it?'

'What, me? I was nowhere near. You heard him. He confessed.'

'Yes, but he had no choice. God alone knows.' John turns away. 'Could you not rub along with the little wretch, he being a townsman of yours?'

'People from Putney don't like each other. You know it.'

'You're as twisty as a skewer, Thomas. Where will you end up?'

Whitehall, it seems. The king lays down his quill. He rubs together the tips of his fingers; right, done, *deo gratias*. Rafe whisks the paperwork away. Each stroke of the pen will translate into a stroke of the axe. Like the eel boy, they will understand that if Thomas Cromwell says, 'You did it,' you did it. No use arguing. It only prolongs the pain.

Outside the room he says to Rafe, 'Get those warrants to the Tower before he changes his mind.'

'Sir ...?' Rafe's glance, puzzled, travels to his master's hand. He is holding – how did it get there? – the king's penknife, 'HR' picked out in letters of jet. Ah, he says, I had better ... Rafe says, I will, I'll take it back to him, and he says, no, you see those papers into Kingston's hands, then you can get home to Helen before it's dark.

Rafe goes; one parting glance over his shoulder, flash of pallor above a swirl of black. He, Cromwell, moves back towards his master, the knife in his grip. He stands in the doorway, words on his lips: Majesty, I find I have this knife in my hand, though it belongs to you.

But Henry is at prayer. Beside the table, he is kneeling, uncushioned, on the stone floor: his eyes closed. Lips move: *salve, regina*. The mild evening is draped around him, the rosy light.

He drops the king's penknife on the table and walks away. Not backing, as one does, from the presence of the monarch, but assured as a man in his own house, turning from someone in midconversation, quitting the room and leaving the door open.

Last night young Dick Purser had said to him, 'Master, is the queen really guilty? Did she really go to it with all those brave fellows?'

No use to say, she is not on trial for that, but for treason. A month from now, it is only the bawdry and lechery that folk will remember. 'You want my opinion?' He had passed his hand over his face. 'You see, Dick, it is why we have courts of law, and judges, and juries ... to protect us from the tyranny of one man's opinion.'

Outside the king's chamber, gentlemen servants had tried to converge on him, but he distanced them with an outstretched palm.

'Go in to the king, he is praying but I dare say he will soon want his supper.' He was irritated; if Henry has a mind to fall to his knees and beseech the Blessed Virgin, someone should have foreseen it and provided a hassock. 'Light a fire, the dew is falling. Later he may ask for music ...'

Clément Janequin, his psalms. The duets of Francesco Spinacino, the saltarellos of Dalza the Milanese: the *pavane alla venetiana, pavane alla ferrarese*: a new toccata from Capirola, quickly rehearsed from a manuscript decorated at its edges with the images of apes and leaping hares. The galliard, the basse-dance, *Chansons nouvelles en musique à quatre parties*: four parties now dead, or dead in effect, and five if you count George Boleyn. On other light evenings, the musicians will ease themselves to the royal threshold: the jellies go out, and the fruits roasted in honey, and as the waiters depart, the consort arrives, one with lute in hand: a single note, shivering, is drawn from a string tightened to a seraph key. With Norris, Brereton, and Weston gone, other gentlemen, chosen by Thomas Cromwell, will take their places in the privy chamber, close to the person of the king. But old servants are the best, the ones who know when you need to sing and when you need to pray. Will death stop them jotting their names on the roster, pricking their names on the list: six weeks off and six weeks on? By the third week in May, their heads are in the street. Autumn will come, the days shortening, and the shade of Harry Norris will slide back to his tasks, bobbing in a corner like a spider on his silk. There is a place, a sequestered place in the imagination, where the eel boy is always waiting to be whipped, where George Boleyn is always in his prison room, always rising in welcome: Master Cromwell, I knew you would come. As George had stood, his hands held out, an image had stirred inside him, and he was elsewhere: in some other enclosed space, the light failing, as if a shutter had half-closed. Above him a shadow, like the outstretched wing of an angel; blood in his mouth, and the curve not of feathers but of stone: and a chill, a deep chill in the marrow. A stone arch, a cellar, a crypt, where someone is waiting in the dark: someone who has apprehended pain for so long that he walks towards it, arms open, relieved that it is here at last.

He remembers himself at eighteen years of age, a shattered creature crawling from the battlefield, creeping through Italy till he came to rest – or a halt, anyway – at the gate of the Frescobaldi banking house. He did not know then whose house it was, only that he needed shelter. He had seen the city's saint drawn on walls – the city's patron, one should say: Hercules as an infant, crushing a snake in his fist; Hercules as a hero cleaning out the Augean stables with his bucket and his rake. So when the gate opened to his knock he crawled inside. 'My name?' he told the steward. 'My name is Ercole, I can labour.'

Now when he recalls himself, helpless on the cobbles, he sees himself blackened as he crawls, as if escaping from a burning building. He walks the rooms of the manor at Mortlake, Lord Cromwell on home ground, the wash of the river familiar as the waters of his mother's womb. He douses his light at last, and sleeps, and dreams he stands, wrapped in his cloak of night, on a wharf where the burning boats have fired the quays.

Towards morning, banging at the gate wakes the household. He rises, prays briefly, and goes down to see what the noise is about. It is Richmond's people, come from St James's to say the young duke is dead.

He says, 'Is someone on the road to tell the king?' (For once, this is not his role: Mortlake to the Dover road, one has not wings.) 'Alert my lord archbishop. He should be ready to go to the king's side.'

He thinks, Henry will say this is God's punishment on him, for allowing the bishops to make new articles of faith. For stripping the number of the sacraments away.

'Ensure word goes up-country to my lady Clinton. Remember the feelings of a mother, tell her gently – not banging on the gate and shouting it to the skies.'

Seventeen years back, when the king's son was born, he himself had not been at court or anywhere near it, and so he had to rely on others to tell him about those days. Francis Bryan saw Bessie Blount when she first came into the queen's household, fair as a goddess and not yet fourteen. The king would not touch her at that age; the most lenient confessor would have shaken his jowls at it. Henry danced with her, and waited a year or two, always mindful of Charles Brandon bustling behind him, ready to snap her up. Then Queen Katherine had to watch her as her little maid of honour filled out, plump and smiling and sick every morning. Katherine said nothing, only praising her glowing skin. Why, she had said, I think our little Bessie is in love.

Bessie was whisked away before her belly showed. Her family were sensible of the honour and hopeful of a son for the king. It was the cardinal who arranged everything. The king never saw her after-wards – perhaps once, after the child was born. He received the compliments, insincere, of the ambassadors: this shows your Highness well capable of siring a boy, and surely God will not long deny your Highness the consolation of one born in wedlock? But everybody knew Katherine's courses had stopped, and she would not bear another child.

It was Wolsey who set up a household for the infant, who found the new mother an honourable marriage, who filtered the funds through – the land grants and honours. Perhaps he looked after Bessie too well. Ten years on, with his power slipping away, his enemies unlocked their chest brimming with slights and derelictions, and out crawled a musty slander. They alleged that – taking their pattern from Bessie Blount – all the maids in England wished to become concu-bines. Harlots had flocked to the king's vicinity, they said, hoping for rich rewards.

It appears, the cardinal had said dryly, I must add to my crimes the degradation of the married state, the corruption of virgins and the valorisation of pimps everywhere.

It is not, and never has been, the custom of the kings of England to attend the burials of their sons or their wives. At the death of Prince Arthur, the chief mourner was the Duke of Norfolk's forebear, so word comes from the king that it would be fitting to follow custom, and for the rites to be arranged by the Howard that is now. And since Fitzroy was under the guardianship of the present duke, and married to his daughter, it seems proper that he should lie at Thetford, among the duke's own ancestors. Instructions are that the removal is to be in a closed cart, the whole matter handled in silence.

'What is Henry doing?' Chapuys says. 'He cannot hope to conceal that his son has died, can he?'

He says, 'Eustache, I cannot tell you about the king's state of mind. I am employed to make laws and mind the treasury. For the rest he has the archbishop.'

'That dubious fellow.'

He looks at him sharply to see what he knows. 'Heretic,' Chapuys says. Oh, only that, he thinks. He is relieved. The ambassador turns back for a parting shot. 'Richmond's death is not a bad thing for the interests of the Princess Mary.' He smirks. 'Your bride-to-be.'

His familars gather at the Rolls House. Call-Me says, 'My lord Privy Seal … you recall that day you went over to St James's with Richard Riche? When Fitzroy was first taken ill? You sent Riche out of the sickroom, he told me. What happened? May I ask?'

He thinks, the son spoke treason against the father. But it doesn't matter now.

Wriothesley says, 'Richmond feared he had been poisoned. I heard him say so.'

'For God's sake, don't start that up,' Rafe Sadler says. 'Or I'll give you a slap.'

'And so you could, little man, if you stood on a box.' Call-Me decides to take it in good part; he is too interested in plots to be diverted. 'If Richmond had been named in the succession bill, there would have been grounds for suspicion against Mary's people. And even as it is, knowing Mary's nature …'

Rafe says, 'Never mind her nature. The king is reconciled with her. It cost our master no little trouble.'

'Reconciled?' Wriothesley snorts. 'She has been forced to bow her knee. Do you think she will forgive? I do not.'

Gregory begs, 'Boys, don't fight. No one is poisoned. Surely.'

He says to Wriothesley, 'Think what you like, but don't go dragging this rumour around the Inns of Court. Or wherever it is you go.'

'Or the brothels of Southwark,' Rafe says under his breath.

'Do you?' Gregory is interested.

Rafe asks, 'What are we going to say to Henry?'

It is the only question left. He must get down to Kent, and say something. Forty-five years on this earth, twenty-seven of them as King of England – and all he has to show for it are three bastard children, one of them now a corpse.

He goes to the Tower to see Meg Douglas, in his pocket a recent example of her verse. 'Shall I read to you?'

Recognising her handwriting, she is startled. 'How did you get that?'

> 'Now may I mourn as one of late
> Driven by force from my delight
> And cannot see my lonely mate
> To whom forever my heart is plight.'

'I think you still don't understand,' he says. 'There was no plighting. You can't afford plighting. Your state was grave last week, my lady, but this week it is worse.'

'Because Richmond is dead.' She looks up. 'That takes me nearer the throne. He is no longer in my way.'

God help her, she supposes that gives her some greater leverage. He says, 'Can you imagine the king's doleful state? They say he cannot speak for sorrow. He has been struck dumb for two days.'

She says nothing. He throws the paper down in front of her. She has written her name under the verse, what she thinks is her name now: *Margaret Howard.* 'I have told the king how you were beguiled and misled. But now your eyes are opened and you are heartily sorry for what you have done. You repudiate Lord Thomas Howard, and you wish never to see him or speak to him again.'

'But that is not true.'

'It will be true, in time.'

'I cannot live without Lord Thomas.'

'You will find you can.'

'*You* don't know,' she says.

He wants to ask her, what did you think would come out of this? That you would sit in a turret, and Tom Truth come riding over the hills, his lyre slung behind his saddle? And you at the high window, letting down your strawberry tresses? When Mary Fitzroy stood guard outside the door, did you know how your beau would secure you, with a brutal thrust that made you bleed? Did you know how he would use and spoil you?

She says, 'My lady mother has written to me from Scotland. She says I must obey my uncle the king in all things. If I do not she will disown me.'

'She is the king's own sister, she understands him. After the summer we have passed, do you not think he is sensitive to his honour? You have chosen an evil hour to fall in love.'

He thinks, you have no notion how hard I am working for you. Neither had the Lady Mary. She ought to marry me, really, out of gratitude. So should you.

Constable Kingston is waiting for him outside. 'Sir William,' he tells him, 'I still have hopes Jane will be crowned this summer. So move Lady Meg to the Garden Tower. She must live in apprehension till I can frame the king's mind to mercy, and that will not be a while yet.'

'Myself,' Kingston says, 'I would stop these letters going between. But I am told it is your pleasure your man Martin should act Cupid. Why encourage it, if you are trying to stop the king proceeding against her?'

'I want their verses for the book.'

Perhaps Kingston thinks he means the statute book. Or a prayer book. 'The book of poems,' he says. The burning sighs. The frozen heart. Better the frozen heart than the perils of the thaw.

Kingston says, 'Lord Thomas is a harmless young man in himself.' There is something almost timid in Kingston's bearing: this man of singular experience, fishing for some inkling of what comes next.

'Pray God the archbishop can console the king in this last blow of fate. They fall so fast, I do not know how he endures it.'

It is dusk when he arrives at the Palace of St James, and at the news of his arrival, servants gather in whispering assemblies, hushing each other. The officers already wear mourning. The menials, in their livery of yellow and blue, have tied black bands about their sleeves. But all colours are fading to subfusc, the yellow bruised, the blue deepening to indigo. A man begs him, 'Sir, my lord of Surrey is in the stableyard. He is picking the best horses for himself, and we are afraid we will be blamed.'

He quickens his step. The servant speeds along with him. 'What will happen to us? To the household?'

'I will take as many as I can. The king will be good to you.'

He feels no confidence in the latter. The king's response to his son's death, so far as one can understand it, is not sorrow but a jealous rage, as if he had been cheated of something. Norfolk has applied to him for better instructions: 'Cromwell, what am I to do here? Closed cart? What does that imply? Shall I have to build a monument at my own expense? Or does Henry want me to shovel the boy into some common pit, like a churl who wears homespun and dines on a boiled onion?'

In the stableyard, he finds young Surrey, standing by as the groom Colins leads out Richmond's black jennet. She is a gleaming and well-muscled creature of Spanish breed, nimble-footed in trappings of black velvet.

Surrey's eyes flicker over him. No greeting. 'He would have wanted me to have the beast.'

'You must account to the king for what you take to your use. But no one will demur, if you clear it with my lord's master of the horse.'

'Giles will give me no trouble,' Surrey says. 'Besides, where is he?'

'At his prayers, I hazard.'

'I thought you did not believe in prayers for the dead?'

'Perhaps Giles Foster does.'

Black elongates the young man's spider limbs. As he turns, a red-gloved hand on the horse's mane, a low shaft of sunlight catches him and he glitters, head to toe, as a web glints with dew. On closer inspection, it proves he is sewn over with diamonds. He should have thrown a cloak around himself, even at the risk of dimming his lustre; high-bred though the jennet is, she still smells of horse. Surrey reaches for the bridle. 'Will you step out of my way, Cromwell? I want to walk her.'

He does not move. 'It would be charity in you, as you and my lord were so brotherly, to give employment to some in his household.'

'I suppose you have taken your pick already? I should have thought your retinue was bloated enough. I see your livery everywhere about the town. You employ some stout ruffians, Cromwell. I have never seen such evil countenances, and such readiness to fight, as I see in your people.'

It is true that he employs men who by reason of their dubious histories cannot find another master. He does not feel equal to explaining this to Surrey. He says, 'I grant you, appearances are often against my boys. But I do not believe they will fight unless for good cause.'

'Not even if provoked?'

'Ah – in that case I could not say.'

He thinks, I could snap you in two, boy. He runs a hand along the jennet's gleaming hide; the beast stirs, and he finds the tender place between the ears, rubs it. Surrey is crying: he buries his face in the bright saddle-cloth emblazoned with the dead boy's arms. 'He was my friend,' he says. 'But you, Cromwell, you would not understand it – the friendship that is amongst men of ancient lineage and noble blood.'

I understand, he thinks, your nose is running like any stable-lad's. 'Your father would not like to see you weep. Take this like a Christian man, sir. Richmond is gone where no harm can touch him, nor spoil the flower of his youth. He was a king's son, but he will find a father in Heaven.'

Surrey's face is mottled: tears, rage. 'Cromwell, I wish I were dead,' he says. 'No, I take it back. I wish you were dead.'

He remembers the breakup of York Place: the rattle of treasure into the chests of other men, the scramble onto the river. He has many of Wolsey's people among his own. The dukes took others. I wonder, he thinks, if Charles Brandon retains that clown who used to keep the hearth and chimneys at Esher? It gives him satisfaction, to think of Suffolk being smoked like a herring, from the year 1529 and every winter till now: and from now, unto the ending of the world.

He answers a summons from Jane the queen: finds her with a book in her lap, a Book of Hours. He thinks, I know that volume. It belonged to the other one.

Jane holds out the book. 'This is hers, Anne Boleyn's. She and the king passed it between them. The king has written an inscription, under the Man of Sorrows.'

He takes the book from her. Christ is kneeling, his flesh gory from head to heels, each bleeding cut fine as a wire. The picture is set within a border of peapods and ripe strawberries: the king has written some lines in French. 'Lady Rochford has kindly translated it for me,' Jane says. '*I am yours, Henry R, forever.* And then she replied to him.'

He cannot see the reply.

'Look under the Annunciation,' Jane says. 'She had hope, of course, in those days. She thought she could bear a son.'

He finds the picture. A coy virgin with lowered eyes is getting good news: the angel of the lord is right behind her.

Jane recites, '*By daily proof you shall me find/To be to you both loving and kind.* Do you think she was kind to him?'

'Not often.'

Jane's hand moves over the book's binding, as if it were a living creature she is soothing. 'Sometimes, when the king has, so to speak, visited me, then he falls asleep in my bed. But he soon wakes because he has bad dreams. Then he kneels by the bed. He cries out, *mea culpa, mea culpa, mea maxima culpa.* To that he appends Latin I do not follow. Then the gentlemen of the privy chamber come, and walk him back to his own chamber.'

'And you, madam, I trust you then take your rest?'

Jane nods to Mary Shelton, who stands at her elbow. Mary curt-seys and goes out, giving him a weary smile.

'You all like Shelton,' Jane says. 'The king likes her.' She waits till the door is closed. 'My ladies say that if a wife does not take pleasure in the act, she will not get a child. Is that true?'

Jane waits. It seems that, humbly, she would wait all day: she knows she asks questions to which answers are not likely.

He says, 'Perhaps consult with your lady mother? Or one of the elder dames here at court might advise you – the Countess of Salisbury?'

'They will have forgotten. They are old.'

'Your lady sister, then. Because she has two fine infants, I hear.'

'Bess puts heart into me. She tells me, say an *Ave*, Jane, and the king will soon spend. She tells me she did not have much joy in her own marriage bed. With Oughtred it was like a military manoeuvre. Brisk.'

He bursts out laughing. Sometimes you forget she is a queen. 'He did not beat a drum, I hope?'

'No, but she always knew when he was on his way. Bess says, she wouldn't mind a bouncing new husband. A willing young one whom she could teach. But the infants come when they will, she says, pleas-ure or not, and never mind what the physicians say.' She holds out her hands for the book. 'Forget this. I should not have asked you. You can go to the king now. Today he is not dressed as a Turk.'

In the king's privy chamber he is surprised to meet Rafe. 'You are on the rota, Master Sadler?'

An esquire says, waspish, 'Master Sadler has his own rota. He is always here.'

'He talks about my lord of Norfolk,' Rafe says. 'He is angry with him. And he has sent for Richmond's inventories.'

'Meg Douglas, does he say …?'

'Not inclined to mercy.'

'Right,' he says.

* * *

A Genoese tailor is draping the king in black velvet. He greets the man, motioning him out. Henry says, 'You practise still that Italian tongue.'

And its variants. The king knows enough Italian to sing an amorous ballad, but not enough to talk about money.

The tailor retreats, bowing, folds of night draped across his arms. 'I am amazed,' the king says, 'that the Duke of Norfolk should so far forget himself as to ignore my wishes. I said a closed cart. I said, discretion. Now I hear that black riders went before.'

'He did not want to dishonour a king's son.'

'He defied my intentions.'

'He did not perfectly understand what they were.'

Henry stares at him: that's no excuse. 'Tell him I shall send him to the Tower.'

'I durst not take that message.' He surprises himself – because, as he delivers this useful lie, he smiles.

Henry is disarmed – like someone who discovers a child's fear, and sees an easy means to dispel it. 'If you fear Thomas Howard, then of course I shall relieve you of your task. I did not think you feared anyone. You should not, my lord. You have my authority.'

'The Tower is filling up,' he says. 'Your lady sister has written from Scotland, begging that her daughter's life be spared.'

'I own Scotland,' Henry says. 'After Flodden I should have taken it back.'

He thinks, you did not have the men or the money. You did not have me. 'The cardinal used to say, marriages work better than wars. If you want a kingdom, write a poem, pick some flowers, put on your bonnet and go wooing.'

'Good advice,' Henry says, 'for any prince whose heart is his own. Or one who has the disposal of other hearts. But if princesses dispose of themselves to men of no fortune, only because they like their verses, then I do not know what world we live in any more.'

'I move you to mercy,' he says.

'My niece is a shame and a disgrace. She gave herself to the first man who asked her. She gave what was mine to give.'

He thinks, I wish Cranmer were here. It is the bishop's task to show how sins can be forgiven or redefined: to prove how adultery is not adultery, and killing no murder. It is he who holds the key to the walled garden of the king's mind; he knows its shady walks, its allées, its rank corners where sunbeams never creep. 'It seems to me,' he says, 'if a word is given lightly, in haste, by a young person, without the advice of sober friends, under the intoxication of love, without knowledge of where it will lead ... I ask myself, sir, does God in His wisdom not wink at such a promise?'

'God is not mocked,' Henry says. 'As St Paul is pleased to tell us, men reap what they sow, and women too. To take an oath and not to mean it, that is blasphemy. And if words are no more than breath, if words are air ... if they are not bonds, if they are not honour ...'

'I speak of lovers. Not princes.'

The king turns his face away. 'True, there is a difference.' A pause. 'There are great lords and rash young women who have cause to be grateful to you, my lord Cromwell.'

He inclines his head. He thinks, Wriothesley will be amazed, that once again I have let Norfolk wriggle away, when I have him on the hook. He imagines himself shouting through to Thomas Avery, who does his accounts: invoice him for my fee, mercy is not gratis.

The king indicates a bundle of papers – inventories, as Rafe had said. He leafs through. 'See Lady Mary gets the silver plate from Richmond's household. The gold plate to me, of course.' He turns the pages. 'These sables and the lambskins, they should be sent to my officers of the Wardrobe. The tapestries ... Moses found in the bulrushes ... the plagues of Egypt ... Moses leading his people through the deserts of Sinai ... Make sure my son's household stuff does not leak away to his mother's people. I have done a great deal for Bessie – Lady Clinton, I should say – and am not inclined to do more. And beware of Norfolk's daughter too – I want her goods listed, so we are sure they are not suddenly augmented by what should come to me.'

'She will be due a settlement, sir. She is my lord of Richmond's widow, even if she is still a maid.'

Henry snorts. 'You wonder if she could be a maid, when she has embroiled herself in this affair of my niece, and filthied her own name. What should a virgin know of assignations, of back stairs and greased locks?'

So this is how it will be. He will use Mary Fitzroy's misjudgement to cheat her of her dues and enrich the treasury. There could be worse punishments.

'Let her father take her back to his own country,' Henry says, 'and see she lives chaste. A convent would be best.' He glances down at the lists. Satin coats fringed with silver; habits of green velvet, to ride in spring through the woodlands when blossom smothers the bough. An image of St Dorothea with a basket and garland; Margaret of Antioch stamping on a dragon; George stamping on a dragon also, with his sword, spear and shield, an ostrich feather on his head. Spoons, chalices, bowls, censers, pyxes, holy water stoups; gold chains with enamelled white roses, red roses with ruby hearts. It is the king's pleasure to read out the inventories, as if he is reading them to his dead son: I gave you life, and I gave you all this.

'A small salt carved of beryl.' Henry frowns. 'The cover set with a ruby, its foot garnished with pearls and stones. They do not say what stones. And I do not recall it.'

'A new year's gift from my lord cardinal. The year escapes me.'

The king looks up. 'How unlike you. I understand Surrey took the black jennet.'

'And its tack.'

'Tell Giles Foster I want the bay and the sorrel.'

'Sir.' He bows his head.

'Mary Fitzroy may have geldings, to take her wherever she is going.' A sour smile. 'You think me heartless? Giving and receiving, when my son is bundled off to lie among strangers? But as the psalmist bids me, *placebo Domino in regione vivorum*. I will please our Lord in the land of the living, since it is only in the land of the living that we can do anything at all.' Henry looks into the distance. 'I hear my cousin Reginald Pole has been called to Rome. The Pope has charged him to lead a crusade against me. He is to visit the French court and stir them into action.'

'I wonder how?' The French armies have just marched into the land of Savoy. Their king has broken two treaties, so the Emperor is after his blood. François has more to do than attend on Reynold when he rolls up, lugging his volumes of canon law and bleating about his ancient lineage.

He says, 'The French will do nothing for him. And the Pope has not given him ships, nor money, nor men.'

'But he has fortified him with spiritual power.' Henry's mouth twists. 'He is to take to the road.'

Henry fed this ingrate, Pole. But now he feels the poisoned lash of the Plantagenet tail, he feels the bite of the back-fanged snake. Henry leans forward. He seems to choke. You can almost feel his heart galloping – his face is as pink as Easter veal. With one flat hand he slaps the arm of his chair. 'Traitor,' he says. 'Traitor. I want him dead.'

He waits for the fit to pass. Says, 'The wars your father fought are not over yet. But I assure you, sir – means may be found in Italy, to rid a traitorous subject. Wherever Pole moves, my people will follow.'

Henry looks away. 'Do what you must. I have told you before this, how Pole's family laid a curse, after young Warwick was beheaded. My brother Arthur died at fifteen. My son Richmond, at seventeen.'

The king used to explain his lack of heirs by saying he had married his wife unlawfully. Now it seems the Poles are to blame. It is the more useful explanation, as things stand; there is no juice left in the other one.

'You saw Margaret Pole at L'Erber,' Henry says. 'Or so I am informed. Keep going there. I should not doubt the whole family, I suppose. Yet I do.'

The king makes a signal. He bows himself out. Henry calls after him, '*Dieu vous garde.*'

He is glad Henry did not tax him on his visit to Margaret Pole. He does not want to say he went there to see Bess Darrell. He does not want to raise Wyatt's name. The king says a man is forgiven, but that does not mean a man's offence is forgot: and a woman can be pulled down, and stifle in his wreckage. The countess had left him alone with Bess, and her sewing. But then, as he was leaving, a servant intercepted him: My lady countess will see you.

The servant had led him to a panelled closet, the countess's private oratory. Here, you were shut away from the noises of the city – hooves on the cobbles, shouts of draymen, clattering and hammering from the workshops beside the walls. A table was set up for Mass, draped with rich brocade; the altarpiece was of silver, shining indistinct figures going about pious lives. It reminded him of one Anselma had, in Antwerp years ago. Though as Lady Salisbury is one of the richest dames in England, it is likely hers is of greater value.

Margaret Pole had turned to him. 'I hope you have not left Mistress Darrell in tears?'

'Why would I?'

She had unlocked her writing box. 'Here.'

'Is this your son's own hand?'

'He has those about him who do the office of secretary. Italians, perhaps. I do not know their names.'

No, he thinks, but I do.

'Believe me, Master Cromwell, I am no traitor. Why would I be? Henry has done everything for me. It has been a slow and painful path, from that low place I occupied when my father Clarence was attainted, to the honour I now enjoy.'

'Surely you cannot remember your father. You cannot have been five years old.'

'Even a child knows when one goes to prison and never comes out. My father did not die by the axe, he – God knows how he died, but I trust he was shrived, he did not lack a priest or die in his sin. I learned early, what treason was, and what follows it. I have seen four reigns – my uncle King Edward, my uncle the usurper, then the first Henry Tudor, and now his present Majesty, whose name I have reason to bless.'

He is reading Pole's letter. It is bitter, as she says.

238

'I scarcely knew my poor brother Warwick. He was a child when Henry Tudor shut him away.'

'To keep the peace,' he says.

'To secure the throne. Our blood being so near it, and so much nearer, in truth, than his.'

'But the Tudor won the battle. God favoured his army. He won England in the field.'

'And none of us,' she said sharply, 'ever contested his victory. When my brother was led to the scaffold, I was quick with child, but I would have come to court to petition for him. I would have begged to wear mourning for him, and observe the proper rites, in which I would have found some solace, I dare say – but one does not pray for a traitor's soul, nor wear black for him. At a traitor's demise, one must smile.'

'I do not think the old king would have required that.'

'You did not know him. In those days no one was safe. When the Henry that is now came to the throne – well, then we thought we had come to the promised land. To right all wrongs, was his express desire: to make restitution, to see justice done. I had been widowed then for years. When my husband died I had to borrow money to bury him. But Henry restored me – in fortune, in title. He and Katherine bestowed on me the inestimable favour of making me governor to their daughter, their only child, trusting in me to fit her either for the office of consort to some great prince, or to rule as a prince in her own right. Henry favoured and promoted my sons –'

'And they all married rich heiresses,' he said. 'Except Reynold, who as we know has his eye on a greater prize.'

She had positioned herself with her back to him, staring down into the courtyard. Whatever was going on there, she found it of interest. 'I do not understand my son. I concede he has behaved with foolish ingratitude. But he is innocent of any greater design. He is drawn to chastity, to a celibate life. He would not wish to marry.'

'Not even a king's daughter?'

'You must not judge others by yourself, Cromwell.'

She turned her head, to see that blow hit home.

'All these years,' he said, 'you have learned to dissimulate. You say it yourself – you smile when you wish to weep. It must work the other way – weep when you would like to smile? So though you appear abashed by what Reynold has done, how can the king know you are sincere?'

She spread out her hands. 'I can only appeal to the history that lies between us. I am a feeble woman, who never wore plate armour, nor links of mail. I have no breastplate, but faith in God. I have mounted no defence against my detractors – but trusted in the king, and in his skill to recognise those who are fit for his company and service.'

'But now you see me,' he said, 'in his company and service. And you wonder if Henry knows anything at all.'

'You are useful to him. How could I doubt it? And I did not mean to deprive you of your title just now. I am elderly and it takes one a while to become accustomed to new usages. We think of you as plain Master Cromwell.'

'Well,' he had said cheerfully, 'if you could learn to think the Tudors rightful kings of England – and you say you could – I am sure you can come to think of me as Lord Privy Seal. And should I ever forget that I was born one of the lower sort, I will presume upon our friendship, madam, and beg you to remind me.'

That jolts you, he thought: 'our friendship': that sickens your stomach. That a Putney boy should presume! He says, 'You claim that your son is not ambitious to rule. But others may be ambitious for him. Others may plan and intrigue for him, at home and abroad.'

Her eyes dart like birds in their nest of violet shadow. 'I? You mean, I would do it? You accuse me?'

'Great families are subject to reversals. For a decade, they climb; then their enemies hurl them down; then they overthrow their enemies, and lead them in a Roman triumph, in chains. It used to be that, if you and your kind stuck doggedly to the wheel of fortune, you would rise as far as you had fallen. But then comes a fellow like me, and knocks you clean off the wheel. Be advised, I can do it.'

'There is a proverb,' she said, 'the truth of which is hallowed by time. "He who climbs higher than he should, falls lower than he would."'

'A feeble saying, and feebly expressed. It leans on that same conceit, the wheel. What I say is, these are new times. New engines drive them. Still,' he smiled, 'I congratulate you. You have said what my lord of Norfolk would say, but he dare not.'

'The duke is a time-server,' she said coldly. 'He forgets, there were lords of Norfolk, before Howards held that title.'

'But there were no lords Cromwell. Not before this. You hope there may be none after. But it is the present you must reckon with. You cannot pray nor curse me away – your women's weapons are no use against me, nor the weapons used by priests, I am proof against them too. If the men of your family would relish an open fight, I am ready – I will fight any day for Henry against papists and traitors.'

Stock-still against the window's light, she had stood with hands clasped, her voice frigid. 'I am glad we have spoken plain. What Reynold has done against the king – God knows, I have never felt so sharp a sorrow; not when his father died, not when some other of my children have died. I shall write to him and advertise him of this. And I am sure you will read my letter by some means, either before it leaves these shores or after – so I shall not detain you now, while I write it. But I shall counsel you, my lord, and I beg you to hear me out. You speak of new times and new engines. These engines may rust before you have wheeled them to the fight. Do not join battle with the noble families of England. You have lost before you ride out. Who are you? You are one man. Who follows you? Only carrion crows, bone-pickers. Do not stop moving, or they will eat you alive.'

The low civil tone in which the countess said this had left him without a rejoinder. She had inclined her head, and walked out of the room.

He possessed the ground. The writing box gaped open; but she was right, he had no interest in its contents.

Outside his escort waited, marshalled by Richard Cromwell. His people carry clubs and daggers, and are ready to move on anyone who casts them a second glance. From Dowgate it's but a step to Austin Friars, but death threats come in daily, some of them in verse. The Londoners who jostle them, the Londoners whose indifferent eyes skim over them, see no more than a sober merchant with his household about him, hurrying to a ward meeting or guild dinner. But there are those who have his features engraved in memory: so they claim, when they threaten to strike him down as he walks. Thank God I am not memorable, he thinks. One coarse-featured sway-belly, like my father in his prime: better clothes, though.

He says to Richard, 'I have no illusions about the countess. Her sons have been feeding our secrets to the Emperor for years. Young Geoffrey Pole, the brother – he was so often at Chapuys's house that Eustache had to beg him to stay away.'

The bell at All Hallows gives tongue, then St Mary's after it. Richard says, 'But you can see why the king fights to think well of them. It was he who restored their fortunes, and he does not want to take himself for a fool.'

St John Baptist rings out; then Swithun strikes up; further off, the bells at Paul's. Across the street Richard shouts: 'Humphrey Monmouth, or do my eyes deceive?'

The merchant, his old friend, halloos in reply. With his companion, he threads between two carts, steps over a stream of horse piss. He, Cromwell, claps their shoulders: 'Will you come up to Canonbury to hunt?'

'I will hunt with you,' Robert Packington says. 'Old man Monmouth can come and watch.'

Monmouth elbows him. 'Old man! You'll not see forty again, sir! I shall ride out with my falcon in your company, Thomas.'

It is a usual conversation. They raise the name of Tyndale, as he knew they would. He says courteously that he has done all he can through official channels, and now awaits the outcome. He turns the subject – the family, are they all well? But Packington turns it back: 'Any visitors from Antwerp?'

'The usual,' Richard says, cautious.

'No one new?'

He says, 'No one who can tell us anything we don't know.'

They part with hearty farewells. The merchants go chattering away. He and Richard walk on, silent. He says to Richard, 'What?'

'They sound as if they are planning a surprise. Perhaps it's a present?'

He doesn't need to say, I don't like surprises.

Richard looks at him sideways. 'So will you? Kill Reynold?'

'Not in the street,' he says.

It is a conversation for Austin Friars: for his private rooms. He says, 'Francis Bryan would do it. He would rise to a challenge. Make a name for himself. He must sometimes wonder, what is the point of my life?'

'Bryan?' Richard makes a tippling motion.

'True.' He thinks, what other desperate men do I know?

'I'll go.'

Fear touches him. 'No.'

'I would need a company of rogues, but from what you say I could find them easy, in any Italian town. There are some gentlemen who might try to manage the business from afar. Now, I am not saying I would put the knife in myself. But I am saying I would see it done.'

'I need you here, Richard,' he says. God knows how much. 'Tom Wyatt would do it. The king would forgive him everything. He would make him an earl.'

Richard hesitates. 'The people about Pole … they might turn him. There are some subtle wits at Rome. I love Tom Wyatt, no man more, but he is not proof against sudden persuasion.'

He says, 'When we ride to Kent to join with the king's party, we will visit Allington, you and me, whether the king goes there or no. Sir Henry writes that he is failing. I am his executor, and should consult with him. And Tom Wyatt would be glad to see you.'

Richard slides a paper out of his pocket. 'This came.' He has been carrying it near his person. 'Another verse. Not stolen. Offered freely.'

This time he knows it: Wyatt and none other. It is not strange if, once again, he laments those lost. Call it two and a half months – late May to Lammas-tide. The dead are no longer fresh, but copper-green flesh is still adherent to their bones. The verse is about slippage, fall, reversal of fortune, the casting down of the great by the great: around the throne thunder rolls, *circa regna tonat*; even as he sits under his canopy of estate, the king hears it, he feels it shudder in the stone flags, he feels its reverberation in the bone. He pictures the bolts, hurled by the gods, falling through the crystal spheres where angels sit and pick the fleas from their wings: hurtling, spinning and plunging till, with a roar of white flame, they crash down on Whitehall and fire the roofs; till they rattle the skeleton teeth of the abbey's dead, melt the glass in the workshops of Southwark, and fry the fish in the Thames.

> The Bell Tower showed me such sight
> That in my head sticks day and night.
> There did I learn out of a grate …

He cannot tell if Wyatt writes *lean* or *learn*. From the Bell Tower, no use to lean: you cannot see the scaffold on Tower Hill. But then, what had he to learn? He could not be ignorant of what was to pass. He did not think the men would come back with their heads on their shoulders.

He thinks, I didn't have to go to the Bell Tower. This sorry procession to extinction – it was always in my sight. Chapuys had said, 'You went to your house and dreamed it, then it came to pass.'

On the day of Anne's death, Gregory saw Wyatt standing at a window; Wyatt looked down at him and made no signal. Did he watch the deer on her last run, her heart labouring, her gait failing? One supposed his eyes were inward, his gaze trained on nothing: where nothing soon would be. He has an image in his mind – and either it is a distant memory, or it is inserted there by a verse – of Wyatt's hands scratched and bleeding, a tangle of roses in his grasp.

Wreckage (II)

But surely, he thinks, it is Wriothesley I remember, at Canonbury: standing at the foot of the tower in the garden, the light fading, a sheaf of peonies in his hands.

They are in Kent, and the king calls him at dawn: he comes in, the locks rattling open, to free his prince from the oppressions of the night. Henry sits in his nightgown on a gilded and fringed stool, while a pale, perfect morning dawns outside the panes, and his features emerge from shadow, as if God were making him for the occasion.

The king begins, as he often does, as if they had just been speaking, and for some slight cause had broken off: a door opening, or a spark flying from the fire. He says, 'In the days when I wanted her, and could not have her, when we were apart, Anne Boleyn and I, let us say I was at Greenwich, she was here in Kent – in those days I used to see her standing before me, smiling, just as if she were real, as real,' the king stretches his hand out, 'as real as you, Cromwell. But now I know she was never truly there. Not in the way I thought she was.'

The room smells sweetly, of lavender and pooled beeswax. Below the window, across the gardens, a boy is singing.

> 'The knight knocked at the castle gate
> The lady marvelled who was thereat.'

Henry lifts his head, listening. He sings:

> 'She asked him what was his name
> He said, Desire, your man, madame.'

When he steps forward into the full light, he sees Henry is crying silently, tears running down his cheeks. 'The archbishop has given me a saying to guide me. It comes from the book of Samuel. "When the child was yet alive, I fasted and wept … But now he is dead, why should I fast? Can I bring him back again? I shall go to him, but he shall not return to me."'

Some fool comes in with a ewer of hot water. He waves the man back again. 'A child's loss is grievous, sir; it is as if we drag their corpses with us, all our days. But it is best to lay down your sorrow in some safe and consecrated place, and then walk on, looking to better times.'

'I thought I had been punished enough,' Henry says. 'But it seems I will never be done being punished.'

'Sir –'

'You cannot know. You have only lost daughters, not sons. When my own day comes …'

He waits. He cannot guess how the king will conclude.

'… you understand my wishes, and should you survive me I charge you to honour them. I wish to be buried in the tomb that the cardinal prepared for himself.'

He inclines his head. There is a sarcophagus of black touchstone, in which the cardinal never lay. All the parts are preserved, laid up in store. They await use, by someone who values himself in the sight of God and man, and wishes his name continued. Wolsey brought the artist over. Benedetto worked on it year after year, but as soon as he put in his account, the cardinal thought of something else. There are twelve bronze saints, and putti bearing shields emblazoned with the Wolsey arms. There are sober angels who bear in their hands pillars and crosses, and dancing angels with curly hair, their garments float-ing about them as they caper and skip.

'You should be glad, Crumb,' Henry says. 'You always want to save money.'

'Only if it sits with your Majesty's honour.'

'The angel who bears the cardinal's hat,' Henry says, 'he will bear a crown instead. The griffins at the feet – I thought they might be wreathed in roses. Golden roses.'

'I'll talk to Benedetto.'

The artist has never gone home. Perhaps he has been expecting the cardinal to rise from the dead, with fresh suggestions? By now one of the skipping angels has developed a crack, between the fingers of his left hand. Benedetto says, no one will know, Tommaso. Not when he's gilded and dancing up there on his pillar. But I'll know, he says.

The king tells him, 'Erasmus is dead.'

'So I hear.'

'I saw him first when he came to Eltham when I was a child. You would have seen him at Thomas More's house, no doubt.'

The great man's eyes passed over him, over Thomas Cromwell: saw him and forgot him. He says, 'He civilised us.'

The king says, 'Then he died with work to do.'

Henry seems frightened of himself, frightened of what he might say or do next. He seems weary, as if he might leave off being king, and just walk out into the street and take his chances.

The knowledge of this collapse of morale must be kept from the court. William Fitzwilliam catches him, outside the king's door. 'Before we left London,' Fitz says, 'he told me he thought he would have no more children.'

'Hush,' he says. 'He is ashamed of himself. He thinks he is done for, only because he cannot follow the chase as he did when he was young.'

This summer, the king will not hunt on horseback. The game will be driven to him as he stands in the butts, crossbow loaded, poised to shoot. He can ride well enough, keeping an ambling pace, but not across rough country, because of the jolting to his leg.

'It seems to me,' Fitzwilliam says, 'that he has some principle of rotation in his head, by which he humiliates his councillors in turn.'

'True. At the moment it is Norfolk's turn.'

'At the council board he walks about behind us. He hovers like a cutpurse. If I met such a man in Southwark, I would turn and knock the felon down.'

He laughs. 'But what would you be doing in Southwark, Fitz?'

'When he gets himself behind us, we must rise and kick our stools away and turn and face him, which throws us off, makes us forget what we were saying – and then, if we address him, is it kneeling or standing?'

'Kneeling is safest.'

'You don't.' Fitz sounds accusing. 'Or not so much as you did.'

'I have too much business with him. He knows not to cripple me.'

'Even the cardinal knelt.'

'A churchman. He was trained to it.'

The cardinal, in his days as master of the realm, had spoken of God as if He were a distant policy adviser from whom he heard quarterly: gnomic in his pronouncements, sometimes forgetful, but worth a retainer on account of his experience. At times he sent Him special requests, which the less well-connected call prayers; and always, until the last months of his life, God fell over Himself to make sure Tom Wolsey had what he wanted. But then he prayed, Make me humble; God said, Sir, your request comes too late.

His servant John Gostwick has been checking the inventories of the Duke of Richmond. Among Fitzroy's effects he finds a doll: no wooden mammet for a common child to play with, but the lively image of a prince.

'Item: a great baby lying in a box of wood, having a gown of white cloth of silver and a kirtle of green velvet, the gown tied with small aglets of gold, and a small pair of beads of gold and a small chain and a collar about the neck of gold.'

Gostwick had called him to see it: he stood looking down at the likeness of the dead boy. 'Wolsey gave him this. Keep it carefully, in case the king wishes to have his son in remembrance.' The infant, he recalled, did not know his own father; the king gave me titles, Richmond had said, but the cardinal gave me a striped silk ball.

The summer passes. The king's entourage winds through the leafy shires. In the deep woodlands, where the king may not venture, you meet the wily shades of boars and wolves, extinct forms: the stag who, between his antlers, bears the cross of Christ. He says to Fitzwilliam, 'If he cannot hunt, we must teach him to pray.'

On the last day of July they are at Allington Castle. The king has wondered aloud if it might be time for Thomas Wyatt to receive the honour of knighthood. His father would like to see it, he says, as he enters into his old age, and whatever has lain between us, Wyatt and I, it is forgot; I know his faithful mind to me.

What he disliked was the short silence, among the gentlemen of the privy chamber, when the king mentioned Wyatt's name.

Henry Wyatt says to him, 'Thomas, I doubt I shall see another winter.' One by one, those gentlemen depart, who served the king's father, whose memories stretch back to King Edward and the days of the scorpion; men bruised in the wars, hacked in the field, impoverished, starved out, driven into exile; men who stood on foreign quays and swore great oaths to God, their worldly goods in sacks at their feet. Men who sequestered themselves in musty libraries for twenty years and emerged possessed of inconvenient truths about England. Men who learned to walk again, after they had been stretched on the rack.

When the men that were then look at the men that are now, they see companies of pretty painted knights, ambling through the meadows of plenty, through the pastures of a forty-year peace. Not, of course, if you live on the Scots border, where the raiding and feuding never stops, or on the Kent coast within sight of France, where you hear the war drums across the Narrow Sea. But in the realm's heart there is a quiet our forefathers never knew. Just see how England is breeding: go out into the town, and the faces you see are those of children, apprentices, shining young maids.

Don't look back, he had told the king: yet he too is guilty of retrospection as the light fades, in that hour in winter or summer before they bring in the candles, when earth and sky melt, when the fluttering heart of the bird on the bough calms and slows, and the night-walking animals stir and stretch and rouse, and the eyes of cats shine in the dark, when colour bleeds from sleeve and gown into the darkening air; when the page grows dim and letter forms elide and slip into other conformations, so that as the page is turned the old story slides from sight and a strange and slippery confluence of ink begins to flow. You look back into your past and say, is this story mine; this land? Is that flitting figure mine, that shape easing itself through alleys, evader of the curfew, fugitive from the day? Is this my life, or my neighbour's conflated with mine, or a life I have dreamed and prayed for; is this my essence, twisting into a taper's flame, or have I slipped the limits of myself – slipped into eternity, like honey from a spoon? Have I dreamt myself, undone myself, have I forgotten too well; must I apply to Bishop Stephen, who will tell me how transgression follows me, assures me that my sins seek me out; even as I slide into sleep, my past pads after me, paws on the flagstones, pit-pat: water in a basin of alabaster, cool in the heat of the Florentine afternoon.

Time was when the cardinal knelt in the dirt, and he saw he was mortal, flawed and old. On Putney Heath, Harry Norris stared down at him, bemused, and his people had to hoist him on his mule; his heart and will had failed him, and with his heart, his joints. The jester Patch stood by cracking jokes, and he almost struck him, he should have struck him – but then how would that have helped the cardinal, his goods confiscated, his chain of office torn from his neck, and now his fool rolled in the Surrey mud with his skull cracked?

When they came to Esher, to the empty house, he had climbed to the top of the gatehouse, wanting to know if they were pursued. New-built when Wayneflete held the see of Winchester, improved by my lord cardinal, no place was more pleasant, when it was staffed and scrubbed; when the fires were blazing and the beds made and the arras hung, when the buffet was stacked with gold and silver plate; when meat was slapped and seared, fruit chopped and skewered and basted in butter, and all the air perfumed with scorching and sweetness. No one had known, even yesterday, how brutally they would set his master on the road, on the river, propel him to these gaunt rooms, the ovens cold, the fires ash, the thick walls not so much repelling the cold as encasing it, like a reliquary.

From the top of Wayneflete's tower, the countryside beneath him was more imagined than real, stretching away in the darkness. It will soon be All Hallows, he thought. It seemed to him time had shuddered and slowed, as if the transit of heavenly bodies was retarded by the catastrophe that had overtaken his master and all England. It was drizzling. There were lights in the river. As he climbed down, the voices of those below curled up to him – rounded, as if in song. But when someone spoke his name – 'Thomas Cromwell' – it was very close, as if in his ear.

Some trick the building has, he thought. The staircase was a spiral of brick, and he had seen it by day, flesh-coloured, flowing from floor to floor. In the dimness where the torch-light failed, the brick was the hue of stale blood, but each twist held a slit of light, like a promise. Delivered to the foot, he emerged and blinked, a child born into a harsh world.

They had found candles to light the lower chamber. 'Who will cook my supper, Tom?' the cardinal enquired.

'I will, I can cook.'

'Come here, you're cobwebbed.' It was George Cavendish, one of the cardinal's gentlemen. 'Allow me, Thomas.'

He let George brush him down, passive as an animal: his eyes on his master, a bereft old man in borrowed clothes. He stood with his back to the brick, feeling the beating of his own heart: waiting to see what he would do next.

PART TWO

I

Augmentation
London, Autumn 1536

The dead man comes out of the Well with Two Buckets, wipes his mouth on the back of his hand, and stands looking up and down the street. He pulls up his hood, checks to see who is watching him, then strides towards the great gate of Austin Friars.

There is a new guard, who lays a hand on the visitor, and rifles through his wallet of papers. 'Blade?'

The corpse stretches out his arms, pacific, allows himself to be patted down. An elder porter steps out. 'We know the gentleman. In you go, Father Barnes.'

Inside they say, 'His lordship's expecting you.' The corpse runs upstairs.

Go back ten years. Winter, 1526, the friar Robert Barnes is brought before Wolsey on suspicion of heresy. Through a frozen day, no light but the ice-light from standing pools, Barnes stands in an anteroom, clad in the black habit of his order. Beneath it, his flesh creeps. The cardinal, they tell him, is making his preparations. What kind of preparations could they be?

Christmas Eve last, at St Edward's in Cambridge, Barnes preached at midnight Mass against the pomp and wealth of the church. It is impossible to do that, obviously, without preaching against the pomp and wealth of the cardinal.

Now it's February: *dies irae*. As he waits the cardinal's people watch him, and a low flame sputters in the grate. 'Cold,' Friar Barnes says.

'Didn't you bring your own firewood?' There is a rustle from the onlookers, a snigger. Barnes moves, edging away from the cardinal's ruffian.

In Wolsey's room a great fire blazes. Barnes stands away from it, against the painted wall. 'Prior Robert,' Wolsey says. 'Come where you feel the heat, man.'

He feels he has walked into a joke, set up to torment him. 'I am not here on trial,' he bursts out. 'Your man Cromwell is out there, taunting me, talking about firewood.'

'Of course you are not on trial.' The cardinal is civil. His purple silks flash in air smoky with resins. 'They say you are a heretic, yet it seems you have no difficulty with the teachings of the church. Your only difficulty is with me.'

Outside, a bell pierces frozen air. A man comes in with a tray of spiced wine. The cardinal pours it himself, from a jug gaudily enamelled with a Tudor rose. 'So what do you want me to do, Barnes? You want me to leave off the state and ceremony which honours God, and to go in homespun? You want me to keep a miser's table, and serve pease pudding to ambassadors? You want me to melt down my silver crosses, and give the money to the poor? The poor, which will piss it against the wall?'

There is a pause. After a time, faintly, Barnes says, 'Yes.'

The ruffian Cromwell has come in behind him and is leaning against the door. Wolsey says, 'I am sorry to see a scholar ruin himself. You must grasp that it is no use to avoid heresy, only to fall into sedition. Oppose the church, you will burn at Smithfield. Oppose the state, you will choke at Tyburn – and for present purposes, I am the church and I am also the state. But both fates are avoidable, if you repent now.'

Prior Barnes begins to shake. The interrogatory stare of the cardinal is enough to bring a man to his knees. 'Your Grace, pardon me. I do no harm. Truly. I could not kill a cat.'

The man Cromwell laughs. Barnes blushes; he is ashamed of his own words. The cardinal says, 'There are four bishops coming presently to examine you. All men who drown kittens for their pleasant recreation. For my part, I will be good to you, Dr Barnes – as much for the sake of your university as for yourself; my secretary Stephen Gardiner has been earnest with me in that regard. If you satisfy the bishops with your answers – please make them brief, and make them humble – I will recommend you do penance. But it must be public. Then afterwards there will be a good deal of fasting and praying, but you won't mind that, will you? Of course you cannot continue as prior of your house. You must quit Cambridge.'

'My lord cardinal –'

The cardinal turns his face, mild: 'What? Drink up, Dr Barnes. And take the chance. You only get one.'

Ejected from the warmth, Barnes weeps like a woman, his face to the wall. Wolsey has not raised his voice, but he is broken by the encounter. Thomas Cromwell walks up to him. 'Dry your tears. You can make a better story to tell among your friends. You can boast you gave bold answers. Confounded him.'

Barnes huddles into himself. He finds Cromwell incomprehensible. He looks like the kind of fellow who chucks drunks out of taverns.

On Shrove Tuesday, the friar abases himself on the flags at Paul's, and Wolsey looks down on him from his golden throne. A score of great churchmen, in their vestments stiff and bright with gems, watch as Barnes kneels among certain merchants of the Steelyard, foreigners, who have been trapped by Thomas More with heretic books. They have been led through the streets on donkeys, set backwards in the saddle with their faces to the tail. Torn sheets of the writings of Luther are pinned to their coats, and now flap like grey rags. Lashed to their backs, as to his own, are faggots, dry sticks tied up for kindling – it is to remind them the stake is ready, if they offend again. Like Dr Barnes, they have recanted. If they backslide they will die in terror and pain, in public, and their ashes will be thrown on a midden.

Outside the church, a crowd has gathered. Their faces rain-blurred as if melting, their forms indistinct in winter light, men are tented under oiled canvases that seem to rest on their shoulders, making them a beast with many legs. 'Stand aside,' officers call. Big baskets are lugged and bumped into the centre of the crowd. Their contents are tipped out; they make a brave enough pile, heaped on a gridiron. One of the executioner's apprentices sets a torch to them. His fellows poke at the books with iron bars, to let air into the pile, and under their skilled attention the pages ignite, despite the sheeting rain. The suspect men are herded together and driven round and round the fire, close enough to flinch from the heat, their faces jerking away as sparks fly into their eyes. The texts sigh as the paper curls, and disintegrate into a mute sludge.

Dr Barnes is sent to a friary in the city of London. His keeping is none too strait, and he is allowed visitors. One day Thomas Cromwell comes in. 'I live near here. Come to supper.' On the bench he drops a copy of William Tyndale's Testament, single sheets loosely tied. 'Arrived from Antwerp,' he says. Barnes looks up. The cardinal's heretic, he thinks.

'I have twenty copies. I can get more.'

It is not long before the Bishop of London suspects where the Testaments are coming from. Another difficult interview: but with Bishop Tunstall, who is not by choice a persecutor. Barnes is not as overawed as he was by Wolsey. 'How would I bring in Tyndale's books? I go nowhere. I see no one.'

He gambles that Cromwell's name will not be raised. Nor is it. Tunstall just shakes his head, and presently sends him to Northamptonshire. It's a long way from any port. You can't run from there, out of the cardinal's jurisdiction. Nor can your fellow gospellers visit you, without all the countryside knows it.

One night Barnes steals out of the monastery where he is confined. Next day in his cell the monks find a letter, addressed to the cardinal, in which the miserable man says he means to drown himself. On the riverbank they find his folded habit. No body is found, but the poor sinner has made his intention clear.

And that's the last of Robert Barnes: till the times change, and the Pope goes down, and he surfaces in a new England, his past failures washed away.

'Come in, old ghost,' the cardinal's heretic says. 'God's work is marvellous. You bobbing up from your watery grave.'

'You never tire of the jest,' Barnes says.

'But your feet not even damp!'

Barnes was never in the river. He swam up from his ruse somewhere in the Low Countries, and found friends, protectors, brothers in Christ. Years pass, he comes back proficient in many tongues; the world turns, and now he is a chaplain to the king, and carries his letters abroad. 'And Tunstall gone up to Durham,' his host says. 'And my lord cardinal dead.' He sits back in his chair. 'And me a lord.'

'Brought you these.' Barnes lays engravings on the table. Fat Martin.

'You spoil me,' Lord Cromwell says.

In the older portraits, Luther is spiritual, attenuated. In the newer ones, porky. His tonsure grew out years ago. Sometimes he wears a beard. Barnes tells him, 'When the papists burn his books they pin his picture on top, as if it were Martin himself. But the country people in Germany, the simple people, they believe his image can resist the fire.'

Lord Cromwell stabs one likeness with a finger. 'I notice he wears a halo.'

'That is not his choice. He does not set up as a saint. But it is wonderful, what the printers can do. All Europe knows his features. Every ploughboy.'

'Is that a good idea?'

'His life has been attempted many a time. Once,' Barnes smiles, 'by a physician who could make himself invisible.'

'Oh, those,' he says. Secret assassins with scalpels of air. 'I have been looking over my shoulder for invisible men since Wolsey's day. I've got ears like a fox and my head on a swivel. One sniff of a papist or a Yorkshireman and it swings right round and eyeballs him.' He broods over the engravings. 'Is his temper not improved?'

'Worse, I would say. Vain and touchy as a woman.'

Luther fleshes out, since he wed an ex-nun. Marriage doesn't have the same effect on our archbishop. Cranmer remains lean and pallid. 'Because he must be worried,' Barnes says. 'In case the king finds out.'

'The king already knows.'

'Likely he does. But I mean, in case he finds himself in a position where he cannot deny the knowledge.'

Our king is vehemently opposed to clerical marriage. Cranmer wed when he was among the Germans, brought Grete back, keeps her secluded. Celibates are busy gossips; many would pull Cranmer down if they could. But then they have their own secrets, that do not bear telling: their mistresses, their children. He says, 'We work it all between us, Cranmer and I. The archbishop tells Henry how to be good, and I tell him how to be king. We do not cut across each other. We try to persuade him that great kings are good kings, and vice versa.'

Barnes says, 'Luther speaks frankly to rulers. Harshly, if need be.'

'But in the end he defers to them: as he must.' He examines Luther's homely features, and lays him face-down. 'Look, Rob, we do what we can do. We are in concord, Cranmer and myself. We are leaving Henry his rituals and he is giving us the scriptures. I think it is a good trade.'

'It seems to me,' Barnes says, 'our prince thinks the purpose of scripture is to allow him to marry new wives. You claim he will license a Bible, so why does he delay?'

He sweeps the engravings together like a pack of cards and tucks them in his writing box. 'Thomas More used to say, all translators crave something from their text, and if they do not find it they will put it there. The king will not let us use Tyndale's version. We are obliged to pass it off, give other men the credit.'

'If Henry is waiting for a translation with God's thumbprint on it, he will wait a long time. Luther would labour three or four weeks on a single phrase. I never thought he would get his work out, and yet two years back at the book fair in Leipzig he was selling a complete

Bible for under three guilders – and they have reprinted twice since then. Why should the Germans have God's word, and not Englishmen? You may stare at the text till your eyes bleed, consume a stack of paper as high as Paul's steeple – but I tell you, no word is the last word.'

It is true. No text stays clean. Yet one must part with it, send it to the printer. The trick is to get them to set the line right to the edge of the page. It does not make for a good appearance, but no white space means no perversion by marginalia.

'You will forgive me if I am indignant,' Barnes says. 'I have been toiling these many years for the king, trying to patch up an alliance, trying to come into some agreement with the German princes and their divines – and the news from England comes, and you have cut the ground from under me.'

By cutting off the queen's head. True. It is autumn, and Barnes is still shocked. 'She, who believed in the Word.'

'She was a Howard,' he says. 'You know what Howards believe in. Themselves.'

'Cranmer doesn't believe she was guilty.'

'Cranmer is like me. He believes what the king believes.'

'That is not true either.' Barnes is bubbling like the hot springs at Viterbo. 'They know in Germany that Cranmer is a Lutheran – whatever he may say to Henry. Cranmer is the only card I hold. I have waited and waited for some word from our English bishops that I can represent as an advance on papist superstition, and at last they issue their ten articles – and they give with one hand, take with the other. Every word is ambiguous.'

'Yes,' he says.

'They mean everything and nothing.'

'You can say to the Germans … how to phrase it? … that though the articles are a statement of our English faith, they are not a *complete* statement.'

Barnes rolls his eyes. 'You send me out naked. If you want allies, you must offer something in return.'

It is more than five years since the German princes formed a league, which they call the Schmalkald League, to defend themselves against the Emperor, who is their overlord. As England needs friends, people to stand with her against the Pope, who better than these princes? Like Henry, they have offered to lead their subjects out of darkness. If an evangelical alliance were also a diplomatic alliance, there is a chance of a new Europe, with new rules. But for now we are still playing by the old ones: setting France against Emperor, one great power against the other, seeing our safety only in their disputes, trembling whenever they come into amity; sneakily trying to disrupt their treaties and stir up mistrust, and bending our efforts to provoke, belie and betray. It is not work for a great nation. Barnes says, 'It is up to you, my lord, to show the king how things could be different, and better.'

'But he doesn't like different!' He is exasperated now. 'I think, Rob, as we have been keeping the gospel alive in your absence, you must let us judge the best way to proceed.'

'You talk as if I had been travelling for my own pleasure. It has all been on the king's business, and a sad business it is. Folk in Germany believe we are living through the Last Days.'

'They've been saying that for ten years or more. If you talk to Henry about the Last Days he thinks you're threatening him. And that never does any good.'

It is difficult to be at ease, he thinks, with men who believe that, since the misunderstanding in Eden, we have had neither reason nor will of our own. 'The king says if, as Luther holds, our only salvation comes through faith in Christ, who has elected some of us, not others, to life eternal, and if our works are so besmirched as to be entirely useless in God's eyes, and cannot help us to salvation – then why should any man do charity to his neighbour?'

'Works follow election,' Barnes says. 'They do not precede it. It is simple enough. The man who is saved will show it, by his Christian life.'

'Do you think I am saved?' he says. 'I am covered in lamp black and my hands smell of coin, and when I see myself in a glass I see grime – I suppose that is the beginning of wisdom? About my fallen state, I have no choice but agree. I must meddle with matters that corrupt – it is my office. In the golden age the earth yielded all we required, but now we must dig for it, quarry it, blast it, we must drive the world, we must gear and grind it, roll and hammer and pulp it. There must be dinners cooked, Rob. There must be slates chalked, and ink set to page, and money made and bargains struck, and we must give the poor the means to work and eat. I bear in mind that there are cities abroad where the magistrates have done much good, with setting up hospitals, relieving the indigent, helping young tradesmen with loans to get a wife and a workshop. I know Luther turns his face from what ameliorates our sad condition. But citizens do not miss monks and their charity, if the city looks after them. And I believe, I do believe, that a man who serves the commonweal and does his duty gets a blessing for it, and I do not believe –'

He breaks off, before the magnitude of what he does not believe. 'I sin,' he says, 'I repent, I lapse, I sin again, I repent and I look to Christ to perfect my imperfection. I cling to faith but I will not give up works. My master Wolsey taught me, try everything. Discard no possibility. Keep all channels open.'

'You cite your cardinal? In these times?'

'Admit it.' He laughs. 'You were terrified of him, Rob.'

Barnes leaves him. He looks downcast and is muttering about Dun Scotus. A worldly man, a clever man, but he is afraid to be in England now: as if she were Ultima Thule, where earth, air and water mix to form a jellied broth, and a night lasts six months, and the people dye themselves blue. There was a day, before Wolsey, when the princes of Europe no more regarded England than they regarded this soup-land, where they had never set foot. England bred sheep and sheep sustained it, but the women were said to be loose and the men bloody-minded; if they were not killing abroad, they were killing at home. The cardinal, out of his great ingenuity, had found some way to turn this reputation to use. He made his country count: he, with his guile and his well-placed bribes, his sorcerer's wit and his conjur-er's wiles, his skills to make armies and bullion from thin air, to conjure weaponry from mist. I hold the balance, gentlemen, he would say: in any little war of yours, I may intervene, or not. The King of England has deep coffers, he would lie, and a race of warriors at his back: your Englishman is so martial in his character that he sleeps in harness, and every clerk has a broadsword at his side, and every scrivener will stick you with a penknife, and even the ploughman's horse paws the ground.

And so for a year or two it became a question: what does England think? What will England do? France must solicit her: the Emperor must apply. War itself, the cardinal preferred to avoid. Henry on French soil, curvetting on his steed, his visor lowered, his armour a blaze of gold: that is as far as it went, if you add in a few sordid engagements that consisted in churning up the mud and blowing trumpets. If war is a craft, the cardinal would say, peace is a consummate and blessed art. His peace talks cost as much as most campaigns. His diplomacy was the talk of Constantinople. His treaties were the glory of the west.

But once Henry began divorcing his wife, spitting in the Emperor's eye, all this advantage was lost. The Pope's bull of excommunication hangs over Henry like a blade on a human hair. To be excommunicate is to be a leper. If the bull is implemented, the king and his ministers will be the target of murderers, who carry the Pope's commission. His subjects will have a sacred duty to depose him. Invading troops will come with a blessing, and the sins incidental to any invasion – rapes, robberies – will be allowed for and wiped out in advance.

Lord Cromwell gets up every day – Austin Friars, his rooms at court, his house at Stepney, the Rolls House at Chancery Lane – and he tries to think of a way to stop this happening. This week, France and the Emperor are at war. Next week who knows? Circumstances alter fast, and before news can cross the Narrow Sea they have altered again. Even now – with the king twice widowed and newly-married – our people in Rome have a wedge in the door, keeping it open a crack: still maintaining a dialogue, and passing cash with a wink. The curia must keep hope alive, that England might return to the fold. The great thing is to make sure the bull remains in suspension.

Meanwhile, we must assume the worst case: Charles or François, one or both, will walk in and wipe their boots in Whitehall.

There are now three kinds of people in the world. There are those who give Lord Cromwell his proper title. There are flatterers, who called him 'my lord' when he wasn't. And there are begrudgers, who won't call him 'my lord' now he is.

Gregory trails him: 'Do you think if my mother had lived, she would have liked being called Lady Cromwell?'

'I do suppose any woman would.' He halts, papers in his hands: looks Gregory over. 'How would it be if we were to stretch out a hand to the Duke of Norfolk, and help him in his trouble?'

The duke has said to him, for God's sake, my lord, work something with the king, to put me back in his grace. Is it my fault Richmond is dead?

'Call-Me,' he says, 'send our people to Norfolk's people, and make them know that if they were to invite Gregory to hunt this summer, I would look favourably on such an invitation.'

'What, me?' Gregory says.

Richard says, 'Not as if you were doing anything else.'

Gregory digests it. 'They say it is good hunting country at Kenninghall. I suppose I can do it. But before I go, I would like to know when I am to get a stepmother.'

He frowns: stepmother?

'You promised,' Gregory says. 'You swore to us, you would step out of here and wed the first woman you met, to clear yourself of any charge you mean to match with Lady Mary. So did you? Have you? Who was she?'

'Oh, I remember,' he says. 'It was William Parr's niece, Kate. Lady Latimer, as she is now. Unfortunately.'

'We agreed a husband is no obstacle,' Gregory says. 'Though is not Latimer her second? She does not keep them when they are worn in, I warrant. What did she say to your suit?'

'She asked him to dine,' Rafe says. 'We were witness.'

'She took his hand,' Richard says. 'She drew him aside, most tender.'

'I think,' Mr Wriothesley adds, 'she would have kissed him, if we had not been right behind them gaping and nudging each other, and grinning and mincing like apes.'

'I have come,' Lady Latimer had said, 'to see the new queen. I have come to introduce my sister Anne Parr, and ask if she can have a position.'

'I am glad to see you back at court, my lady. If your sister is as handsome as you, she will do well.'

There is a stifled giggle from his attendants. He pretends not to hear it. Kate Latimer is a sweet-faced, snub-nosed young woman, five-and-twenty. Her family are courtiers by blood. Maud Parr, her lady mother, served Queen Katherine for many a year; William her uncle is an Esquire of the Body.

'I will speak to Lady Rutland for your sister, though I don't know if Jane can take anyone else. Lady Lisle sends me a reminder by every boat. If her daughters are not placed, I shall soon feel her wrath, blowing out of Calais on a cutting wind.'

'Oh, the Bassett girls.' Kate bites her lip: considers the applicants, as if they were parading before her. 'The queen should not feel obliged to take more than one. Put in a word for my sister, will you? And come and dine this week at Charterhouse Yard. Lord Latimer is here under sufferance, and chafing to get back to his summer's sport. I want some conversation, before he can gallop me back north.'

Latimer is a papist, he suspects: but, so far, loyal. 'How do you like Snape Castle?'

She wrinkles her nose. 'Well, you know. It's Yorkshire.' She touches his sleeve, nods towards a window embrasure. 'We seem to be amusing your boys.'

'Oh, they are a foolish set of youths. They cannot keep their countenance at the sight of a pretty woman.'

Out of line of sight, she drops her head, as if they were going to discuss her velvet shoes. 'Tyndale?' she whispers.

For a moment he thinks he has misheard. Then, 'Still alive,' he says.

'But out of hope.' She nods. 'We hear you have done what is possible. Now he must suffer, as the godly must. Till they go to a better world than this.'

He looks at Lady Latimer with new eyes. 'I beg you to trust no one here at court.'

'And you, trust no one in Yorkshire.'

He breathes in the warm scent of her skin: rose oil, cloves. He looks out of the window. 'I never did.'

'If the king intends to crown Jane, he should do it in York. Show his power there. It would be timely.' For the benefit of passers-by she raises her voice. 'Advertise us which day you will come. We should like to do all honour to you.' She glances over her shoulder. 'Send one of those silly fellows with a message.'

She seems to have caught on to the joke, because she turns at the end of the gallery and blows him a kiss.

August, he is in Kent; his duties follow him, the boy Mathew bundling up his papers as he did at Wolf Hall, and Christophe riding at his elbow, a club slung at his saddle to beat off assailants. 'Have you heard of fire-pots?' he demands, as they pass under the dripping trees. 'One fills them with ardent substance and then launches them in a sling. Such a weapon might reach Gardineur, who knows? Flying across the sea to ignite him.'

He says, reminiscing, 'We made those in Italy when I was a boy. We used to seal the sulphur in with pig fat. I dare say there are better ways now.'

'Pig fat is king,' Christophe says. 'When are we making them?'

At Allington Castle, the master looks as if he has only weeks to live. 'This last summer,' Sir Henry says, 'I could not sleep for the thought of my boy lying at the Tower. I knew you would not suffer him to be mistreated. But you could not watch over him all the hours, with great business of state toward.' His hand trembles; a drop of wine falls on the ledger before him. 'Oh, by the Rood!' Sir Henry dabs at the page.

'Here. Let me.' He moves the book from danger. The old man sighs. 'I trust Tom has learned to live quiet. I hope it will content him

267

now, and he be well to keep.' Sir Henry's eyes close. 'To be master of Allington in my stead, and all its pleasant ways and walks. My chases and woods. My flowery meads.'

Thomas Wyatt says, send me abroad. Send me abroad in the king's service. I will go anywhere. I want to be out of the realm.

He lays the papers down and sits by the old man as he dozes. *Lauda finem*, he thinks: praise the end. He thinks of the lioness that stalked Tom Wyatt, out in the courtyard: where the scent of evening flowers drifts, instead of her feral breath. Sir Henry opens an eye and says, 'He'll gamble the shirt off his back, unless you nail it to him. He'll sell the place off, or lose it at some gaming house. And be borrowing from you, Thomas Cromwell, before my corpse is cold.'

As he travels, he signs off on the paperwork to give Rafe a clutch of Essex manors belonging to William Brereton, deceased. In accordance with the king's wishes, he redirects the possessions and holdings of young Richmond. Charles Brandon receives munificent grants. Henry Courtenay, the Marquis of Exeter, is given a slice of Dorset to secure his loyalties and keep his wife Gertrude content. A portion of the county of Devon goes to William Fitzwilliam, and the land and buildings of Waverley Abbey; it was the first house of the Cistercian monks when they came into England, but the site has always been likely to flood, the coffers are exhausted and there are but thirteen monks to be paid off. Fitz is granted manors in Hampshire and Sussex, set on firmer ground; he needs to support his new dignities, as he is promoted Lord Admiral.

It's another disappointment for the Duke of Norfolk. The post had been his once. Having given it up to young Richmond, he hoped to get it back now he is dead. But the king says, William Fitzwilliam is more use to me, a steadfast man who tells me the truth.

The king's new family must be augmented, with leases and licences. Tom Seymour sails among the ladies, scattering smiles like posies; he wears a doublet of hyacinth, a curtmantel of violet velvet. Edward Seymour seeks out the company of black-gowned savants to learn how he can be useful to the realm. All agree he is an improvement on the last royal brother – though as Gregory says, if he can only keep from tupping his sister, it puts him ahead of George Boleyn.

Edward Seymour invites him to his town house and shows him a painting that occupies a whole wall. It portrays all the Seymours that grace the records, right back to where writing began: other Seymours, imagined ones, carry the line back to paradise, situated top centre. Far-sighted ancestors wear plate armour, years before its manufacture. They carry broadswords, poll axes, horseman's hammers and maces. Their brides are represented by their family emblems. Give or take a beard, generations of Seymours bear a marked family resemblance: that is, they look like Edward. They shelter under their coats of arms as if standing out of the rain.

As for the queen herself – Henry doesn't know how to reward her, what to give her. She is endowed with castles, manors, rents, services, privileges, liberties and franchises. Her letters patent are inscribed in gilt, illuminated with the king's picture: in which he is younger, fresh-faced, clean-shaven, as if Jane has wiped away the last ten years. Henry has made exhaustive enquiries into the state of her body and soul. He is satisfied that no man except a brother or close cousin has so much as kissed her cheek. When she confesses to her chaplain, it takes five minutes. She may as well be transparent, for all she has to hide. And the king takes all her attention. Katherine had her little apes, Anne her spaniels, but Jane has only her husband. She treats him with great deference, and carefully, as if he might snap; but she treats him cheerfully, as he himself, Cromwell, tries to do. Above all, she treats him as if everything he wants to do is perfectly normal. And in gratitude for the gold and precious stones, she smiles slowly and blinks at him, as if she were a lass whose lover has cut her a slice of apple, and offered it to her on the point of his blade.

Before he lays down his pen, Lord Cromwell remembers Lady Latimer with a manor in Northamptonshire.

As summer ends Gregory returns, tousled, sun-browned. 'My lord Norfolk was good to me. When he saw me sit down to my book, he said, "Gregory Cromwell, are you not done with learning yet?" I said, "No, my lord – I have set aside Linacre's Grammars, but now I must look into Littleton's New Tenures, and be educated in the law. Also," I told him, "my father said to me lately, 'Are you acquainted with the Seven Wise Men of Greece?' And when I said no, he said, 'Look you be acquainted with them by September.'" So my lord of Norfolk said, "Seven wise men be buggered, I never knew them myself, and I lack no parts that become a sage. Leave off your book, lad, and get out there into the sunshine, I'll make it right with your father.'"

He nods. 'So he did.' Thinks, I cannot fault the scrawny old reprobate, he has been genial to my boy.

'But his son …' Gregory says. 'Surrey was a surly host. He spoke Italian at me. I am not perfect in that tongue, but a man knows when he is being insulted.'

'True. Especially in Italian.'

'Surrey says you are a sectary. A heretic. You say there is not one God but three. You say Christ was not God, or God was not Christ. You are a sacramentarian, he says. That is, one who does not think infants should be baptised. Surrey pretends to favour the gospel himself, but it is only to provoke his father. My lord Norfolk curses the day laymen began to read the scriptures. "Blessed are the meek!" he says. "With all respect to our Saviour, you don't want that notion to get around an army camp." So the more he hates the Bible, the more Surrey loves it.'

He nods. Fathers and sons. At the age when lords were perched up on their first quiet pony, he was playing in the forge within range of flailing hooves. 'Just let him get kicked once,' Walter used to say, 'and he'll learn.' He did get kicked, but he doesn't know if he learned.

Gregory says, 'Mary Fitzroy is at Kenninghall with her family. She scolds night and day about her settlement from Richmond's estate. She has all the figures in a book, what she should have as his relict. The duke is surprised she has such a good wit, he has barely spoken to her till now, he does not think a man should dally in idle talk with daughters. She says, "If you will not go to the king and get my settlement, I will turn to Lord Cromwell, he is gentleness itself to widows."'

Mr Wriothesley suppresses a snort of laughter. But then when Gregory has cantered off, Call-Me follows him into his closet and says, 'You want Gregory to be wed. Have you thought of Mary Fitzroy? You could secure the duke's friendship for ever.'

'That's a turnabout, from you. You said I should destroy him.'

Mr Wriothesley looks penitent. 'I did not understand your methods.'

Norfolk depends on him now, to speak up for him to the king. Henry glowers whenever he hears Norfolk's name. The row over Tom Truth, and Richmond's death, his scant poor burial … the king's grievances have accumulated. Norfolk sees himself in the Tower. By the gridiron of St Lawrence, I never deserved such treatment, the duke says. When did I ever thwart Henry or cut against him? Always my loyalty, always my best endeavours, my money and my men and my prayers. *I am full full full*, he writes, *of choler and anger*. When you read his letters, you picture tongues of fire bursting from his head.

As for Norfolk's daughter, 'Not for us,' he tells Wriothesley. 'Norfolk will look higher. The Howards don't think about the future, not the way we do. They want it to look like the past.'

Seven Wise Men, he tells Gregory: here are their sayings. Moderation in all things, nothing to excess (those two are the same, wisdom can be repetitious). Know yourself. Know your opportunity. Look ahead. Don't try for the impossible. And Bias of Priene: *pleistoi anthropoi kakoi*, most men are bad.

This summer, the Court of Augmentations is busy turning monks into money. Only the small houses are dissolved: the court has capacity for more work, should Henry wish it. When its clerks move into their new rooms at Westminster they will have a garden, where they can recreate themselves in fresh air and sit amid birdsong and the fragrance of the herb beds. Yarrow and camomile comfort the scrupulous, who stay late re-adding the columns. Betony cures a headache, blue borage lightens the heart. Oculus Christi, infused, is good to bathe the eyes of those who spend long hours at their books, and the scent of a rosemary hedge strengthens the memory.

Bishop Hugh Latimer says to him, it were pity the monasteries should close and the poor gain nothing from it. But it is not likely the pauper will lay his head where Father Abbot once reposed. More likely a gentleman will knock down Father Abbot's house, and build himself a bigger house with the stone. No doubt it is good policy in the king, not to keep all the gain for himself. The Pope's name is taken out of the service book, but parishes have simply glued strips of paper over it, thinking the world will turn and Rome rise again. But once the lands are given out, no subject will want to give them back to the church. Prayers may be rewritten, but not leases. Hearts may revert to Rome, but the money never will.

So even after Henry dies, he thinks, our work is safe. After a generation, the name of Pope itself will be blotted out of memory, and no one will ever believe we bowed to stocks of wood and prayed to plaster. The English will see God in daylight, not hidden in a cloud of incense; they will hear his word from a minister who faces them, instead of turning his back and muttering in a foreign tongue. We will have good-living clergy, who counsel the ignorant and help the unfortunate, instead of a scum of half-literate monks squatting in the dust with their cassocks hauled up, playing knucklebones for farthings and trying to see up women's skirts. We will have an end to images, the simpering virgin saints with their greensick faces, and Christ with the wound in his side gaping like a whore's gash. The faithful will cherish their Saviour in their inner heart, instead of gawping at him painted above their heads, like a swinging inn sign. We will break the shrines, Hugh Latimer says, and found schools. Turn out the monks and buy horn books, alphabet books for little hands. We will draw out the living God from his false depictions. God is not his gown, he is not his coat, he is not shreds of flesh or nails or thorns. He is not trapped in a jewelled monstrance or in a window's glass. But dwells in the human heart. Even in the Duke of Norfolk's.

As the days shorten Norfolk writes to him, to ask him to be an executor of his will. Not that he thinks of dying; but of course, *sic transit gloria mundi*, and he will be five-and-sixty soon, though he doesn't know where the time has gone. He seeks a meeting, at the convenience of the Lord Privy Seal. He wants to talk about Mary Fitzroy. 'It's a shame that Richmond didn't go and die a few weeks sooner. For then the king could have wed my daughter, who is some of the best blood in the kingdom, instead of John Seymour's girl. And my girl is a maid, you know, pure as the day she was christened, for I never let Richmond near her.'

It is precisely because the match was not consummated that the king is saying it was no marriage, so the bride does not merit a pay-out. But as the duke is so well-disposed, he does not interrupt him with that news. 'You know who came to see me?' Norfolk says. 'The Emperor's man. Begged audience. Wanted to give me money. Well,' the duke says benignly, 'that's all in order. I used to have a pension from the Emperor, till my niece came along and fouled up every reasonable arrangement.'

'Then your Grace is restored to your rights,' he says gravely.

The duke eyes him. 'Have I you to thank?'

He waves it away. 'Chapuys well understands your great lineage and your long experience. He knows what you are and will always be, to both the king and the commonwealth.'

'That may be,' the duke says. 'But he doesn't regard them as much as the dinners you give him. He speaks about you as if you have all to rule. Cremuel this, Cremuel that. Still. You have done me service. I acknowledge it.' The duke stumps away on his little legs.

In answer to his summons, Master Holbein comes. He trails with him traces of his occupation, the scents of linseed and lavender oil, pine-resin and rabbit-skin glue. 'Now you are a milord, shall I paint you again?'

'I am content with what you did before.' If a portrait may serve as an act of concealment, then he has effected one, he and Hans between them. He says, 'I thought I might have a whole wall of portraits. The past kings of England.'

Hans sucks his lip. 'How far you wish to go back?'

'Back before King Harry who conquered France. Before his father Bolingbroke.'

'You wish to include those murdered?'

'If it does not take up too much space.'

Hans crucifies himself against the wall, then spins about and about, using his wing span to measure it. 'You can build a new room if need be.' Below the window, the tramp of bricklayers: scaffolding is lashed together, dust rises into the air. 'Write them down, their names. You want a picture of Henry? You standing beside him, whispering sums of money?'

He knows what Hans is hinting at. If Henry is to be painted this year, he wants the commission. Hans says, 'He can no longer ride hard, nor play at tennis. So look now.' He pats his belly.

'True. The king is augmented.'

Hans strides along the gallery, squaring off with his hands the notional space for each king. 'When you come home from the court you will come in and greet them. They will say, "God bless you, Thomas," as if they were your uncles. You do this because you have no people of your own.'

True again. 'I wish you had painted my wife.'

'Why? She was pretty?'

'No.'

If he had been able to afford Hans when his wife and daughters were alive he could have painted them as he had Thomas More's family, along with their house spaniels and any other little pets they had then: he with his book in hand, and Gregory playing with a child-sized sword, and his daughters with their coral beads. He can almost see the picture; his eyes move around it, to where Richard Cromwell leans on the back of his chair, and Rafe Sadler sits to the right of the frame with abacus and quill, and a door is open for Call-Me to come in when he pleases. When he tries to bring the faces of his girls to mind, he cannot do it. He knows memory tricks but they don't help with this. Children change so fast. Grace changed every day. Even Liz's face is a blurred oval beneath her cap. He imagines telling her, 'A German is coming to draw us, and we shall be doubled, as if we carried a mirror.' When you went to Chelsea you made your bow to the Lord Chancellor – the one seated on the wall, wearing the grave expression of the councillor. Then the real one would sidle up, with his blue chin and his frayed wool gown, rubbing his cold hands and letting you know you were interrupting him. Thomas More looking at you twice: a dirty look both times.

He says, 'Hans, I am not expecting you to paint these kings yourself. Send a boy. It doesn't matter what the faces look like, because nobody knows.'

They shake hands on it. There is nothing against the recreation of the dead, as long as they are plausible. He, Lord Cromwell, will provide bed and board for two apprentices, who will stay till the kings are dried and hung, and Hans will charge for materials, and a nominal sum for labour, 'but rich man's rates', Hans says. He digs a finger into his patron's plush person, and goes out, whistling.

His jester Anthony comes to him: 'Sir, when was it heard of, that a man was fool to the Lord Privy Seal, and was not hung with silver bells?'

'Good idea,' Richard Cromwell says. 'You can ring them to let us know when you make a joke.'

'I may be the saddest jester born,' Anthony says, 'but I don't go parading around the taverns and giving your secrets away, and I am cheaper than Will Somer, that is the king's fool now, for he has a man to attend on him, and I need no keeper. Except in the spring when I am melancholy, and need someone to keep me away from sharp knives, and streams and ponds where I might drown myself.'

Will Somer is a hunchback who falls asleep while he is talking. He sits at table and slam goes his head, right down into his platter. He is not safe in the street; if he did not have a servant to check him he might fall under the wheels of a cart. He might slump to the ground while he is mounting a stile, his feet entangled, his hair trailing in mud. Every moment of his day is interpenetrated with night, and when he sinks to the ground in the precincts of the court, spaniels run up and peer at him, and wave their tails as they lick his ears. Somer is harmless, an innocent. But the man Sexton, or Patch, remains in Nicholas Carew's house, where they say he tells stories about the queen that was, calling her a harlot, and for each slander Carew augments his living; and the ingrate talks about the cardinal too, his former master, and defames him every waking hour.

He says to Anthony, 'Tell Thomas Avery to give you a budget. Then you can buy your own bells.'

Three great ships, it is reported, have docked in the river port of Seville, and are unloading treasure from Peru to swell the coffers of the Emperor: whose forces now advance into Picardy, into the territory of the King of France. King Henry offers his services as mediator, and declares he will remain neutral. 'By which he means,' Chapuys says, 'he will go to the side that promises him most and costs him least. That is what he means by neutrality.'

He says, 'What prince would do anything else? He must seize his advantage.'

'But then,' Chapuys says, 'Henry talks so much of his honour.'

'Oh,' he says, 'they all do.'

The Venetian ambassador, Signor Zuccato, calls on him beaming with pleasure, to explain the Senate has voted him fifty ducats for the purchase of horses – a perquisite all former ambassadors have enjoyed, but which in his case had unaccountably been forgotten. So the Venetian can hunt if he likes, cantering after the king and Madamma Jane into the dappled misty mornings. There have been years of hunting *par force*: while gentlemen lie abed the questers are at work to find a runnable stag, who stirs in the glade and wakes and sniffs the air of a new day. When the beast is chosen the hounds are relayed on the line of his run, grey and lemon and tawny and white; and when the hart is unharboured, the huntsman feels the grass where he lay – if it is cold, if it is warm. At sun-up the chase begins. Hart may ruse and he may flee, he may plunge into the chilly stream, but the hounds run on and never change, till he is brought to bay, and as they run they revile him, baying their taunts in a language he can understand, calling him a varlet and a knave: and the hunters cry *ho moy, cy va, ho sto, mon amy: sa cy avaunt, so ho*. And when the sword strikes him, through the shoulder into the heart, then hart is turned on his back, his antlers in the earth; and the horn, which has blown mote and recheat and prise, now blows mort. When he is unmade, disassembled, then the hounds are thrown bread soaked in his blood, and certain bones, cast aside for crows, are called the raven's fee; and the head is set on a spear and carried home, foremost, as it was in life.

But this year, to save the king hard riding and so he may enjoy the society of delicate ladies, the harts are driven to the hunters where they stand against the trees, dressed in silken green, their crossbows in hand. Henry, dragging his new weight, is easily fatigued, his face furrowed sometimes by pain from his leg, which his servants bind every morning as tight as he may endure, bandaging round and round the patch of fragility where the damage strikes into the bone. The queen is silent beside him, her steady eye on the deer. If the quarry should swerve to left or right it takes discipline for the hunters to hold fire lest they wound each other; if the beast cannot be shot head on, it is better to let him break through the line, then place the arrow forward to anticipate his path. If the kill is not clean the hunter tracks the wounded hart, knowing by the quality, colour and thickness of the blood how long the pursuit will last. Hunters, it is said, live longer than other men; they sweat hard and stay lean; when they fall into bed at night they are tired beyond all temptation; and when they die, they go to Heaven.

II

The Five Wounds
London, Autumn 1536

Rumours of Tyndale's death seep through England as smoke leaks through thatch. Are we to believe them? The privy chamber gentlemen say that the king has asked the Emperor for assurances – one sovereign to another – that this Englishman is really dead. But if such an assurance is given or denied, it is not in any document that passes across his desk. 'I thought we got everything,' Call-Me says tetchily.

When our people abroad write to the king, they send a copy to my lord Privy Seal – often with a covering note that says more than the original. Henry likes to treat with monarchs brother to brother; 'Crumb,' he says, 'I cannot fault your management of my affairs at home, but some matters should lie between princes only, and I cannot ask my fellow kings to deal with you, because ...' The king looks into the distance, perhaps trying to imagine Putney. 'Not that you can help it.'

Some maintain Tyndale is still alive, and his keepers are trying to torment him into a spectacular public recantation. But our Antwerp contacts are silent. Perhaps we are missing something, and news is encoded in some merchant's invoice? Call-Me-Risley says, 'In Venice they have men who spend every day working at ciphers. The more they do it, the better they get.'

'I'm sure that could be arranged for you,' Rafe says. 'But then Lord Cromwell would put you on a *per diem*, and you would not get the fees from the office of the Signet, and what would Mistress Call-Me say about that? She would not put her views in cipher – they would hear her scolding in Calais.'

Henry is restless; as if trying to prolong the summer, he tows Jane from house to house. He tries to make sure either he or Rafe is by the king's side. He says to Chapuys, 'These talks with the Scots – they will never happen. Henry will not go further north than York. He apprehends bad food and bandits and no proper baths. And the King of Scots will not come south, for the same reasons.'

They are at Whitehall. Chapuys joins him in a window embrasure. The ambassador's entourage backs off, but he feels them watching. 'Is Tyndale truly burned?'

'Henry has not spoken to you? He knows your attachment to that heretic.'

'I couldn't abide the man,' he says. 'Nobody could.'

But then, we didn't require Tyndale for a supper guest, or a companion in a game of bowls. We required him for the health of our souls. Tyndale knew God's word and carried a light to guide us through the marsh of interpretation, so we would not be lost – as Tyndale himself put it – like a traveller tricked by Robin Goodfellow, and left stripped and shoeless in the wastes.

Ambassador Chapuys, you notice, has not exactly said he is dead; he has only let him fall, as it were naturally, into the past tense.

He visits the convent at Shaftesbury as a private gentleman, as if attending on Sir Richard Riche, the Chancellor of Augmentations: with Christophe, as a boy attending him. Begging the favour of an interview with Dame Elizabeth Zouche, he expects to be kept waiting, and he is.

'Laughable,' Riche says, gloomily. 'You the second man in the church. And me, who I am.'

'King Alfred founded this abbey,' he tells Christophe. 'They are rich because they have the bones of Edward the Martyr.'

'What tricks do they do?' Christophe asks.

'The usual miracles,' Riche says. 'Perhaps we shall witness one.'

Christophe sees to the horses and trundles out to the kitchen, seeking some young sister to feed him bread and honey. He and Riche are kept in an anteroom. Their entertainment is a painted cloth of St Catherine, suffering on her wheel. They listen to the sounds of the busy house and the town outside, till increased agitation in the air tells them their ruse is detected: scampering feet, a slamming door, a call of 'Dame Elizabeth? Madam?' Shaftesbury is a town of twelve churches, too many for the inhabitants. When they ring their bells, the streets quake.

'So,' says the abbess, 'you have come yourself, Lord Cromwell.'

'You know my face, madam.'

'One of the gentlemen of the district has a portrait of you. He keeps it on display.'

'I hope he does. It would be no good in his cellar. You visit many gentlemen?'

Her eyes flick up at him. 'On the business of the house.'

'What else? Did the painter do me justice?'

She surveys him. 'He did you charity.'

'What you have seen is a copy of a copy. Each version is worse. My son thinks I look like a murderer.'

The abbess is enjoying herself. 'We lead such a quiet and blessed life here, I am not sure I have seen one for comparison.' She stands up. 'But you will want to get on. You have come to see Sister Dorothea.'

As he follows her she says, 'Why is Richard Riche here? We are as wealthy, praise God, as any house of religion in the realm. I understood Sir Richard's business is with houses of lesser value.'

'We like to keep our figures current.'

'I have been abbess for thirty years. Any question about our worth, ask me.'

'Riche likes it on paper.'

'I give you warning,' Dame Elizabeth says. 'And you can carry the warning to the king. I will not surrender this house. Not this year, nor next, nor any year this side of Heaven.'

He holds up his hands. 'The king has no thought of it.'

'Here.' She pushes a door open. 'Wolsey's daughter.'

Dorothea half-rises. With a gesture, he bids her sit. 'Madam, how do you? I have brought gifts.'

They are in a side room, small and sunless. He permits himself a single long look. She is not like the cardinal. Her mother's daughter? She is pleasant enough to look at, though she cannot fetch up a smile. Perhaps she is thinking, where have you been these years past?

He says, 'I saw you once when you were a little child. You will not remember me.'

She does not reach out for her presents, so he places them in her lap. She unties the bundle, glances at the books and lays them aside. But she picks up a kerchief of fine linen, and holds it to the light. It is worked with the three apples of St Dorothea, and with wreaths, sprigs and blossoms, the lily and the rose.

'One of my household made it to honour you. Rafe Sadler's wife – you may have heard your father speak of young Sadler?'

'No. Who is he?'

He takes out of his pocket a letter. It is from John Clancey, a gentleman-servant to the cardinal, who acted for her father in placing her here. He has had the letter for some time, and he has formed the habit, not of carrying it around, but of knowing where it is.

'Clancey tells me you want to continue in this life. But I think, you were very young when you made your vows.'

Her head is bent over the kerchief, studying the work. 'So I can be dispensed?'

'You are free to go.'

'Go where?' she asks.

'You are welcome in my house.'

'Live with you?' The chill in her tone pushes him backwards, even in the cramped space. She folds up the kerchief, so the design is hidden. 'How is my brother Thomas Winter?'

'He is well and provided for.'

'By you?'

'It is the least I can do for the cardinal. When your brother is next in England, I could arrange for you to meet.'

'We would have nothing to say to each other. He a scholar. I a poor nun.'

'I would keep him in my house and gladly. But for the sake of his studies he would rather live abroad.'

'A cardinal's son has no place in England. In Italy, I am told, he would be well accepted.'

'In Italy he would be Pope.'

She turns her shoulder. Very well, he thinks. No more jokes.

'When Anne Boleyn came down,' she says, 'we believed true religion would be restored. The whole summer has passed, and now we doubt it.'

'True religion was never left off,' he says. 'You have had no opportunity to see the king's manner of life – so you imagine the court spends its days in masques and dancing. Not so, I assure you. The king hears three Masses in daylight hours. He keeps all the feasts of the church, as ever he did. Fasting is observed, and the meatless days. We scant nothing.'

'We hear the sacraments are to be put down. And that all monks and nuns will be dispersed. Dame Elizabeth is sure the king will take our house in the end. Then how would we live?'

'There are no such plans,' he says. 'But if that were to occur, you would be pensioned. I believe your abbess would bargain hard.'

'But what would we do, without our sisters in religion? We cannot go back to our families, if our families are dead.' She flushes. 'Or even if they are alive, they might not want us.'

He must be patient. 'Dorothea, there is no need to weep. You are imagining harms that could never touch you.'

He thinks, should I embrace her? A king's daughter has cried on my shoulder – or she would have, if I had stayed still.

'I have come here to give you good assurances,' he says. 'I understand this place is all you have known till now. But you have all your life before you.'

283

'Clancey brought me and left me here under his name. Everybody knew I was Wolsey's daughter. It was not my choice to come, but no more is it my choice to leave. I do not wish to be turned out to beg my bread.'

This is women, he thinks – they must enact some scene, to wring tears from themselves and you. I have already offered her my house.

'I will make you an annuity,' he says.

'I will not take it.'

He brushes that aside; it is the kind of thing that people say. 'Or I will find you suitors, if you could like marriage.'

'Marriage?' She is incredulous.

He laughs. 'You have heard of that blessed state?'

'A bastard daughter? The bastard daughter of a disgraced priest? And no looks, even?'

He thinks, a good dowry would make you a beauty. But that is not what she wants to hear. 'Trust me, you are a lovely young woman. Till now, no good man has held up a mirror, for you to see yourself through his eyes. Once you have clothes and ornaments, you will be a welcome sight for a bridegroom. I know the best merchants, and I know the fashions at the French court, and in Italy. I have dressed ...' He breaks off. I have dressed two queens.

She appraises him. 'I am sure your eye is expert.'

'Or if you would consider me, I could, I myself –'

He stops. He is appalled. That is not at all what he meant to say.

She is staring at him. You cannot take back such a word. 'I'll marry you, mistress, if you'll have me. I am, you may not know this, I am a long time a widower. I lack graces of person, but I lack nothing else. I am rich and likely to grow richer, so your want of fortune is no obstacle to me. I have good houses. You would find me generous. I look after my family.' He hears his own voice, recommending himself as if he were a servant, urging his merits on this shocked young woman. 'I have no children to burden you, except Gregory, who is almost grown and will be married himself soon. I would like more children. Or not, as you wished. If you want a marriage in name only, so you have a place in the world, then for your father's sake I would be prepared …' He falters.

She crosses to the small window, and stares out of it furiously. There is nothing to see but a wall. 'In name only? I do not understand you. Are you offering to marry me or not?'

'You are alone in the world, and so am I. For your father's sake I would cherish you. Who knows, you might grow fond of me. And if you did not, then – you would still have a home and a protector, and I would make no other demand on you.'

'That is because you have a mistress?'

He does not answer.

'Several, perhaps,' she says, as if to herself. 'It is true you have everything to commend you – if you were a buyer and I were for sale. You have money to buy any article, thanks to my father, who gave you your start in life.'

My start in life, he thinks: madam, you cannot imagine it. He feels bereft, injured, cold. Why should she have a stony heart towards him? Many times, that long winter at Esher, he had settled the cardinal's debts. They were sums you would pay out of your pocket, but still: there were butchers, bargemen, rat-killers, men who make poultices for horses, purveyors of horoscopes and salt fish. And there had been other disbursements, that never went through the books: buying off the spies, for instance, that Norfolk had put in the household. 'Your father was a liberal master,' he says. 'I owe him much that cannot be cast into figures. It was he who explained to me the king's business. How things really work, not how people say they work. Not the custom, but the practice.'

'Certainly,' she says, 'it was he who brought you to the king's notice. With the result that we see.'

He thinks, she does not like my proposal, she does not. I should never have spoken, I know in my bones it is wrong; I am too old, and besides, so close to her father as I was, perhaps it seems to her we are related, almost as if she is my sister. He says, 'Dorothea, tell me what it needs, to make you safe and comfortable. Forget I spoke of marriage.' Despite himself, he smiles. He can't stop himself trying to charm her. 'There is still a way forward. Though you find my person defective.'

'Your person is not defective,' she says. 'At least, not so defective as your nature and your deeds.'

He is still smiling. 'You do not like my proceedings against the religious. I can understand that.'

'Many of my sisters are keen to cast off their habits. If the house were dissolved they would go tomorrow. Dame Elizabeth does not speak ill of you. She says you are fair in your dealings.'

'Well, then ... I think it is my religion itself you do not like. I love the gospel and will follow it. Your father understood that.'

'He understood everything,' she says. 'He understood you betrayed him.'

He gapes at her. He, Lord Cromwell. He who is never surprised.

'When my father was in exile, and forced to go north, he wrote certain letters, out of his desperation to have the king's favour again – letters begging the King of France to intercede for him. And he appealed to the queen – I mean Katherine, the queen that was – to forgive their differences and stand his friend.'

'So much is true, but –'

'You saw to it that those letters reached the Duke of Norfolk. You put upon them an evil construction, which they should never have borne. And Norfolk put them into the hand of the king, and so the damage was done.'

He cannot speak. Till he says, 'You are much mistaken.'

She is shaking with rage. 'You had your men in my father's household in the north, do you deny it?'

'They were there to serve him, to help him. Madam –'

'They were there to spy on him. To goad him, to provoke him into rash actions and rash statements, which your master the duke then shaped into treason.'

'Jesus,' he says. 'You think Norfolk is my master? I was no man's servant but Wolsey's.'

Be calm, he says to himself: not like a hasty gardener, who tugs out the weed but leaves the root in the ground. He asks her, 'Who told you this, and how long have you believed it?'

'I have always believed it. And always shall, whatever denial you make.'

'If I were to bring you proofs that you are wrong? Written proofs?'

'Forgery is among your talents, I hear.'

'You hear too much. You listen to the wrong people.'

'You are angry. Innocence is tranquil.'

Don't speak to me of innocence, he thinks. I pulled down certain men who insulted your father, as an example to others – call them innocent, if your definition stretches. I ripped them from their gambling and dancing and tennis play. I made each one a bridegroom: I married them to crimes they had barely imagined, and walked them to their wedding breakfast with the headsman. I heard young Weston beg for his life. I held George Boleyn as he wept and called on Jesus. I heard Mark whimper behind a locked door; I thought, Mark is a feeble child, I will go down and free him, but then I thought, no, it is his turn to suffer.

'If you are of this fixed opinion,' he says, 'then I shall not trouble you more. Since you hold it against all evidence and reason, how can I oppose it? I would swear an oath, I would do it gladly, but you would think –'

'I would know you were a perjurer. I have been told, by those I trust, there is no faith or truth in Cromwell.'

He says, 'When those you trust abandon you – Dorothea, come to me. I will never refuse you. I loved your father next to God, and any child of his body, or any soul who was true to him, may command me to any service. No risk, no cost, no effort too great.'

'Take this with you,' she says. She holds out the kerchief. 'And these books, whatever they are.'

He picks up the gifts and leaves her. He stands outside the room. He leans against the wall, his eyes resting on a picture, where a twisted man adheres to a tree, and bleeds from head, hands and heart.

Richard Riche bustles up: 'Sir?'

Christophe's face is stricken. 'Master, what has she said?'

'I believe I have not cried since Esher,' he says. 'Since All Souls' Eve.'

Riche says, 'Have you not? You surprise me. The king's great trials have not drawn a tear?'

'No.' He tries to smile. 'When he is vexed the king cries enough for two men, so I thought my efforts needless.'

'And what provokes this now?' Riche asks. 'If I may ask? With all respect?'

'False accusation.'

'Bitter,' Riche says.

'Richard, you do not think I betrayed the cardinal, do you?'

Riche blinks. 'It never crossed my mind. You didn't, did you?'

He thinks, Riche would not fault me, if I had betrayed him: what use is a fallen magnate? He says, 'If not for me, the cardinal would have been killed in those days of his first disgrace, or if he had lived he would have lived a beggar. I put myself in hazard for him, my house and all I had. If I treated with Norfolk, it was only to speak for my master. I did not like Thomas Howard then and I do not now, and I was never his man and never will be, and if he came to me for a post as a pot boy I would not employ him.'

'Nor I,' says Christophe. 'I would kick him in a ditch.'

'When I wept,' he says, 'that day at Esher – my wife lately dead and my daughters, the ashes cold in the grates, the wind howling through every crack – then the dead souls came out of purgatory, blowing around the courtyards and rattling at the shutters to be let in. That was what we believed in those days. What many believed.'

'I still,' Christophe says.

'I do not believe I shall cry again,' he says. 'I am done with tears.' He hears his own voice, running on. 'Do you know, when Wolsey was in the north, a fellow came to me, a factor for the cloth merchants: "The cardinal owes us over a thousand pounds." I said, "Be exact." He said, "One thousand and fifty-four pounds and some odd pence." I said, "Will you remit the pence, for the love you bear him?" He said, "My masters have remitted and remitted, supplying cloth for vestments out of their piety and at no profit to themselves – and we are talking about cloth of gold."'

He thinks, I tried by every means to save my master: I tried by exhortation, by prayer, and when that failed, I tried accountancy. Riche is wondering at him, but he cannot stop. 'He said to me, this fellow, "The cardinal has owed the merchant Cavalcanti the sum of eighty-seven pounds, standing over these seven years, for richest cloth of gold at thirty shillings a yard, 311½ yards: and of the lesser quality, 195½ yards." He said, "The whole order was left at York Place – I have the delivery note. The cardinal claims the king will pay," he said to me – "but I think we shall see doomsday sooner than that."'

'Sir,' Christophe says, 'sit down on this chest. Using that handkerchief you may wipe your eyes.'

He looks at the green leaves, the loving stitches Helen has made, to give pleasure to a stranger. 'So I said to Cavalcanti's man, "Very well, I acknowledge the debt, all but five hundred marks – for the merchants swore they would give that sum to the cardinal, to have his friendship – and no doubt it will do them good at the Last Judgement." But he said, "The sum was already knocked off, you cannot have it twice." And I had to concede it.'

He sits down on the chest. Christophe says, 'Sir, do not weep any more. You said you would not.'

'After Harry Percy went up to Cawood with a warrant, the cardinal was set on the road without time to pay his debts. The apothecary came to me with a bill for medicines – useless, for the patient was dying.'

'They are not paid by results,' Riche says.

'Once he was dead, the wolves closed in. Basden the fishmonger claimed he was owed for three thousand stockfish. "Since when?" I said.'

'Sir ...' Riche says.

'Bay salt too – but why would any kitchen buy salt at one mark the bushel?' He looks around him. 'The girl is right. There was rank ingratitude, there was false dealing, there was perjury, defamation and theft. But I was true to Wolsey, or God strike me down.'

A bell is ringing. He can hear the nuns begin to stir, gathering to say their office. He says, 'I should have gone up to Yorkshire with him. I should have been with him when he died. I should not have let the king get in my way.'

'My lord,' Riche says, his tone hushed, 'the king is not in our way. He *is* our way.'

He says, 'I shall go back in to Dorothea. I shall explain it to her.'

Christophe says, 'You cannot undo what she has been believing for so long. Let it rest.'

'Good advice, on the whole,' Riche says. 'My lord, that was the Vespers bell. We had best be on the road, unless we incline to spend a night here. I have parted on good terms with the abbess, I find her a reasonable woman and well-found in the law – these women surprise one. I have the figures. So for now I have done here – if you have.'

'I have done,' he says. '*Allons.*'

He remembers the false prophetess, the nun Eliza Barton. She said she could find the dead for you, if you gave her enough money. She searched Heaven and Hell, she said, and never found Wolsey, till she found him at last in a place that was no place, seated among the unborn.

In London, he twists the embroidered kerchief in his hand. Rafe comes; 'You can give this back to Helen.'

'I hear,' Rafe says gently, 'you were ill-received.'

'You counselled me,' he says, 'you and my nephew – you said, you must let the cardinal go. Whether I would or no, he was prised away from me. But I did not know he would go as far as he has gone now.' His hand describes the space of the room. 'I am used to his visits. I see him in my mind. I ask his advice. He is dead but I make him work.'

'He will come again, sir, when you need him.'

He shakes his head. Dorothea has rewritten his story. She has made him strange to himself. 'Who could have told her I betrayed her father – except her father himself?'

Rafe says, 'So much expenditure of time, of goods, of prayers … surely he knew your devotion?'

We must hope so. You can persuade the quick to think again, but you cannot remake your reputation with the dead.

'I see now I should have asked her more questions. *Your master the duke*, she said. By God, I'd rather work for Patch.'

Rafe puts his finger to his lips. 'You know what the cardinal used to say. Walls have eyes and ears.'

As if he is not safe in his own house. But then, Sadler is a more cautious man than he will ever be.

And Riche? Riche tells his story all around Lincoln's Inn, and the courts of Westminster, and the guildsmen's houses in the city: boasts of him, or so he hears. 'Lord Cromwell had all the figures in his head. Stockfish, bay salt, I know not what. Even though he was stricken, at Wolsey's girl insulting him. I fear he has been grievously slandered, and who knows who is at the root of it, when he has so many enemies? And yet he has a remarkable mind,' Riche says reverently, 'remarkable. I think if writing were rubbed out, and all the records of government erased, he would carry them in his head, with all the laws of England, precedent and clause. And I am a fortunate man, to stand his friend, and to have been able to work a little to soothe his temper. Yes, I am glad I was standing by. Praise God,' says Richard Riche, 'I learn from him every day.'

Returned from Shaftesbury, body and mind, he opens letters from Gardiner in France, saying that the dauphin is dead: an unexplained fever, three days' duration. Henry, who so recently lost a son of his own, offers his sympathies, and the court goes into black. No hardship for Lord Cromwell: black's what he's in. He appears at many gaudy occasions – as a courtier he cannot help it – but he would not want his brothers in the city to say, 'These days Cromwell is wholly in crimson,' or 'He has taken to purple as if he were a bishop.'

The news from France is soon corrected. Not that the dauphin is alive, rather that his death was in no way natural. But, he asks, why would anyone trouble to poison the boy? François has other sons.

The French embassy maintains silence. Anthony walks through Austin Friars, ringing his new silver bells and crying, 'God be thanked, one Frenchman less!' The sound fades behind closed doors, up staircases, through distant galleries. 'One less, who cares how?'

The sound echoes: who-who, an owl's cry: how-how, the hound's call. Austin Friars is augmented, growing into a palace. Builders bang and hammer from dawn. Richard Cromwell walks in with a roll of drawings in his hand. 'Our neighbour Stow is bad-mouthing you all over London. You know he has a summerhouse? Our boys have put it on rollers and run it twenty feet back on his own side. He says we're stealing his land. I sent a message, compliments to Master Stow and may we have sight of his plans?'

He looks up. 'I know where my boundaries are. He lays a serious charge and I take it ill.'

'So go fuck himself,' Christophe suggests.

They scarcely knew Christophe was in the room. But there he squats in the corner, like a gargoyle fallen off a church. He remembers the boy saying, that day when they rode up to Kimbolton, 'I will kill a Pole for you. I will kill a Pole when you require it.'

He thinks, if Christophe can be in my room undetected, I am sure he could weasel in to Reginald's household. He says to Richard, 'It is time I saw about him. Having him stopped.'

'Stow?' Richard is surprised. 'A stiff letter will do it.'

'Pole. Reynold. As you suggested, it may take a knife.'

But then, he would be sorry if Christophe should end his days screaming in some hell-hole, probed and burned by Italian tortures. The French also are devoted to pain; they say you never get the truth without it. The rumour is that they have arrested a man for poisoning their prince, but they are coaxing him for the while, because they believe he will confess to some master-plot. Subtle methods have their place. But any interrogator would look at Christophe and see subtlety as wasted. 'Christophe,' he says, 'if ever –' He shakes his head. 'No, never mind.'

If I do employ him, he vows, I will tell him to bawl out, 'Thomas Cromwell's man,' before they can burn or stretch him. Why not? I will take the blame. My list of sins is so extensive that the recording angel has run out of tablets, and sits in the corner with his quill blunted, wailing and ripping out his curls.

'Come on,' he says. 'Get your coat, Richard. We're going outside to tramp up and down our line and put down markers for a stone wall as high as two men. And our friend Stow can sit behind it and howl.'

In Lincolnshire, in the east of England, the rumour has been spreading these three weeks that the king is dead. Drinkers gathering at alehouses claim that the councillors are keeping it a secret, so they can continue to levy taxes in the king's name, and spend the proceeds on their pleasures. Rafe says, 'Has anyone told Henry he's dead? I think he ought to know, and I think it should come from someone more senior than me.'

Rafe yawns. He has been with the king at Windsor all week and he has never been in bed before midnight. Henry lingers over paperwork, accepting it from his hand in the morning but calling him in after supper to confer, keeping him standing while he frowns over the dispatches. There are rumours of unrest up in Westmorland; anything that happens near the border, Henry says, you can depend upon the Scots to make it worse. The King of Scots has taken ship, sailed away to France to find a bride, but the winds have driven him back on his own shore. Meanwhile the Emperor offers Henry a joint enterprise against France. Charles is fitting out a fleet of warships. As proof of our commitment, he would like cash on the table.

He says to Chapuys, 'No wonder your master comes cap-in-hand. Why does he never have ready money? And he pays out such huge sums in interest.'

'He ought to have you managing his cash,' Chapuys says. 'Come on now, Thomas – show willing. My master pays you a pension. We do not fee you for nothing.'

'That is what the French say too. How can I please you both?'

Chapuys waves a hand. 'I too would take their bounty. Now you are a lord, you have heavy expenses. But we all know that you are the

Emperor's man in your heart. Think of the advantages to your merchants that would be forfeit, if my master was provoked against them. Be mindful of the losses, if my master were to close his ports to Englishmen.'

He smiles. Chapuys is always threatening him with blockades and bankruptcy. 'The difficulty is that my prince no longer trusts yours. Time was when your master promised to kick out King François and give my king half his territory. And Henry, good soul, believed him. But then, while we were polishing up our French so we could address our new subjects, Charles was talking to them behind our back and patching up a treaty. We are not fools twice. This time, we would need some great assurances, before we laid out a penny.'

'Make a marriage with us,' Chapuys coaxes. 'Lady Mary says she is not inclined to matrimony, but she would be glad, I believe, to be reunited with her own bloodline. My master will offer his own nephew, the Portuguese prince. Dom Luis is a fine young man, she could do no better.'

'The King of France has sons.'

'Mary will not take a Frenchman,' Chapuys says.

'That is not what she says to me.'

The king is still keeping his newly-beloved daughter at arm's length. It is understood that when Jane the queen is crowned, that will be the time for her to come to court, making a great entrance. Meanwhile Mary seems tranquil, ordering new clothes and trotting through the leafy days on Pomegranate and other mounts her friend Lord Cromwell has supplied. She has plenty money for her privy purse – thanks again to her friend – and seems content to encounter her royal father by pre-arrangement, for a day here and there: for supper, and a turn in the gardens when the sun is not too high for a virgin's complexion. Henry has begged her, 'Tell me the truth, daughter. When you acknowledged me as what I am, head of the church, did someone prompt you, or constrain you, or urge you to say one thing and mean another? Or did you do it of your own free will?'

He would like to divert the king from this line of questioning. It drives Mary deeper into evasion. Chapuys has told her to send to

Rome for the Pope's pardon, for statements she made in favour of her father. She made them, she argues, under duress.

But in Rome they argue, reasonably enough, that Mary's declarations were public, and any retraction would need to be public too. She would have to tell Henry, to his face, that she has changed her mind.

Then where would she be? Dead.

Mr Wriothesley says, my lord, you should challenge her. You know where her loyalty lies: to Rome, and to her dead mother. If the ignorant populace are in thrall to an Italian warlord who sets himself up as God's deputy, surely a king's daughter should know better? Surely by now, the world and all she has seen has knocked off the shackles of her upbringing, and allowed her to walk a straight path towards reason?

But he does not dispute with Mary. He simply repeats to her, madam, obedience is your refuge. Be consistent in it. With consistency comes peace of mind, and peace of mind is what you need.

Amen to that, she says. She looks grave. Just make my father's wishes known to me, Lord Cromwell. I will perform them.

'Mary says,' he tells Chapuys, 'that she will marry a Portuguese prince, or a French prince, any prince her father selects. But please note, Eustache, she does not say at any point, "But if I had my choice, I would take for my bridegroom the Lord Privy Seal."'

The ambassador chuckles – a rusty little sound, like a key grating in a lock – and holds out his hands as if to say, guilty.

Luckily for Chapuys, gossip is not a capital crime.

When the first reports of trouble come in, he is at Windsor with the king. The days are still fine and it is warm in the sun. It is Michaelmas, and through the realm there are processions, with the banners of Our Lady and the angels and saints. All summer, a ban on sermons has been in force, to keep the peace. The ban is lifted for the feast. From the town of Louth in Lincolnshire – a shire of no great fame – there are reports of crowds gathering after Mass. They do not disperse even at dusk.

You know those nights, in market towns. A little money jangling in the pocket, and old companions stumbling through the streets, arms entwined. Youths carolling under a sailing moon, daring each other to leap a ditch or break into an empty house. If it rained they'd go in. But the weather holds. Darkness falls and the marketplace is still packed. Leather flasks are passed hand to hand. Stale grudges are let out for air. Wiping of mouths, spitting at feet. Any quarrel will do, for apprentices looking for a brawl. The clubs and knives come out.

Nine o'clock, a chill in the air. A few masters pick up staves and trot shoulder to shoulder to face down the boys. 'Sore heads tomorrow, lads! Come on now, get home while your legs will carry you.'

Shog off, say the apprentices. We will break your pates.

Their masters say, almost sorrowful, do you not think we were young once? All right, stay out and starve. See if we care.

Through the hours of darkness the townsfolk hear hallooing from the marketplace – some fool tootling on a trumpet, another bashing a drum. The sun rises on cobbles plastered with puke. The marauders stretch, piss against a wall and go looking for pies. They ransack a baker's stall, and by ten o'clock they have broached a cask of wine, making cups of their hollow palms.

Last night they stole the watchman's rattle, and knocked the watchman down. Now they go rattling through the streets, proclaiming the ballad of Worse-was-it-Never. There was a former age, it seems, when wives were chaste and pedlars honest, when roses bloomed at Christmas and every pot bubbled with fat self-renewing capons. If these times are not those times, who is to blame? Londoners, probably. Members of Parliament. Reforming bishops. People who use English to talk to God.

Word spreads. On the farms around, labourers see the chance of a holiday. Faces blackened, some wearing women's attire, they set off to town, picking up any edged tool that could act as a weapon. From the marketplace you can see them coming, kicking up a cloud of dust.

Old men anywhere in England will tell you about the drunken exploits of harvests past. Rebel ballads sung by our grandfathers need small adaptation now. We are taxed till we cry, we must live till we die, we be looted and swindled and cheated and dwindled ... *O, Worse was it Never!*

Farmers bolt their grain stores. The magistrates are alert. Burgers withdraw indoors, securing their warehouses. In the square some rascal sways on top of a husting, viewing the rural troops as they roll in. 'Pledge yourselves to me – Captain Poverty is my name.' The bell-ringers, elbowed and threatened, tumble into the parish church and ring the bells backward. At this signal, the world turns upside down.

Morning brings Richard Riche riding from London to Windsor with rumours of assault on officials of the Court of Augmentations. 'Our men are in Louth, sir – gone in to value the treasures at St James's church, which you know is a very rich one.'

He pictures the spire rising three hundred feet, holding up the Lincolnshire sky, clouds draped about it like wet washing. It takes two days to ride from here to Lincolnshire, sparing nor horse nor man. Even as Riche is talking, new messengers are bellowing below: rural gawpers, clay on their boots. How did such folk get here, within the castle walls? They call up, 'Is it true the king is dead?'

He comes down the stair towards them. 'Who says so?'

'All the east believes it. He died at midsummer. A puppet lies in his bed and wears his crown.'

'So who rules?'

'Cromwell, sir. He means to pull down all the parish churches. He will melt the crucifixes for cannon, to fire on the poor folk of England. Taxes will be tenpence in every shilling, and no man shall have a fowl in his pot but he pay a levy on it. There will be no bread next winter but made of pease flour and beans, and the commons shall be poisoned by it and lie in the fields like blown sheep, with no priest to confess them.'

'Wipe your feet,' he tells them. 'I shall bring you to a dead king, and you may kneel and beg his pardon.'

The messenger is cowed. 'We do but report what we have heard.'

'That's how wars start.' Somewhere out of sight a man is singing, voice echoing around the stones:

> 'Now God defend and make an end
> Their crimes to mend:
> From Crum and Cram and Cramuel
> St Luke deliver such to Hell.
> God send me well!'

He thinks, I believe that's Sexton. I thought the pest was crushed. 'Who is Cromwell?' he asks the messengers. 'What manner of man do you take him to be?'

Sir, they say, do you not know him? He is the devil in guise of a knave. He wears a hat and under it his horns.

As the trouble spreads from the town of Louth throughout the shire, the king demands, without result, the immediate attendance of Sir Thump and Lord Mump, Lord Stumble and Sheriff Bumble. It is still the hunting season, and they cannot be got to his side for three, four days. First, messengers must go and tell them of the disturbances to the peace. Then they must say, 'Lincolnshire up? What the devil do you mean, *up*?' Then they must instruct their stewards, they must kiss their wives, they must make their general adieux …

'Come in, cousin Richard,' the king calls. 'I need my family. No one else rallies to me in my need.'

At this point he, Thomas Cromwell, could say 'I told you so.' Last year he had argued, if we are closing houses of religion, let us deal with them case by case: no need to frighten the people with a bill in Parliament. But Riche had insisted, no, no, no, we should have the clarity of statute. Lord Audley had said, 'Cromwell, you cannot do everything as you did it in the cardinal's time. Would not such a programme take us the rest of our lives?'

He had closed his eyes: 'My lord, I suggested dealing with the houses individually. I did not suggest "one at a time". That is different.'

But he was overruled. They beat the drum for their intentions: and now look! The king at Windsor wants familar faces about him. His boys are edged onto benches where the great magnates of the realm are used to sit. When the archbishop comes in, dusty from the road, they are at a loss to find an episcopal sort of chair.

'Why are you here?' he asks: politely enough. 'You were not looked for.'

'Because of the songs,' Cranmer says. '*Crum and Cram and Cramuel.* Do they think there is you, my lord, and me, and then some third person compounded of both?'

'It is a mystery. Like the Trinity.'

It seems the trouble is not confined to a distant shire. Cranmer says, 'There are placards hung through Lambeth. I am not safe in my house. Hugh Latimer has been threatened. I hear in Lincolnshire they have attacked Bishop Longland's servants.'

John Longland is a cautious, rigid, unsmiling man, who helped the king to get free from his first marriage: not popular on that account, in his own see or through the realm. The upset is worse than Cranmer knows. In Horncastle – it is well-witnessed – one of Longland's men has been bludgeoned to death, the parish clergy cheering as he gasped his life out; and a man who calls himself Captain Cobbler is strutting with the victim's coat on his back.

'My lord archbishop, you should know that I am in the songs too,' Richard Riche says. 'I hear my name is reviled.'

'It would be,' Richard Cromwell says. 'It's a fine name for a rhyme. *Flitch, pitch, ditch.*'

He says to Cranmer, 'Perhaps withdraw to the country for a week or two?'

'Well, if the country were safe,' Cranmer murmurs. 'I am afraid there are papists in my own household. If they travel about with me, where shall I go? But London is your business, my lord. If this contagion is spreading, you must look to it.'

'*Switch, twitch, hitch,*' Richard says.

'Hush,' Fitzwilliam says. 'The king is here.'

Mr Wriothesley is a pace behind the king; he has a new doublet of sea-green satin, in which he glows like a Venetian, and delicately he edges aside the quills and penknives of smaller men, to mark out a place for himself. Rafe Sadler, harassed in his old grey riding coat, nudges himself onto a bench end.

'My lord archbishop!' the king says. 'No, do not kneel! It is I should kneel to you.'

'Why?' Richard Cromwell whispers. 'What sin has he done now?'

He suppresses a smile. King and prelate tussle; Cranmer is set on his feet. 'Well, gentlemen,' the king says, 'the news is poor hearing. I would incline to mercy if this brawl were to end now, with no further harm to gentlemen's property nor insult to the crown.' He sighs: Henry the Well-Beloved. 'They fear the winter, poor devils. Reassure them that should there be scarcities, no one will profit from their distress. Proclaim a fixed price for grain if you must. Set up a commission to investigate hoarding. My lord Privy Seal knows what to do, he will remember how the cardinal used to deal with such matters in his day. Offer the malcontents a free pardon, but only if they disperse now.'

'I counsel you against leniency,' Fitzwilliam says. 'If this should spread to Yorkshire, and north to the border, we are all in peril.'

He leans forward. 'May I alert my lord of Norfolk? He could turn out his tenants and quiet the eastern shires.'

'Keep Thomas Howard away from me,' the king says.

Riche says, 'With respect, Majesty, it is towards the rebels we would send him. Not towards your sacred person.'

The king is annoyed. 'I think I can rely on my officers in those parts. If need be, my lord of Suffolk has a sufficient power.'

Wriothesley holds up a dispatch. 'It is stated here that wherever they gather they are chanting, "Bread or Blood". They have sworn oaths. What oaths,' he consults his papers, 'we await advisement.'

Fitzwilliam says, 'Saving your Majesty, the reason for these riots – it is not just about filling their bellies. They want their monks back.'

'Their monks are not gone,' Richard Riche says. 'I wish to God they were, and the revenue from the great houses free to use.'

Under the table, he – Lord Cromwell – kicks Riche's ankle.

Fitzwilliam says, 'They ask for the old worship to be restored. The Pope to have his primacy.'

'They ask for all things to be as they were in times past,' Wriothesley says. 'And God knows, even my lord cardinal would have found that outwith his powers, to make time flow backwards.'

'But their saints are eternal,' Fitzwilliam says, 'or so they think. They want them back, those our injunctions have taken away. They are asking for St Wilfred. They want Crispin and Crispianus, and the virgin Agatha. They want Giles and Swithin, and all the harvest saints. They would rather have a holiday than get the crops in, and they would rather parade with banners than set the winter wheat.' He says, 'They believe that if you harvest on saints' days, your hands drop off. The fruits of learning may one day be seen in England, but let me advertise you, they are not seen yet.'

Cranmer says, 'I understand they are burning books.'

'Poor men do not rise without leaders,' he says. 'Let no man tell me they do.'

Letters come in. The seals are broken. The king tosses the papers down as he reads: 'Here, Wriothesley. Give my lord Cromwell sight of this.'

Call-Me is reading over the king's shoulder. 'As you say, Lord Cromwell, certain gentlemen are leading the *canaille*. We have names.'

'But the gentlemen protest they are enforced?'

'Haled out of bed in the middle of the night,' Wriothesley says. 'Nightcaps on their heads.'

'One has heard of it before,' he says. Their wives screaming, and country folk with torches aloft in their hands, threatening to fire the barns unless the gentlemen saddle up and lead them to the king. These broils begin the same, and from age to age they end the same. The gentry pardoned, and the poor dangling from trees.

He says, 'I will send a message up-country to Lord Talbot. Tell him to turn out his people and get himself to Nottingham with the strongest company he can find. Hold the castle, and from there he can move either by Mansfield towards Lincoln, or up to Yorkshire if –'

The king says, 'Sadler, send to Greenwich for my armour.'

There is a babble of protest: no, sire, do not risk your sacred person! For Lincolnshire? God forbid.

'If the common folk are saying I am dead, what choice have I?'

Cranmer says, 'The malcontents aim at your councillors, not your Majesty's person. To whom they declare themselves loyal – but such rebels always do. I know what they intend for me. If they come south I shall be burned.'

'Lord Cromwell's head is their chief demand,' Wriothesley says. 'They believe my lord has practised some device or sorcery on the king. As the cardinal did before him.'

He says, 'I am offended for my prince, that they deem him no more than a child to be led.'

'By God, I am offended too,' Henry says. He has read all the news that comes in, but only now does he seem to take it in – flushed, his fist thumping the table. 'I take it ill to be instructed by the folk of Lincolnshire, which is one of the most brute and beastly shires in the realm. How do they presume to dictate what men I keep about me? Let them understand this. When I choose a humble man for my councillor, HE IS NO MORE HUMBLE. Who will advise me, when Lord Cromwell is put down? Will these rebels do it? Colin Clump and Peter Pisspiddle, and old Grandpa Gaphead and his goat?'

'No, they will not,' the archbishop murmurs.

'Will Robin Ragbag raise the revenues?' the king asks.

'Or Simple Simon draft a law?' Riche pipes up as if he cannot help himself. Henry glares at the interruption. His voice rises. 'I made my minister, and by God I will maintain him. If I say Cromwell is a lord, he is a lord. And if I say Cromwell's heirs are to follow me and rule England, by God they will do it, or I shall come out of my grave and want to know why.'

There is a silence.

The king rises. 'Keep me informed.'

Master Wriothesley steps out of the king's way, watching him with solemn eyes.

'I go to shoot,' Henry says. He rolls away with his gentlemen, to the archery butts below the royal apartments. 'Keep my eye in,' he calls. His voice trails after him, and is lost in the afternoon.

The council disperses, except the archbishop: except Fitzwilliam, and except Richard Riche, who sticks at the table, frowning and leafing through his papers, and Wriothesley, who leans over him, whispering. It is settled that Charles Brandon will stop whatever he is doing, take men and restore order in Lincolnshire. Charles is a brisk man for this sort of thing, and we rely on him not to be too heavy-handed with the poorer sort. Lord Chancellor Audley, now on his way to Windsor, should be sent back to his own parts, in case any spark blown south should start a fire in Essex.

'So, Crumb, how does it feel?' Fitzwilliam asks him. 'To be the heir presumptive to England?'

He waves the joke away. 'But he proclaimed you!' Fitz says. 'Sir Richard Riche, you are witness.'

A non-committal grunt from Riche, head low over his notes. Fitz says, 'The king by himself can appoint you, since he made his new law for the succession. Certainly Parliament can make you king – what think you, Riche?'

Suppose Parliament were to pass an act saying that I, Richard Riche, should be king? If Riche hears an echo from Thomas More's day, it does not distract him. 'Riche will not look up,' Fitz says. 'I must be wrong. I am no lawyer, am I? Still, my ears did not deceive me. He named you next king, Crumb. And I have thought that, of late, young Gregory had a very princely air about him.'

'It is since he came back from Kenninghall,' he says. 'He enjoyed his summer with Norfolk.'

'If this business spreads,' Fitz says, 'we will have to unleash Uncle Norfolk, whether Harry wants him or no. He has the forces in the east, and he is a power in the north.'

Riche says, not pausing in his scribbling, 'Anyone you can pull back from Ireland?'

'We're barely holding the Pale,' he says. 'I would abandon the wretched place, except it would let our enemies in Europe set up camp on our doorstep. My lord archbishop,' he turns to Cranmer, 'you must take your lady out of London. Keep her safe at some small house of yours –'

The archbishop emits a shriek – muffled, like Jonah's inside the whale.

Riche cuts him off. 'Oh, peace, my lord archbishop. We all know you have married a wife.'

Fitz says, 'We all know.'

'No one here would betray you,' Riche says. 'The king holds you in high esteem, and if he does not choose to know, we do not choose to tell him.'

'I pray God to move his heart,' the archbishop says, 'so he relents, and understands matrimony as a blessing no man should be denied.'

'He likes it himself,' Fitzwilliam says. 'You would think he would like it for others.'

'Give him time,' he says. 'And Riche, I know you are keen for work, you Augmentations men, and I am sorry I kicked you under the table, but I do not want the king to say we pushed him or led him where he did not want to go.'

'But we have a plan?' Riche says. 'For the great houses to be dissolved?'

'Oh, we always have a plan.'

Call-Me straightens up from his conference with Riche's papers: glimpsing himself in the window, he studies his wavering shape and adjusts the angle of his cap. 'My lord archbishop, you should comfort your lady that all will be well. I hear she does not speak our language. That must make her start at shadows. The rebels will not come here.'

'No?' Cranmer says. 'You will not talk it away, Wriothesley. It is no light matter and I believe we are ill-prepared. I do not believe this is the action of a few malcontent men. You will find the Emperor's finger in the pie. You will find certain familiars of his Majesty, who look to a future without him. They will proclaim Mary if they can get her, and then we shall have war. You need not mince matters with me,

Mr Wriothesley. I have seen the worst men can do, to their fellow men and to women. In Germany I have seen a battlefield. I have not spent all my life at Cambridge.'

He turns his back on the archbishop and walks to the window. He can see the king and his gentlemen at their sport, in a haze of late sunshine. On the opposite bank, out of sight through the trees, the scholars of Eton are conning their book, and filing to oratory and chapel to pray for their founder, King Henry VI of blessed memory.

Riche has joined him, silent at his elbow. Far below them, he sees a shifting glitter, like salmon skin, against the afternoon: it is the queen in a dress of silver grey, brought out to watch the sport. 'She looks – cushioned,' Riche says.

'She is a great doer at the table, that is all. She is not with child. Lady Rochford tells me when her courses come. No husband more anxious than I.'

'The other one was skin and bone at the last. A thin old woman.'

The king looks up, as if he knows he is being watched. He turns and waves: Lord Cromwell, come out to play?

He holds up a letter, just arrived: scratches his head to show he is busy making sense of it. The sunshine has faded, and the river light is green; the king, swimming in it, thrusts out his lip to mimic a sulky child. Then he plucks off his hat and points with it towards Datchet: I shall come in when the light fails.

'October already!' people say. 'Where did the summer go?'

Helen has sewn another kerchief, in place of that he carried to Shaftesbury. She has sewn the laurel, which lives for ever, and the ivy, continual in its green.

An order goes to the London guilds to muster men and arm them. Beacons set by the rebels are seen across the river Humber. It is certain Yorkshire will rise. 'Rely on my lord Cromwell to placate them,' Fitzwilliam says, smiling. 'In Yorkshire they treasure his good word.'

The king raises an eyebrow. He must explain – an activity he dislikes. 'In former times, Majesty, they used to threaten my life.'

Mr Wriothesley adds, 'My lord Privy Seal was detested, for his service to the cardinal.'

'Sir,' Riche says, 'had we not better heed the archbishop's words, and secure the person of the Lady Mary?'

'What do you suggest?' he asks Riche. 'Chaining her up?'

The king looks uneasy. 'I would not for the world that rebels use my daughter against me. Keep watch on her, will you?'

He says, 'She's watched.'

In London they halt all large gatherings, including Sunday games. Horses are requisitioned, the garrison at the Tower reinforced. Let merchants buy up stocks of wool and finished cloth and keep the outworkers of Essex employed, as well as apprentices in the city: we know about idle hands. Masters should look well to their servants. All the priests and friars should deliver up any arms they possess to the city – save they may keep a knife for cutting their meat at table.

Wriothesley comes to him: you need to go to the Tower and get the king's gold plate and start turning it into coin. Then back here to Windsor, quick as you can.

He says, I am going to see Chapuys.

It is said that a servant of his called Bellowe, a trusted clerk, has been captured and blinded. They have skinned a new-dead bull, sewn Bellowe in its hide, then loosed dogs.

He pictures Bellowe, as he was. Presumably his own father would not know him now. Only God will recognise him, restoring his features at the general resurrection.

He thinks, how can they know the dogs are hungry enough? Do they whip them into pens and starve them? Even his own watchdogs would not eat a living man.

The ambassador says, 'I understand the Duke of Norferk is in London, and in a fever to see you. *Alack, where is Cremuel?* One would think the duke is in love.'

'He wants me to put him back in credit with the king.'

'Henry thinks he has disrespected the corpse of the poor little

Fitzroy,' the ambassador says. 'The king asked for no pomp, so the duke tips his dead bastard in a wagon.'

'It gives you something to amuse the Emperor with. In your dispatches.'

'I myself think Norferk was angry with the boy for dying. What about Madame Jane, is Henry tired of her yet?'

'You see, this is how my master is traduced,' he says. 'Fickleness is not his vice – even you must allow that. He was with Katherine twenty years. He waited seven years for Boleyn.'

'There were concubines, of course. Although, what king is without them? There was Richmond's mother. And the Boleyn sister who he bedded before Anne. The court is speculating who will come next. They say Norferk will put his daughter forward. He must get use out of her, and perhaps it would pique Henry's appetite, to penetrate the widow of his dead son.'

'Eustache …' he says.

'I see you are out of humour.'

'It's the scent of treason in the air. It makes my eyes water. It sets my teeth on edge.'

Grievous, Chapuys murmurs.

'If your master means to send aid to our rebels, he has left it late in the year.'

'Ah, you call them rebels. I thought it was merely a few turnips, sodden with drink? What interest could my master have in their proceedings?'

'None. Unless he has received bad advice. Through your usual bad sources.'

He imagines upending Lord Montague and other Poles, and smacking the soles of their feet till their secrets spill out of their mouths. He imagines laying a clasp-knife to the heart of Nicholas Carew, prising it open like an oyster. He imagines shaking Gertrude Courtenay, till treason drops from her like falling leaves. Slicing the cranium of her husband, the Marquis of Exeter, and stirring a forefinger in the murk of his intentions.

'I shall not regret this business if it brings the traitors out,' he says.

Chapuys is shocked. 'You cannot mean the princess!'

'Any approaches, Mary must report to me. Any letters, they must come straight from her hand to mine.'

'By the way,' the ambassador says, 'I hear that the Courtenays have taken in Thomas Guiett's woman. It is a charity.'

'A duty. Bess Darrell gave all she had to Katherine in her trouble.'

'An angel's face,' Chapuys says, 'and an angel's disposition. Ah, Thomas, it is always the women who suffer. Those tender creatures whose protection God has given into our hands.'

'I told Mary, I have done all for her that I will do. Let her move one inch towards the rebels, and I will cut off her head.'

'Truly, Thomas?' The ambassador smiles. 'We know this game, you and I. It is your duty to come here and boast to me of the strength of the king's forces, and say how he is loved throughout the land. And it is my duty to exclaim, "Cremuel, what kind of imbecile do you take me for?" You know what I must say, and I know what you must say. Why do we not, as the tennis players say, cut to the chase?'

'Very well,' he says. 'Let me say something new. If your master subverts my king in his own country, I will find means to make him suffer, by uniting my king with the princes of Germany, who are your master's subjects – or he thinks they are.'

'I doubt it, *mon cher*,' the ambassador says cheerfully. 'All your talks so far have come to nothing. Henry may hate the Pope, but he hates Luther worse. You once told me you hated him yourself. I believe you incline to the Swiss heretics, for whom the host is but a piece of bread.'

'You are my confessor?'

'You have a great many secrets. You and your archbishop.'

He thinks, if Chapuys knows Cranmer has a wife, he will keep it back till it can do most damage.

'Bread can be more than one thing,' he says. 'Anything can.'

'If Henry were to destroy you for heresy, it would be ...' Chapuys thinks about it. 'It would be a tragedy, Thomas.'

'You would come to Smithfield to see me burned.'

'That would be my painful duty.'

'Painful my arse. You'd buy a new hat.'

Chapuys laughs. 'Forgive me,' he says. 'I sympathise with you. At such a time you must feel the inferiority of your birth – which at other times' – a courtly nod – 'is not evident. Your rivals at court can turn out their tenantry, and arm them from their caches of weaponry that they have owned time out of mind. But you have no retainers of your own. You can expend some of your wealth, no doubt. Yet the cost of keeping even one soldier in the field, especially if he is mounted, and at this end of the season, fodder so dear ... I do not care to estimate, but figures come easily to you. Of course, you could go and fight yourself –'

'My soldiering days are done.'

'But no one would follow you. Not even the Londoners. They want noble captains. In Italy there are charcoal-burners and ostlers who have founded honourable houses and left great names. But England has its own rules.'

Not prayer nor Bible verse, nor scholarship nor wit, nor grant under seal nor statute law can alter the fact of villain blood. Not all his craft and guile can make him a Howard, or a Cheney or a Fitzwilliam, a Stanley or even a Seymour: not even in an emergency. He says, 'Ambassador, I must leave you and cross the river to see Norfolk. Or his heart will break.'

Chapuys says, 'He is chafing to be at the rebels. Any glory going, he wants to get it. He wants to slaughter somebody, even if it's only tanners and plumbers. He is in high spirits, I hear. He thinks this affair will bring you down.'

When he goes to the Norfolk stronghold in Lambeth, he takes an entourage: Rafe Sadler, Call-Me. He hopes Gregory's presence will ease matters.

The duke's great hall is like an armourers' shop and Thomas Howard, batting to and fro, looks more worn and gristly than ever, like a man who has chewed and digested himself. 'Cromwell! No time to talk to you. I'm only here to get my orders direct and then get on the road. North, east, I will go where the king commands, I have six hundred armed and ready to ride, I have five cannon – five, and they are all mine. I have artillery –'

'No, my lord,' he says.

'And I can whistle up another fifteen hundred men in short order.' The duke pounds Gregory's shoulder. 'Well, lad! Are you saddled and armed? Oh, I tell you, Cromwell, he's a wise quick piece, this young fellow! What a summer we had of it! He spares no horseflesh, eh? Let's hope he doesn't go at the women so hard!'

Speaking of women ... but no, he thinks, I will mention his duchess later. First to disabuse him. 'Gregory stays at home,' he says. 'But the king has given a command to my nephew Richard. He is taking cannon from the Tower. The king has declared a muster in Bedfordshire, at Ampthill.'

'So thereto I proceed,' says the duke. 'Is Harry going to the Tower?'

'Staying at Windsor.'

'Probably wise. In olden times, I was once told, the rabble pulled the Archbishop of Canterbury out of the Tower, and cut off his head. But Windsor should stand against rebels and all else, the wrath of God excepted. It should be strong enough to keep out these piddle-wits, if every gentleman in the realm does his part. How many can you turn out, Cromwell?'

'One hundred,' he says.

He wishes the ground would open and swallow him.

'One hundred,' the duke repeats. 'Clerks, are they?'

He is sending his builders from Austin Friars, and his cooks. Cooks are belligerent men, they are worth two. But to equip them he will need to go begging to the London armourers, and pay whatever they charge. He says, 'Everything I have is at the king's disposal.'

'I should hope so,' Norfolk says. 'Since everything comes from him in the first place. No disrespect, my lord. But your father was a pauper, all know.'

'Not a pauper, my lord. A roisterer, I concede. It was not money we lacked, so much as peace of mind.'

The duke grunts. 'You can handle a weapon, therefore. I hear you've killed men.'

'Who hasn't?'

At his back, he feels Call-Me stiffen in alarm.

'Not without cause, I dare say,' the duke concedes. 'And as God gave you other talents, beside the ruffian kind, it is proper to use them for the commonweal.'

The duke is doing his best to be civil. He is straining every sinew, as he paces and twitches and breaks off to bellow an order to a man at arms. But whiffs of hostility come from him – he can no more help it than a manure heap can help stinking. 'You can tell the king from me,' he says, 'that if his forces are extended in the north, he will be hard put to hold down the east country too.'

'Which is why it is the king's pleasure –' Wriothesley begins.

The duke turns on him. 'I'm talking to Cromwell. Who has been to war, which is more than you have, sir.'

'We have enjoyed the benefits of a forty-year peace,' Wriothesley says, 'under the most sagacious of kings.'

Norfolk glares. 'To maintain which, every gentleman must lead their tenants, and maintain his right and title – which we are right glad to do, and God defend our cause. This will find out traitors, I assure you.'

His eyes meet the duke's: those indented, fiery pits. 'I hear some of these rural stuffwits are proclaiming Mary,' the duke says. 'God knows who has stirred them towards that treason, but we can make a shrewd guess. If she moves an inch towards the rebels, I will not speak for her, I will not defend her, I will do naught.'

'Nor I,' he says.

'If the Scots were to come down ...' The duke gnaws his lip. 'We need every strong man. We need every brute who can wield a staff and every gentleman who can sit a horse. Henry wouldn't let my nephew out of the Tower, would he?'

'Tom Truth? No.'

'I only hope the king knows I had no part in his folly.'

It is a question, really; but he turns aside, and says to the duke, 'So the king's pleasure is – as Master Wriothesley here hoped to explain – that you linger neither in London nor near his person, but repair to your own country, there to ensure quietness –'

The fiery pits glint. 'What? There are no rebels in my country!'

'You must see there are not,' Rafe Sadler says. 'For now, my lord Suffolk takes command of the king's forces.'

'Brandon? That horsekeeper? By St Jude,' says the duke. 'Am I to be set aside? Me, of the best blood this nation affords?'

'It is all one, my lord,' Rafe says. 'Blood, I mean. We all come of the same parentage, if you go back far enough.'

'Any priest will tell you,' he says gravely.

The duke glares. He knows this is true. But he would prefer if there had been a special Adam and Eve, as forebears to the Howards. 'What about my son?' he says. 'What about Surrey? It appears I have offended his Majesty, God knows how, but surely he will not rebuff my son's service?'

'He says he'll see,' Call-Me says.

'See?' The duke is simmering. 'See? I had better ride to Windsor and meet my sovereign face to face. For I doubt not you misreport him.' Call-Me opens his mouth, but the duke says, 'One more word, and I'll gralloch you, Wriothesley. The king knows he has no more faithful servant in England than Thomas Howard.'

'My advice, my lord – if you will hear it –'

But the duke will not. 'I have followed the Tudor's words in every matter – as ever I shall, so help me God. Yet what fortune falls to me? The monasteries are pulled down, and every little jack and knave is paid. But where is my reward?'

'If you want abbeys,' Gregory says, 'you must apply to Richard Riche. The Master of Augmentations.'

'Apply?' The duke fairly spits the word. 'Why should I apply for what should be granted as of right?'

'It reminds me,' he says, 'I have a letter from my lady your duchess. She says it is four years now since you separated.'

'Aye. Best years of my life,' the duke says.

'She complains of scant living.'

'Her choice.'

'You don't want her back, but you don't want to maintain her?'

'Let her family keep her.'

'Sir, it is shameful,' Rafe says. His face flushes. 'Forgive me, but I cannot fail to speak, when I hear of a woman misused.'

The duke shoves his face into Rafe's. 'We all know about your woman, Sadler. We know you bought her out of a brothel, and so well-used they handed her over for the pence in a pauper's pocket.'

Rafe says, 'If you were not an old man, I would strike you.'

He, Lord Cromwell, steps between them. The duke says, 'I'll stick you, Sadler. I'll spit you like a pullet.'

'My lord,' he says, 'if there is anything I can do, to hasten your return to favour – count on me.'

The duke whirls away, cursing. 'You know in the north parts they use your name to frighten children? Be quiet, they say, or we'll fetch Cromwell.'

'Do they?' he says. '*Lord* Cromwell would be more polite.'

'Your title is still a novelty,' the duke says, 'and change is slow up there. Their view is, the fellow will be dead before we have to use it.'

As they cross the river on his barge, rain drives into their faces, and the flag with his coat of arms whips about its pole; the statue of Becket on the wall of the archbishop's palace is barely visible through the spray, but Bastings his bargemaster salutes the saint just the same.

'I'll have that traitor down,' he says. 'One day soon.'

'But sir, the rivermen hold him lucky.'

'You make your own luck,' he says.

They sit under the canopy. 'That was ill-considered,' he tells Rafe. 'Face-and-brace with the duke?'

'I have only done one foolish thing in my life,' Rafe says. 'I mean, in marrying Helen. And since those who have seen her know I was truly wise, I have not even that to set in my account. Therefore while I am still young enough, I am looking to run into danger. So I know how it feels.'

'Because we are not fighting men,' Wriothesley says, laughing. 'We must try our manhood where we find the opportunity.'

'Give me notice of the next time,' he says. 'And keep Uncle Norfolk out of it.'

He broods. He will stand up each one of his men against Norfolk's – cooks or clerks or masons. He will stand up himself, against the duke. Norfolk has tenants, but he has cash. If the duke has ancient blood, he has stomach. If the duke is an impregnable fortress, then he is a siege engine, he is God's catapult, he is the Warwolf; he is the trebuchet and the mangonel, crashing boulders into the walls and chucking body parts over them. People will tell him that the duke's walls are unbreachable, like the walls of Caerphilly, like Maynooth. But he believes there is no fortress that cannot be undermined or betrayed from within. He doesn't want Norfolk dead. He wants him alive and conformable. He wants him grateful.

He says to Wriothesley, 'Tell Riche. Treat with the duke for his requirements. Find out what abbeys he has in view.'

'I believed he maintained the old ways,' Wriothesley says. 'I hear he hates the scriptures. Now he is asking for profit from the monks' fall?'

'The Howards were merchants once,' he says.

Wriothesley says, 'I suspect we were all merchants once.'

'One hears,' Rafe says, 'that in Lincolnshire monks have come out with battle-axes, and are leading the rebel columns. The king says their vows will not save them, when the broil is over he will hang them up in their habits.'

They disembark. The steps are half under water, it threatens to lap over their boots. Richard will be lucky if he can get his cannon north of Enfield, he thinks, before he is bogged down. The rebels are now advancing on Lincoln. They are said to be ten thousand men mounted and armed, with another thirty thousand behind them, and their ranks increasing by five hundred every day.

'Let me go with Richard,' Gregory begs. 'For the honour of our house. Or with Fitzwilliam – he will have me in his train. He is keen to be killing rebels, he says he will eat them with salt.'

'You apply to your book, Master Gregory,' Richard says. 'You are not done learning yet. And look after your father.'

He has to get back to Windsor to the king. Government must still go forward, it does not stop because we are raising an army. Henry insists he will go up to Ampthill to the muster, and all must try to dissuade him. For the next weeks – who knows, perhaps for ever – he, Thomas Cromwell, will be on the sodden road west of London, or on the swollen river, while his carpenters and spit-boys and glaziers fight north and east through their own morass. He thinks of all the roads of the kingdom swilling into trackless mud, into drench and mire.

He goes out to say goodbye to Thurston. His chief cook is resolved to go with Master Richard to pepper some traitors, but he is tearful as he stands polishing a knife, turning it about, a glint on the blade. 'I remember your little lass Anne,' he says, 'when she came looking for eggs to paint. I offered her a brown egg from the bantam, and she says to me, "Thurston," – or rather, "Master Thurston," she says – "I want to paint the cardinal in his scarlet hat, and you give me this egg? Do you say to me he has a head the size of a thumbnail, and a complexion like a Moor? You must do better," she says. "Only a good-sized egg will answer, and a milk-white shell." You could not have put it better yourself.' Thurston blows his nose on his apron. 'God rest her. A milk-white shell.'

When he thinks of his daughters now it is as very little girls, clinging to their mother's skirts. He eases them away from him, to wherever the dead live now. He sits alone, under a blue ceiling newly painted with stars, in a chamber suited to the head of a house: lofty, airy, draughty. He closes the shutter, pulls his chair to the fire. He knows these eastern towns. Horncastle, Louth itself, Boston where he did much business when he was young, going to Rome once to represent their pious guild. He knows people in Lincoln who will report to him, and he has advance notice, from the rebels' camp, of their demands. He remembers Norfolk saying to him once, 'Give a pike to some tosswit and he is more dangerous than the greatest general, because he has nothing to lose.' If his informants are correct, the rebels are writing lists of demands, and what they demand – along with the restoration of the Golden Age – are amendments of certain laws that bear on inheritance, how they can dispose of their goods in their wills. These are not the concerns of simple people. What has Hob or Hick to leave behind him, but some bad debts and broken shoes? No: these are the complaints of small landowners, and men who don't like to pay their taxes. Men who want to be petty kings in their shires, who want the women to curtsey as they pass through the marketplace. I know these paltry gods, he thinks. We had them in Putney. They have them everywhere.

From the fireplace wall, there is a scrape and scratch. The spaniel at his feet scrambles up and shakes herself, her nose raised and twitching, her eyes shining in merriment; the marmoset is stirring in his night-box, and the dog hopes he will venture out. He remembers a lightless November afternoon: Anne Boleyn, her *moue* of distaste as she pulled her sleeve away from the tiny paw reaching for her hand. 'Who sent it? I don't want it. Because Katherine coveted such creatures does not mean I do.'

Someone in pity had made it a little wool jacket, and like a nervous petitioner the creature was shredding it with its nails: it shrank and twitched under the lady's hostile glance. 'I'll take it,' he said. 'It will thrive with me, I keep my houses warm.'

'Do you? How?' Anne was shivering even in her ermine.

'Smaller rooms, madam. You would not want those.'

She made a wry face. Cranmer had once said, she is afraid of what she has begun. 'Perhaps I shall give it all up,' she said. She pulled at the fur of her cuff, tugging gently as if to show what she would lose. 'Perhaps the king can never marry me, and I am a fool to think he can. Perhaps I shall give it all up, Cremuel, and come and live in your warm house with you.'

The town of Beverley is the first place north of the Humber to join the rebel cause. Thomas Percy, who is the Earl of Northumberland's brother, brings five thousand rebels down from the north-east. A one-eyed lawyer called Aske is leading the commons of Yorkshire.

First he said he was loath to do it, he said he was pressed – but that is what such chancers say. It is Aske who calls the rebellion a pilgrimage to the king: sometimes he calls it a pilgrimage for grace. He gives the rebels their emblem, raising over their ranks a banner of the Five Wounds. This is how Christ died: two nails in the hands and two in the feet, heart pierced by a lance.

The web of treason is sticky in the palm, and leaves its bloody smear: the pukers on the Louth cobbles, the fat confederates in the north, the abbots wiping their grease on their napkins and raising a glass of gore: the Scots, the French, Chapuys *mon cher*, Gardiner plotting in Paris, Pole at his dusty prie-dieu. When this is done, who will be master and who will be man? He pictures Norfolk in his armoury, polishing the plate: diligent he rubs, till he can see his swimming face. The king's companions are prepared to march. So scented, the courtiers, so urbane: the rustle of silk, the soundless tread of padded shoes. But slaughter is their trade. Like butchers in the shambles, it is what they were reared for. Peace, to them, is just the interval between wars. Now the stuff for masques, for interludes, is swept away. It is no more time to dance. The perfumed paw picks up the sword. The lute falls silent. The drum begins to beat.

By mid-October, the king's hand falls on Lincolnshire. Richard Cromwell writes to him from Stamford, where Charles Brandon has arrived with his power, and Francis Bryan with three hundred horse. The commons sue for pardon, and will hand over their ringleaders. Captain Cobbler is stripped of his borrowed coat. But can we send Charles north, to meet the next onslaught? Not unless we want trouble to break out again behind him.

Meanwhile, the storm-lashed King of Scotland has made landfall among the French. He has been seen at twilight in a lodging near Dieppe, his gentlemen about him, his manners so easy and free that no one knows who is gentleman and who is king: 'I do not think,' Henry says, 'that anyone could entertain a similar doubt in my case, and even if I were to dissemble' – he laughs – 'I doubt I would pass as a common fellow, unless I were to assume some disguise, and even then …' Scotland's ships lie at anchor in the bay, while James himself takes the Paris road, with the intention of marrying a French princess and thereby doing mischief to his English neighbour.

It is a pity James did not linger in Dieppe. It might have killed him. The townsfolk complain of a pest brought over from Rye. Contagion and false news cannot be stayed by officers of the excise.

Wriothesley says, 'Bishop Gardiner applies for instructions: how shall he bear himself if, as our ambassador, he should meet the King of Scots?'

He says, 'He should congratulate James on escaping the dangers of the deep. He has been on his voyage a good while.'

The king says, 'Tell Gardiner to do James no more honour than he must. I am, as all know, the rightful ruler of Scotland.'

Behind the king's back he makes a sign to Call-Me: you can leave that out of your letter.

'And if the French ask about the commotion in our shires,' the king says, 'let Gardiner assure them that I have an army at my command that is ready to humble any prince in Europe, and then have puissance remaining, for a second battle and a third.'

He can imagine with what shrugging, grimacing and eye-rolling this news will be received by François. 'Though the Tudor claims he has a hundred thousand men, all know he has but a fraction of that, and cannot trust his own commanders: or if he can trust some of them, he does not know which.'

And when you think about it, François will say, what did it take, fifty years back, to invade England and overthrow Crookback? A rabble of two thousand mercenaries, led by a man whose name no one knew.

Henry says, 'You can tell Gardiner, and any other person who enquires, that I will go against the rebels with the whole armed might of England, and so reduce them that their heirs will have to creep over the earth where they lie, and puzzle out their fragments with a magnifying glass.'

But meanwhile, what will he do? He will negotiate.

* * *

At Windsor, the king picks through his Italian songbook. The autumn rain beats at the glass. Dead leaves whisk through the air. *A la guerra, a la guerra, Ch'amor non vol più pace ...*

The king says, 'Where is Thomas Wyatt?'

'In Kent, sir. Raising his tenants.'

'How many can he fetch?'

'A hundred and fifty. Perhaps two hundred.'

A la guerra ... Love wants no more peace.

'How is Sir Henry Wyatt?'

'Dying, sir.'

'Will he leave me anything?'

'His son, sir. Begging as his last request that you will favour him.'

Tom Wyatt: his ardour, his faith, his verse.

The king says, 'Will Lord Montague bring his people to the muster?'

'He needs only a day's warning, sir.' He thinks, it will be interesting to see if he takes the field himself.

'Where is his brother Reginald?'

'Just left Venice.'

'For?' The king finishes his thought. 'Perhaps for Rome. In Rome they will be triumphing over me now.

'*Questa guerra è mortale*,' the king sings. 'Cromwell, I have forgot the words.

> 'Io non trovo arma forte
> Che vetar possa morte ...'

What weapon is strong enough, to shield me from death? He leafs through the manuscript, which is illuminated with larkspur, vine leaves and leaping hares. '*I am the tree the wind casts down, because it has no roots ...*' And Scaramella goes to war, boot and buckler, lance and shield.

Five wounds. Wife. Children. Master. Dorothea with her needle, straight between his ribs. One withheld? A man might survive them if they were evenly spaced, and he knew the direction from which they would come.

The king says, 'How many can Edward Seymour turn out?'

'Two hundred, sir.'

'And the Courtenays? My lord Exeter?'

'Five hundred, sir.'

'Richard Riche?'

'Forty.'

'Forty,' the king says. 'He is only a lawyer, of course.'

'I have ordered every coastal district to keep a strait watch for alien ships.'

The king plucks his lute string. '*Perché un viver duro e grave, Grave e dur morir conviene …*' My life hard, my death bitter, a ship that is wrecked upon a rock.

Prophets – and we are awash with them, though their better forecasts are made after the event – have assured us that this year the waters of Albion will run with blood. When he closes his eyes he can see the flow: not a river tumbling and bursting its banks, not a torrent roaring over stones, but a channel that is oily, crimson, a narrow slick rivulet, boiling beneath its surface: a slow, seeping, unstoppable flood.

In Yorkshire they sing that old complaint from John Ball's day:

> Now pride reigns in every place, and
> greed not shy to show its face,
> And lechery with never shame, and
> gluttony with never blame.
> Envy reigns with reason, and sloth is ever
> in season.
> God help us for now is the time.

III

Vile Blood

London, Autumn–Winter 1536

Aske: he is a petty gentleman, but the king places him at once – second cousin to Harry Percy, and kin to the Cliffords of Skipton Castle. Mr Wriothesley, newly attuned to the king's mind, marvels at Henry's knowledge of obscure family ties. In calling the process of the rebels a pilgrimage, Aske lends it the colour of piety. The aim of the Pilgrims, at divers times stated, is to have vile blood drained from the king's council, and the nobility of England set up again; to have Christ's laws kept, and restitution for injuries (as they call them) done to the church. Aske enforces an oath on those who come in his path.

He knows Robert Aske – to nod to, anyway. He is a member of Gray's Inn, sometimes in London on business for the Percy family. Being a lawyer, Aske cannot claim ignorance. He is aware it is a gross presumption to offer oaths in the name of the king. And he must foresee – for he must be acquainted with the chronicles – what the end will be: how rank the puddle in which he swims and will one day sink.

We have all grown up on tales of Jack Straw and John Amend-All – those brave days when the commons marched on London and killed the judges and foreigners. They pissed in rich men's beds, tore up their poetry books, and used altar cloths to wipe their arses. Their leaders were mean clerks and spoiled priests, Straw and Miller and Carter and Tyler, none of whom went by their right names; as for Amend-All, he is immortal, a self-made man green as spring, who noses up from his common grave whenever mutiny stirs. These rebels wrecked palaces and stormed the Tower of London itself. They smashed whatever they could find to smash – there were not so many mirrors in those days. On Cheapside they set a chopping block, and demanded the heads of fifteen of the king's councillors, including the Lord Privy Seal. If they could not catch the men they were hunting, they hung up their coats instead and shot them with arrows.

In those days the King of England was a child. There was no good governance. Labourers and craftsmen were oppressed by statute, every trade on a set wage, whatever the price of grain. They endured the poll tax – no wonder that they set the heads of its begetters on spikes. Yet all the while, like Robert Aske, they called themselves loyal subjects, and shouted, 'God bless our king.'

It is a hundred and fifty years since that broil. It is eighty years or more since Jack Cade called himself Captain of Kent and led his rabble to London Bridge. But to the *rustici*, you might as well say it happened last Easter, or before the Conquest. They say they want no taxes and will pay none, and they protest against imposts never levied and never imagined. And as the king says to him – when did you hear of a tax so light and pleasant that every man clamoured to pay it?

The common folk of England live on songs and tales and alehouse jokes. Spending their pence on candles to burn before holy images, they live in the dark, and in the dark take fright. Let us say a calf is born dead. By the time the tale crosses a field, it is a calf with two heads. Cross a stream, and it is a calf with two heads, chanting backwards in Latin, and some friar is charging a shilling for a charm against it. So it goes, in half a day, from abortion to Antichrist: and somehow, everybody is poorer except the priests. Pastors warn their flock that if they do not send tribute to Rome, trees will walk and crops will blight. They make them dread the fire of Purgatory, which eats to the bone; they ask, can you bear to see your dead folk burning – your helpless old mother, your dead little children, bound in agony and screaming for your prayers?

Now it is hard for them to hear the gospel news: there is no Purgatory, only Judgement. God is not a market trader, selling mercy by the pound. You cannot buy salvation, nor can you delegate a monk to work out your salvation for you.

'In Lincolnshire,' Mr Wriothesley says, 'they believed the Pope was coming to their aid, in his own person.'

The king snorts. 'They may as well say, a giraffe is coming. They do not know what a pope is.'

Perhaps they do not know what a king is either. Their leaders tell them that Henry has made himself God. Now if a child falls sick between Truro and Newcastle, they lay it at the king's door; if a well dries, if the butter spoils, if a bucket leaks: everything that is out of joint with them, from a fall of hailstones to a cricked neck, they blame on the court and council. Their grievances run like streams underground, welling up from the Scots border to Dover, till the whole land is flooded with nonsense. How is it some verse against Cromwell, sung in the street in Falmouth, is chanted next day in Chester? The further he travels from London, the stranger Cromwell gets. In Essex he is a scheming swindler, a blasphemer and renegade Jew. Spread him east to Lincoln and he is notorious for his knowledge of poisons. In the dales of Yorkshire he is a magus, with the stars and moon on his coat, while in Carlisle he is a ghoul who steals children and eats their hearts.

He, Lord Cromwell, goes to London, to keep his hand on the city. The rebels have no cannon, but London's walls are ornamental these days, you could knock them down with a dirty look. The Pilgrims boast they will strip the city bare and carry the glitter back to their caves. London dreads the north. Old people recall how Richard the usurper brought his outlanders down, bare-legged and wild-eyed, their speech uncouth, their actions worse: they burned ledgers for fuel, and would kill a man's geese in his own backyard.

At the Rolls House and Austin Friars, he receives the city worthies, to soothe them and spur them on. At the Tower he ships out the king's armaments and melts plate into coin. Then he hurries back to Windsor to parse true and false news and head the king's council; whoever is notionally in charge, he writes the agenda. All information that comes in, if it is fresh, is wrong: if it is stale, it is possibly accurate, but also useless. Every order that goes out from the king contains its countermand: if this has occurred, do that, but if you are delayed or deceived, by no means do the other, but write and ask us. Be cautious but don't delay. Strike boldly, but not too expensively. Use your judgement, but refer all to the king. The commanders in Lincoln, in Ampthill, in Yorkshire are trying to will themselves inside the heads of the councillors in Windsor, while the councillors strain to see far-off rills and bogs, dells and crags, cattle droves and goat tracks: terrain they have never visited, even in dreams.

Luckily, Lord Cromwell has been everywhere. He knows the eastern ports, the castles on the high fells. For the cardinal he used to ride to Durham. He could go north himself, get more certain news, and escort some of the king's treasure to pay the troops. 'But suppose they seized your person?' Mr Wriothesley says. 'Suppose they asked a ransom?'

'How much do you think Henry would pay? He should set my value against what I bring in to the treasury.'

Richard Riche frowns. 'And he should estimate, my lord, what you might bring in years to come, should God spare you.'

Call-Me suppresses a smile. Riche says, 'Why the sneer, Wriothesley?'

'It is not for any rebel to know Lord Cromwell's worth.'

Riche turns on him. 'You are not named in their songs, are you? Obscurity has its merits.'

Gregory says encouragingly, 'They will hate you once they know you, Call-Me.'

He says, 'I am sure you have deserved ill of them. They cannot find a rhyme for you, that's all. They are worse poets than Tom Truth.'

An army must be supplied. With the king's forces go the harness-makers and blacksmiths, the armourers, purveyors of soup kettles, bowstrings, blankets, buckets, trivets, rivets: and unless they are to go unpaid you need clerks to keep accounts, and the clerks need ink-horns and parchment and wax for seals. Each man in the field needs ale or beer, bacon and beef, salt fish and cheese, biscuits baked and not too old, peas or beans to boil in salt liquor, and a pot to boil them in. To get these things you need ready cash in a strong-box. When you are at war a promise will not do.

And as for the greater business of the realm – it does not stop because some arsewipes in the shires are waving pitchforks. Marriages are made and children born, and children grow and need new gowns, new household goods and minders. It is time Anne Boleyn's child began learning her letters. The Lady Mary longs for an infant of her own to love and in default she tries to love her half-sister; the child cannot be blamed, she says, for what her mother was. As her features emerge from baby flesh, Eliza is beginning to resemble less a piglet and more the king, so these days no one suggests she is Norris's by-blow. No child should be left floating queasily, in the space between fathers. She is still a bastard, of course. But even a bastard daughter has value on the marriage market, if the King of England acknowledges her: so her education should be that of a princess.

He has arranged a stipend for a young woman, Cat Champernowne, whom he knows to be kind and a good Latinist. He trusts Eliza will live to thank him. It is important a child's first tutor should be gentle and like a mother, so the child is not afraid of making mistakes. Look at Gregory, who now promises so well. His first tutor was Margaret Vernon, who was prioress at Little Marlow – a small house which closed this summer. Margaret has visited him in London, to exclaim over her pupil, his height, his looks, his manners. 'Where have the years gone? It seems only yesterday since he was learning his Pater Noster.'

No one should think he hates nuns, or monks either. Many of them have been his friends. He used to ride up to Little Marlow, making business in the neighbourhood. His mother-in-law Mercy said, 'What does she look like, this Margaret Vernon?'

He understood the question. 'She's not young.'

Gregory prospered with her. Now she must prosper in her turn. He makes a note: Margaret Vernon to Malling, Kent. Malling is a solid house, she will be well enough there: for as long as Malling lasts.

He thinks of Dorothea. He draws a monster in the margin of his papers. He thinks about Dr Agostino and his potions. If there is a mystery about the cardinal's death, he is no nearer to solving it. The solution, he must suppose, lies in the heart of the king.

When he goes to the queen's private apartments with Rafe and Call-Me, he finds her seated as usual among her women. Today everybody is sewing and no one singing; the queen's neckline is edged with goldsmiths' work, from which depend single fat pearls in the shape of tears. 'Highness,' he says, 'why not ask the king to fetch Lady Mary here?'

'That would cheer us up,' Jane Rochford says. 'She is famous for her japes.'

The women hide their smiles. He says, 'I think Lady Mary's health would improve with gentle company.'

'Do you?' Rochford says. 'I suppose it were pity if she went on praying till she wore out her knees. In the country one loses any looks one has.'

'Lady Rochford speaks from experience,' says Edward Seymour's wife.

Rochford says, 'If Mary is here with us, the rebels cannot take her. Nor she, for that matter, resort to them.'

'She would never do so,' he says. 'I have her pledge.'

Rochford folds her hands, smiling.

Jane the queen says, 'I would like her company, myself. I could ask the king. But he is displeased with me. Because I am not, yet.'

'With child,' Jane Rochford supplies.

The queen says, 'I hear agates are helpful. You lay them next the skin.'

'No doubt the Wardrobe will have some,' Rafe says. 'If not, we will get them. In Cornwall you can practically pick them up in the street.'

The queen looks surprised. 'In Cornwall? Do they have a street?'

Call-Me steps forward. 'If I may suggest, my lord Privy Seal? We might rehearse her Highness in a pretty speech? We might approach his Majesty by first praising him.'

Sound, he thinks. Let's try it. '"Sir,"' he begins, '"you have raised me to a sphere apart."'

'He has,' Jane says. 'And I heartily congratulate you, Lord Cromwell.'

'No, your Highness,' Jane Rochford explains. 'That is not what Cromwell says, that is what you say. "Sir, you have been pleased to set me above all other Englishwomen."'

'"I all unworthy,"' Wriothesley offers.

'"I unworthy,"' he says, 'that's very good – "exalting me into a sphere apart. With whom then can I be at ease? There is no lady of my rank with whom I can share a confidence."'

'Then continue,' Rafe suggests, '"Sir, out of your liberality and generous, fatherly heart, please to let the Lady Mary come to court, so that I may have comfort in her society, and be merry."'

'Let me try it,' Jane says. She takes a breath. '*Sir, out of your liberality* … Is it his liberality, or his something else?'

'Liberality has a fine ring to it,' Rafe urges.

'Then we'll proceed with liberality,' Jane says, 'and see where it gets us. But Lord Cromwell, I must raise a matter with you –' She nods to the ladies. They exchange glances and withdraw. Rafe, Wriothesley, both fall back. For a moment, unspeaking, the queen watches her court recede. Then she detaches from her girdle a small flask for rosewater. 'It is of great antiquity,' she says. 'The king gave it me. He says it is Roman.'

The glass in his hand is darkened, fragile as air. 'It's possible.'

'Once it contained a sacred relic. He did not say of which saint.' As if anticipating his question she says, 'I don't ask. I wait to be told.'

'I do the same.'

'The king tells me his dreams.' He wonders at the expression of dread on her face. 'He talks about when he was a child.'

'Women want to know about a man's childhood.' It had not struck him before, but he has never known a woman shun an anecdote, however mendacious.

'It is because they wish to love them,' Jane says. 'They cannot always love the man, but they think they could love the child he was.'

He feels unease. The glass is only a diversion – but from what? 'The king was a very handsome child,' he says. 'So it is reported.'

'Lady Rochford,' the queen says, 'could you stand off, please? No – further off. With the other ladies. Thank you.' She turns her face to him, her expression opening like a flower. 'He talks about his brother Arthur. He thinks he killed him.'

He is startled into simplicity. 'He didn't kill him. He just died.'

'He killed him with envy – with wishing against him. Even when he was very young, when he was Duke of York, he wished to be a king himself, even if not King of England. It was his intention, he says, to reconquer France, then Arthur would give it him as a reward.'

'Highness, wishes do not kill people.'

'Nor prayers?' Jane says. 'It is wicked to pray for our advantage at the expense of another. But we cannot always help what comes into our head.'

He says, 'There must be a mechanism. Like a gun or a knife or a disease.'

'But then, Henry says, he imagined all the misfortunes that might overtake his French war. Such as flux, mud, penury.'

'That was sage, in one so young.'

'But he thought, I should like to be a king anyway. And God read his heart. And so Arthur died, and Henry inherited all his brother's dignities and titles, and married Katherine his wife.'

'Or tried to marry her,' he says. He feels tired. 'It was not a real marriage, of course, that is established.'

'And Arthur never came home,' Jane says, 'but lies in a tomb at Worcester cathedral, where they left him at dead of winter. And Henry never goes to see him.'

After a moment she says, 'My lord? You are going to stand there and not speak?'

He says, 'Why now?' Cranmer and I believed we had vanquished that spectre: in one winter's night of persuasion and prayer, refined Arthur into thin air. But it seems Henry withheld something. We took him for the helpless victim of a spirit, rudely appearing. We did not know his shame fetched it.

He says, 'If the king raises the matter I shall say it was a child's fantasy, and he should dwell on it no more.'

'Thank you. I tried my brother, Lord Hertford, in this matter. But he said, "Tush, sister, superstition."'

'Did he?' He smiles.

'You may go,' the queen says. 'If anyone asks what we spoke of, tell them I wanted to show you the glass and know about the Romans. I do not believe everything the king tells me.'

Rafe and Call-Me follow him out. They are twitching with curiosity. Call-Me says, 'Do you think she will make bold and ask? About Mary?'

Rafe says, 'I hope she will, because if Mary is here, no misunderstandings can arise, about who she meets or writes to.'

'You see?' Lady Rochford is behind them. 'Even your own people do not trust Mary. But she will come with all speed. I hear she pines for you, Lord Cromwell.'

He takes her arm and steers her away. She is his ally, like it or not. She snaps, 'I have deserved gentler treatment at your hands. And at the queen's, I may say.'

He lets go. She rubs her arm, as if he had injured her. He thinks, if wishes were death, I would be superfluous to the state. Henry hated both his wives at divers times, but they spitefully lived on, until God put an end to one, the French executioner to the other. Henry could not wish them away, for all his power. Only I could do that. It is I who tell him who he can marry and unmarry and who he can marry next, and who and how to kill.

But perhaps it will not matter, he thinks. Perhaps the Yorkshiremen will come and slay us all.

The queen makes her request before Henry in sight of the court. Note his alert face, the modest inclination of her head. 'Sir,' she begins, 'out of my unworthiness, you have been – what? – liberal. I am in a sphere. Please to bring the Lady Mary to court. I may have comfort in her society, and share a confidence.'

Henry looks at her in tender bewilderment. 'Are you lonely, sweetheart? Of course we will have her, if it will make you merry.'

'Merry. That was the word I forgot.' Jane does not smile. She sinks low to the ground, collapsed inside a stiff tent of brocade and satin. 'Will you hear me?'

What now? He tries to catch Rochford's eye, but the whole assembly is staring at the queen. 'My heart is moved, sir, by the divisions that arise between your subjects and your most sacred self.'

There is a rustle of consternation. This is not Jane's own language, surely?

Henry gazes at her. 'I take these words as they are meant. A queen has a double duty. As a wife, she feels for her husband when he is troubled. As a queen, she feels as a subject to her lord.'

'I am only a woman,' Jane says. 'I do not presume to be wiser than your Grace. But my heart misgives when honourable and devout customs are left off, sanctified by usage since the world began. We must cherish them, as a son or daughter will cherish an aged father.'

Henry frowns. 'What customs?'

'Nan!' he says to Edward's wife. 'Nan, quick.'

Lady Seymour steps forward, 'Madam –'

Jane says, 'Your people want the Pope of Rome. They want the statues they have known all their lives, and blessed candles, and holy days.'

Nan Seymour is urgent: 'Madam –'

'Let her be,' Henry says. 'She should be instructed, and who but I should do it? How is it, that for all the preachers who set forth the king's supremacy, for all that has been said and written, there are still those who do not grasp that the Bishop of Rome is merely a foreign prince, out to conquer if he can? Madam, I will have no alien interfere with my rule, and I will allow no traitor to shelter behind the cross of Christ.'

Jane says, 'They think you will take their silver crosses and turn them into coin.'

Henry says, 'The simple people may believe it, but who leads them to do so? What manner of pastors are they, the priests and abbots who break their oath to me, and are first in the fray, swords in their hands?'

'They would still pray for the king,' Jane says, as if bargaining, 'if they could pray for the Pope too.'

He thinks, I must end this if the king will not. 'Madam, there can be no double jurisdiction. Either the king rules, or Rome.'

'And it is not a question,' Wriothesley warns.

Henry says, 'Her Grace will withdraw.'

Jane is shaking. 'They are too much burdened with taxes.'

The king leans forward. 'The burdens of tax do not rest on the shoulders of labourers, or small husbandmen. Dives, the rich man, knows and has always known how to pass off his interests as the interests of Lazarus, the beggar.'

Jane stares at him. 'Yes. Possibly. I do not understand the subsidy or the revenue. But my lord – take care of your thoughts as well as your deeds. What you say by night haunts you by day, and what you refuse by day will return by night.'

Nan Seymour takes one arm, Jane Rochford takes the other; they lift her to her feet. The king says, 'Jane, understand this – I dispose for my subjects, body and soul. A prince answers before the strait court of Heaven for his proceedings, and when he dies will be judged by standards of which ordinary men are quit. God gives him graces: God gives him wisdom, policy and prudence, and these virtues are his to exercise, by methods of which he is the only arbiter. I am the earthly shepherd of God's sheep. It is a prince's part to provide not only for noble families but for obscure ones, and not only for scholars and magistrates but for the untutored and the poor, for the whole commonwealth of his people – both for their corporeal welfare, and their spiritual good.' He adds, benign, 'The duty is laid on me, and the world shall see me discharge it.'

'Amen to that,' Mr Wriothesley says. The courtiers clasp their hands together – they would applaud, if the king gave the nod. The Lord Chancellor murmurs, 'Eloquence, sir.' There is a rumble of appreciation from Sampson, Bishop of Chichester; the Earl of Oxford, who is Lord Chamberlain, sighs like a farm-girl in a feather bed.

The king says, 'We are willing to consider all lawful petitions. Willing to spare any ceremony or image, if it is not baneful. However.'

He lifts his eyes, and positions his gaze deliberately above the head of his wife. 'When you are fruitful, that will be the time we give ear to your complaint.'

As the women draw Jane away, 'Follow,' he says curtly, to Rafe, to Call-Me. He wants this crowd dispersed. It is like when a cart overturns in the street. 'Pass along,' the constables shout. 'Nothing to see, pass on.'

Wriothesley catches his arm. 'Has Carew been with her? Or the Courtenays?'

'Perhaps,' he says, 'it proceeds from her own misled and gentle heart. She lacks good companions. I wish her sister Bess Oughtred might be got from the north.'

Rafe slaps his arm to alert him: Lady Rochford at sword's length. She says, 'I hope you don't blame *me*.'

He says, 'It hadn't occurred to me. But now that you mention it …'

He thinks, you have destroyed one queen, is one enough?

Richard Cromwell writes from the town of Lincoln, which has now been seized back for the king. The gentlemen are disappointed that the foe has melted away. They went out to shed blood, not to parlay. Richard feels cheated himself, it is clear. The work he does, doorkeeper to his uncle, is not warlike enough for his nature.

Charles Brandon, to pin Lincolnshire down, will need to reserve a force and keep it in the field for the duration. 'What is Charles doing?' the king says. 'I hope he is not too lenient. He should make an example of these beasts. Their women will creep to him, I suppose, and sue for pardon. Charles cannot abide to see a woman weep.'

'We are none of us indifferent to it,' he says. Henry stares at him.

It has never been possible to count the king's subjects – not with certainty. Only the angels know how many are baptised and how many buried. We have the muster rolls of years past to see what each district can marshal: what archers, pikemen, how many horse and foot; how many helmets and coats of mail, what spears, war hammers, poll axes, swords; what gentlemen they have to lead them, whether novices or veterans. But we do not have windows into hearts, to say who is true. There is no single enemy, there is no one place he is; when one head is cut off then, Hydra-like, he grows another. They are rising in Cumberland and Westmorland and as far south as Derbyshire. In the towns of north Yorkshire they gather ten thousand strong. From Durham they descend with the banner of St Cuthbert, streaming silks of crimson and white. In Cumberland, four captains go in procession with relics before them. They have trumpeters, and heralds crying out their names: Captains Pity and Charity, Poverty and Faith.

He has their true names: Rob Mounsey and Tom Burbeck, Gilbert Whelpdale, John Beck. Captain Cobbler, the great traitor of Louth, is a shoemaker by trade, as his name may well attest: under his real name, Nicholas Melton, he will answer when the day comes. Meanwhile we can guess, from reports reliable and unreliable, that in the north fifty thousand men are in the field. There is no army the king can command or deploy that can meet, outmanoeuvre or halt such a force.

So: talking must hold the rebels back. But by now the king hardly wants to talk. He does not ask if the rebels' demands are reasonable. He says he is their sovereign and they have no right to make any demands at all.

At his palace in Kenninghall, the Duke of Norfolk chafes and fumes, igniting himself like one of the rebel beacons, firing off several letters a day. He burns to fight: release him to go north; he will go tonight, by God, he will not be stayed! He will even serve under Brandon, he pleads. In Windsor young men pass the duke's letters around, smirking: they are all Lord Cromwell's servants, his *discepoli*, flocked after him from London. They see out the day with him, eating and drinking and talking of God and man till the candles burn down; and they see it in with him, keen as little dogs that scratch your door at first light.

The weather is not fit to hunt, so the grooms who keep the king's outer apartments do not stir much before six. They rise by custom, by regulation, for unless he is sick or at the chase the king's mornings are the same. The grooms rouse the esquires of the body, who take up their pallets, wash and dress themselves and carry in the king's under-linen. It is they who hear the king's first words each day, his first prayers, and report any special requests he has, so Lord Cromwell may see them on their way to fulfilment. One day Henry says, his voice sleepy, 'Could you fetch Norris?'

They gape at each other. Each man struck dumb. The king pushes back the coverlet, as if impatient.

'Sir,' one ventures, 'Norris is dead.'

The king yawns. 'What?' He spoke out of his dream, and as his feet hit the floor, he has forgotten it.

But the grooms stumble out, babbling: 'My lord Cromwell ...'

'He must have been half-asleep. But tell me if he asks for Norris again.'

Mr Wriothesley laughs. 'Why, are you going to supply him?'

Riche says, 'You cannot raise the dead.'

'No? That's not my experience.'

He nods to the esquires: they bow in their turn, and go in to Henry with their perfumes and linen cloths. It is their honour to rub down the king's person till his skin is tender and pink, then raise the lids of cedar chests and shake out his shirts, soft as April air. All those garments are gone long since, that Katherine embroidered with Spanish blackwork, and now they are stitched by paid and proficient hands, with lions and laurel crowns.

Hovering beyond the door, inventories in hand, is the Yeoman of the Wardrobe. A page bears a box of jewellery so the king can make choice; but first the king sits on his velvet stool for his barber. While his beard is trimmed and his hair combed his physicians come in, and gather in a black knot with their basins and urine flasks. They smell his breath, and enquire into his sleep and dreams.

The poor labourer owns his sleep and his stool, and can sell his piss to the fuller, whereas the king's piss and stool is the property of all England, and every fantasy that disturbs his night hours is recorded somewhere in a book of dreams, which is written in the clouds massing over the fields and forests of his realm: every stir of lust, every frightful waking. Should he be costive, he is ordered a potion; should his bowel be loose, its product is taken away in a bowl under an embroidered cloth. They can only judge what is within him, by what comes out: a pity he is not made of glass.

Then a signal passes room to room, hot water comes in a silver ewer, and cloths of diamond weave and the softest nap: scissors clink in a basin, and the most deft of the esquires cleans and re-bandages the sore leg. The process brings tears to the king's eyes. He jerks his chin away, and studies the tapestry or the ceiling. 'All done, sir,' they say, as if to a little child.

Unsteadily, he stands: is Cromwell there, any news? In his closet he kneels at his prie-dieu, his chaplain ready beyond the lattice. The king's prayers are Latin prayers, and his hand beats his breast: his head bows, for we are all sinners, we sin as we breathe. Why is it when our eyes water with pain our mouth fills with the taste of phlegm and blood? Why do tears sting, after they have been blinked away? With a creak of wood he stands, leaving the cleric in a private cloud of incense: and as soon as he leaves his inner rooms, a laundress creeps in for yesterday's shirts and the soiled bandages, and the king's bed is unmade, the sheets tossed onto the floor, his velvet coverlets shaken and folded: beating and scrubbing begins, scouring, for no speck of dust can ever come under his eye, lurking in the pinions of a carved angel, or in the plaster curls of a Wild Man, or between the toes of a marble god.

Once the king leaves his inner rooms and enters his privy chamber, his natural body unites to his body politic: here he is dressed and presented to the world, a bulky, new-barbered man scented with rose oil. As rebels run free in the north, and the members break faith with the head, a kind of mutiny or civil war has broken out in the king's body.

The doctors stop him: 'Lord Cromwell, you have influence with our sovereign: could you persuade him to rise earlier from table?'

'Not I,' he says. A man who is accustomed to hard riding will fatten when he leaves off, and he knows it from his own person. When he was young in the cardinal's service he would ride forty miles a day, forty the next, forty the day after: many horses but only one Cromwell. These days he is coddled by clerks who chase about at his whim. He says, I am fifty, and even at thirty I was never lean. He does not take his belly, as the king does, as an insult to God's design, nor dwell on days when he did great exploits in the saddle. After Mass the king sits with Gregory working through the score sheets from old tournaments. Their voices are low and absorbed, their heads together, decoding the notches on the staff: jousts are transcribed like music, the anthems of violent and passionate men. 'See where he misses.' Henry's fingers stab the line. 'That is not because he is unskilful, but because he is aiming for the head.'

'It is chancier, sir,' his son says.

'But here he aims lower and begins to succeed. Two hits, and on the third he breaks his lance. Atteint, atteint – and then, broken on the body.'

The joust is not his model for public affairs. You don't want your opponent to see you coming. The last thing you want is a tent and a flag. Mr Wriothesley complains of the time wasted. 'I see it makes him happy, impressing young Gregory. But as far as business is concerned, not enough is done to justify the royal hour.'

The king flaps the score sheets down. 'I could have made a living at it, riding through Europe, one tournament to another, if I had not been called to rule.' His hands knead Gregory's shoulders: 'Look how this young master is putting on muscle.' He ruffles his hair. 'Daily practice is what I advise. If you cannot get into the tilt yard, still you can wear your armour for an hour. That way, you start to bear the weight as if it were a silk jerkin.'

'Sir, even on a Sunday?' Gregory says.

'Ask your father.' The king winks. 'He is over the church, you know. I know him for an unholy fellow, making up accounts on the Sabbath, rattling away on an abacus and taking his pleasure. So why should you not have your sport? There is nothing like the wearing of harness, for any man who wishes to be lean as well as strong. With the heat inside, surplus runs from you like fat from a spit-roast.'

There are those who believe – and perhaps the king is one of them – that the health of the land depends on the health of its prince, and on his beauty besides. If you speak of an ordinary man you might say, 'He cannot help his face.' But a king must learn to help it. If he is ugly, so is the commonwealth. If the king is sick, so is his realm. Old men will tell you how the king's grandfather King Edward grew soft in middle age, his eye always rolling in the direction of any woman at court, wife or maid, under the age of thirty. He lolled on a daybed with supple flesh, while his own brothers plotted against him, and when one brother was dead the other plotted alone: so golden a prince, lucky on the battlefield, blessed by God, was spoiled by sloth and neglect of business, because you cannot have your hand on your ministers when your fingers are creeping up a cunt. Even King Edward's sons, two likely young sprigs, were pulled out like weeds and their corpses thrown God knows where.

He tells the doctors, 'You forget the king is a newly married man. A man who wishes to produce strong children cannot do it on a vegetable diet.'

True, the doctors say, but neither can he eat as much as he did when he exercised every day. Not without an imbalance of the humours and congestion in the organs, a sluggish digestion and a fat liver.

Afternoon: he sits with the king in his library, where books are kept in great chests, volumes covered with embroidered velvet or scented leather, emblazoned with the royal arms or the badges of former owners. When our forefathers defeated the French under Great Harry, we shipped their manuscripts home across the sea. They were mirrors for princes, texts that prescribed how to be a king: they were written for kings to read.

'Great Harry was not only a soldier,' the king says. 'He took his harp on campaign. He composed songs, but all of them are lost.'

In the king's prayer book is portrayed King David, who plays his harp. Turn the page: David studies his psalter – it is an edition, in miniature, of the volume our king now holds. His red beard curled, his gown loose, the King of Israel sits at his leisure, holding in his hand the very book in which he is pictured.

'Come, Gregory,' the king says. 'You are fond of stories of Merlin. My father had many books made about him. Choose and read.'

'Are you not afraid of him?' Gregory says. 'His prophecies?'

'Not I,' the king says. 'Merlin has been killing me these ten years. I have had my bones rotted and my head cankered, and as for London Bridge, I cannot count how many times it has crumbled, and this very castle in which we now sit washed downriver and into the sea. I am inclined now to doubt when I hear his pronouncements.'

'Wizards are made like other men,' Gregory says. 'Offer Merlin an abbey. It could not hurt.'

'Tell the Master of Augmentations,' the king says, laughing. 'I shall like to see Riche's face.'

He is surprised the king does not burn such books. Merlin is popular in certain quarters, and you can see why he gets so much credit. He foretold a day would come when churches would be flattened and monks forced to marry; where German heathens sat at table with the king, and true noblemen were herded starving from the hall. But of course, Merlin also said that the river Usk would boil, and that bears would hatch out of eggs; that the soil of the future would become so rich that men would leave farm work and spend their days in fornication.

The scholar John Leland, the king's antiquary, is travelling through the land looking to see what the monks have, that might be good for the king's own libraries. He himself, on his journeys for Wolsey, would ask to see anything of interest. Often as not, he would meet with stony-eyed exclusion: 'Sir, I regret that text was lost years ago.' Or, 'Ah, no, Master Cromwell, I fear the worm has got it.'

He says, 'They thought I might steal their prizes for the cardinal.'

'He was known to be acquisitive,' the king says.

He looks away. Sometimes the king speaks well of Wolsey. Sometimes not.

The king says, 'What happened to the cardinal's books of conjuring?'

'I have no memory of them, sir.'

'Perhaps my lord Norfolk took them,' Gregory says. 'He took most things.'

The king says, 'Is it true that Wolsey had the spirit of Oberon bound to him, to serve for a term of years?'

'I don't credit such tales, Majesty. They're only to get money out of you.'

'I only partly credit them myself,' Henry says. 'But Oberon is a very powerful spirit.' The king stirs, he rubs his leg, he gets to his feet. 'Walk,' he says.

Mr Wriothesley falls in with them, and Richard Riche. The king cannot wander about his palace by himself. The yeomen of the guard, who assemble in the watching chamber, are supposed to line his route. Where is the queen? In her own apartments, among the women: but her offence forgiven. 'She pities the poor,' the king says. 'It is a woman's part. I would not have her otherwise. And she hates all talk of war. She fears for my person. It is largely to soothe her that I have not gone north myself.'

He sees Wriothesley and Riche exchange a glance. Riche says, 'Your Majesty has never been north, I think? Though what reason to go now, of course – among ingrates who more regard their goblins than their God?'

The king says, 'A man who has reigned twenty-eight years, not passing a day without the cares of state, should be able to place his faith in his liegemen. Among the northern lords I mistrust Lord Dacre, but not only he. I thought I could count on Lord Darcy, yet even as he prates of his loyalty he complains of his rupture and his stiff joints.' The king looks down from the oriel window, over the new terrace. 'Let us hope he can oil himself and go into action, but now he tells me that at Pontefract the garrison is under strength, they have no guns, they cannot feed all who flock there, and the walls are falling down. Why does he tell me this, except to discourage me?' The rain slashes against the window. 'And the Earl of Derby – it is known there are malcontents in his train and they hate you, Cromwell – besides, all Stanleys are turncoats, they will watch to see which way the battle goes before they join it. Now Henry Clifford –'

'Our strength in the border,' Riche puts in.

The king frowns. 'His tenants grumble against him even in years of plenty, so will they obey him now?'

'Clifford is a hard man,' he says. 'Even Norfolk says he is a hard man, but we can count on him. As also Lord Talbot with his great train –'

'Always our mainstay,' Riche offers. *Our?*

The king says, 'Talbot is another ancient man – but yes, loyal to me and mine.' He stops, grimaces. 'Norfolk, I suppose, must be permitted to ride north.'

Norfolk's father was seventy when he sliced up the Scots at Flodden. Our duke has some seven years left, to do anything as famous as that. 'Norfolk will work hard for your favour,' he admits. 'He relishes a battle, even if it is only country folk. He thinks we have enjoyed peace too long.'

'I tell you what it is, the loyalty of the Howards.' Henry limps; he puts out a hand to steady himself against the Lord Privy Seal. 'John Howard, who was grandfather to the Norfolk that is now, was known to declare that if a stock of wood or a standing stone were King of England, he would defend its title – if it were named so by Parliament.'

'It shows a high regard for the standing of Parliament,' Richard Riche murmurs.

'But he fought against my father!' The king turns on Riche. 'Do you not comprehend that, you dolt? He took Richard Plantagenet for king.'

Riche draws back into himself so far that he seems to be trying to retract into his ribs, like a man squeezed by Skeffington's Daughter. He begins his apologies, but he – Lord Cromwell – cuts him off. Young men, and Riche is young enough, do not understand that to this very day, nothing in this kingdom counts so much as how your forefathers behaved on the field at Bosworth.

'The Howards made a grievous error there,' Mr Wriothesley says. 'And it cost them their dukedom.' He is so keen to distance himself from Riche's folly that he has passed to the other side of the king and appears to be hanging on his elbow.

'The present Howard keeps before him that example,' he says. 'He would never offend.'

'Well, he does offend,' Henry says. 'And I perceive that you, Riche, do not know what a king is. A king is made by God, not Parliament. Parliament proclaims his title, furbishes his authority – but where in the scriptures does it mention Parliament? *Contra*, there are numerous mentions of what submission the subject owes to his prince, and of how the powers that be are ordained of God. If these Pilgrims cleaved to true religion as they claim, they would know this. And they would beg pardon on their knees and straightway go home.'

'And would you pardon them, sir?' Mr Wriothesley asks.

'Stand further off, Call-Me,' the king snaps. 'I don't like to be crowded.'

Mr Wriothesley's mouth drops open. Call-Me? How has this private joke rolled into the public sphere? Henry is displeased; he signals to them to fall behind, and limps on alone, into the darkening afternoon.

'I perceive your fingers were a-twitch for pen and paper,' he says to Riche. 'But he has said it all once, and he will say it again.'

There are things the king has not voiced, yet must suspect: that behind the banner of the Five Wounds, there are other invisible banners, sewn with the emblems of the Courtenays and Poles. Gentlemen of ancient houses have turned out to defend the Tudor – but they must be watched closely, their deeds as well as words. Some captured rebels have freely confessed that they hope the Pope will send another king, Reginald Pole by name, who will wed the Princess Mary, and turn her father Henry out to beg. The Pilgrims claim they crusade for the Virgin in her innocence and purity. But knowingly or not, they serve the pride of Gertrude Courtenay and Margaret Pole – the young woman who would like to be queen of England, the old woman who deems she already is.

'Sir,' Richard Riche pulls at his elbow, 'I have notification – that is, I am required – I am advertised that I could be useful, that I should go up to York, that I should show myself –'

'Why don't you do that?' he says. 'York might be safer than here.'

Mid-October: at Lincoln Richard Cromwell is now encamped with Fitzwilliam and Francis Bryan. He is called into every council, and gives Fitz credit for it. Other lords would prefer to keep him out, but Fitzwilliam stands our fast friend, he writes: no one may speak ill of Cromwells, in his presence. He writes that Bryan hopes to encounter Aske in single combat: two one-eyed men grappling for glory, as in tales of old. He writes he misses his home and his uncle: 'Comfort my poor wife.'

He wonders, should he bring Frances under his own roof? He is not short of roofs; she might go to Stepney or Mortlake. If any malcontents should penetrate London, they would attack Austin Friars. God knows what they would expect to find. A great heap of treasure: confiscated chalices winking with gems. Precious relics, such as twigs from the burning bush, and a box of the manna that fell on the Israelites in the desert.

He writes to Richard in his own hand: here we are all well if not contented, Mrs Richard is impatient for your return as am I but the king must be served, temperately, carefully. At idle times, while you are waiting for action to begin, do not let your companions draw you into games of chance. If you refuse they will jeer, look at Cromwell's nephew, he is not good for the money: but if you take part, they will find some excuse to brand you a cheat. We are agreed Norfolk and his son must join the campaign; but if you come in young Surrey's path, get out of it, he will work you a mischief if he can. Do not be drawn by any slander to myself. They will say what they must to provoke you, at a time when every man's weapon is ready in his hand.

He ends each day buried under a weight of dispatches; with every piece of news that comes in, he seems to know less. If Aske were fighting in your own cause, you would call him a robust captain, and godly too, because he directs his ragbag army to pay for what it takes from the country people. But do his soldiers heed him? Or have they run beyond his control? Loyal gentlemen fleeing the north bring their reports. Aske says, hold back: his sergeants say, march. Aske says, don't ring the bells, his soldiers ring the bells; he says, don't fire the beacon, and they fire it. His own brothers have deserted his side and galloped for sanctuary. And yet they say his rise was foretold in a prophecy. The north has long been expecting him, a one-eyed messiah. How did he lose his eye? No one knows.

Henry says: 'Vile blood: what is it, that these rebels cry it down? There have always been mushroom men.' Grown up overnight, he means. 'Both my father and my grandfather would agree, a common man can be as good a servant as a duke. Being humble-born, they have no interests of their own – only solicitous to serve their master, from whom they derive all their fortune.'

He says, 'If my lord of Norfolk were here, he would tell your Majesty that, having no family, such men have no honour. They will do anything, without scruple.'

'But they have souls to save,' the king says. 'So not *anything*, I do suppose. Did you know Reginald Bray? Bray came from nothing. Worcester grammar school, if I recall. But he was a wise and expert man in my father's cause. The great lords had to be very pleasant to him, for they feared every word he might drop in the king's ear.'

Bray must have been dead thirty years, more; how could he have known him? But the calculations of princes run beyond mortal span. He says, 'I know his resting place, sir.'

Bray is buried here at Windsor, within St George's, which his munificence helped build. (Though so is John Schorne, a priest who conjured the devil into a boot.) He has seen Bray's emblem high in the air, his rebus frozen in stone and glass. I should find one at ground level, he thinks, and abase myself on it. Bray took over the king's finances; he made money for himself by the way. Henry says, 'The labourer is worthy of his hire. Bray went into battle against the Cornish rebels. He acquitted himself gallantly.'

For a clerk, he thinks. Is the king suggesting that he should put down his pen and pick up a sword? Despite all that has been said?

'You remember the Cornish,' Henry says.

He nods. 'I was a boy then.'

'My father took us to the Tower. He had faith in that fortress to stand, even if they looted the city.'

It is not just in the north they hate taxes. At the fringes of the kingdom they do not understand England to be one nation, with borders we all must pay to defend. When the Cornish broke out in rebellion they said they would not pay to secure the north against the Scots, for they did not know what a Scot was. They were led by a lawyer, one Thomas Flamank, and a blacksmith they called An Gof: 'blacksmith' is what it means, his name tells you what he was. Gathering forces as they rolled up-country, they marched towards London, and before them strode a giant, name of Bolster. Possibly he did not lead them but guarded their rear, for nobody saw him – he was always out in front or just behind.

At the Williamses' house in Mortlake, where he ran errands in exchange for his dinner, they poured scorn on giants, roaring with laughter as they told the story of one of Bolster's Cornish mates, a sad and lonely giant who played quoits on Sundays with his only friend, a spry lad called Jack. One day the giant patted Jack on his pate, and his fingers went through the bone as if it were piecrust. The giant's cries made the welkin ring, while Jack's brains ran down his chin like gravy.

He told his sister Bet, 'Giants were descended from Cain, who killed his brother. There were hordes of them on the earth before they drowned in Noah's flood. They were tall, but not so tall their heads came above the water.'

Bet said nothing.

He said, 'Trojan Brutus fought those that survived, and put them to the sword. He was the mighty man who invented London.'

Bet said nothing again.

'Bolster?' he said. 'Is that really his name? Because that's ridiculous.'

Bet said, 'Are you going to tell him that to his face?'

The more nobody saw Bolster, the more the fear of him grew. He was ten foot tall, or twelve foot, with arms like the sails of a windmill and iron-shod feet that could burst a head like a grape. In Putney, their homes stood in the path of the rebels; and he a boy, some twelve or thirteen years old, stood ready to knock hell out of Bolster's kneecaps.

In that commotion time, Walter turned a shrewd penny, outfitting his friends in third-hand armour, bashing breastplates into shape. Privately he said he feared not, because he knew about the Cornishmen's ale. It takes twenty-four hours to make, and they brew it wherever they camp. They down it by the pail, creamy brown and fizzing, and it gets you drunk like nothing else. Then it makes you spew all next day.

At Blackheath the rebels were destroyed by the king's army. Many knights were made on the battlefield that day. An Gof and the lawyer were hanged and quartered, their bloody parts sent back to be displayed where they were born. But Bolster was never hanged. No gallows would be strong enough. The world is wide and he is in it somewhere. Perhaps he lies fathoms deep, breathing through his gills like a fish, till he is ready to swim up to the light and begin his career afresh. A giant is not used to inaction. Nor is my lord Privy Seal. This frustration, this constraint, as the last of the leaves fall and the early frosts begin, takes him back to his early life, before Bolster was thought of, and before he set his foot on the ladder to rise in the world: before he knew there was a ladder: back to the days when other people were in charge of his fate: before he knew there was fate: when he thought there was only the smithy, the brewery, the wharves, the river, and even London seemed distant to him, or, to speak truth, he had no idea of distance: when he was no more than seven years old, and his uncle John and his father settled his destiny between them, and he said scarcely a word.

His uncle John said: 'I tell you what, brother. Thomas is no use to you yet, he is only underfoot. So why don't you let me train him up?'

They're inside the doorway of the brewhouse. The smell blankets him. He comes up to John's elbow. His father is moving in the dimness, heaving some chests around; he wonders what's in them.

'Oh, just stand there, brother!' Walter says. 'Just stand there and watch a man break his back!'

John says, 'Do me courtesy of listening when I speak to you.'

Walter dumps the box he is hauling. 'What?'

'Let me take Tom to Lambeth. The kitchen steward's a good friend to me.'

'You want to make him into a cook? No lad of mine will be known as Platterface.'

'He won't be bound,' John says. 'What harm?'

'I suppose he can make me a posset in my old age. Stew a fowl. All right.' Walter laughs. He thinks he'll never be old. He thinks he'll always have teeth. 'Mind, Tom, obey your uncle, or you'll be baked in a pie.'

'You'll be minced.' John slaps him around the head to seal the agreement. Already there's something solid about him, that inclines people to cuff and slap him, perhaps because it makes a satisfying noise. But as they walk away, John says, 'You need a skill, Tom. You don't want to be like your dad, good at nothing but trouble.'

He says, 'There's a box under his bed with three padlocks.'

'Gold, I don't doubt,' John says. 'Where from I don't like to think. But take him out of his parish, and how would he thrive? They all know him in Putney and none dares cross him. But let him walk abroad without his bully boys, then it's a different tale.'

Think of that. For the first time, he imagines Walter through the eyes of an indifferent stranger: sees a squat bruiser, unshaven, his belt holding him together. A scoffing, jeering ruffian, looking for a fight; and being Walter, he never looks far. Everybody's agin him and hoping to do him down, filch what's his. Filch them first, is Walter's maxim, and that's how he thrives. He clip-clops through life to the sound of other people grieving: sniffing out weakness, anybody sad or lost, so he can inflict them.

He says to John, 'Everybody in Mortlake knows my dad. Everybody in Wimbledon. I'll get the smithy when he's dead.'

'What's going to kill Walter,' his uncle asks, 'unless the hangman? You'll be a labourer till you're thirty if you wait on him. I can't teach you his business, but I can teach you mine. You need a trade you can carry with you. Even in a foreign country folk always want cooks.'

'I wouldn't know their dishes,' he says.

'A light hand with a sauce, and you're welcome anywhere.' John sniffs. 'I'd like to see Walter make a cream sauce. The bugger would curdle as soon as he looked at it.'

He thinks, my uncle is jealous. My father is a famous fighter, and he's only good at flouring things.

But he says, my good uncle, I would like to learn your trade, where do we begin?

Mid-month: Lord Clifford is besieged at Carlisle. The Duke of Norfolk is at Ampthill with the king's forces, and with him Henry Courtenay, the Marquis of Exeter: with the marquis, though the marquis does not know it, are men watching him, on Lord Cromwell's behalf. Norfolk has got what he wants – a troop of men at his back, the king's commission in his saddlebag – yet still he grouches in every letter he sends. Mr Wriothesley opens them, and interprets the content to the king.

The rebels are aiming for York and the mayor believes the city is too divided to resist. The rumour is that its archbishop has already fled. Robert Aske has called down the rebels from north Yorkshire to join his host. They say they will restore houses of religion in the territory they capture. Mr Wriothesley says, I told you so. I told you, when the monks go, we should knock the buildings down after them.

He, Thomas Cromwell, goes from Windsor to London, road or river, to and from at the king's behest – he might as well be with the armies, so uneasy his bed, so spare his diet. Even when he is on the road he feels he is still within the castle, trapped in the royal hour, the royal day. The king is querulous when he is not in his presence – he is still Master Secretary, after all, and everything works through and by him. But the king's first need is coin. His dishes and chalices must be sacrificed, weighty gold chains signed out of the Jewel House never to return. He has never believed metal should be left to lose its lustre, or weigh down the persons of great men – it should circulate as money and multiply. But, he says to Call-Me, I would like to meet a competent alchemist this fall, or a princess who could spin gold out of straw.

In Windsor the town hugs the castle walls, and what were market stalls in King Edward's day are dwellings now, dirty infills like dens for dwarves, clustering up to the castle ditch. The streets are packed with tradespeople come to try their luck, see what they can sell to the court, for within the castle's tight precincts they grow nothing, can't even stock a carp pond. All day wagons rumble uphill, across the cobbles and through the great gate, so noble folk must edge aside to give carters a path. He hears that sermons have been preached in the town in favour of the Pilgrims. He slips money to a few boys of his choosing so they can stand in line at stalls and get the gossip, and later filter into the Windsor taverns, jostling with the customers of Thameside harlots. Afterwards they seek out a priest, see what kind of confessions he likes to hear, then put it to him bald: are these rebels holy, Father? Should we take their part?

So much travelling in the cold and wet, and he wakes up aching. His dreams are oppressive: he finds himself at a landing stage, the opposite bank out of view. The river widening, nothing but the grey still water stretching away, polished pewter reflecting a silver sky: no bank in view because there is no bank, because the water has become eternity, because his flesh is dissolved in it; because his stories merge, all memories flatten to one.

His uncle John says, mind, young Thomas: if you are going to learn, you can't go running up and down the riverbank, you have to be where we can find you. Because when Archbishop Morton – Cardinal Morton, he is now – has visitors from Rome, they're not replete with a dish of split peas, they expect to eat songbirds basted in honey. We can't say to them, well, Monsignors, unfortunately the boy who catches larks has gone home to Putney, because his father's entered in a shin-kicking contest, and Tom is holding his coat and taking the bets.

It was not easy to leave Putney. There were matters that called him back; he was a boy, you whistled for him and he came. Men planned a robbery and besought him to go through a window for them, and open up the house.

'No,' he said.

'No?' said the brigands. 'Why not?'

'Because I fear God's punishment.'

The chief robber said, 'You should more fear my fist.' And showed it to him.

Besides, they said, why would God notice a boy like you? Why would He care if you go through Mildred Dyer's window, she being a widow with a store of money, and none but a lapdog to defend her, a cur we can kick away, or easy break its neck?

He thought, God regards every sparrow that falls. From listening at a sermon, he had this text by heart. God regards Mildred Dyer. God regards her dog Pippin. He said, 'I disdain you. You are the sort who need strong drink before you dare jump a puddle, and on the day you are hanged my friends will laugh at you while you kick.'

The chief robber deployed his fist then, pinning him against the wall and pounding his head till the others cried, 'Edwin, he's not worth it.'

He did not remember the pain, perhaps did not feel it. But he remembered the taint of the man's breath.

'Who did that?' Walter said, when he took his injuries home. 'All angels help me,' he said, when he heard the story. 'Next time someone invites you to a robbery, say no in a civil fashion. Tell them you've a job on somewhere else – it's only common courtesy.'

As he grew up, he grew into caution: to a degree. He sinned, he sinned greatly, but usually he picked his time. He saw a woman forced, and he said and did nothing. He saw a man's eyes put out of their sockets, because he had witnessed what he should not: Jesu, he'd said, would it not have made more sense to slit his tongue? One day when he was brought up against the frontier of Walter's schemes – some frontier he was unwilling to cross – he had said, 'Father, do you not know right from wrong?'

Walter's face grew dark. But he said in a tone mild in the circumstances, 'Listen, son, this is what I know: right is what you can get away with, and wrong is what they whip you for. As I'm sure life will instruct you, by and by, if your father's precept and example can't get it through your skull.'

The thief Edwin had said, while he sucked his knuckles, 'Be glad of that, boy, a gift from me. You may go begging for a beating hereafter: Satan himself wouldn't soil his paws.'

On 16 October the rebels enter York. York is the second city in the realm. England is collapsing in on herself, like a house of straw.

When the news comes he is in London, scraping together ten thousand pounds so Norfolk can pay his troops. A message comes from Wriothesley: the king wants him, wants to see him as soon as humanly possible. Another letter follows, another …

When he arrives at Windsor a knot of councillors surges around him, long-faced. The king is at prayer. In his private closet? No, he is addressing God from a grander place, the chapel of St George's.

Bishop Sampson says, 'Cromwell, he waits on you.'

'But you have told him? That York is lost?' Only in that moment does it strike him that they might have held back the news for him to break.

But it appears Rafe Sadler has done it: Rafe is with him now. Oxford says, 'I doubt the king will blame you too much, my lord.'

For the fall of York? How could he be to blame? But someone must be …

Lord Audley says, 'I doubt even Wolsey could have changed the wind these last weeks.'

No? Wolsey would not have fled York, like the present archbishop. He says, 'No rebel would have dared to rise within a hundred miles of my lord cardinal. Active force would have met him, if he did.'

To St George's, then. He pushes through the councillors. 'Come on, Call-Me.'

Wriothesley says, striding beside him, 'Death has made the cardinal invincible, sir?'

'So it appears.' Though Wolsey never speaks to him now. Since he came back from Shaftesbury he is without company or advice. The cardinal bounces in the clouds, where the Faithful Departed giggle at our miscalculations. The dead are magnified in our eyes, while we to them appear as ants. They look down on us from the mists, like mystic beasts on spires, and they sail above us like flags.

The king is in the chantry chapel, high above the Garter stalls. He climbs, and on the tight spiral of the stair the chambers of his heart squeeze small. From here, he knows, the king looks down on his ancestors, at the murdered King Henry – sixth of that name – in his tomb.

He ducks into the low doorway. The king is kneeling, back rigid, seemingly at prayer. Rafe Sadler is kneeling behind him, as far away as the space will allow. Rafe turns up his face, imploring; as he, Lord Cromwell, passes him, he flips his cap over his eyes.

There is a cushion; it's better than the bare boards. For some time he kneels in silence, directly behind his monarch.

In Florence, he thinks, I played at *calcio*. It is a game of many players, more a mêlée than a sport. The young men of family would turn out their stouter servants, twenty or thirty to each team. Mad Englishman, he: his excuse being that, as his Tuscan was not perfect, he did not know the rules.

He can hear the king's breath, his sigh. Henry knows he is there: he gives himself away by a twitch of the muscles at the back of his neck.

Ten minutes into the game you would be bloodied, the ball itself basted in snot and sand and gore, your breath short, your long bones juddering, your feet stamped to a paste and your hair yanked out in handfuls: but you never noticed or cared, once you got hold of the ball. Forward you charged, ball tucked against you, a whoop of triumph sailing over the rooftops; but when you had run ten paces, some bellowing lunatic would hack you behind the knees.

Henry puts his hand to his nape, like someone who has been brushed by a gnat. His sacred head half-turns; he lifts his gaze, wary. 'Crumb?' he says. As if it were the start of a prayer: though one with no particular efficacy.

He waits. The king heaves a deeper sigh: a groan.

Mother of Sorrows, the game hurt when it stopped. Though when you were playing, you never felt a thing.

Henry crosses himself, and begins to struggle to his feet. Would a hand to help him be welcome, or bitten?

'York? How can York fall?' When the king turns his face it is dismayed: as if somebody has cut a gash in it, opened his brain to the light.

Rafe, in the shadows, stands behind him.

He scoops up his cushion. It is embroidered gold on crimson: 'HA HA', it says. *Henricus Rex. Anna Regina.*

Rafe takes it from him as if it were hot.

If this were Florence, he thinks, I would boot that cushion over Santa Croce. Her memory with it.

The king says, 'Tonight I shall dine in the great hall.'

'Majesty,' he says.

'I must appear in great ...' the king falters ... 'glory, you understand me? Where is the Mirror of Naples?'

'Whitehall, sir.'

He thinks Henry will say, take a guard and fetch it. The king takes no heed of distance or weather. He wants to blaze before his subjects in the great pearl and diamond that was the treasure of France.

'Whitehall?' Henry says. 'Never mind.' It appears he only has to think of the Mirror to feel glorified. He always says, when the French ask for it back, 'Tell François my claim to that country is stronger than his. One day I shall ask for more than jewels.'

'We shall need the trumpeters.' Henry's voice is small in the great spaces of the chapel. 'Rafe, are you lurking there? My duty and my love to the queen's grace. If she pleases to wear the sleeves with my monogram that Ibgrave sent in June, I shall wear the matching doublet.'

Far below them – in the mirror of time you can see them – the Garter knights weep in their stalls, their dead skulls rattling inside feathered helms. But the king straightens his shoulders, tilts up his chin. Later Rafe will say, 'You have to admire how he took the news, when York fell. You would have thought someone had given him a thousand pounds, instead of a kick in the teeth.'

By suppertime he is so harassed by messengers that he has to send Rafe to whisper in the king's ear and beseech pardon for his absence. They say the mayor of York has got the treasure out of the city, but can he keep it safe? The Pilgrims will be able to finance their cause from what remains, fleecing the rich citizens. Within York's walls are crammed forty parish churches, a dozen great houses of religion untouched by the Court of Augmentations. That the place seethes with papists, he has long known; but where would York be, or any of those great wool towns, if he did not work continually to patch up peace with the Emperor, to keep their ports open, and if he did not represent their cause, persistently, to the merchants of the Hanse? If he met Aske he would ask him, how is it in the interest of the north, to threaten those who can best prosper your people?

He says to Rafe, 'Lucky the King of Scots has gone to France. If he were at home, he might be mustering to come down on us.'

The word from Paris is that James has not yet married a wife. Instead he is doing a lot of shopping.

Rafe says, 'James has left his council at home to govern. They have an eye to their opportunity, I suppose. I do not know if they would venture to declare war.'

They don't have to declare it. At *calcio*, nobody ever declared war. The result was wreckage, all the same: a field strewn with teeth, and (one had heard of it) gouged eyes. No one was actually stabbed but sometimes, inadvertently, players fell onto each other's knives.

Letters done. He sands his papers. Tonight I can no more. 'I'm hungry, Call-Me. Perhaps it is not too late to join our master.'

At the end of the great hall where servants sit and boast, he can see Christophe hard at work. Christophe tells people he has been to Constantinople, where he advised the Sultan. At his palace in the twisting lanes of that metropolis, perfumed fans would agitate the air, and plump women, in their skins as God made them, would lie about on divans, with nothing to do all day but work a curl around their forefinger and wait for Mustafa Cromwell to come home, and call for sherbet and virgins.

But in Windsor the light is low outside, and grouped about the king in their furs, his senior councillors: Audley the Lord Chancellor, John de Vere Earl of Oxford; a bishop or two. At the queen's right hand, Lady Mary is seated. Mary's eyes pass over him. No signal, except a faint pursing of the lips. On the queen's other hand is the Marchioness of Exeter, Gertrude Courtenay. It is her office to hold the queen's fingerbowl, should she require it, while Lady Mary hands her napkin. Glancing down the hall to Gertrude's entourage, he sees Bess Darrell, and Bess Darrell sees him.

He approaches the king. About his neck, as deputy for the Mirror of Naples, Henry is wearing a rough-cut diamond the size of a large walnut. His doublet of crimson satin is sewn all over with gold and pearls, picking out the queen's initial. Jane's crimson sleeves are stiff with matching letters: H, H, H again.

Without looking at him, Henry stretches out an arm for a bundle of dispatches. The king's attention is fixed on some fantastical tale being trotted out by – blood of Christ, how did he come here? – Master Sexton the jester.

'I thought you had forbidden him the court, sir?'

Henry's smile is wary. 'True, I boxed his ears. But poor fellow, he has no other way to earn a living. Will Somer is sick. He has a colic. I have recommended oil of bitter almonds. An Italian remedy, I think?'

Sexton skips across the floor, chanting:

> 'Will is sick and ill at ease
> I am full sorry for Will's disease.'

The king says, 'Have you not had your supper? Take your places.'

'Has he washed his hands?' Sexton bawls. 'Go lower, Tom. Which is the table for shearsmen? Which is the table for the blacksmith's lad? Go lower. Keep walking. Trot on till you get to Putney.'

'Master Wriothesley,' the king says, 'my scribe. Take your seat ...'

'What, Wriothesley?' Sexton bawls. 'My ink-horn, my splot, my blotch? Frig him, ladies, and he spurts ink. Tell me, Blotch, where's your friend Riche? What do they call him, Sir Purse?'

Call-Me turns pink. He takes his place. It can only be moments before the king checks Sexton from such bawdy talk, which is never to his taste, let alone that of his wife and his maiden daughter. The ladies will not understand his crudities, of course. Gregory used to call Riche 'Purse', but Gregory was young then – he didn't know it means a cunt. Unless, of course, he did.

Sexton lurches towards them. 'What, Purse is among the Pilgrims? We may never see him again, which would not make you cry, would it, Master Blot? No, Blot brooks no rival – he would be glad if the rebels cooked and ate Purse, and spat out what they could not stomach. All know how he betrayed Thomas More. I wonder any gentleman speaks to him.' He rolls his eyes around the company. 'I wonder even Cromwell speaks to him.'

There is some incautious sniggering. The king frowns. But Master Sexton bowls on. 'The commons cry for bread, Majesty. Why not give them Crumb?'

The queen moves a hand to cover her mouth. Her embroidered sleeves flash initials: H, H, H. Lady Mary is looking at the table linen with some attention, as if it needed darning. Henry says, 'The fellow is impertinent, but you must take it in good part, my lord.'

'The Pilgrims will crumb you,' Sexton shouts. 'They will crumb you till you are crumbed back to flour.'

The king says, 'Do not answer, it will goad him.'

'If the Emperor comes you will be crumbed and fried. You will be sizzled like the heretic Tyndale.'

He should heed the king's word, yet he must speak: 'We do not know for certain that Tyndale is burned.'

Sexton says, 'I could smell him from here.'

* * *

Bess Darrell is a flitting presence by candlelight, a wraith. He cannot help but belly out her gown with the shape of the child that never was.

'My lord Privy Seal.' She considers him. 'Creeping about the apartments of the ladies, by night.'

'See me as Master Secretary. In that capacity I get everywhere.'

She laughs. 'So your friend is at court.' Mary, she means. 'She is a dangerous friend to have.'

'How is that?' He is playing stupid: feeling out the rumours.

'She thinks you have offered to make her queen one day. She thinks you have an understanding. Tacit, of course.'

Hardly an offer, he says, indifferent, but she says, 'Do not disdain the rumour. It may buy you a little credit with the Poles or the Courtenays, and you may need it one day.'

'Why, do they think the Tudors will go down? Do they say so?'

'Never in my hearing. But my mistress Gertrude hopes the king will take advice and put the government into the hands of honest men. If abusing Lord Cromwell were treason, you could hang her tomorrow.'

'I could hang half the peerage. I am glad your marchioness is at court, under our eye. Though I can think of people I would rather look at.'

'Can you?' She is teasing him. 'Meg Douglas?'

'Oh yes,' he says. 'I like her so well I keep her under lock and key. But tell me, does Mary confide in your mistress?'

'Mary says nothing to anybody. She bides her time.'

Bess's face raised to his: a sweetly encouraging face, her eyes warm. Does she think he will speak out for Mary's rights and damn himself? He would not put it past this young woman to hold a double hand in the game. He turns away: 'Are the Courtenays good to you? They have not reproached you about Wyatt?'

She lays a flat hand on her person. 'There is no sign Wyatt was ever here. The Courtenays do not mention his name.'

He thinks, they are persons of limited capacity and Wyatt is too hard for them to fathom. Bess says, 'Verses are written to damn him.

They circulate here at court. Because in the spring he stood with you, and not with the Boleyns.

'To counterfeit a merry mood
In mourning mind I think it best.
But once in rain I wore a hood
Well were they wet that barehead stood.

'Blood,' she says. 'The precipitation of our age. They think he walked away and left his friends to die. I wonder where those five gentlemen are now? For that matter, I wonder where Wyatt is.'

'With the king's army. I cannot be more exact, we are all like planets driven out of our courses. But I hear he does great deeds with his Kentish men. Does he not write to you?'

'Of course. But you know Wyatt. He would not put a date or place, he would not like to be pinned to it. He does not say anything usual, like "Commend me to my friends," or "My heart is your home for ever."'

'I am sure it is. Who would not grant you the freehold?' She darts a smile over her shoulder and melts into the darkness, as fleetly as she came. He rubs his fingers together, as if he had tried to catch at her linen and caught a spider's web instead.

He has almost gained his own door when another woman steps into his path, a candle in her hand. Jane Rochford is as precise and fresh as if she were going to Matins. 'Cromwell? Where have you been? She wants to see you.'

'The queen? At this hour?'

'The Lady Mary.' Rochford laughs. 'She is her father's daughter. She does not sleep, so why should anyone else?'

Mary wears a furred nightgown of stiff crimson brocade. 'I hope they are keeping you warm,' he says. 'And well-provisioned?'

He had told the household officers, block out the draughts, build up her fires, send in extra fuel: bread, wine and boiled meats to go to her chamber each day at dawn.

She says, 'The great breakfast is needless now. If you remember, it was so that I did not have to dine in the hall in company, and sit lower than little Eliza. In those days when my title was degraded, and Eliza was styled princess.'

She does not ask him to sit. He would not, anyway. He says, 'We have worked so much between us that I forget some of our ploys. I must ask you, my lady – you have not been approached?'

'The rebels may use my name, but they have no permission from me.'

Which is to say, yes, I have been approached. And as he moves towards her – he, Lord Cromwell – she does not move, except that with a little hitch she draws her nightgown together, hiding the white of her linen; and at once lets it go, as if she knew the gesture to be ridiculous. He is close enough to touch the cloth of her gown, but of course he does not. 'You favour that crimson, I perceive, you and the queen both – may I ask, is it from Genoa?'

'I believe so. The queen sent her brother Edward to Hunsdon, to see what apparel I needed. I said, my father's favour is clothing enough, but he begged me to ask for whatever I wished. Edward Seymour is a fine gentleman. It is a pity he is a heretic.'

'Edward is guided by the king, as are we all.'

God forgive me, he thinks, but she is exhausting. And starved of touch, her rank forbids it.

She says, 'I hear the council is discussing a marriage for me. With the young Duke of Orléans.'

'The French are discussing it. I'm not sure we are.'

The French will not take her unless Henry makes her his heir. This, of course, he will not do; but could some compromise be reached, a French marriage would detach her once and for all from the Emperor and the Spanish. Therefore, we are talking.

He says, 'You see yourself with a Spanish husband, very likely.'

She hesitates. 'The king is such a good father that he would not marry me against my own wishes.'

Answer the question, he thinks. She turns her back on him, as if incidentally. 'And your own care of me has been so tender that it is like that of a father.'

He can see her face in a glass, only she does not know that. Someone has made her aware that we are linked, if only by rumour. She is warning me off. Well, he thinks, I am warning her. 'Would you not like to marry an Englishman?'

'Who?' The question jumps out at him.

She stares at him through the mirror. Her heart is in her mouth. Let's leave it there.

A restless supper: a worse grace. He can hear the rain on the leads, its trickle and swirl. *Well were they wet that barehead stood ...* His meal lies heavy, and as he goes to his desk – the last messages have come in from Yorkshire – he finds himself thinking of his spectacular bed: the king has given him a set of covers and bed hangings, purple woven with silver tissue, emblazoned with the royal arms. You are mine asleep or awake, Henry is saying: like a lover. You could keep a troop of horse in the field on what the gift has cost him, but Henry must feel he is worth the expense. He lights another candle, and calls in Christophe to build up the fire. He has used up his court allocation of coals and wood but he says, hang the expense, say it's for me, and if anybody queries it, just knock them down, will you?

Christophe grins. I fetch Rafe to talk to you? Or someone to sing? But he says, no, no, I must get to this, it won't wait; but then he rests his head on his hand and perhaps dozes, and he is now here, now there: now lit by the tentative flicker from the hearth, now by the sunlight on the water of the Thames at Lambeth, forty-odd years back: but what is forty years, in the life of a river?

I kept this back for you, Uncle John says. Got to eat it when it's just warm. Too hot or too cold and you don't get the beauty of it. A cook has to learn. It can't always be leftovers.

It is an aromatic custard in a white dish. He saw the gooseberries earlier, tiny bubbles of green glass, sour as a friar on a fast day. For this dish you need fresh hens' eggs and a pitcher of cream; you need to be a prince of the church to afford the sugar.

His uncle stands over him. The custard quakes in waves of sweetness and spice.

'Nutmeg,' he says. 'Mace. Cumin.'

'Now taste it.'

'And rosewater.'

John's smile is a benediction. 'Nothing is so green as a summer in England, Thomas. Those who have voyaged yearn for it. They dream of a bowl such as this.'

On the silk road; in the heat of the plains where neither rill nor brook trickles in three days' march; in the fortified towns of barbarians, where you can cook an egg by cracking it on the stones; in the places at the edge of the map, where the lines blur and the paper frays: by Mother Mary, says the traveller, by the maidenhead of St Agatha, I wish I were in Lambeth and had a dish of gooseberries and a spoon.

He shakes his head. This dish lacks some final flourish ... He pictures himself, forty years on, standing where John stands now. He is the master-cook, he wears velvet: he never goes near a flour bag, nor flying hot oil: papers in hand, he issues his orders, and at his behest a boy who looks very like himself tosses slivers of almonds in a latten pan; then he spoons them into the cream, freckling it.

And then he might, if he had made an elderflower cordial, venture to add a drop or two.

The boy he can see has his own curly head, his skinned knuckles, his feet cold on the stone-flagged floor. He wears a patched jerkin of sad colour. Beneath his clothes are the prints of his father's fingers: bruises reversing nature, turning from the autumn black-purple of the elderberry to the pale yellow-white of the flowers.

All his flesh is dappled with these shadows. Walter can't help it, John says, he lashes out. Our own father may God acquit him was the same.

If you go out on a morning in late June, after the dew has burned off, you can pick the finest elderberries from the top of the bushes, employing a hooked stick or giant to help you. When you have carried them home, you spill them by handfuls onto a scrubbed tabletop. Breathing in their honeyed scent, you sift them for the best-formed blossoms, your fingertips gentle; then you paint each petal with white of egg. If you dip them in sugar, which as the servant of a rich man you can afford to do, you can keep them a year. On a cheerless November day, when the idea of summer has dropped out of the world, you can lay the crystallised petals on the surface of a cake, each one a five-pointed star: to enchant the eye of a lady, or to tempt the jaded palate of a king.

19 October, the city of Hull capitulates to the rebels. In Doncaster, mayor and chief citizens are compelled to take the Pilgrim oath. In the chapel at Windsor, the dead knights in their Garter stalls bow over their shame in an agony of colic that no oil of almonds will ease: inside their helms they moan, earls of Lancaster and earls of March, Bohuns and Beauchamps, Mowbrays and Veres, Nevilles and Percys, Cliffords and Talbots and Fitzalans and Howards, and that great servant of the state, Reginald Bray himself. There are more dead than living; why can they not fight?

When evening comes a blue light fades in the north windows, and the river is sucked into the darkness, as if into a universal sea. The south windows are shuttered, the courts below fall quiet, and the watch is changed at the foot of the king's privy stair. The tapers are brought in, and mirrored sconces redirect a shivering light; the king's private rooms, painted and gilded, shine like a jewel box.

The king says, 'I remember my father's passing ... Bishop Fox came to me at Evensong: "The king your father is dead: God save your Majesty." I said, at what hour did his soul depart? And Fox never answered. I guessed by that my father had lain untended, cooling in his death sweat, while his councillors plotted at their leisure. For two whole days after that, his ministers pretended he was still alive.'

He thinks, they meant well. They wanted everything ready for a smooth accession.

'Think how they had to dissimulate,' the king says, 'walking around Greenwich with unaltered countenance. I could not have done it myself, being a natural man, incapable of deception. You see

361

how, my lord, by the time my councillors proclaimed me, they had already started lying to me. As soon as you are king, nobody tells you the truth.'

'I might ...' he says.

'You might mollify it,' Henry says. 'Or tell what truths you think I can bear. Though I will not say, "My lord, I want truth unadorned." I will not make that claim. I have my share of human vanity.'

He is afraid Gregory will laugh.

Henry says, 'I wanted two months of my eighteenth birthday, so they named my grandmother regent. But then on Midsummer Day, Katherine and I were crowned together.'

The songs tonight are Spanish: a boy sings about contests with the Moors, airs less martial than melancholy. Messages are brought to the Moorish king: God keep your Majesty, here is bad news. *Las nuevas que, rey, sabras/no son nuevas de alegria ...* The notation is strange to him, the voice part inked in red.

Henry says, 'You know when you see a little child placed on a chair, its legs dangling? You smile and pity the child, do you not? Imagine a young man placed on a throne ... you feel as if your feet are in the air, like that ...'

He sees Gregory smile. He thinks of Helen, before she was Rafe's wife, bringing her little children to Austin Friars and setting them on a bench, their legs thrust straight out before them.

The king says, 'My father said that the surest sign that Heaven favoured his reign was the birth of a prince so soon after his marriage to my sainted mother. In January they were wed, and in September they had Arthur in the cradle. It is no sin, you know, to go to bed once you are betrothed, or if it is a sin, it can easily be absolved. They were blessed with a numerous family after. I remember us together at Eltham, gathered in the great hall, the day Erasmus came to see us.'

'May God rest him,' Gregory says. He hopes Erasmus will not rise, to write more books.

The king's hand moves to cross himself; his jewels catch the light. 'I would be eight years old, I think, a bonny child and a toward wit. I sat under the canopy of estate, and to my right my sister Margaret, being about ten years old, already betrothed to Scotland. My sister Mary on my other hand, her hair white like angels' hair. And Edmund still a babe, he was held in some great lady's arms I suppose. I had another sister, Elizabeth, three years old when she died, I have no memory of her, but they said she was as lovely as Mary, and a great pity she died, for she could have been married thereafter, with advantage to our polity. Edmund himself lived not long after. And my sister Mary is dead now. And Arthur. There is only myself left. And Margaret, far beyond the border.'

It is hard to know whether the king is congratulating himself, or commiserating with himself. His lips are stained by many cups of a strong and sweet malvasia; he blots with his napkin, eyes distant. 'The burden of kingship,' he says, 'no man can imagine it. All my life, to be a prince: to be observed to be a prince; all eyes to be set on me; to be an exemplar of virtue, of discretion, of excellence in learning; to have a mind young and vigorous yet as wise as Solomon; to take pleasure in what others have designed for my pleasure, or be thought ungrateful; to discipline all my appetites, to unmake myself as a man in order to make myself as a king; to waste not a minute lest I be seen to waste it; for idleness, no excuses; always alert to prove, always to show, that I am worthy of the place God appointed me ... When I was a young man I suppose I showed the calf of my leg to an ambassador and said, "There, has your French king a calf as good as that?" And my words were reported, and all Europe laughed at me, a vain idle boy, and no doubt people laugh still. But being young I asked myself, if God had formed François better than me, which prince did He favour most?'

Thomas More had said once, can a king be your friend? He thinks, the first time I came into Henry's presence, it was like the Fox and the Lion. I trembled at the sight. But the second time, I crept a bit nearer and had a good look. And what did I see? I saw his solitude. And like Fox to Lion, I stepped right up and parleyed with him, and never looked back.

The king says, 'I have got no good of my sister Margaret or her marriage with the Scot. She has been a trouble and an expense all her life. And see now her daughter going the same way, intriguing with Tom Truth.'

He has been hoping the king will be good to Meg Douglas, and let her move from the Tower to some easier custody; now, he sees, is not the time to broach it.

'They are saying in the north that you want to marry her.'

Gregory is caught unawares: 'What?'

'You need not deny it,' the king says. 'I tell everyone, Cromwell would not presume. Not even in his dreams.'

He feels obliged to state, 'Nor do I.'

The king says, 'Do you know, there are some who claim the old Scots king did not die at Flodden? They believe he escaped the battle-field and took ship to become a pilgrim in the Holy Land. He has been seen in Jerusalem.'

'Only in fantasy,' he says. 'Did not Lord Dacre, who knew him, inspect his naked remains? And my lord of Norfolk will tell you, you could put your fist through the holes in his surcoat where the blades had pierced him.'

Henry says, 'I was winning battles in France at the time, I cannot know. But I wonder if princes do die, as common men die. I feel my father watches what I do.'

'Then surely, sir, he sees your difficulties, and admires your resolution?'

'How can I know that? If the dead can see us, be sure they do not like the world to change from what they knew. Nor do they like their power disrespected. Norfolk's father took credit for Flodden, but in Durham they credit St Cuthbert with the victory. They march behind his banners now.'

The king holds up a hand to the lute player: 'Thank you, leave us.' The boy stuffs his music back into his budget and goes out backwards. The king picks up his own lute. Oh shining moon light me all the night … *Ay luna tan bella*, light me to the sierra. He says, 'I loved Katherine. Did you know that? Despite all that ensued.'

He thinks, if he forgets the words I cannot assist him here. Though it is a fair bet that the night will cloud up at some point and hide the moon. The ladies look down from the towers of the Alhambra. The horsemen curvet below, on white mounts with gilded hooves, pennants streaming from their lances. All the troupe, Moors and Christians both, file together into the antique darkness, a blur of gold against the night: cities are besieged and cities fall, warriors burn with the fires of love and are consumed.

Henry sings: *I am the dark girl, the rose without thorn.* He says, 'Katherine claimed she loved me. So why did she try to destroy me?'

He makes no answer. He has mastered silence, but to better effect than More.

The king's eyes rest on him. 'The children who died in her womb, I think they did not want to be born, they did not care to live in this peevish world. But where did they go? They say there is no salvation for the unbaptised. Some think God would not be so cruel. And God is not as cruel as man. God would not sew a man in a cow's hide, and set dogs on him.'

His servant John Bellowe is alive, it transpires. Richard Cromwell has seen him, and patched him up and set him to work again. It is true he was taken prisoner, roughly used, and set in the stocks at Louth. But he is not blinded or mauled by dogs. He hopes no one explains to Bellowe the death they thought he had died. Hearing such a tale, a man might lose his confidence in his fellow man.

The old king's advisers, he thinks, knew trade and the law. Bray died in his bed. But his protégés, Empson and Dudley, were arrested before they knew the old king's soul had passed. They were haled out of their houses and dragged through the April dawn along Candlewick Street and Eastcheap and so to prison. They were charged with the crime of massing troops in the capital, plotting to seize the person of the young Henry. It was an unlikely charge. They fell because the people hated them. They were the old king's bad angels, but God he knows, they kept him in funds.

There are moments when as he goes about his duties he feels a fierce exultation – he, Cromwell, Lord Privy Seal. But he would never admit it to any person: they would lecture him about the mutability of fortune. Look at his life: does he need a reminder? He says to Rafe, vanity compels us to to pretend we plan every step. But when the cardinal came down I stood before the lords of England like a naked child waiting for the whip. I sent you oiling to Norfolk, 'Can Master Cromwell have a seat in the Parliament house, he will do much good for your lordship?' Christ, yes, Rafe says, I thought he would have kicked me to Ipswich.

There is a time to be silent. There is a time to talk for your life. He saw Henry's need and he filled it, but you must never let a prince know he needs you; he does not like to think he has incurred a debt to a subject. Like the old king's ministers, he labours day and night for his prince's increase. The Italian Niccolò says that when a prince has such a servant, he should treat him with respect and kindness, advance him to honours and promote his fortune. Perhaps when the book is put into English our prince will read it.

In Sienna you may see a fresco, where Good Government is set out on the wall, so that everyone can see what peace looks like. Peace is a woman: she is a blonde; her hair is braided, and her head leans upon her hand, which is turned so that you see the tender white skin of her inner arm. Her dress is of a fabric so fine that, when it falls away from her breasts, it skims the length of her body and drifts into graceful pleats and folds, into an area of mystery between her relaxed, parted legs. Her feet are bare: they look intelligent, like hands.

On the opposite wall, Bad Government has taken Peace by the hair. She is panicked, screaming, jerked to her knees.

He remembers the great jars in Florence, their cool curve under his hand; they seemed to him to be speaking to each other, edging closer so their sides touched and chimed. Oil and wine, in jars with sounding depths; bread and wine, God's body; the torn manchet loaves at the tables of the rich, fine white bread while the poor eat barley, rye. At Windsor in the king's chamber a gentleman brings in more tapers; the light flutters across the ceiling like an influx of cherubim. The king consults the songbook. He sings that he burns without surcease: a mountain girl, unloved, a maid from Estremadura.

He and Rafe exchange glances. Rafe, who knows the Spanish tongue well, looks as baffled as he is. Henry says, 'Crumb, have you talked to my daughter? You know the French have offered for her?'

'I find their approaches tepid. Not to mention offensive. They assume your Majesty will not have a son, when all likelihood is that you will.'

'Write to Gardiner,' Henry says. 'He can tell François we are not interested.' He bends his head over his lute again. 'Though perhaps we should get Mary wed before her bloom fades entirely. She is not like her mother. Katherine was a beautiful creature, at her age.'

Call-Me says, 'The French must have a spy among the queen's women. I swear they know when she has her courses.'

'That will be Jane Rochford,' he says.

'You know that, sir?'

'No,' Rafe says. 'But Lord Cromwell is a gambling man.'

Their supper tonight was lamprey pies and whiting and Suffolk cheese, and pheasants killed with their own hawks. You rise from table and it is as if you have been invited to a feast by a magician in a tale. You think you have been in the king's chamber two hours but when you step outside, seven centuries have passed.

As October enters its third week, Lord Darcy surrenders Pontefract Castle to the rebels. The distinguished men who have sheltered there – among them Sir William Gascoigne, Sir Robert Constable, and Edmund Lee, Archbishop of York – are compelled to take the Pilgrim oath.

He has channels open, across the Narrow Sea. Among the French councillors are those who urge the Pope to sieze the moment and publish his bull of excommunication. Once it is public, all Henry's subjects will be loosed to join the rebellion. He says to Rafe, 'Put the word out to the gentlemen in the privy chamber, and let them spread it among their friends – if I find any have written to Rome, I shall take it as proof of treason without further enquiry.' He says, 'Our hope now is that the Bishop of Rome will not act because he cannot understand what is happening in the north country. How should he? We hardly know ourselves. And if Pole is advising him, he can scarcely know Pontefract from the kingdom of Cockaigne.'

The king sends Lancaster Herald to Pontefract with a proclamation. Robert Aske refuses to let him read out his message, but civilly offers him safe conduct out of the castle and town. He and his Pilgrims will stay true to their cause, they say, and will march on London.

Norfolk has proceeded from his home at Kenninghall to Cambridge, from Cambridge to the north. He claims he is grieved to the heart at the actions of Lord Darcy, who by blood or marriage is related to the greatest families of the north, and who appears to have declared for the Pilgrims. Surely there is a misunderstanding? Space must be left around this magnate, so later he can claim he has been misunderstood.

Darcy sets himself up as the bluff old soldier, but his nature is double. The cardinal was good to him; Darcy betrayed the cardinal, drawing up the indictment that fed the king's anger. He swears great oaths that he is true, but these three years past he has been talking to Chapuys, enquiring as to the chances of troops from the Emperor.

Garlanded by praise for his fidelity from the Lord Privy Seal, the aged Lord Talbot is ordered to march towards Doncaster. Now the fightback has begun: though the prescription is to avoid any actual fighting, swerve engagement where possible. What is essential is to secure the bridges and the main highways, pen the Pilgrims north of Trent. At Windsor he sits by the king, working out what terms will entice the foe. It is for him, the vile Cromwell, to make the king's language emollient. Offer what you must, to induce the bands to disperse. Corrupt them from within. Set gentleman against servant, rustic against monk. They have no common bond but their banner, and what is it? Painted cloth.

Norfolk writes he neither eats nor sleeps, except in the saddle. For an hour he gets his head down and he is roused three times, each time by fools bringing in messages that contradict each other. 'Take in good part whatever promises I shall make unto the rebels ... for surely I shall observe no part thereof ...'

I will, the duke indicates, lie for England. Send me approved lies by the next courier. Send them by your fastest horse.

Near Doncaster, the Pilgrims halt their army. The duke halts his puny forces. His heart is broken, he complains, at having to talk to these traitors, instead of plough them under; all the same, he meets their leaders, listens to their complaints. Norfolk gives a safe-conduct to two Pilgrims, gentlemen, to take a petition to the king.

Truce, then. Temporary, conditional ... But I believe, he tells his boys, Aske's nerve has failed. The heart within his breast, which is no soldier's heart, quakes at the bloodshed in prospect. Once they sit to talk, the Pilgrims lose the impulsion that has brought them so far, their confidence in their own crude strength. The winds of November will bluster through their tents; where they camp, the district will grow hostile; food will grow scarce for man and horse; their water pails will ice over in the night; boots will crack: good order will break down, disease break out. Our pockets are deeper, after all, our arguments more baffling, and we have better guns. We will temporise, and winter will come, and it will be over.

Some hours before the king retires, the groom of the bedchamber calls in four yeomen of the bedchamber, and four yeomen from the Wardrobe of the Beds bring in the king's sheets. The straw mattress that forms the first layer of his bedding is pricked all over with a dagger, before a cover is stretched across it; while they prick and stretch, the yeomen pray for the king, to come safe through the rigours of the night ahead. When the canvas is taut, one of them seats himself on the bedframe, topples backwards most reverently, draws up his unshod feet, and rolls the width of the bed; pauses, and rolls back. If the gentlemen are satisfied there is nothing sharp or noxious beneath, the feather beds are laid down and pummelled all over: you hear the steady thud of fist on down. All eight yeomen, moving in step, stretch taut the sheets and blankets, and as they tuck in each corner, they make the sign of the cross. The fur coverlet follows, a soft swish and slither; then the curtains are drawn around the bed, and a page sits down to guard it.

So the king's long day closes. If he decides to go in to the queen, then a procession escorts him to her door in his night robes. During

daylight hours, he is so bejewelled that it hurts to look at him; he is
the sun. But when he strips off his nightgown stiffly pearled, he is a
phantom in white linen, and beneath his shroud his skin. To breed
kings in a line of kings, he must become a naked man, and do what
every pauper does, and every dog. Outside the door his gentlemen
wait till he is finished. They try not to think of the maidenly queen,
her blushes and sighs, and the king, his grunts of pleasure, his sweat
while he ruts. Let us pray for his good success. He must fertilise the
whole nation. If he is impotent, every Englishman falters, and
foreigners will come by night and cuckold us.

When the king returns to his chamber, they bring a ewer of warm
water, his toothpowder, his night-bonnet. In the glass he sees himself
for the last time today, and glimpses the young prince he was, bowing
out: king of hearts and Defender of the Faith. And in the place where
he stood, a bloated man in middle age: 'Oh Lord, I am working hard
in the field, and the field of my labours is myself.'

Gregory says, 'Father, when the king sent me to look for Merlin
books, I lifted up the lid of a chest, and what did I see? I saw three
volumes, on their binding the badge of the falcon, and the letters
"AB". I ask myself, does the king know they are there?'

He puts his finger to his lips.

Gregory says, 'I think it might be like Cranmer's wife. He
knows and does not know. All of us can do this. But kings in higher
degree.'

They are going to bed themselves; but he has one last mission.
'Kitchens,' he says.

'You are still hungry?' His son looks incredulous.

On the stairs he meets Rafe, with papers in his hand and tomorrow's agenda swimming in his eyes. 'You wish you were at home
with Helen,' he says.

Rafe pinches the bridge of his nose, blinks as if to dispel sleep.
'What about you, master – another tryst with a lady?'

'No, but I have a *billet doux*. Norfolk writes every hour.'

Rafe says, 'The king says tonight, if it will hold off the rebels,
Norfolk can promise Jane will be crowned in York. It would be to

the city's profit, so they will be keen, the king thinks. And if Norfolk is forced to it, he may offer a parliament in the north.'

'They want to push me off my patch. They believe, get Cromwell outside London and his power will falter.'

Rafe says, 'I don't think the king wants to go to York any more than you do. But every week Norfolk gains by promises is a week nearer winter.'

He wonders why rebels would disperse on a promise. Himself, he would want performance.

Rafe yawns. 'Call-Me has listed the names of all gentlemen who have been sworn by the Pilgrims. Did you know Lord Latimer is among them? Perhaps the king will hang him, and you can marry Kate Parr. In furtherance of your vow.'

'Shame on you!' he says. 'When you know I am pledged to the Lady Mary, and to Margaret Douglas. I swear I will not marry below royal degree.'

Outside the king's room the nightwatch is set; but his gentlemen, as they leave him, place his sword by his bed, with a lighted candle. In the last instance, a king must defend himself.

At Windsor there has never been enough space for the kitchens, so they are always throwing up some lean-to in the courts around, and such temporary arrangements have been subsiding and leaking fumes since Adam was a lad. He wants to know if they have damped their fires and cleaned their pans, and see it with his own eyes: no point saving your king from rebels if he is burned up by grease from a loyal turnspit. He swoops in on odd nights to catch them out – just as, on odd days without warning, he arrives at the Tower Mint and weighs their gold coins.

A mist is rising; he rubs his hands against the cold. He knows these back-courts; in all the king's houses he knows them, the forgotten yards and unpatrolled snickets. In a corner where a wall-torch burns, he sees the jester Sexton alone in a pool of light, scuffling a deerskin football against a wall. 'Sexton? Why are you abroad?'

Sexton scoops up the ball. 'No curfew in Patchtown.'

'You have no business in the kitchens.'

Sexton huddles the ball against his chest. 'You never know where you'll find a joke, do you?'

He lunges, knocks the ball out of the man's grasp, tosses it up and catches it. 'Your head, Patch.' A slap of his palm sends it over the wall. He hears a yelp from the darkness; some stranger has had a shock.

Returning, he sees there is a guard set outside his door. The man says, good night and God bless you. The shapes of other men, armed, occupy each recess.

Christophe is sitting up for him. His spaniel is snoring; the marmoset is huddled close to the embers, chattering to himself. When he first brought the creature in, the king had said, 'Beware, Lord Cromwell, my father had a little monkey that got hold of one of his books of memoranda, and tore it to shreds with his nails and teeth. They pieced the fragments together, but no one could read the result. And so it falls out that today there are gentlemen in luxury, who would have been beggars if my father had sent them their tax bills, and others snug in their parlours who would have been clapped in a strait prison, if the monkey had not altered their fate.'

'Gregory is abed already,' Christophe yawns, then absently kisses his cheek: 'Do not sit up writing, sir.'

Christophe rolls towards his pallet, pulling off his jerkin, scratching himself as he goes. Alone, he – Lord Cromwell – takes the knife from under his shirt, and sets it down. If some north country ogre burst up the stair, would he defend his son, or his son defend him? As the king says, Gregory promises brawn and sinew, the keen level eye of the sportsman, the set jaw of a man accustomed to the weight of a helm. But still like a child he whispers in the dark: 'The king would see Anne's books if he pleased. Kings can see through stone walls, and hear remarks passed in the reign of Uther Pendragon. They feel more than common men – as the spider feels the finger before the finger touches it. A king is more like an animal in certain regards, but do not say I said so, it might be ill-taken.'

His head hits the pillow. 'Might it?' he says. 'Well, perhaps you should err on the side of caution. Men have lost their heads for less.'

You think of the prince as living on an exalted plane, finer and higher than other men. But perhaps Gregory has a point: is a prince even human? If you add him up, does the total make a man? He is made of shards and broken fragments of the past, of prophecies and of the dreams of his ancestral line. The tides of history break inside him, their current threatens to carry him away. His blood is not his own, but ancient blood. His dreams are not his own, but the dreams of all England: the dark forest, deserted heath; the stir in the leaves, the dragon's footprint; the hand breaking the waters of a lake. His forefathers interrupt his sleep to castigate, to warn, to shake their heads in mute disappointment. At a prince's coronation, God transfigures him, his human faults falling away, his human capacities increased; but that burst of light has to last him. That instant's transfusion of grace must sustain him for thirty years, forty years, for the rest of his mortal life.

He lies sleepless: Baron Cromwell, Lord Privy Seal, his mind ranging across country over the dales and rivers to where the factious in their encampments stir in their sleep and curse his name. It ranges west, far west, beyond the river Tamar, to where the sons of Cornishmen cold-sweat and heave, their ale foaming through their blood, and where Bolster in his sea cave blows giant bubbles in the midnight deeps, and dreams of swimming up for air; of planting his giant feet on hill and dale, fording the rivers in spate and demolishing the bridges with his heels; of marching to London, to net the ministers of the king, and snap their necks, and grind them up like spices to sprinkle on his porridge.

A giant cannot imagine what it is like to be a man of ordinary height. He cannot enter into their feelings. He never learns to bargain, or deceive: why would he, when he gets his way simply by cracking his knuckles?

When you are a child you think you have to kill the giant, but as you grow up you think different. Suppose you meet him by chance one day: you about your common business, picking up sticks or inspecting your rabbit traps, and he taking the air at the entrance to his cave, or toiling on a mountainside to uproot great oaks. Giants are lonely; they don't know any other giants. Sometimes they want a boy like Jack to amuse them, to run errands and teach them songs.

Conquer your awe then, grab your chance. If you know how to talk to a giant it works like a spell. The monster becomes your creature. He thinks you serve him, but in fact you serve yourself.

He is restless – he, Lord Cromwell. He gets out of bed. Opens the shutter. Rain. He shields a candle flame with his hand. His head bobs against the ceiling. But he is not the giant – he is sprightly Jack. You leave your home and head east, you cross the sea, you think Bolster is behind you, but he is ahead. Wherever you arrive, he has arrived first. It's here at Windsor, the swollen Thames surging under your walls, the water gurgling in downspouts and ditches – it's here, after all the years, you find your confluence.

In his spare moments he is studying to improve his Greek. Old Bishop Fisher was in his seventies when he began the language, and he is not to be bested by a dead prelate. In a year or two, he wishes to be able to join the divines in their subtle dissection of each point of translation. This week he is reading a book of letters written by the philosophers and soldiers of those ancient times; though you wonder Alexander the Great had time for letters. Our king does not care to write his own – his writing seems to turn back on itself, so after long labour he makes no progress. Instead he corrects the manuscripts of others, or makes marginal notes of a startling nature. Probably the great Macedonian was the same – no doubt he laid aside his lyre and murmured the gist of his message, and a slave inscribed it, the Thomas Wriothesley of his day: bowing in a tent on a day of still heat, the perfume of frankincense masking the reek of elephants on the move.

Long ago in Venice he bought this book, trusting sometime he would have leisure for study. It is from the Aldus workshop, with his dolphin mark: clean, though one page marred by a thumbprint from its first owner. Sometimes he wonders who he was, and why he would part with such a work. Perhaps he is dead and his heirs sold his book, thumbprint and all. Or perhaps he lost interest in the ancient world and turned his mind back to business; tomorrow morning he will be strolling to the piazza with a basket and a street-child to carry it, shopping for olives and pumpkins, pine-nuts and garlic.

When he was an infant, Thomas was afraid of the river: of high tide as it crept around his ankles. He feared it would burst its banks and widen like the sky above us – he had no other way of thinking of it, for he had never seen the sea. He thought the river should be walled off to keep the streets safe, or banks built, to allow men to walk dry-shod above it and view its rising. Imagine then when he came to Venice. The child stirred inside him, crying, 'Look, look what it's done! I told you so!'

In Venice he saw, by torchlight, the whole of Heaven painted, and high above the canal a woman's face brooding in the space between planets. He went back in daylight to view it better, and saw the world painted on a wall, with scaly landmasses and blue oceans; forests where deer sprang from coverts, where nymphs with the heads of birds sang in the trees. He saw a rider richly dressed riding into the distance, his horse's shoes turned back to the onlooker; the hoof prints are impressed in memory, while the rider fades into an avenue of fallen columns, diminishing to a dot and vanishing from view.

Sometimes Henry says to him, 'Still at the antique letters, Lord Cromwell? What did you learn today?'

He says, 'I learned that *ars longa, vita brevis*: I learned how to say it in Greek.'

'That is Hippocrates,' Henry says. 'He tells us, life is short and our task so great that we will die before we can ...'

The king breaks off. It is an offence for his subjects to speculate about his death or predict it, but it is not an offence for him to speak of it himself; yet he looks chary, as if he thinks it should be. '"Life is short and art is long, the opportunity sudden and fleeting: experiment dangerous, judgement difficult." I think I have the sense of it.'

He bows. 'I am the better instructed, sir.'

Daily, daily, one must practise the courtier's art, and nightly, the art of governance: and never get it right. Chaucer says it in our own English tongue. 'The lyf so short, the craft so long to lerne.'

Just before 5 a.m. on Monday, 13 November, the merchant Robert Packington, a member of Parliament, leaves his house in the City of London to attend early Mass. A thick mist blankets the streets around Cheapside, and bells are ringing from all the parishes nearby. As Packington crosses towards the church of St Thomas of Acon, he falls to the ground. Some day-labourers, gathered on Soper's Lane waiting for hire, will claim to have heard a boom, a blast, a crack, or a soft detonation like a giant's fist punching a cushion.

Other churchgoers are close behind. They sprint towards the fallen man, shouting, and the labourers shout too, and the noise brings the neighbours into the street, lanterns in their hands, nightcaps on their heads, faces gaping, blankets thrown over their shoulders. By the time they reach Packington he is dead. Looming out of the mist, a woman screams, 'Help! Murder!' Men run for the watch.

A crowd gathers. Packington is recognised: he is well-known in the Mercers' Company and one of our chief citizens. A surgeon arrives, and identifies the wound as a gunshot wound. No one saw the assailant.

Before seven o'clock he, Lord Cromwell, is under siege at Austin Friars. I can tell you nothing, he says, shouldering through the crowd of guildsmen; I just want witnesses. Where did the attacker come from? In what direction go? And how, in so thick a mist, did he pick out Packington? Because we suppose Packington was his target – you do not crack at random at good men going to Mass.

'Fetch Stephen Vaughan,' he says. He has brought his trusted friend over, to keep an eye on the Mint, and he is the man for this business, as for all business requiring sternness and a quick eye; and he has known Packington for years. The coroner comes down with his clerks. The news is broken to the dead man's brothers. The Lord Mayor puts up a reward for information. Packington's friends add to it. Meanwhile the labourers have carried the body back to the dead man's house, and someone has paid them to scrub the blood away. Packington cannot have known he was shot. The surgeon says he would have felt nothing, unless the sensation of flying as West Cheap came up to meet him. He would have been dead before he could say a Pater Noster.

No one saw a strange man in the street. No one saw fire in the murk – as it might be, the match-flare for an arquebus. No one was seen carrying a parcel or wrapping, that could have disguised an arquebus. It seems possible a pistol was employed, that a man could carry in his coat and fire with one hand; moreover, a wheel-lock device, which needs no flare. There are few such weapons in London. Some countries have banned them, but that does not weigh with felons. If the pistol is still with its owner, it convicts him. If it was hidden, it will soon be found. Unless, of course, it's at the bottom of the river: in which case he is not just a whoreson, but a whoreson with a rich paymaster, to toss such a weapon away.

Packington was a gospeller, he was a Bible man, these many years he has travelled between here and Flanders, not only on cloth business but on the business of scripture; he carried Testaments home, when it was death to do it. 'He saw Tyndale just before –' a mercer tells him, and he holds up a palm: 'I cannot hear what you are telling me. If you met Tyndale yourself I must not know.' I am your brother in Christ, he thinks, but I am also the king's servant.

By noon he, the Lord Privy Seal, has visited Packington's widow, a daughter of the Skinners' Company. Rob had two stepchildren with her, and five of his own from his first marriage; the city wants to know who will make decisions for them. Chief Justice Baldwin, father of Robert's first wife, steps forward as their guardian. 'Guard yourself, Cromwell,' the judge tells him. 'I doubt not this killer has stalked you and you have never seen him.'

'What remedy?' he says.

'Body armour?' Baldwin says.

He has worn it before, in times of civic excitement, under his court robes. It is hot and as the day wears on it becomes a hoop around the ribs and a band tightening the heart. It is the same feeling you get when you are standing before the king, agenda in your hand, twenty items on it and every one crucial – and the king decides to talk about the medicinal properties of lilies. You think you might choke; you feel the ache of being bound to your desk while your nephew rides east, while Wyatt rides north, while Norfolk in some distant tent makes the fate of the commonwealth. And now he is told he is not safe in his own streets – not in his own house, not in his own bed, where Walter stands at the bedpost, sneering at him and fingering the king's purple and silver curtains.

It is no distance from Austin Friars to where Packington fell. He sits down in the parlour of the woman who cried 'Murder!' He listens to her recitation of her morning, from first opening an eye to the moment she ran into the street. But it is clear she saw nothing: except in a dream, she says, two or three nights back, where she saw the city on fire. Outside a restless crowd mutters and gossips on the spot: as if the gunman might come back and do it again, so they can witness. The labourers from Soper's Lane have changed their story. They now remember a tall man wrapped in a cloak, clutching something under it, and incanting to himself as he crossed the road.

Judge Baldwin is unstrung by the morning's events. 'Tall man in a cloak? How does that aid us? We did not think it was a naked dwarf did the deed.'

'But Lord Cromwell,' the men plead, 'he looked Italian.'

'How does an Italian look, in a thick fog?'

They shuffle their feet. He gives them some coins anyway, for showing willing. 'You're too soft,' Baldwin says, but he says, have mercy, Baldwin, they are only boys, and they carried the corpse – in acting as good citizens, they lost their earnings for the day.

'Listen, Cromwell. You don't get a good name among the lowly by sharing their concerns and handing out coin. You get their respect by overlooking them, as if you did not understand their sort, and your own belly had never been empty.'

'I could not so belie myself.'

'I'm not telling you what to do. I'm telling you how it is.'

Vaughan says, 'Do not advise my lord how to be lordly. A great man is open-handed.'

The labourers follow them, encouraged to more suggestions: perhaps the miscreant was a Yorkshireman? 'We would walk in the procession for the obsequy, sirs, if we got black gowns and four-pence. Pity he was felled on his way into church, and not his way out, for he might have flown straight to paradise and be looking down on us now.'

There is no Purgatory for Packington. He will rest quiet till, at the end of time, he takes a final boat to meet his God. A pity to have survived so many sea crossings, and Thomas More's persecutions, and the simmering fury of the London clergy, only to come to grief outside your own front door. There is no time to mourn, though the dead man has been his friend these many years. By ten o'clock the mist has dispersed, a pale sun shining from a clear sky. By the Angelus bell it is grey again, but for an hour the air is sprinkled with flakes of gold, as if Heaven has thrown some lustre on dead Packington. Funeral in two days, the family are told, three at most. Father Robert Barnes to preach. It's what the dead man would have wanted.

It's a miscalculation. Barnes's sermon is so inflammatory that he has no choice but to take him into custody. Better in my hands, he says, than in the Bishop of London's prison. The city has not forgot the case of Richard Hunne. It may be twenty-five years, or nearly that, but the shame is still fresh. This godly merchant, shut up in the Lollards' Tower, was found hanged: never was there such a hanging, with blood on the flags and blood on the walls. The authorities claimed Hunne had killed himself, in despair at his own heresies. The stool on which he was supposed to have balanced was well beyond reach of his feet.

At Windsor he stands at a casement with Henry, watching the rain. The wind moans in the chimney. The room seems drained of light, as if each window were a device for sucking it out and dribbling it feebly into the day outside.

The king says, 'Brighter? In the west? Do you think?'

'Not really.'

Henry sighs. 'The eye of faith, it must be.'

It occurs to him that he has answered absently, as if to a child or a member of his own household. Henry is fretful, his mind hopping here and there, and when he is in this humour it is best to keep your head low, like a birdcatcher. 'Do you know what I liked best this summer?' the king says. He corrects himself: 'I mean the summer before? I liked Wolf Hall. Once in a while every prince wishes he could lay aside his duties, and live for a year as a private gentleman. Because a gentleman bides content; he dances in the great barn decked with garlands, he sees the harvest home and knows every harvester by name.'

He says nothing. He has the boy Rob in his service, down in Wiltshire reporting on who comes and goes. Not that he suspects the Seymours, but it is no harm to have a source. The king says, 'I was innocent in those days. I did not understand the Boleyns and their treason. But once I did understand it, and cleared them out of the court, I thought everything would be better. Yet here I am, one summer passed and one winter passing, my son Fitzroy is dead, I have bastardised both my daughters, I have no heir and, as far as I understand, no hope of one. My subjects are in rebellion, my coffers are empty, and my cradle empty too. So tell me, Thomas, how is this better? How am I better off than this time last year? Last year, my subjects were not shot down in the street.'

Still he says nothing. We must trust the gale of self-pity will blow itself out, and presently it does. Henry straightens up. 'There are thirty thousand loyal men advancing on the town.' Pontefract, he means. 'Fear not, my lord. It will soon be back in our hands.'

Henry puts a hand on his shoulder. In that anointed palm there is *vertu*. Once consecrated, a king can heal. So why does he not feel healed?

As they bow themselves out Mr Wriothesley says, 'You were at a loss there, I think. You did not utter, sir.'

He says, 'Leave the king long enough, and he will start to cheer himself up. You must not crowd him, Call-Me. Did he not tell you so?'

* * *

When he goes to the Tower to see Barnes, it is without the body armour: it will stop a dagger, but it would not have saved Packington, and why would it save him? No breastplate but Jesus, and Thomas Avery as clerk. It is another foggy day, and it has not lifted by afternoon: rain just holding off, but the air as damp as if the afternoon had been rubbed with snails.

Barnes is at his books, but at the sound of the key he jumps up in alarm: a volume skitters away from him, he tries to catch it, picks it up from the floor and comes upright with his face red.

'Are they looking after you?'

Barnes falls back to his stool. 'Every time I hear footsteps in the passage, my heart ...' He taps the table, a broken rhythm. He sees Lord Cromwell is not alone: 'Who is this?'

'A good Christian. So be at your ease.'

'Ease?' Barnes laughs.

Avery says, 'This custody is for your protection.'

'You think it is I who needs protection? What about Cromwell here? Perhaps we should all take each other into custody?'

'As soon as my lord has the city quiet, you will be free.'

Barnes is himself again, tidying the papers before him. 'Most men would not believe you. But your master said the same when he locked up Wyatt – you will soon be free. And he kept his word. Though why he would extend himself for such a saucy fellow, I cannot imagine. Wyatt is hardly a promoter of God's cause.'

'But he is no papist,' Avery says. 'He saw their manners in Italy.'

'The Pope will unleash his terror now,' Barnes says. 'This is only the beginning. Where is that ingrate Pole? Or have you lost sight of him?'

'Still in Rome. They say Farnese lodges him above his own chamber, and means to make him a cardinal.'

'He should refuse,' Barnes says.

'Did anyone ever refuse to be made a cardinal?'

Barnes says, 'I thought you would have worked him some mischief weeks back, when he was in Sienna. If Thomas More can reach out his hand to strike at Tyndale, being himself dead, then I think that you, being a quick and vigorous man, should be able to strike down Reginald.'

He says, 'I like my life to be full of interest, Father Barnes. Nothing about killing interests me. And Reynold's heart was not always cankered.'

As soon as he unravels the conspiracies of such people – unknotting them with a casual hand, and deliberately looking the other way – they insist on entangling themselves again, and whistling and shouting till they get his attention. Margaret Pole, the renegade's mother, is in her castle at Warblington: too near the coast for his comfort. He imagines her in a tower with a mirror, signalling to boats at sea, which land and discharge the enemy. If it takes just one man to shoot dead a member of Parliament, it takes just one to shoot dead a king; his heart can burst like a common heart. The spot where Packington died is five minutes from the gate of Margaret Pole's town house; for all we know, the killer issued from behind her wall.

Barnes says, 'I hear that Henry put on a bold face with the Pilgrims' delegates. But that in private, he is very much afraid.'

In truth, it was all he could do to stop Henry apologising to the envoys, who came to Windsor and will travel back under safe-conduct. The king declared to them that, contrary to their belief, he had as many noble advisers now as at the beginning of his reign: he offered to name them, earl by earl, baron by baron, so the north country men could count up for themselves. That is not the way forward, he had thought. But at the king's command, he withdrew and left the field clear for his sovereign to exercise his charm.

He says to Barnes, 'The king believes his subjects are loyal for love of him. He is not by nature inclined to believe they conspire.'

'But you are training him to believe it?'

'Only a fool sees plots where there are none. Any crime may begin in impulse – a rash man, an angry man, a fool the worse for drink. But an impulse will not sustain rebellion. Nor can anyone rebel alone. It needs forethought. It needs confederacy. By the nature of the thing, there is conspiracy.'

'Then Henry must learn to help his good nature,' Barnes says. 'Unless you teach him to deploy it towards our German friends. Or the Swiss pastors. Thomas, all their goodwill is wasting away. They are tired of talks without result. Every chance of alliance is there, if we strike agreement on doctrine. But without a helping hand, England will go down.'

Picture Albion: a lonely ship on the ocean, the feet of her crew perpetually damp. The wind adverse, the storm blowing, the ports closed against her by chains stretched across the harbour mouths. The ignorant and fantastical people of the north say Henry is the Mouldwarp, the king that was and the king to come. He is a thousand years old, a rough and scaly man, chill like a brute from the sea. His subjects drive him out, and he drowns in his own tidal waters. When you think of him, fear touches you in the pit of the stomach; it is an old fear, a dragon fear; it is from childhood. He says to Avery, 'Would you leave us? It is for –'

'My own safety. I know.' Avery bows; pulls the door behind him as he goes.

'A good young man,' he says to Barnes. 'I trust him with my life, but some things he should not hear.'

'Things about our dread sovereign,' Barnes says. 'Do you dread him? I do. As much for what he will not do, as what he might. For his hesitations, which ruin us.'

'I think I make an advance. When I was first in his service he thought of our Zürich friends as no more than blasphemers who eat sausage in Lent. And Luther, he believed he was the son of a demon, who foams at the mouth when Mass is said. But what you must remember about the king – he was brought up to heed priests and to ask forgiveness for everything he does. You may kick out the confessors and tell him he is justified, but he still has a priest in the head.'

'He must be enraged with you,' Barnes says bluntly.

'Yes, though he tries to disguise it. He is angry that he has to defend me for my vile blood. But he cannot cast me off. Or it will seem as if he has allowed rebels to dictate to him.'

'That is poor security. To think you hold office at their pleasure.'

'It's all I have, Rob.' He gets up, stretches. 'I am going to see Tom Truth now.'

'Oh yes,' Barnes says, 'the fornicator. What I hear is, he makes extravagant promises to any keepers who will bring him to Margaret Douglas and leave him there an hour. But the keepers laugh at him. They don't trust his money.'

'I ought to get myself locked up,' he says. 'Then I might learn a thing or two.'

'Don't say it.' Barnes touches his crucifix. 'Shall I bless you?'

'Oh,' he says, 'don't put yourself out.'

He bursts out laughing: he feels light, no plate armour, no chain links, only the knife under his shirt. He has removed Margaret Douglas to the convent at Sion, put her under the care of the abbess. But perhaps her lover does not know that.

His old friend Martin is waiting to escort him. 'Lord Thomas sets up for a poet, Martin. What do you think?'

'Not one-tenth of Mr Wyatt's wit. Nor his application to the page.'

'You are becoming acquainted with the highest in the land.'

'Amongst whom I count yourself,' Martin says reverently. 'Though I trust it shall be many a day before I see you here.'

'Why not trust it will be never?' Avery says.

Martin is startled. 'I meant no ill-will. I am ever grateful to his lordship.'

Thomas Avery disburses the customary coins, for Lord Cromwell's godchild.

Tom Truth, unshaven for two days and unprepared for visitors, doesn't know whether to spit at him or kneel to him. It has perplexed better men. 'Sit down,' he tells him. Avery looks into his portfolio and passes him a paper. 'From Lady Margaret. May I read?

'And tho that I be banished him fro'
His speech, his sight and company,
Yet will I, in spite of his foe,
Him love, and keep my fantasy.'

Tom Truth lurches at him. He straightens his arm and fends him off.

'Give me that!' Truth comes at him again. He grips a handful of the lover's jacket and dumps him down on a stool.

'Do what they will, and do their worst,
For all they do is vanity,
For asunder my heart shall burst,
Surer than change my fantasy.'

He passes the paper back to Avery. 'By her "foe", do you think she means me? I hope not, considering I saved her life. She told me she was done with you, my lord, but it seems not.'

Lord Thomas jumps up. He is ready for him. Again he puts him down. 'Wait – I have also a verse from you to her.

'Thus fare ye well, my wordly treasure,
Desiring God that, of his grace,
To send in time his will and pleasure,
And shortly to get us out of this place.'

He raises an eyebrow. 'Are you going somewhere?'

Truth is winded. That was a hard dunt in the belly.

'Well,' he says, 'let us say you simply wanted a rhyme.'

'The king should release me.' Truth rearranges himself, his crumpled person. 'As matters stand in the north, he needs every man.'

'Every man he can trust.'

'The Yorkshiremen have you on the run. Their abbots will curse you.'

'Curses with me have none effect, because I give them no credit. They may curse till they combust.'

Truth says, 'My brother Norfolk will speak for me to the king.'

'I think the duke has forgot you. He is busy with the rebels. Not fighting. Bargaining.'

'Is he?' Truth looks mortified.

'We are outnumbered in the field. He has no choice but to give way.'

'He will not keep promises to low men,' Truth says. 'He will not be bound. No more will the king be bound to you, Cromwell. The harder you try to bind him by your deeds, the more he will detest you. I pity you, for there is no way forward for you. He will hate you for your successes as much as your failures.'

Truth has done some thinking, while he has been locked away. He says, 'I make sure that my successes are the king's, while my failures are my own.'

'But you cannot do without the Howards,' Tom Truth says. 'You cannot rule without noble blood. And my brother Norfolk would rather fight in an honourable contest –'

He interrupts him: 'Honour is a luxury, when someone is trying in earnest to kill you. Your brother knows that. As for you, your bad verse will choke you. I need not lift a finger. There are some prisoners I forbid to have paper. I might forbid you. For your own good, of course.'

He gets up. Avery steps out of his way. At the door a spirit jumps up and intercepts him: George Boleyn, arms gripping him, head heavy on his shoulder, tears seeping into his linen and leaving a residual salt damp that lasts till he can change his shirt.

By the first week of December, any sympathy for the rebels – sympathy which he has retained, for their ignorance – has melted away. Their communications from the peace talks are vomitous torrents of insult and threat. The commanders are obliged to exclude Richard Cromwell from the sessions, as the rebels will not sit down with him. All Cromwells, they declare, should be killed or banished. Parliament has no authority to dissolve abbeys – and it is not a real parliament anyway, because it is packed with the king's sycophants and elbow-hangers.

All this – and yet they expect a general pardon. They will get it, because their numbers are so great, even though they do not spare the king himself, reminding him that a prince who rules without virtue can be deposed, and they do not find any virtue in his adherence to Cromwell. They mention Edward II, Richard II: kings murdered by their own subjects, because they kept favourites, persons of high ambition and low morals. To compare Lord Cromwell, as they do, to Piers Gaveston … when their jibes are read out, certain councillors bite their lips, others turn their faces away. Because you would not feel it safe to laugh, if you had seen the king's white face.

Richard Riche says privately, perhaps it is an argument why the king should show himself to his subjects in the north. They would soon perceive he is not the sort of man who keeps a catamite. And that, even if he were, he would not so use the Lord Privy Seal.

He says, it is not for any unnatural vice that the people hated Gaveston: it was because he was base-born, and the king made him an earl. It was because the king made him rich, and he went in silks. But then, he was not English-born: that weighed too, with the ignorant.

Do not mock Ricardo Riche. At least, not to his face. He has stood up well to the hatred directed at him in recent weeks. He understands that there are sins that governors may, perhaps must, commit. The commandments for a prince are not the same as those that govern his subjects. He must lie for his country's good. We do not need a translation from the Italian, to understand that.

The rebels call him, Lord Cromwell, a Lollard. It is a term almost antique, though when he was young, men and women were burned for it. He hears a woman's voice in the air, on a breeze blown from his childhood: 'A Loller, that's one who says the God on the altar is a piece of bread.'

He is small; his belly is empty; he is far from home. Motherly, she takes his hand as they are jostled in the crowd: 'Stick by me, sweetheart.' She bats at the men in front of them, their solid wall of backs, and they part for her, saying, 'Sister, watch out, you'll have that child trampled!'

'Let us through,' she says, 'he's come a long way. Show him how the filthy creature dies, the enemy of God, so he gets a good view and remembers it when he is a man grown.'

Some memories from his childhood he can entertain. John in his kitchen, even Walter in his forge, all accompanied by the smell of burning. But when a memory like this rises up – and in truth there is no other like this – he slaps it down like a man killing a mole with a shovel.

The king tells his council – savouring the moment – 'I mean to invite our chief Pilgrim to join us for Christmas.'

Aske? There are gasps of surprise – simulated, as Lord Cromwell has taken care to prepare the councillors. After all, it's his idea.

'It is Aske who has chief credit with the rebels,' the king says. 'I shall probe his heart and stomach. And he will see that I am a monarch both generous and just.'

The only danger – and we cannot get around it – is that Aske will also see that Henry is not the puissant warrior of ten years ago, and he will carry word back to Yorkshire. The king wishes to be known as Henry, Mirror of Justice. But perhaps he will be known as Henry the Bad Leg.

Still: the game is worth the candle, and there is nothing to lose from sport with the chief Pilgrim. In our forefathers' time, the rebel Jack Cade had a good run before he was quartered, and his fractions sent back to his shire. The king will dandle Aske like an infant. Large presents, large promises: a gold chain and a crimson jacket. He will overawe him: trust the king for that. A man's dealings with Henry are a measure of him. They are a mirror to his weaknesses and vanities. You believe you are a man of ready address, you have rehearsed the encounter in your mind, but such is the overwhelming effect of his presence that you are overcome by holy fear and not able to utter a word.

'What shall I do, sir?' he says. 'I should not meet Aske.'

'Keep the feast with your own people.' The king adds: 'Be at your Stepney house. Then if I want you, you can get to Whitehall in an hour.'

He, the Lord Privy Seal, instructs Bishop Gardiner in France to quash the rumours that are rolling abroad. It is not true that Henry is besieged in Windsor Castle. Nor that he, or any Cromwell, has been stabbed to death in London on Chancery Lane. On the contrary, Cromwells are looking forward to the feast. Richard returns from the north; he comes with the plaudits of his senior commanders, Suffolk and Fitzwilliam.

By mid-month the rebel armies are dissolving themselves. Aske is to come to court under safe-conduct. News comes that the King of Scotland has compacted for his match with the French king's daughter; he and Madeleine will be married at Notre Dame on New Year's Day. The match will see hearty accord between Scotland and France, which is much to our disadvantage. 'What can I do but wish him joy?' the king says. He dictates a letter, waving aside offers to phrase it for him. 'Having certain knowledge ... your determination and conclusion for marriage ... daughter of our dearest brother and perpetual ally the French king ... *et cetera, et cetera* ... congratulate with you in the same ... desire Almighty God to send you issue and fruit thereof ...' the king's voice drips disdain, 'that may be to your satisfaction and to the weal, utility, and comfort of your realm.'

'Bravo, sir,' Wriothesley says. 'A wonderful powerful phrasing.'

The king says, 'James has already nine bastards that I know of.'

Edward Seymour: 'Majesty, I think he shall have no issue by Madeleine. I hear she is dying.'

'Then why would Scotland want her?'

No one answers. Perhaps to have a daughter, any daughter, of so great a king. And to get a hundred thousand crowns, which is more money than James has seen in his life. The king says, 'We will see how she likes the voyage to Caledonia, and the rough manners when she gets there.' But his voice yearns for her: 'They say she is beautiful ...'

'James must have wooed her with jewels,' he says, 'because he cannot speak the simplest word of French. All that shopping was not for nothing.'

'So does Madeleine speak Scots?' Henry says. 'That seems hardly possible. Would you not want to talk to your wife? Have some companionship with her? Still, he will not need her instruction in the bedchamber. He seems to know his business there.'

At Stepney, hedgerow berries are humble jewels, bright as beads of blood. The walls are hung with pine boughs, and the great wreaths of vines take two men to carry and hang; they were woven in autumn, when the branches would still flex. Blossoms from the drying rooms are bundled and gilded and ribboned, and as the weather grows dry and sharp, the panelled rooms fill at dawn and sunset with washes of blush-coloured light. He has been waiting for a clear day to see the apple trees pruned, and he goes out with his gardeners. 'Do not venture on the ladders, sir. Do you stand back, and watch the shape as we cut.'

The middle of the tree we call the crown. We take out any shoots that are frictious against each other, those that are growing back-wards, inwards, any way they shouldn't. We thin the new shoots and as we cut we are aiming for the shape of a goblet. When the balance is right, we clip the shoots, cutting back to an outward-facing bud. By three in the afternoon, though sweat is running in channels inside our jerkins, our gloved hands are stiff as clods and our voices in the air are faint, like birdsong in a distant paradise. We say, all done lads, and we get under cover and warm our hands around hot spiced ale. We have come through queasy days, his gardeners say. Please God all our builders and our cooks will be back with us for the feast, and Mr Richard in his glory.

We raise a cup to the warriors, picking their way south through the frightened shires. Then we sing a song, and cross ourselves, and pray for the apple trees. Indoors, we unlock the room called Christmas, with its costumes for mermen and magi and talking animals. We fit together the spikes of the great star that hangs in the hall.

What survives from this year past? Rafe's garden at midsummer, the lusty cries of the child Thomas issuing from an open window; Helen's tender face. The ambassador in his tower at Canonbury, fading into twilight. Night falling on the rock of Windsor Castle, as on a mountain slope.

In back alleys not yards from where the martyr Packington died, sailors offer nutmegs stolen from their ships' holds at three times the November price – which is already a duke's ransom. To show seasonal goodwill, a party of London rascals have set on members of the French embassy as they are enjoying a Christmas drink at the Cock and Keys in Fleet Street. They chase them, shouting 'Down with the French dogs!' The day ends with one dead Frenchman and another in a grave condition from stab wounds.

Gifts by the cartload roll up to his door: fat swans, partridges, pheasants. And Ambassador Chapuys, chuckling at the misfortunes of the French. He sits him down over a quiet supper and evades his close questions about the north. They are not really questions; because of his links with Darcy and other slippery souls, Eustache probably has better information than we do.

'Well,' the ambassador says, 'the writers of the almanacs said this would be a great year for secrets.'

He grunts. 'Greater for expenses.'

'Henry must eat his Christmas dinner from pewter. All his plate is melted down to coin.'

He shrugs. 'We have a great host to pay off. We must have turned out fifty thousand, at short notice.'

Chapuys does not believe the king had fifty thousand men, but all the same he cannot help working out the expenditure.

'I tell you, Eustache,' he says, 'you are much deceived about Englishmen, their temper. You talk to the wrong people. The Poles and the Courtenays don't know what is happening, I know what is happening. The Emperor boasts of what he will do here when his troops come. But Charles will do naught, because it is a bad precedent when a prince helps another prince's subjects to rebel. It gives his own people the idea they might do the same.'

'Go on thinking that,' Chapuys says, 'if you find it comfortable.'

They eat in contemplative silence: spiced venison, teal, partridges, and oranges thin-sliced like sunbursts. A shaft of light makes its way over the fallen snow, picking a path to the year ahead. The court rides through the city of Westminster and east to Greenwich, a moving trail of darkness against the frost. The Thames is a long glimmer of ice: a road in a frozen desert, a trail into our future, a highway for our God.

When the ambassador leaves him, it is three in the afternoon and feels much later. He sits down in gathering dusk to work through his day-books, compile his memoranda for the first council meetings of the new year. Christophe brings him wine in a goblet of Venetian glass. He says, 'This belonged to the cardinal. I bought it from the Duke of Norfolk.'

He buys the cardinal's property when he can, wherever he sees it, hangings and plate and books from his library: the new owners feel so guilty at the sight of him that they do not refuse his offer, which he pitches insultingly low. If things are not for sale he gets them back somehow. Look at this tapestry, under which he now sits, which depicts the Queen of Sheba in bold colours and gilt thread, her mild face like the face of a woman he once knew. Wolsey owned this hanging; the king took it when Wolsey fell: one day, in an overflow of generosity, the king gave it to him. Or, as he thinks of it, gave it back.

'Sometimes,' he says to Christophe, 'I am like you, I imagine other lives I might have had.' If Henry has a princely double, perhaps he has one as well, leading a safer life in Constantinople. Compared to Henry, a sultan is placid.

'I could have been a Frenchman like you,' he tells Christophe. 'I could have been a Lowlander.'

Christophe glances at the wall. 'If you had married that woven lady.' He does not mean the Queen of Sheba: that would be more outrageous than marrying the Princess Mary. He means Anselma, the Antwerp widow whose likeness has got into the weave. Maybe it is not so surprising to find her there. A master must have models. Perhaps the man who made the design passed her one day, running with a message to the quayside, or glimpsed her as they left Mass together at the church of Onze-Lieve-Vrouwe: and thought, who is that supple widow, with that slab of an English on her arm?

He says to Christophe, 'Will you bring The Book Called Henry? I think I will write down my thoughts. And more lights, if you will.'

'Do not miss your supper,' Christophe says. He sees how his household are trying to take care of him. Fussing over me, he says, as if you were my godparents.

He takes up his pen. God bless the work.

> You cannot anticipate or fully know the king. Thomas
> More did not grasp this. This is why I am alive and he
> is dead.

This is not a book you could take to the printer. It must be for the eyes of the few.

> Your enemies will continually belie you, and fix you
> with the blame for the malfeasance of others or for
> simple misfortune. Save your breath: any exculpation
> is too late. Do not be weakened by regret, and do not
> let regret weaken the king. Sometimes a king must act
> on imperfect information, and afterwards sanctify his
> impulses.

He thinks, suppose I fell ill, and were like to die? What would I do with the book then?

> Do not be afraid to ask for what you want. Ask and it
> shall be granted: but first cost it out. The king wishes
> to appear magnanimous at the least expense to himself.
> This is a reasonable position for a ruler to adopt.

I could leave it to Gregory or my nephew or to Rafe Sadler. But I will not leave it to Ricardo or Call Me. I doubt if there is much I can teach them. Or much they can learn.

> The king believes that even if he were not king, he
> would still be a great man. This is because God likes
> him.

He needs to be liked and he needs to be right. But
above all he needs to be listened to, with very close
attention.

Never enter a contest of wills with the king.

Do not flatter him. Instead, give him something he can
take credit for.

Ask him questions to which you know the answers.
Do not ask him the other sort of question.

This year has been what every year is: one long royal day, from the
king's first stirring to his slumber. Yet it has drawn to one singular
moment, as glass concentrates the rays of the sun. Time has distilled
to a single heartbeat, to the instant of the cut: the Frenchman with his
sword, his perfectly calibrated motion. Then the women holding up
their hands, their fingers stiff with loathing; bending their backs,
lugging the corpse away, tears glistening on their cheeks.

In the old stories, a great mirror is set before the palace of the king.
It is as wide as the sky, and three thousand warriors guard it. It is
reached by five-and-twenty steps of porphyry and serpentine. Even
by night they guard it, when it reflects nothing but a kingdom blan-
keted in darkness, and perhaps the faint etched line of a star.

Keep your eyes clear. Remember he is a king first and a
man second. This is where Anne went wrong. She
began to think he was only a man.

He looks up. The room is empty, except for those who do not count.
At such moments the phantom Wolsey would walk in, and peer over
his shoulder, and tell him what to write, large white hands with their
glinting rings heavy on his shoulders.

Sometimes he needs to imagine how it would have been, if the
Cornish had come to Putney, bellowing and drooling and trampling

everything in their path. Sion Madoc's dad had told him, 'They'll take a child like you and roast him on a spit.' He had laughed and said, 'I'll spit their arses.' In his black heart he wished for them, he wanted to hear their tread. Hear it, and you don't have to imagine it. Let the face of their giant crest the rise; or just see the crown of his head, and then you don't have to think about him any more, you don't have to picture him, you know the worst: walk with him one red mile, as he tears apart the neighbours and tosses their limbs into ditches.

And what then? Either he kills you, or you are one of those left, picking up remnants of Putney and gathering it into baskets.

> Do not turn your back on the king. This is not just a matter of protocol.

He is about to close the book, but he dips his pen, adds a final line:

> Try and keep cheerful.

PART THREE

I

The Bleach Fields
Spring 1537

When you become a great man, you meet kinsfolk you never knew you had. Strangers turn up at your door claiming to know more about you than you know yourself. They say that your father helped them in their misfortunes – unlikely – or that your mother, God rest her, knew their mother well. Sometimes they claim you owe them money.

So when among a crowd of petitioners he sees a woman who looks familiar, he takes her for a Cromwell of some sort. Seeing her again next day, and it appearing she has no protector, he has her fetched in.

She is a young woman, robust, sober. Good wool, he thinks, looking at her gown. He does not look at her, as looking at women gets him into trouble. 'I am sorry you had to come back for a second day. As you see, half of England is out there.'

'It has been a longer wait than you know, sir.' Her English is fluent, her accent Antwerp. 'I have come from over the sea, from Meester Vaughan's household.'

'You should have said so, they would have brought you in at once. You have a letter?'

'No letter.'

Messages that can't be put in writing are usually bad news. But she seems unperturbed: her eyes sweep over his coat of arms painted on the wall, and the set of pictures made by Holbein's apprentices. 'Who are those?'

'Princes of England.'

'You recall so many?'

He laughs. 'They are long gone. We have invented them.'

'Why?'

'As a reminder that men become dust, but the realm is continued.'

'You like to think about old days?'

'I suppose I do.' I prefer the common history, he thinks: in my own life and times, certain themes must be elided.

Her questions are simple ones, her manner open, and surely her message is nothing – snippets of Antwerp gossip too trivial for a courier. Still, he is interested to sweep them up. 'Christophe, wine for this young lady – will you take some wafers and spices, some raisins? An apple?'

'It was by eating of an apple that sin came into the world.' But she smiles as she says it, and as she takes her seat, raises her eyes to the Queen of Sheba, behind him on the wall: where she with her kindly expression and modest diadem offers a cup to the wisest of kings.

Her eyes flit to his face. She looks shocked. 'Where did you get that tapestry?'

'Our king gave it to me. For my services.'

Her glance moves back. 'And where did he get it?'

'From my patron, Wolsey.'

'And where did he get it?'

'Brussels.'

She looks as if she is calculating its value. 'So you did not have it made yourself?'

'It would have been beyond my means. I was not always a rich man. You see that it is Sheba and Solomon. You know your scriptures, I venture.'

She says, 'Also I know my mother.'

The cup in his hand is part-way to his lips.

She says, 'I am Anselma's child. I do not know how she is in this tapestry, but we can ask ourselves that some other day.'

He rises to his feet. 'You are welcome. I did not even know that lady had a daughter. I also have asked myself how it came about that her picture is in this weave. It is for her sake I always coveted it. I would look and look, and one day the king said to me, "Thomas, I think this lady should go and live with you." He turns back to her, smiling. 'So your father must be –'

He knows who Anselma married, after he left her to return to London. He knows the man's banking house, his family. Yet his name has always stuck in his throat.

She says, 'I know the gentleman you mean. My mother married him after I was born.'

He frowns. 'So he is not your father?'

'No,' she says. 'You are.'

He puts down his cup.

'Look at me,' she says. 'Do you not see yourself?'

Her sectioned apple lies on her plate; he studies its green peel; he studies the plate beneath it, blue and white, Italian, the design half-hidden by the fruit. His mind completes the hidden picture.

She says, 'I came because I heard from Meester Vaughan there was revolt here, and that you were in danger from certain pilgrims. I wanted to see you, even if it was only once.'

He thinks of his daughter Anne following him upstairs, her stocky little form wobbling, her fat hands reaching out. He says, 'My daughters are dead.'

'I am informed.'

By Vaughan, of course. What more has he told her? And what less? He says, 'How is this possible?'

'Secrets can be kept.'

'Evidently.' In his experience, secrets do not keep. Perhaps that flat watery country is less leaky than this.

She says, 'It was my mother's wish that after you left Antwerp you should not be troubled. When I would ask her, "Where is my father?" she would say, "Gone over the sea." When I was a little child I thought you were one of those men who sails to the new-found lands, and brings back treasure.'

He turns his back to give himself a moment to arrange his face. He looks at the tapestry as if he had never seen it before: as if he were taxed to unpick it and reweave it. It is usual to show Sheba gazing at

Solomon. Hans, for instance, has made a picture in which the monarch wears the face and garments of our own king, and the onlooker sees the back of Sheba's head. But Anselma looks you frankly in the face; she has turned away from the Israelite, as if behind her smile lies boredom.

She says, 'You are thinking, I am not much like my mother.'

More like me, poor girl. 'You are aware that until this moment I did not know you lived?'

'I have shocked you. I am sorry.'

'You must allow me time to understand it … Your mother bore you after I crossed the sea, and said not a word to me?'

'That was her resolve.'

'But why did she not write, when she knew her condition? Why bear it alone? Of course,' he sighs, 'you cannot answer that. Such matters are not discussed with children, are they? But I would have come back. I would have married her. Tell her –'

'My mother is dead. A cold on her chest this winter.'

In the pause he consults his heart: it registers nothing, except the trace of the pen that, in the Book of Life, lightly inks a fate. It is the fate of a woman he knew in another country. And she not young, either.

His daughter says, 'My mother always spoke well of you. Though she did not speak of you much. She said, Jenneke, I do not want him to regard you as a mistake he must pay for; he was a young man far from home, and I a widow, and both of us wanted company. But as you say, a child never hears the whole of these matters, and that is why I have come to find out for myself what manner of man you are. Are you glad to see me?'

'I am amazed,' he says. 'How could I have a daughter and not know it? When she was carrying you, how did she hide you?'

She shrugs. 'As women do. She went away. She made a journey. I was born in another town.'

'And she married the banker.'

'Yes, it was a good chance for her. He was a kind man and made her no reproach, but he had sons from his first wife, he had no need of an Englishman's daughter. I stayed with the nuns, who were good to me. Then my mother took me to Stephen Vaughan. Teach her English, she said, against the day.'

Against the day when the secret comes out. 'How could Stephen know and say nothing?' Each word she speaks seems to deepen his bewilderment. Though he has heard, of course, of cases like this. Men like him, who have been travellers; men like him who are not celibate saints: one day they are going about their lawful occasions and there is a knock on the door, and 'Guess who?' It was a joke with the cardinal, who claimed he had spawned bastards everywhere: whenever some squat rascal heaved into view, he would say, 'Look, Thomas, one of yours.'

No joke now. He says, 'You know Stephen Vaughan is here in London?'

'He will scold me,' she says. 'He intended to pick his good time and tell you himself. He said, Cromwell rises in the world, he has the ear of the king; he defends the gospel, he protects our sisters and brothers, and we should not carry fuel to the flames. He said, no name is too bad for his enemies to smear him – and if they know about you, Jenneke, they will call him a whoremaster too.'

'True,' he says.

'But then he said, you do not want to be a nun, Jenneke, nuns are finished; so it is time you were wed. And your husband will need to know who you are, or we can make but a poor bargain – you are a bastard, but you are not just any bastard. We must sound out my lord your father, we must prepare him. But then this trouble broke out. And I did not want to wait any longer.'

When he held out his hands to her, she had not risen to take them; she had kept her seat and kept her countenance, and he admires her for it. He searches for Anselma in her but can only find himself. He thinks, why did you not come early? Time was when I was a different sort of man. Time was, I would bound into my own house and run upstairs singing. Even last year I was different, before I met Wolsey's daughter: before she cut me to the quick, and the wound healed and scarred.

He asks, 'Your mother had more children? With the banker?'

'No. But she lacked nothing. Nor did I. The nuns taught me what a woman needs to know. Later, many of them who were wise women read the books of Erasmus, his New Testament, and became wiser still. Perhaps you knew him?'

'No, not I. I only know his books. Though he came to London and stayed with Thomas More. Outstayed his welcome, Lady Alice said.'

'More had a wife?' She digests this. 'I thought he was some kind of monk.' She puts down her plate; she has eaten most of her apple, so now the platter shows the blue townscape beneath: campaniles, castellated towers, bridges over fast-flowing water. He has spoken of More without thinking – the name hovers at everyone's lips these days, you would hardly think the man was dead; to hear the chit-chat about him, you would expect to meet him as you hurry down Cheap. 'You are a Bible woman?'

'I am instructed.'

'And you know – forgive me, I do not know what Stephen has told you – but you know it is my cause, it is my chief endeavour –'

'The English scripture. I am advised.' She says, 'Meester Vaughan tells me your father was a brewer, trading in wool also, having a sound business, and connected to a good family called Villems, who were towards the law.'

'Williams,' he says. 'We say it so.' He considers. 'All that is true.'

Enough said, perhaps? She doesn't need to hear about Walter.

'These people have helped you to your fortune? The family Williams?'

She is a quick learner. Already she seems less foreign than when she entered the room. He says, 'Wolsey helped me. But perhaps Stephen has not told you who Wolsey is?'

'A worldly prelate. Dead.'

'You see my coat of arms, painted there on the wall? Those black birds are called choughs. They were the cardinal's emblem.'

'Does it not anger his enemies to see them there?'

'Yes. Oh, yes. But, you see, they have to grit their teeth and stifle their curses. They have to bow their heads and endure it and say, "I trust you are in health, Lord Cromwell?" They have to fetch up a smile for me. And bend the knee.'

'You are proud.' She gazes at him. 'Your person is very fine, and I like very well your house. I was told, your father is the first citizen of London. I did not believe it but I believe it now. I have stood outside a day or two. I wanted to look at you and judge.'

That seems reasonable. 'I am encouraged that you decided to come in.'

'Who would not be curious to see such a great household? Especially if your father is in it.'

He feels he ought to make some statement, some apology – some lengthy explanation, why all is not as it seems – but already he hears footsteps and voices outside his door, his people will be thinking this young woman has taken enough of his time. He says, 'When you work for Henry Tudor you have no choice in how you appear. You must be a courtier, you cannot look like a clerk. And the common people, outside the gate, you must show them you have the king's favour. They only understand what they see plain. If you put on no show, they take you for nothing.'

He wants her to know, I was happy in my lawyer's black. But is that true? He thinks, I used it for concealment. That does not mean I was content. Did I not have a doublet of purple satin, long before the cardinal came down?

The door opens. It is Thomas Avery. He stares at the visitor. 'Christ in Heaven, Jenneke, what are you doing here?'

'Thomas Avery, this is my daughter.'

The young man stands with a folio slapped to his chest, his eyes on Jenneke. 'I know.'

When Jenneke has gone he calls Avery in and bids him sit; he would give him an apple if he wanted one, and they are good Charterhouse apples too. 'I am not angry,' he says. 'Come, Thomas Avery, you are a Putney boy, my people knew your people, we should deal straight with each other.'

'None of that follows,' Thomas Avery says warily. 'Putney people are as crooked as anywhere. Worse.'

'I mean, we should be at ease with each other.'

Avery looks at him as if to say, do you have any idea how impossible that is?

'You saw her, did you not, at Stephen's house, when I sent you over to learn his trade? You came back and talked about her. Jenneke, you said. The name so often on your lips, I thought you were in love with her.'

Avery says nothing. His hands lie still, unoccupied.

'I thought, we will make this work for Avery – even if she is an orphan with no money, Stephen and I will manage it between us. But then you ceased to speak of the girl and I thought – God help me – I thought perhaps she had died, and so I did not speak of her either. I waited for news. And now …'

He feels he is reaching for the truth but failing to grasp it. A dead thing has proved quick: it is as if Anselma is one of those statues monks keep, that moves its eyes, jerking them in their orbits; or reaches out a wooden hand, and adjusts its cerulean robe.

Avery says, 'Sir, I came home from Antwerp with Jenneke's picture in my mind as clear as if she stood before me, and in this very room I took your measure, I studied your features, I crossed the sea again and studied hers. You can see she resembles you, and I could not miss it. I put the question to Mr Vaughan. He said, Avery, you have it right, but be very secret. I saw I had trespassed in private business. Vaughan said, I will not ask you to take an oath, for that should not be done except in the gravest cases, and I suppose it will come out one day – but let it not be through you.'

'And you kept my secret. That I did not know myself.' He considers Avery. 'Well, if you can keep one secret, you can keep another.' The boy stirs, reaching for paper, but he raises a palm: 'Sit still and listen. I am going to tell you where my money is.'

Avery is surprised. 'Well, sir, I talk to your receivers and your surveyors. Your officers are all confidential with me. If they were hiding anything, I would know.'

'I applaud your diligence. But there are other funds.'

'Ah.' Avery thinks about it. 'Abroad?'

He inclines his head.

'Why?'

'Against the day.'

'But has not the king said – you will pardon me, sir, but the whole city talks of it – "I will not part from my Lord Privy Seal, not for no man on earth"?'

'That is what he has said.'

Avery looks down at his feet. 'We know the love his Majesty bears you. We see the fruits of it daily. But we fear the country will rise again, and who knows how the world will turn? Not that we doubt our sovereign, his word – but who was in greater favour than my lord cardinal in his day?'

'His example is before me.' Though not his ghostly person: not since Shaftesbury. 'So if one day the Duke of Suffolk and the Duke of Norfolk storm in here, breaking my locks and splintering my chests, and wrecking like the devils at the sack of Rome, I want you, Thomas Avery, halfway down the street, and not so much as "What do you?" Do not even stop to curse them, just run. As soon as you can get a letter abroad, send to those names I shall tell you. Then if Henry lays hands on what is mine, he will think he has the whole, but he will be – let us not say he will be deceived, for I would not deceive my king – let us say he will be less than fully informed.' He watches Avery. 'You can do it? Or the task lies too heavy?'

The boy nods.

'Good.' Because Richard is of too hot a temper for such a post-mortem task. And Rafe is assumed to know all my business, he thinks, and I should not like his loyalty divided, as he is the king's servant now and must answer to him. He says, 'Gregory is still young. He would need help. And now it seems I have a young woman to provide for as well.'

'Where has she gone, sir?'

'To seek Vaughan. I wonder what she will tell him.'

He would be glad to have Avery in his family. But he is no longer free – he is pledged to the daughter of Thacker, the steward. They keep close, the Austin Friars boys: perhaps there will be one of them spare for his daughter to wed. Though something in Jenneke's manner tells him that she has not come to stay. She came to satisfy her curiosity and set eyes on the father who is a great man. Perhaps as a child she watched for his ship coming up the Scheldt. But those days are long gone and childhood is over.

Aske's safe-conduct is good till Twelfth Night. At Greenwich during the Christmas season, the king has asked the rebel leader to write an account of the outrages in the north – from the first hint of trouble in the autumn, to his winter journey under flag of truce.

Aske is two or three days about his task, sustained by prime beef, claret and banked fires. The product is conveyed to my lord Privy Seal. He is spending his holiday dealing with letters from Calais, where the population has been swelled by an influx from beyond the Pale of men and their families pressing to become English denizens. Grain is short this winter and herring go four for a penny, therefore some plan will have to be made to feed the town. No use waiting for the governor to do it. Lisle can't boil an egg.

My lord Privy Seal lays aside his letters to read Aske's tale of the Pilgrims. 'What a marvellous little book,' he says at last. 'I wonder that a lawyer should be so free with the ink.' Aske talks about himself like a man in a storybook. 'The said Aske', he calls himself. He says what he did in the rebellion, but he doesn't say why.

'Aske has seen the king,' says my lord Privy Seal. 'The king has seen Aske. He has served his purpose. Now get him back to Yorkshire.'

Aske must be conveyed promptly, with the king's offer of a general pardon, in order to quash rumours that on the one hand he has been hanged, and on the other hand promoted to high office. No loyal subject could turn down Christmas with his king. But the visit has compromised him: it will be easy for the Yorkshiremen to say the court has bought him. In any event, it is futile to believe Aske alone can command the towns and shires. The banner of the Five Wounds has even been seen in Cornwall, where they say it was brought back by some real pilgrims, who had walked right across the country to the shrine at Walsingham in Norfolk.

Does this not show the nature of the pilgrim trade? In my lord Privy Seal's view, nothing comes of trailing from shire to shire to pray. You can pray at home. It costs you less, you don't get robbed on the road, and you don't spread diseases or carry them back to your native country. Besides, Walsingham is useless, the king says. 'I went there to pray for my son I had with Katherine, but he only lived two months. Still, Jane wanted to go. Women are fanciful and set store by shrines. She prayed for her womb to quicken but ... There you are,' the king says. 'Nothing's happened yet.'

As part of his peace offer, the king has committed himself to a progress through the north. At Whitsuntide in York he will open a parliament and crown Jane: or Michaelmas, at the latest. Convocation will sit in York too, so the northern church can have its say in how we worship God, instead of being quashed by Canterbury and told what to think and how to pray. Ahead of the king's coming, the Duke of Norfolk will arrive to guarantee order, and deal out justice to anyone who breaches the newly-established peace. Norfolk will have the title of the King's Lieutenant, and he will not come with an army, but only his ducal train. Meanwhile those gentlemen who have taken part with the rabble, voluntarily or not, are required to get themselves into the king's presence to make their explanations and receive their pardons man to man.

But when the north empties of its chief leaders, every tanner and butcher pushes to the fore, inscribing rebel proclamations and nailing them to church doors. The Earl of Cumberland writes it is dangerous for a messenger to be taken with a letter addressed to Cromwell – whatever the content, he will be murdered. The wars are bitter, in pulpit and in print, in guildhall and market square: name-calling, placarding, brawling. Royal couriers and even the heralds are attacked on the roads, their office not respected. Since they meet the Pilgrims' immediate demands, the king's offers are enough to buy a truce. But with regard to their request to turn time backwards, nothing is done and nothing can be done.

The crown is anxious about its income this year; he, the Lord Privy Seal, meets with the treasury to plumb the depths of the deficit from the north, where taxes due last September are still unpaid. Rafe Sadler leaves mid-January on a mission to Scotland – he is meeting our king's sister Margaret, who is seeking to annul her third marriage. On the road he sees how uneasy is the king's peace. At Darlington, forty men with clubs come and stand outside his inn, with no good intent. 'So Rafe is having a dangerous time after all,' says my lord Privy Seal. 'He thought his life was too quiet.'

Rafe talks down the Darlington men, addressing them from the window of his inn, shivering as the wind slices: out of sight below the sill he grips a dagger. Lucky they don't know Rafe is like a son to Cromwell, or they would haul him out and make short work of him. Worse is ahead, he fears, from the Scots. Besides, experience assists him: forty armed Yorkshiremen do not equal Henry on a bad day.

'Wait till the king gets among them,' my lord Privy Seal says with relish. But only part of him believes the king will go.

We are all concerned about our friends in the north. When Lord Latimer set out for London, to give an account of his conduct in last year's broils, a rebel host entered Snape Castle and took his wife Kate hostage. There is eye-rolling and elbowing among the young clerks at the Rolls and at Austin Friars: 'Our master will ride to her rescue – he must, she is his bride-elect.'

According to the northerners, it is the king's niece Margaret Douglas who is his bride-elect, and he is aiming to be named the king's heir.

He says, 'This Douglas marriage, is this instead of the Princess Mary, or as well? The rebels think I am a heretic, but surely they know I am not an infidel, to have a wife in every house?'

Gregory says, 'I think I should have some choice in my step-mother, but nobody asks me what I think. These ladies are none of them much my senior. And anyway,' he says, puzzled, 'why do people think my lord father will outlive Henry, to reign after him? It does not say much for Dr Butts and his art.'

The news of his father's bastard, Gregory has received with equanimity. He is glad to have a sister again. 'When my father is king,' he says, 'and wed to Latimer's wife Kate, and to Meg Douglas and Mary Tudor, you will be the Princess Jenneke, and you and I shall harness a gold chariot with white horses, and speed like Phoebus through Whitehall, and throw buns to the populace. The populace will say, "They are plain-looking folk, but see how their faces shine!" And eat up their buns, and bless us as we hurtle past. Surely you will stay with us? What can Antwerp offer, next to the prospects here?'

When he has cleared an afternoon, he sits with his daughter, the snow-light filtering into his workroom: 'These books?' she says.

'Law books.'

She nods. 'It was your trade.'

He asks her, 'How is Antwerp now? I try to picture it. I heard about the fire at Onze-Lieve-Vrouwe church. I hear that the roof fell in.'

'It was a catastrophe,' she says. He is pleased that she knows the word. 'It started with one candle. All the timbers from the transept fell, and destroyed the chapels below. Some of us said it was God destroying idols.'

'When I came back here I was homesick for Antwerp,' he says. 'I was settled among its customs, and I would have stayed there, for not much encouragement. You must believe me – if I had understood your mother to be with child, I would not have left her. I would not have dragged her to England – you see, I was returning home after many years, and I had no patron, and no sure livelihood.'

He sees himself then: sleek young Italian, face attentive, eyes busy. What's left of that boy? Only his glance around a room to note the exits, his dislike of having people moving behind him. Now he settles into a chair when he sits in it. His hands – formerly busy with knife and quill, taking down the words of other people – now rest lightly one in the other, right fist in left palm. He looks as if he is praying; but with a slight shift of posture – a straightening of the shoulders, a dip of the chin – he looks as if he is spoiling for a fight.

He says to his daughter, 'I forgive Stephen Vaughan, I must, because he meant for the best, even though it would have been a consolation for me to have you here with me. Such things happen. Misunderstandings. Partings.'

'It is through Stephen Vaughan I know you,' she says. 'He talked of you, long before I had reason to listen. He would not admire a soft man or a foolish man. He loves you next to God.'

'Do people know who you are? In Antwerp?'

'Some guess. You are well-remembered in the town.'

No doubt he is. The English merchants would say, go out, Thomas, and hear the gossip. Tell us what our neighbours are saying; when they put their heads together and use Antwerp expressions, what are we missing? He wore in those days an air of dazed amiability, the new boy keen to learn. 'What can Antwerp offer?' Gregory has asked Jenneke, and once he had asked it himself. In Italy you thought, this is all I want: this misty view from belvedere or turret, this blue, this gold; this heat filtered through leaves, this mosaic across which the light shifts, where ancient eyes look back at me. It was true there were aspects of Italy he preferred to forget. What can you learn from the memory of hunger and pain, of destitution and flight? He remembers the day when his only task was to drag himself undercover before it was too cold to sleep in the streets. But in Florence his fortunes turned. It was there – and in Venice, in Rome – that he had learned to be sly and sidelong, always vigilant, always ready to take offence or pretend it, ready also to back off with a soft word when the odds were against him. He learned to walk by night, to whisper, to bow to magnificos; to step forward at the right time, with the right hint or suggestion made in a low voice, so magnifico can take the credit.

But then he was restless. He thought, what next? And when he set foot in Antwerp he thought, there is more to want and more to know. The sky so wide and the land so flat, possibilities stretching out before you. In Italy you learned cunning, but in Antwerp, flexibility.

And besides, the shopping! Just step out of your door and you can get a diamond or a broom, you can get knives, candlesticks and keys, ironwork to suit the expert eye. They make soap and glass, they cure fish and they deal in alum and promissory notes. You can buy pepper and ginger, aniseed and cumin, saffron and rice, almonds and figs; you can buy vats and pots, combs and mirrors, cotton and silk, aloes and myrrh.

Already he had friends in the city. On the day he first sailed from England, a boy, he had met a merchant family with their samples of wool, and they had seen the marks of his father's boot on his face. We shall not forget you, they said, there is a bed for you whenever God brings you to our town. The years rolled by: 'Good Lord!' they said, when he knocked at the door. 'It's Thomas! He is grown up! He is an Italian now!'

In Antwerp, the more tongues you could master, the more you could succeed. If he lacked a phrase in one language, he had it in another, and his earnest vehemence made up for any gaps. He sought out, as he had in Italy, the company of sober elders, whose table talk was refined and who would give away their wisdom to a young foreigner who admired them, one who asks questions, questions, and looks impressed by the replies. Such dignitaries always need a repository for their secrets, just as they need a man who will take a confidential dispatch and be back with an answer before you notice he's gone. The drawback is that one must consent to their indoor lives: no *calcio*, just polite archery on a Sunday. The courtyards where one trades in wool and money may be open to the sky, yet they cannot help but smell of tallow, ink and dinners, seeped into the wool of dark winter garments: he would walk, and under the shadow of the Steen with its warehouses take a breath of river air, and imagine the great world beyond. There were some hundred of his countrymen – Englishmen, that is – dwelling in or around their English House; they lived side by side with the Castilian nation, the Portuguese and the Germans, but they were cherished by the city because they paid so well for their privileges. When their ships came in they had first use of the crane at the docks, powered by a man treading inside a wheel. He asked one of the Antwerpers, 'Does it have a name?'

A baffled look. 'We call it the crane.'

He thought, if a cannon has a name, if a bell has a name, the crane should have a name too.

413

'It is not unreasonable,' he said coolly.

The Flemish fellow said, laughing, 'We can call it Thomas if you like.'

'By the way,' he muttered, as he walked away, 'it would work a lot better if you had men treading the outside, not the inside.'

No use trying to disturb the fixed notions of a strange city. But he is a man who thinks about lifting heavy weights, about winches, beams and pulleys, and about joints, how to make them frictionless.

Of course they gossiped about him, when he moved into Anselma's house. She undertook to show him the country and introduce him to people who could do him good, relatives of hers. One day they went to Ghent together and stepped into the church of John the Baptist to say a prayer. It is only on a feast of the church that they open the doors of the great altarpiece to show you the crowds of angels and prophets flocking to the Lamb of God. Instead they saw the donors of the piece, portrayed on the outer doors. They were a careworn couple, she purse-featured, he bald: but no doubt full of grace. He thought, give it thirty years, and that could be us. I would have forgotten my English and be entirely a Fleming: a stout burger, persuading younger legs to run to the wharves for me, or climb up to high places to see if my ships are coming in.

The church was bustling and noisy, but they could hear each other whisper: their heads close, her fingers sliding into his palm. Their breath mingled; she leaned against him, soft and warm. He said, 'Make me good, O Lord, but not yet.'

She laughed, and he said, 'Not me. Augustine.'

Yet the day came when she told him, 'Time to sail, Thomas. You are my past now, and I am yours.'

He goes to the Tower to interview Robert Kendall, the vicar of Louth, the first begetter of the trouble in Lincolnshire: the pardon does not extend to such principal offenders as he. Clouds stack over the town in grey-blue fortresses of air, battered by the wind as if by cannon-fire. Mr Wriothesley attends him. He misses Rafe, but Rafe is heading to Newcastle, to await his safe-conduct over the border.

Reginald Pole has left Rome, in his new cardinal's hat. Now that peace has broken out, he has missed his chance to invade and lead the English, though the Scots have made clear they would have been ready to come to his aid. When Lord Cromwell hears Pole is en route to Paris, Francis Bryan crosses the Narrow Sea with a demand for his extradition. Reginald reaches the French capital to find the king is elsewhere. Thwarted and scanted, blocked and barred, he skulks off towards Imperial territory: but our man in Brussels has already persuaded the Emperor's regent not to receive him.

The new cardinal's relations – his mother Lady Salisbury, his brother Lord Montague – still protest they abhor his foolery. All they want is to see Reginald conformable and loyal to the Tudors, as they are and ever shall be. To hear them talk, if they saw Reginald in his red hat, they would snatch it off and spit in it.

Mr Polo, the Spanish call him. It makes my lord Privy Seal laugh.

'I hear you have had a visitor, Cromwell,' the Imperial ambassador says.

'Oh yes? Why don't you tell me all about it, Eustache?'

The ambassador waves a hand. 'Naturally the neighbours talk. It is not every day they see the Queen of Sheba's daughter with her travelling bag.'

Their dinner comes in: in deference to the cold, a thick ragout of mutton, and an ox-tongue pie heavy with mace. '*Ça va, Christophe?*' the ambassador enquires, but Christophe only grunts; he is wondering how much of the pie they might chance to leave.

'I wish it were spring,' Chapuys says. 'I am like the Israelites in the desert, I long for the melons and cucumbers of Egypt.' He sighs. '*Mon cher*, you must not blame me if your amours are of interest to all Europe. Hitherto, observers have been frustrated by your extreme discretion.'

'It is a stale sin,' he says. 'If it was ever a sin at all.'

Chapuys serves himself a little ragout. The scent of dried sage fills the room. 'You think your Lutheran God will understand?'

'I tire of telling you I am not a Lutheran.'

'Rest from your labours, for I shall never believe it,' Chapuys says cheerfully. 'Certainly you are a sectary of some sort. Perhaps one of those who oppose the baptism of infants?'

He chews a little, his eyes on Chapuys. This is the rumour young Surrey has spread, and other ill-wishers; it is the way to ruin him with Henry, and the ambassador knows it. 'Christophe,' he calls, 'where's that capon?' He puts down his napkin. 'Is it likely?' he says to Chapuys. 'How could I profess such a creed, and remain the servant of a Christian commonwealth? Those people oppose the payment of taxes. They oppose the taking of oaths. They oppose books and writing and music.'

'Yet they say this sect has crept in everywhere in Calais. And Lord Lisle cannot do much against it.'

Christophe bears in the capons, the flesh cubed and seethed in red wine, the sauce thickened with breadcrumbs.

'This is a very brown repast,' Chapuys says, 'but it tastes better than it looks.'

'Soon it will be Lent. Then you will be crying for the fleshpots of Egypt, and never mind the melons and cucumbers.'

The ambassador dabs his mouth. 'What will you do with your new daughter? Marry her quietly, I suppose, with a good dowry. You will confess to the world who she is?'

'I shall have a hard time to hide it, with you shouting it through the streets.'

'It is a miracle,' Chapuys says. 'Like Lazarus. Though one wonders, was he truly welcome?'

It has crossed his mind before now. Were his family pleased to see him, or did they think he had been too self-important, in violating the laws of nature?

'What does she want, actually?' Chapuys asks.

'Just to see me. She says she will not stay.'

'Back to the heretics' refuge?'

'Antwerp is hardly that. Your Emperor keeps his hand on it.'

'As I understand it, the whole place is hollow. There are tunnels and cellars, a whole city underground, and from the surface you would not know it was there. Of course, you will have been in them yourself, in your young days?'

'Naturally. Because they are warehouses. Nothing more.'

Chapuys says, 'If you want to keep your daughter in England, you will have to tempt her. You must unlock your chests and spend your money. Is there a woman in this world who will refuse a string of pearls, or a border of goldsmiths' work?'

In Antwerp you open a door that you think leads to another room. Instead, plunging at your feet is a stair down into the earth. You strain your eyes into the darkness. You creep like a snail, your shoulder brushing the wall to steady you, a foot feeling for the edge of the step. Yet within weeks, you can run up and down easily, your feet knowing exactly where to go.

But only in your own house. On another man's steps, look out.

Austin Friars, January: his daughter turns over, in a flood of splintered sunlight, the Book of Hours that belonged to Lizzie Wycks. 'Your wife, what was she like?'

What can he tell her? We were practical people, who did each other acts of practical kindness; she died and I missed her. Her affections were deep and stern and when she spoke to the children about their derelictions she would say, 'I tell you this for your own good.' When she went into company she wore a gable hood like a woman of fashion but when she was at home she wore a housewife's coif. She was a maker of lists, a tabulator of stores: servants careless as they are, a woman must always be taking stock. She kept a list of his sins, in the pocket of her apron: took it out and checked it from time to time.

When his children were born, the house was entirely given over to women. Elizabeth was well-furnished with cousins and godsibs. They knew his family, his history, and perhaps they did not think he could rise above it. He was very pleasant to them, very mild. One day he heard a cousin say to Liz, 'He tries really hard, your husband.' He could not hear Liz's muffled response. For all he knew she might have said, 'He tries really hard but he consistently fails.'

When they married he had said to her, one thing I guarantee: no woman of mine will be poor. He had hoped to be a good husband, to be provident, faithful. He was exceptionally provident and mostly faithful. By the time Grace was born he was working for Wolsey every hour. The cousins would look at him warily when he came in: where have you been? As if it must be somewhere nefarious. They were waiting to see another self: the wolf that lives in man, his father Walter bristling through his skin.

By the time he returned from Antwerp, Walter was a man of consequence in the district. Formerly he had enlarged his land-holdings by kicking over his neighbours' boundary-markers, but now he had acres by lawful purchase, and he had invested in his brewery, even tempting a Lowlander over to teach him to improve his beer, for the art was well-mastered there. His brother-in-law Morgan had said, 'Thomas, you should go to Putney and see your dad now. You should see the belly on him. You should see the hat he's got, now he's a churchwarden.'

'If you recommend it,' he'd said, 'I'll go and have a look.'

The day came. Before he caught sight of Walter, the neighbours caught sight of him. Word spread. Some gawper said, 'It's bloody little Put-an-edge-on-it. Where's he been, do you think?'

He did not feel a need to answer.

'Show his face here!' a woman said. 'He must think we have short memories!'

He had nothing to say.

'We thought you were dead,' a fellow exclaimed.

He did not correct him.

Then he looked up and Walter was rolling towards him. He wasn't wearing the hat but he was wearing the belly. It didn't soften him. He might be sober and shaven, but he still looked as if he would knock you down as soon as blink.

The smithy was still there, not that Walter did the work these days; when he held out his hand it was pink and clean and you would have to look close to see the burn marks.

He, Thomas, prowled around the premises. Tools in their racks; a leather apron on a peg, with the stench of the tannery still about it.

Or perhaps he imagines that: sweat, salt, shit, all the savours of his early life. Walter said, 'Taking inventory, are you? I'm not dead yet, boy.'

He made no answer.

'You moving back?' Walter asked.

'No.'

'We not good enough for you?'

'No.'

People are always prompting you, you notice, to forgive and forget. They are always urging you, do as your father did, boy: be what your father was. Young men claim they want change, they want freedom, but the truth is, freedom just confuses them and change makes them quake. Set them on the open road with a purse and a fair wind, and before they've gone a mile they are crying for a master: they must be indentured, they must be in bond, they must have someone to obey.

He would like to be the exception. He has travelled a mile and more. But perhaps he isn't that different from the mass of men. As a boy, before he ran away, all he wanted was to be his father – Walter, but tidier. He had thought, one day the old man will keel over and get buried: then I, Thomas, will be master of the brewery and runner of the sheep, and I'll hand the smithy work to boys I'll train, only because of lack of hours in the week. There's something about a smithy (it's the warmth) that draws in all the idlers of the district on a winter's day, and they stand around gossiping, till the light drains from the sky, and the colours of burning, cherry red to pale straw, are replaced by a sky of slate, by the moon heeled underfoot by late drinkers heading home. The day gone, and what's to show for it? Rose-headed nails or brads, hooks, skewers, stakes, bolts, holdfasts, bars.

In Florence, and then in Antwerp, Walter patrolled his dreams: he would wake up belly churning, awash with rage. But still, he came home to Putney. When Walter died the neighbourhood mourned his loss: the new, reformed Walter. He believed in Purgatory in those days, and though he paid a priest to pray for Walter's soul, he hoped

Purgatory had a good strong lock on the door. He sees no need for Walter's grandchildren to put him in their prayers.

Anne is a child who grizzles and wails, a trouble to the wet nurse: greedy, Liz says. She always wants something but nobody knows what it is. All of us are born into sin, our souls already besmirched: Anne illustrates it, the picture of infant turpitude. She creates spillages and knocks objects flying. She sits on the stairs outside the room where he is working, till he brings her in and she sits under the table with the dog, twisting Bella's fur into spirals, humming to herself; till he says, 'For God's sake, daughter, can't you read a book?'

'Not yet,' she says. 'When I'm six.'

'How old are you now?' (He loses track.)

'I don't know.'

It is a good enough answer. Why would she know, if he doesn't? He brings her out from under the table, and says he'll teach her. 'But I should warn you,' she says, 'I'm not fit to have a book.' She speaks in her mother's voice. 'Give that child anything and she destroys it. You'd think she was brought up in a midden. Look at the state of her.'

When Anne applies to her needle, beads of blood decorate her work. Liz says, she'd be better with a cobbler's awl, except a cobbler wouldn't be so chatty. He will not let his wife strike her; Anne cannot be faulted for diligence, and for the rest he feels she should not be faulted. 'I suppose she will outgrow it,' Liz says. As Gregory will outgrow his bad dreams, in which demons who live south of the river try to bribe the guards to let them across the bridge; or knock down the watermen and commandeer their barges, leaving them bloody smudges on the quays; or simply wade through the black tide and pad the streets with their webbed feet, looking for Gregory Cromwell to chew and digest.

When Gregory commands a story he wants the same one over and over, till he can take it away and murmur it, his private possession: the fair knights Gawain and Galahad, or the giants Grip and Wade. But Anne shouts, 'Oh, we killed that beast yesterday, isn't there a worser?' What next, she says, what next? The world is burning under her hand. She lives in intense striving, her earnest little face creased with concentration: the women say, don't frown like that, Anne, you'll stay that way and then no one will marry you.

Before Advent he made the peacock wings for Grace, working with a penknife and a fine brush, sticking feather to fabric with bluebell-root glue. 'Sad work to be doing by candlelight,' Liz had said. But the days were short and there was no choice if she was to have them for the Christmas play. He prayed he would not be called away before the job was done; he was always out making money for the cardinal. He would have liked Grace to know it was for her that he was so often on the road, to provide for her future: but how would she understand that, when he never comes home, if he comes at all, till the fires are damped and all God's people sound asleep? Sometimes he would stand by the door of the room where she was bundled into bed with Anne and a young servant, the three entwined like puppies. Once, once only in all the nights, she had raised her head and looked at him from the darkness, her eyes open wide and the flicker of the candlelight inside them; perhaps she thought he was in her dream, as she was in his. She wore no expression, nothing he could later recall: he remembered only the shape of the bedcurtain, a curve of shadow; the glow of a white sleeve, a white face, and the flame in her eyes.

Jenneke says, 'It was a cruel time for you, the children dead so young. I ask myself, why did you not begin another family?'

'I had Gregory.'

'But why did you not marry again?'

He doesn't know why. Perhaps because he didn't want to have to give an account of himself, to say what he was thinking. It didn't matter in Lizzie's day, because he only had the usual thoughts. Some men can make a tidy parcel of their past and hand it over; not he. But when he looks at Jenneke he cannot help but imagine other histories. If he and Anselma had wed, would they have had only one child? Or is he more potent than the banker? In this reconfiguration of circumstance, Gregory would be unborn. His soul would be bobbing around in the somewhere, still waiting for a body. Anne and Grace, likewise, would never have been conceived. And this house would not have been his house. The day not his day, when they told him his wife was dead, and the day not his day, when his daughters were sewn into their shrouds and carried to burial: two lost little girls, weighing nothing, owning nothing, leaving barely a memory behind.

'So what have you done since?' his daughter asks. 'About women?'

'You are blunt.'

'An Englishwoman would not ask?'

'Not out loud. She would wonder. And listen to gossip. And add to it. Invent something.'

'Better to say the truth. Of course,' she says, 'one buys women. No doubt your people arrange it for you. They are in awe of you.'

'I am in awe of myself,' he says. 'I never know what I will do next.'

He goes to court: in his bag are plans for war machines. Better he has the king's ear in these matters than Norfolk, whose ideas are old-fashioned.

But the gentlemen grooms intercept him: there are six French merchants with the king, with chests full of fabrics and ready-made garments – they have guessed at his measurements. 'He is trying on all their stock,' the grooms warn. Their faces say plainly, stop him, Lord Cromwell, before he spends the cost of a castle, or fritters away some cannon.

It is a day of raw cold, a metal light. But great fires are blazing in the king's chambers, and the scent of pine and amber floats towards him on a warm cloud. 'Come and get warm, Thomas,' the king says. 'Come and look at what these fellows have brought.' His face is alight with innocent pleasure.

The merchants murmur and make him a bow. They have thrown open the lids of their travelling chests and are spreading out their stock: not only embroidered garments but looking glasses and gemstones. They show the king a standing cup whose lid is topped by a naked boy riding a dolphin. They unfurl a needlework panel four yards long, and line up with it plastered across their persons. The king's eyes pass left to right over Susanna going to bathe, the Elders spying from the bushes. They offer a child's cap garnished with gold buttons in the shape of the sun in splendour; the king smiles and perches it on his fingers, saying, 'If only I had a child to fit it.'

Mr Wriothesley's eyes signal to his: distract the king, please. 'Ah, you have dog collars!' he exclaims: as if dog collars were his only thought.

'Let us see,' the king says. 'Ah, this is pretty, it would look well on little Pumpkin!' He says to the Frenchmen, almost shyly, it is my wife the queen's pet, Lord Cromwell got her from Calais.

At once, they write him down for a velvet collar, six shillings, and making further curtseys draw out bags, and disgorge crucifixes and clocks and puppets and masks, topaz rings and tortoiseshell bowls. Kneeling, they offer bracelets enamelled with the signs of the zodiac, and a picture of the Blessed Virgin standing on a carpet of fleur-de-lys, her immortal child in the crook of one arm and a sceptre in the other. They lay out chessmen and cases of knives, and the king's hand reaches out, as if to set the board or test a blade. From a linen shroud the Frenchmen draw a *jeu d'esprit* – a pair of sleeves in grass-green, embroidered with deep-red strawberries: to each berry there is a dewdrop, a diamond clear as water.

'Oh.' The king glances away, to dilute their sweetness. He is pink with desire. 'But I am too old for those.'

'Never!' The French speak as one man. Call-Me joins the chorus. He keeps quiet. The king is right, the sleeves are meant for a tender youth, like Gregory or the late Fitzroy. But you can see how Henry's mouth waters.

A hush falls on the Frenchmen. It is the signal, he knows, that they have arrived at their best item. Their captain gestures the youngest of them forward. The Frenchman stoops over a chest; he clicks a key in its lock; he pauses, then draws out and floats into the air something like a swathe of evening sky, or a thousand peacocks, or a vestment for an archangel. Murmuring in delight, they flourish, they spread, they caress the gorgeous vestment: 'We designed it expressly for you, your Majesty. No other prince in Europe could carry this off.'

The king is entranced. 'I may as well try it, since you've come so far.' His face is shadowed by a sea-green ripple. 'We call it *pavonazzo*,' the Frenchman says: a turn of the wrist, and the cloth flows in liquid iridescence, turning from sea-green to azure to sapphire. The king shines like Leviathan, upheaved from the ocean bed. He takes a breath at the sight of himself.

They mention a sum. The king laughs, incredulous. But you can see him edging towards the purchase. Mr Wriothesley, brave man, makes an ah-hem. The king acknowledges it with a flicker of his blue eye, then he grimaces, cunning as any old miser: 'It is a pauper king who stands before you, messieurs. I have spent all my money on the wars.'

'Really, Majesty?' The Frenchmen look at each other; you can be certain one or more of them are spies. 'We thought it was only a spit-spat,' their captain says, 'some far-flung agitation of no import, and no more to your puissance than a flea-bite.'

'At least,' one adds, 'that is what Monseigneur Cremuel is telling the world.'

Even while the false Frenchman is saying it, he is sliding other wares from a leather bag soft as a virgin's sigh. It crosses his mind that in Harry Norris's day, they would not have got access: unless of course Norris was taking a percentage.

The sun has come out, a white haze infiltrating the forenoon. It emboldens the merchants, who hold up their mirrors, and walk around the room with them: as they angle them, they catch little off-cuts of the king's person, and with each caprice of the light, he dazzles himself.

Yet still Henry hesitates. 'Come, Majesty,' they say. 'We are giving you first refusal. Think how you will feel if one of your courtiers were to buy it – it would be a humiliation for any prince.'

An inspiration seizes the king: 'You know my vessel the *Mary Rose* is enlarged? I mean to make her carry more ordnance, and to build some new warships – two or three. I believe those are the drawings, that the Lord Privy Seal has in his bag.'

Mr Wriothesley grins. Warships: the message cannot fail to be carried home to France. 'So you see I may not commit great sums for my adornment,' the king says. 'It would wrong the commonweal.'

The dealers begin to gibber. Sweat starts out of their brows. He realises that even their captain must answer to a master, and he dare not take these wares back unsold. If the King of England will not buy, where next: the Emperor, the Sultan? Add in the expense of the voyage; factor in that the goods may look fingered.

What he really has in his bag, besides the war machines, is an excitable proclamation from the north, urging a new Pilgrim effort. '*Wherefore now is the time to arise, or else never, and go proceed with our pilgrimage for grace …*'

He steps forward. 'My lord Cromwell?' the king says.

He whispers in Henry's ear: *caveat emptor*, sir, and by the way – let me at these pedlars.

'I know,' Henry says aloud. 'I will.'

But Thomas, he whispers: I want it all. I want Susanna and the Elders, and the chessmen, and the puppets, and the strawberry sleeves. And in that *pavonazzo*, I like myself much better than I did.

'Watch this,' he whispers to Call-Me. He follows the Frenchmen out. Safely beyond the closed door, he throws an idiomatic fit: what do they take him for? What fraud is this they are trying to perpetrate, on one of Christendom's great potentates? Do they not fear for their souls, passing off such trash? Our Lord Jesus Christ, if he saw them, would personally hurl them out of the Temple and break their teeth: and as it seems Jesus is not here, he will gladly do it himself.

'But Milord Cremuel,' the Frenchmen moan. One begs, 'Magnificence, lend your king the money.'

They reduce their demands, drooping with anxiety and fatigue.

'I'll have your total in writing,' he says. 'Five copies, please.'

They blanch. They are afraid he means to pay them with a warrant, which they must then present, and sue for payment, and wait till quarter-day. 'We dare not go back without money in hand,' they say. 'We will be skinned alive.'

'Cash, then,' he says, indifferent. 'But a third off the price.'

They brighten. The compliments begin. 'We will make you a present, of course, my lord – this mulberry satin would do much to enliven your complexion?'

He considers it. It's something, not to be purple-faced like old Darcy. Not to be drawn and jaundiced, like Francis Bryan. Yes, he agrees, that hue has a certain appeal.

Call-Me says, 'Be careful, sir.' With the colour, he thinks he means. He wants to unroll the bolt, see it in the piece, how it changes with the light, but this is not the place. 'You can come to my house,' he says. 'And those vanities you did not show the king you can show to me.' He turns away. 'Mr Wriothesley, do you have my list, my remembrances there? We should get back to our meeting, we have a dozen items to work through before we can let his Majesty have his morning back. And we must talk about the new warships of course.'

When after Vespers he goes back to the king with papers to sign, he tells him how much money he has saved him. 'Did you?' Henry says. 'I thought I had driven a bargain, but there you are.' The king's brow has cleared. He looks five years younger than before the Frenchmen came; it's almost worth the expense. 'I want some new clothes,' he says, 'because I think of being painted. Speak to Master Hans for me.'

'Gladly,' he says. He goes out smiling: good news for once.

Before he left court after the Christmas season, the king gave the rebel Aske a coat of crimson, which ill became him, especially when he blushed red with pride. Departing homewards, Aske left it at an inn, the Cardinal's Hat, with other stuff too heavy to port to Yorkshire. Perhaps he did not want his gruff compeers in the fells to see him tricked out like a dancing monkey. The outer man, Henry knows, shows the inner man to the world; and if he knows it, how much more does Master Hans. He paints your shell and he does not put his sticky fingers on your soul; when he draws you in preparation, he makes a note of the colours you wear, in a tiny hand that looks like stitching along a seam. Hans has waited for a big commission, and here it is: as the Boleyns used to say, *le temps viendra*.

The rebels say, *Wherefore now is the time to rise, or else we shall all be undone: Wherefore forward! forward! forward! Now forward on pain of death, forward now or else never.*

* * *

His daughter says, 'I want to tell you about Tyndale, how he died.'

It is twilight; they sit together in an alcove. 'You saw it with your own eyes?'

'Tyndale wanted witnesses. People who would not look away. Have you ever seen a man burned?'

He says, 'In the king's service, yes, I regret.' Henry controls what you look at; you cannot direct the angle of your gaze. 'I have seen a woman burned.' He feels a tightness in his chest. 'But that was a long time ago. She died for Wyclif's book. It was an old Bible. She was what they call a Lollard, and many such folk were poor and could not read, and so they learned the scriptures by heart. But she whose death I witnessed – this heretic, as they termed her – she was not poor, and not unfriended. It was only that, I being a child, and seeing her bare-headed and in a smock, and seeing their base usage of her, I took her for a beggar.'

She interrupts him. 'You were a child? Who took you to see such a sight?'

'I brought myself. Wandering through the city, to Smithfield. It is open ground, where folk suffer even to this day. My family did not know or care where I was. My mother was dead.'

In deference to her English, which is good but not perfect, he is speaking simply; a lesson for me, he thinks, a lesson for us all, to converse with Jenneke. Never have events seemed so plain: no nuance, but a clear noonday light. She says, 'Stephen Vaughan has told me of how he first met Master Tyndale. He says it was at your instruction.'

'I hoped at that time Tyndale would come back to England. Be reconciled with the king.'

'They did not stay within doors,' she says, 'because walls have eyes and ears. They went out to the fields – not the *schuttershoven* where they practise with their arrows, I mean the … the *raamhoven* – the bleach fields?'

'Ah,' he says, 'not bleach fields, you mean the tenter-grounds. Where they pin out the cloth to dry.'

But she has put in his mind an image of Tyndale strolling in the open air, the ground dissolving into a pale radiance, the city walls whispering into vapour: his shabby cross-grained countryman trans-figured, and Meester Vaughan beside him, hood pulled up, his secret instructions hugged to his heart.

'Tyndale lodged with the merchant Poyntz,' she says. 'He lived quiet, like the poor apostles, working to make his Bible, and he sought no payment for the great pains he took. The merchants fed him, they gave him a little money in his hand, and out of that he gave charity. He made no trouble, so the city magistrates were content.'

'Your overlords, of course, were aware of him.' The Emperor's black double eagle flies over the walls; Antwerp is not a free city, though it has free men in it.

She says, 'He was careful, he drew no attention. The English language is not much understood of them, nor did they know his face. But then the man Phillips came, the man who sold him.'

'Harry Phillips,' he says. 'Yes.'

'You know him?'

'I know who paid him. Everybody knows.'

'Meester Poyntz misliked this person. From the first he warned, beware of that one, you do not know his intentions. But Tyndale was not of that suspicious sort. His mind was only on his book. No one who knew him would have given him away. Only a stranger, and a paid stranger. Phillips learned his habits, where he would walk and with whom converse. He enquired, how far along with his holy work? Then he took the word to Brussels. The councillors did not listen at first but he had money to buy their attention. He brought them papers of Tyndale that he had stolen, letters, and he put them into Latin so that those councillors could understand, and always he was urging how the Emperor would recognise their services, and reward them. And so they decided to seize up Tyndale. They waited for a day when the quarter was empty, when all the merchants were out of town, gone to the Easter market at Bergen. They wished, you understand, to do it quietly and without any disturbance on the street.'

'Poyntz would be away,' he says. 'Everybody.'

'You will hear he was taken outside the English merchants' house. This is not true. It was outside the house of Poyntz.'

'The first news is always wrong,' he says.

'Phillips led the soldiers, and they blocked the way. He pointed: "That is the heretic, take him." The good man went with them like a lamb. Even the soldiers pitied him.'

That narrow place, he can picture it as if he stood there. He has lived and worked in that same net of streets. He sees Tyndale – a little man, irate – turning desperate between gate and wall.

'When they returned from Bergen the English merchants made their protest. But they could not do anything.'

'Thomas More paid for Tyndale's death,' he says. 'He vowed he would follow him to the world's end. He planned it from his prison, and he had plenty of time, the king was patient with More and so was I. You must not think he was straitly confined. His friends sent his dinners in. He had good wine and good fires and good books. He had visitors. Letters came and went.'

'I would have kept him closer,' she says.

'We were remiss, I see that now. Killing Thomas More did not avail because the payments were already in the pocket of that shabby knave Phillips.'

Early dark has fallen. He rises, lights a candle, closes the shutter against a night of steel-tipped stars. His daughter's eyes follow him, every move. She would make a good witness, he thinks. 'Thomas More wrote his epitaph in his lifetime,' he tells her. 'He was that sort of man.' Words, words, just words. 'He wanted it engraved in stone: *Terrible to heretics*. He was proud of what he did. He thought if you let the people read God's word for themselves, Christendom would fall apart. There would be no more government, no more justice.'

'He believed this? Truly?'

'That we needed the constraint of ignorance? Yes.'

'He did not give much credit to his fellow man.'

'But then – I dare say that unless you knew him you could not understand – his own sins lay heavy on him. And at the end, I think he had lost faith in his own arguments. Those people who now claim to be his followers – he would not recognise the painted papist they make of him. I can remember a time when he was no great friend of

429

popes. And you know that blood-truffler Stokesley is still at work? Stokesley who is Bishop of London, I mean. It was a protégé of his that was vicar of Louth – that is in the east country, where these late troubles broke out. It all goes back to More.'

She frowns. So many names, too many; too much geography, the terrain of a strange land. 'Nothing ended with his death,' he says. 'It only began. When he was alive and Lord Chancellor, Stokesley used to aid him, raiding houses, hauling men and women to prison.'

'Dismiss this bishop. You have power.'

'Not that much.'

'Shall I see him?'

'Stokesley?' He is amused. 'If you like. He is a blustering fellow. Not worth the seeing, in my opinion. I have better bishops to show you. And noble dames, if you like. And their lords.'

'Shall I see Henry, where he is throned?'

He hesitates. 'Tell me about Tyndale. After his arrest.'

'He was not hurt in prison. I can say at least that. They respected his scholarship and they tried by reason to convince him. They treated him as a Christian man.'

More, he thinks, would have tormented him with bitter words and with scourges.

'He wrote much in his own defence. They brought against him the worst people they had.' She spits out their names. 'Dufief, who is a corrupt lawyer. Tapper. Doye, Jacques Masson. All the great papists of Leuven.'

'They wanted to destroy him in argument,' he says. 'I admit, I have wanted that myself. If he would have come to the king's side in his great matter – I mean, the matter of his marriage – he would have been safe, perhaps sitting here with us now. I tried to save him, but I am only a private man. I was not even Lord Cromwell then. The Emperor did not heed my appeals.'

'Your king might have saved him,' she says, 'but he would not. Some would ask why, when your ears are open to the gospel, you would serve such a master.'

'Who else should I serve? A man cannot be masterless.'

The door opens. Young Mathew. Letters. 'Put them there.'

'They stay for an answer, sir.'

'Leave them. Say I am with my daughter.'

'I should say that?' Mathew asks. 'As you please, sir.' He goes out.

She says, 'My tale is almost done. Tyndale gave no ground. They could not shake him. All the weary months they say he prayed for his gaolers, and I believe we shall presently hear that some of them were brought to Christ.'

'That would be good hearing.' More likely, he thinks, they stripped his cell after he was gone, stealing even a threadbare coat or candle-end. 'They say he tried to work even while he was shut up.' He imagines the word of God, damp and slimy, slipping from the page and pooling on the stone flags.

'I can't see that could be possible.'

She says, 'He left certain writings behind him, in the city, in the secret places of the wall.'

'Who has them? I shall buy them.'

'I cannot tell you. Your king might rip them from your hands.'

True, he thinks.

'We thought they would burn him as soon as the trial was done, but they kept him a little space – to give him more chance to recant, we suppose. Then we thought they might burn him inside the prison, but it was done in the market. They chained him to the stake, and put a halter around his neck. They arranged this mercy, as they call it – to be strangled first. They make a hole in the stake – do you know this? – and pass the rope through, so the executioner is behind him, and when the flame is set, he heaves backwards on the rope, and so kills the good soul. But often of course he does not.'

'I have heard he was not dead when the fire reached him. That he spoke from the flames. He said, "Lord, open the King of England's eyes."'

She says, 'He spoke nothing. How could he speak? He was choked. He stirred and moved and cried with the pain.' She is angry. 'Who is King Henry, to occupy his last thought? And what is England – except the realm that turned its back on him?'

They sit in silence. Tyndale has left us his New Testament and some of the Old; the Law and the Prophets, the records of Israel's fearful wars, God's long campaigns against His chosen people. 'The king sees ...' he begins. But he lapses into silence. Smoke is what he sees; hears the distant bellowing of a crowd. 'He sees that an English church needs a Bible. We have worked long to bring him to it. We have agreed a translation, and it is Tyndale's, as far as we have his work, but it goes under another scholar's name. We have put Henry's own image on the title page. We want him to see himself there. We need him to set forth a Bible under his own licence, and set the scriptures up in every church, for all to read who can. We need to get it out in such numbers that it can never be recalled or suppressed. When the people read it there will be no more of these armed and murdering Pilgrims. They will see with their own eyes that nowhere in the scripture does it mention penances and popes and purgatory and cloisters and beads and blessed candles, or ceremonies and relics –'

'Not even priests,' she says.

Not even priests. Though we do not stress that point to Henry.

'Jenneke,' he says, 'you have come so far to bear witness. Now it is done, you will not abandon me? This place is strange to you now but you will soon feel at home. I will make you a marriage, if you think you could love an Englishman.'

Sometimes it is years before we can see who are the heroes in an affair and who are the victims. Martyrs don't reckon with the results of their actions. How can they, when their mind is only on how to endure pain? A month after Tyndale, the merchant Poyntz himself was arrested, on the word of Harry Phillips. Poyntz was accused of being a Lutheran and he would likely have burned, but he escaped and is now in London. His wife Anna has refused to join him. Why should she leave her life, her language, to dwell with a man whose name is besmirched and who has abandoned her and his children, and whose livelihood has gone too?

As for Phillips: with Thomas More dead, he is seeking other paymasters. He has been in Rome, and our man there, Gregory Casale, reports him trying to worm into the Pope's favour by claiming to be one of More's relations. Now he is in Paris, they say, looking for who he might destroy. Phillips is plausible, none more: a witty, conversible young man, easy to like, with a bagful of hard-luck tales, and a treasury of names he can mention from his time at Oxford. It is easy to see how he insinuates himself, the ever-helpful youth with his mastery of several tongues.

He says, 'Do not go back, daughter. Life will be harder. Antwerp will be less free. The city magistrates – the sway they thought they had, they do not have. There will be more arrests. The printers must take care.'

There are more English books printed in Antwerp than in London, but those who print without a licence are branded, sometimes an eye is gouged out or a hand cut off. And informers are everywhere. Even, no doubt, amongst our own merchants.

He says, 'Your mother –'

'The Queen of Sheba?' She smiles.

'– she knows this is her home, Austin Friars. I never move her. If I quit this house for the summer I roll her up and put her in store.'

Anselma's woollen self has never aged. But he fears if she is carried too much across country, her features may fuzz and blur. She came into his house only after his wife was dead. He is not the sort to run two women at once, or, like Thomas More, to marry a second wife before the sheets of the first are cold.

The fire is low; he throws a log on it. 'My wife's mother, Mercy, she is aged now. A house needs a mistress. I am always hearing that I am about to marry, but I never seem to do it.'

He pictures Meg Douglas swishing across his threshold. Or Kate Latimer, which seems a lot more likely, if old Latimer would go and die. He pictures Mary Tudor blundering in, flailing around her as she did at Hunsdon, her tiny feet grinding his Venetian goblets to dust.

'Or you could live with Gregory,' he says.

'Gregory has a house?'

'He will have. I will marry him this year.'

'He knows?'

'No,' he says shortly. 'I shall tell him when I have found a bride.'

'Would it be the same with me? This Englishman you say I might wed?'

He looks up. 'I will give you your choice of bridegroom, of course. Gregory is my heir, it is not the same. I will make you a good settlement.'

She says, 'I am like poor Anna Calva. Poyntz's wife. She would not live among strangers.'

'But think of Ruth, in the Bible. She adapted herself.'

She laughs. 'You mistake those times for these? We live in the last days, they at the dawn of the world.'

So. She is one of those who think, what is the use of marrying, or giving in marriage? These are the end times.

He thinks of Wolsey's daughter, knocking him back. He is not sure he has got up again.

'I shall leave you,' she says. 'I mean, for tonight only. I shall not go without a goodbye.'

She came to tell a story, and she has done it; to see a father, and she has seen one: what's to keep her now?

Lazarus, of course, died twice. The second time it was for good and all. Travelling east for his bank once, he visited his second and final tomb. It is guarded by ferocious monks, who stick a collecting bowl in your face and make you empty your pockets to see something that, after all, is only proof that miracles do not last. The crippled man walks, but only twice around the churchyard before he collapses in a flailing of limbs. The blind man sees, but the faces he knew in his young days are altered; and when he asks for a mirror, he doesn't recognise himself at all.

After his daughter has left, Mr Wriothesley comes in. 'So what about Harry Phillips? Could she tell you anything you didn't know?'

He says, 'I see he is a useful man. And mobile.'

'One might send him after Polo. I do not think Phillips is a papist, sir, for all his pretences. I think he will work for anybody.'

He nods. 'But I fear only direct force will do for Polo, and a man like Phillips leaves the killing to others.' He pauses. 'But no harm to sound Phillips out. Interest him a little. One never knows if there might be a use for him.'

'After all,' Call-Me says, 'you employ Dr Agostino. Even though –'

'Yes.' He cuts him off. He uses him even though he suspects him of selling the cardinal. Dr Agostino travels Europe, and sends much useful intelligence back.

He thinks of Tyndale in the bleach fields, his human sins whited-out, speaking from within a haze of smoke. He thinks of the river at Advent, its frozen path. There is a poet who writes of winter wars, where sound is frozen. The soil beneath the snow seals in the noise of stampeding feet, the clank of harness, the pleas of prisoners, the groans of the dying. When the first rays of spring warm the ground, the misery begins to thaw. Groans and cries are unloosed, and last season's blood makes the waters foul.

Now Tyndale has put on the armour of light. On the last day he will rise in a silver mist, with the broken and the burned, men and women remaking themselves from the ash pile: with Little Bilney and young John Frith, with the lawyers and the scholars and those who could barely read or read not at all but only listen; with Richard Hunne who was hanged in the Lollards' Tower, and all those martyrs from the years before we were born, who set forth Wyclif's book. He will clasp hands with Joan Boughton, whom he, the Lord Privy Seal, saw burned to bone when he was a boy. In those blessed days the whole of creation will shine, but till then we see through a glass darkly, not face to face.

Somewhere – or Nowhere, perhaps – there is a society ruled by philosophers. They have clean hands and pure hearts. But even in the metropolis of light there are middens and manure-heaps, swarming with flies. Even in the republic of virtue you need a man who will shovel up the shit, and somewhere it is written that Cromwell is his name.

II
The Image of the King
Spring–Summer 1537

Hans does not like the *pavonazzo*. You cannot have a king who is purple from one angle, blue from another, green from a third, who shines and shimmers wetly as if evading the artist. Stick to crimson, sir, Hans says: it is my earnest loyal advice.

The king has not decided yet what kind of portrait he wants. He might ask for anything, from a picture that covers a wall to a miniature you can hold in your palm. But he agrees to be crimson. Each ruby is a tiny kindling fire.

In the kitchen at the Rolls House, the Lord Privy Seal holds a white basin, within it a pool of green oil, in which he is dipping pieces of bread, and giving them to passing boys to taste. Mathew, bustling in for his portion, sneezes loud enough to crack an egg. 'That will be the plague,' Thurston says.

'Too early for plague.'

'Then I blame our diet. Englishmen were never made to eat fish. Salt water gets in your brain. A German can live on vegetables, he eats what he calls crowte. A Frenchman eats roots and herbs – if he's famished you just turn him out to grass. But an Englishman is bred on bacon and beef.'

'An Englishman may ask,' Mathew says, 'why we still have Lent. Now we've kicked the Pope out, you would think we could enjoy a dish of tripe every day.'

'The season will be easier this year,' he says. 'We can have eggs. Cheese. The king allows it.'

'Naught but yellow and white,' Thurston says.

The French and the Emperor are fighting by land and sea. Their war makes fish scarce, and that's the only reason the king makes a concession. Cranmer complains that at the royal court even the minor feasts of the church are held with all the old superstitious ceremonies. How then can he convince the simple people to labour on saints' days, instead of drinking ale under a hedge: to till and sow, instead of playing skittles?

'There are willing butchers enough,' Thurston says. 'A man can purchase flesh even on Good Friday, if he has a shilling and a good wit.'

He holds up a palm. 'If I knew the names of willing butchers, I'd have to close them down.'

'Our master is second to God,' Mathew says, chewing. 'First comes the king, God's deputy, and then comes our master, deputy to the king.' He licks his fingers. 'Sir, they are saying the French have given you a big present. I mean, not a lion or a fighting horse. A present of money.'

He relishes the last fragment of bread, sacramentally: pepper, grass: Chapuys sent the oil. 'The king's not averse to us getting our living,' he tells Mathew. 'It's how it's always been. We frighten the French, and they give us money. The king himself has a pension from them, from old King Edward's time. Not that they're good payers.'

Mathew's brow clears. 'As long as it's true. If it were a slander, we'd have to wallop them.' He sniffs and goes out, with a speculative slap of fist into palm.

'I've no strength to beat anybody,' Thurston says. 'An egg won't do it for me. I want a rib of beef. I could kill Christ for a taste of bacon. I reckon that was Eve's sin – she never erred for an apple, she went wrong for a fat rasher.'

'Oh, stop it,' he says. 'You'll make me weep.'

And yet, you wonder who thought of this arrangement: the blind haul from Christ's birthday, through freeze and sleet to Candlemas, and then weeks of penance, raw meatless days till Easter. Mid-March the trees will leaf and the birds sing, but you can't eat beauty. Thurston says, 'It's all right for His Holy Majesty, I avow he stuffs himself with sugar. He calls for mead and malmsey, and drinks the cellars dry.'

In the blink of an eye, in the space of an Ave, he is somewhere else: he is at Launde Abbey, on the cardinal's business: on a day of buzzing heat, a young fellow laughing with the monks in a garden. This abbey, where he ate honey scented with thyme, stands in the heart of England, far from the dangers of salt water. It basks in woods and fields, and summer or winter the air is sweet. When he visited for the cardinal he looked at figures as he was bidden, but he found it so blessed a spot that he could not see it through the grid or lattice of an account book. Now he thinks: I'll have Launde for myself, when its surrender comes. I'll build a house, and live there when I'm old, far from the court and council. It's time I had something I want.

He thinks, I need to go back to the Charterhouse, the London Charterhouse, to lock myself once more in argument with those monks: men unused to speech, hermit-like, but eloquent in their dislike of what they call the king's pretensions to rule their spiritual lives. Henry is only a man, they say: but he says, what else is the Bishop of Rome but a man, and not a fine example either?

He has pleaded with the king to keep the Charterhouse open. There is no abuse and no slackness there, and they never eat meat, not once in the year, but subsist on the fruit and herbs they grow for themselves. I will turn them to us, he has said, a little and a little. But that doesn't seem to be happening. When he thinks of the blindness of these earnest men, he wants to weep. When he thinks of Farnese, the present Pope – Cardinal Cunt, as the Romans used to call him – he wants to cross the seas and mountains and grab him by the throat.

The third week in February, the court attends the christening of Edward Seymour's daughter. She is his first child with his present wife, and she is to be called Jane, after the ornament of the family; the queen stands her godmother. Tradition keeps the king from such an occasion, though he looks forlorn. 'Bring my jewel back safe, my lord.'

You wonder about these traditions, that shut out a king from occasions of common rejoicing. What law puts him, at a queen's coronation, at a dizzying height above the action in a prayer closet? As his subjects roar *gloria in excelsis*, he watches through a squint.

Henry kisses the queen heartily before she descends the water stair, a pale doll wrapped in sables. Lady Mary is the other godmother; the godfather, the Lord Privy Seal. Under the canopy of the queen's barge, he makes small talk with the ladies. Audley makes efforts at an impromptu council meeting, but he ignores him; he can talk to the Lord Chancellor any time.

They are no sooner on the queen's barge than they disembark at the pier of Chester Place. No notice of the event has been given to the Londoners. All the same a crowd gathers, and cheers for Lady Mary as she is handed to dry land. As for Jane, they look on with indifference, giving their voices neither for nor against. They know she's not Anne Boleyn. Nor is she the dead woman they still call Queen Katherine. But he has given money to women in the crowd, and when they shout 'God bless Queen Jane,' there is a chorus in support. People will shout anything, he thinks, once you start it up. That's how it must have been in Lincolnshire, when the tumult began. Some rustic bleats 'Follow the crosses!' and the whole county is up.

The crowd recognise him. They call out: 'Cold enough for you, Tom?' He is a stout godfather, wrapped in black lamb and lynx fur. You cannot say the Londoners like him, but they know he has done good work in defending the city, and that he has vowed to buy and store arms himself for their defence. No doubt they prefer him to a Yorkshire looter. A stray voice pipes, 'Cromwell, king of London!'

His stomach lurches. His head turns. 'Friend, if you love me, sing some other tune.'

A consort of musicians meets them, piping them indoors. Garlands of painted roses lead them into the gallery. The christening party inspect the Seymour ancestors, painted on the wall. Today's bundle of linen must be added into the picture – perhaps down at her parents' feet, her red crinkled face like a flower on the forest floor.

Mary has been silent on the short journey. Her face looks wan under her gable hood. When she sheds her cloak, he sees she has fixed to her gown the pendant Hans cast: a ring, after all, was not practicable. At the font she touches it, as they stand side by side: 'You see I am wearing your verses, in praise of obedience. Though my father gave them me, I know their origin.'

He inclines his head. 'Madam.'

'And thank you for my Valentine's gift. You use me beyond my deserts.'

'You look very well today,' he lies. 'Crimson is your favourite colour, I think?'

She murmurs, 'Do not make light of what you did for me.'

Why would I, he thinks, when it nearly killed me?

'You saved me, my lord, when I was drowning in folly. When I was almost past recovery.' Her voice runs on, rehearsing her gratitude. But she won't look at him, he notices. Her eyes are everywhere, but never on him.

Chester Place belongs to the ancient bishopric, and Seymour is even now wrangling over the lease. A shame if he has to move now he has had the ancestors painted, and the chapel reglazed at his own expense. Winter light filters through the plumage of the Seymour phoenix; the slumbering fire beneath the feathers is so deep a red you want to warm your hands at the glow. Glass angels coo and flutter: they hold tabors and shawms, scourges and crowns of thorns. Some hold hammer and nails, to nail God to the cross: Easter will arrive, and the Man of Sorrows must bleed.

Little Mistress Jane cries heartily at the font. It is a sign, the ladies claim, that the devil is departing. 'Women are fanciful,' Edward Seymour says, his tone fond. His wife Nan holds court from her great bed, where they go to kiss her and give her presents. They give money to the wet nurse, and to the midwife for seeing Nan safe, and then they take wine and wafers.

All the talk is of heirs and new-borns. Sir Richard Riche has been augmented, after the birth of many daughters, by a son at last. With stout independence, in a year when all the boys are Henry, he has called his baby Robert, and talks of him excitedly, as a sturdy child and likely to live. Any increase in Riche's benevolence is of public interest. The treason of certain northern abbots makes it sure that their houses will be pulled down, and Sir Richard will be pleasantly placed to hand out the assets. Meanwhile the news from Calais is that Lady Lisle is pregnant, her child expected late spring, early summer. It seems like a miracle, the couple have been without offspring so long. Lisle is an ageing man, of course, but Honor had seven children with her first husband, though she married him when he was fifty-three already.

The Seymours show no pleasure at the news. They have old law suits with the Lisles, so they don't care for additions to the family. But noble dames write doting letters to Honor, looking forward to welcoming a little Plantagenet into the world. Arthur Lisle may be a bastard, but he is still old King Edward's blood.

He spies Lord Lisle's man of business, bobbing on the edge of the gathering: 'Spying, Husee?'

'I bring a christening gift, sir. From my lord and my lady over the sea.'

He has some fellow-feeling for John Husee. Lady Lisle runs him ragged with her shopping lists, and she never wants to pay for anything, so he is constantly begging for credit: and he remembers his own early days, when the Marchioness of Dorset used to send him out for orient pearls, with only the price of oysters in his purse.

The Lord Chancellor heaves in view: 'Ho, Husee! I hear in Calais there is nothing but singing all the day. And Lisle dancing as if he never knew what gout was.'

Husee makes a reverence. 'I am explaining to my lord Privy Seal, sir – I have to list everything my lady Beauchamp has, for her lying-in, so my lady can get the same.'

'Oh, I see that,' Audley says. 'She would not want any less for herself, in terms of her hangings, her gold plate, and so forth.'

'My lady wondered,' Husee says, 'if she should come over for her confinement, so the child can be born on English soil.'

He, Lord Cromwell, rolls his eyes. 'Calais is English soil. As the Lord Deputy's wife, I hope she grasps that.'

Husee turns to him. 'But if she's to be confined there, she wants the silver font sent from Canterbury. Can you put in a word, sir?'

'I'd send the archbishop to carry it, if Lisle would bestir himself. I hear of two priests preaching treason through the streets, and the governor turns his head and does naught. Tell him to truss them up and put them on a boat, addressed to me at the Tower.'

He thinks, if Cranmer turned up, font or no, Honor would bar the door. She would sprinkle holy water on the threshold, and throw blessed salt in his eyes.

'I hear Lady Beauchamp has ermine caps,' Husee says. 'And if I could get the embroidery pattern for her nightgowns, my lady would be well pleased with me.'

Clearly we can expect no business to be done in Calais this year. Arthur Lisle defers to his wife, and he will never cross her while she is in pup. He says, 'I mean it, Husee, you tell your master – either he catches me those priests, or he must come himself to answer for them. I am not patient for ever. Perhaps your lady mistress encourages him to slack his duty, but tell him I am watching him. I will have him out of his post and at the gallows' foot, if he tries to play me for a fool.'

Husee sucks his lip. 'I'll tell him.'

'Look out,' Audley says. 'The queen.' He steps back, clutching his bonnet to his chest, as if Jane were a runaway horse. 'Madam – we are speaking of Lady Lisle. Her great hopes of an heir.'

'Marvellous, isn't it?' Jane sounds bored.

'May God in His own good time make your Highness a happy mother too. Your sister-in-law sets a glad example.'

'Does she?' Jane is puzzled. 'I shall hardly be a happy mother, if I have a girl. I should think I will be sent back to Wolf Hall in a basket, like a fowl unsold on market day. What do you think, Lord Audley?'

She turns away. Audley's jaw drops.

He looks around. 'My lady Rochford, spare me a moment?'

Nothing urgent in his tone. Can he have mistaken Jane's meaning? A pregnant woman will not usually stand godmother to another woman's child, as she deems her future too precarious. He steers Lady Rochford aside. 'It is true her courses have not come,' she murmurs. Like Mary, Jane Rochford won't look at him – her eyes are on the guests. 'Her titties are swollen. She won't speak till she's sure. Let's hope it's stuck fast, eh?'

He stares at the queen. 'Let me know when she decides to tell Henry.'

'Yes,' Jane Rochford says, 'make sure you are at hand. He will be in a humour to hand out favours. He might give you ... whatever it is you lack. Though that's not much, is it, my lord Privy Seal?'

Five minutes, and the whisper has spread. Edward Seymour has his sister by the elbow: 'I believe you have hope. Your Highness.'

'We all have hope,' Jane says sweetly.

Edward looks as if he would slap her: playing games, at a time like this! 'We have waited long enough, sister.'

'Oh, Edward.' She sighs. 'You are so eager for promotion.'

'When are you safe to speak?'

He, Cromwell, says, 'Highness, why delay?'

'Because ...' The queen contemplates her reasons. 'Because once the king has hope of a son, what will there be, to make him say his prayers?'

He and Edward exchange glances. She's right. Whenever one of his queens has been with child, Henry has always been sure it is a male. Once he has an heir in the womb, once he can say again, 'God is pleased with me,' what will there be to refrain Henry from every desire? He might free all the prisoners in the Tower. Or he might go to war on a whim. King François is in the field himself, reports say: laying sieges, ordering up the big guns. Henry grunts and colours when he speaks of it. His leg is sore, and Thurston is right: the more miserable he is, the more sugar he requires.

He puts his hand on Edward's arm. 'Listen to your lady sister. Say nothing yet.'

In idle moments he has been planning a cake he could give the king for Easter: a huge marzipan one, gilded balls on top. Perhaps he will keep it for when the news comes out.

Jane's eyes are like deep ponds on a still day.

As the short afternoon darkens, he is back at the Rolls House, writing letters to Flanders. They say Pole has spent all his money, and the Pope has given him none: but still Reginald struts, with his title of papal legate, trying to sell the idea of an invasion of England. Lord Darcy, and no doubt some other of the rebel lords, have sent him letters; we do not need to read them, to know the rebels take Pole for their king in exile.

Now he has learned through back channels that Pole is asking to talk to him: Reginald wants him to cross over to Calais, then meet on Imperial territory, both parties with safe-conduct. He, Lord Cromwell, has thought it wise to bring the matter into daylight: so he loses his temper in the council chamber, shouting that if he should find himself in a room with the traitor Pole, only one can emerge alive.

The king had watched him, head tilted, as if sceptical about his sudden passion. To reinforce it the Lord Privy Seal had shaken his fist in the direction of Dover. Richard Riche had gaped at him, and the Lord Chancellor dropped his penknife in shock.

He sands his papers. The prospect of an heir, he thinks, will strike Pole a blow to the heart. Though if Jane is in a happy condition, it changes our plans. The king will want to stay by her side this summer. He will never go north. There will be no coronation in York.

Christophe comes in. 'That Mathew, sneezing,' he says. 'If he has a disease, you will not be able to go to court.'

At any time, the king is always afraid of contagion. And now, of course, every precaution will be necessary.

Christophe says, 'Call-Me is here for his supper.'

He thinks, Mary looks at me as if she doesn't know who I am.

* * *

Supper is pike, with rosemary and fried onions. Call-Me says, 'I hear when Rafe is done in Scotland he will go to France.'

'I shall try to get him home first. Helen says she is sick for the sight of him. She is expecting a child in the autumn.'

'I suppose by now she knows the signs,' Call-Me says. 'It seems they took a liking to Rafe, the Scots?'

'Who would not like Rafe? He goes to France now with messages to King James. James lingers there, does he not?'

'Rafe will meet Bishop Gardiner while he is in Paris. He cannot avoid it. Gardiner is asking for his recall.'

He pokes his fish around the plate. 'God forgive me, but I wonder why He ever made pike?'

Mr Wriothesley extracts a bone. 'I imagine the bishop's return would be as welcome to your lordship as hemlock in a salad.'

He sighs. 'It will be a while before we taste salad. I hear from France there will be no cherries till July.'

Christophe brings almonds and dried fruit. Mr Wriothesley says, 'I perceive how the Lady Mary is continually applying to you for money and favours. Lady Rochford says,' he smiles, 'that Mary avoids looking at you, only for the great love she bears you. You are too dazzling a sight for her maiden eyes.'

'We have to be gracious to Lady Rochford,' he says. 'Without her, the king and queen might not be married. Anne Boleyn would still be queen.'

And our heir unconceived. It appears that despite his sharp ears, Call-Me has not caught on to the day's most important news, because he only wants to talk about Calais. 'Lisle is careless. You do well to warn him, sir. It is not only papists he is harbouring. It is sectaries, they say. Sacramentaries.'

'So Chapuys tells me.' He eats a fig, meditatively. 'I'd rather be in bed with a scorpion than with Honor Lisle.'

'I too,' Christophe says loyally, coming in with cheese. 'I would squash her beneath my foot. Are you sitting up writing your king book tonight?'

Call-Me turns a curious glance on him. But he does not ask.

* * *

When the northern lords have made their excuses for their conduct during the winter past, the king sends them home wearing the badge of St George. He decrees the red cross a mark of allegiance for all men who have a coat to pin it on: wear a red ribbon, or sew a red thread that connects you to your sovereign. Because though the rebels are stood down, and the weapons confiscated, there is no truce in the war of words. The south calls the north traitorous; the north calls the south heretical. The north says, you have abused us for a thousand years: all we represent is a barrier between you and the Scots, a wall of corpses to delay them, while you have time to lock up your wives and daughters and put your gold in store.

The southerners say, have you ever been to Dover? Have you ever stood on the cliffs and seen the lights on the French coast, and considered how narrow is the Narrow Sea – how much we risk, and how much we pay, to save you from the slavers and pirates and barbarians who have been battering our shores since shores were thought of?

He says to the king, in the north they have contempt for the king's peace, they want to administer their own murders. If Norfolk cannot subdue them they will fall into their old savagery, where each eye or limb or life itself is costed out, and all flesh has a price. In our forefathers' time a nobleman's life was worth six times that of a man who followed the plough. The rich man can slaughter as he pleases, if his pocket can bear the fines, but the poor man cannot afford one murder across his lifetime. We repudiate this, he tells the king: we say a man of violence cannot go free because his cousin is the judge, no more than a wealthy sinner can make up for his sins by founding a monastery. Before God and the law, all men are equal.

It takes a generation, he says, to reconcile heads and hearts. Englishmen of every shire are wedded to what their nurses told them. They do not like to think too hard, or disturb the plan of the world that exists inside their heads, and they will not accept change unless it puts them in better ease. But new times are coming. Gregory's children – and, he adds quickly, your Majesty's children yet to be born – will never have known their country in thrall to an old fraud in Rome. They will not put their faith in the teeth and bones of the dead, or in holy water, ashes and wax. When they can read the Bible for themselves, they will be closer to God than to their own skin. They will speak His language, and He theirs. They will see that a prince exists not to sit a horse in a plumed helmet, but – as your Majesty always says – to care for his subjects, body and soul. The scriptures enjoin obedience to earthly powers, and so we stick by our prince through thick and thin. We do not reject part of his polity. We take him as a whole, consider him God's anointed, and suppose God is keeping an eye on him.

Until these blessed days dawn, 'Let's have peace,' he says: 'Peace is cheap.' Everyone agrees the north must be governed better, but by whom? Thomas Cromwell thinks we need able men, but the Duke of Norfolk thinks we need noble men.

When fresh insurrection breaks out, it is led by a man who owes the Lord Privy Seal a great deal of money. His name is Francis Bigod: a boy in Wolsey's household, an Oxford scholar, zealous for the gospel till lately; a man on friendly terms with our archbishop, with Hugh Latimer, with Robert Barnes; on friendliest terms of all with my lord Cromwell. So what does it mean, what can it mean, that such a man is riding about the countryside talking wild and waving a sword, swearing to take back Hull for the rebels, seize the town of Beverley, launch a force against the port of Scarborough? He is tired of people asking him, what does it mean, and whence comes this? Did you quarrel? As if he were responsible for Bigod's bloody caprice.

He can only say, Bigod asked some strange things of me lately. He asked how the king could be responsible for our souls: as if there were some other candidate on earth, better qualified. He asked if he, Bigod, could preach in the pulpit, like a priest. When I said no, he asked, could he be ordained a priest? Though he was married?

He is brainsick, perhaps, his wits turned. But his folly will undo his countrymen, leading them to the fight through weather in which only a novice would campaign. And Bigod is not so mad he cannot be responsible for his actions. The king's pardon was once and once only: after that, martial law.

* * *

Hans comes to him. 'He has decided he wants a wall painting.'

'Is that more difficult?'

Hans rubs his beard. He wants to talk terms; he wants to go on the royal books, with board and lodging and a workspace at Whitehall for the life of this project and beyond. He asks for a guarantee of thirty pounds a year, and then he will turn down other commissions and call himself painter to the King of England.

'Thirty?' He frowns. But after all, Hans has a mistress and two children to keep, apart from his family over the sea.

Hans says, 'There is a piece of wall in the privy chamber here, I measure it at twenty-two feet.'

'The privy chamber? That's where he wants it?'

'I should hardly put it there without his permission.'

'I thought he would want it in the presence chamber. To awe the whole world.'

'No. He just wants to awe you. And his attending gentlemen. And I suppose any poor foreigner he brings in for a tour.'

Of course, the privy chamber is not as private these days as its name implies. The king does not reckon to be alone there. If he wants solitude, or the company of one or two, he finds himself a sanctum in every house: a corner room where he tunes a lute, or a secret book store up a winding stair.

Hans says, 'I do not mind if few people see it, as long as the right people see it. I plan to place his head' – he indicates above his own head, 'about here. No harm to give him an extra inch or so.'

'In the leg,' he suggests, 'not the body. Or you mean elsewhere?'

Han sniggers. 'I will draw him with gown well-parted, so the world can see the wonder. A generous wad of quilting.'

'How big will it be? The painting, I mean.'

Hans stretches his arms then wheels about, demonstrating in space. 'He wonders if he should have his father painted too.'

'In the same picture?'

'It can be done.'

And his mother, why not? A line of kings and queens, stretching into the blue distance. And an unborn child hovering, like a shadow of a bird against glass.

'So he must be available to me,' Hans says. 'For drawings. They must be detailed, it will take time. Afterwards I can dispense with his body. He need not be present. I can meet separately with his clothes.'

'You did not give me that choice when you painted me.'

'But I failed with you,' Hans says curtly. 'You should have been painted by some other master, a dead one, for God He knows, you looked dead. You know Antonello, that fellow from Messina? He would have dragged some expression out of you.'

He has seen this master's work. When Antonello painted the grandees of Venice, he captured the sceptical raised eyebrow, the flicker of a sour smile. But the Venetians didn't like his work; he knew too much about them.

'By the way,' Hans says, 'how is your daughter?'

'Gone home.' He intends to say no more.

'She did not like England? Or she did not like you?'

Hans, he thinks, has likely known about Jenneke for years. It would explain certain snatches of conversation, broken off: sideways glances, sly. 'Hans,' he says, 'don't ask questions unless you know what to do with the answers.'

March, 1537: day by day, at the Tower and at the Rolls House, the Lord Privy Seal unpicks the events of the year past. With witnesses, with interrogatories before him, with clerks and Mr Wriothesley, he is laying bare, day by day and name by name, the machinery of revolt.

'So you say you were coerced into rebellion? That you took an oath against your will? Please name the rebels who resorted to you, and say when. How were they armed? Did they use force against your person? Did they threaten force against your person? You say your horses were seized, your thatch fired, your wife insulted – you have witnesses? You allege the rebels set fire to your property, which included movable goods to the value of …? You did not have an inventory? Ah, I see, they burned your inventory. And what did you do, to counter their threats? Did you not send messages to your friends for help? You did, and they did not stir? Why not? What had you done to them, to cause them to abandon you?'

Mr Wriothesley wears the sables sent him as a present by our man in Brussels. Christophe builds up the fire. He, Lord Privy Seal, now keeps his own wine store here at the Tower. He has a strongroom, to lock up the interrogatories, so no one can interfere with them overnight, writing between the lines. Helpers come in and out – Augmentations men, his relative John ap Rice, and a useful cleric called Edmund Bonner, a fussy, clucking little man with an eye for the ladies and an ear for gossip. The bishops, still working on their new statement of doctrine, send him weighty folios every night: from the snivelling wrecks at the Tower, he goes home to number the sacraments. The interrogations grind on through the spring. For every answer he has six questions. He is willing to pinch a man with pains, if nothing else will work, though the threat will do more, and he regards it as a defeat if he has to call for chains and heated irons.

Wriothesley has not his patience: but then, he is young, and he has a family he would like to see sometimes. He will touch his elbow: 'Sir, this is a mild pain, and we have a stubborn rebel before us, and it is late. I believe he can stand more.'

But he thinks, no, none of us can stand anything. Scrape our skin, and beneath it there is an infant, howling.

He says, 'You could try listening. That's how you find things out.'

'But if he says nothing?'

'Then listen to his silence.' Listen through his silence. Imagine what you could give him, to make him speak – instead of what you could take away. Perhaps he must die, and he knows that; but some deaths can be faced and some not. What is it worth, to be spared castration, and the apprehension of it? You could offer him the shock of the axe, the carpet of blood, not the panic of half-hanging and the agony of the knife in the bowel. It is all about anticipation, he tells Call-Me. Give him something to live for, or offer him a death that spares him shame. Assure him that, whether or not he helps us, the king will pay his debts and look after his family: such small mercies can make a felon weep and break his will.

In no other country could this happen. In the domains of François or Charles there would be no truces, negotiations, or sessions of question and answer that stretch from Advent to Trinity. Once apprehended the noble suspects would be tortured and killed and the common dead would be butchered and lie under the open sky. He says, where we cannot avoid severity, we can still temper justice with mercy. Where loyal men have been despoiled of property, the crown will compensate them. Where the king has been well-served, there must be rewards. Where his authority has been held in contempt, retribution must be swift and public. In the north Norfolk hangs truce-breakers from the trees. He hangs them in chains if he can get them, but iron is so dear, and rope will do. Their wives come by night to cut them down, but the king says any women who are caught must be straitly punished. He wishes the corpses to hang there through Easter and into the warm weather: as you hang a maggoty crow on a fence, as an example to other birds not to steal your crops. In London, heads are spiked on the bridge, and limbs of traitors are nailed to the gates. But the cold weather stops them rotting and the citizens are sickened by the sight.

By the middle of February young Bigod is captured. His captains are in ward. Tyburn waits for them, in season: no rush. The summer will clean up the winter's spoilage. Thomas Cromwell will never recover the money he is owed. Nor will Henry learn he should bury the dead.

He sends for Thomas Wyatt to see him at the Rolls House. Like every loyal gentleman he has been in the saddle against the rebels, but there is another task for him. He has long begged to be sent out of the kingdom. Now he is going as ambassador to the Emperor. It means pursuing Charles across Europe summer and winter: an ideal posting for a restless man. The role needs honest force and honeyed words, and a certain willingness to obfuscate about the intentions of the King of England: and as Wyatt says that to him nothing is ever clear, and no truth is a single truth, he seems the man for the job.

The Emperor continues to urge that Lady Mary should marry the brother of the Portuguese king. He recommends Dom Luis as wise, discreet and loving. He will be content to reside in England, rather than carry the princess from her native land.

'Wyatt,' he says, 'ask the Emperor how much he will pay us for Mary. Put it suavely – but do not be misled if he names great sums, ask him how he will secure the debt. The king will not part with her for promises.'

'You don't want this match,' Wyatt says.

'More to the point, she doesn't.'

'What do you want?'

'Only to protect her.'

'The king needs a friend in Europe,' Wyatt says. 'The kind of special friend he can only get through a marriage.'

'The king could get a troop of friends in Switzerland, and among the German princes. All we need is to agree a bare statement of doctrine, and we will have allies enough.' He frowns. 'And if a marriage must be made, better Eliza than Mary.'

'You are a long thinker, my lord. The young lady is, what, four this year?'

'So it cannot be consummated,' he says. 'Not for ten years – and that would be early. Twelve years, if we plead she is delicate. It will not be a true marriage, so if it turns out not to serve us we can set it aside.'

'You guard Mary's virginity,' Wyatt says.

He shrugs.

'You were her Valentine. Wriothesley is telling everyone how he carried a handsome present to her.'

At the court's annual feast – Wyatt well knows – we draw lots for our Valentine. So no one is left out, young or old.

'One never knows with Cremuello,' Wyatt says. 'I remember when the rumour was that you were making your addresses to one Mistress Seymour, who is now queen.'

Cold as a stone he says, 'What gave rise to that idea?'

'She would have been better off,' Wyatt says.

'The queen is not unhappy.'

'You would know, my lord. You know much about women that is hidden from the rest of us. How to advance them. How to undo them.'

Last summer, then, abrades Wyatt's temper, frays his inner peace. Though he has slipped the noose, he must be unpicking the rope, shredding the fibres in his fingers. 'Wyatt,' he says, 'such talk will undo me. Is that your intention?'

'Put yourself in my place. In every conversation we have held for a twelvemonth, I have had to ask myself, is he trying to save me, or is he trying to drown me? Am I precious cargo, or thrown overboard?'

'Well, proof of the pudding,' he says. (Let the poet do what he can with that image.) 'You are still breathing.'

'And yours till my last breath.' Wyatt stands up and stretches. 'I would follow you to the ends of Christendom. Whither go I now, chasing Carolus.'

Wyatt seeks himself in the mirror. In some invisible adjustment, his finger brushes the feather in his cap. 'Look after Bess Darrell while I'm gone.'

He takes a day off, and walks the grounds of Austin Friars with his gardeners, Mercy Prior leaning on his arm. The wood of the garden arbour is sodden to the touch and the walls have grown plump pillows of moss. The stakes that support his young trees seem to be quivering with their own, green inner life.

He invites Richard Riche to supper, to ask what can be done for the other Bess – Lady Oughtred. 'Her husband left her mean provision. She wants a house of her own.'

'The Seymour family has deserved well of the king,' Call-Me says. 'Riche, you might help her to some abbey?'

Riche says, 'You will find she is positioning herself for a new marriage. I am surprised, sir, your friends among the ladies have not mentioned it. She will look high, and quite proper she should. The Earl of Oxford is mentioned.'

John de Vere is an old widower: two wives killed under him already. He is the fifteenth earl. Imagine, he thinks, being the fifteenth anything.

Thurston has tried a new cod dish – garlic, saffron, fennel. Just white and yellow, as he said: it looks as if they've sicked it up. 'I hear you will have Quarr Abbey,' he says to Call-Me. 'Good rents for you from the manors. And the woods are worth a clear hundred pounds, are they not?'

Ten monks at Quarr, all of whom desire continuance in their vows. Some thirty-eight persons waiting on them. White stone, sea views, fifty-five pounds of debt: not a large house, but there are lands in Devon that, obligations discharged, should come to Call-Me within six months. 'I am thinking about Launde for myself,' he says.

Riche says, 'Launde will not come down yet. It is worth four hundred a year.'

'I can wait.'

He watches the platter of fish go out. He is struck by a happy thought, and it has nothing to do with abbeys at all.

He seeks an audience with the queen. 'When is your sister Bess coming to court? You will need her company through these next months.'

'I suppose so,' Jane says. She counts on her fingers. 'It seems a long time to October.'

There is a rustle that spreads from where she sits, through the room, through the court, through England and across the sea. At last, the news is public.

'My lord Beauchamp, I felicitate all your family,' the court says. Edward's handsome face relaxes into smiles; he bows and passes on, as if in a radiant cloud, to send a message down to Wolf Hall and a message to his brother Tom, who is with the king's fleet.

Now the space around the queen becomes a blessed space. All displeasant airs and discordant sounds must be banished. The jelly creature within her flinches at harsh words or bright lights and Jane must be protected from them, as from strong sunlight or draughts.

Only the finest cloth must touch her skin, and no scents assail her but the sweetness of summer grass and the light spice scent of petals. The paws of attending lapdogs must be wiped before they can impose on her person. No courtiers who sneeze or cough, or who know anyone who sneezes or coughs, must come in her vicinity. Only beautiful sights must meet her eyes: though, he says to her, 'We cannot do anything about me, madam.'

When the king meets his council the gentlemen pound the table in their glee. 'A great day for our nation,' they shout, and 'This will astonish the Emperor,' and 'This will put France's great nose out of joint.'

Henry says, 'There is no need the news should go out to the common sort.' He sounds strained. 'Not yet awhile.'

'I think it is out,' Fitzwilliam says, 'and not a man or woman in England who does not wish your Majesty well and pray on his knees nightly that the queen will give you a sturdy boy.'

Henry says, 'I wish the cardinal were –' He breaks off. He, Thomas Cromwell, looks down at the documents on the table. The council rises, the babble of congratulation still floating in the air. 'Fitz, stay,' Henry says. 'Cromwell?'

The noise recedes: laughter below; laughter above, perhaps, the cardinal applauding from somewhere beyond the *primum mobile*. The dead watch us, zealous in old causes.

The king says, 'Jane wants to make a pilgrimage to Becket's shrine.' He frowns. Canterbury does not hold good memories: it was where the prophetess Eliza Barton rose up, and gripped his arm and told him he would soon be dead.

Yet Barton was hanged. And Henry flourishes. God confound all false prophets! 'Of course we will go,' Henry says. 'The queen must go where she likes, while she can safely travel. Even so far as Wolf Hall, if she has a fantasy to it. But my lord – my lord Privy Seal?'

He wants to put his hand on the king's shoulder, as he sits sweating in a cold room; the lords of the council have taken the cheer and the warmth with them, and there is no power in the stray shafts of spring sun that trace a shivering line down the wall.

The king says, 'I am a man who … my hopes … after so long … and I want to be sure …'

Fitz raises his eyebrows.

'When I married the queen, that is, before I married her … I need not remind you of the circumstances, but rest assured that though I was hasty, yet I am constant in my affections –'

'Spit it out, sir,' Fitzwilliam says.

'Are we truly married?' Henry says. 'When I entered into that compact, there was nothing to impede or frustrate it?'

'You mean,' he says, 'nothing about the queen that you should have known?'

Fitz sounds shocked. 'I am sure you found no reason to question that gracious lady's virginity.'

Henry colours faintly. 'Not at all. But are you certain you did all you should, as my councillors? The most diligent enquiries? You can be sure she was absolutely free to enter into matrimony?'

'There was no pre-contract,' Fitz says, 'if that is what troubles your Majesty.'

'But was she not once courted by William Dormer?'

'It was something and nothing,' Fitzwilliam says.

He says, 'It was nothing.'

Fitz says, 'To be blunt, sir, the Dormer family would not come to a settlement. They concluded the Seymours were not –'

'Rich enough,' he finishes.

'So you think there was nothing between them?' The king gets to his feet. 'If you are sure. Because I need to be sure. Because I cannot start hoping again, it will kill me. I have lost Richmond. I never had a son born in wedlock, that lived. I must know that this time I am safe. That no one can question his birthright. I have been patient. Surely God will reward me now.' There is a glitter of tears in his eyes. He, Cromwell, turns away, and Fitzwilliam turns, so they do not see them spill. But the king says, 'I should know you by now, eh, Crumb? If ever a man was thorough, you are that man.'

The king squeezes his shoulder. There is a new magic in the royal touch. It transmits a vision, a vision of what England could be. You imagine the city of London in the days when prophets walk its streets, when angels cluster on gable ends; you look up as you leave your house, hearing their strong wingbeats in the air.

At his first session with Hans, the king can hardly walk for the weight of ornamentation. 'How best to do this, Master Holbein?' His face is solemn, attentive.

Hans waves his hand towards the privy chamber gentlemen, the pages, the hangers-on: it is a motion of erasure.

The room empties. Space clears around the king. 'Can I stay?' he asks.

Henry says, 'You may sit with me, my lord Cromwell, but I don't require conversation.'

He smiles. 'I'll stay if your Majesty will grant me five minutes when Hans is done.'

Henry does not reply. He has fixed his gaze on nothingness and he looks as if he is thinking about God. He, Master Secretary, clears himself off to the window, sits on a stool and looks through his papers. His spaniel flops down at his feet. There is no sound in the room but her gentle snoring, except with the king's every respiration, his garments shift and sigh: as if, a fraction after the king breathes, his clothes breathe too. Behind the silence, he begins to hear other sounds: footsteps above, a scuffling outside the door, a soughing wind that tests the window's glass in its frame. Every so often he glances up at Henry, in case he wants anything. After a time the king grows tired of God, and starts watching his minister instead. 'I wonder you can see to read.'

'I am fortunate.'

'Mm,' the king says. 'You should bathe your eyes with a decoction of rue.'

As he works at his drawing Hans purses his lips and sucks his teeth. He bites down on his lower lip. He hums. As he stands back and lets out his breath there is a sibilance, very nearly a whistle.

The king says, 'We should have music, perhaps.'

'Master Hans is doing his best to supply it,' he says.

Henry says, 'What did you want with me, my lord Privy Seal?'

'To talk about the King of Scots, by your leave. You know he is still in France, he has not set forth with his bride. Her father is apprehensive at the thought of her putting to sea. They say she is so frail you can see through her.'

Henry snorts. 'It is Scotland who is apprehensive. He is quaking. He has been boasting to François he will kick my throne from under me, and now he must reckon with the consequences. He is afraid one of my ships will take him as soon as he is out of port.'

'Indeed, but now he appeals to your Majesty as a gentleman – he wants to shorten the voyage, land with his bride at Dover and have safe conduct to the border.'

Henry says, 'What, have his train eat up everything in their path, and sow sedition as they march? Parade in their strength through the north country, showing their banners? Does he think I'm a fool?'

Hans breaks off humming. He coughs.

Ah well. It is a chance lost, of a meeting between two monarchs, uncle and nephew, who have long avoided each other.

The king's hand rests on the pommel of his dagger: 'Like this?' he says to Hans.

Hans says, 'Perfect.'

Henry eases his shoulders, flexes his knees. Portrait-taking freezes muscle, makes feet hard to manage, makes elbows feel as if they belong to someone else. The harder he tries to hold still, the more the king fidgets. He says, 'I have messages from Ireland. They want you to go over for a season, my lord Cromwell. They think you could bring order. I do suppose you could.'

'So am I to go?'

'No. They might murder you.'

Hans hums.

The king shifts his stance. 'When are the bishops going to utter?'

Since early in the year the bishops have been working on their profession of faith. It is only last July that the ten articles were issued, and gave birth to months of debate. The king hopes a new statement will consolidate opinion. But every time the bishops send Henry some text, he writes over it and makes nonsense of their propositions. Then the papers go back to Thomas Cranmer: who emends the king's emendations, and corrects his syntax while he is about it.

Hans says, 'Would your Majesty be so gracious as to turn his face? Not to Lord Cromwell, to me?'

Henry obeys. He stares at the painter and speaks to his minister: 'Has Lisle's man been here? I marvel Lady Lisle has not taken to her chamber. She must be near her time.'

'Your Majesty will be the first to know.'

Hans says, 'If she has a boy Lord Lisle will shoot off cannon, so if it is a still day they will hear it in Dover and put a rider on the road. I hope the walls of Calais do not fall down.'

'Master,' he whispers, 'you forget yourself. Apply to your trade.'

Sometimes, sitting beside the king – it is late, they are tired, he has been working since first light – he allows his body to confuse with that of Henry, so that their arms, lying contiguous, lose their form and become cloudy like thaw water. He imagines their fingertips graze, his mind meets the royal will: ink dribbles onto the paper. Sometimes the king nods into sleep. He sits by him scarcely breathing, careful as a nursemaid with a fractious brat. Then Henry starts, wakes, yawns; he says, as if he were to blame, 'It is midnight, master!' The past peels away: the king forgets he is 'my lord'; he forgets what he has made him. At dawn, and twilight, when the light is an oyster shell, and again at midnight, bodies change their shape and size, like cats who slide from dormer to gable and vanish into the murk.

But today it is not ten o'clock: a morning in early spring, the light a primrose blur. 'Is it not dinnertime?' the king says, and then, 'What do you hear from Norfolk?'

'That he has a chill. A lax. Each day a flux.'

The king laughs. 'So delicate a soul. Like the Princess Madeleine.'

Hans tuts. 'A solemn countenance, if it sorts with your Majesty? And eyes to me? If my lord Cromwell does anything worth turning around for, I shall let your Majesty know.'

The silence returns. In Florence, he thinks, an artist would make a whole man in a mould. You strip him naked and rub him with grease and close him in a case up to his chin. You pour in plaster and let it set, and when you are ready you take a chisel and open the case like a nut. You draw out the man, his skin rose-red all over, and wash him, then you promise to model his head another day: but you have his form you can use ever after, to make satyrs or saints or gods from Mount Olympus.

Down below in the privy kitchen they are roasting dottrels for dinner. His spaniel starts awake, and runs in excited circles as the savour drifts up. The king's eye follows her; Hans scoops her up and gives her to a menial, saying severely, 'Collect her later, my lord.'

As the hour passes, more and more noise crowds into it: the ring of horseshoes on cobbles, bursts of shouting from distant courtyards, trumpeters clattering past to practice: till finally it seems as if the whole of the court is in there with them. Meanwhile the king's expression changes slowly, as if the moon waxes; so by the time Hans signals that he is done, Henry seems to glow from within. He gathers himself, rearranges his robes. He says, 'I think the queen should be in my picture.'

Hans groans.

The king says, 'Come to me later, Cromwell.'

'How much later, sir?'

No reply: Henry sweeps away. A boy belonging to Hans gathers in the drawings. The king's heads are turned this way and that; his brow is furrowed or clear, his eyes are blank or hostile, but the mouth is always the same, small and set.

'Enough time, Hans?'

'I suppose. I only wanted his head.'

'We should have a lute player next time.'

'With you in the room? You're dangerous to them.'

Mark Smeaton resists oblivion. It is not yet a year, after all. He says, 'I tell you again, I did not hurt Mark.'

'I hear when he left your house his eyeballs hung out on his cheeks.'

Hans does not sound indignant: more curious, as if he imagines making an anatomical drawing.

461

'Witnesses saw him on the scaffold,' he says, 'uninjured. Do not try my patience. And do not try the king's.'

Hans says, 'Henry is easy. He never shows he would like to be elsewhere. He takes it as his duty to be painted. Do you not see? His face shines with the wonder of himself.'

Towards the end of May the queen's child quickens. The *Te Deums* of Trinity Sunday celebrate not only the hope in her womb but the close of the campaigning season. The parish churches ring their bells, cannon are fired at the Tower, and butts of free wine trundle over the cobbles so even the beggars can join in crying, 'God bless our good Queen Jane.' Banners drop from windows, streamers fly from house-tops, thrushes sing, salmon leap, and the dead in London's church-yards jiggle thighbone and knee.

Jane has objected to the taking of her portrait, saying, 'Master Hans will look at me.'

But she has yielded to the king's pleasure, requesting only that Lord Cromwell be present: she seems afraid that the artist will shout at her in a foreign tongue. He makes the introductions and then retreats, so he is out of the painter's eyeline.

'Here?' Jane says.

The queen takes up her stance. Her sister Lady Oughtred, now in attendance, stoops to arrange her skirts. Jane is as stiff as a woman on a catafalque. She stands with her hands clasped over her child, as if keeping it in order. 'It is very correct to breathe,' Hans reminds her. 'And certainly your Highness may sit if she pleases.'

Jane's gaze rests on the middle distance. Her expression is remote and pure. Hans says, 'If your Highness could lift her chin?' He sighs; he shuffles, he walks around the queen, and hums. He is dissatisfied; her face is puffy; he cannot find the bones in it.

Jane speaks only once: 'Is Lady Lisle delivered yet?'

'It cannot be long, madam,' he says, from his seat in the window.

'God send her a good hour,' Lady Oughtred says.

His mind shifts, wanders: he takes a prayer book out of his pocket and thumbs through it, but an image of water, of daylight on water,

begins to flicker and flow between his eyes and the page. He thinks
of a woman sitting upright in a tangle of linen sheets, her breasts bare,
sunlight sliding over her arms. He thinks of himself at nightfall, on
the slippery paving beside the German House in Venice, his friend
Heinrich asking as they step out of their boat: 'You want to see our
goddesses on the wall? You, guard, hold up your torch.'

Almost imperceptibly, Jane's chin has dropped again. Hans
approaches him. It does not matter, he whispers, whether she sits,
stands, kneels, anything she has a fantasy to do; her hands, her
posture, I can fix it later, and we can put her in another gown if she
likes, or paint on different sleeves, we can push her hood back a little,
and as for her jewellery I will give her pieces of my own design,
which will be a good advertisement of my skill, Thomas, do you not
think so? But I must have her face, just for this one hour. So implore
her – spare me a glance.

'The king will want her as she is,' he warns. 'No flattery.'

'It is not my habit.'

'I warrant when he married her,' her sister says, 'she did not look
so much like a mushroom.'

The queen's happy condition is now known all over Europe, and the
Seymour name exalted. It is time he, Cromwell, opened talks with
Edward.

'Your lady sister,' he says. 'Oughtred's widow.'

'Yes,' Edward says.

'Her hand in marriage.'

'Yes?'

'I believe you're talking to the Earl of Oxford? You know he's
older than I am?'

'Is he?' Edward frowns. 'Yes, I dare say.'

'So would Bess not prefer a young lad?'

Edward looks as if something improper has been hinted. 'She
knows her duty.'

'I see it is promotion for you, to marry into the Vere family. Yet
the Seymours are as old a house, I would have thought, old and just

as good, if less rewarded till now. The Veres have more power, but not more estimation.'

'So what are you saying?' Edward is cautious.

'You don't need Oxford to make your fortune. It is already made. And I suggest that a bride could be happier elsewhere.'

'This is a surprise,' Edward says. 'Would you then …?' He closes his eyes as if in prayer. 'That is, are you willing …'

'We are willing,' he says.

'And ready? To talk about money?'

'It is my favourite subject,' he says.

We rough Cromwells, eh? Edward tries to smile.

'But Edward, this could be a great thing,' he says. 'We can make an alliance in blood, as well as in the council chamber. Have no qualms. All the grace and goodwill lie on your side, and the rude substance will come from mine. I will build Bess a new house. While she is waiting she will not be short of a roof over her head – Mortlake is much enlarged, and there is Stepney which is a very pleasant house at any season, and there is Austin Friars of course – all my property is at her disposal, and if there is some house of the king's she has a fancy to, I feel sure that of his kindness he will lend it us. She will have whatever I can give to make her happy.'

Edward says, 'I have heard gentlemen venture – saving your lordship – that Thomas Cromwell is not base-born after all. That you are the natural son of some nobleman.'

He is amused. 'Do they say which one?'

'They reason, how else to explain your talent for ruling men?'

Walter ruled with his fist, he thinks.

'Well, however that may be,' Edward says, 'I shall talk to my sister, and know her mind. And the queen, she will have a view, of course. I don't know what I shall say to the Earl of Oxford …'

'I'll talk to him.'

'Would you?' Edward grasps at that. 'We have come a long way together, my lord,' he says, embracing him, 'since we welcomed you to Wolf Hall.'

He goes home and tells Gregory, 'I have found you a bride.'

'Very well,' Gregory says. 'I shall contain myself in patience till you mention who.'

He hurries on. There are six bishops here to see him, and a delegation from the French embassy. But that night my lord Privy Seal sleeps soundly, under his canopy of violet and silver tissue, beneath a ceiling dusted with gilded stars.

On St George's Day, at the chapter of the Order of the Garter, the king selects the Earl of Cumberland to fill a vacant stall, in exchange for his offices on the Scots border. It is the first, my lord Privy Seal hopes, in a series of tacit bargains that will free up posts in the north country for keen young men he will choose, whose loyalty is not to great families but only to himself and the king.

Cumberland's grandfather was known as the Butcher, and the family has not mellowed since. Generations of raw dealing made his tenants smart; no wonder they turned on him, in the late rebellion. But such magnates, even in our day, are best controlled by offering them rewards. And the Garter is Europe's most ancient order of chivalry, the highest honour the king can bestow.

Mr Wriothesley edges up to him: 'Shall I tell your lordship what the heralds are saying?'

He waits.

'They say that the king is disappointed he must give the Garter to Cumberland. He would rather have filled the vacancy with one he holds more dear.'

The dear one should not have long to fret. Harry Percy has requested the loan of his old house in Hackney; he wants it to die in. The doctors say he will not last the summer, and when he goes, that will free a Garter stall. And when Lord Darcy comes to execution, that will make another vacancy. Mr Wriothesley looks coy. 'Better order your mantles, sir.'

Your mantles of cerulean velvet: sky blue lined with white damask. Hans busies himself at once with new and better designs for Garter insignia: he never lets slip a chance to market his genius. 'I am not your enemy, you know,' Hans says to him. 'Even though I did paint you.'

As Jane lets out her bodices and appears unlaced, she yearns for cherries and peas, but there are none yet. She asks for quails, and the Lisles send them from Calais by the crate. They are fed on the boat and killed at Dover, to keep them as fat as possible, but even so they dwindle on the road, and Jane complains she must have more, and fatter. She eats them rubbed with spices and basted with honey, cracking and sucking the tiny bones. 'She sets into them as if they had done her an injury,' Gregory says. 'Though she looks as if she would only eat curds and whey.'

The king says, 'I like to see a woman show her appetite. The late Katherine, God rest her, when first we were married –' he corrects himself, 'when first we were thought to be married – she would make short work of a duckling. But then later,' he glances away, 'she began to undertake special fasts and penances. Always some strict practice, above the misery prescribed. It was her Spanish blood.'

He thinks, she was praying for us. Offering up her hunger pangs for England.

John Husee brings the quails at seven in the morning. Jane sends word from her suite: roast half for dinner, and we'll have the rest for supper.

He asks Husee, 'Is there no child yet? The king is keen for the outcome. It will warm his heart if Lisle has a son and heir.'

Husee shakes his head. He looks harassed, but then he always does.

'Perhaps Honor has mistaken her reckoning,' Fitzwilliam says. 'What do the doctors advise?'

'They advise patience.'

Fitzwilliam says, 'By the time it is born it will know its letters, and be fit to gnaw a marrowbone and wave a wooden sword.'

In return for quails, and cherries when they are ripe, Jane agrees she will give a position in her household to one of Lady Lisle's daughters. Jane asks them to send two, and whichever she rejects she will place in the train of some other noble lady. She kindly says that the girls may wear out their French apparel, even though English fashion has changed since last year.

But when the girls arrive, Jane looks at them and says, 'Oh, no, no, no, no. I will have that one, but take her away and bring her back dressed more seemly.'

Anne Bassett must have finer linen, so fine the skin shows through. She needs a gable hood, and a girdle sewn thickly with pearls. When she reappears by the queen's side, it is with her hair hidden, her skull squeezed, and in a gown belonging to my lady Sussex.

When next he sees John Husee and hails him, Husee shoots off in the other direction.

Whitehall: he arrives outside the Lady Mary's presence chamber, Gregory attending him. Some grand arrival is in the air. Household folk crowd him, chattering: 'Who is it, Lord Cromwell?' Mary's silk-woman has brought a basket. A boy has come to tune her virginals. A little dwarf woman called Jane is waddling around the chamber: 'Welcome, one and all.'

'Dodd!' He greets Mary's usher. 'Big fish today.' He speaks for everyone to hear. 'A Spanish gentleman has come from the Emperor, to assist Ambassador Chapuys in wooing the Lady Mary.'

One of the queen's ladies, Mary Mounteagle, has coins in a net purse; the queen lost at cards last night, and now pays her debts. Another lady, Nan Zouche, escorts her, as if she might be robbed. Both of them hang on his elbows: 'A Spanish gentleman? Is not Dom Luis a Portuguese?'

'Though it is all the same,' Nan Zouche says. 'All the Emperor's cousins.'

Mounteagle asks, 'Does Dom Luis speak English? If not, Lord Cromwell will have to kneel at their bedside, interpreting.'

'I do not speak Portuguese, so they must make shift,' he says. 'Does the Lady Mary always collect her winnings?'

'Always,' Nan says. 'And she is such a gambler! One day she bet her breakfast on a game of bowls.'

The little woman says, 'I hope the ambassador does not bring her comfits. Her teeth are not sound.' She shows her own. 'Me, I can crack nuts.'

The great men enter to the sound of giggling. The new envoy, Don Diego de Mendoza, is followed by Chapuys, followed in turn by his Flemish bodyguard. Don Diego is one of those men who requires a big space around himself. Chapuys looks jittery: he backs away to allow the new man to be admired, in his plumes and black velvet. Prominently and reverently, Mendoza carries a black-ribboned letter, sealed with the double-headed eagle. 'Lord Cremuel,' he says. 'I have heard a great deal about you.'

'And I,' he says pleasantly, 'feel I know you already. For you must be related to that Mendoza who was ambassador in the cardinal's time?'

'I have that honour.'

'The cardinal locked him up.'

'A violation of every agreed principle of diplomacy,' Mendoza says. The chill in his voice would blight a vineyard. 'I did not know you were at court then.'

'No. As I was the cardinal's man, I have inherited his concerns.'

'But not his methods,' Chapuys says quickly.

It is evident that Eustache is keen to make a success of the encounter. 'You have much in common, gentlemen. Don Diego has been in Italy. At the universities of Padua, and Bologna.'

'You were there, Cremuel?' Mendoza asks.

'Yes, but not at the university.'

'Don Diego knows Arabic,' Chapuys offers.

He is alert. 'Does it take years to learn?'

'Yes,' Don Diego says. 'Years and years.'

He asks, 'Have you brought Dom Luis's portrait for my lady?'

'Just this,' the ambassador says, showing his letter.

'I thought perhaps you had it in miniature, and carried it next to your heart.'

It is obvious that Don Diego is carrying something of which he is painfully aware: as you might be aware if someone slid a hot iron under your shirt. No doubt it is a second letter, perhaps in code.

'There are presents, of course. Which follow by mule,' says Mendoza.

'Because they are large,' Chapuys says.

'Good. Lady Mary has lavish tastes. That's why her father has brought her to court. He could not maintain her in a separate household. She wrote for more money every week.'

'She is generous with her small means,' Chapuys says. 'Charitable.'

'I suppose she lives as befits a princess?' Don Diego says. 'You would not expect her to do other?'

'Ordinarily,' Chapuys advises, 'Lord Cremuel would kick your shin if you spoke her proper title. They call her by her plain name, Mary. But behold – when they are offering her in marriage, we call her "princess" and suddenly,' he smirks, 'Cremuel does not mind at all.'

The door of the chamber opens and out issues Mary's chaplain, in conference with her doctor, a Spaniard. To the chaplain he says, 'How do you, Father Baldwin? How does my lady?' The doctor he greets in his best Castilian: suck on that, Mendoza. 'I will give you a quarter of an hour, ambassador. Then I regret I shall interrupt you.'

Chapuys protests: 'It is hardly time enough for them to pray together.'

'Oh, will they do that?' He smiles.

Dodd the usher bows Mendoza into the presence chamber. 'Has she attendance?' Nan Zouche says, and the two ladies exchange a glance and slip in after the ambassador. The door closes.

Chapuys mutters something. It sounds like, 'Hopeless.'

'I'm sorry, ambassador?' he says.

'I think those ladies are your friends, who have just intruded on the Lady Mary.'

Mary Mounteagle is Brandon's daughter, from one of his many early marriages; yes, he would say they were friends. Nan Zouche – Nan Gainsford, as she was – gave him matter to use against Anne Boleyn.

'How is the queen?' Chapuys says. 'The king must be very anxious.'

'She gives no reason for anxiety.'

'But even so. Given his past losses. They say Edward Seymour is certain of a prince, that he is walking around with his head swelling like a yeasted loaf. Of course, if she has a boy, the Seymour brothers will be promoted – they may come to rival you.'

He cannot see Tom Seymour running the Privy Seal's office. He says, 'I'll have to watch that, won't I?'

'But then I am sure they will be wary,' Chapuys says, 'remembering what you did to the brother of the other one. If I were them, I would hurry back to Wolf Hall and be forgotten.' He chuckles. 'They should become shepherds, or something of that sort.'

He says, 'Don Diego is not very friendly. I thought it was an ambassador's duty?'

'He is fastidious,' Chapuys admits.

He laughs. A hiatus. From behind Mary's closed door, voices too faint to be useful. Chapuys says, 'Mr Call-Me is much in your confidence.'

'Yes, he is growing into consideration.'

'He opens your letters.'

'Someone must. There are too many for one man.'

'He was Gardiner's man,' Chapuys says.

'Gardiner remains in France.'

'And loyalty is to the proximate,' Chapuys says. 'I see.'

He looks over his shoulder. 'A word to the wise?' The ambassador approaches. 'Aske implicated you.'

'What?' Chapuys says.

'Under questioning. And we have letters you sent to Lord Darcy. Going back three years.'

'I protest,' Chapuys says swiftly.

'You claim they are forgeries?'

'I make no claim. I say nothing to them.'

'I know how it is, Eustache. You come to my house and you sit down to supper and you say to me, peace. You go home and light your candle and you write to your master, war.' A pause. 'Lucky for you, I am more clement than the cardinal. I shall not lock you up.' He gestures to the closed door. 'I think that's ten minutes.'

He is as good as his word: kicks his way in like a drunken horse-boy. Gregory and the ambassador are at his heels. As they enter, they hear a scream. A large green parrot is bouncing up and down on its perch. When they wheel around, it laughs.

'It is a present,' Mary says. 'I apologise.'

'Does it speak?'

'I fear it may.'

Mary, he notices, has not asked Don Diego to sit. The ambassador draws up his person: 'My lord, go out, we are not done.'

The parrot sways on its perch, and squeaks like an unoiled wheel. He says, 'I come to remind you of your urgent next engagement.'

Don Diego looks for a second as if he will try to face him down. But Chapuys clears his throat. The moment passes. The Spaniard says, 'My lady, for now we must part.'

'No, do not kneel,' Mary says. 'Haste away – the Lord Privy Seal is holding the door for you.' She extends a hand for the ambassador's kiss. 'I thank you for your good counsel.'

He cedes the door-holding to Gregory, steps into the room. The ambassador passes out with an ill grace: Chapuys follows, making a comical face at him as he passes. He closes the door. The parrot is still scolding. 'It has not taken to the Spaniard,' he says.

Mary says, 'Neither have you.'

He approaches the bird. He sees the slender gold chain that fastens it to a bar. The creature stamps, and raises its wings in threat. 'I used to have a magpie when I was a child. I caught it myself.'

She says, 'I cannot imagine you as a child.'

He thinks, neither can I. I cannot picture myself.

'I tried to teach it to speak,' he says. 'But it flew away, first chance it got.' But not before it said, *Walter is a knave*. He turns to Mary. 'So what passed?'

She is unwilling to divulge. 'He asked me if I meant what I said.'

'Generally? Or specifically?'

'You know well,' she says. An instant flare of passion: her face is alight, as if someone had forced air into her with a bellows. But the next moment, she drops her eyes, an obedient woman, deflated: reverts to her monotone. 'He asked if I meant it, when I said I accepted my father as head of the church, and that he and my mother were never truly married. I said I did. I said I accepted it all. I told him I had taken the advice of my uncle the Emperor, as conveyed to me by Ambassador Chapuys. I told him you, Cromwell, had stood my friend. And if he did not believe me that is not my fault.'

He says, 'But did you tell him how you wrote to the Pope, taking back your statement, and begging to be absolved?'

Her eyes fly to his face.

'No matter,' he says. 'It is another case where I forbear to bring your conduct home to you. I only mention it by way of warning.'

Panic in her voice. 'What do you want?'

'Want? My lady, I only want you to pray for me.'

'Oh, I do,' Mary says. 'But do you know what I have discovered? The king has great power, but he has no power to know me, except through what I say and what I do.'

The parrot has put its head on one side, as if listening.

He says, 'The previous Mendoza was never allowed to be alone with your lady mother. It was for her safety.'

'I think, rather, it was for the safety of the state.'

'Everything we do is for that. Without the king's peace, my lady, we would be in the wilderness with the wild beasts. Or in the oceans with Leviathan.'

He moves about the chamber to put space between them. Zouche and Mounteagle slide back against the wall; if they could weave themselves into the arras, they would do it. The parrot swivels its head to follow him as he moves. 'I suppose the ambassador promised to get you away from these shores.'

Mary looks down at her feet: as if to catch them going somewhere.

'If he did not, then he will. He thinks we will force you into a marriage with the French.'

'I trust my lord father will not do that.'

'I myself have no such intention. I make you no guarantee, his Majesty's will being supreme, but you are better to trust to my efforts than to scrambling down a rope ladder in the dark, and setting to sea in a sieve.'

She turns her face away.

'Give me the letter,' he says. 'The ambassador's letter.'

She takes from the table the fat ribboned packet, the seal broken, and offers it to him. 'Perhaps you would like to read it and then take it to the king?'

'The other letter,' he says.

She hesitates, but only for a moment. Without a word, without glancing at his face, she slides it from her book and gives it him. It lacks a seal. But she has not had time to read it.

'What is your book?' He turns it up to see. It is a Herbal, with a device of a wild man and a wild woman, hairy creatures holding a shield with the printer's initials. 'I have one of these,' he says. 'It is ten years old, it could stand some correction.' He turns the leaves, looking at the woodcuts. 'But there will be other matter for us soon. Archbishop Cranmer is sending me a new translation of the scriptures.'

'Another?' she says wanly. 'It must be the third this year.'

'Cranmer says it is the soundest yet. He is confident your lord father will license it and set it forth.'

'I am not against the scriptures. Do not think so.'

'I will make sure you receive an early copy. You will do well to study the Commandments. Honour thy father. Since thy mother is departed.'

Katherine, God pardon her. Katherine, whom God assoil. Katherine, whose children would not stay within her womb: who is responsible nevertheless for the sorry object before him, her eyes dull, her face swollen with toothache.

He thinks of her Spanish grandmother in shining breastplate, mirror of fate to the infidel. Isabella took the field: Andalusia trembled.

* * *

473

On Whitsun eve, after a voyage so long postponed, the King of Scots makes landfall on his own shore. The French bride looks as if she has heaved up her soul on the deep. She falls to the ground, observers report, scoops up two handfuls of the port of Leith and kisses the soil.

A man called William Dalyvell, a follower of Merlin and King James, is put into the Tower. He has been spreading a prophecy that the King of Scots will swoop down from the north, expel the Tudors and rule two kingdoms. He also says he has seen an angel.

In former ages this would have been a cause for congratulation, but times being what they are, Dalyvell is put on the rack.

The Cornish people petition to have their saints back – those downgraded in recent rulings. Without their regular feasts, the faithful are unstrung from the calendar, awash in a sea of days that are all the same. He thinks it might be permitted; they are ancient saints of small worship. They are scraps of paint-flaked wood, or stumps of weathered stone, who say and do nothing against the king. They are not like your Beckets, whose shrines are swollen with rubies, garnets and carbuncles, as if their blood were bubbling up through the ground.

June, second drawing: 'The king is to stand on this carpet,' Hans decrees. Boys spread it at their feet: his own feet of Spanish leather, the neat red boots of Mr Wriothesley, the distinguished padded toes of Lord Audley and Sir William Fitzwilliam. It is one of the cardinal's carpets; he stoops to uncurl an edge.

'All of them?' the Lord Chancellor asks. 'Together on this carpet? The king, the queen, and his royal parents too?'

Hans gives him a withering look. 'His father I will place behind him. His royal mother, behind the queen that is now.'

He asks, 'How will you show the old king and queen? At what age?'

'In eternity they have no age.'

'There are other pictures to guide you, I suppose.'

'Did we not make you a gallery?' Hans says. 'A whole room of the lost.'

Yes, but that was more like a game, he thinks, a game of kings, their faces like clues in a riddle. No one could point to them as a true or false likeness. They were all so old and they had been gone so long.

Hans begins to pace out the scene. The father here, towards the centre, but Henry in the foreground. Between the two parents I shall place a column, he says, or a piece of marble –

'A sort of altar?' Lord Audley offers.

'He will want verses on it, Hans. Extolling him.'

'Words are for Lord Cromwell to supply.'

'Mr Wriothesley,' he says, 'will you make a note?' But Call-Me is already sketching out suggestions.

They look up as the king comes in. He has to walk the length of the gallery. He seems unbalanced, as if the floor were soft. Fitz whispers something: 'Hush,' he says.

'Ah, Cromwell,' Henry says. 'Lord Chancellor. I hear a rumour that François is dead.'

'I fear untrue,' he says.

The king's face is pale and puffy. He dare not ask if he is in pain. Henry would not want an underling like Hans to hear the question, let alone the answer.

'Better light today,' the king says. 'Norfolk writes to me that in Yorkshire there is a hard frost every morning. When here, the roses are out!'

Call-Me says, 'There is always a hard frost in the region of Norfolk.'

Henry smiles. 'The zephyrs do not play about his person. And young Surrey, he writes, is suffering from a depression of his spirits. Myself I always thought action dispelled melancholy, and I should have thought the Howards would find plenty to do ...'

'The duke should stay up in Yorkshire,' Fitzwilliam says. 'He is as well-accepted among the northern sort as any lord can be.'

Thomas Howard says another winter will kill him. But he can take his chances till September. He would not want to be in London, surely, with the plague's incursions? A hundred and twelve buried last week.

'And what do we hear of Harry Percy?' The king rubs his nose, reflective. He is looking forward to the reversion of the Percy earldom to the crown. 'Send young Sadler, will you, to see how the dying goes?'

From Wriothesley, a stir of mute discontent: not him, Majesty, send me!

'Unless you care to go yourself, my lord Privy Seal? But I think the earl fears you of old, and I do not want to be accused of frightening him to death.'

'I never hurt the earl,' he says. A picture rises to his mind of Call-Me at the deathbed, taking off his coat and turning back his sleeves, picking up a pillow …

The king calls, 'Hans, where are you? We are ready. Today you must finish with the drawing, or you will have to chase me. I shall not linger at Whitehall when I could be hunting.'

The king's tone is hearty; as if he is trying to encourage himself as well as the painter. Hans whistles through his teeth and flaps over his sheets. When stitched together they will cover the wall. The councillors fall back, making space. Fitz murmurs, 'What's the matter with him today? Something's the matter.'

He thinks, the damage has been done since last October. It is cumulative, but we are only noticing now. The rebels have knocked him out of true. He will not be the same again. The king stands alone on the turkey carpet, feet planted on the cobalt stars. His voice reaches out, as if to loop them into his plans: Hampton Court to Woking, to Guildford, to Easthampstead. 'You will hunt with me this summer, my lord Cromwell.'

He moves so fast that he is able to grip the king by his upper arms and steadies him as he sways. Fitz is behind him. 'A seat for the king!' Audley bawls. Cries of distant alarm – how news flies! – then pounding of feet, and servants and courtiers pour in. 'Keep away!' Fitz windmills his arms, bellows as if he were on the battlefield. Wriothesley has a stool, gliding it smoothly under his monarch's haunches. Gingerly, they lower the afflicted man, so he sits gaping, his face working as if he might cry. He and Audley lean in, propping him up. There is a sheen of sweat on Henry's face. He takes out a handkerchief. They huddle to shield him from the ring of faces. 'Have you a pain, sir?' Audley asks. 'Where is your pain?'

'Give me some air,' the sick man says.

They step away; but Henry takes him by the sleeve; he is reeled in. 'My lord,' Henry blots his face, 'this is not the first time we have felt ourselves fall. A humour has got into our legs. A weakness. No, the doctors don't know, any better than we know. But it will get better, it must.'

He sees that the king is furious with himself: a low white fury that makes him tremble. 'Send all these people away. Tell Hans to come tomorrow. Tell them it is only a – no, tell them nothing. Disperse them.'

He thinks the king is done. He eases away from him, straightening up, but the king still holds his sleeve. 'Cromwell, what if it is a girl?'

His heart sinks. 'Then boys will follow.'

The king releases him. 'Where's Fitz?' Henry says, plaintive. 'I want Fitz, send the rest off.'

He turns. No one dares approach. '*Allons*,' he says. Audley falls in with him, Wriothesley treads on his boot heels. They do not speak till they reach the other end of the gallery. Audley casts a glance back. 'We must keep this secret.'

Mr Wriothesley says, 'Of course, my lord.'

He says, 'Not a chance.' The painter has followed them. 'Master Holbein? Bring your drawing. The king's face. Let me see.'

Hans whistles up a boy, who scuffles through the sheets bearing the king's head, till he finds a version the master is content to show. He, Cromwell, puts his thumb on the king's forehead, as if he were smudging him with chrism. 'Turn the head. Turn it full on. Make him look at us.'

'God in Heaven,' Hans says, 'that will be frightening. Turn body and all?'

Frowning face and massive shoulders. Bloated waist, padded cod. Legs like the pillars that hold the globe in place. Legs that could never stagger, feet never lose the path.

* * *

As July comes in Lord Latimer is down from the north, complaining to all who will listen of his sufferings at the hands of the Pilgrims. He will be glad to see much less of Yorkshire; he knows the king's business will force him back, but for the rest of the time he will be content to live on his property in Pershore: and so says his wife Kate.

Lord Latimer wonders why young men hide smiles. What's funny about his wife Kate?

News comes from Scotland that Princess Madeleine is dead. Her triumphant entry into Edinburgh will not now take place. The banners are furled, the pageants dismantled, the silver trumpets laid in their cases.

Henry says, 'Surely James will seek another Frenchwoman. But I do not think François will let him have his younger daughter, to be exposed to the Scottish air. There is the Duchess of Vendôme – though James turned her down once, and I do suppose her people are offended.'

'The Duke of Longueville has died,' he says, 'leaving a widow – a very handsome woman, they say, only three years wed, yet with a son in her arms and another child in the womb. James might look that way.'

But I don't know, he thinks, if she would look at James. The family of Marie de Guise are such lofty people they might not know where Scotland is. Anyway, James will be mourning a while yet. A pension was to come with Madeleine, thirty thousand francs a year; it will not continue with a corpse.

Madeleine was one month shy of her seventeenth birthday. In fairness to the French, they did advise James to choose a more robust bride.

With Lady Oughtred, on a fine evening, he walks in the queen's privy garden. Bess rests her hand on his arm. 'So the marriage, when shall it be?' she asks.

'As soon as you like. But,' he stops and turns her to face him, 'you do like?'

'Oh, yes.' Her eyes are warm. 'I know some would think ...'

'There are disparities, of course. I have talked it over with your brothers. I have not shirked the point.'

'But after all, I am a widow,' she says, 'and not some inexperienced girl.'

He is not sure what she means; but then, why should he expect to understand this young woman's mind? 'My lady, may I ask – it is perhaps too private a matter –'

'Whatever it is, I am bound in obedience to tell you.'

'Well then … I should like to know, do you mourn your husband still?'

She turns her face away; he admires her: her face, like Jane's, has a soft smooth shape, and she has the same habit of dipping her chin, as if taking a covert survey of what's around her.

She says, 'I make no complaint of Oughtred. He was a good husband and I regret his passing. But you will not think me heartless if I say I could also be happy with a different kind of man?' She turns her face up to his, earnest; he sees how she wants to please him. 'I am quite ready to make trial of it.'

'When my wife died,' he says, 'I missed her out of all measure. Considering what my life was then, always riding up the country, over to Antwerp half a dozen times a year, late nights with the cardinal, livery dinners and conclaves at Gray's Inn … sometimes when I'd come in she'd say, "I'm Lizzie Cromwell, have you seen my husband?"'

'Lizzie,' she says. 'Just as well I'm Bess these days. It is the same with all Elizabeths – as we are called, we answer.'

He smiles. 'I won't confuse the two of you.'

'We did suppose, myself and Jane, that you were fond of your wife, because you never took any opportunity you were offered – and Jane says you were friendly with Mary Boleyn, and could have married her if you pleased.'

'Oh, that was just Mary's whim,' he says. 'She wanted to upset her people. Put Uncle Norfolk in a rage. And she thought I would do a good job of that. Mary has a good heart, and they say she suits well with that fellow Stafford she wed. But I thought of her as … God love her, well-used.'

She is anxious. 'But you do not object to a widow?'

'My first wife was a widow.'

'If you had wed Mary Boleyn you would have been related to the king.'

'After a manner.'

'You will be related to him now. Though it has taken longer.'

He thinks, how gentle she is, to give thought to my state of mind. How careful she is, for she has mentioned the old gossip about Mary Boleyn, but never the new gossip about Mary the king's daughter.

He halts; the garden's scents rise around them; he turns her to face him, taking her two hands. 'Let's not talk about the dead. I would rather talk about you. We must dress you up. We must order some silks and velvets. And I thought, emeralds?'

'I lent my jewel box to Jane, when she was so suddenly elevated. I suppose she will give it back now I am to be married.'

'I will talk to people in Antwerp. We could go through the king's man, Cornelius, but I know some setters who do beautiful work, and after all, you won't want to have what your sister has.'

She drops her eyes. 'Jane said you would be generous.'

'You must indulge me. I have no daughters. Though that is not true, I have one, you will have heard.'

'Your Antwerp daughter.'

'But I don't think she cares for such things.'

She lowers her head and smiles. Suddenly she is as shy as her sister. 'My lord, you may indulge me and I shall indulge you. But I shall hardly be your daughter.'

He says gently, 'I had hoped that you would see yourself in that way.'

'Oh, but ...' She stops and puts her hand on his arm. 'It is to be like that? I did not know. As you please, of course ... but you are not so very old, and I had hoped to have your children.'

'Mine?'

He is shocked to the marrow. He, who has been in Rome! Who has been, frankly, everywhere ... 'Bess,' he says, 'we should go inside.'

'Why?'

These Seymours, he thinks, they are like something from the Greek legends. A curse will fall on them. We know Old Sir John tupped his daughter-in-law, but surely she does not think that is the usual arrangement?

'It is late, you are tired, it's cold,' he says. 'And we should not be alone.'

'Why?'

'It could lead to –' He passes his hand over his face. What could it lead to? 'To misunderstandings.'

She says, 'It is barely eight o'clock, the night is warm, and I am as fresh as a milkmaid at dawn.'

'Come in,' he urges her.

'In other respects I agree.' Her voice is icy. 'I think there has been a misunderstanding. I am offering my person to one Cromwell only, the one I marry. But which Cromwell is it meant to be?'

His mind flies back to his conversation with Edward. It lands, light as a fly, and begins to crawl over it: over every meaningful pause, every ellipsis. Were names spoken? Perhaps not. Could Edward have supposed – could Edward have mistaken – yes, he supposes he could.

He lets out his breath. 'So. Well. I am flattered, Bess. That you would even consider it.'

She says firmly: 'I am not at fault.'

'By no means.'

'You are at fault. I listened to what my brother required of me. I made no objection. I never said, what age is Cromwell, and was his father not a tradesman? I just said, Yes, Edward. For the family, Edward. Anything and anyone you command, Edward.'

'I see,' he says. 'I begin to see.'

'I know you are a busy man. But I think you might have paused to explain yourself, so Edward could explain to me. But with no elucidation, I assumed –'

'But why would you? When Gregory is so likely a young man, and of an age to marry?'

'I think you have no idea, my lord, how much your single state is talked of. How much the whole court looks to you to change it. How they speculate, men and women both, that a great and dangerous honour will come your way.'

'It is all just gossip,' he says. 'And you are right that it is dangerous. Dangerous to me, dishonourable to the Lady Mary.'

'Then you would do well to be clear in your mind. Who you will marry. Who you will not.'

He begs, 'Don't tell Gregory. He thinks you have freely accepted him.' A qualm overtakes him. 'You will accept him? Because Bess – my lady – you are relieved, that it is not as you thought?'

A pause, then: 'My lord, I will not tell you whether I am relieved or not. You must puzzle it out. But I dare say you will be too busy to puzzle for long.'

'Gregory will make a tender husband,' he says wretchedly, 'and he will make you proud of him. He is a kind young man and gentle, and he is a good dancer, and he cuts a fine figure in the tilt yard, as fine as the best gentleman with sixteen quarters of nobility on his shield, and the king likes him, and no doubt he will make him a baron very soon and you will once more have your title and style. He is all together better than me –' I, he thinks, who am so soiled in life's battle, so seamed and scarred, so numb, so unwanted, so cold.

'Stop,' she says. 'First, too few words. Now, too many.'

'But you will? You will wed Gregory?'

'Tell me when and where, and I will come in my bridal finery and marry whichever Cromwell presents himself. I am an obliging woman,' she says. 'Though not so obliging as you thought.'

She walks away on the grassy path, but she does not hurry. Her head is down, she appears to be in prayer. He thinks, she will be plain Mistress Cromwell, and she had not reckoned on that. Does she mind? It is not the least part of it, to find you are not only dropped down a generation, but have no title. Yet surely she would prefer the son, with all his prospects before him, to the father who – well, he thinks, I suppose there are prospects before me. No doubt Wriothesley is right, about the Garter. It seems such a thing could never happen, not to Walter's son. Yet so much has happened already, that the most credulous child would never believe.

When he was a boy he used to go door to door offering to sharpen scissors and bodge pans. He would scrub out a henhouse or scour pewter or cut up a carcass if a housewife had come by half a pig unexpectedly. He called all his customers 'my lady'. He saw how it brightened their day. Sometimes it earned him an apple or a half-penny, and once a kiss: and these things were over and above the fee for his services.

His father's friends worked the river, piloting travellers and running ferries from bank to bank. So he did river work too: a hungry, ignorant boy. What did he want with a horn book? As soon as he needed to read, he could read. If there was something worth writing, he could scratch it out. He used to search for treasure in the riverine mud, and plenty treasure he found. Let a gentleman's cap blow off and it will feed a family for a week: it is not the watermarked velvet that you trade, but his cap badge. It could be a gold Becket or Christopher; a flower with enamelled petals; or a jewelled cross, with a garnet where God's head should be. He learned to hide his finds from Walter, and keep the profit for himself.

One night, drunk, Walter said to him, hand slapping his own breast: 'This boat is rowing and rowing, Thomas. I'm rowing to save my life.'

Towards the end of June the Cromwells visit the Seymour household at Twickenham. Gifts are exchanged, they take pleasure trips on the river, and musicians play into the dusk: then by the scent and light of beeswax candles he makes his arrangements with Edward, the head of the house. Edward agrees with him that the young couple should have time together without being overlooked by their elders. They will marry in early August when he, the Privy Seal, sees a two-day gap in his schedule; two days when, we trust, the princes of Europe, instead of clashing in arms, sit with dreaming eyes in the shade, listening to water drop in marble basins.

If Edward Seymour shared his sister's mistake, he does not allude to it: neither of them do. Messages of congratulation pour in, a few of them sincere. Call-Me says, who would have thought Gregory would be so useful to you, as to unite you with the king's family? I always said he would come to good. Once the paperwork is done, the match is as good as made; and with the short scented nights before them, there is no harm if the young couple go to bed. Try and make her happy, he tells Gregory, happier than an old earl ever could: then she never regrets it, never looks back and says, I could have been the Countess of Oxford.

For his son's first household he has ordered majolica ware from Venice, from the masters who work by the church of Barnaba. A rush job, but he looks forward to unpacking the crates, running his finger over the glaze. He has stipulated gods and goddesses: Danaë visited by Zeus, who arrives in the form of a cloudburst. This is no ordinary rain: the bride stands, complacent, as gold plummets down on her, and nuggets roll over her bare arms and thighs and pool as a pile of bullion around her ankles. Never was a lass so augmented; and no bruises either. Bess Seymour will recognise Danaë, and no doubt give her a nod.

The faux-pas is forgotten, he thinks. No reason the girl should speak of it: it would make her seem a fool. He wishes Jenneke might come from Antwerp; he will write, or Gregory will write, but he does not know if she will stir. All the household is braced for celebration. The kitchen can build his major cake at last, topped with balls of gilded marzipan: the one he intended for Easter. They will eat Venetian cakes from the new dishes, some made with pine-nuts and ginger, and some with syrup of violets.

By midsummer the Pilgrims are all dead: hanged or beheaded, along with those who assisted them, excused them, or fed them with money and hope. Bigod, Lord Darcy, and Captain Cobbler himself, the great rebel of Louth; the Abbot of Jervaux, the one-time Abbot of Fountains: some executed at Tyburn, some at the Tower, some sent to be killed in York or Hull. They say old Darcy spent his last days cursing Thomas Cromwell, when he should have been telling his beads. The recalcitrant monks of the London Charterhouse are chained up at Newgate, and in less than a week the plague takes five of them, leaves others dying: dispatched, it seems, by the hand of God.

Harry Percy does not outlast the month of June. Rafe is at his deathbed, where he lies sans sight and speech, yellow as saffron and with belly blown. You would have pitied him, sir, Rafe says, and he says, I am sure I should. Did he mention his wife Mary Talbot?

After a manner, Rafe says. When the onlookers reminded him he had made no provision for her he nodded that yes, he knew: but she was not his wife, never his wife, he was married to Anne Boleyn. And all this he showed them, Rafe says, by pushing away any papers they laid before him, and by a petulant sweep of his hand over his embroidered coverlet: his palm, damp with his last secretions, brushing the emblems of Percy rule, the blue lion and lozenges of gold.

He says, 'His memory was still good, despite his pain, if he remembered Anne Boleyn. I wonder if he remembered the night he walked in to arrest the cardinal?'

The Percys' noble house is now utterly undone. Harry Percy has no offspring, and the king is his heir. His brother Thomas has predeceased him, beheaded for treason in the late broils; his brother Ingram lies in the Tower, under threat of the same.

And Robert Aske is dead. Norfolk supervises the execution. He is hanged in York, from the Clifford Tower, on a market day. Where now his tawny silk jacket with the velvet facings, his crimson satin doublet? Still in London at the Cardinal's Hat. Aske begs to be full dead before he is cut up: the king concedes it.

After that, his mercy appears exhausted. Among the traitors fetched to London is a woman, Margaret Cheney – known as wife to Sir John Bulmer, but really his concubine. It is indecent to cut a woman apart in public or strip her to draw out her entrails, so if guilty of high treason she is burned. He goes to Henry. Asking for quick deaths devolves to him, a duty inherited from the cardinal. For Anne Boleyn he procured not only the swifter end, but the Calais swordsman: she too could have died by fire.

He says, 'Sir, Bulmer's woman is sent to suffer at Smithfield – I know the penalty is specified, but it is not often enforced.'

Henry grunts.

'Consider, sir, she made a guilty plea.'

'She could hardly do other,' the king says. 'No, my lord, there is no help for it, she must endure – it will be an example to other women, should they incline to papistry and rebellion.'

Margaret Cheney is beautiful. He has seen her. She is tender and young. He says, 'Majesty, let me bring her where you can see her.'

Her beauty might move him. He can be moved. We have seen it happen.

Henry says, 'I have no curiosity to see a traitor. Except Pole. I would be curious to see Pole, but you seem unable to get hold of him.'

He bows, withdraws: a failure, twice a failure. He thinks, perhaps Cranmer and I, perhaps if we pleaded on our knees for him to stop the burning … But Cranmer is in the country. In times past, the king's women might have appealed to him, for one of their own sex. But the Lady Mary has been warned stiffly, by him, not to speak for any rebel; and the queen, he supposes, has been told the same by her brother.

He leans against the wall in the privy chamber. He thinks, do not falter, Master Secretary. Have no qualms, my lord Privy Seal; Baron Cromwell, do not fail. You must not soften now.

A young man approaches: 'May I offer you assistance, my lord?'

'Tom Culpeper,' he says. The young fellow bows. Doublet silk, manners honed: by blood, some sort of Howard. Is there no end to them?

The young man says smoothly, 'Messages from Calais, my lord.'

'Lady Lisle is delivered at last?'

'Ah, no, it is not yet her time.'

'Then do not trouble the king. He looks every hour to hear Lisle has a son.'

He brushes past Culpeper, hugging his folio of papers. You cannot falter, he thinks, and you must not. You must crunch up the enemy, flesh, bones and all. You cannot afford to fail, you must bring Henry good news, you must dredge it up from somewhere; he is outwardly

486

serene, but not serene or patient when he wakes in the night, not when his leg pains him in the small hours.

The king has pulled Francis Bryan back from France, saying, 'What's the use? This ingrate Pole always eludes us.' The difficulty is not how to seize his person – it is where. In the Low Countries, jurisdictions lie so close that a man may easily pass from France to Empire and back in a day; territory is so contested that the border can change while a traveller is hearing Mass or taking a nap. But Pole does not hover in mid-air, he is always in someone's jurisdiction. Any violence involved in arresting him could be taken as a hostile act on foreign soil: a provocation to war, or an excuse for it.

But where can Pole go next? Neither France nor the Low Countries will receive him, but they will not extradite him either. He says to Wriothesley, he will go to Italy now. He has missed his chance with our rebels. He will retreat to warmer climes, where his pedigree is applauded, and where with fellow prelates in scarlet he will pace on a white mule, while poor peasants throw money under the hooves.

And that is our chance to kill him, he thinks. For in Italy who owns the night, who can patrol it?

He says, 'I wish I had the man who shot Packington. Were he the greatest papist alive, I would turn him, and send him after Reginald.'

At the Charterhouse – the property now shuttered and barred – lights have appeared at night. Papists spread the word that ghosts walk abroad. 'Probably thieves,' he says to Wriothesley. 'Tell them, set a good watch. All the movables belong to the king.'

But the watchmen see who holds the lights; it is the plague-stricken brothers themselves, tiptoeing the cloisters in their stinking shrouds. They bring dispatches from the world beyond, apparently: they have seen the martyred Bishop Fisher, seated at the right hand of God.

'What about Thomas More?' he says. 'Anybody seen him?'

Revenues from the London Charterhouse should be £642.0s.4d. Riche has the figures. Take all the Carthusians' houses together, and you are looking at the annual sum of £2,947.

'And fifteen shillings, four pence, and one farthing,' says Richard Riche.

He says, 'It seems to me, Sir Richard, that you have done service to the state. You can have the farthing, and spend it on your little pleasures.'

The Lisles' man, John Husee, is never away from his door, jostling with other petitioners and begging for ten minutes. When Richard Cromwell waves him in at last, he has his arms full of maps and account books, but he has the face of a downtrodden spaniel. 'Sir,' he says, 'Lord Lisle's promised abbey – he is desperate to get it signed over.'

'I've said I'll see to it, Husee, and I will. Give all those papers to Master Richard.'

'With respect, sir, my lord – you have been promising to attend to it since last November. My lord is so beleaguered, you would not imagine how his creditors press. And Sir Richard Riche has brought in a delay at every turn. Without a fee Riche will do nothing. And my lord cannot pay his prices.'

'Sit down, Husee,' he says. 'Shall we have a glass to keep up our strength?'

Husee sits, but he shifts on his stool. 'The abbey – my lord trusts to have the rents for the months he has been waiting?'

He sighs. 'I'll talk to Riche. No more delays, I swear. But now, look, Husee, I have always known you for an honest man, so give me an honest answer. Only this morning at early Mass the queen asked me, how does my lady in Calais, is she not a mother yet? By my reckoning, she said, the child should be teething by now.'

To his astonishment, tears fill Husee's eyes. He says, 'My lord, I do not dare to tell you.'

'She has lost it?' Richard says.

'No.' Husee looks wild. 'It has gone away.'

He says, 'I know that prodigies and wonders have been seen in Calais this year. But a child does not vanish before its birth.'

Richard says, 'Is her belly down?'

'No.' Husee rubs his eyes. 'She appears as ripe as ever woman was. But it comes not forth and it comes not forth, and now the midwives say they were in error.'

'We thought she was carrying some fabulous beast,' Richard says. 'But she never conceived, is that not the truth?'

A tear drops on a map of Lisle's new property. He leans across. 'Tell Lord Lisle we will pray his lady will amend.'

'Oh, she must,' Husee says. 'Were she to die, how would we settle her debts? She has wept a salt ocean. My lord set so much store by his heir. But good gentleman that he is, he will love her no less, he only asks her to stop grieving. If I could tell her the abbey were signed over, it would do her heart good.'

'Husee, go away,' Richard says. He sounds tired.

'I will, Master Richard. But by your favour, do not forget the abbey.'

The door closes. 'Christ,' Richard says. 'Who will tell the king?'

'That lucky man sits not far from you.' He lifts the topmost papers from the pile Husee has left. 'If Lisle wants his abbey he needs to find money for the clerks' fees, they will not give him credit.' He scratches his chin. 'I wish John Husee worked for me. He only gets eightpence a day with the Calais garrison, and I warrant Lisle never shows him gratitude. He is a tenacious man.'

Richard says, 'This will strike Henry to the heart.'

He gets up, heavily. His feet seem reluctant to walk. 'I'll make sure he is sitting down, and help at hand.'

Henry does not stagger at the news. He just stares, mute, his colour rising, till he says, 'Gone? Gone where? St Gabriel help and guide us.'

'I have never heard of such a case,' he says, 'nor I suppose have the physicians.'

'Oh, have you not?' Henry's tone is savage. 'If your memory were longer you would know that Katherine misled me in the same fashion. God punish these women, they are serpents!'

'I did not know,' he says. 'I was not here then.' He feels like Tom Thumb, an inch high.

'We were but newly wed,' Henry says. 'What did I know of women and their schemes? She miscarried of one child, but kept her chamber, and claimed she was carrying its twin. Till the imposture was found out.'

'Majesty, was it not an honest mistake?'

'Women are the beginning of all mistakes. Read any of the divines, and they will tell you.' Henry turns and looks at him. 'Always you, Cromwell, with the bad news.'

Tom Thumb is caught in a mousetrap. He is baked in a pudding. He is swallowed by what beast you please, not to emerge till it shits.

'But then, no one else tells the truth,' the king says. 'So how does Lady Lisle now?'

'Weeping.'

'She may well. My poor uncle.' A pause. 'Send my doctors over.'

Relieved, he bows again. 'Lord Lisle will be indebted.'

Henry says, 'I want to know what is inside her. Some women carry dead flesh in their wombs, they call it a mole, it is not alive and it cannot be born. But sometimes it is sloughed off, it proves to have the features of a monster child, such as hair, or teeth.'

When the king sees the mural Hans has painted, he says nothing. It is not for him to thank a mere artist. But he glitters: not merely augmented, but enhanced.

The queen stands by him, and his hand steals out, and rests on her belly, as if testing what he finds there: as he has many times in the last few days, while she holds her breath and wonders why. On the advice of her brother, her ladies and the doctors, the news from Calais has been kept from her. And she has trained herself not to pull away, but to keep her frame steady and her face as immobile as the face of a marble Madonna. If she shrinks a little now, and averts her eyes, it is from the man on the wall: from his fist planted on his hip, from his hand on the pommel of his dagger, from his belligerent gaze; from his straddled legs, unbandaged calves bulging with muscle; from his bejewelled manhood, with a bow tied on top.

Jane stands herself, caught in her own gaze, crimson and tawny: her painted eyes resting beyond the frame. Behind her, our king's gracious mother, in an old-fashioned hood with long lappets. And leaning on the altar which bears his son's praises, the pale invader who carried his banners from the sea to the altar at Paul's: narrow-faced, narrow of shoulder, his robe twitched across his person, his hand half-concealed by the ermine lining his great sleeve. Four-square in front of him, his son seems twice his girth; he could tuck mother and father both inside his jacket, he could swallow them whole.

'By the saints you were right,' Hans whispers, 'when you said I should turn him to face us.' He seems awed by his own creation. 'Jesus Maria. He looks as if he would spring out of the frame and trample you.'

'I wish France could see this,' Henry tells the company. 'Or the Emperor. Or the King of Scots.'

'There can be copies, Majesty,' Hans says, modestly. Mirrors of his lively image: ever larger, more active with every telling.

'Come, Jane.' The king plucks his eyes away. 'We are done here. Time to be off to the country.'

Like a cottager he takes his wife by the hand, and kisses her mouth. My dear darling, I to Esher, you to Hampton Court. I to pleasure, you to pain: but not just yet.

August: the Lady Mary requests a greyhound to course with the royal party, and so before the sport begins he is taking her one: pure white, clean-limbed, with a small proud head and a green and white collar of plaited leather. Himself, Richard his nephew, Gregory his son – soon to be a happy bridegroom – and Edward Seymour, Lord Beauchamp – soon to be a happy brother-in-law. And as their escort, Dick Purser to lead the hound, and the boy Mathew, in his Cromwell livery coat; and a score of followers who have tagged along.

Lord Beauchamp frowns at the boy Mathew. 'Did you not use to be my man, down at Wolf Hall?'

'Aye, sir. But I came to seek my fortune, and I have found it.'

'I am at fault,' he says. 'I drew the boy from his rustic innocence.'

'Country mouse to town rat,' Dick Purser says, shoving Mathew in the back.

'Stop that,' he says. 'Arrange your faces. Here is Norfolk's boy.'

A blazing day, a young lord in orange satin: Surrey advances, his long limbs flying, his eyes screwed up, his hands beating the air like a man in a cloud of mosquitoes; the court is swarming with rumours about his father, and all of them sting.

'Seymour!' the young man yells.

I shall speak first, he thinks, the soul of courtesy – 'My lord, I see you have quit Kenninghall –'

'You are not wrong,' Surrey says.

'– and the court is the gainer.'

Surrey is upon them. His father is right, he looks ill: his face has fallen in. 'My business is with Lord Beauchamp. I have nothing to say to you.'

Edward Seymour says, 'Surrey, stand where you are.'

'Or take a pace back,' Richard Cromwell says. 'I sincerely advise it.'

'I stop where I please,' Surrey says. 'Do not tell me where to stop.'

'Armed like a man,' Richard says, 'yet talks like a three-year-old.'

Surrey does step back, as if he wants to view them better: the servants in their grey marbled coats, Gregory and Richard and Seymour in their peacock silks, and Lord Cromwell in his indigo gown, body solid beneath its soft folds. The greyhound steps sideways, grizzles and yaps, and Dick Purser bundles her backwards for fear she should snap: how tempting must be Surrey's thigh, the tender flesh in its flashing hose. Surrey jerks a thumb at him – at the Lord Privy Seal: 'Seymour, are you so in love with this churl's money that you drag your family name through the mire? When they told me of this match you have made I could scarce believe it – not even of you.'

'He means me,' Gregory says. 'I am the match.'

'Aye, you,' Surrey says, 'you squat little clod.' He whips around, long body glinting like a viper's and ready to bite. 'What evil persuasion is this, Seymour, to marry your sister to these shearsmen, these sheep-runners – I ask you, what disparagement is it, to your own family's coat of arms, and to the name of the late Oughtred, so worthy a man –'

'Oughtred is dead,' Gregory says. 'He is well dead, worthy or not.'

'He sees you!' Surrey yelps.

'And I see you, you sorry piece of work.' Now Richard Cromwell steps forward. He does not touch Surrey, but he locks his gaze.

He, Lord Cromwell, pats a hand to his own chest: there is his knife, but no man must draw. He sees the pain that clouds Surrey's face – belligerence, bewilderment. 'Surrey, you are not yourself.' As he speaks he takes Richard by the elbow to hold him back. 'Your lord father has told me you are mourning still for young Richmond, God rest him.'

'It is a year,' Surrey says, 'a year my friend has been mouldering in his tomb at Thetford – and blackguards like you left to run above ground. I come here and the whole court is buzzing like a muckheap in a sty. I dare say there are a score of rascals who would perjure themselves to pull the Howards down. They are so eaten by envy that they would consent to have both their legs broken if they could see us take a fall.'

'You will take a fall anyway,' Richard says, 'if you do not back off.'

'My father could be king of the north. All the great families support him. But witness his loyalty. He has refused all offers to turn his coat –'

'Has he?' Edward says. 'Offers from whom?'

'And where are the rewards for him? Does he not deserve more rewards and greater than any other subject? Instead, we of noble blood must stand by and watch knaves filching manors from those who have owned them time out of mind, and trusting to mingle their seed with the finest blood this land affords. What does the king do, keeping about him such a set of common thieves and dip-pockets? Thrusting out of his council gentlemen of high birth –'

He puts his hand on Surrey's arm. Surrey dashes it away. 'Cromwell, you plan to murder all noblemen. One by one you will cut off our heads till only vile blood is left in England, and then you will have all to rule.'

'This is my quarrel,' Edward Seymour says. He steps up to Surrey, lays a soldier's hand on orange satin and silver fringing. Surrey lurches forward, hand on his dagger. The dog barks in panic. The boy Mathew shouts, 'No blades, Spindle-shanks.'

My lord Privy Seal roars, 'Drop your hands all. Hands at your sides.' Shocked, they do it – but Surrey flails overarm, and the boy Mathew throws up a hand and then sags against his master. A bright spatter of blood drops to the tiles.

Surrey steps back, aghast. His face is smeared with sweat and tears. Richard twitches the dagger out of his hand. It was like disarming a child, he will say later. He will recall how the young man's fingers felt: numb, cold and blue.

Mathew has righted himself. Furiously he sucks the wound in his palm. The greyhound licks the floor: vile blood. 'A scratch,' the boy claims, but his blood runs down his chin.

Gregory takes out a handkerchief. 'Here, Mathew.' The youth Culpeper has appeared, alarmed, and other gentlemen, sprinting from gallery and guard chamber.

Richard says, 'Are the tendons cut?'

'Culpeper, run and seek a surgeon,' Gregory says. In the hubbub he notes his son's ease of manner.

Edward says, 'An inch, Surrey, and you would have severed his veins at the wrist, a defenceless lad who never did you harm.'

'Well, he called him spindle-shanks,' Gregory says. 'And so do I.'

Surrey rubs his face and glares at Gregory. 'Meet me in the fields, Cromwell – or no, I will not fight you, you are not my match, find some nobleman to fight for you if you can, and I will skewer him and you may come and collect his carcass at your pleasure.'

'You'll skewer nobody, boy,' Richard says. 'You won't be able to skewer your own dinner. You won't have a right hand to pick your nose with.'

'What?' Surrey says.

Edward says, 'It is forbidden to draw blood within the precincts of the court. Any such action is a threat to the sovereign.'

'He's not here,' Surrey says stupidly.

'The queen is here,' Richard says. 'With a child in her womb. So is the king's maiden daughter.'

He says soberly, 'My lords, gentlemen, you are all witness. One blow was struck, and my lord Surrey struck it.'

Edward says, 'Surrey, you know the penalty.'

The dog's tongue diligently polishes the tiles at their feet. Surrey gazes at his right hand, holding it before him. It is limp, as if already it does not belong to him. 'I did not mean to wound him. I only meant to make a show. And he is not much hurt, is he?'

Mathew begins to agree. But Surrey turns on him: 'Mathew – is that your name? I am sure I know you under another.'

No doubt, he thinks. From some household under suspicion, where he waits at table or carries coals: hands clean or hands dirty, working for the safety of the realm.

Richard says, 'It does not matter if he has as many names as the God of the Jews. It is not a servant you have injured, it is the king's peace.'

Surrey's hand goes to his purse. 'Let me give the boy some recompense.'

'Offer it to the king.' Seymour looks as grim as if he is presiding over the punishment already. 'Your father will be shocked to his marrow when he hears this. He will know the punishment laid down – and you Howards, you always say that old customs should be kept.'

There is a method for it: ten men are required. The sergeant surgeon with his instrument; the sergeant of the wood-yard with mallet and block. The master cook, who brings the butcher's knife; the sergeant of the larder, who knows how meat should be cut; the sergeant ferrer, with irons to sear the wound; the yeoman from the chandlery, with waxed cloths; the yeoman of the scullery, with a dish of coals to heat the searing iron, a chafing dish to cool them; the sergeant of the cellar with wine and ale; the sergeant of the ewery with basin and towels. And the sergeant of the poultry, with a cock, its legs strung, struggling and squawking as he holds it against the block and strikes off its head.

When the fowl has been sacrificed the right arm of the offender is bared. His forearm is laid down. The butcher fits the blade to the joint. A prayer is said. Then the sword hand is severed, the veins seared, and the body of the collapsed offender is rolled onto a cloth and carried away.

He takes two days off for the wedding, as promised: leaving the king at his hunting lodge in Sunninghill on 1 August, heading to Mortlake on 2 August for the ceremony next day, and back with the king in Windsor by the fifth. It is a modest wedding, not one of those that ape the nobility; but the sun shines on the bride and groom, and the guests are in high good humour. 'Where's Call-Me?' Gregory asks.

He has to draw his son aside. 'At home. His little boy has died.'

'God save us. Does the king know?'

Gregory is a courtier, he thinks: he is what I have made him: his mind goes first to the king, to whether the news might frighten him or put him in a bilious humour.

He says, 'The king need not be told. He does not usually enquire after our sons and daughters.' He has not, for instance, alluded to Jenneke, though someone must have told him all about her. 'I do not think he knows how many children Wriothesley has, and it would be a pity if the first he heard of William was his decease.'

They are at Mortlake: Cromwells *en fête*, in their old country. What would Walter say, if he knew his grandson was the king's brother-in-law? Though it was Walter who used to claim the Cromwells were gentry. He said he could show parchments about it, but then he said that rats had eaten them. Walter said, your mother came from good stock, Staffordshire, Derbyshire, places up north; no paupers they. This may be true. But these strangers who write to him, claiming kin; what if he had made a claim on them, when he was a boy? They would likely have kicked him downstairs. Prised his fingers from the ironwork of their gate.

Gregory says, 'Surrey lies under a heavy sentence. Perhaps the king would pardon him, as a wedding gift to me?'

'Three points,' he says. 'First, I am hoping he will give you an abbey. Second, you are not the person offended – it is the crown that is offended, this is not a private matter. Third – I thought you hated Surrey.'

'He hates me,' Gregory says. 'That is different. Though I am not squat, am I?'

'By no measure,' he says. 'You are happy? You and Bess do not seem shy of each other.'

'Yes, I am happy,' his son says. 'We are both happy. So please not to look at her, sir. Converse with her when others are present, and do not write to her. I ask this of you. I have never asked anything much.'

His heart misgives. She has told him, then. 'Gregory,' he says, 'I do not defend myself. I should have made myself clear.' He looks at his son and sees he must say more. 'It was only out of duty she consented, when she thought I was the groom, for surely I could never be preferred, not to a goodly young man like you – and as for how the muddle came about – Seymour, you know he can be brisk. One gentleman going past another in conversation, it can happen.'

'Other things can happen. But do not let them.'

He feels himself flush. 'I am a man of honour.'

Gregory will say, what honour is that? The Putney sort?

'I mean,' he says, 'I am a man of my word.'

'So many words,' Gregory says. 'So many words and oaths and deeds, that when folk read of them in time to come they will hardly believe such a man as Lord Cromwell walked the earth. You do everything. You have everything. You are everything. So I beg you, grant me an inch of your broad earth, Father, and leave my wife to me.'

Gregory is going. But then he turns. 'Bess says she could not eat her breakfast.'

'It is a big day for her.'

'She says it means she has conceived already. It is how it took her before, when she was carrying both her children.'

'Congratulations, Gregory. You are a man of action.'

He wants to stand up and embrace his son, but perhaps not. They have never had a harsh word till today, he thinks, and perhaps what has passed is less harsh than sad: that a son can think evil of his father, as if he is a stranger and you cannot tell what he might do; as if he is a traveller on the road, who might bless your journey and cheer you on, or equally rob you and roll you in a ditch. 'Gregory, I am glad with all my heart. Do not tell Bess I know, she might take it amiss.'

'Anything else?' Gregory says.

'Yes. It will be the back end of the year before the world needs to know, and meanwhile, it is another thing not to tell the king.'

Henry will think, why so easy for some? How are children so cheap they are left on doorsteps to be scooped up and parented by the parish, and yet the King of England is begging God for one solitary boy? How are they got so easy that a hot kiss in a garden arbour springs fertile desire, and leads to the font and the chrisom cloth when we have scarcely blessed the wedding bed?

'And also,' he says, 'we do not want it said, Cromwell's son is so keen to be at his bride he does not wait for the blessing of holy church.'

'It would be true,' Gregory says. 'I did not wait for it. I do not give a fig for their blessing. What do priests know about marriage? The king bars them from it. It is time they were put out of the business entirely. They have no more to do there than cripples in a footrace.'

'I'll not argue with that. Though I wish them able-bodied.'

'Oh, the archbishop is your friend,' Gregory says. 'I sometimes wonder what Cranmer will do in Heaven, where there is no marriage or giving in marriage. He will have no pastime.'

'Do not talk about Cranmer's wife.'

'I know,' Gregory says. 'It goes into the big box of secrets, where an ogre squats on the lid.'

A late-spring child, he thinks. I shall be a grandfer. If we can get through next winter.

'Go and find your bride,' he says. 'You have left her too long.' But then: 'Gregory? You are the master in your household – you are the head of it and there is not a soul will doubt it.'

And I like wandering Odysseus, salt-hardened, befogged, making my long way home to a house full of raucous strangers. When I see ordinary happiness the horizon tilts and I see something else. And now I sound like a dotard, saying 'If we can get through next winter.' As if I were Uncle Norfolk, claiming the damp will finish me.

On his next mission he takes Fitzwilliam with him: they chase Henry up-country, find him sulking indoors on a wet day, and looking, except that he is seated, much as he does on the mural at Whitehall: less ornamented, but with the same glare. All the same, he seems glad to see them: 'Thomas! You were to hunt with me, I thought. I have been expecting you. But now the weather turns.'

He opens his mouth to tell the king about the heap of papers on his desk at home. Henry says, 'What is this we hear, that France and the Emperor have stopped fighting? Can it be true?'

'They will be fighting again next week,' Fitzwilliam says, 'depend upon it. But Majesty, we are here about young Surrey. You cannot cut off his hand, you know.'

The king says, 'I expect Thomas Howard has written to you? Begging?'

True. You can see the stains seeping through the paper: sweat, tears, bile. Good Lord Cromwell, stand my friend: exert yourself for Thomas Howard, who is your daily beadsman, your debtor for life. Let my foolish son suffer any punishment, but not maiming, a Howard cannot live without his sword hand ...

'Norfolk thinks you bear much credit with me,' Henry says. 'That whatever you say, I will do. He thinks me your minion, my lord Privy Seal.'

He cannot think of an answer. Not a safe one.

Henry says, 'Why should I not punish Surrey according to custom? Let me hear your reasoning.'

Because, Fitzwilliam says. Because it is almost worse to maim a nobleman, than to kill him. It savours of barbarity, or at best of an alien code.

He, Thomas Cromwell, takes up the theme: because he is young, and experience will temper his pride. Because your Majesty is far-seeing, sagacious, and merciful.

'Merciful,' Henry says. 'Not soft-hearted.' He stirs crossly. 'I know the Howards and what they are. They expect prizes, when they should expect forfeits. I have kept Tom Truth alive, have I not, when I might have cut off his head for his knavery with my niece?'

He says, 'My advice, sir – let Surrey sweat for a space. It is a lesson he will not forget. And he will be in your debt thereafter.'

'Yes, but you always say this, Cromwell. You say, remit them, and they will behave better. Three years back Edward Courtenay's wife entertained that false prophetess, Barton – ah, you said, forgive her, she is but a woman and weak. I believe now she intrigues again.'

Fitzwilliam says, 'Courtenay's wife is clear of present offence, to my mind. And if she is not, Cromwell will soon know, for he has a woman in her household.'

'And the Pole family? Whom I prospered? Whom I restored in blood, whom I plucked from penury and disgrace? How am I repaid? By Reginald parading around Europe calling me the Antichrist.'

He says, 'Perhaps there must be a new policy. But – craving your Majesty's favour in this – we will not start it by cutting off Surrey's hand.'

Fitz says, 'I beg you, do not lightly shed ancient blood.'

'Ancient blood?' The king laughs. 'Was there not a Howard who was a lawyer at Lynn?'

'Majesty, that is true.' It was some 250 years back, and what is that but the blink of an eye, in a land where the heads of giants emerge from the treetops?

He thinks of them: Bolster, Grip and Wade. He watches Henry. He is about to yield, he thinks, and spare the boy; but Surrey should be aware. The king is like the shrike or butcher bird, who sings in imitation of a harmless seed-eater to lure his prey, then impales it on a thorn and digests it at his leisure. He says, 'Saving your Majesty, I believe if you go back far enough we were all lawyers. At Lynn or some other place.'

'And not long before that, we were all beasts.' Henry smiles, but his smile fades. 'Send the boy to Windsor. He must stay within the bounds. He may take his exercise in the park, but tell him he will be watched. When we come there ourselves, he need not approach us till we give him leave.' He stares into space. 'My lord Cromwell, it is blessed work, to reconcile great families. But you do not imagine Norfolk will ever be your friend, do you?'

'No,' he says. 'And it is not to please him that I ask for mercy.'

'I see. It is not to please him. Yet I hear you are talking to him about the great priory at Lewes? Howard territory, and yours too I think?'

The king has been in a huddle with Richard Riche: asking what gentleman wants which abbey, and why. Lisle, for instance, has tried to get Beaulieu, Southwick and Waverley, before settling for a modest Devon property. He, Cromwell, has been buying up land in the county of Sussex: terrain where he means to push the Howards, to nudge up against them, run his borders with theirs. 'I thought that when Lewes comes down, if your Majesty is not averse, the prior's lodging might be rebuilt to make a house for my son.'

The king's anger has drained away. He has remembered to be the Well-Beloved. 'Gregory and his wife should expect every kindness at my hand. Only, my lord, such a great church as there is at Lewes, will it not take many months to pull it down?'

'I'm not going to pull it down. I'm going to blow it up.'

'Really?' The king looks respectful.

'I know an Italian. He is confident it can be done.'

'Come to me after supper,' Henry says. 'Bring drawings.' He looks as excited as a child.

When the chapter of the Order of the Garter is held in the king's closet at Windsor, the king runs his eye along the list and says what everybody is primed to hear: 'One place we will keep for the prince who will soon be born to us, by God's grace. The other is for the Lord Privy Seal.'

A muffled – what? The gentlemen rustle in acknowledgement but cannot bring themselves, for a moment, to applaud. They knew it was going to happen. But they are still shocked. A brewer's son: it takes time to get used to it.

He kneels before the king and makes an eloquent thanks. Henry lowers over his head his Garter collar, a thirty-ounce chain of gold knots and enamelled roses. Affixed to it is the Garter badge, with the image of St George, a golden saint astride a golden horse. 'Stand up, my lord,' the king whispers.

Only the dragon is missing: not killed, he thinks but sated, lolling, curled up in the hot sun. His sister Kat used to tell him about a dragon that ate seven women every Saturday, not sparing them even in Lent.

Henry says, 'You are entered into a sacred brotherhood now. All you need to know of the rites to come, my lord Exeter here will tell you. Or Nicholas Carew, or any of these most noble confreres of mine. I hold them all next my heart, as I do you, my dear Thomas. I hope you will live many years to enjoy your new state.'

There is a sort of groaning, a heavy banging, which signifies the knights' assent. Henry Courtenay, the Marquis of Exeter, is laggard in joining in. The ceremony is to come: late August. In Europe the peace holds. The king says the gospel may be given to the people, this new translation is fit: and the bishops sign off on their deliberations, and send both of them to the printer.

The night before the Garter ceremony, he rides to Windsor, where the canons receive him kindly. But they are hesitant, he perceives, afraid of offending the recruit. My lord, one advises gently, tonight you should think on your failures and derelictions, and make confession if you will: tomorrow you must be perfect, for tomorrow you enter into this order where, if all the knights happened to gather, you would be joined in procession with the kings of France and Scotland, and Charles the Holy Roman Emperor himself.

Do you know, a man from the Wardrobe asks him, the king still has young Richmond's Garter robes stored here? They are hanging up. If he came down from Heaven, he could step right into them.

In one of the canons' houses, painted foliage grows over the wall: Tudor roses with giant pomegranates. These are the only licit paintings of such fruits, the canon tells him, and why are they so? Because there, you see, above the door, is the image of Arthur, Prince of

Wales, portrayed as he was when he took his Spanish bride: and there she is herself, indicated by the image of the wheel, on which St Catherine was martyred. And we have always said, we canons, the paintings are very clean and fine and we can keep them without penalty or fear, because though our king has denied he was married to the Princess of Aragon, he has never denied she was married to his brother.

'But all that is a long time ago,' he says.

'Really,' the canon says, 'you think so? It does not seem so very long ago to me.'

In the precincts there has been a song school, for as long as anyone can remember. As he searches out the old queen's image above him, he can hear the children learning a motet, and the sound leads him out into the splash of sunlight, under ancient walls. He has seen them in their schoolroom, a nest of chirping birds, little bodies huddled together, their voices soaring above their circumstances: when their voices break, who will they be, will they live meanly? They will be music masters and teach the virginals to oafish boys with thick fingers, to simpering girls who toss their heads and try to see their reflections in the window. They will sing in church on a Sunday: verses of the new gospel, perhaps. He has such children in his own household, though they are not so polished as the king's performers. In the song school the notes are painted on the wall so the whole group can learn at once. When they are well learned, the notes are whitewashed over. But none of the songs vanish. They sink deep, receding through the plaster, abiding in the wall.

Tomorrow there must be no mishaps, so they walk him through: Lord Exeter, Carew, William Fitzwilliam an encouraging presence at his shoulder. Everything is laid at hand: his cerulean mantle, his feathered hat. He has billed the king for eighteen yards of crimson velvet and nine yards of white sarcenet. Everything is ready to furnish his stall: his helm, cushion, banner, all as prescribed in the statutes. The knights will process to St George's Chapel, then in the chapter house they will take away his cloak and he will put on his surcoat, and receive his sword. Then he will walk to the quire, head bare, supporters at each side, and there place his hand on the gospel and take the oath. Then, they say, you may ascend to your appointed stall, and Garter Herald – who will be standing just there, please note – he will hand your mantle to your supporters and they will place it on your shoulders. Then they will take your collar and – be ready – they will put it over your head. Then the blessing is read, beseeching St George that he will guide you through the prosperities and adversities of this world.

That's what we want, he thinks: help in prosperity. We can brace ourselves for the seven lean years. But when the fat years come, are we prepared? We never know how to take it when our life begins to be charmed.

I failed with Jenneke, he thinks. I had her and I let her go, I was handed a precious vessel and I dropped it in shock. I was not prepared for the past to yield such sweet fruit: I was busy painting it out, whitewashing my wall for what was to come.

The Marquis of Exeter says sharply, 'Have I your attention, my lord? When the blessing is read, you take the book of statutes in your hand. Then put on your cap. Bow to the altar. Bow to the king's stall. Then take your place, among the illustrious knights.'

Those present, those absent. Those quick and those dead.

It is hard for Exeter to call him 'my lord'. It sticks in the Courtenay craw. Four years back, he thinks, I salvaged you and Gertrude your wife, and now the king suspects me of too much forbearance; he thinks I am trying to make friends of you people. You and Lord Montague, you are sprinting to the end of your silken rope. One more step, then see if I favour you.

That night he prays and goes to bed early. I am not ill, he says to Christophe, do not fret. He needs a space in which he can watch the future shaping itself, as dusk steals over the river and the park, smudges the forms of ancient trees: there are nightingales in the copses, but we will not hear them again this year. Tomorrow, all eyes will turn, not to the Garter stall he fills, but to the vacancy, where a prince as yet unborn reaches for the statute book, and bows his blind head in its caul. Why does the future feel so much like the past, the uncanny clammy touch of it, the rustle of bridal sheet or shroud, the crackle of fire in a shuttered room? Like breath misting glass, like the nightingale's trace on the air, like a wreath of incense, like vapour, like water, like scampering feet and laughter in the dark ... furiously, he wills himself into sleep. But he is tired of trying to wake up different. In stories there are folk who, observed at dawn or dusk in some open, watery space, are seen to flit and twist in the air like spirits, or fledge leather wings through their flesh. Yet he is no such wizard. He is not a snake who can slip his skin. He is what the mirror makes, when it assembles him each day: Jolly Tom from Putney. Unless you have a better idea?

The morning of his installation he is awake early. He should lie rigid, he thinks, like an effigy on a tomb, waiting for the ritual to commence. But instead he climbs out of bed. He needs a candle, till he doesn't; when he lowers the shutter a wan light filters through. A knight of the Garter begins his day as any other man – pissing, stretching, rubbing his blue chin. If you are alert to the workings of the household it is hard to go back to sleep after dawn. The noise only ceases in the darkest hours; hemmed in by the town below, the castle is supplied by wagons that rumble constantly over the cobbles and in at the great gate. And as you make your way about those precincts, point to point, the ages joust and clash: as if armoured monarchs were colliding, a wall built by a Henry driving into a wall built by an Edward who is long ago dust. All these holy kings gone to their rest: time is battering their works like siege engines, and when you descend a step you are walking on another layer of the past.

He wants a walk, perhaps to exchange a good morning with some fellow creature who will dissipate his dreams. The kitchens, the larder, are stirring, ready for goods inward. Men rub their eyes and sleepwalk past each other as if swimming in a grey sea: no one speaks, they merely blink and swerve him as if they were skimming through his dreams, or he through theirs. When he hears footsteps, purposive, descending, he follows them. Down and down, to a stone-floored room, where a deep gutter runs with brown water, burbling like a running stream.

When he was a child at Lambeth he saw the coupage, as the dead animals were carried in, beef and sheep and pig. He learned to stand still as blades sang in the air and whistled past his ears. He grew to relish the company of men who feel a cleaver fit their hands, who plunge skewers into shy flesh, who split and spit and haul great joints with flesh-hooks. He saw beasts disassembled, becoming dinner; witnessed the household officers shovel up their perquisites and portions, neck and scrag-end, forelegs, feet, trotters and tripes, the calf's head, the sheep's heart. He learned to sweep out the sawdust clogged with blood and swab down the slabs where lung and liver clump, to chase the jelly particles stained with gore. He learned to do it all without a contraction of the gut: to do it calmly, to do it without feeling. Twilight coupage or dawn, the light is the same, grey-streaked, wine-dark: the butchers pass without seeing him, eyes front, their burdens hoisted on their shoulders.

Get out of their way: he moves back against the wall. They ignore him, in the dimness taking him perhaps for some inventory clerk. Still they tread, with their cadavers the size of men, eyes on their feet, their heads bent and hooded, silent, undeterred, squishing the gore from their bloody boots, around the winding stair and, guided by the sound of rushing waters, down into the dark.

III

Broken on the Body
London, Autumn 1537

What is a woman's life? Do not think, because she is not a man, she does not fight. The bedchamber is her tilting ground, where she shows her colours, and her theatre of war is the sealed room where she gives birth.

She knows she may not come alive out of that bloody chamber. Before her lying-in, if she is prudent, she settles her affairs. If she dies, she will be lamented and forgotten. If the child dies, she will be blamed. If she lives, she must hide her wounds. Her injuries are secret, and her sisters talk about them behind the hand. It is Eve's sin, the long continuing punishment it incurred, that tears at her from the inside and shreds her. Whereas we bless an old soldier and give him alms, pitying his blind or limbless state, we do not make heroes of women mangled in the struggle to give birth. If she seems so injured that she can have no more children, we commiserate with her husband.

In the long summer days, before her seclusion begins, Jane walks in the queen's privy garden. All traces of Anne Boleyn, who occupied her rooms before her, have been erased, and a new gallery, with a view of the river, built to connect Jane's rooms to the royal nursery. Her condition can in no wise be compared to Lady Lisle's. The creature inside her is alive and kicking. It stirs and flutters, you can almost hear it complain: here I am stifled beneath my dam's skirts, while the trees are in full leaf and the living stroll across the lawns.

507

As her time of delivery approaches, a woman will lay out a fortune for a thread of Mary's girdle. In labour she will pin prayers to her smock, prayers tested by her foremothers. When the smock is blood-ied, the midwife will plaster the parchment against the skin of her domed belly, or tie it to her wrist. The perspiring woman will sip water from a jug over which her friends have recited the litany of the saints. The Mother of God will help her, when the midwives cannot. Eve undid us, but Mary by her joys and sorrows helps us to salvation: the pearl without price, the rose without a thorn.

When Mary gave birth to her Saviour and ours, did she suffer as other mothers do? The divines have sundry opinions, but women think she did. They think she shared their queasy, trembling hours, even though she was a virgin when she conceived, a virgin when she carried: even a virgin when redemption burst out of her, in an unholy gush of fluids. Afterwards, Mary was sealed up again, caulked tight against man's incursions. And yet she became the fountain from which the whole world drinks. She protects against plague, and teaches the hard-hearted how to feel, the dry-eyed to drop a tear. She pities the sailor tossed on the salt wave, and saves even thieves and fornicators from punishment. She comes to us when we have only an hour to live, to warn us to say our prayers.

But all over England virgins are crumbling. Our Lady of Ipswich must go down. Our Lady of Walsingham, which we call Falsingham, must be taken away in a cart. Our Lady of Worcester is stripped of her coat and her silver shoes. The vessels containing her breast-milk are smashed, and found to contain chalk. And where her eyes move, and weep tears of blood, we know now that the blood is animal blood and her eyes are worked on wires.

There is a great book that tells you what to do when a royal birth is pending. It is in a clerk's hand but the marginal notes were made by Margaret Beaufort, the old king's mother. Having been at court in the reign of King Edward, and witnessing the birth of his ten chil-dren, she was clear that the Tudors should adopt the same protocol.

'That creak-kneed saint,' Henry says. 'She had me in terror when I was a child.'

'Still, we must carry through her ordinances, sir. Ladies do not like any change.'

His new daughter Bess keeps him informed of all that passes in the queen's chambers. Gregory does not like to be parted from his bride, but these are no ordinary days, and besides, he has already done to her all a groom hopes to do. Edward Seymour becomes more taut-featured by the day, as expectation works on him. He goes down to Wolf Hall to hunt. The game is excellent this year, he writes: my dear friend Cromwell, I wish you were here.

It has been a dangerous summer. For fear of plague the queen keeps a reduced household. The king lives separate at Esher, also with small state. A messenger called Bolde, who goes daily between Rafe and the Cromwells, is taken with an unknown distemper and must be isolated till he improves or dies. Rafe has often instructed Bolde face to face, and so the king suggests he avoid the court; but then Henry forgets and asks irritably, 'Where's young Sadler?'

For God's sake, Rafe writes, do not let the king forget me, or some rival steal into my place. From my years of discretion you have nourished, brought me up and admired me. Do not let me slip and slide now.

The king does not want to be without Cromwell, as the mornings grow misty and the first chill lies on the air. Come and be near me, he says. Spend your days with me. Maybe just, to keep to the rules, sleep under another roof at night. He obeys. He makes sure to talk every day about young Sadler, how he misses the light of the king's countenance. He writes to Edward that his visit to Wolf Hall will have to wait. The king calls him Tom Cromwell. He calls him Crumb. He walks through the garden at Esher, his arm about his councillor's neck, and says, 'I have hopes of this child. If I could have three wishes, like a man in a tale, I would wish for a prince, bonny and well-doing, and I would wish for myself to live long enough to guide him to man's estate. Do you think you will make old bones, Crumb?'

'I don't know,' he says frankly. 'I have a fever I brought home from Italy. They say it weakens the heart.'

'And you work too hard,' Henry says: as if he were not the cause of the work. 'If I die before my time, Crumb, you must ...'

Do it, he thinks. Draw up a paper. Make me regent.

'You must –' Henry breaks off: he breathes in the green air. 'So soft an evening,' he says. 'I wish summer might last for ever.'

He thinks, write it now. I will go back in the house and get paper. We can lean against a tree and make a draft.

'Sir?' he prompts him. 'I must ...?'

We can seal it later, he thinks.

Henry turns and gazes at him. 'You must pray for me.'

They ride and hunt: Sunninghill, Easthampstead, Guildford. The king's leg is better. He can make fifteen miles a day. In the mornings he hears Mass before he rides. In the evenings he tunes his lute and sings. He sends love tokens to his wife. Sometimes he talks about when he was young, about his brothers who have died. Then his spirits rally and he laughs and jokes like a good fellow among his friends. He sings a ditty Walter Cromwell used to sing: *O peace, ye make me spill my ale ...*

Where did he hear that? No women are assaulted in the king's version, and the words are cleaner.

On 16 September Jane takes to her chamber to rest and wait. Dr Butts is waiting too, but he and the other doctors will keep their distance till her pains begin. What usages the women have among themselves, we dare not enquire. As our preachers make it clear, we do not prohibit statues of our Lord's mother, nor prayers directed through her. She is our intercessor, our mediatrix at the court of Heaven. Only remember she is not a goddess but human, a woman who scours pots and peels roots and brings the cattle in: surprised by the angel, she is weighed down by her gravid state, and exhausted by the journey before her, the nights with no certain shelter.

From behind the papist virgin with her silver shoes there creeps another woman, poor, her feet bare and calloused, her swarthy face plastered with the dust of the road. Her belly is heavy with salvation

510

and the weight drags and makes her back ache. When night comes she draws warmth not from ermine or sable but from the hide and hair of farm animals, as she squats among them in the straw; she suffers the first pangs of labour on a night of cutting cold, under a sky pierced by white stars.

Two of our best men, Dr Wilson and Mr Heath, are sent to Brussels to the renegade Pole: experienced negotiators, they are to convey to him that the king's offer holds – if he will return to England and live as an honest subject, he can be pardoned yet. He, the Lord Privy Seal, is unsure how long the king's offer will last, and whether it is an efflux of generosity or an arrant deception. But he instructs the envoys as he himself is instructed, counselling them to give the traitor no title but 'Mr Pole'.

He says to Wolsey, 'How do you like it, this upstart calling himself the Cardinal of England?' But his dead master has no opinion.

The queen is two days and three nights in labour. On the second day, a solemn procession of city worthies wends to Paul's to pray for her, and the people join them, standing in the street with their beads, some kneeling, some crying out for pardon for the king for denying our Holy Father in Rome; some saying he is the Mouldwarp, and will see no offspring, and others proclaiming that Lady Mary is his heir, because she is the child of a true princess. The city officers move among them, taking some into custody. But most are let go before curfew, their ignorance pardoned. This is not a week for whipping, or cutting off ears.

Some doubt the efficacy of prayer at such times. Why should God spare one woman and not another? But by the time forty-eight hours have passed, what is there but prayer? If the king's child is lost, nothing will persuade him that it is mischance. Kings are subject to fate, not luck. Accidents don't happen: dooms overtake them. Gregory says, if the king does not like the outcome he will quarrel with God again. He may tear up his own ordinances, and the gospels now in press may never see the light of day.

If the Lord Privy Seal were on Jane's threshold, he could catechise her doctors as they pass in and out. But the messenger Bolde has died, and he dare not go to court lest he carry infection.

He occupies himself with monastic pensions, and with writing to Tom Wyatt, now with the Emperor. Wyatt has been found out in a careless error. He has failed to present to Charles the letters sent by the Lady Mary, in which she describes her present state of unhindered bliss, and stresses she is and always will be her father's servant. It's strange, Wriothesley says, because Wyatt doesn't make mistakes, does he? Or not simple ones.

It is hard to explain. But he and Wriothesley have covered for Wyatt, so Henry knows nothing about it. We do not want Wyatt's embassy to fail. Wyatt above any man can feel out the Emperor's intentions. This peace that Charles and François are supposed to be making: do they not need a mediator, arbitrator? Better they should ask England, than turn to the Pope. We need, somehow, to force our way into the process.

Anyway, treaty or no, Emperor and France will fight no more this year. Winter will soon be here. Nor will the north country rise.

Though the Hydra was never a fair opponent. It lurked in caves, and could only be killed in daylight.

Jane gives birth on 12 October, at two in the morning. The courier makes good time and they wake him with the news. 'Man or maid?' he asks, and they tell him. By eight o'clock all London knows it. At nine o'clock they sing *Te Deum* at Paul's. It is St Edward's Eve, and the child will be named for the saint. Rafe has been ordered back to court. The queen's official letter goes out in his hand, phrased as if she had gripped the quill and scrawled it herself: *grace of Almighty … a prince, conceived in most lawful matrimony … joyous and glad tidings … universal wealth, quiet and tranquillity of this whole realm …*

Tranquillity? All day they fire off guns at the Tower, as if to puncture the clouds. There are feasts in every alley. The generous merchants of the Steelyard get the poor folk drunk on beer. The horns, bagpipes and drums continue long after dark. He thinks, Rafe should have printed 'most lawful matrimony' in big red letters: especially for those copies that travel, bound with silk tags and weighty seals, to the papal court, to France and to the Emperor. He whispers to the air, 'Shall I read it aloud, my lord cardinal?' For who knows if ghosts can read? The cardinal is quiet: not a chuckle. The air is empty: not a stir.

Now all the lords of the kingdom gallop to share the glory. They head to Hampton Court for the christening, but they must leave their retainers at home. The plague is in Kingston and Windsor. Movements are restricted. Even a duke must manage with only six men to guard and serve him. Strangers are barred. Delivery men must quit the precincts as soon as they have dropped off their loads, and the royal nursery be scrubbed out twice a day.

The queen is upsitting, the women say. She has lost much blood but she is bright-eyed. She says, 'Are there quails? I am very hungry.' A light diet, madam, they urge. Jane tries to clamber out of bed, white feet feeling for the carpet. No, no, no, they say, putting her back: not for days and days, madam.

There are rumours the king will make earls. That he himself will be Earl of Kent, or Hampton: an old title revived, or a new one created, for Honest Tom. On the day of the christening the queen is carried in a chair into the public spaces of the palace. The christening itself, by tradition, is another event the king and queen do not attend in person: they are in the precincts but not at the font. I am tired of these traditions, he thinks. It is time they were turned out of doors. It is traditional to rob travellers as they come down Shooter's Hill: is it laudable therefore?

It is an evening ceremony. Henry is enthroned, Jane by his side, and receives his liegemen, their congratulations, prayers and presents. He inventories the presents and gives them to the Wardrobe to carry away, or consigns them to the Jewel House, or notes that a certain gold cup or chain should go to the mint to be examined and weighed. The nobility of England process, with prayers and tapers, towards the Chapel Royal. They have swaddled Jane in furs and velvet, and before he joins the procession he sees her hand thread out and push away the wrappings from her throat, as if they irritated her. They have placed a prayer book on her knees, but she does not look at it. From time to time she says a word to the king, and Henry cranes forward to hear her. He sees her turn her head to the window, away from the blaze of banked candles, as if she would rather be outside in the autumn night.

He is in the procession: he is of it, amid the hot breath and scent of herbs. Gertrude Courtenay has the honour of bearing the babe at the font. Her husband the Marquis of Exeter stands next her, and the Duke of Suffolk. 'Well done, Crumb,' Suffolk says. He is handing out the same compliment to every man, as if the whole of England had set the seed. 'Well done, Seymour.' The young Lady Elizabeth travels in Edward Seymour's arms, a jewelled vessel of chrism in her hands; she looks about her, and when something interests her she bucks in Seymour's arms and kicks his ribs. Nicholas Carew and Francis Bryan, his brother-in-law, stand by the font with ceremonial towels; from Bryan's eye-patch, a lewd green wink. Tom Seymour holds a cloth of gold over the babe, embroidered with the arms and achievements of the Prince of Wales. The prince himself is a sweet nut in a shell; you take it on trust he is there, at the centre of the yards of tasselling and fringing and furs. He must be heavy, for Gertrude falters, and Norfolk, jostling her elbow, steadies the baby's head – in that single moment expert and tender. Then the duke grins around the company with his yellow teeth: masters, you see my exile is over? The birth will reconcile all quarrels.

The font has been mounted on a plinth. The great men and their wives in the body of the chapel cannot see much, their view blocked by a canopy and the bodies of those who are even greater than they are. He is one of this number; the Lady Mary, who is godmother, is at his elbow. In a murmur she speaks to him: 'My heart rejoices for my father's sake. I feel a burden is lifted. I am lighter today than I can ever remember.'

She thinks, no doubt, I will never be queen now. The prince is robust and likely to live, and no reason why Jane should not give us a Duke of York, and many more princes to follow. Mary says so, pious, and he does not know if she means what she says.

He bends his head to speak below the music: 'Do you know we are to have a new French ambassador?'

The trumpets shrill. Mary mouths something, shakes her head. 'Louis de Perreau, the Sieur de Castillon. As soon as he arrives he will come to you to pay his respects. He will revive the project of your marrying the Duke of Orléans.'

'But Mendoza is still here!' she says. 'Offering Dom Luis.'

'Yes, but Mendoza does not have the authority to conclude anything. So your father has told him he is wasting our time.'

Mary looks away. The procession is re-forming. It is almost midnight. Tapers are carried before them, as they retrace their path through the palace, to unravel, to fall back into their separate orbits, earl and earl, duke and duke, taken to bed by their own people. A day or two later the news comes of what rewards the king will give, and he finds he has been left out. Edward Seymour is to be Earl of Hertford. Tom Seymour is knighted and promoted to the king's privy chamber. Fitzwilliam is to be Earl of Southampton. Cromwell remains Cromwell.

Why Fitzwilliam, above him? Old friendship, no doubt: old usage. Fitzwilliam has sense and wit, speaks plain and to the point. But without a clerk at his elbow he is like Brandon, he cannot spell the days of the week. How will such men as he engage with sophisters like Gardiner, like Reginald Pole, who have spent their lives in the business of chop-logic? Whereas he, Lord Privy Seal, is no scholar, but will thrash through any text and give you the gist. If you set him to orate, he will do it extempore. Bid him draft a law and he will draw it tight as a miser's purse.

Mr Wriothesley says, 'Are you disappointed, sir? If your services were properly requited, you would be a duke.'

'And after all,' Richard Riche says, 'you have the income to sustain such a dignity.'

'You have the Garter, sir,' Rafe says. 'It should be enough for a rational man.'

He combs back through his recent dealings with the king. It is Pole, he thinks: I did not have him killed when I said I could, nor did

I bring him bound and whimpering to Henry's feet. Nothing a minister does, or fails to do, escapes the king. Like a judge or a keen spectator at a joust, he notes when a blow goes wide or when a lance is broken on the body. He sees his council in session, observing like a man from a watchtower as battle commences and blood spreads across the field. He grants latitude to his ministers – yet he sets a hedge of expectation around them, invisible but painful as blackthorn. You know when you have brushed against it.

Two days after the christening the queen is reported fevered and nauseous. The doctors go to and fro, and as they come out the priests go in. We thought when the child was born the waiting was over, but the waiting comes now.

Henry has intended to move back to Esher, to spare work for his reduced household, and he does not know whether to go or stay. The queen weakens and is given the last rites. It does not mean she will die, Henry says: the sacrament is given to strengthen her. Overwrought, he paces and prays and talks. It is true that his mother, when her last daughter was born, lay ill for a week and lost her fight. But it is also true that his sister Margaret, near death for nine days in childbed, recovered and is now stout and hale and likely to be amongst us for years yet. The superstitious sort say that it was because her husband the King of Scots made a pilgrimage to St Ninian's shrine at the Galloway coast; they say he went on foot 120 miles. I would walk to Jerusalem, Henry says, but pilgrimages are vain: God keep Jane, if I cannot.

Certain priests about the king make a note of his words, with time and date: the king says out of his own mouth, though pilgrimages are vain, anointing is a sacrament. Last year the seven sacraments were reduced to three, and now we are back to seven; it seems the four that were lost have been found again. The bishops have said so in their book. Or have they? It is difficult to know. It is always going back to the printer, for corrections and additions. They call it the Bishops' Book, but soon, laymen grumble, each bishop will have his own. You used to know what you had to do and what you had to pay out, to guarantee eternal bliss. But nowadays you can hardly tell feast from fast.

He, the Lord Privy Seal, has no remit to be in the queen's part of the palace, and if he were, no one would tell him what was going on. He returns to St James's, to the house in the fields that Henry has lent him, away from infectious crowds. Later his daughter-in-law will say, in the last hours Jane did not always know us. Then at times she did know us, and would try to sit up, and we would give her thin wine to sustain her, but she spilled more than she drank.

The prince sucks well at his wet nurse, the sick woman is told. He is to be Earl of Cornwall, as well as Prince of Wales. She signifies with a nod of her head that she is content.

When he lived in Florence the Portinari family showed him a Nativity, painted for them in Bruges some twenty years back. It is a painting with doors, which open on winter. Within its span, time collapses and many different things happen at once, that could not happen in an unblessed human life. In the painting the past is present, the future happens now. Mary was untouched by man, and so remains; yet once, and now, and always, the angel stands over her, the holy spirit batters her heart, her side, her womb. At the centre of the picture the helpless babe lies on earth, new-born, white as a grub, and shepherds and angels have fallen back to give space to the new mother, while up on the hill, the still-pregnant Virgin greets her sister, St Elizabeth, and on another eminence, far in the future, Mary and Joseph and the donkey trundle towards Egypt.

Who can look at this picture and believe this Blessed Lady suffered labour pains? She looks solemn, impressed by what she has produced. Wrapped in red, attending her, is Margaret of Antioch, the patron of childbirth, and at her feet is the dragon that, at an earlier stage in her career, had swallowed her. Here is the Magdalene with the spikenard jar; here St Anthony, with bell. The shepherds, with their peasant faces, can hardly contain their excitement. The whole of our future is compressed between their joined hands. The angels are not young. They look shrewd; their wings shimmer with peacock eyes. The three kings are coming over the hill. Their journey is almost over, but they don't know it yet.

It is a lie, he thinks: the painless birth, the safety of Egypt, the piety of the kneeling patrons who have painted themselves into the story. He believes the king wants to scramble onto a fast horse: away he spurs, over that same mountaintop, where out of sight a new day dawns, where the past has ceased to repeat itself, caught up in a loop, a stitch, a noose. He left Katherine at Windsor and went hunting and never came back. At Greenwich with Anne he rose from his seat at the tournament, mounted his horse and rode to London, with Henry Norris beside him. He strode away and took the horse's bridle, he mounted up and he never glanced in his wife's direction, he never saw her again. He leaves his queens, before they can leave him.

Henry's entourage, a small riding household, are alert for his departure. Yet he stays, when hope has gone. At eight o'clock, 24 October, he goes to the queen's bedchamber and takes his last look. Her breathing labours. The doctors withdraw, their art and craft failed. What is a woman's life? It is dew in April, that falls on the grass.

At St James's, very late, they bring in a letter: 'It is from Norferk,' Christophe says. 'Written this eve, his messenger says.' He drops it as if it were soiled.

He breaks the seal. *I pray you to be here early to comfort our good master, for as for our mistress there is no likelihood of her life, the more pity …*

He too drops the letter. Then he picks it up and gives it to the boy Mathew to file. His mind travels the road, the river. There is banked filthy mud, there is snow on the ground, there is thaw water running and the Thames overstraining its banks: the cardinal is at Esher, the Parliament is planning to ruin him, and he, a square plain figure in worsted, tries to keep his hat on his head and his head down, while the black north wind plunders and beats him like a thief, and rolls him nightly, howling, in a ditch.

'What time is it?'

Christophe looks at him in pity: 'You hear the midnight bell?'

He thinks, if Jane had married me, she would be alive now; I would have managed it better.

When he gets back from court he walks into his workroom and sits unspeaking at his table. Mr Wriothesley says, 'You seem angry, sir?'

Call-Me has arrived with scant ceremony, tossing his hat down on a stool and rummaging in a chest for papers. Rafe says, 'Who would not be angry, at the loss of so fair a creature? My lord considers her keepers to have been negligent. He believes they suffered her to take cold, and eat such things as her fancy dictated.'

'I wish I had been at Hampton Court,' he says. 'When they told me to stay away I should not have listened.'

Wriothesley says, 'Perhaps, sir, you are angry because you wish you had kept Gregory in reserve, where his marriage could do you most good. As the prince's uncle he will of course be of consequence, but if the queen had lived, and given the king more sons, then you and all your house would have been great men for ever.'

Call-Me knocks together his bundles of papers and nods himself out. 'I am going to write to Tom Wyatt,' he says, turning and holding the doorframe. 'He had better see to his duties, for I cannot do my duty if I cover for him any more. And I shall give him notice his dispatches make my head ache – there is no need to put every triviality in cipher.'

'Right,' Rafe says. 'Save it for the big lies?'

Wriothesley says, 'Wyatt scrambles his wits without point or purpose. Everything is a plot, to him.'

Rafe calls, 'Close the door.'

They wait till they hear he has gone downstairs. Rafe says, 'We must forgive him. I wonder how he would be if his wife had died, and not his son.'

He says, 'He looks older. Or am I imagining it?'

'I am very sorry for him. I remember when my first Thomas died. But even so ...'

Wriothesley has entered into public duties, where you cannot let your private sorrows show, not even by an increased hauteur with petitioners, or impatience with women and underlings: still less with

519

the Lord Privy Seal. He shrugs it off. He says, 'I give thanks that Helen is safely delivered, Rafe. And I hope your new son will live to serve his prince as you have served the king, so happily and well.'

For Rafe has slipped back to his place at the king's side, drawing only a distant nod and 'All better at home, Sadler?' It was the king himself, solicitous for a mother-to-be, who had advised Rafe to send Helen to Kent, away from the pestilence: but now he has forgotten to ask after her. Rafe's child is a boy, and they are calling him Edward, but all other Edwards are naught, in the king's exultation at his heir: he stands over the cradle, marvelling at what God has bestowed. But then he remembers the queen, a husk now eviscerated by the embalmers, tapers burning day and night around her bier, the prayers never ceasing, the syllables pit-pattering, the sorrows and joys of Our Lady, her mysteries, her worship and praise.

Already Jane's household is being broken up. Her brooches and bracelets, her jewelled buttons, girdles, pomanders, her miniature pictures set in tablets; the Wardrobe takes them back, or they are given to her friends. Her manors and farms, her woodlands, chases and parks, go back to the king from whom they came, and her body, after her embalming and lying in state, goes back to God her maker. It is a long time since I first saw her, the king says, a lily among roses: I consider all the time wasted, till I made her my bride.

It is only two summers past that the king held her hand in the garden at Wolf Hall, her small paw swallowed in his palm: two summers since he, my lord Privy Seal, greeted her in a slippery dawn light, stiff and timid in her new carnation gown. This winter he will see the carnation cloth again, worn by Gregory's wife, as she lets out her bodices to accommodate her growing child. Bess says she is not afraid. Jane was lucky and unlucky, she says: lucky to become queen of England, unlucky to die of it. They will always make ballads about her, Bess says. And the king will give her a magnificent tomb, he says, in which he may lie with her in time to come. But I would rather be alive, Bess says, than have a great name: would not you, Lord Cromwell?

Gregory says, 'My lord father, who will you let the king marry next?'

PART FOUR

I

Nonsuch

Winter 1537–Spring 1538

'My lord?' a boy says. 'A gravedigger is here.'

He looks up from his papers. 'Tell him to come back for me in ten years.'

The boy is flustered. 'He's brought a sack, sir. I'll send him up.'

His neighbours at Austin Friars think he is in charge of everything, from framing the laws to propping cellars and cleaning drains. Go to the city surveyors, he says: but they say, Yes, sir, but if you would just walk around the corner and cast an eye? For I swear my boundary stone has been moved, my foundations are cracking, my lights are obscured.

Today's will be a problem of bodies stacking up, the ground too hard to dig. You should try not to die at the turn of the year. Hang on through the season of marzipan and mulled ale. You might even see spring.

The visitor pulls off his cap. He stares around; he sees a low-lit expanse, with nothing in it but Lord Cromwell before the barber gets to him, the Queen of Sheba hanging on the wall behind. Painted on the ceiling, the stars in their courses; on his desk, like a low winter sun, a dried orange.

The gravedigger has left the door open to a rising babble from below. 'It sounds as if you've brought the whole street with you. What's in your sack?'

523

The man huddles it against him. He wants to tell his tale and tell it in order. 'My lord, I woke up this morning about four o'clock. I had such a wambling in my belly ...'

Lord Cromwell settles himself inside his furs, with a soft grunt like a heavy cat. He unwinds in his imagination the sexton's morning. The sloth with which he pushes off his blanket and rises from pallet bed. The odiferous splash of his urine. The icy shock of water to his face. His mumbled prayers, *Salve Regina* and God bless our king. His shirt and jerkin and patched coat, his draught of small ale. Then out he goes, spade in hand, to break the ground in the frozen hour.

In the churchyard a dozen neighbours are gathered. 'Get over here with that shovel,' they shout. One poor torch gives a wavering light. The parish clerk is pulling and tugging at a bundle, half in and half out of the ground.

The sexton hastens over. One swipe and he has the thing out. It is a winding sheet, muddied and torn. 'We took it for a babe, my lord,' he says. 'New-born and scantly buried.'

'That is not the infant, in your sack?'

Clods of earth shake to the floor as the man lays the sack on the table. He opens its neck and, like a witch midwife, extracts a baby, naked and cold to the touch. It is life-sized and made of wax.

Lord Cromwell rises. 'Let me see it.' His palm follows the curve of the skull. The face is a blank slope, as if its features have been sheared off. He touches the blunt hands, the toeless feet like tiny hooves. Below the slope of the belly the wax has been crudely scooped and scrolled to make a cock and balls. Iron nails have been forced into the flesh where heart and lungs would be. They have been skewered deep, leaving a friable rim around each entry point.

The man is afraid. 'Turn it about, sir.'

Into the back's broad plane, its maker has ripped a Tudor rose.

'It is the prince,' the sexton says. His voice is awed. 'It is his image. It is made to waste and kill him.'

'You know conjurers, then?'

'Not I, sir. I am an honest man.'

He goes to the door. 'Christophe! Is Mr Wriothesley out of bed? My compliments to him, and will he go with this fellow and see where this thing was discovered, and find out who put it there?'

He pulls the sack over the babe's head. Says to the sexton, 'Spread word no further.'

Christophe comes in. 'Half London knows. You hear the *canaille* below, making moan as if their mothers were dead.'

'Give them bread and ale, and get them back to their occupations.'

'I can see the monster?' Christophe peers into the sack. He makes a face.

He, Lord Cromwell, goes to the window, opens the shutter. A diffident area of grey; you cannot call it light. 'Christophe?' he says. 'Tell Mr Wriothesley to wrap up warm.'

In less than two years, two queens have died in England, but under circumstances that have prevented the usual rites. There has been no court mourning since the king lost his mother, which must be some thirty-five years ago. Fortunately, his grandmother Margaret Beaufort left us full notes on what to do: weddings, christenings, funerals, she had it pat. The Duke of Norfolk is called on to supervise the rites, with the help of Garter Herald. The king goes into white, his court-iers into black.

On All Souls' Eve, while Jane the Queen is still lying in state, news comes from the Tower of the death of Lord Thomas Howard. He was out of hope, his keepers say, which made him prey to any passing malaise. Lady Meg Douglas, his paramour, has been permitted by the king to join the court for the mourning period. If through the first week of November her face is swollen and blurred by tears, we need not take it that she was still attached to the late Lord Thomas; we can interpret it as sorrow for our gentle mistress. All the ladies are needed for the vigil, svelte in black, their heads bowed. They kneel on silk cushions, their closed eyelids fluttering, incense floating around them in clouds. Their hands are joined, except when two fingers delicately tap their breasts, or sign a cross at forehead and lips. In what manner they pray for the late queen, no one should enquire. The dead woman's body is never left alone. Lady Mary leads the prayers by day. By night they leave her to the priests.

By the time Jane is taken to Windsor for her burial, the rumour outside the gates is that the king had her cut open while she was alive. She could not be delivered of her child, so 'Save my son!' he ordered. From Cornwall to Durham, they are singing ballads about it. How the babe and his father prosper, and the mother lies in clay.

In the first days of mourning the king has sequestered himself, as a king ought, seeing no one but his confessors and the archbishop, who comes to pray with him.

The council conduct their business alone. Wanting to ask one question and ask it urgently, they look nobly intent, like men trying to hold back a fart. Finally, some lord pipes up: 'My lord Cromwell, when might our noble sovereign, having regard to the parlous state of the succession –'

'Right,' he says. 'I'll go and ask him, shall I?'

He gets up heavily. 'Mind my papers,' he says to Edward Seymour. Collecting Call-Me to watch his back, he sets off towards the privy chamber. Marching smartly by his side, the Duke of Norfolk; beside him, the duke's son Surrey, so elongated by black that his legs seem to be multiplied like the legs of a great spider.

'Well,' Norfolk says, 'it falls to you to get him through this, Cromwell. Through it and out the other side and a married man again. No disrespect to our lord prince, but we all know how easily a babe is snuffed out.' He scowls. 'So have you got a list?'

'Of course he has a list,' Call-Me says. 'But he has more reverence than to produce it, my lord.'

Surrey is treading on his father's heels. Like Meg Douglas, he has been permitted to return to court to join the mourning. 'Do not speak to the Lord Privy Seal,' Norfolk orders him. 'Do not even glance at him, boy, or you will incur my displeasure.'

Surrey casts up his eyes to the gilded roses on the ceiling. He sighs, shifts from foot to foot, fidgets his dagger in its scabbard. Short of taking out his privy member and waving it, there is no more he could do to establish his presence.

'It seems to us,' Mr Wriothesley says, 'the king is not ready to talk about a new wife. As your lordship says, it falls on my lord Cromwell, so let him pick his time.'

'Let that time be soon,' young Surrey snaps. 'Or my father will force the point.'

'What did I tell you? Silence!' Norfolk glares at his son. 'The king's grieving. Of course he's grieving. Lovely lady, who wouldn't? But the Emperor and France are creeping close to a treaty, which is very displeasant to us; what would make them quarrel, faster than a marriage? Let Henry claim a bride from France. We can stipulate not only a good sum of money with the girl, but military aid, should Charles attempt anything against us.' He rubs the tip of his nose. 'We are all very sorry about the queen, of course. But it can turn to advantage. All is for the taking, Cromwell.'

'Though not your taking,' Surrey says.

'Cease, sirrah!' Norfolk roars.

'My lord Privy Seal would prefer –' Wriothesley says.

Norfolk cuts him off. 'We know what he'd prefer. Marriage with some gospeller's daughter. But that will not happen, and you know why? Because it derogates from the honour of our sovereign. Henry wears a crown imperial. He is beholden to none. But the best of these Germans is a mere prince's daughter, and the Emperor is their overlord – whatever they pretend.'

'The king is free to choose a lady of any rank,' Mr Wriothesley says. 'He could choose one of his own subjects. That has been known.'

He says to Norfolk, 'I will not put a foot forward in this matter unless I have the council behind me, and Parliament too.'

'Oh, I trust you,' Norfolk says. 'I do not think you will go venturing on your own, my lord Privy Seal.'

'Or your head will fly off,' Surrey says.

'My lord –' he is hovering, '– I must go in to the king.'

'Let me come in with you,' the duke says.

'Introduce you suddenly?' he says. 'Like a surprise?'

'Say I am right outside. Say I offer fatherly comfort and counsel.'

'My lord father,' Surrey says, 'do not let these fellows impede –'

Irritated, he puts his palm on Surrey's chest, stops him dead. 'And look, I need no blade,' he says.

They walk away. He shrugs. 'I'm human.'

'Of course.' Call-Me makes it sound like a warm endorsement. 'What do you hear from Cleves?'

'No great praise, neither of the lady's face nor person. Though I am not discouraged. No one has had much opportunity of seeing her, these people keep their women very close. She sounds amiable. The age is right. And the Cleves councillors are keen, I hear.'

Keen enough to keep her off the market. Anna. Twenty-two years old. Never married.

The king is waiting: heavy-faced, heavy-eyed. He turns his head, and it seems like an effort. 'There you are, Crumb.'

'Norfolk would like an audience. He threatens to talk to you like a father.'

'Does he?' Henry dredges up a smile. 'Let us hope I turn out better than young Surrey. I shall try to be a credit to him.'

'He says it is your duty to marry again.'

Henry looks into the middle distance. 'I could be well content to live chaste my remaining days.'

'Parliament will also petition your Majesty.'

'Then I must set aside my own wishes, I suppose.' The king sighs. 'What do we hear of the widow, Madame de Longueville? I feel I could be interested in her, if in any lady. The noble house of Guise would be flattered by an approach.'

Marie de Guise has been described to him: a bouncing, vivid redhead with two young sons, her husband six months buried. 'They say she is very tall.'

'I am very tall myself.'

He thinks, we could send Hans to paint her, and measure her at the same time. 'There is a difficulty, Majesty. The King of Scots wants her.'

Henry is glacial. 'I do not call that a difficulty.'

'Her family might stick over the dowry.'

'What, haggle with me?' The king is annoyed. 'There are other Frenchwomen. And I have not yet said I will marry at all. I will not get such a pearl as Jane again.' He rubs his eyes. 'Talk to me again in a week, my lord. I will try to make you a better answer.'

Fresh from watching by the corpse, stiff-kneed and bored and cross, Jane Rochford steps into his path. 'I have need of instruction.'

He stops. Smiles slowly at her. 'Will you take it?'

'We ladies do not know how to order ourselves without a mistress. Do we stay or go?'

The queen's household is broken up, and Lady Mary set to withdraw to Hunsdon, or some other place. If there is no queen's side at court, there is no need for women at all. 'But if we are all sent away,' Lady Rochford says, 'what will we do in case of a sudden bride?'

'Look to the direction of your seniors,' he says. 'Lady Surrey. Lady Rutland.'

'When shall I be senior enough to count?' She is waspish. 'I have served three queens now, and I trust to serve a fourth.'

'Uncle Norfolk wants a Frenchwoman,' he says.

She laughs. 'The French must have bribed him. I thought he would offer a Howard. The old dowager duchess, across the river at Lambeth, she has a houseful of girls.'

'Perhaps none of them are ripe for breeding?'

'I dare say the king would be trying to marry Bess Seymour, if she had not wed your son. One woman in a family is never enough for him. Has not Jane other sisters? I know there are Bible texts against it. But the king rules over the church now. And we know what he thinks of the scriptures. "Read on, masters, there's always another verse!"'

'Your reckless tongue,' he says. 'I may not always be able to save you.'

'Save me? Is that what you do?' Jane Rochford shakes out her black skirts, and rubs her back to ease its ache. Sometimes he sees an expression of concentration in her eyes, as if she is trying to fathom where she mistook her turning. You leave a trail of bread and the ravens eat it. You drop cherry stones, and they grow into trees. 'Are they happy,' she asks idly, 'your newly-weds? Bess looks as if she carries a secret. She has the shadow of a double chin. Unless I mistake, you are on the way to becoming a grandfather.'

He is at that age when one loses old friends. November saw Humphrey Monmouth's funeral; he wanted to follow the burial party himself, but Rafe said, 'Careful, sir, Monmouth was Tyndale's protector once: do not antagonise the king, do not take a risk for the sake of a dead man.'

Other mourners brought him word of what passed: a simple inter-ment, before dawn. Monmouth refused candles or papist emblems, but he left money in his will for sermons. He wanted no funeral bell, but provided for the bell-ringers to have their fee: which was like him, a man who considered the humble and the poor.

He, the Lord Privy Seal, had packed up the silver cup Monmouth bequeathed him, and ridden down to Mortlake to be at home with Gregory and his wife. He gave notice that for the next fortnight he would see no one, do no business but the king's. Till now, Cromwell no more refused work than a dog refuses mutton. But he had felt bruised: not only by the queen's loss, but by his failure to lay hold of Reynold.

Henry says, 'You promised me you would put an end to Pole. When he returns to Italy, you told me, I will have him struck down as he leaves his lodging, or ambushed on the road.'

'Majesty, I do not know how to intercept a man who is never where he is expected. My people wait for him at some chosen place, but then he falls from his horse, and is carried into a refuge, and is three days nursing his bruises. We anticipate him at the next town, then we hear he has missed the way, wandered off in a circle, and ended where he began. He is too stupid to be killed.'

Henry says, 'You'll have to learn to be stupid too, won't you, Crumb?'

* * *

He is bound to show his face, whether he feels better or not, at the Christmas court at Greenwich. It is a small court still in black, where Master Johan the tumbler tries to raise a smile. Rather than music and dancing, there are plays, mounted and devised to pique the king's interest: masques with fantasy castles, with princesses inside them. The king's eye follows Margaret Skipwith, a blithe little maid of honour. 'He wouldn't, would he?' the Lord Chancellor says. 'He wouldn't give the Lady Mary a stepmother younger than herself?'

The Lord Chancellor chirps, 'Anne Bassett is a pleasant sight – Lady Lisle's girl.'

'She has enjoyed a French upbringing,' he says. 'Like Anne Boleyn.'

Audley frowns. 'But she seems a biddable wench, and I have seen him looking at her, and her English is fluent enough.'

'She cannot write it,' he says. 'She can barely write in French.'

'What?' Audley goggles at him. 'You read her letters? Little Anne Bassett?'

Of course he does. He needs to know everything that goes into Calais, or comes out. On the chance of unguarded information, he can endure accounts of what buttons and fringes Mistress Bassett craves, and what cramp rings and ribbons Lady Lisle sends.

He says, 'The king will not be happy with a maid of sixteen, whatever he thinks. He needs a woman of competent age, who will get on briskly with breeding, and knows how to keep him entertained meanwhile.'

He turns his attention back to the play. There is a party of boys from Eton, and Charles Brandon's players, and Lord Exeter's men. Sometimes Pride and Folly speak, as if they were persons: Humblewise and Good Council answer them, in verse.

The common people who gather in inn yards and barns have plays of their own. Not a village that does not boast King Arthur on a hobby horse, or Robin Hood. *Robin Hood in greenwood stood/ Good yeoman was he.* He wears garments of the same colour as the trees, so he can steal like a sprite through copse and dell. He takes to wife one Marion; they make their promises beneath the green bough. He ambushes friars who deviate from the beaten track, knowing them by the scent of cheap wine and loose women that creeps before them through the sweet air; their bags are full of money, screwed out of poor folk for pretended forgiveness of their sins.

Robin Hood sings ballads about his deeds while he is doing them. A hundred times he escapes the noose and the sword. In the end he is betrayed and bled to death by a false prioress. His blood runs into the soil, red into green, and another Robin springs up, to wear his jacket and bear a quiver of arrows at his back.

The man who takes Robin's role must be broad in the shoulder. He must speak with some accent of education, not mouthing his lines like Arthur Cobbler. If he plays with skill in his home village, he will be asked to the next: and so to the town, where he will become famous.

There are other outlaws whose deeds are renowned: Clym of the Clough, Adam Bell, Will Scarlet, Reynold Greenleaf and Little John. Old stories can be rewritten. It is good to get such personages harnessed in the king's cause. Besides the green men we recruit knights of old, like Sir Bevis of Hampton and Guy of Warwick: they cross the plains and forests on intelligent horses which sometimes talk.

All these men have a reason for leaving home. Sometimes they are booted out of it, by the malice of a stepmother or a witch; sometimes they are wrongfully set up for a crime. If traduced, they will strive to clear their names; if betrayed, they cannot rest till they have revenged. In the course of their wanderings they battle giants. They are sold to pirates. They are locked up and they burst the locks. They hide in caves with hermits. They lead armies against Rome. Sometimes they go mad, and no wonder. They get the girl and lose her again – or else, at the point of consummation, she turns into an animal, or her flesh falls to ash.

But in stories the odds are evened. The devil knocks down our hero, and up he gets. The outcast is restored to his rights. The youngest brother, called simple, becomes the richest of all. The gruel-fed serf feasts on the sweet flesh of the roe, and the swine boy strides from his hovel and builds a crystal house.

He calls up John Bale: a Carmelite, eloquent and embittered, who has thrown off his habit and married a wife. Could you, he asks, write a play about the villainous Archbishop Becket, who defied his king? About the sorry end he came to, knocked on the head like a calf by three stout and loyal knights?

'A play in English?'

'Latin is no good to us here.'

Bale asks for time to think about it. At court, Queen Jane's Players give their final performance, before their troupe is broken up.

At Candlemas the court goes out of mourning and the talk is of an Imperial bride: Christina, Duchess of Milan, the Emperor's niece. 'A very pretty little widow,' Chapuys calls her: married at twelve to Francesco Sforza, widowed at sixteen, believed still a virgin.

Christina's father was once King of Denmark, but was dethroned. At present Denmark has a Lutheran king, who has seen the Bible translated, and has already made links with the German princes. The Emperor aims to bring him down, and perhaps put Christina in his place. Though England would lament the loss of an ally against the Pope, she might gain, through Christina, not only Denmark but Sweden and Norway, those fields of snow and ice with their harbours and great shining shoals; their waters where a thousand whales can feast on cod and bring a thousand friends, and still tomorrow there are more fish than there were yesterday. And their forests of which we hear, stretching in low lines below bare mountains, with store of timber for building ships.

Besides, they say she is of a sweet disposition and might suit him.

'I would emphasise the sweetness,' Fitzwilliam says. 'The rest is conjecture.' He pinches the bridge of his nose. 'You could feel out the terrain, Crumb.'

Sometimes the king, in playing chess, hesitates with a piece in his hand, while in his head he plays out a series of fantasy moves, which he would never attempt in life. As black to his white, one must simply wait it out; Henry is more averse to risk than he pretends. After long deliberation, a nudge to a bishop is the most he ventures, or a pawn unleashed to its limit.

Now the king's negotiators are ready, the canon lawyers and linguists, the theologians and the accountants. In a dozen cities of France and the Low Countries, quartering Europe from Lisbon to Düsseldorf, they will meet with their peers, earnest and expert men, their dark garments relieved by a single, weighty gold chain: men who are followed by their own line of clerks with folios, with maps and charters, with trees of precedence and lineage. When negotiations are at their stickiest, the team can be reinforced by emissaries from home, bringing news of the king's good health and his hopeful disposition to whichever match is in question.

He, the minister, must move on all fronts: bustle from board to board, pushing six queens at once. In the space of hours, the game may be kicked over. One might bring arrangements to a point, only to be knocked back by a coup within some foreign chancellery. Or just as you are signing off the finances, the girl might die. Sometimes a returned envoy will say, 'Go yourself, Lord Cromwell, you would speed the business along.' But he sets his face against it. His appearance in any foreign city would cause amazement and consternation and lead to inflated expectations, lending too much weight to one set of negotiations at the expense of others.

February, the king sends Philip Hoby into France. Hoby is a gentleman of the privy chamber: a gospeller, good-looking and keen, and well-briefed by himself, the Lord Privy Seal. The king thinks he has a chance of Madame de Longueville, despite the King of Scots' claims that they are affianced. But there is no harm in looking at her sister, Louise. There is another sister, Renée, who they say is bound for a convent; perhaps she could be enticed from her beads by the prospect of becoming Queen of England?

And while Hoby is across the sea, he might call on the Duke of Lorraine's daughter. Don't fret, he tells his clerks, you don't need to remember all these ladies individually: not till the king chooses one, and changes her fate. They are all cousins, mostly papists, and mostly called Marie or Anne.

The Duchess Christina is at the court in Brussels, with her aunt, who is regent in those parts for her brother the Emperor. Early in March, he commissions Hans to go out with Hoby and paint her. On 12 March, Hans is granted a three-hour sitting.

'I think,' Henry says, when he sees the drawing, 'that we might have a little music tonight.'

Christina is straight and tall, clear-eyed. When I have made the painting, Hans says, you will see she is so young she has dew on her. She is grave, she is poised: but there is a hint of a smile. You imagine she might put down the gloves that she twists in her fingers, and slide a warm palm against yours. Our envoy Hutton says she has three languages besides Latin. She speaks softly, gently, in all of them, and lisps a little.

The king craves her, the privy chamber gentlemen tell him. He says we should remember her in our prayers, as if she is our queen already.

But also he says, 'Madame de Longueville has red hair. So I would feel I knew her, as if she were my family. And she has a tried and tested womb.' He looks at Christina's drawing again. 'Now I do not know which lady to love.'

'Yon Christina has a look of my niece Mary Shelton,' Norfolk says.

'I think he has had enough of your nieces,' Charles Brandon says.

But Shelton is still free. Henry always liked her. He could wed her right away. Thomas Boleyn is soon back at court, perhaps to press the case: they are very close, these families, very greedy. Boleyn is still Earl of Wiltshire despite all. He is grey, drawn, less flesh on him than doctors like to see. He wears his Garter badge and a gold chain, but he wears them against the subdued garments of a private gentleman, and neither he nor his small entourage boast nor strut nor pick fights with the servants of the Seymours. He speaks to my lord Privy Seal in a low confidential tone, as if they were old friends. 'We have seen such times, Lord Cromwell,' he says, 'if I consider what has befallen in England, since my late daughter came up – we have seen events crowded into a week, that in ordinary times would have sustained the chroniclers for a decade.'

Rather than waste time he, Lord Cromwell, decides to force the point: 'Majesty, you are thinking of Mistress Shelton?'

Henry smiles. 'Perhaps it is time she was married. Though not necessarily to me.'

He bows himself out. The king is not in a mood to confirm or deny. He thinks, the late Harry Norris had a daughter, did he not? She must be of age now to come to court. Useless to say to her, stay away; stay in the country, keep yourself intact. Brides frisk like silly sheep to the slaughter; like martyrs to the circus, when they hear the lion roar.

The new French ambassador, Castillon, presents himself. He is one of those good fellows who parade their honesty, always showing you the palms of his hands.

He looks him up and down. 'Monsieur, I think your accord with the Emperor, it is only a winter truce?'

Monsieur Castillon sighs. 'We must try to settle a permanent peace, when the chance offers. My master is keen to show the world he is a Christian king.'

'Mine too,' he says. 'But I wish François would show a little more warmth about our marrying a Frenchwoman.'

'You are not set against it? Personally?'

'I only want to make my king happy.'

Castillon says, 'Your king must be very clear what he offers.'

'You can talk to me about that. I do the money.'

'But I am speaking of a pact, a military alliance –'

'Talk to Norfolk. He does the soldiers.'

'Norferk is far more friendly to us than you.'

'Perhaps because you pay him more, ambassador.'

In dealing with the French he always feels he wants Wolsey's advice. The French were terrified of the cardinal. They called him *le cardinal pacifique*, in the hope he wouldn't smite them.

* * *

Since new year, the rich and fertile county of Kent has been swept by rumours of the king's death, which are passed between the patrons of the Checkers in Canterbury, and carried by fish-sellers door to door. They say he is dead of a flux, a fever, a cough, and that it is a pity he did not die seven years back. They also say that a tax will be placed on every horned beast, as well as a poll tax on their owners, and it will be set high so as to enrich Thomas Cromwell, and bring honest farmers to their knees.

Anyone spreading such a rumour can expect to be nailed to the pillory by his ear on market day. But the origin of such lies can seldom be traced. Nor has he found who made the wax child. Mr Wriothesley had followed a trail of names, but they led to ruined or empty houses, or to men who call up such a blizzard of nonsense when questioned that you are driven out of their workshops, your head aching from verbiage and mercury fumes. The London wizards bear a grudge against Lord Cromwell, and no wonder. He has watched them since the cardinal's death. He has confiscated their alembics and retorts, their snakeskins and secret bottles containing homunculi, their orbs and robes and wands. He has impounded their *Clavicula Salomonis* for calling up the dead, and read their texts in mirror writing; he has tossed to his code-breakers their almanacs in unknown tongues. Anyone who wishes may open his chests and inspect their cloaks of invisibility: which they claim he has converted to his own use.

The north is quiet as winter ends. But then from York comes a report of one Mabel Brigge, attempting to witch Henry to death. She is a widow, aged thirty-two, so robust that every year when Lent comes her neighbours pay her to fast for them. For a fee, she will fast for a godly purpose, like the recovery of a sick child. But she will also make a black fast, that aims to waste its victim. Now she is fasting against the king and the Duke of Norfolk. Every hour Brigge goes without food, king and duke will dwindle.

'She is not fasting against me?' the Lord Privy Seal asks. He is surprised.

But his informants say, 'She has seen the duke face to face. She feels she knows him. She says he is a promise-breaker. She says he has spoiled the north.'

When the duke hears this he will be spurring north to hang Brigge in person. The king has flesh enough to see out any widow, but Norfolk has not an ounce to spare. You know my will and testament, Norfolk writes, that I gave you in a box? Send it back to me, Crumb, I must remake it. I am so short of money I shall have to sell land, and that comes hard. For God's sake put some abbeys my way.

He, Lord Cromwell, almost rips up the paper in a rage. Has he not just made a bargain with the duke for the abbey at Castle Acre? Can nothing sate the brute?

February goes out with stormy weather, bringing down the west pier at Dover. In far-off lands they are preparing for war: the Venetians and the Emperor are to go against the Turks, with the Pope's loud encouragement. But with a scent of spring in the English air, Lord Cromwell feels more himself. In the council chamber he is the focus of calm, though the king continues skittish, contrary. Henry says, 'I will open my mind to you,' and you can see him busily packing its contents into strongboxes, like a man stowing his assets against thieves. He says, 'Do feel you can speak freely to me,' and already he is adding up the bill. Gregory says, 'He is a king after all, he does not think as we think, he does not know what we know. I would be afraid to argue with him as you do, father, lest God strike me dead.'

I argue, he says, to make him argue back: to make him say what he thinks and what he wants. Seven years I have stood at his elbow while he sets a course. I found him in low water, the cardinal gone who was captain of his ship: bereft of good advice, gnawed by intermittent lusts, frustrated by his advisers, hamstrung by his own laws. I filled his treasury, made his coinage sound; I packed off his old wife and got him a new one of his choosing; while I did this I soothed his temper and told him jokes. If like a princess in a fairy tale I could have spun a babe from straw, I would have worked a year of nights. But he has his prince now. He has paid a price for him, but good fortune never comes free. It is time he knew that; it is time he grew up.

Besides, there is reason to be cheerful. Even when the king has expressed a desire to be alone, he will call in Lord Cromwell to debate a text with him, or idly throw dice. Those councillors are unwelcome now, who hulloo as if they were on the hunting field, or talk to a solitary and sorrowing man as if they were addressing a troop from horseback. He needs a voice pitched low, a listening ear: when he talks of how women have made him suffer, he needs someone who will not show incredulity.

If you wonder if Lord Cromwell is succeeding, look how he and his people are augmented. Mr Richard is seized of abbeys in the county of Huntingdon. He means to seat himself at Hinchingbrooke Priory, after rebuilding work of course, and establish himself in that county as a beacon of loyalty to the king; while at the same time, Mr Gregory is set up in east Sussex.

The great abbey at Lewes brings with it a generous spread of houses and estates. Gregory will be sworn in as a justice of the peace, and he will have all the help and comfort and advice he needs while he feels his way into his role as one of the chief gentlemen of the region. The aim is for him to be able to host the king this summer, so rebuilding must hurtle along. Giovanni Portinari is assembling his demolition crew, ready to take down the church. He, Lord Cromwell, imagines the apple blossom shaking from the boughs, and the flight of the doves from their cotes: stone heads of devils and angels springing from the stonework as if fired from cannon, their shards rolling underfoot. The bell metal alone should fetch seven hundred pounds.

In March his grandchild Henry is born, and christened in the old font at Mortlake. Well, Master Gregory, the king says, you make a father with great speed! The child is healthy, the mother in good spirits, and Lady Mary is godmother. She does not come to Mortlake herself but she sends a gold cup and gifts to the midwife and nurses.

Lady Bryan has our prince safe, wrapped so tight in his gilded swaddling bands that no nail can pierce him nor pin sneak between his ribs. One day when Edward is King of England, we hope Henry Cromwell will be by his side, his first cousin.

By March, the Emperor is willing to open talks about Christina. The two Imperial envoys, Chapuys and Mendoza, are invited to Hampton Court as privileged guests. They visit the prince, and pay their respect to Lady Mary and Lady Eliza. Lady Mary plays proficiently on the lute. Asked for a private interview, she politely declines it. Eliza squeaks a pretty Latin verse, in which she has been rehearsed by Cat Champernowne, his appointee.

Next day Chapuys sends him a present of two hundred sweet oranges. He ships half down to Sussex for his son and grandson, and walks around Whitehall giving the rest out. The Bishop of Tarbes, newly arrived to join the French embassy, encounters him in air made lively by their zest. 'Do not pretend to be glad to see me, Cremuel,' the bishop says. 'I know the Imperialists make you great offers –'

'They give me oranges,' he says.

'I hear that since last year you are much enriched from spoiling the monks – you and your son and your nephew Mr Richard. In England you write the laws to suit the robber.'

Ambassador Castillon puts a restraining hand on his colleague. Then he turns, glad of a diversion. 'My lord Norferk!'

Norfolk nods towards the king's door: 'He in there, Cromwell? Take me in.'

He says to the Frenchmen, 'My lord is like a poor foundling these days. For ever wheedling and beseeching. *Take me in, take me in.*'

Norfolk leaps as if pricked with a bodkin. 'Do you do this for pleasure, Cromwell? Do you obstruct me so you can work me into a fit of choler?'

'You work yourself,' he says coolly.

'Who are you to advise on a royal wife? You are nothing but an old widower, you cannot get a woman because you think yourself fit for a princess and you will not take less.'

He sees, from the corner of his eye, the two Frenchmen exchange glances. He turns on the duke. 'And is the king to be advised on marriage by a wife-beater?'

Sweat springs from Norfolk's brow. This is what they have come to, for all the friendship they swore last autumn – standing outside the king's privy chamber bawling insults.

'Make way, make way!' call the ushers. Henry emerges. He eyes Norfolk. The duke sinks to one knee. The king ignores him. 'Messieurs, my lord Cromwell – come in.'

They begin well enough, Castillon hinting he has a surprise: 'A proposal about the Lady Mary, that I think will be very gratifying to your Majesty.'

'I am all ears,' Henry says. 'Lord Cromwell, likewise, is all ears.'

'Majesty,' Castillon says, 'our dauphin is already wed – but could not Lady Mary marry my master's second son?'

The king groans. 'We have been here before. Cromwell, tell him.'

He says, 'Your master wanted a guarantee that Lady Mary would succeed to the throne.'

Castillon bows. 'You have a son and heir now, of course. But the Lady Mary's virtues are known throughout Christendom. So what could be more pleasant than a double wedding, father and daughter? The king will be honoured to give you any French lady you choose.'

The king says, 'Not excepting his daughter Marguerite?'

The ambassador is ready. 'If a year or two were allowed, till she is sixteen, perhaps ...'

'I am forty-six,' Henry says. 'I am not seeking a companion for my old age. If I am to marry, I should do it now. Madame de Longueville would suit me. She cannot really mean to marry the King of Scots. Such a stupid, beggarly knave –'

Castillon is taken aback. 'James will wed her before the summer. The promise is firm.'

'But is it free?' Henry asks. 'Hearts should be free. Milord Cremuel will tell you. He is a great promoter of love matches.'

Tarbes says, 'Try to understand this. My king regards James of Scotland as his own son. He will not break a promise that knits our two lands in their ancient amity.'

Castillon urges, 'Why not consider the Duchess of Vendôme?'

He does not wait for the king, but cuts in: 'James saw her and did not like her. Why should we?'

The king says, 'I do not want to take a lady I have not seen. The thing touches me too near.' He raises a finger, and lays it precisely beneath his collarbone, on the puff of white linen that shows above the buttercup yellow of his jacket. 'Perhaps she and some other ladies could come to Calais? Then I might make the crossing, and see them for myself.'

'What?' Castillon can no longer contain himself. 'Do you think it is a horse fair? You want us to trot them out like fillies, the noblest dames of France? Perhaps your Majesty would like to mount them too, before making choice?'

He says, solemn, 'If they are virgins on arrival, we will send them back intact. I swear it.'

'Excuse,' Tarbes says curtly. Red in the face, the ambassadors turn aside to mutter to each other. He wishes now that Norfolk were here, to see his show.

The ambassadors turn back. 'No,' Tarbes says. 'No meeting.'

'A pity,' he says, 'since the king and I are going to Calais anyway. From there we will pass to the Emperor's territory, to meet with Christina and her councillors. We mean to take Lady Mary – and Lady Eliza too, if her keepers do not object to the voyage for her.'

He feels Henry's gaze swivel to him: will we, do we?

'Then I wish you joy of the Duchess of Milan,' Castillon says. 'I hear she is very much afraid of what awaits her, and is begging the Emperor to marry her anywhere but England. Has your Majesty considered that it might be difficult to find any lady to marry you at all?'

'Why?' the king asks.

'Because you kill your wives.'

'Take that back,' he says. He is standing, so are the ambassadors; he thinks, there may be two of you, but I kill giants.

Castillon turns to Henry. His voice shakes. 'You say your first wife died in the course of nature, but many believe you poisoned her.

Your second match was widely deplored, but no one imagined you would end it with a beheading. Now it is said – even by Cremuel, in fact especially by he – that your third wife perished of neglect in her childbed.'

He says, 'I should not have said that.'

'No, you should not,' Henry says mildly. 'My dear ambassadors, you cannot understand – you do not know our court or our ways – Cremuel worked not a little in the making of my marriage with Jane. The whole realm has reason to be grateful that he did so. Cremuel's son is married to the queen's sister. He feels to her as to his own kin. After her death, his shock and sorrow caused him to speak in haste. There was no neglect. How could there be?'

'Our position is –' Tarbes begins.

'Your position is back on the boat,' he says, 'unless we hear an abject and prompt apology.'

Henry holds up a hand. 'Peace. The ambassadors have some right on their side. I have been ill-fated.' He bows his head, then looks up from under his brows. 'But I do not lack offers.'

He says, 'Be assured, gentlemen – we are at a point, with the Duchess of Milan.'

'At a point?' Castillon is outraged. 'Cremuel, why do you not pack your bags and present yourself to the Emperor as his own true servant? You serve him better than you serve the King of England.'

Henry says dryly, 'I find myself satisfied.'

He says, 'Even if my king does not take Christina, he will marry into Portugal. And Lady Mary will wed their prince Dom Luis. What could be more pleasant than a double wedding?'

It is hard to know whether the ambassadors are dismissed, or whether they dismiss themselves. But on the threshold, Castillon stops, defiant: 'My master and the Emperor mean to extend their truce till midsummer. Mary will lose her chance. Dom Luis will marry my master's daughter – with whom, I tell you, he will be delighted.'

They are gone. The door closes after them. The king says, 'They should stop trying to frighten me. I have been king nearly thirty years and they should know it does no good.'

543

They have been speaking French, and continue to do so, as the footsteps fade.

'So, Cremuel,' Henry says, 'I hope you will not run away to Charles, but stay.'

Henry's eyes are on his portrait of himself, massive, on the wall of the chamber. His own eyes consult the image of his master. 'What should I want with the Emperor, were he emperor of all the world? Your Majesty is the only prince. The mirror and the light of other kings.'

Henry repeats the phrase, as if cherishing it: the mirror and the light. He says, 'You know, Crumb, I may from time to time reprove you. I may belittle you. I may even speak roughly.'

He bows.

'It is for show,' Henry says. 'So they think we are divided. But take it in good part. Whatever you hear, at home or abroad, I repose my faith in you.' He smiles. 'When one speaks French, one finds oneself saying *Cremuel*. It is hard to resist.'

'And Norferk,' he says. 'And Guillaume Fitzguillaume.'

The dead queens blink at him, from behind their broken mirrors.

Did you ever hear of St Derfel? No shame to you if you did not. He is called 'the strong' or 'the valiant', and was one of Arthur's knights; he built many churches in Wales, and at length retired to a monastery and died in his bed.

In a church in the diocese of St Asaph stands his effigy, a giant made of painted wood, astride a giant stag. Derfel is a jointed figure, with mobile eyes that blink. The Welsh believe he can bring souls out of Hell, and on his feast day in April they come five hundred strong, with cattle, horses, women and children to be blessed. For the priests it is a prime money-making proposition.

Hugh Latimer has suggested a bonfire of statues at Paul's or Tyburn or Smithfield. But Derfel is a special case: his legend says that if you set fire to him, a forest will burn down. For safety's sake you could just hack him up; but best not in front of the local people.

He sends his man Elis Price to deal with it. Elis comes of a noble Welsh house; he worked with his father, in the cardinal's time. Just bring me Derfel, he tells him, leave the stag behind.

Monks go down fast this spring. Beaulieu. Battle. Robertsbridge. Woburn and Chertsey. Lenton, where the prior is executed for treason. The monks present themselves as having lived like beggars, in garments ragged and patched, and without firewood or food stores. They have sold the firewood, of course, they have sold the grain, and unless you are swift on their trail they will pawn or bury their treasures.

Objects retrieved are sent to him: seals with the faces of abbesses and bearded theynes; a crozier with a head of ivory, bearing the face of Christ; herbals and missals, and long-hoarded silver coins decorated with the heads of petty kings. He saves for himself a map of the world, its four corners stalked by lions. He keeps it for a memento of the earth as it used to be.

They bring him compendia of superstitions, the ghost-books kept by monks, and at Austin Friars (or wherever he finds himself this spring) they read aloud after supper: when the nights are growing lighter even the jittery can stand the strain. They make him laugh: a ghost in the form of a haystack? A ghost that helps a poor man carry a sack of beans?

The purpose of ghost stories is extortion, generally: to frighten poor folk into paying for prayers and charms to protect them. He reads of a man who, on pilgrimage to Spain, met the half-formed corpse of his son, miscarried at six months. The pilgrim does not know his child, but the child, a tallow-coloured object in a shroud, is able to speak out and claim his father.

He rolls up the parchment and says, destroy this tale. And let's give thanks we have a living prince at last.

He thinks about Derfel, his powers. Why would you want the damned fetched back from Hell? There's a reason God put them where they are.

* * *

The end of April, the king's doctors seek a consultation with certain councillors: two earls and himself, Privy Seal. Fitzwilliam says, 'Is this about the bad leg?'

'The King's Majesty's wound,' Dr Butts corrects. 'We try to keep it open to keep it clean. But it tries to close.'

'It is its nature,' Dr Cromer explains. 'We fear a crisis approaches. Dead matter trapped within.'

'What do you advise?' Edward Seymour asks.

The doctors look at each other. 'What we always advise. We must thin his blood. He should keep a spare diet. Water his wine. Gentle motion only.'

'Hopeless,' Fitz says. 'It is the hunting season.'

The king is planning a progress. Essex, then north as far as Hunsdon, to see the little prince.

'He needs to keep the leg up,' Cromer says. 'Can you not talk to him, Lord Cromwell? You are very great with him these days, everybody says.'

'So they do.' Does Fitzwilliam sound galled, or is that imagination?

He says, 'There was a professor at Padua who worked out the recipe for a long life.'

'I suppose it did not involve jaunting around Essex,' Cromer says.

'One must eat the meat of the viper, nutritious and light. And drink blood.'

'Animal blood?' Edward Seymour is repelled.

'No, human. And when you have got your foaming beaker of it, you powder it with gemstones, just as one powders milk with nutmeg. The professor was called to Constantinople, where –'

'He lived to be 120 and became the Sultan?' Fitzwilliam asks.

'Sadly not. He failed in one of his cures and the Ottomans sawed him in half.'

'St Luke protect us!' Cromer exclaims.

He thinks, I must be ready for Henry's death. But how shall I be ready? I cannot imagine.

* * *

In the king's absence, he sits down to new duties. All over the realm our castles are being surveyed and repaired. The king will ride ten miles but his minister's mind will range three hundred. Fortifying costs money and he has to find it.

Thomas Cranmer comes to see him. 'Two items, Thomas.'

'How are you?' he asks. The archbishop still looks as if he has a pain behind his eyes.

Cranmer puts down his folios: no small talk. 'First, Mary Fitzroy. Her husband Richmond has been dead a year and she has not had her settlement. The king has said to me, Look here, my lord archbishop, you know the marriage was not consummated? So she and my son were not properly married, and I need not pay out.'

'And what did you say?'

'I said, "Of course they were married – in the sight of God and man. You must pay what is due, and do it quickly." So he sulked.' Cranmer opens his folio. 'They say that as his lord father got older, he cared for nothing but money. Henry is going the same way.'

Even the cardinal had his areas of illusion where Henry was concerned. It seems Cranmer has none. Yet he agrees to carry Henry's conscience, which is burden enough for a whole bench of bishops.

'Second item, Father Forrest,' Cranmer says. 'Katherine's confessor, when she was queen. He praises all popish ceremonies, and preaches clean contrary to scripture. He has abused the king's patience these five years and more. Now I fear he must burn. I will bring him to Paul's Cross. Hugh Latimer begs to preach to him. He believes he can bring the sinner to Christ. And at a hopeful sign, we will unloose his bonds.' Cranmer's tone is dry, precise; but his hands shake. 'I hope he will abjure. He is a man near seventy.'

He has been watching Forrest for years. 'The king would not trust his penitence. If you do not burn him I will hang him.'

Cranmer says, 'The council must witness his death. So that the ambassadors note it, so the smoke is smelled in Rome. You yourself must be there. And Bishop Stokesley.'

'Oh, the Bishop of London will come,' he says. 'Never doubt him. He will close his eyes and breathe in the stench, and he will pretend it is you and me and Robert Barnes on the pyre. I do not trust him any more than I trust Stephen Gardiner.'

Gardiner is coming home. He gives such offence to Frenchmen that we dare not keep him as our envoy. The quarrels of great men are copied on the Paris streets. Gardiner's boys are taunted when they step out of doors: 'Call yourself fighters? You are timid as mice. You came here with an army, and you let a girl throw you out.'

'Yes,' the English boys shout, 'and we took your witch Joan and burned her, and all your victories did not save her from our fire.'

Joan the Maid was consumed by flame in 1431. You would think they would find a fresher taunt. But even the market wives curse our ambassadors, and throw ordure on their best clothes.

Stephen should learn to be immune to insults, he says. Look at me, I take them as compliments. Norfolk calls me vile blood. The north calls me a heretic and a thief. The eel boy in Putney used to say to me, 'Yah, Thomas Cromwell, you miserable gibbet-bait, you toss-brain, you remnant, you crumb: your mother died rather than look at you longer.'

As the Duke of Norfolk would say, the old insults are the best.

'You Irish,' the eel boy would say, 'you flying smut from Satan's forge; I'll pillock you, I'll fillet you, I'll set your hair on fire.'

And in reply he said naught. He never said, 'I'll spit you, I'll stab you, I'll carve out your bloody beating heart.'

Till, of course, he did.

The king is up-country when news comes of his collapse. He, Cromwell, takes an escort and rides at once.

It crosses his mind, of course: make for the coast before they block the ports. If Henry dies, what friends have you? Whichever way you go you could be stopped on the road. By the Courtenays, if they can move fast, rallying troops for Mary. By Margaret Pole, by her son Montague. By Norfolk, his forces galloping cross-country.

We have been here before, the king dead or near-dead: the tilt yard at Greenwich, January 1536, with Henry shelled of his armour: the roaring of his injured horse, the shouts and prayers, the clamour of denunciation and blame. He feels once again a needle-tip of panic, working under his breastbone.

But at journey's end only a single figure comes out to greet him: Butts, looking bone-weary: 'Still alive,' he says.

'Lord Jesus.' He falls from his saddle.

Butts is drying his hands on a linen towel, its hem embroidered with a pattern of periwinkles. 'His Majesty rose from the table, and then fell under it. We drew him out black in the face, breath short and rapid. He coughed up blood, and I think that saved him, for then he drew breath. You must not go in. He is too weak.'

'Let me pass,' he says.

The silken lout Culpeper is hovering around the king, with a knot of physicians and chaplains. He recalls Henry asking once, 'Why is it that whenever disaster strikes there is a Howard in the room?'

The boy says slyly, 'We needed you earlier, Lord Cromwell. I heard how at Greenwich the other year, you raised his Majesty from the dead.'

'I had the honour,' he says curtly.

Around the king's person there is a smell of liniment and incense. Henry is propped by a mound of pillows, his bandaged leg bulky beneath a damask cover. His cheeks are fallen in and his colour bad. He blinks: 'Cromwell, there you are.' His voice is weak. 'In your absence, I fear we took a tumble.'

The royal 'we'. No other person was involved.

'Have you any letters from Wyatt?' Henry pushes the covers off. His leg is fatly bandaged. 'I have nothing this week. And nothing from Hutton in Brussels either. Is someone stopping our messengers, or are they reporting straight to you these days? Who is the king, you or me?'

Our sovereign lord is back, he thinks; for an hour speechless and choking, but now imperious: the mirror of all rulers, his flickering light scarcely visible against the sunlight of a May morning.

Henry says, 'Cromwell, I remember Greenwich. When I. When you.' He cannot easily speak of his death. 'I do not remember the fall.

549

Only blackness. I thought myself extinct. My senses were stopped. I believe I saw angels.'

He thinks, at the time you said not.

Inside a tent the king was stretched out his full length, pale as paper. Henry Norris was intoning the prayers for the dead. The Duke of Suffolk was bawling like a teething babe. Outside the Boleyns were shouting their own names, and Uncle Norfolk was bellowing that he was in charge now: '*Me, me, me.*'

'Yesterday,' the king says, 'you were far away, and I thought I should die alone.'

He recalls the howling surge of servants and lords, his bellowing for quiet; his palm on the king's chest, the pounding of his own heart. Then beneath the horsehair padding of the king's jacket, a fibrillation, like a scamper of shrews' paws. After a second, Henry gasped; he groaned; he coughed violently, and uttered, 'Thomas Cromwell.' The shocked lords wailed, 'Lie down, lie down!' but Henry levered himself upright; his eyes turned, and took in the scene. Alive again, he looked at England. He saw her dark valleys and green fields, her broad silver waters, her nightingale woods. He saw her just laws, her free people, he heard their prayers.

Dr Butts is back, a urine flask in hand. 'Majesty, you must not think of transacting business today.'

'No?' Henry says. 'Then who will rule, Dr Butts?'

It sounds like a civil enquiry. But it makes the doctor step back.

'We are talking of my fall at Greenwich,' Henry says. 'Reminiscing.' He spits the word out.

Butts says, 'God protect your Majesty.'

'He did,' Henry says. 'I heard every man in that tent believed I was dead, except Cromwell. He stood over me and felt the beating of my heart, when others had given me up.'

He thinks, I could not allow you to be dead. Who had we for sovereign? Mary, a papist, who would have killed all your ministers? Eliza, still in the cradle? The unborn child in Anne's womb? And how is it better now? I still have no plan, I have no route out, I have no affinity, I have no backers, I have no troops, no right, no claim. He thinks, Henry should give me the regency, give it me now. Set it down and seal it: multiple copies.

The king says, 'I suppose now the embassies will be spreading it to the world that I am dead again.'

'If you will spare me, I will go back to Westminster. I will visit the ambassadors in person and assure them I have seen you alive with my own eyes.'

'Oh, and they'll believe *you*,' the king says. A fit of coughing shakes him. Butts says, 'My lord Privy Seal, enough for now.'

'The poisoned vapours from the wound rose right up to my brain,' Henry says. 'But tell them – I don't know – tell them I had a megrim. A fall. A fright. Tell them I will be back in the saddle within days.'

Henry raises a hand to dismiss him. Versions multiply as soon as a tale is told. He knows his own story: at Greenwich the royal heart fluttering, faint as a god's breath in a glass bubble. He recalls himself praying, but others recall him doubling his fist and pounding the king's chest hard enough to split his ribcage. And Christophe, who was at his side all that wretched hour, claims he bounced the king's person up and down by the shoulders; that he seized him by the ears and bellowed into his face: 'Breathe, you fucker, breathe!'

May comes, and the king is planning a dynasty. 'If I could get Madame de Longueville, I am sure she would give me a house full of sons, which would be a great comfort to England, if anything but good came to Edward. Our first son together would be Duke of York. The next would be Duke of Gloucester. Our third, I think, Duke of Somerset.'

Fitzwilliam says, 'Have you forgotten she is pledged to Scotland?'

Henry never forgets anything. But sometimes he believes a king's caprice can alter reality.

The King of France, it is said, is proceeding to Nice, where he will meet the Emperor. It seems the only way to break their amity is for Henry to choose a bride from one party, thereby insulting the other.

His councillors caution, 'No haste, Majesty. As soon as you choose, you forfeit advantage. You can marry only once.'

'Can he?' Fitzwilliam mutters. 'This is Henry we're talking about.'

Henry says, 'Cromwell, I want you to entertain Ambassador Castillon. You were too brisk, threatening to knock him down. Now you must mend the damage. I want you to use emollient words. Feast him. If you want anything from my larder or pantry, just say the word.'

Lately he has been tormenting Thurston with a design for a spit driven by a system of gears and pulleys, which uses the fire's draught to turn the meat at a steady speed. '*Voilà,*' he says, impaling a chicken. But Thurston turns down his mouth: there are plenty of boys, so wherefore a machine?

Boys produce burnt bits, he says. Or some parts cooked, some raw. This way, you have a regulated action. Stoke up the fire, and the faster it goes, the faster the spit turns. Bank down the fire, and –

Try again, master, Thurston says. The machinery is so much bigger than yon pitiful pullet.

When Castillon and the king's councillors arrive, they sit down to turbot, baked guinea fowl, and a cress salad dressed with vinegar and oil. The salmon is roasted with orange zest, and young fowl deboned and baked into what the English call Lombard pasties, though he never met a Lombard who knew aught of them.

Once they are alone, the ambassador drops his napkin, like someone discarding a flag of truce. 'The leg will not heal, you know. Next time he will not be so lucky, nor will you.'

He does not answer. It seems his silence leads to a certain overconfidence on Castillon's part. When next in the king's presence he comports himself like a tavern companion, recommending Madame Louise, the sister of Madame de Longueville. 'Take her, Majesty, she is better-looking than her sister. Besides, the elder is a widow, the younger a maid. You will be the first to go there. You can shape the passage to your measure.'

Henry guffaws. He slaps the ambassador on the back. He swings away, his back to the Frenchman, the smile wiped from his face. 'I cannot abide bawdy talk,' he whispers. He calls over his shoulder,

'Excuse me, ambassador, if I leave you. My chaplains attend me to Mass.'

A day or two later the king is away again with a hunting party. Rafe is with him, and Richard Cromwell rides between, back and forth with letters and messages better not trusted to paper. When Richard arrives at Waltham, he is told the French ambassador is there before him, and that he must wait; then that various councillors have been summoned to see the king; then that he must stay overnight.

Rafe, covered in apologies, takes Richard's letters in, saying he will put them in the king's hand himself. Richard says, 'Don't apologise for *him*, Rafe. It is no fault of yours. What does he think he is about?'

Richard is incredulous. It is without precedent, for Cromwell business to be deferred.

Next day Richard rides back with his letters answered. 'But I don't like it, sir,' he says. 'Norfolk was there by the king's side, strutting like a player king; for two pins I would have wrung his neck. Surrey with him, the pricklet. Both of them giving out how the king was displeased with you, finding you favour the Emperor. Norfolk was linking arms with the Frenchman. They only wanted a fiddler and they could have danced.'

What's Henry up to? I may belittle you, he said. I may reprove you. But do not be misled. My trust is in you.

He takes out The Book Called Henry. (He keeps it under lock and key.) He wonders if he has any advice for himself. But all he sees is how much white space there is, blank pages uninscribed.

At Father Forrest's burning are present, besides himself and Thomas Cranmer, the Lord Mayor of London; Audley the Lord Chancellor; Charles Brandon Duke of Suffolk; Thomas Howard Duke of Norfolk; Edward Seymour, in his dignity as Earl of Hertford; Bishop Stokesley, of course. They are at Smithfield for eight in the morning. Forrest is brought from Newgate, drawn on a hurdle, wearing his Franciscan habit. He is set on a platform to hear Hugh Latimer's sermon.

Hugh talks for an hour but he might as well be pissing in the wind. Forrest has the strength to cast his words back at him, saying he has been a monk since he was seventeen years old, and a Catholic since he was baptised, and that he, Latimer, is no Catholic, for only those who obey the Pope are members of God's universal family: at which the crowd groan. The rest of what he says cannot well be heard, but at a signal the officers pull him from the platform and carry him to the stake, his feet off the ground. He hangs limp, mouthing prayers.

Now there is a flourish of trumpets, a beating of drums, and into the arena comes the Welsh idol Derfel. Eight men bear him, which is needless, but it makes a show; and in mockery of his pretensions to strength, the idol is bound with ropes. The crowd laugh and sing. It is said Derfel can burn a forest; let's see if he will. At a word of command, he is set down, upright. At another word, his limbs jerk, his eyes wink, his wooden arms rise imploringly to Heaven. 'To the devil with him!' the crowd call. The officers dismember Derfel, take up their hatchets and begin to reduce him to firewood.

Father Forrest has now let slip every chance the king and Cranmer and Hugh Latimer have offered. He has chosen his dreadful end and must endure. Thomas More used to say that it hardly made a man brave to agree to burn, once he was bound to the stake. He, the Lord Privy Seal, calls out, 'Forrest! Ask pardon of the king!'

For this is what Forrest has omitted to do. This is what every offender does, though he feels himself to be guiltless, in order to mitigate the wrath that may fall on those who he leaves behind: so that the king will heed their pleas, and not strip them of all they have.

But Forrest is a celibate. He has no sons and daughters, or none that he knows. And as he is a friar, and they do not own property, he has nothing for the king to take. All he owns is his habit, now tattered, and his skin, muscles, fat and bone.

'Beg pardon of your king!' he calls out: he, Cromwell. He does not know if Forrest can hear him.

He thinks, it is too late to stop it now. A martyr may burn fast or slow. The faggots may be dry and stacked high, so he is hidden from the crowd and the flames take him in minutes and he dies in a roar of heat. But since Forrest has refused even a word of contrition, this will be a slow burning. The friar is hoisted by a chain around his waist, and the fire is set below him, at his feet.

Dry-eyed he watches, and watches everything. He does not steal one glance at the faces of his fellow councillors. He thinks, there must have been some point at which we could have bargained with Forrest. There must have been something we could have offered, to make him yield a point and save himself this agony. It is against his nature to think that no bargain can be struck. Everybody wants something, if only for the pain to stop.

When the heat reaches him Forrest draws up his blistered bare feet. He contorts himself, screaming, but is obliged to let down his legs into the fire. He draws them up again, he twists in his chain, he roars, and Derfel crackles merrily; and this stage seems to last for a long time, the flames reaching ever upward, and the man's efforts to escape them ever more feeble, until at last he hangs and does not resist, and his upper body begins to burn. The friar raises his arms, which have been left free, as if he is clawing towards Heaven. The fibres of his body are shortened and shrivelling, his limbs contorting whether he will or no, so that what seems like an act of adoration to his papist God is only a sign that he is *in extremis*: and at a signal, the execution- ers step forward and with long iron poles reach into the flames, hook the roasting torso from its chain, and pitch it into the fire below. It goes with a scream from the spectators, a rush and spurt of flame; then we hear no more from Father Forrest. No more from warrior Derfel, the great idol of Wales: he is ash. Cranmer says, close to his ear, 'It is over, I believe.'

Edward Seymour looks as if he will spew. 'You have not seen this before?' he asks him. 'I have seen it too often.'

The official party begins to disperse. What does one do for the rest of the day? Work, of course. 'A cruel death,' one of the guildsmen says. He says, 'A cruel life, brother.'

* * *

The day he saw a woman burned, he was – what – eight years old? He was run away, or so he told himself: he had travelled from his home in Putney by foot and by cart, spending one night in a hedge. Next day he begged some bread and milk at a back door, and got a ride on a boat that put him down by the wharves under the Tower. He meant to go on a ship and be a sailor, but seeing the crowds surging in their gaiety he forgot his purpose. He said, 'Is it Bartholomew Fair?'

A man laughed at him. But a woman said, 'He's only little, Will.' She looked down at him. 'Holy Mary, your face could do with a wash.'

He did not like to say he had wakened in a hedge. Will said, 'What's your name?'

'Harry.' He offered his hand. 'I'm a blacksmith by trade. You, Will?'

The man grasped his hand and squeezed it. Too late, he realised Will meant to torture him; it was his idea of a jest. He thought his bones would crack, but on his face he retained an expression of polite indifference. Will dropped his hand as if in disgust. Tough lad, he said.

The woman said, 'Come with us, young Master Harry, stick by me.'

Clinging to the woman's apron, he stood fast in the heave of the crowd. She patted his shoulder and then let her hand rest there – as if she were his godmother, or somebody who wished him well. 'Here comes the city!' a man yelled. A trumpet announced a procession: men of dignity bearing staves of office, wearing gold chains. He had never seen such men, except in a dream. He saw the swing of good wool and the sheen on velvet coats, and a bishop arrayed like a sunburst, a gold cross carried before him. 'You'll have seen a hanging?' Will said.

'Oh, many a one,' he boasted.

Will said, 'Well, this isn't a hanging.'

When they dragged the old woman forth, battered and bound, he looked up into the face of his godmother and said, 'What's she done?'

'Harry, you need to see her sizzle,' his godmother said. 'She is a Loller.'

Will said testily, 'Lollard. Have it right.'

The godmother ignored him. 'She is of the devil's party, eighty years old and steeped in sin.' She raised her voice above the roar. 'Let this boy through!'

Some made way, thinking it a pious work to show a child a burning. Still, the crowd thickened. Some were praying aloud but others were eating yeast buns. Standing behind him, his guardian no longer smelled of the linen press but of excitement and heat. He twisted back towards her; he wanted to bury his head in her waist, to lock his arms around her. He knew he must forbear, or Will would squeeze his neck as he had squeezed his hand; and seeing him turn, thinking he was trying to get away, Will shoved him: 'This boy is a heathen. What parish spawned you?'

Caution made him say, 'I don't have a parish.'

'Everybody has a parish,' Will scoffed. But then the crowd began to bellow out prayers. A preacher shouted above them. He said the pain of earthly fire was but a feather touch, a May morning, a mother's caress, when compared with the agony of the flames of Hell.

When the fire was set the multitude carried him forward. He tried to swim against its tide, crying out for his godmother, but his voice was lost. He saw people's backs, but he smelled human flesh. You had to breathe it in, till the wind changed. Some weakly folk wailed, others were sick at their own feet.

Afterwards when the excitement was done, the Loller reduced to bone, rendered to fat, to paste, the dignitaries departed and the ordinary spectators began to break up and go their ways. Some were drunk, swaying with arms linked, hullooing and pumping their fists and shouting as if they were at a bullfight. Others were sober, gathering in muttering groups. They had homes to go to: he, not. Putney seemed distant, as if it were a place in a story. 'In a town by a river dwelled one Thomas Cromwell, with his father Walter and his dog. One day he strayed away, to seek his fortune in a foreign land ...'

He wondered how long it would take him to reverse the story. Putney was clear the other side of London, and you are not always lucky, you do not always get a ride; and if they knew where he had been and what he had seen, surely every man and woman would curse him.

It came into his mind to go under the stand where the dignitaries had been, and live in it as in a house. Nobody stopped him. Nobody saw him. The sawn planks for his roof, he sat cross-legged on the damp ground. Time passed. He was aware of persons who waited on the fringes of the spectacle, as if waiting for the field to empty. One had a basin, another a basket. Still they lingered, as if afraid. The executioners returned with their iron bars, whistling, and smashed up the bones that were left, raking through the remnants.

Crouching in his new dwelling, he watched them as if from a great distance. His body felt cramped and frozen. The bones of his hand throbbed where Will had squeezed them. It came on to rain and the men dropped their tools and sought shelter. Water dripped between the planks above his head. He counted the drops. He caught them in his cupped hand and he drank them. He felt them run inside him and freeze to ice.

When the bones were shattered the officers wiped off their crowbars on the grass, pulled up their hoods and tramped from the field. They did not look directly at those waiting with basin and basket. But one of them spoke over his shoulder: 'All yours, brothers.'

The men called brothers began to grub and scrape the ground. He crept out, telling them his name – Master Harry, blacksmith – and informing them of all that had passed. We know, they said, we saw. They said, this lady died for God's word, Harry, and we are come to gather what remains. They smeared on the back of his hand a long streak of fat and ash. Remember this day, they said, as long as it pleases God to give you life.

He told them what the priest had informed him, about the feeble nature of earthly fire, how it was a cooling draught compared to the raging flames below. He rolled up his sleeve and showed them the puckered streak of flesh where he had seared himself at the forge. A woman said, that must have hurt you sore, sweetheart. He said, it is no hardship to a man to have a scar. My dad has many a one. 'You go home now, son,' a man said to him.

He said, 'I don't know how.'

They went their ways. He returned to his dwelling house under the stand. The sickness had quelled and he was hungry. He thought, the heel of a loaf would do me. He knew that in time he would have to sally out and steal something, but for now he must be quiet and still, because what if the men came back to pull down his house? They might haul him out, saying, 'Here is a Lollard boy.' They might start another fire and throw him on it, as a man throws a last bundle on a cart.

No one came. The light was waning. He was not afraid of the old woman's ghost, but he was aware of company. In the smoke that still lingered, he could see certain shapes, low and slinking. At a distance but looping closer, the dogs of London.

To see them was to know their histories. Not one of them, he supposed, had name, kennel nor master. They were scabbed and scarred and limping, bowed and worn like shadows. For hours they must have lurked, keeping their distance, chins on their paws, drooling. When the officers were at work they dared not advance, for fear of stones thrown or a slingshot that would blind an eye. They were shivering with fright, but hunger made them brave: it made them dare all, while the smell of burned meat lay heavy on the air.

At first they came on their bellies. Then they rose to a crouch, their backs still dished, quivering with fear but always forward. They circled; they lifted their muzzles and sniffed the wind. They licked their lips. They drew nearer. Their eyes passed over him. They would have been afraid of the city dignitaries, of the officers, but they were not afraid of him, a ragged boy. The circle tightened. At any sound they crouched, froze. But still they closed in.

The Lollard was lean pickings, no more fat on her than a needle. When they realised nothing was left but her smell, would they turn on him? Chunk of Putney flesh: one can bite out his throat and lick his blood.

The space under the stand was tall enough for him to stand. The dogs raised their hackles. They hesitated for a moment; then came on, teeth bared.

His pockets were empty. He had no weapon, not even a pebble. He took a breath. He lurched forward with a shout: *fuckoffbeasts-youfuckoffand die.*

The dogs checked. They bolted, they scrambled backwards. But then they halted. They melted into their hunched, lumpen forms, and watched him. Then once again they formed a loop and began to creep towards him, flat to the ground, muzzles towards the stake. Will had asked him, What do you want so far from home, a child like you? A priest had said: 'God sees into the righteous heart: He leads us to Sion.'

He threw up his arms, yelling, cursing. He pitched from under the stand, his left arm flailing, his right arm stretched towards the dogs as if to give them a blessing: but he made the horn sign at them, he made the fig.

He turned his back on the execution ground. He began to stumble away from the day he had passed: dazed, blundering westwards, knowing yesterday he walked with the sun behind him, till the world giddily swung, and a crowd swamped him and swept him up, and a godmother took him by the hand and towed him through it, saying, 'Let this child to the front, he needs to see her suffer, hereafter it will make him a saint.'

It was not the first crime he had seen, but it was the first punishment. Much later he learned the woman's name, Joan Boughton. She was no beggar, as she appeared, but a woman of education; a lord mayor of London had been among her folk.

Nothing protects you, nothing. In the last ditch, not rank, nor kin. Nothing between you and the fire.

In a day or two he fetched up back in Putney. These were the first nights he spent in the open, but not the last. At home they had not missed him. His father hit him, but that was usual. Whatever dereliction had driven him to run, they had forgot it; soon it was subsumed in his next fault, because he could not help but sin: he was of all God's creatures, his dad said, the most wretched. He did not wait for the priest to tell him more: Walter's bellow was loud in his ear.

It was years before he realised the boy who went to Smithfield was not the one who came home. The child Thomas still crouched under the stand, vigilant as the dogs, his hands cupped to catch the rain-water, the icy drops on his palm. It is a work he has never undertaken, to go back and retrieve himself. He can see that small figure, at the wrong end of time; he can feel the heave of its ribs as it tries to cry without uttering. He can see and feel, without pitying the child; only suspect that, to keep the streets tidy, someone ought to collect it and send it home.

Summer approaches. The French ambassador says to him, 'Limping, my lord Cremuel?'

'I got an injury long ago in your country's service. The leg some-times lets me down.'

Castillon says, 'I wonder your king does not think you are mock-ing him.'

Leave that to the King of Scots. The second week of June, Madame de Longueville lands at the town of Fife, and is met by James and his nobles. She looks bonny; she has had a luckier voyage than the Princess Madeleine. With the blessings and acclamation of their countrymen on both sides, she and James ride to their wedding.

The Emperor, meanwhile, seems to have cooled towards the project of our marriage with Christina. The king tells our man in Brussels to spend whatever money it takes, to make it happen. But it is spelled out to the English that since their king was formerly married to Katherine of Aragon, who was Christina's near kin, they will need a dispensation from the Pope. In which matter, Ambassador Mendoza says, you may find you have made a difficulty for yourself.

Archbishop Cranmer says, I wish all this diplomacy would stop, this casting of Master Hans to the four winds and this bandying of women's honour. The king's bride should be someone he knows and feels he can love. Because Henry thinks marriage should not be contracted without love. He used to sing a song about it in

Katherine's day: *I hurt no man, I do no wrong/Love true where I did marry ...*

But the council says, if a king makes a love-match once in his life, count him lucky. He can't expect to do it again and again.

Since the king cannot have a wife he occupies himself in building. A new palace is to arise in Surrey, not far from Hampton Court. It is designed to create hunting grounds stretching many miles. At first it seems that a modest lodge will do, but then the king decides it will be one of the wonders of the world. He indents for Italian craftsmen and fetches in all the building stone from the demolition of Merton Abbey. He clears the manor house that stands already, with its farms, barns and stables, and knocks down the ancient parish church. He buys up tracts of adjacent manors. He orders a thousand loads of timber and begins building brick kilns.

Thomas Lord Cromwell, Vicegerent and Privy Seal, no longer has time to oversee the king's building. He is able to advise on the choice of Italians, but the king is pleased to place Rafe Sadler in charge of the project. Anything Cromwell does for the king, Sadler and Thomas Wriothesley will be able to do: in time, and between them. He has trained them, encouraged them, written them as versions of himself: Rafe as the plain text, and Mr Wriothesley in cipher.

The building of the marvel goes on through the summer of 1538. When the king has a new wife he will place her in it, as a jewel in its setting. Meanwhile, separated from us by the Narrow Sea, the ladies of Europe watch the misty land through crystal mirrors; down the winding flowery path the messengers of the king advance, on high-stepping white steeds. In the old stories, princesses are never too old or too young or too papist. They wait patiently for the prince seven years and more, while he does his valiant deeds, and they spin out their fates from a single thread, growing the while their long golden hair.

Sometimes the king weeps for his late wife. Where shall we find a lady so benign, so meek, and so comely as Jane? As he cannot he amuses himself with the creation of the new palace, the rarest ever seen: and the name of the palace is Nonsuch.

II

Corpus Christi

June–December 1538

Wyatt has followed the Emperor from the shores of Spain to Nice, where Charles has disembarked to meet the Pope and the King of France. Their meeting is like some ill-starred conjunction in the heavens, which we could forecast but not prevent. Early June, Wyatt is in England, pacing a room at St James's. The Lord Privy Seal, sitting in a splash of weak sun, follows him with his eyes.

'I saw Farnese,' Wyatt says. 'Close enough to spit. With Polo leaning on his shoulder, conspiring in his papal ear. I should have spitted him on my dagger, and carried home his collops.'

Wherever the Emperor goes, Wyatt jolts after him, with his household of twenty or so young gallants: all armed, all poets, all lovers, all dicers. From Nice, Charles has sent him home with an enticement. If Lady Mary will marry Dom Luis, he will settle the duchy of Milan on them: Milan, his greatest prize, over which he and François have fought for years.

'But he will never give up Milan,' Wyatt says. 'Not this side of the Last Judgement. And they are asking for an outrageous sum with Mary. The king should offer two-thirds.'

Always a good rule of thumb: knock a third off, see what answer you get. Wyatt says, 'But then I don't know if the king intends to let Mary go. Or if he even intends to marry himself, or is just playing a game with them all, and keeping Hans employed.'

He shrugs: I do not know anything.

563

'I hate Spain,' Wyatt says. 'I would prefer the lowest cell in Newgate. And I cannot understand the Emperor. I cannot read him in any language. I hear the words he says, but nothing that lies between them. His face never changes. Sometimes he admits me every day. Sometimes I arrive and his servants shut me out. I think, have I committed some breach of manners? Is it reasonable to stand outside his presence chamber two days, or three, or until they sweep me out with the rushes? If I am told to quit his realm, do I pay my bills and leave my compliments, or do I run in the clothes I stand up in?'

'It is prince's tricks,' he says. 'Three days in a row Henry gives the French a private audience. Then he ignores them for a week.'

'When he shuts me out I write my dispatches. I translate Seneca. I keep no company with women, whatever you hear, but with a skin of bad wine and the gospel. In Spain the women are cloistered. Husbands kill you on suspicion. If the Earl of Worcester were Spanish, you and his wife would be skewered and mouldy in your graves.'

'I never had to do with Worcester's wife,' he says. 'But it is just as when I say "I am not a Lutheran." Nobody believes me.'

'The Inquisitors in Toledo think all Englishmen are Lutherans. They have tried to put spies in my house. They offered money to my servants. Letters were stolen.'

'I have warned you, lock up what you write. Prose or verse.'

Wyatt looks uneasy. 'At first I thought it was you.'

He would not deny it; he has a man with Wyatt, as he has men with Gardiner in France. He sighs: 'It is as much for your protection as anything else. My agents would not steal your letters, only read them at your desk. I am surprised at the freedom the Emperor gives the Inquisitors. Do not provoke them. You should show your face at Mass.'

'No greater beadsman,' Wyatt says. 'I can mop and mow to an altar with the best of them.'

Heresy knows no borders, the Inquisitors declare. No traveller of any nation is exempt from our enquiries. And what could the King of England do, if they threw his envoy in a dungeon? He could make representations; but meanwhile, they could have bored a needle through our envoy's tongue, or pulled out his fingernails.

A clerk comes in with a sheaf of papers. 'From Sir Richard Riche, my lord. He said, never hesitate, but go straight in. This will rejoice Lord Cromwell, he said.'

He says to Wyatt, 'I am augmented. I am to have the priory at Michelham. Gregory and I are writing our names on the chalk hills of Sussex. You too will have your reward.' Even if posthumously, he thinks.

Wyatt watches the clerk out. He sits down. 'Last year in France – Henry does not know this – Pole approached me. He sent presents. And a letter, wrapped around a flask of good wine.'

'And?'

'I read the letter. Francis Bryan drank the wine.'

'Ah, Francis. How did he take to Nice?'

'He gambled,' Wyatt says, 'as ever. The town stank like Hell, it was crammed to the rafters with papists, but Francis thrives on it. He plays for high stakes with the chancellors of great men, their familiar creatures, and he sleeps with their women. I could not prosper without him. I would learn nothing.' Wyatt hesitates. 'It seems to me I could approach our man Pole. I could contrive a meeting.'

He nods. 'But remember no one has authorised you to make contact. I have not. The king has not.'

Wyatt curses. 'When I am face to face with my opportunity, must I refuse it? What am I to do – send back to Westminster for instructions? Has Henry no faith in my judgement? If he wants an envoy, he should send who he trusts, and trust who he sends. And if he wants words and no deeds, let him choose some other man. I would kill Pole as soon as look at him.'

'Well, that would terminate your embassy, for sure.' He averts his face. 'As it is, Henry will send you back, no matter how you squall.'

'Then do one thing for me,' Wyatt says. 'Call home that runt Edmund Bonner. He has trotted after me from Spain into France and I swear the next time we take ship I will overboard him.'

The fat little priest is newly popular with the king. 'We sent Bonner to help you against the theologians. We thought he would strengthen your embassy. We meant well, I swear it.'

'I would rather live in a rats' nest than lodge with him. I have never met a man so quick to take offence, and so quick to give it. He makes me sweat with shame. I do not understand why either you or the king would promote such a ball of tallow.'

He is silent on that. 'You would not like to go to France instead? To replace Gardiner? I mean to put some friend as ambassador in his place.'

Wyatt smiles, as if puzzled. 'I am that friend?'

There is a tap at the door. It is Dick Purser. He pulls off his cap. 'Master, the present from Danzig is here.'

He slaps his hands on the desk. 'Alive?'

'Three alive. Let us hope not all of them after one kind. None of us are minded to pick them up and see if they have pintles.'

'I'm coming,' he says. And to Wyatt, 'We are done?'

'If you knew the long empty days when I talk to you in my head …'

'Then stay to supper.'

'And the long empty nights,' Wyatt says.

The presents from Danzig are sad huddles of fur, their eyes bright hostile points; they shiver as if they have a fever. 'Get them in the pond,' he says, dismayed.

Wyatt peers down at them. 'What are they? Beaver?'

'Not seen since our grandfathers' time. I want to breed them. Fishermen will be against it.'

He shrugs. It's always the wrong bits of the past people want back. With their dams, these busy animals can divert and slow the waters of streams likely to flood. No human ingenuity can match theirs, and it is a pity they were ever hunted. Wyatt says, 'What else will you bring back? Wolves?'

We do not need more predators. We do not need wild boar, though they make good sport. But we need to keep our rivers in their courses, and we need to plant trees, if we are going to cut them down at the present rate: for timber frames for merchants' houses, for palaces for princes; for ships to sail against the Pope and the Emperor, and all the world in league against us.

In the long twilight Wyatt says to him: 'I have learned one thing in Spain. They have a poison so virulent that one drop on an arrowhead can kill. I wonder if I should get some for our purpose.'

'Oh, I would sooner an honest murder,' he says. He pictures Pole felled on the highway, his minions fleeing like piglets from the butcher. 'I think of cleaving his cardinal's hat in twain. Slicing his pate, as Becket's was sliced.'

Outside the window rises an English moon, yellow as a slice of Banbury cheese. Wyatt says, 'I must get down to Allington and see about my affairs. I do not have your skill in choosing deputies to guard my interests. My son is fifteen now, and if the worst befell, what have I to leave him?'

'On paper you are rich.'

'Oh, paper,' Wyatt says. 'I think it was not by a serpent, but by paper and ink that evil came into the world. Such lies are written of me, in and out of cipher, that I think, this time Thomas Cromwell will show me the door. But you do not.'

He does not answer. Wyatt says abruptly, 'I want to see Bess Darrell.'

'If the Courtenays were to be at their house in Horsley, the king's business might take you that way. She has wit enough to meet you day or night.'

Wyatt has never mentioned the phantom child who saved his life. But its absence hovers, a mild haze, behind Wyatt's shoulder where his guardian angel skulks.

He stands up. 'I shall not see you again before you sail. I wish you a swift passage. I hold you in my prayers.'

They walk out together into a warm misty evening. At the gate Anthony is sitting with the porters. He is a melancholy sight, his hollow chest, his bowed head, his spindly legs stuck out in front of him.

'Anthony, I thought you were in Stepney.' To Wyatt he says, unnecessarily, 'This is my fool.'

Anthony is wearing his working suit of stripes and patches. Wyatt passes him with a glance, and as the fool raises an arm in salutation, his silver bells chime.

Wyatt leaves to resume his embassy just after the feast of Corpus Christi. On 21 June he writes from the dockside at Hythe. No ship can leave, the winds are so stiff. All day it has been blowing, and it means to blow all night, but tomorrow, the mariners say, it will have blown itself out. Early, he hopes to set sail.

He, Lord Cromwell, thinks back to their parting: Wyatt's eyes begged him to say, you need not go back to Spain, I will plead you have done your utmost. But Henry would answer, 'I will be the judge of that.' The king knows Wyatt's uses. He is able to read sighs, construe by contraries. His word is just what a diplomat's word should be: as clear as glass and as unstable as water.

Wyatt thinks himself shrewd, but he does not grasp what friendship is, as the world goes now. Friendship swears it will stand and never alter, but when the weather changes men change their coat. Not every man has a price in money: some will betray you for a kind word from a great man, others will forswear your company because they see you limp, or lose your footing, or hesitate once in a while. He says to Rafe and to Call-Me, I urge you both, undertake no course without deep thought: but learn to think very fast.

The Emperor and François, in the absence of the English envoy, have made what they call a Ten-Year Truce. It is well into July before he, Cromwell, can obtain a copy of the terms. Then he and all the councillors see how little England has been regarded. Wyatt writes to him, 'The king has been left out of the cart's arse.' That makes him laugh, the thought of Henry sacked and tied for market, forgotten in a farmyard and forlorn in the rain.

Our official reaction to the treaty is disbelief. Instead of the Ten-Year Truce we call it the Ten-Minute Truce. Henry says, 'Why does Charles think the King of France will keep faith with him, when he does not keep faith with me? He has broken every ancient agreement between his realm and ours. The King of France and the King of England have always delivered up each other's rebels. So why has he not delivered up Pole?'

He, Lord Cromwell, sighs. 'Gardiner has ill-served us in that regard. It is high time he came home.'

'When he does, send him to his diocese,' the king says. 'We do not want him near our person.'

All my envoys have let me down, Henry complains. They know how peace threatens our interests, and yet they could not stop it. 'Francis Bryan said he would trap Pole. But he has disappointed me. Like you, Cromwell.'

If the treaty lasts our peril is extreme. Charles has always seen himself as conqueror of Constantinople. But quicker would be conquest of England, and with France as his ally it would be simple enough and cheap. Only consider the friends he has waiting for him, as soon as he sets foot on our soil: the old Plantagenet families, with their retainers armed and ready. Pole's people, the Courtenays.

Wyatt has been deceived by the Emperor. England has been deceived by both Emperor and France. Henry is furious. Nothing will console him but theology.

A delegation comes from the German princes, with high hopes of friendship, of compromises that will allow our churches to make common cause against the devil and the Pope. The king's team of negotiators includes Robert Barnes, who is familiar with the Germans and with whom they make good cheer. But also it includes the Bishop of Durham, Cuthbert Tunstall, fetched down from his see in the north to strengthen the hand of those who say, 'Slowly, slowly, sometimes no change is best.'

Tunstall is a subtle man, experienced, congenial. It is dismaying how the king favours him, conferring with him as he rides from house to house; he does not let the godly Germans get in the way of his hunting. Dr Butts says, I suppose we should allow the king to ride, while he is able. But at every house where he intends a stay, Butts situates a surgeon.

The Lutherans tell Henry, your Majesty well knows we have made a League; it is not to attack anyone, only to secure us against the Emperor. If you will take part, you can be our head, we will make you Protector of our confederacy.

Through the summer the teams are locked in conference. Rafe Sadler takes minutes and relays them to the king. He himself, Thomas Cromwell, keeps a distance from their unsuccess. He knows the king will never agree that clergy may marry, or that laymen should receive Christ as both bread and wine. We cannot agree on the nature of Christ's body, what is fact and what is allegory, what is human and what is divine. Can God be baked into bread? When we consume the host, why do we not hear the cracking of his bones? Is he still God, when he churns in our guts? And what if a dog eats him, is he still God then?

Corpus Christi is a miracle. It is a mystery. Once consecrated, the host contains your God, alive: the wine is his blood. You cannot hope to understand it but you must believe it. And if you fail to believe it you must keep quiet, because your failure can kill you.

The Germans do not enjoy their summer. They complain there are rats pounding across the floor of their lodgings, and where they sleep is next to the kitchen, so they are afraid their clothes smell of smoke and burnt fat. He could lodge them himself, but he would not go so far. He would not go far at all with Brother Martin. He is sending young men to study in Zürich, his mind drawn by the teaching of the learned doctors there. Hugh Latimer says the God of England worketh all, and under Him worketh Cromwell. But he keeps his eye on the prize: the English Bible. With this good book in your hands, God speaks to you as your father and mother spoke, as your nurse: and if you cannot read, others will read it for you, in this close, this loving, this familiar tongue.

The king has given permission for the Bible – what remains is to create and distribute it. He needs one to each parish, placed where the people have access. He needs copies by the thousand, not by the dozen. His friend the scholar Miles Coverdale takes charge of a revision, aiming to print in Paris. The French printers are the quickest in Europe. But the Inquisition operates there too.

Formerly he would have printed in Antwerp. But Charles is the master of those territories and Charles is in his killing vein. You sit down with his ambassadors, with Mendoza, with Chapuys; you pass a pleasant evening, you talk about books, you enjoy good food and a little music. But never forget: their regime buries women alive.

When the German doctors go home in September, it is with the king's praise for their piety and learning. They should come back, Henry says; the door is open. That month he, the Vicegerent, makes new ordinances for the church. An end to pilgrimages. An end to the Angelus bell, which causes the people to kneel in the fields. No lights burning before statues or pictures. The images themselves remain, except the idols that the people furnish with oatcakes and ale; and the spangled, red-lipped Virgins who wear silver shoes when poor women go barefoot.

In autumn, too, he brings in a way of counting people. Each parish must start a register to record baptisms, marriages and burials. From now on his countrymen will know who they are and where they come from, who their cousins are and what their grandfather was called. Uncle Norfolk and his peers have heralds to tell them their lineage. The Poles, the Courtenays, the Veres and the Talbots, they have arms and devices. Their ancestors are buried beneath their own effigies, and even before noblemen learned to write, they had tame priests to record their lives. But the butcher or ploughman, the shepherd or shoemaker's apprentice – for all he knows, he might have grown in a wood like a toadstool.

His friends ask: 'What do you hear from Antwerp, from your lady daughter?'

He turns the conversation. He does not want to talk about Jenneke. He thinks, I may not be much of a father but she knows where to find me. If she sends a message it will reach me. Vaughan's people will send it on the shortest route. But the Cromwell name is no protection to her, rather the reverse, and her faith – if she believes we are living through the last days – is a danger to him and to all her kin.

In high summer, he follows the king on his progress through Kent. At Dover they meet Lord Lisle, come over to importune the king about abbeys. 'Talk to Riche,' the king says, bored.

'Riche?' Lord Lisle says. 'There never was such a dip-pocket as he! He wants a shilling to say good morning to you!'

'He's a lawyer,' the king says, 'how else do they make their shillings?'

The king is at his ease with Lisle, who was a kindly uncle to him when he was young. But Lisle's hair of Plantagenet red has faded to russet and now to grey, and age has dimmed him. 'Well, Cromwell,' he says; and pats himself down, as if he were looking for a coin to offer. 'I have your letters daily,' he says, 'but we do not often encounter, do we?'

'Sadly not,' he says. 'I trust her ladyship is mended?'

Lisle manages a doleful smile. 'Her belly is down at last. Poor soul, I never saw a lady more disappointed with her condition.'

'I want to buy her land at Painswick,' he says. 'I will make her a good offer.'

Lisle is amused. 'You think you could do with a slice of Gloucestershire, do you? Sussex does not satisfy your appetite? Majesty, is there no stopping these new men?'

'I hope not,' the king says. 'I rely on them, sir.'

Lisle rocks back on his heels. 'I don't know that we're selling.'

The king laughs like a boy. 'Uncle, what a lot you don't know!'

Henry is in an affable mood, though he is drawing up plans to build forts. I will talk to anyone, he says – talking is cheap, unless it involves the meeting of kings, and even that, he suggests to François, might be managed in a quiet way: why don't we rendezvous outside Calais? He is still eager to inspect French brides. Perhaps François could bring a selection?

François, his tone dry, says that he sees no point in a meeting. Henry says, 'Cromwell, François is in breach of his treaty obligations. He owes me four years' pension. Tell the French that if they do not disburse I will invade them.'

The councillors, alarmed, scurry after him: 'Cromwell, tell them no such thing!'

Another day, 'Call Chapuys in,' the king says. Multiple marriages are on the table: if Mary takes Dom Luis, not only will we throw in young Eliza as a makeweight, but Lady Margaret Douglas can wed some ally of the Emperor, perhaps in Italy. The king will also offer Mary Fitzroy, his dead son's widow. Chapuys and Mendoza are invited to the palace at Richmond to spend a day with Lady Mary. Once again Mary performs on the lute. Chapuys reports, 'She speaks fondly of her friend Cremuel.' He adds in a low voice, smiling, 'She seems confident you will save her from any unwanted bridegroom.'

With the visit, Mendoza's mission is over. The king gives him a farewell banquet. 'The Emperor has paid his London expenses,' Chapuys says, sulking. 'And no doubt rewarded him richly. Whereas months have gone by when I have not seen a penny, and am forced to take out loans.'

But now, the French and Imperial ambassadors are meeting and comparing notes, not just about the meanness of their princes but about the games played by the English king and his ministers. They say, our sovereigns are allies now, so why not we? 'We are issued more news of the infant Edouard,' Castillon says. 'We are told he has four teeth. We are terrified, Cremuel.'

The king says, let the ambassadors know I mean to talk to the Duke of Cleves, about his sister. Let us stir them up a little, alarm them. Let them understand, Cromwell, that a match with Cleves has many advantages for me.

As our prince approaches twelve months of age, it is time to appoint his dry nurse. That done, with Mr Wriothesley and on a spare sheet of paper, he works out how to spend the king's revenue. He wants twenty thousand marks for the repair of harbours and castles. For the comfort of the poor and sick, Henry will need to refound the hospitals that the monks used to run, and he will need ten thousand marks to get that under way. Then he plans to ask for five thousand marks for employing men without work to mend the highways.

'You do not give up that notion,' Wriothesley says.

He tried it before and Parliament would not support it. The king was more favourable. It becomes any prince to look after those without resources, and find them an honest life. Though probably, he says to Mr Wriothesley, King Arthur never occupied himself with such matters. In his day, castles repaired themselves, and all beggars were Christ in disguise.

Our man in Brussels, Hutton, is dead. Mr Wriothesley must get over there, the king says: help Hutton's widow wrap up her affairs and travel back to England, and get himself into the confidence of the Emperor's regent, the Queen of Hungary. The regent likes a handsome man, and Mr Wriothesley is both handsome and eloquent. And it is time for Hans to get on the road again. With him goes Philip Hoby of the privy chamber, to play the lover on his monarch's behalf. He must set forth Henry's qualities: his liberality, his clemency, his peaceable nature. Is Philip well-briefed? He, Cromwell, draws him aside.

'Philip, when you go to see one of these ladies – French, Imperial, it is indifferent – you must seem, when you are ushered into her presence, to be silenced by utter astonishment. Your eyes must dart away from her, as if in panic; and then slowly, slowly – as if you hardly dare do it – you must raise your eyes to her face.'

'Yes, I see,' Philip Hoby says.

'And then, once again, you look away. But this time, as if it pained you to do it. Drop your gaze, Philip, and look at your boots, and make a heavy sigh.'

Philip is unable to help himself; he makes one.

'Next, you stammer through the courtesies. But once again, lose your composure. You pat your person, you search your bag – "Ah, here is my brief!" – all the time, you are aquiver, Philip. You take out your letter. Your fingers fumble. You read: "My master says", and so forth, "Our council asserts …"'

'I keep losing my place, do I?'

'Then you cast the paper aside, as a thing you scorn. You burst out: "Madam, I must speak. Reports allude to the brightness of your eye, the sweetness of your lip, the freshness of your youthful complexion. Yet those reports fail to capture even a particle of the loveliness it is now my privilege to behold."

'At this point, Philip,' he says, 'you must put your hand on your heart. What she must perceive is, "Ah, this envoy is in love with me!"

'She will smile on you. She will pity you. Look abashed, but let her draw you out. "Alas, madam, you are for princes, not for such a humble man as I be. Yet I could be consoled, if I saw you Queen of England – matched with so noble, so puissant, and so benign a prince." While she is fluttering, move quick. Get her to agree to a portrait.'

'Get Hans in,' Philip says. 'I see.'

He claps him on the shoulder. 'I have faith in you.'

Rafe says, 'Sir, now I have heard how these things are managed, I am surprised you have no wife yourself. I am surprised you have not a thousand wives.'

Late summer he rides down to Lewes to see Gregory and his grandson. Plague has not only prevented the king's visit but forced his son's household from the abbey site. But Gregory has refuges within a few miles, a choice of quiet and commodious manor houses. The baby thrives. The marriage, one judges, is happy. Poor Jane is lost, but her sister keeps her value. The young prince needs good uncles and protectors: Edward Seymour remains a councillor, and his brother Tom is in the privy chamber.

If Gregory still thinks about the misunderstanding over his bride, he shows no sign of concern. Father and son ride out together in the evening, the sun a perfect crimson orb above the line of the downs. The sky has become a mirror, against which the sun moves: light without shadow, like the light at the beginning of the world. Gregory's chatter stills; the creak of harness, the breathing of the horses, seems to muffle itself, so they move in silence, outlined against silver, tall against the sky; and as the upland fades into a pillowy distance, he feels himself riding into nowhere, a blank, where only memory stirs.

He thinks of those who he has known who have died by fire, as if they have fallen into the sun. Little Bilney; the sour and obstinate Tyndale; the young and tender John Frith.

When they ride down to their supper, the light is the colour of pigeons' feathers. He hands over his horse and puts on his public face. The gentry of east Sussex must be entertained, both early and late. Bess is a practised hostess, having filled the role for her first husband. Gregory is ebullient, good company, but still eager to listen and learn; his eyes travel often to his father's face. 'I wish Richard were here,' Gregory says. But Richard is setting up his household in Huntingdonshire, augmented by several abbeys. Around November, he thinks, I shall want Richard myself, to help me at the Tower.

At the end of August he arrests Geoffrey Pole. He is the youngest of the tribe and the least trusted – by his family, by his prince, and by himself.

He is in no hurry with Geoffrey. He is housed in circumstances that befit a gentleman who is cousin to the king. He is sure Reginald Pole can read the signal he sends. Reginald still has time to save his family. He can come home, and meet Henry face to face.

In the meantime he consults his memory and his files. He looks out reports from people close to the Poles: chaplains, servants, messengers and go-betweens. He sifts through papers from the days when the false prophetess arose in Kent and was entertained by the Courtenays. He combs through his transcript of the talks he had with Francis Bryan, two years back when he held him in the Tower. Francis is a mine of implication. His least word is a treasure trove of hints for the suspicious mind.

He is preparing to bring down two of the richest and most noble families in England. They have land all over the southern and western counties. If the Emperor invades he will set one of them on the throne: either Montague, Pole's brother, or Henry Courtenay, the Marquis of Exeter. If they choose to make Mary queen, it will be for her mother's sake; they will marry her into one family or the other, and make her their puppet, dancing between them.

The grandees of England claim descent from emperors and angels. To them, Henry Tudor is the son of Welsh horse-thieves: a parvenu, a usurper, a man to whom oaths may be broken.

In Canterbury, early July, he and the king had watched the new Becket play, devised by his man John Bale and acted by Lord Cromwell's Men. Some are survivors from George Boleyn's troupe. Some are young actors, not afraid of fresh plots, nor superstitious about putting new lines in the mouths of the dead.

Becket is England's saint, more proximate than St George. He was a real man, unlike some saints destroyed this summer; he was a Londoner, native of Cheapside. Before he was born his mother dreamed the river Thames was flowing through her body. She dreamed that her baby was out of her already, and lay on a purple blanket, looking up at the roof; the blanket unfolded by itself, and overspilled the bed, and overspilled the room, and she walked backwards, holding its hem, until she was walking to the rim of the universe, among the moon and stars.

Some say Becket's mother was a Saracen princess, but more likely she was a draper's daughter. Her son came from nothing, and rose by the king's favour to be Lord Chancellor, archbishop too. But once elevated he scorned princes, believing the old lie that popes are set above them; he thought all priests were above the law. When his king cried out against him, four loyal knights departed to Canterbury, to show him his errors.

These knights left their arms under a mulberry tree, and walked empty-handed to meet the archbishop. But finding him arrogant, hard-hearted and incapable of amendment, they picked up their weapons and pursued him into the cathedral, their metal feet ringing on the stonework. Becket could have hidden in the roof or crypt. Instead he stood by the altar of St Benedict, awaiting his dispatch.

The knights struck him with the flat of the sword, ordering him off holy ground. But Becket held up his hands and rolled his eyes to Heaven, swearing he would die where he stood. The first blow drew blood, which the archbishop wiped off with his sleeve. A second blow split his skull and brought him to his knees. He toppled forward, face down, and the broadsword of Richard le Breton swiped off the top of his skull. Then Sir Hugh de Morville planted his foot on the neck of the dying man, raked out the brains, and smeared them over the flags; adding, as a man of sense would, 'Now he will not get up again.'

As soon as the townspeople knew the killing was done, they crowded into the abbey, wailing and crying out against the knights. The monks crammed the corpse in a stone coffin and buried it in haste. But they took care to mark the spot where Becket died. The miracles began after two days. Frozen arms jerked in their sockets. Cripples danced. Hot as a devil's fart, word rattled around Europe that the knave was a martyr for our Holy Mother Church, whereas really he was a martyr for his own pride. Within two years the Pope made him a saint. The clamour for relics began. His blood, diluted so only the memory of it remained, was sold through the known world. The spot the monks had marked became his shrine. Even the lice from his hair shirt were sacred. Fifty years after his death his remains were placed inside a new and rich feretory, on a platform behind the high altar. Soon the faithful had plated the chest in gold and studded it with gemstones. The King of France gave a ruby the size of a hen's egg. Queen Katherine was often a pilgrim here. The Emperor Charles has prayed to the bones.

As for the guilty knights, they went to Rome and grovelled. The Pope sent them to the Holy Land to serve, knowing they would never come back alive. Becket was a vengeful man and his rancour did not die with him. In a Kentish town where the folk had laughed at him, he caused a generation of children to be born with tails. And in another place where he had been slighted he banished all the nightingales, so that to this day their song is never heard, neither by lover nor poet.

Each season the people of Canterbury re-enact Becket's death: it is the monkish version, because till now no other kind of history has been available. Crowds line the streets – excited, as if the tale might come out different this year. Hot pasties are sold. There are processions with drummers and pipes, and then the show begins. The knights get tuppence and some beer, but the lad who plays the saint gets a shilling, for the knights make him suffer, smashing him on the flags as the old archbishop was smashed. As Becket calls on Christ, a child crouching behind the altar squirts the scene with pig's blood. The actor is carried away. Then everybody gets drunk.

September: he himself, Lord Cromwell, arrives in Canterbury and calls together the worthies. These are not easy times for you gentlemen, but you must know that the king hates your saint, and if you want to keep your town's privileges you will show him your loyalty by keeping the streets quiet. It is true you will lose money when the pilgrims stop coming. But gentlemen, build up trade: don't cry on my shoulder, when here you are in rich wool country, surrounded by great harbours. You cannot continue an abuse which is an affront to reason, just because folk from overseas come by the thousand to gawp at it.

The town is full. He stays at the prior's lodgings, but every room is taken at the Porpoise, the Dolphin and the Mitre, at the Sun, the Crown and the Checker. The Bull Inn has even filled the bad rooms at the back, that overlook the shambles on Butchery Lane. The monks have had plenty of notice. They are not offering any resistance. They are only glad the priory itself is to remain open – or rather, be refounded by the king. Becket's shrine is not the first to be broken. The method is to strip the precious metals and gems, weigh and value them, and arrange transport to the king's treasury. Then, rebury the supposed saint in some decent but obscure spot.

On a fine autumn night they clear the precincts of the cathedral. Prior Goldwell begs to be excused the exhumation and retires to bed. The Vicegerent's party sits by the hearth till the small hours. When the night office is done, the hour for Lauds approaching, he gives the nod to Dr Layton, his commissioner.

A young monk leads them by a short route to the burial site. Keys turn behind them, bolts are slammed, bars dropped into their guards. The vast nave stretches away, a black and echoing expanse in which he has set men with dogs. He can hear their scrambling paws and their panting as they strain at their leashes. These are ban-dogs. Their jaws are like vices. They will nab any intruder and have him on the floor screaming. 'Sweeper!' their keepers call. 'Sturdy!' 'Diamond!' 'Jack!'

The monks of the advance party have lit torches around the tomb. He walks towards the light. He counts his witnesses: Layton's clerks, the chosen townsfolk. He wants every man where he can see him, no one loitering in the cavernous space. 'Loose the dogs.'

In the space of a breath, the black void fills with snarling. 'Jesu,' Christophe says. 'They sound like roving demons.'

He puts out a hand and finds the boy's shoulder. 'Stick close.' Even a Frenchman knows the legends of the shrine. As for those huddled bystanders from the town – guild officials, aldermen – they have been brought up on stories of those who, mishandling a saint's relics, were consumed by plague or leprosy, or were choked by invisible nooses and died twitching on the floor.

'We are ready,' he says. A monk is walking towards him and his eye catches the glint of metal. His hand flies to his chest, to his knife. But as the man steps into the flicker of light he sees it is not a weapon he is holding but Becket's skull. He has it tucked against his robes, as if it were a shy pet animal that feels the cold.

'Give it here,' he says. A cap of silver holds together the crazed fragments of bone. The lips of thousands have grazed this relic; but he is a whore's client with no time for kissing. He holds Becket up, eye to hollow eye; he looks into his vacancy. He turns the skull up, to see where it was chopped from the backbone. There is no record that the four knights cut off Becket's head. His admirers did that, later.

'Shall we have a look at the rest of him?' Dr Layton asks.

Now that the jewels and gilding are prised off, what rests on the flags is a serviceable iron chest, such as our forefathers used time out of mind. His fingertips graze its surface: common rust. 'Jesus, Layton,' he says, 'the monks missed a chance here, they could have scraped down the rust every spring and sold it for more than you could charge for powdered unicorn.'

'Hold up a light,' Layton says.

The chest has been sealed around with lead. 'See if it is still tight.' A workman crouches and examines the seal, feeling his way along the join. Dr Layton squats beside him: 'You would swear it has not been disturbed in years, my lord.'

Their anxiety is that the bones have been stolen by some dissident monk: that they have been sent by a courier to Rome, or tucked in some private ossuary till old times come again. But if the seal is intact, 'I could have been in my feather bed, Dr Layton.'

'Oh, I would not miss this,' Layton says. 'Not personally.'

The workman straightens up. 'Shall we do off the lid, sirs?'

A monk says, 'God in His mercy protect us.'

He is aware that some of the witnesses are retreating from the circle. 'Don't go too far, or the dogs will have you.' The workman is a stonemason, and has brought his own bag of tools. A blacksmith, he thinks, made them all. Some nameless smith three centuries past melted the lead to make the seal which we will now split and rip. He says, give us a chisel. He fingers the business end, passes it back. Some smiths cannot make chisels, or punches either – they have to re-dress them after every job. Walter used to say, you must wait, wait, wait, till the colour fades from sunset-red to ash. It's the last three hammer blows that count.

Each blow rings. One, two, three. He would rip open the chest himself, but: dignity of his office, the king's Vicegerent, Cromwell of Wimbledon, Lord Keeper of the Privy Seal. Knight of the Garter.

The mason exhales as he stands up. He walks around the chest and repositions himself, kneeling.

'Another torch,' he says. The flames lick, sway, and behind him there is a cry: 'Up there!' He whirls around, a black storm of velvet and fur. The dogs set up a thunderous barking. High above, a shape cuts through the space, swaying. He glimpses the edge of a wing – the outline, against the heights, of a huge bird or bat.

Cowled monks plummet to their knees. A body goes down and a head hits the flags. He calls for more light. Lanterns bob in the nave. The handlers whip back the dogs. 'Oh, by the thighs of Mary!' shouts

581

Christophe. High in the roof, thrown across the scaffolding, a stone-mason has left his coat. It stretches its arms, as if swimming through the black air.

The fallen man is slapped about the face and levered to the vertical. He is led away, shaking, by two fellow witnesses who will dine out on it for years. There is some uncertain laughter.

'I suppose that's not your coat?' Layton asks the mason.

The man shakes his head. He would cross himself if not encumbered with a chisel in hand. 'By St Barbara, I swear it moved,' a monk exclaims.

He says mildly, 'Masters, as you see, it is but a garment.'

Are these Englishmen? Are these the conquerors of Agincourt? Fear jumps and runs like fleas under the skin. Someone trundles up with a long pole and a short ladder, and prods at the coat as if it were a hanged man subject to indignities by the state. He says to the mason, 'Master? Will you proceed?'

Three more blows. Each one shuddering its way into the body, making the heart pound. 'Crowbar,' he says.

When the lid of the chest moves, a smell creeps out, a stench like a plague pit. It is like a knock with a cudgel. Every man steps back. He has a flask of *aqua vitae* in his coat. He takes a swig from it and passes it to Christophe. The boy gulps, coughs. 'I am on fire,' he says gratefully. 'Why did you not give me this before?'

'I am ready,' the mason says. 'Assist me, sirs?'

One-two-three: master and man heave the lid aside, upending it on the ground. Dr Layton is at his shoulder. In the shadows the monks trample and snuffle and pray out loud.

Inside the chest there is not enough to make a man. The saint's ribs are gone, unless ribs are what form this residue; his fingers dust through it. The long bones have been crossed – forearm and shin, thigh bone and the thick bone from the upper arm. They form a square: laid in the centre of it, a skull.

The mason says, 'Christ alive! Shall I, sir? Or will you?'

'You,' he says. 'Hold up so all can see. If I do it myself they will not believe it. They will think it is a conjuring trick.'

Arm raised aloft, the workman displays the skull. The witnesses gasp. The dogs set up a roar. Their shapes plunge and dart. 'Down, down!' their keepers shout. Only the cloth man hangs overhead, serene.

Well, says Dr Layton, either the silver skull is Becket or this one is; no saint is so special he has two heads.

The stench, he notices, is dissipating, or dispersing into a general foulness: the cooling sweat of fear, the fasting breath of early morning. He could swear some monk has pissed himself – or let us say it is one of the brutes running in the nave. He can pick out their shapes now, their muscular bouncing frames, their open jaws and lolling tongues. He turns up the skull between his hands. His fingers explore the calvarium. They emerge through the battered eye sockets. 'Well – whence comes this second relic?'

If this is Becket's skull, who is the nameless wretch in the silver cap, kissed more in death than in life, the lips of princesses pressed to his noddle? Did he die of an ague? Did he choke on a plum stone? Did the monks say, 'Nobody owns this fellow, we'll make him into a Becket?' Then bump his cadaver into a yard, and go at it with a hatchet?

He lays the naked skull back in the chest, between the crossed bones. This shrine is as thorough a forgery as you will get, he remarks. We do not even know if these are Becket's, these thighs, these shins. There could be any number of confused corpses here.

How cold it has grown: as if the year had leapt from leaf-fall to Advent. Dr Layton rubs his hands. 'Are we done, my lord? I will make a note of everything we have found. I have witnessed with my own eyes.'

The bell rings for the dawn office. When they step out into the air, they can see their breath. The stars fade around them. 'My lord Cromwell,' one of the monks says, 'we have prepared ...'

'Another tomb will not be needed. The king wants the bones.'

The man gapes at him. Only the cloister's long discipline stops him from crying out in distress. 'He will not be buried here?'

'Prise the silver from the skull,' he says. 'Have it weighed and list it with the other metal. Put what remains back into the chest, with the other skull, and indeed any more skulls you may turn up; it would not surprise me if that treacherous knave had six heads. I shall take the chest with me today. Give it to Monsieur Christophe here. You need not reseal it.'

The dogs are chained, led away – whining and grumbling, but wagging the stumps of their docked tails. After their night's work they are hungry for breakfast. As are we all, if we can cough up the poison from our throats. 'Give me that flask again?' Christophe says.

He passes it over. 'Keep it.' He pulls Christophe close and says in his ear, 'Get the bones to Austin Friars. If anyone asks where they are, they went on a cart and you never saw them after.'

He thinks, I want to be able to locate the knave at a moment's notice. The king spits at the name of Becket, but give him a year or two and he may change his mind, and make him a saint again. Sad, but those are the times.

The king has approved new injunctions this month. The Bible is to be read, the people are to learn their Commandments and their Creed, the priest is to teach them, a little and a little every week. 'But my lord Cromwell,' the king says, 'do not make my church strange to the people. Keep those images worthy of reverence. Retain all laudable ceremonies. Do not outrage my subjects with new and alien practices.'

The Germans say, 'We know you are on our side, Cromwell, no matter your caution.' Hugh Latimer says, 'More honest men have been promoted under you, these last five years, than in a hundred years before.' Thomas Cranmer says, 'You have given everything for the gospel: you have risked everything, everything you have and are.' Robert Barnes says, 'Suppose the king is losing his nerve?'

He feels as if their words are echoing in his head. He walks away. He is very tired: bone-weary, he says to himself. He wonders, where is my daughter Jenneke this morning? He feels as if he is drunk, as if he had emptied the flask himself; and he remembers a day, Putney, the riverbank, long ago, walking home in the dawn: he sees himself as if from the treetops, swaying from side to side, a small striving figure in the white light, with a taste of vomit in his mouth.

October brings Stephen Gardiner: rolling up from Dover with his baggage, aware he returns from France under a cloud. Bess Darrell, listening to the talk in papist houses, is sure that someone within our French embassy had contact with Reginald Pole last year, and told him where to move to avoid the king's agents. It would be neat to find Stephen was the traitor. The bishop has always been a stout defender of the king's title of Supreme Head. But those who know him have long believed what he says is different from what he thinks.

It has been good work to keep Gardiner out of England for three years. Now he sets Bonner, who is to succeed him as our envoy, to truffle through Stephen's files for any trace of those mishaps that occur in a diplomat's life. Bonner takes to it with relish. To give him rank, he has been promoted Bishop of Hereford, and can hardly believe his luck. His letters from France are gleeful, yet full of rancour and complaint, couched in phrases that make my lord Privy Seal laugh. His predecessor, he reports, was obstructive in the handover, and leaves behind him an embassy guest list that shows how much he enjoyed papist company. And his common table talk was how the king could be reconciled to Rome without losing face: and how he, Stephen Gardiner, Bishop of Winchester, was the man who would bring it about.

'Look,' he says to Rafe: he hands over Bonner's letter. What caterpillars these men be, who digest all before them, who fatten on the king's favour, who bite jagged holes in the commonwealth. They cocoon in dusty corners; one day they will split their casing and emerge in gaudy, flaunting their Roman vestments.

Bonner complains of Wyatt too. Wyatt was rude to him when they were in Spain, insufferable when they were in Nice. He was secretive. He was nonchalant when they were in peril. His housekeeping is extravagant: harlots pass in and out of the lodgings of his entourage. And also, Bonner says, Wyatt bears a grudge against the king about his imprisonment two years back, a grudge which he often airs.

He finds that believable. He finds it natural. A petty clerk like Bonner, he will never understand a man like Wyatt, unconstrained in action or speech. I have always been surprised, Richard Riche says, that Wyatt should be an ambassador. He seems to me to come from a former age, when such gallantries as his did not have to pass through the king's accounts.

Francis Bryan has crawled back to England sick enough to die. The king has kicked him out of the privy chamber, though Bryan swears all his excesses have been in England's service. His people take him off to the country, and write to Lord Cromwell begging for a kind word. 'You know you would miss him sorely,' Richard Cromwell says. 'Anytime you don't know what to do, you say, "Arrest Sir Francis Bryan!"'

He has nothing against Francis, personally. It is only out of a sort of affection that he calls him the Vicar of Hell. And it nettles him, that men are applying for his offices even before he is dead. He writes him a letter to encourage him to live, and he asks Dr Layton to send him some of the excellent pears he grows at his rectory at Harrow-on-the-Hill.

Mr Wriothesley, passing through Antwerp, carries a letter to Jenneke. He is unsurprised when he receives no reply: if she perceives a risk she should not take it. He thinks of her; he sees her sitting under the tapestry where her mother is in the weave; he sees her bold and bright on the page, when Anselma is a faded text. Her visit marks her place in the book of his life – a book which falls back into loose leaves. Printers can read as if through a mirror. It is their trade. Their fingers are nimble and their eye keen. But examine any book and you will see that some characters are upside down, some transposed.

November: the feasts of All Souls and All Saints. In the last few days William Fitzwilliam has been six times to the Tower to see Geoffrey Pole. Fitzwilliam has not hurt him, though he has mentioned the possibility of doing so. After the first interrogation, having somehow obtained a blade, the prisoner stabbed himself in the chest.

Nephew Richard goes to see the prisoner. He adds his persuasions to Fitzwilliam's. Just tell us everything, he says to Geoffrey; it couldn't be simpler. Open your heart, and throw yourself on the king's mercy. Do it before my uncle gets here.

Finally he, Lord Cromwell, arrives himself. 'How is Geoffrey today?'

The gaoler Martin says, 'Well enough. For a man with a hole in him.'

They had brought in surgeons, who declared it a small hole, and that in a week you would hardly see the mark. They had brought Geoffrey's wife, Lady Constance. After the visit she left by boat, tear-streaked and panic-stricken, exclaiming that Geoffrey would ruin his whole family. Fitzwilliam said, 'We should bring Constance before the council, she clearly knows a good deal. But my lord Privy Seal should talk to her first, he always makes progress with the ladies.'

Geoffrey has been cleanly kept these weeks. No one has insulted him, or spoken to him less than deferentially. But since his interrogations began, he has been taken lower, and his chamber smells stale. He has not been eating, his eyes are hollow. Seeing his visitor, he struggles up from his bed. Good manners, or alarm? 'Cromwell,' he says.

'I hear you punctured yourself.' He shakes his head. 'Dear God, Geoffrey, what were you thinking? Do you need to lie down again, or can you sit?'

Geoffrey looks at his stool dubiously, as if it might be a trick. Martin assists him to it.

'Fitzwilliam has been here,' Geoffrey says. 'With fifty-nine questions. Who would put fifty-nine questions? Why not sixty, I ask myself. He had a pattern drawn on his paper, and he made to write between the lines. I said to myself, this is some device of Cromwell's.'

It seems the grid on the paper has filled the prisoner with dread. It makes no more sense to him than a heptagram or other figure drawn by a magician. 'It's only to help the clerks,' he says. He sits down opposite Geoffrey, drawing his coat about him. 'It helps them record the dates and places and who was present when treason was spoken, or some treasonable act set in train. It is a help to us when the conspiracy is a big one. Especially when many of the wretches are related to each other and have similar names. You remember the Holy Maid? We used a device of that sort, when we questioned her.'

'The woman Barton? You harp on that still? Barton is hanged.'

It is Geoffrey's first flash of spirit; his hands tremble on the tabletop.

'Yes, she is good and dead,' he says. 'A poor simple country girl, who would never have thought of treason if the monks at Canterbury had not corrupted her. She forecast the king's death, and the death of his queen that was then. She foretold my death too. We were all dying and damned, she said – myself, my little nieces, the maid who brought her dinner when she lodged with me, and the spaniel who lay on her feet at night and kept them warm.'

'You lodged her?' Geoffrey is shocked. 'I did not know that. What did you do to her?'

He leans forward. 'Your family are lucky you were not all hanged with her. You were mired in Barton's schemes up to your necks, you and the Courtenays both. The king was merciful because he respected your ancient blood. But you know what I think of it. I respect it no more than I do your dung.' He looks up. 'Martin, I want two candles please.'

It is a fine afternoon, and though the window is small, there is a wan silver light outside. Geoffrey starts in his skin: 'Jesu, do not burn me!'

'Beeswax, Martin,' he says. 'A small size.'

Tallow would do, to burn a man. As the thought penetrates, he sees Geoffrey's shoulders ease. He says, 'I thought you and I understood each other.'

'Who can understand you, Cromwell?'

'I have been feeing you for years. And now I find you have wasted my substance. I paid you to watch your family and yet you appear to know nothing of their dealings. Is it negligence, or lack of capacity, or do you play me false?' When the man does not answer he says, 'Call it question sixty.'

Martin brings the candles and a pricket stand. 'Geoffrey,' he says, 'the French merchants have a custom they call the *vente à la bougie*. Suppose you have something to sell. It may be bales of wool, it may be a book, it may be a castle. All interested parties gather, there is some discussion, perhaps a glass of wine, and then the bidding begins, and lasts while the first candle burns. Martin, will you light one?'

'I know nothing of this practice,' Geoffrey says. 'I have never heard of it.'

'That is why I am explaining it to you. When the first candle is burned down, the bidding ceases. But then, who wants to make a hasty bargain? Buyer or seller, a man needs thinking time. A second candle is lit. There may be higher bids. When the second candle goes out the deal is done.'

A grating laugh. 'Do they not know their minds, these merchant friends of yours?'

'Oh, they are not my friends,' he says innocently. 'They are just divers Frenchmen, I don't know them personally. But I know how it works. The second candle tends to drive the bids up. A man thinks, I have put my best offer on the table ... but regret overcomes him, as he sees his chances melt away. He searches his pockets, taps his friends for a loan – he finds that his best offer is far better than he thought. Now, you have offered us a few scant pence. I think you are good for a thousand pounds. Dig into your resources, and find what you have that will persuade me.'

'What do I get?' Geoffrey says.

'*Caveat emptor*,' he says. 'This is the good part. You have to bid blind.'

He has a satchel of paperwork with him. While the candle is wasting and Geoffrey is sweating, he takes out a bundle and lays it on the table. Martin comes in and out with ink and sand and each time the gaoler goes out of the room Geoffrey follows him with his eyes, as if Martin's presence offered him some protection. 'Forgive me,' he says to Geoffrey, 'if I make use of the time. There is a letter here I must attend to, from Bishop Latimer. He is at Hailes Abbey, finding out one of their frauds. It is what they call the Holy Blood.'

Geoffrey Pole's hand twitches. At the mention of this very sacred residue, he wants to cross himself. But he does not think it would be wise.

'Latimer says it's some sort of gum. But if shown the coins of simple folk, it becomes liquid.' He returns to Hugh's letter. 'Don't hesitate to interrupt me when you are ready to bid.'

The next paper in his bundle should properly go to Richard Riche at the Court of Augmentations, as it relates to the surrender of the nunnery at Malling. But pinned to it is a note to him, from the abbess in her own hand. She is Margaret Vernon, Gregory's old tutor: she who so tenderly taught him to write his name and say his Ave. I'm coming to see you, she writes. I'm coming Friday. I can't travel up from Kent in one day. I'm getting old. I'll have to stop with you overnight.

'Martin,' he says, 'I feel in my bones that my friend will soon make me an offer. Bring my lord Southampton's interrogatories. So they are ready to my hand.'

'Southampton.' Geoffrey invests it with a sneer. 'It put him out of countenance, when I called him by his plain name Fitzwilliam.'

'I understand that. If I were made an earl, I would expect you to address me as one.'

'You?' Geoffrey laughs. 'That were a world where fishes walk.'

'And trees sing,' he agrees. 'I shall put questions now. You will offer answers. I shall see if I can accept them.'

'You have no proof,' Pole bursts out. 'All you allege is words, words, words. But you cannot prove any of them were ever spoken.'

'I have letters.'

'My brother burns his letters.'

'Your brother Montague? I wonder why? A heap of ashes may be eloquent.'

It is now late in the afternoon. He glances through Fitzwilliam's notes, and allows a silence to blossom. He feels Pole watching him. The first candle is spent and Martin, glancing at him for permission, kindles the second from its stub. 'This is what they call *le dernier feu*. While the light lasts, I am accepting bids.'

'I will not play your game.'

'It is a serious transaction, I assure you. I am still in the market. Help me fill in the grid. Part of it is done but you will see,' he holds the paper up, 'there are spaces. If between us we can complete it, I will offer you your life. It will be on my terms, not yours, but still it will be your life. You may live quiet. Away from the court. I am not a hard man. You will have a competence. Enough to live as a gentleman.'

Let Pole wrestle with that. He picks up Margaret Vernon's letter. She wishes to strike a bargain. Let me sell off one of the abbey manors, I'll pay the sisters their pensions out of it yearly, and settle up with the servants. What's left will be my portion for life. Enough for a woman on her own. I know people who will give me a home.

He thinks, I do not seem able to help women. Dorothea. My daughter. Lady Rochford. They present me with their pain and longing. They tell me they are lost and confused and fatherless and out of hope. I give them money. Or in the case of the king's daughter, a horse, a jewel, a piece of advice.

The sun has slid away. *Le dernier feu* burns orange. 'Speak to me, Geoffrey. When the last fire is done we will be in the dark. Then I will break your legs. And that will be just the start of it.'

Pole leaps up from his stool. A jolt rocks the table and the draught he makes causes the flame to buckle. He, the Lord Privy Seal, reaches out, closes a hand round the candlestick; it is a cheap thing, tarnished pewter. 'Steady!' he says. 'Do not shorten your time. You may still trade. No? Then will you fetch the frame, Martin?'

'The frame?' Geoffrey says. 'What is that?'

'It is a sort of vice, in which we clamp the limb to be broken.'

Martin, uncertain, does not move. 'I am sure, sir,' he says to Pole, 'you would not want my lord to go to that trouble.'

'Observe the candle,' he suggests.

'Mother Mary protect me,' Pole says.

'She will not.' His tone is bored. Outside the moon is rising. His mind keeps straying back to Margaret and her letter. 'Do you know,' he says to Geoffrey, 'I'm weary of this. Fetch the mallets as well, Martin.'

He settles back to his papers. What Margaret Vernon asks is unusual but not unreasonable. Her terms are precise – she is a woman who knows some law – and her figures look sound at first glance. Geoffrey on his stool is trying to make himself narrow. His shoulders are drawn up, his eyes closed. If you laid your hand on him you would feel every pulse in his body jumping.

Martin comes in. 'Is this what you require, sir? The frame is on its way.'

He had imagined a wooden-headed mallet, short-handled, for tapping in the wedges to hold the limb rigid. What Martin has brought is another kind of instrument, a weapon not a tool, with a handle three foot long. 'That would smash the head of a Scot,' he says admiringly. He stands up and takes it from Martin. 'Just the one? It will do for now.'

The weapon's head is solid and cold against his palm. He tests the weight of the whole, holding it away from him, at a right angle to the stone flags. Then he drops his arm and swings the hammer, experimentally. He likes the sensation. The pleasant sway of the body; the moment of balance, control, then the growing impulsion, the motion from the heels up. It takes you beyond yourself, into a pleasant giddiness, such as you might feel with a woman: a lightness, when you reach the point of no return.

The noise when the hammer hits the wall is enough to wake the dead. It knocks Geoffrey's stool from under him, jerks him to his feet. 'Jesus!'

While the light is still quivering, while their ears are still ringing, he says, 'We can start without the frames. Perhaps they are in use elsewhere. Martin, will you gather up those papers? They are the king's affairs, and I would not want blood on them.' With his right hand he grips the hammer and with his left he pinches out the candle.

Later, outside, Martin leans against the wall, shaky. 'You said, fetch the frame. I thought, Mother Mary, what does he mean, I don't know any frame.'

'There are such things. I have seen them. Not here. In other prisons.'

'I can imagine them,' Martin says.

'So could Geoffrey.'

In the room behind them the prisoner weeps. There is no damage, not even a scrape to his shins. 'But would you do it?' Martin says.

There is little light: only one torch burning in its bracket. Somewhere a drip of water, actively corroding stone. It is the smell of these places that is the worst, the enclosed, stale air, the metallic tang of fresh blood, the sour reek of piss. 'I mean,' Martin says, 'could you smash a man's limbs, then go home to your supper and your family?'

'I haven't a family.'

'No,' Martin says. 'Begging your pardon. I know you haven't.'

'Although,' he says, remembering, 'I am a grandfather now.'

'I've seen people hung up,' Martin says.

'Sooner or later, you see everything.' He feels a weight in his chest; it is dull, the shape of the hammer head. He wishes he were back in time, before Geoffrey started to talk. He wants to swing the hammer again. The head was large and it diffused the impact, so it barely jarred.

'When they're hung by their wrists their own weight does it,' Martin says. 'You might say, they torment themselves.'

The manacles get you a result within twenty minutes. The cold sweat starts out of the man as if from a faucet. If you're short of time you can hang weights on his feet. You're across the room, your pen poised, when he breaks; no point being awash in other people's body fluids. Once you've taken down the first, virgin words of his confession, words that are green and sweet, the gaolers come and swab the snot, the tears, the loose stools that creep down his legs.

'There is a rack.' Martin indicates with his head. 'It is used. I've been in earshot.'

It is a nice question. Do you let the fellow scream? Some men who are used to the work say it is the prisoner's own wails that drive up the terror and make him speak. Others feel it's not worthwhile, for it agitates those who overhear; there are always clerks on hand, or gentlemen councillors, who may be sickened by the racket. In these cases, some means may be used, short of suffocating the prisoner, to stifle the noise. He says, 'The Spanish, when they burn what they call a heretic, they parade the poor soul through the streets. They sheet him in white, and shave his head and sometimes his eyebrows, so that he looks more like a puppet than a human. They put a taper in his hand, as if he were lighting the fire for himself. They promenade him across the cobbles with his feet bleeding and papers pinned to him proclaiming his heresy, and the monks process behind him with their silver crosses and their psalms. And the people line the streets to see it, the market squares. But when the whole city has viewed the spectacle, they burn him in private in some prison yard, with a gag in his mouth.'

'You have been in Spain, sir?'

'No, but Thomas Wyatt has told me, and when Wyatt tells you, it is as good as witnessing.'

Martin looks respectful. 'If your lordship recalls, I had the privilege to serve Master Wyatt when he was last in ward. Generous and open-handed.'

'Generous to a fault,' he says. 'Look, do not let Geoffrey injure himself again. Turn his clothes inside out and make sure he has not so much as a pin. He will give us no trouble now. The king will not inflict pains on any man from a noble house. I cannot think it has ever been done, not in his reign. But can they rely on that? The king has done a number of things that have never been done before.'

'He has not done the dungeon work,' Martin says.

Or mopped the floor afterwards. Or, on the execution ground, shaken adherent flesh from chains. He asks, 'What persuaded you into this trade?'

'A man must get a living.'

'You could have been an honest farmer.'

'And kill pigs?'

Sow seed, that's what he was thinking. Harvest the grain. There is a pure, clean world, where men subsist on milk and apples, and bread so white and soft it is like eating light. He says, 'William Fitzwilliam is on his way. And Richard Riche, and Richard my nephew. Now Geoffrey is babbling, they will be able to fill in the grid. And we can do as we like hereafter with his kin. A good day's work, I call it.' And all from smashing a mallet against a wall. 'When they're done, take Geoffrey upstairs. Give him his supper, if he can eat it. Cut up his meat for him.'

Martin looks chastened. 'When we took his knife away, he threatened to hang himself from a beam.'

'I am not afraid of that.' It would take a resolution he doubts Geoffrey could summon. 'Still, if he does, it is no great matter. Though it must be clear it is by his own hand.'

'Do you want me to give him a rope?'

'I wouldn't go that far.'

Soon reinforcements arrive, with a brace of clerks carrying ink-horn and paper. 'You boys stay out in the fresh air,' he tells the clerks. 'Or do you follow Martin here, he will get you some ale. Richard Riche will write for us, won't you? I have another sixty-two questions for Geoffrey. If we get tired we'll whistle for you.'

The clerks look grateful. He watches them out of the passage and waits till they mount the twisting stair. He says, 'Geoffrey will talk around the point. He will blizzard you with "I swear it was October but it could have been March," and "I believe it was in Sussex or else it was in Yorkshire," and "It might have been my mother or it might have been the Wife of Bath." Nail him down on threats to the king himself – threatening his councillors, that is no news, we know his brother Montague hates us. Chapuys is one of the chief doers in their plots, and that is no news either. But I think the King of France is deeper in this than a brother monarch should be.'

'If François invaded,' Richard Cromwell says, 'I believe he would put the King of Scots on our throne.'

'Yes. But Exeter's people don't know that. Or the Poles. They have such pride of their persons. They think they will all be kings.'

'I fear we lack proof against Exeter,' Fitzwilliam says. 'He is a cautious man, he destroys his traces. Geoffrey will give us enough on his own family, but –'

'But it will stretch,' Riche says. 'They are known confederates, the two houses.'

'You recall I have a woman with the Courtenays,' he says.

Riche says, 'What, some laundrymaid?'

Fitz laughs: 'Leave Cromwell to his devices.'

Riche says, 'I do not see how the Lady Mary can be left out of it this time. Surely, if they were planning to make use of her, she cannot be ignorant of that?'

'That were great pity,' Fitzwilliam says. 'To see a princess destroyed, on suspicion.'

He says, 'They abuse her trust. She would never strike down her own father.'

'We have been here before,' Riche says. 'You are too lenient. You do not see her nature, sir.'

'What did you do to Geoffrey?' Fitzwilliam asks.

He bundles his papers under his arm. They are strung with twine, Margaret Vernon's note with the rest. He had run her figures in his head, while Pole was confessing. 'I made a noise,' he says.

He thinks, I took up residence in the pit of his stomach. What do I ever do?

A week on, he will hear what the people of London are saying: that Gregory Pole was tortured at the Tower: that he was strapped to a grid, and it was heated, so he was grilled like St Lawrence the martyr. That Thomas Cromwell did it all.

He is shocked when he sees Margaret Vernon. It is disconcerting to see her dressed like a burgess's wife, although he himself has recommended nuns lay aside their habits. Fashion is shifting. Women are showing their hair again. Margaret's is silver. He asks her, 'What colour was it before?'

'No especial colour. Mouse.'

They are at Austin Friars in the parlour. She has been waiting for him. He feels he should have changed his own clothes. He feels there might be blood on them, though no blood has been shed at the Tower. Geoffrey has admitted he planned to go abroad, with a band of men to join his brother Reginald. He speaks of confederacies in closets and in garden arbours, plots over supper and after Mass. He reports dubious talk overheard: from Thomas More's family, from Bishop Stokesley. The ripples spread wider, wider with each whispered phrase. Signing off his statement for the day, he begs the king's mercy. At the foot of the page he scribbles, *Geoffrey Pole your humble slave.*

Margaret says, 'You are stouter, Thomas. You look as if you don't get any fresh air.'

'Sometimes I try to get out with my falcons,' he says. 'But the king might call me back at any time. The Venetians, you know, they draw a line on their ships to see that they don't overload them. I have no load line. Or none that the king can see.'

'You don't have enough help? All these boys ...'

He thinks, no one can help. It's just Henry and Cromwell, Cromwell and Henry. 'Once I took Michaelmas Day off, because it is a lawyers' holiday, but the king objected. His reasoning is, he doesn't get a day off, every day he has to rule. I say, but Majesty, you are divinely anointed, you are granted a special grace that means you are never tired. He says, it's thirty years since I was crowned. It must have run out.'

'You ought to have a wife.'

'Well, get me one. If you know a comfortable woman, send her my way. I do not want for fortune so she need not bring a penny, she needs no great wit and she need not be young. All I stipulate is that she not be a papist, and subvert my household.'

Margaret laughs. 'What a pity, because soon there will be a pack of young women turned out of their cloister, but I fear some of them cleave to Rome. Not I. I took my oath to the king and meant it.'

He says, 'I think the king will not allow a woman to marry, if she has been a nun. Not if she was sworn and professed.'

'So where would he have my sisters live? Southwark, in the stews?'

He wants to beg her, don't be angry. Angry people fill my life. 'You should go and see Gregory. If you want a home, he would welcome you. I am sure he would be pleased for you to teach his son as you taught him.'

She shakes her head. 'I shall set up housekeeping with some of my sisters. We shall be unruly women, with no master.'

'You will give scandal,' he says.

'We are too old for it. Folk will pity us, and leave apples on our doorstep. They will come to us for poultices and lucky charms. All the same,' her face softens, 'I should like to see my little boy.'

'My wife – Elizabeth – she used to be jealous of you.'

Margaret says calmly, 'There was no need.'

He thinks, if it could be held that Katherine of Aragon was no wife, if it could be held that Anne Boleyn was no wife, might it not be discovered that Margaret Vernon was no nun? Could we not find an error in the paperwork? Then she would be free.

But what's the point? he thinks. She would die and leave me. Or I would die and leave her. It's not worth it. Nobody's worth it.

In the first week of November he arrests Lord Montague and the Marquis of Exeter. He detains Constance, Geoffrey's wife, and Gertrude, the marchioness, and some other of the king's old friends. He sends Fitzwilliam down to Margaret Pole at her castle in Sussex. Keep at it, he says: question her day and night if you have to.

But Fitz gets nothing from the countess. Her answers, he says, are earnest, vehement and precise. She denies any wrongdoing or intent to do wrong. When Fitzwilliam calls her son Reginald an ingrate bastard, she says, not a bastard, no: I was ever true to my lord husband, I was a wife beyond reproach.

She admits that when she knew Reginald had evaded harm, she expressed relief: she is his mother, after all. Yes, she knows that he despises her for keeping faith with the Tudors. Does she know he has said he will tread her under his feet? She purses her lips. 'I know, and must abide it.'

Fitzwilliam tells Margaret Pole to pack her bags. He means to bring her on a litter to his own house at Cowdray. When he tells her that her household goods are to be inventoried, she knows her long run of good fortune is over; the wheel has turned, and she is going down. For the first time, Fitz says, dismay shows on her face. But that is nothing to the dismay on the face of Lady Fitzwilliam, when he tells her the Countess of Salisbury will be living with them, for how long no one knows.

He himself, at the Tower, questions Margaret's eldest son. Detached, disdainful, Montague often declines to reply. 'My lord, witnesses have heard you say you never liked the king, not from boyhood.'

Montague shrugs: as if to say, that is my privilege.

'False reports have come out of your household, that parish churches are to be pulled down. You know there is no rumour more calculated to bring simple people out under arms. Why did you not intervene?'

'It is hard to stop rumours,' Montague says. 'If you can do it, let me know your method. I assure you, it was not I who started them.'

'Did you say ...' he consults his papers, '... that the king killed his first wife by unkindness? That he next married a harlot? That he bred a bastard?'

'Women's things.'

'Did you say the Turk is a better Christian than the king?'

'Did Geoffrey tell you that?' Montague laughs.

He presses on: has Montague conferred with Lord Exeter, as to how many men they can raise between them? Has he said it is not enough to kill the king's councillors, one must also aim at their head? And is this not plain treason?

'I suppose it would be,' Montague says.

He goes to the Marquis of Exeter. He has fewer cards in his hand, and Exeter knows it. But both the Poles and the Courtenays, in recent years, have dismissed any servants they suspected of favouring the new learning, or of Bible reading. They have dug, therefore, a deep well of resentment on which he may draw. It takes just a little time to fetch up the bucket.

He says, 'Lord Exeter, you have been in company where the king has been called a beast.'

Exeter sighs. 'Is this the best poor Geoffrey can do?'

'You have said, the king and Cromwell are alike, they disdain the whole realm to get what they want.'

Exeter rolls his eyes.

'Have you not said, "All the king's pretensed authority cannot cure his sore leg"? Have you not said, "His leg will kill him one day"? Have you not said, "When Henry dies, then goodnight Master Cromwell"?'

Exeter makes no reply.

'Have you not said, "We may have a prince but he will soon be dead, the whole Tudor line is accursed"?'

Exeter bridles: 'I do not deal in curses.'

'No,' he says. 'Women's things. Perhaps your wife does?'

Richard Cromwell steps in. Has Lord Exeter not taken abbey lands?

Yes.

Accepted them of his own free will?

Yes.

Excused himself, saying God will forgive him, as they will all be restored to the monks one day?

Silence.

'How could that be?' Richard asks.

'By a reversal of policy,' Exeter says. 'The king might repent.'

'Or join again with Rome?'

'You cannot rule it out.'

He smashes his hand down on the table. 'Believe me, I can.'

He talks to Gertrude, Exeter's wife. She is the man of the household, a bold and enterprising woman, constantly seeking to advance the family she has married into. Her stepmother was Spanish, one of Katherine's ladies; no wonder she is drawn, he observes, to the company of the Emperor's ambassador, Chapuys. No wonder they confide in each other.

It is hard to abash Gertrude. He has let her go free before, so she thinks he is soft-hearted. 'I beg the king to stay his hand,' he tells her. 'God knows, my lady, he has been merciful in your case. Myself, I always hope folk will amend.' He looks at her, sorrowful. 'I am often disappointed.'

He walks out. Says to his people, 'We must lay hold of the child. I mean, Exeter's son.'

They stare at him. He says, 'When have you known the king harm a child? But all the same, fetch him.'

Richard Cromwell says, 'We cannot risk Exeter's heir being taken out of the country, to gather supporters abroad.'

'And bring in Montague's son too,' he says. 'Henry Pole is of like age.'

It is a cataclysm. They are down, the great families, falling like skittles when a giant bowls; swept from the shelves like jugs in an earthquake.

Bess Darrell is brought to the Tower. No one raises an eyebrow over it, since all Gertrude's women are questioned. Bess is her angel self: her golden hair, her eyes of cornflower blue. She gives him facts on paper, letters she has copied. She gives him samples of treason embroidered: the pansy for Pole, the marigold for Mary. But when he has done with her she asks, 'What now? Must I go back and live amongst these people? What shall I say, when they ask me what I told Cromwell?'

'Say you told me your dreams.'

They set great store by dreams, these families. They are always writing them down under seal and sending them to each other by fast courier. Many nights, it seems, they dream the king is dead. Sometimes they dream Jane Seymour comes in her shroud, to tell the king she hates him and he is damned.

He says, 'You cannot go back among the Courtenays because they will not exist. When you leave here you will go to Allington.'

She looks up. 'And what will I do there?'

'Live and make no stir.'

'You will bring Wyatt home?'

He nods. 'Though I cannot say when.'

'They say the king is not satisfied with him.'

'He is not satisfied with any of us.'

601

He thinks, we do not even know that Wyatt is still alive. But I trust his skill in locating his peril and moving away from it. Or not, if stasis is best: Wyatt stood while a lioness stalked him.

Bess Darrell says, 'Lord Montague calls England a prison. He says it has been a prison these last six years.'

'Too kind a gaol for him to leave,' he says. 'They sicken me. They are cowards. If he had flown across the sea to Reginald, at least I would respect him. He would have shown himself a man, to be taken under arms.'

'It would have made your task easier,' Bess says. 'No doubt of their treason then. But apart from what I have supplied, you have nothing but Geoffrey's nonsense, and hearsay and rumour and kitchen boys' gossip. They will not oblige you, Montague and Exeter, unless you rip their treason out of them, and you cannot do that.'

'I am very ingenious,' he says sadly. 'And your testimony is a great help.'

'But think, my lord. If you call a traitor everyone who has voiced a dislike of the king or his proceedings, who does that leave alive?'

'Me,' he says. Henry and Cromwell. Cromwell and Henry.

'Exeter thinks the world will turn,' Bess says. 'He knows Henry is afraid of excommunication. He thinks a show of force will bring him back to Rome.'

'He will not turn,' he says. 'Too much has been said and done in England. The king cannot resist change even if he would. Let me live another year or two, and I will make sure what we have done can never be undone, not by any power on earth. And even if Henry does turn, I will not turn. I will make good my cause in my own person. I am not too old to take a sword in my hand.'

'You would take arms against Henry?' She seems entertained, more than shocked.

'I did not say that.'

She looks down at her hands, wearing Wyatt's ring. 'Oh, I think you did.'

* * *

Mid-November: with the first foul weather, you may witness a Cambridge man, a priest, committing a slow public suicide. One man, taking on the king: one puny challenger against the giant, his person small as a crumb, his weapons straw.

His name is John Lambert, though he was born Nicholson. He was ordained priest, and knew Little Bilney, who converted him to the gospel. He went to Antwerp, chaplain to the English merchants; his path crossed every dangerous path, Tyndale's included. Thomas More, he says, tricked him back to England. Then old Archbishop Warham – Canterbury, that was – hauled him up for heresy, charging him in forty-five articles, which he rebutted. Yes, he admitted, he had studied Luther's work, and he found himself the better man for it. He agreed with Luther that it was lawful for a priest to marry. The question of free will, he called too hard a matter for a simple man. But he believed only Christ, not priests, could forgive sin. Scripture has all we need, he said. We do not need the extra rules Rome has made up.

In the middle of the hearing, Warham died. The case was allowed to lapse. But the passage of four, five years has not made Lambert cautious. At Austin Friars – no clerks present, no record kept – Thomas Cranmer has reasoned with him. He, Thomas Cromwell, has argued with him fiercely. And Robert Barnes has stood by, his face pinched with dislike and fear: bursting out at last, 'You – whatever you call yourself – Lambert, Nicholson – you will ruin us all.'

Cranmer had said, 'We do not quarrel with your views –'

'Yes, we do,' Barnes said.

'Well then, we do – but the chief thing is, be circumspect. Be patient.'

'What, wait till you crawl in my direction? Play the man, Cranmer, stand up for the truth. You know it now, in your heart.'

Barnes says, 'Lambert, you question baptism itself –'

'There is baptism in the scriptures. But not of infants.'

'– and you question the eucharist, the sacrament of the altar. Now, if you do that, if you do it openly, I cannot protect you and I will not, and he,' he points to the archbishop, 'will not, and he,' – he points to the Lord Privy Seal – 'he will not either.'

'I tell you what I will do,' Lambert says. 'I will spare you torment. I will go over your heads. I will put my case to the king himself. He is head of the church. Let Henry judge me.'

The king – let no man be astonished – has risen to the challenge. At Whitehall he will debate with Lambert in public. 'Cromwell, are the ambassadors coming?'

Europe calls the king a heretic – so now let Europe see and hear him defend our common faith. Pole asserts he is inferior in learning to men like More and Fisher, the blessed dead. He will show the contrary. Rows of benches are set out for the spectators.

'Pray God the king does not get a fall,' Rafe Sadler says. 'Lambert is a student of languages. He can cite the scriptures in tongues ancient and modern.'

He is rueful. 'I always told the king, English is enough.'

He thinks, for every point Lambert scores, I will smart.

He has done his best to deter Henry from putting on this show. He does not need to answer Lambert, he tells him – he has bishops to take care of it. But Henry is not listening. It is only the day before the debate that he senses the discomfort of his advisers. 'What, do you fear for me? I am well able for any heretic. And I must carry the torch of faith high, where my friends and enemies can see it.'

He says, and when will your Majesty begin to carry it? 'About noon,' Henry says. 'And by twilight we should be done.'

Early on the morning of the hearing, he receives Lisle's wife, over from Calais. There is no one, other than Stephen Gardiner, whom he would less like to see before breakfast.

He knows Lady Lisle dislikes him. She dislikes what he is – a jack-in-office – and makes him feel that his manner, his address, gives him away as a pot-boy. All the same, she chatters gaily about the terms on which she will sell him her Gloucestershire property. You would think all was merry in Calais; she does not mention the stream of disaffected informants who roll up to his various houses, some of them still green from the sea-crossing. She does not mention the folk in custody at the Tower, though surely they are cousins of hers; all these people are related. Only she says, 'I hear you are busy, Lord Cromwell. Never too busy to get land, are you? I said to my husband, depend upon it, Cromwell will make time for me. He wants what I have.'

'How is my lord Lisle? John Husee says he is melancholy.'

'It would cheer him to have reward for long service.'

'The king has offered him two hundred pounds a year.'

'I would it were four hundred.'

He suppresses a smile. 'I will ask. I promise nothing.'

'If the king speeds well with the heretic, he will be in a giving humour come this evening. Well,' she gets up, 'I must speed away myself. The sooner I am back in Calais, the better my lord will like it. He says he would rather lose a hundred pounds than spend a week without me.'

'If he had it to lose,' he says, before he thinks.

'That's up to you,' she says. 'Try and work it, won't you, Master Cromwell?' She laughs, excuses herself. 'My lord, I should say.'

'Yes, you should,' he says. 'You should know by now.'

'I mean no slight. What the king has made you, that thing you are. But do you wonder my lord is miserable? So many nobodies are enriched, while we must scrape.'

Lady Lisle cannot get women to serve her, she is so demanding. But old Lisle is in love with her, he thinks: his hard, bright, selfish bride.

It is gone ten o'clock. At Westminster the bishops are waiting: the members of the king's council, the gentlemen of the privy chamber, the mayor, the aldermen, officers of the London guilds. Christophe helps him into his coat. 'Bishop Gardineur will be with you,' he reminds him. 'Today he will enjoy himself, for surely this poor Lambert will burn? For who can deny baptism? Before St Christophe was baptised, he was a dog's-head cannibal. His name was not Christophe, but Abominable. After he was baptised he was human, and could pray. Before, he could only bark.'

He says, 'I know your name is not really Christophe. You had another. Fabrice, was it not?'

'Christophe was my Calais name. On Calkwell Street. Before Fabrice I was Benoît, a very good little boy. But it does not matter what I was christened. I have forgot.'

He thinks, it is not baptism that will undo Lambert, it is *corpus Christi*, it is the body of Christ.

Stephen Gardiner, sweeping in: he checks his pace, they halt, they square up; they do off their hats to each other, respectful men, elaborately polite. But with Stephen, politeness only ever lasts a blink.

'I don't know what you have been doing in my absence,' Stephen says. 'I don't know why you would tolerate an anabaptist. Unless of course you are one.'

In fantasy, he takes off his coat again. He rolls up his sleeves, and punches Stephen on the nose. It is dismaying to him, that Stephen has been gone three years, and his urge to knock him down is as strong as ever.

'Is it likely?' he says. 'These people you call anabaptists will take no oaths. They will serve no kings. Not only do they deny the commonwealth their labour, the magistrate their obedience, but they deny the child his book. They love ignorance. They say we live in the last days, so why learn anything? Why tend crops, why store grain: there is no need of a harvest.'

'Oh well,' Gardiner says, 'one sees their point, if Christ's coming is imminent. Which I do not believe. But I thought you might.'

'You know I have nothing to do with this sect.'

'Perhaps not.' Stephen smiles. 'After all, you take conspicuous thought for the morrow. You lay up treasure on earth, don't you? Indeed you do little else.'

'Now you are back in the jurisdiction,' he says, 'you will see what I do.'

* * *

At midday the king comes in, announced by trumpets. The day is dark but Henry is wearing white from head to foot. He looks like a mountain that one hears of in fables, made of solid ice.

The king takes his place on the dais beneath his canopy of estate. The tiered benches are packed. The clergy sit at the king's right hand, his noblemen on his left. The hall is hung in splendour, a blur of pennants and flags, and tapestry has been brought from the Wardrobe, so that giant Bible figures preside over the scene: Daniel, Job, Solomon without Sheba.

He, the Vicegerent, takes his seat. Bishop Tunstall gives him a courteous nod. Bishop Stokesley glares. Dr Barnes appears like a graven image. Cranmer seems to have shrunk. Hugh Latimer keeps leaping up and down, running to this one and that, tapping shoulders, whispering, passing notes. He says to Cranmer, 'Has Hugh briefed the king?'

'We have all briefed him.' Cranmer seems surprised. 'Have not you?'

'I would not presume. He is closer to God than I am.'

When they bring John Lambert in, his step is firm, his face resolute. But as he looks around him, takes in the grandeur of the hall, you can see he is overwhelmed. He stares at the king, at his shining slopes, and then begins an obeisance – he does not know whether to bow or kneel.

He, Thomas Cromwell, sees Dr Barnes smile. He hears Stokesley shift on his bench, a smug rustle. He swings around and glares: 'A little charity?'

'Hush,' Cranmer says.

They have built a platform so Lambert can be seen from all parts of the hall. He stops before it, like a horse that has seen a shadow in the trees. Urged to mount the steps, he creeps up as if it were a scaffold. He faces the king. His head turns, seeking faces he knows, but when he finds them, in the dim light of noon, he finds them stony.

Henry leans forward. This hearing has no precedent, therefore no rules, but the king has decided to run it like a courtroom. 'Your name?'

John Lambert is used to defending himself in small rooms. He is courageous, but he is not a man who has ever had to rise to an occasion: and here is his king, the maker of occasions.

His voice seems faint, as if it is coming from another era. 'I was born John Nicholson. But I am known as John Lambert.'

'What?' The king is shocked. 'You have two names?'

Lambert recoils. He sinks onto one knee.

Gardiner murmurs, 'Wise move, fellow.'

The king says, 'I would not trust a man with two names, even if he were my own brother.'

Lambert is taken aback by the king's plain speaking. Did he expect a learned oration? That is to come: but Henry moves, unerringly, to the ground of their quarrel. 'The body of Christ. Is it present in the sacrament?'

When the king says *corpus Christi*, he puts his hand to his hat, in reverence.

Lambert observes the gesture. His shoulders hunch. 'Your Majesty being so well-learned, a prince of rare sagacity –'

'Lambert, Nicholson,' the king says, 'I did not come here to be flattered. Just answer.'

'St Augustine says …'

'I know about Augustine. I want to hear from you.'

Lambert flinches. He is kneeling now and he does not know at what point he can stand up. It is a form of torture he has devised for himself. The king glares at him. 'Well? What do you say? Is it Christ's flesh, His blood?'

'No,' Lambert says.

Stephen Gardiner slaps his knee, lightly. Bishop Stokesley says, 'May as well set fire to him now. Why drag it out?'

The king's face flushes. 'What about women, Lambert – is it lawful for a woman to teach?'

'In case of necessity,' Lambert says. The bishops groan.

And the word 'minister', the king demands, what does he take to be its meaning? The word 'church'? The word 'penance'? Should the faithful make private confession? Does he think priests may marry?

'Yes,' Lambert says. 'Any man should, if he has not the gift of chastity. St Paul is clear in the matter.'

Robert Barnes says, excuse me. He gets up, blundering over the feet of the learned divines.

'My lord archbishop,' the king says, 'will you stand up now, and show Lambert or Nicholson why he is wrong?'

Cranmer rises. Cuthbert Tunstall leans forward: 'My lord Cromwell, why does Lambert have two names? It seems to trouble the king as much as his heresies.'

'I believe he changed it to evade persecution.'

'Hmm.' Tunstall sits back. 'He had better have changed his views.'

Cranmer is on his feet. His manner is tentative: 'Brother Lambert ...'

The people at the back shout they cannot hear.

Robert Barnes has returned. Excuse me, lords, pardon me: blundering over their feet again. He looks sick. Perhaps he has been. Cranmer says, 'Brother Lambert, I am going to show you some passages in scripture which I believe prove you wrong, and if you admit my texts well-founded, then I think you must concede to my opinion and the king's. But if –'

Stephen Gardiner is shifting in his seat. While Cranmer makes his case he keeps up a buzz of commentary, no doubt too low for the king to hear. Bishop Shaxton shushes him. Hugh Latimer glares at him. Stephen ignores them, and even before Cranmer has finished he is on his feet.

Cuthbert Tunstall says, 'My lord of Winchester, I believe I am listed to speak next?'

Gardiner bares his teeth.

Tunstall looks about for help. 'Gentlemen?'

Cranmer slumps in his chair. Hugh Latimer says, 'Perhaps the Vicegerent is next?'

He, Cromwell, holds up a palm: not I.

Bishop Shaxton is waving the list. 'You are number six, Gardiner. Sit down!'

The Bishop of Winchester takes no notice at all. He just carries on, talking a man to death, tripping him and goading him into the flames where he will scream and bleed.

Two o'clock. The king is magisterial. He is nimble, he is trenchant; he is, at times, humble. He does not want to kill Lambert, that is of no interest to him. He wants to out-reason him: so that in the end, Lambert will crumple and confess: 'Sire, you are the better theologian: I am instructed, enlightened and saved by you.'

You would not hear François engage with a subject in close debate, nor would he be capable of it. You would not find the Emperor fighting to save the life of a miserable subject. They would bring in their Inquisitors, and break Lambert in the torture room.

He, Cromwell, thinks of the tournament, the score sheet, the record of each atteint: *broken on the body*. Each time the king collects his horse and couches his lance, he pauses, makes Lambert some kind of offer. A prospect of mercy. Your life – if you withdraw, concede, and then beg. Asked if he believes in Purgatory, Lambert says, 'I believe in tribulation. One may go through Purgatory in this world.'

'It is a trick,' Hugh Latimer mutters. 'The king does not believe in Purgatory himself.'

'Well, not today,' Gardiner says.

Three o'clock: piss break. Origen cited, St Jerome, Chrysostom, the prophet Isaiah. Outside, Gardiner says, 'I cannot think why the old charges against Lambert were ever dropped. A change of archbishop is no excuse. You should have been on top of that, Cromwell.'

Stokesley says, 'You don't seem to be taking much interest in the case, my lord Privy Seal.'

'I wonder why,' Gardiner says. He spies Latimer. 'What about you, are you profiting from the king's learning?'

Hugh growls like a terrier before a bull.

It takes some time for all the spectators to file to their places, to cease coughing and settle. Then all eyes turn to him, the king's Vicegerent. He lurches to his feet. 'Majesty, having heard your reasoning, and that of the bishops, I have nothing to add, and I do not think anything is wanting.'

'What?' Gardiner says behind him. 'Nothing is wanting? Go on, Cromwell, reason on the case. You think no one wants to hear you? I want to hear you.'

The king glares. Gardiner throws up his hands, as if in apology.

It is Lambert's turn to speak. And turns are observed – except by Stephen. Lambert has negotiated himself from his knees to his feet, but four hours have gone by and nobody has offered him a chair. Twilight: his shoulders sag. The torches come in. As their light plays over the faces of the bishops, the king says, 'It is time, Lambert. You have heard all these learned men. So now, what do you think? Have we persuaded you? Will you live or die?'

Lambert says, 'I commend my soul into God's hands. My body, into your Majesty's. I submit to your judgement. I rest in your clemency.'

Don't, he thinks. Not there.

Henry says, 'You hold the sacrament of the altar to be a puppet show.'

'No,' Lambert says.

The king holds up a hand. 'You say it is an illusion. That it is an image only, or figure. You are confounded by one text, the words of Jesus: *Hoc est corpus meum*. It is the plainest text of all. I will not be a patron to heretics. My lord Cromwell, read the sentence against this man.'

He picks up the documents. In such cases they are prepared in advance. Stokesley says he alone has burned fifty heretics, and even if he is just bragging, there is a form for the next part of the procedure that is well-rehearsed. He stands.

'Give it good and loud,' Stokesley says. 'Let us hear you at last, my lord Cromwell. Leave the wretch in no doubt as to his fate.'

After the edict is read, the guards take Lambert out. The king inclines his head to his audience, with the sober piety of a churchman: which, for this afternoon, he has been. When he lifts his chin, his expression is exalted.

At a signal, the trumpeters step into the hall. They blow a fanfare to see the king out. Six trumpeters. Sixteen pence each. Eight shillings for the treasury to find. The king is thinking of forming a new guard, called the Gentlemen Spears, with new livery. The way he's going, he'll want trumpeters every hour.

Barely six o'clock, but black night outside. The winter has taken its iron grip. 'That was grim,' Rafe says.

He agrees. 'Poor fellow.'

Rafe says, 'I did not mean Lambert. He brought it on himself.'

'I believe Gardiner brought it on him.' He is angry. 'He sets his claws back on English soil and this occurs. I think he has been to the king behind my back. I think he has been pulling at his sleeve – telling him how the French are disgusted at our reformation, how the Emperor is appalled – how he must prove himself a good Roman at heart. As if his great cause is some silly quarrel that can be patched within a fortnight, and seven years' work dismissed –'

'It is too late now for a speech,' Rafe says.

His household guard is here, ready to take him home. The crowds are dispersing. The fanfares are done, the trumpeters are strolling away. He calls them over, reaches in his pocket to give them some drinking money. They touch their caps to him. He turns back to Rafe. 'I hope it does not seem I disdained the king's efforts. I did not. He reasoned very well.'

Rafe says, 'It appeared that you did not know what to do.'

He thinks, I did know. But I didn't do it. I could have given my voice for Lambert. Or at least walked out.

'Barnes played the hypocrite,' he says. 'But for the grace of God he would be standing there himself, accused.'

Rafe says, 'Rob has done himself no harm today.'

Rafe leaves the rest unsaid. They go out into the cold. He thinks, I could have quoted, I could have cited. What has all my reading been for?

He puts his arm across Rafe's shoulders. Rafe never fleshes; he is no hunter nor tennis-player, he is meagre as a boy, breakable.

'Never fear,' he says. 'We shall prosper, son.' The cold stings their faces.

It is not many days till the burning. He sends to Lambert food and drink, words of consolation and pity, but he asks himself, how can these be received? He knows I did not speak for him. I sat in the cockpit among those eager hard-eyed men, with the taste of blood in their mouths, and I did not lift a finger. Or raise my voice, except to read the sentence. But if the king would not consult me, what could I do? In all of The Book Called Henry, there is no precedent for it.

John Lambert's end is a grand occasion. At Smithfield there are stands for the dignitaries, hung with the emblems of England, furnished with plush cushions. Every councillor is on parade, who is not actually sick in bed: each man hung with his chains of office, and the Garter badge for the elite. Seats with the best view are reserved for the principal ambassadors, for Castillon and Chapuys.

The day is a fiesta of pain. He has never seen a man suffer so. A spectator cannot make his eyes blind. He can only close them for moments together. He thinks, thank God that Gregory is safe down in Sussex. He could not look when Anne Boleyn died, and that was but a heartbeat: less.

Lambert is an hour dying. At his side, attending my lord Privy Seal, is a small boy, Thomas Cromwell, alias Harry Smith. There is a smear of ash on his bare arm; his body, beneath his jerkin, is cloudy with bruises.

In the starlit hour, Cranmer comes to see him. A pastoral visit. 'You are not well?'

He will not admit to that. 'Awake at all hours,' he says. 'It is Master Traitor Pole, he makes so much paperwork with his machinations.'

The archbishop looks helpless himself, exhausted. He, Lord Cromwell, calls for wine for him, for food if he will take it: a capon's wing, plums. Cranmer shuffles in his chair. He blows his nose. He says, 'You know, what we have begun will not come to fruition in one generation. You are past fifty. And I, not much less.'

'Gardiner asked if I thought we were living in the last days.'

Cranmer darts a glance at him. 'But you do not. Surely.' The archbishop is biting his lip, like a man lifting a splinter with a needle.

'I can see why good men want to believe that Christ is coming. We want His justice, when justice seems so long delayed.'

'You think Lambert did not have justice?'

He looks up. It is not a trap.

He says, 'You can't pick and choose, if you serve a prince, week to week or cause to cause. Sometimes all you can do is lessen the damage. But here we failed.'

Cranmer says, 'We must not make Thomas More's mistake. He thought Henry's conscience was his to command.'

The door opens. Cranmer starts. 'Ah, Christophe –'

Christophe puts down a platter. 'I think my master ought to have a holiday.'

'Beyond my remit,' Cranmer says faintly. 'You know, when I was a boy I did suppose an archbishop could do anything. I supposed he could do miracles.'

'I never gave it a thought,' he says. 'Christophe, bring fruit.'

The boy trundles out. He says, 'The light of Christ leads us to some murky places.'

The archbishop is looking at his roast fowl. He says, 'I cannot touch flesh. Not this evening.'

He says, 'Have you ever seen a hawk keep killing, when the prey is dead?'

Cranmer flinches. 'No,' he says, 'no. I think the king was ... he surprised me ... he was judicious, he was, at times, he was almost ... fatherly.'

Ripping and stamping, rage in the eye. Sipping blood from the body cavity, then slashing again at the flesh.

'Fatherly,' he says. 'Yes, he was.'

He thinks, after I saw Joan Boughton burned, I went home to my little life and I did not know if it was true or if I had dreamed it. I wondered if I might see her in the street, an elderly body about her business, going with her basket to buy cloves and apples for a pie.

Cranmer says, 'But what else could we have done? Lambert chose his answers. It lay within his power to make others.'

'I do not think it did.'

Cranmer considers that. To fill the silence he asks him, 'How is your lady?'

'Grete?' Cranmer speaks as if he had other wives, one or two. 'Grete is afraid. And tired of hiding. I assured her when I brought her to England that the king would be brought to a different opinion, and that we would be able to live freely like any couple. But as it is ...'

His voice dies away. We are living on borrowed time, in small rooms, a bag always packed, an ear always alert; we sleep lightly and some nights hardly at all.

He says to Cranmer, 'So what now? After this? If the king can burn this man he can burn us. What shall I do?'

'Maintain your rule as long as you can. For the gospel's sake I shall do the same.'

'What use is our rule, if we could not save John Lambert?'

'We could not save John Frith. Yet look at all we have been able to do, since Frith went into the fire. We could not save Tyndale, but we could save his book.'

True. Dead men are at work. Their cause is not lost. They labour on, screened from us by smoke.

When Cranmer has gone his household supply him with candles and wine and draw his door closed. They subdue their voices and walk as if wearing felt slippers. He takes a fresh sheet of paper and begins to write a letter. *To my very loving friend Sir Thomas Wyatt, knight, the king's ambassador with the Emperor.*

He writes, *The king's Majesty, my lord prince's grace, my ladies his daughters, and the rest of his council be all merry and in good prosperity ...*

When I was a young man, he thinks, I needed all my strength. Pity was a luxury I might one day afford, like fine white bread or a book; a sound roof over my head, a light of amber or blue glass, a ring for my finger; an ell of pearled brocade, a lute, a beechwood fire; a safe hand to light it.

The xvith day of this present …

Origen says for each man God makes a scroll, which is rolled and hidden in the heart. God inscribes with a quill, a reed, a bone.

… the king's Majesty, for the reverence of the holy sacrament of the altar …

He thinks of adding, our monarch wore white. Head to toe he shone. Like a mirror. Like a light. He writes, *I wish the princes of Europe could have seen it, heard it – with what gravity he strove for the conversion of this poor miserable wretch …*

His hand moves across the paper, the ink unites with its weave. The firelight stirs, a candle flame bows and blurs. He remembers riding with Gregory across the downs, under a silver sky: the light without shadow, like the light at the beginning of the world.

If those princes had been with me today, he writes, they would have seen Henry's learning and marvelled at it. They would have witnessed his judgement, his policy: they would have seen him as – he lifts his pen for an instant from the page – *the mirror and light of all other kings and princes in Christendom.*

Among his papers he still has a verse from Tom Truth's pen. It has become loose from its poem, but he has it by heart.

> But since my fancy leads her so
> And leads my friendship from the light
> And walketh me darkling to and fro
> While other friends may walk in sight …

Even the worst poets, from time to time, hit on a felicitous phrasing. You can see the flicker, as the human form passes from light to dark and back again. He looks around the room. The subdued glow of the turkey carpet. His books bound in kidskin and calf. The silver plate, reflecting himself to himself: the mirror and light of all councillors that are in Christendom.

He puts down his pen. He thinks, this letter will not do, tomorrow I will fill in the gaps; or perhaps not, tomorrow they want me at the Tower. He is too tired, too shaken, too riven by horror and desolation to describe in any detail the judgement of Lambert, let alone his last day. He writes, *I doubt not some of your friends who have leisure shall by their letters advertise you of the whole discourse …*

Let them. He closes his eyes. What does God see? Cromwell in the fifty-fourth year of his age, in all his weight and gravitas, his bulk wrapped in wool and fur? Or a mere flicker, an illusion, a spark beneath a shoe, a spit in the ocean, a feather in a desert, a wisp, a phantom, a needle in a haystack? If Henry is the mirror, he is the pale actor who sheds no lustre of his own, but spins in a reflected light. If the light moves he is gone.

When I was in Italy, he thinks, I saw Virgins painted on every wall, I saw in every fresco the sponged blood-colour of Christ's robe. I saw the sinuous tempter that winds from a branch, and Adam's face as he was tempted. I saw that the serpent was a woman, and about her face were curls of silver-gilt; I saw her writhe about the green bough, saw it sway under her coils. I saw the lamentation of Heaven over Christ crucified, angels flying and crying at the same time. I saw torturers nimble as dancers hurling stones at St Stephen, and I saw the martyr's bored face as he waited for death. I saw a dead child cast in bronze, standing over its own corpse: and all these pictures, images, I took into myself, as some kind of prophecy or sign. But I have known men and women, better than me and closer to grace, who have meditated on every splinter of the cross, till they forget who and what they are, and observe the Saviour's blood, running in the soaked fibres of the wood. Till they believe themselves no longer captive to misfortune nor crime, nor in thrall to a useless sacrifice in an alien land. Till they see Christ's cross is the tree of life, and the truth breaks inside them, and they are saved.

He sands his paper. Puts down his pen. I believe, but I do not believe enough. I said to Lambert, my prayers are with you, but in the end I only prayed for myself, that I might not suffer the same death.

III
Inheritance
December 1538

His scheme of registration is badly taken. Recording baptisms, the people say, will enable the king to tax us in our infancy. Recording weddings will allow him to impose a levy on every bride and groom. Given notice of funerals, Cromwell's commissioners will attend to pluck the pennies off the corpse's lids.

Cromwell is laying his plans, they say, to steal our firewood, our chickens and our spoons. He means to impound our millstone, tax cauldrons and stewpots, weight the beam, tamper with the baker's scales, and fix liquid measures in his favour. The man is like a weasel, who eats his own weight every day. You do not see him coming, he makes himself so small he can pass through a wedding ring. His eyes are open all night. He dances to baffle his prey then sucks out their brains. His lair is in the dens of the vanquished and he lines it with their fur.

Ambassador Chapuys seeks an interview. He is agitated. 'Thomas, do you know what they are saying in Rome? They say that when you broke Becket's shrine you took his bones and shot them out of a cannon. Surely it cannot be true?'

'Ambassador, if only I had thought of it ...'

Chapuys says, 'You are lucky you do not serve that King Henry who had Becket murdered. The chronicles state he would roll on the floor in his rages, and foam at the mouth like a mad dog.'

At Lambeth Palace they had a statue of Becket perched in the outer wall, looking over the river. Now Cranmer has taken it down and the place is empty. His bargemaster says, 'I've been saluting that knave since I was a boy.'

'Time you stopped then, Bastings.'

'My father before me. His father before him. I expect habit will keep me to it.'

Bastings spits over the side. In the days when he was a little lad at Putney, he used to think boatmen spat for luck. But his uncle John told him that they do it to alert their gods, who look up through the tides at the underside of vessels, and see the leaks not yet sprung.

When he was fourteen he thought all the time about the river. When it rained he thought, good, more water, carrying me away to the sea.

The Thames is swollen; it is the kind of weather that washes the corpses out of St Olave's churchyard, and sends them swimming on a frothy tide. Safely home, he unlocks the box where he keeps his dead wife's prayer book. He locates the image of Becket and cuts out the page. He does it delicately, with a thin-bladed knife. He turns over the pages and looks at each picture. He sees Mary dead and carried in procession, with the Jews darting out to shake the bier and trample underfoot the rose-garlands of the mourners. He sees Christ scourged at the pillar, His white fish body writhing from the flail.

At Austin Friars the strongrooms and cellars are filling with relics. There is a stack of handkerchiefs neatly hemmed by the Blessed Virgin and a piece of the rope with which Judas hanged himself. Madonnas have been through by the half-dozen, some on their way to be burned, others axed; our Lady of Caversham nudges St Ann of Buxton, St Modwen giggles in their train. It reminds him of the days before Anne Boleyn came down, when the ladies clustered together, sliding dangerous thoughts through painted lips, and rolling their painted eyes. In a box there is a livid two-inch piece of gristle, which is the ear of Malchus, servant to Israel's high priest – cut off by St Peter at the time of our Saviour's arrest. Becket's bones lie in their plain box. Only a clever surgeon, and possibly not even he, could tell you whether they are the bones of a martyr or of an animal.

* * *

While her kinsfolk are interrogated at the Tower, Margaret Pole remains in custody at Fitzwilliam's house. When Fitzwilliam goes from home, his wife Mabel makes him take her with him. She will not stay alone under that cold Plantagenet eye.

Once a thorough search is made of Margaret's castle at Warblington, papers come to hand which perhaps she wishes were burned.

'And I doubt not,' Castillon says gaily, 'that more will come to hand, as you require them.'

Chapuys says, 'Cremuel is happy enough if the evidence follows the trial.'

'Margaret Pole is not on trial,' he says, expressionless.

She is the head of the family. It is she who carries the bloodline. She will never walk free again, but time will take care of her; he does not relish explaining to the ambassadors why the king chose the headsman, to rid an ancient lady. Geoffrey's wife Constance is not to be charged. He has left Thomas More's family out of the indictments, and Bishop Stokesley: for now. The net spreads wide, but at its extremities it is cobweb-thin.

Riche says, 'We have no actual thing against them, to convict them of treason. No actions. Only words. But we have done it before. We have done it under the statute.'

Our law of treason is capacious. It encompasses words and bad intentions. We let More bring himself down that way, we let the Boleyns do it. Is a man a victim, who walks onto a knife? Are you innocent, if you set up the damage for yourself?

'Thank you, Riche,' he says, 'for your confidence.' But it is up to him, as ever, to make sure the king does nothing he regrets.

Henry says: 'Lord Montague and Lord Exeter have worked against me seven years past. They have perverted my daughter Mary to their cause. Her safety ensured,' he inclines his head, 'only by your efforts, my lord Cromwell.'

He waits: allowing the king to hold a trial inside his head. At last he says, 'Geoffrey Pole, sir? Without Geoffrey's help we would have not much matter to stand up in court.'

'A pardon, I suppose. Hold him for now.'

He makes a note. There is no doubt as to the outcome of the trials. 'Will your Majesty grant them grace as to the manner of their deaths?'

'Noble blood,' Henry says. 'I cannot send them to Tyburn, though God knows – would François be as merciful? Would the Emperor endure to be laughed at, as I have been? Because they did laugh at me, my sore leg. Said it would kill me. And if it did not, they would speed nature. I ask myself, what would they have done to my son Edward? The day he was baptised, Gertrude Courtenay carried him in her arms. She held him against her heart. How could she, with such malice in it? God knows she has deserved a death.'

'No, sir,' he says firmly. 'We will spare the women. By themselves they can do nothing. Gertrude may be lodged at the Tower in a chamber near her son. He is still of a tender age. And Henry Pole is not yet ten.'

'They will be companions for each other,' Henry says. 'They can walk in the gardens. They can have a target to practise archery. Who knows? A time may come when they can be let go. Though I hope my son's heart will not be as soft, to nourish traitors decade after decade. In truth, I hope none of my heirs will have hearts as pitiful as mine.'

The captive children will need to be shown occasionally to witnesses, so no one can say they have been disappeared, like King Edward's heirs. As with those tender princes, it is inheritance condemns them. Though he, Thomas Cromwell, has nothing to say against inheritance. Already the name of his grandson Henry is beginning to appear on title deeds. And the child as yet has no teeth.

In early December the order goes to the Tower: bring up the bodies for trial. Henry Courtenay, Marquis of Exeter, is condemned, and Lord Montague too, led to the scaffold at Tower Hill on a day of howling wind and heavy rain.

Geoffrey Pole will be released before spring. He is pardoned by the king, but not by himself. On the fourth day of Christmas he tries to kill himself again, this time by eating a cushion. The feathers fail to choke him.

For the season the king goes to Greenwich as usual. The Pope's bull of excommunication is now to be carried by Reginald Pole through Europe, and for a man doomed to Hell, Henry keeps a merry court. From Brussels, our envoy Mr Wriothesley writes he has seen Christina. He never thought he could like a woman as tall as himself, but he does like her, and he understands the king would not object to a tall bride. When Christina smiles, dimples appear in her cheek and chin. He thinks she would smile more often if she were given cause. When he asks her how she would like to be Queen of England, she says, alas, it is not for her to decide.

Henry shows off her picture. Everyone who sees it smiles. 'She looks kind,' the king says wistfully. 'What if she is not so white as Jane? Jane was white as Staffordshire alabaster.'

All souls must make the passage, Dante tells us. They flock on the riverbank to wait their turn: the mild, the defenceless, crossing in the weak light.

On the last day of 1538 Nicholas Carew is arrested: the king's Master of the Horse, old Carve-Away, the hero of the tilting ground. A cache of letters in possession of Gertrude Courtenay shows him as one who has not only urged on the conspirators but broken the king's confidence repeatedly over the years, revealing freely what is done and said in the privy chamber.

Henry says sadly, 'The cardinal always warned me against Carew. I didn't listen. I should listen to my advisers, shouldn't I?'

He feels it is not for him to comment.

'Carew was always a partisan of my wife. I mean, of Katherine. Then of Mary, crying up her rights.' Henry is thoughtful. 'Carew's wife is still a beautiful woman.'

He almost drops his papers. He imagines the words dragged out of him: Majesty, I know you had to do with Eliza Bryan in your young days, but you cannot order a man's death and then marry his widow. King David sent Uriah into battle to be killed: thereafter, he impregnated Bathsheba, who gave birth to a dying child.

He thinks, somebody else will have to tell him. Lord Audley. Fitz. I have had enough of refraining him from what will hurt him, slapping away his hand like a nursemaid.

The king says, 'I gave Lady Carew diamonds and pearls. I never saw her wear them. I suppose Nicholas locked them away in his coffers.'

He says, 'His coffers will be emptied now. They will come back to the Wardrobe. By your Majesty's leave I will send Master Cornelius to make a special inventory.'

'Yes, do that.' Henry looks into the distance. 'These men, you know, Carew, Lord Exeter – they were the friends of my youth.'

He bows, waits, then begins to withdraw. The end of the Round Table, he thinks. Henry says, 'Reginald called me the enemy of the human race.'

The boy Mathew comes to him: 'My lord, an old woman has brought a nightingale in a cage. I gave her one mark.'

Christophe says, 'You gave her one mark, for a singing bird? You rustic dolt. My lord should send you back to Wiltshire. I suppose it is all the entertainment you are used to, down at Wolf Hall.'

Nicholas Carew is held in custody, pending his indictment on Valentine's Day. The king does not mention his name again.

> Ou sont les gracieux galans
> Que je suivoye ou temps jadiz,
> Si bien chantans, si bien parlans,
> Si plaisans en faiz et en diz?

Such singers, such dancers, their words and deeds false to the core: when our prince went hunting they whispered to each other, 'When will the Tudor break his neck?'

The gaoler Martin tells him that Carew has begun to read the gospel. He laments the life he has led, and wishes to be a new man. 'Will you not do something for him, sir? Now he has come over to us?'

Before Lambert was burned he would have protested against the trial of a fellow evangelist, thinking it his duty to prevent it, knowing that until he had done his utmost his conscience would not rest. But he has got over that now.

They say the cardinal in the days of his power had a wax image of the king, which he talked to and bent to his will. He keeps a waxen Henry in the corner of his imagination, painted in bright colours and fitted with gilt shoes. He lives with it but he doesn't talk to it. He is afraid it will answer back.

PART FIVE

I

Ascension Day
Spring–Summer 1539

'Call-Me wants a picture of the king,' Rafe says. 'We must get one on the first boat. He needs to show it to Christina.'

Does Call-Me know his business? It seems perilous, to open a gap between a young girl's fantasy and a man who is past his prime. But then, she must have heard Henry described, by those whose pleasure it is to rip up her dreams.

He sits with Rafe and goes through a sheaf of drawings. Sometimes a child emerges from behind the king's eyes: an alert little boy, who expects the world to do him pleasure. Henry owns more than a hundred looking-glasses. If they had a memory, we could send one that reflected the prince as he was at Christina's age: tumbling curls, broad shoulders, damask skin.

Henry rides up to Waltham to see his little prince. Edward's limbs are firm and sturdy. No spells or conjurations have withered him. His pallor he gets from his mother, his shy blue eyes and pointed chin. His coats are of tawny and crimson, his winter gowns lined with miniver and trimmed with ermine. He makes full use of his Christmas present from the old Earl of Essex – a rattle combined with a bell. The Earl of Essex is stone deaf.

Every dispatch from Wriothesley reassures us that yes, he knows his business. He visits Christina in her chambers hung with damask and black velvet. The atmosphere is hushed: our handsome envoy whispers to her, enticing. The king's character, he tells her, is naturally benevolent. In all his reign, few have heard angry words fall from his lips.

Christina's colour rises, Call-Me says. She looks as if someone has tickled her.

Majesty, he advises, take her on any terms: you cannot do better.

But Call-Me is chagrined that the courtiers in Brussels do not understand his lineage. They imply that anyone who serves Cromwell must be of base degree himself. He assures them that he is proud to walk behind the Lord Privy Seal, carrying his pen, ink and paper. He doesn't mind their aspersions, he says.

Rafe says, 'He does mind, really.' Call-Me has always been touchy, quick to take offence; easily rattled, and proud of his good blood. But the new year has begun well for him, because he has laid hands on that coveted master-spy, Harry Phillips.

How did this happen? Phillips has simply walked into our embassy and handed himself over. He craves Henry's pardon for anything he has done or seemed to do against England and Englishmen. Now he is ready to tell the truth about his life, and is able to lead us straight to Master Traitor Pole. And then, Wriothesley believes, Phillips can be interrogated and turned, sent back into Europe to work our will – drawing the king's enemies gradually towards him, then spilling them into the hands of the executioner.

Call-Me's dispatch has scarcely been read at Westminster when he is obliged to write a follow-up. Though placed under guard, Harry Phillips has absconded in the night, taking with him a bag of money belonging to our English delegation.

Call-Me has spent four futile months standing in anterooms and absorbing insults, and now a trickster has gulled him. He is eaten up with humiliation, gnawed with anxiety till he knows if the king and council blame him. He should bear the blame, of course. But his fellow envoys write home on his behalf: for God's sake, comfort him, my lord Cromwell – he will be ill if you do not give him a good word. Never was son so anxious to please his father, as Mr Wriothesley is to please you.

Perhaps it will be a lesson to him, Rafe says, not to think he has the most penetrating wit in Europe: to realise he can be as big a fool as the rest of us.

It is a cold winter. No sooner have floods abated than the first snows blanket us. In the warmth of Toledo, the Emperor and the King of France ratify their treaty. They mean this concord to last their life-times, they say, and they swear to make no agreement with England – marital, military – without the support of the other. Which will not, of course, forthcome. Who can deal with an excommunicate king? No Christian man can give him bread if he is starving – let alone provide him with a wife.

Henry's subjects are now released from their obedience to him. The Pope reminds the faithful that for sectaries and schismatics, the normal rules are suspended. You may break your contracts with them and seize their goods. All Englishmen abroad, whether students, merchants or ambassadors, are at risk of arrest. It is true there has been no formal declaration of hostilities. But it feels like war. The King of Scots is preening himself; he thinks that if France invades, they will partition the kingdom and give him the north, if not the whole.

The men around our king live by what they call honour: skill in arms, prowess on the battlefield. Their appetite is not slaked by the cutting up of northern rebels, or the attrition of border feuding. Norfolk calls war *business*. 'If we have business with the French,' he says, or 'Should some business with Charles ensue …' Now church bells are cast into cannon, ploughshares beaten into swords, the cross of Christ becomes a bludgeon, a club to beat out the brains of the opposition. What's ink in Whitehall is blood in the borderlands, what's a quibble in the law courts is a stabbing in the streets. Mild monkish blessings are turned to curses, and the giggling of courtiers tails off into an uneasy hush. Each man is watching the other, for signs of treason, signs of weakness. You cannot greet the world in the morning with anything less than ferocity, or by evening you will be destroyed.

It is not our custom in England to maintain a standing army. Using former church revenues, we could raise one. But then Henry would want to use it, as monarchs do, to carry war beyond the seas: which, Master Secretary says, is a thing I will never permit. For our defence we can mobilise swiftly. Ready cash oils the wheels. The best men are appointed in every region, to draw up muster rolls, build beacons, recruit gunners, captain ordnance. Can our friends in Cleves, the king asks, send a hundred expert cannoneers?

The king's ships stand in the Thames: the *Jesus* and the *John Baptist*, the *Peter*, the *Minion*, the *Primrose* and the *Sweepstake*, the *Lyon*, the *Trinity*, the *Valentine*; the *Mary Rose* and the *Mary Boleyn*. The king's tabletop is papered with charts and plans. He draws forts and blockhouses, and he, Cromwell, sends out surveyors to map the coastline. All the maps are to be sent to the king. He dreams of laying them out in Westminster Hall, a pattern of these islands.

The message to the world is: we can withstand a sudden invasion, and we can sustain a long war. He, Cromwell, writes letters into Europe, explaining the recent executions. Every prince will under-stand that the dead men were dynasts; Henry is keeping his line safe. Within a year our country will be a giant fortress, guns trained on the sea lanes: more like a castle than a realm.

A castle is a world in little. Everyone inside it must work together. If it falls it is because it is betrayed from within. The Duke of Norfolk rides north, to stamp out sedition where the king's writ is weakest: a querulous old man, taking to the winter roads. 'Take your time,' he advises: he, Lord Cromwell.

'I've no choice, have I?' Norfolk snarls. But then he turns, relent-ing: 'Look here. When you write to me, you need not address me as "your Grace". It doesn't seem fitting these days. You being what you are.'

He bows. Perhaps Norfolk has received a prompt from the king? 'Most humbly I acknowledge your lordship's condescension.'

But, he thinks, I won't start calling you Tom. He never sees the duke with a sword at his side, without imagining himself run through: 'Beg pardon, Lord Cromwell, was that your heart?'

The king says, 'Ask the German princes what they will do for us, if we find ourselves under attack. Ask them to send engineers. If they must send more scholars, naturally we will receive them, but our need is for fighting men.'

You can hire soldiers, of course. The king's father hired the army that knocked the throne from under Crookback. They will fight as long as they are paid or rewarded with plunder, but they will not stir one foot unless they hear the chink of coin. He, Cromwell, puts out scouts through Germany and Italy. He is not interested in a poxy rabble of Irishmen or Scots, only in proven captains from nations where war is a science.

This winter the council sits every day. The king presides, except when he rides off in person to inspect the Channel ports. The exigency has given him a new briskness, a vigour. 'My lords, I am weary of reading long letters. You must digest them for me. Unless they come from my brother kings, when I shall read them entire.'

The King of Scotland sends his compliments, and asks for a lion. A lion! 'The temerity of the man!' the councillors exclaim. 'The presumption!'

'I have plenty of lions, I suppose,' the king says mildly, 'in the cages at the Tower. I would not refuse to do him pleasure. My lord Cromwell, will you see to that?'

Someone laughs, and stifles the laugh. Any odd tasks, the king always says they are Cromwell business. And they always are.

The king's council is smaller now. It is compacted to an effective body, so there are no makeweights. But every man who sits has a strong will and strong interests. The king begs for concord amongst his advisers. But Henry himself cannot walk a line: he leans violently one way, then violently the other, and it takes a robust man to support him. Intemperate councillors fail. We have all seen Gardiner flouncing from the royal presence, looking like a plaice, with his mouth turned down and his underlip thrust out.

The king's temper is no mystery. The astrologers say it is his moon in Aries that makes him explosive, confrontational – but really what matters is the state of his leg. Some days it hurts more, some days less, but there are no days it does not hurt at all. As the king's doctors remark, the ailments of great men have too little credit, when their lives are passed in view. They inherit thrones, but so much else. When the Emperor speaks, his words rattle like pebbles in the cavern of his overshot jaw. François is paying for his sins: he has lost so many teeth to the mercury cure that his wishes are expressed as spit, and his parts are ulcerated in a fashion that would repulse the lowest whore.

He is repulsed by François himself. In Paris his new Bibles have been seized and his printers warned off. He thought he had bribed enough people to keep the Inquisitors at bay. Now, perhaps, they expect him to pay a ransom for the type? Perhaps he will, as he has paid out so much already. He calls in Ambassador Castillon, and asks that François, as a favour, release the unbound sheets. Perhaps the day may come when François wants a favour in turn?

In letters home Castillon begs for his recall. He is afraid that, if hostilities break out, Henry and Cromwell will kill him. He refers to 'the king and his milord' – as if there is only one milord in England.

Meanwhile he, the Vicegerent, arranges to set up his print shop at Greyfriars, where he can walk in and see what is done day by day. It will be safer, if slower. In one bad week, he says to Rafe, your life's work can be shot out of the water.

Around Candlemas, coming in to the king, he finds him sitting at twilight over his books; Henry raises his head and looks at him with a faint puzzlement, as if he has never seen him before. Then the king seems to shake himself and says, 'You look cold, Thomas, come to the fire. I was thinking that sometimes we should pray together. How do you pray, my lord? Do you begin with your Pater Noster, or do you repeat a psalm, or do you say words of your own devising?'

He looks closely at the king and sees the question is not a trap. He says, 'I praise God as master of our ship. No tempest will sink us.'

The king grants licence for one John Misseldon, alchemist, to return to England from his stay beyond the seas. He may practise his craft as long as he does not resort to the dark arts. 'Sooner or later,' he warns the king, 'all such men grow desperate, and then they turn to necromancy.'

I also, he thinks. I sit at my desk day after day, waiting for the cardinal to whisper in my ear.

Before February ends we are locked into crisis. Only Lord Lisle does not seem to know it. John Husee, salt-sprayed from the crossing, drips into his waiting chamber. 'Husee,' he says, 'since Edward Seymour has been in Calais, I begin to form a picture of how your master falls short.'

'You know he is not well,' Husee says awkwardly.

'Ill enough to be replaced?'

'No, no, please ...' Husee says.

He takes pity on the man. 'I shall send over my nephew Richard to help him.'

'If it please you,' Husee says, 'Lord Edward, Master Richard – they would be described as gospellers –'

'Lord Lisle objects to that?'

If war breaks out, Calais is the first place the enemy will attack. I should go myself and take charge, he thinks. But I don't want to find that, in my absence, the king has panicked and called Norfolk back from the borders, or put a plaice in my seat at the council board.

France and the Emperor give notice that they are withdrawing their ambassadors. Chapuys comes to see him privately, twitching with tension. 'Do not take it as an act of war, I beg you. The Emperor is recalling me only because I know your English manners, and can advise the Duchess Christina – how she should order herself, when she comes over to England to be crowned.'

When he, Lord Cromwell, conveys this to the councillors, the whole table bursts into laughter. Only Call-Me, and perhaps the king, still believe Christina will ever be his bride. Officially, talks are still open. But the Emperor is imposing conditions that make the match impossible. When the duchess's servants visit Wriothesley these days, they flit in by owl-light.

He says, 'The Emperor wants Chapuys back so he can report on our war preparations. But before we release the ambassador, we should make sure we get Wriothesley home safe.'

'Hostages!' the Lord Chancellor says. 'Oh, Mother Mary! What about Wyatt in Spain? I hear the Inquisitors are at his back.'

He has Wyatt's letter in his pocket. Our ambassador writes, *I am at the wall. I cannot endure till March.*

He goes home. His leg is aching and his people have made a special stool to set it on. 'Decrepit,' he says to his nephew Richard.

He sees himself from without, a miniature on vellum: Lord Cromwell in his Later Years. A Flemish tiled floor, a chequerboard of blue and gold; a red velvet gown and inside it a hunched invalid. Richard leans over his chair, a hand on his shoulder. 'What if you are not in your first youth? I shall be glad if at your age I am as sound.'

Christophe says, 'Compare with the king! My lord Admiral, he has been ill since Christmas. Norferk, he is shrivelled like a dried bean.'

Richard says, 'Christophe, respect your betters.'

Christophe says, 'One fears for Call-Me. Suppose they kill him? Or drop him in a deep dungeon?'

This has occurred to him. They could lock the boy in Vilvoorde where they kept Tyndale. Richard Cromwell says, 'You used to have a plan of that fortress. Would we send a troop of men to break him out?'

They glance at each other, turn away again. Probably not.

He limps along to the Tower, where in a broad and pleasant room, a pale fire in the hearth, he converses with Gertrude, Courtenay's widow. For a woman who has just lost her husband to the headsman, she is self-possessed: dry-eyed, and eating almonds from a platter. 'No doubt you fortified yourself with prayer?' he says. 'You cannot have been surprised. You knew everything my lord Exeter said and did against the king. You were in his inner councils.'

'A woman has her own soul to save,' Gertrude says. 'Her husband will not do it for her.'

'Do you know the traitor Pole is now in Spain?'

She offers him an almond. 'Why would I know?'

'He is with the Emperor, urging a crusade against his native land. Then he will go to France again, urging the same. So he turns about and about, snared in his treason.'

Her gaze drifts over his shoulder, as if the wall is more interesting.

'Our ambassador in Spain has begged to return home, but they say, "Tarry, Mr Wyatt." The Inquisitors have begun a process against him. You would not like to be in Wyatt's place.'

'Why would I be? I am not a heretic.'

'Once they detain a suspect he cannot answer to the charge, because he is not allowed to know what it is. Nor is he told who has laid information. He is tortured by methods – well, my lady, I would not sully your ears. In Castile these days, every soul lives in fear.'

'They have nothing to fear from the Holy Office,' she says. 'Not if they are good livers, and go to Mass.'

'They fear their neighbours. Old enemies bring each other down.'

Her eyes move over him. She sees the king's councillor: a genial man, comfortable in his skin. She doesn't see the other man, whom he keeps short-chained to the wall: the man for whom the work of forgetting is strenuous, who dreams of dungeons, cavities and oubliettes. Such men are subject to uprushes of fear which wake them in the night; when they are frightened, they laugh.

'My lord,' she says, 'where is Bess Darrell?'

Judging by her tone, she does not know Bess's evidence helped to ruin her family. He says, 'She is in a happier place.'

Her hand flies to her throat. 'God forgive you – you have not killed her?'

'Do you think I am a brute?'

He is interested in her answer. She says, 'I have wondered why I am still alive myself. They say you do not like killing women, but you killed Anne Boleyn.'

'You do not quarrel with me for that, I suppose?'

'If you are trying to bargain – if you were thinking of trading me, for Mr Wyatt – I am afraid that the Emperor might not …'

'Perhaps you and Margaret Pole?' he says. 'You are right, madam. You make little weight on the scales. Your son is of more interest.'

She looks up. 'Please do not take him from me.'

'When the Emperor decides on his policy to England, we hope that he will consider your welfare, and that of your boy. He says he is always solicitous for the old blood of England.'

She says, 'The Holy Maid – you remember her? You blame me still, because I had dealings with her. I swore then and will swear now, I meant no malice.'

She begins to cry. He gives her a handkerchief. 'You know I have lost little children. My lord husband used to fault me – "Heirs frail as they are, the times so cruel, one son is not enough." She, the Maid – she said she would speak to Our Blessed Lady. She claimed her prayers were heard.'

He remembers Barton on a public scaffold, her broad countrygirl's face chafed by the wind, and a crowd of Londoners gaping up at her. He remembers Thomas More by his side, huddled into a cape and rubbing his raw blue hands; it must have been a winter like this. He says gently, 'Well, they weren't, were they? But thank you for telling me this. The king may think better of you than he does now. A mother's heart. He will understand.'

She blows her nose. He says, 'If you have anything else to tell me, I think confession would ease your soul. About Thomas More, for instance. Or Bishop Fisher.'

'Why? They are dead.'

'In Rome they talk about them as if they had just left the room.'

They take a cup of wine together, served in silver as befits their rank. He takes a courteous leave. A guard takes his arm and guides him down a twisted stair to where an Irish monk squats on straw. Taken on the sea with letters to the Emperor, the prisoner is waiting for the pains of Purgatory to commence. If invaders come, the king's Irish subjects will let them in by the back door.

He asks the gaoler, 'Is he talking?'

'He cracks on he only speaks Irish.'

'Send to Austin Friars. We have interpreters.'

He takes a breath. He walks in on the prisoner, holding the letters salvaged from his purse. Lucky he did not think to cast them into the sea.

If Wriothesley were here he would break the cipher in ten minutes. Wyatt, no doubt, would do it in less. But while they are in the Emperor's hands, it is quicker to break men.

By an order from Brussels, English ships are detained in Lowland ports. But Spanish merchants are leaving London, and he knows how quickly panic spreads among traders; they may speak in different tongues, but money talks to them all.

The king says, if they hold my ships, I will hold theirs; I will board any Spanish vessel in our waters.

There is another way, he says; not better than your Majesty's, but supplementary. He issues a fiat to lift dues and taxes on resident foreigners – put them on par with Englishmen. That, he believes, will induce aliens to see out this storm in harbour, and not to pack their wives and chattels on the next boat.

Call-Me reports a rumour that the young Duke of Cleves has been poisoned by agents of Rome. For God's sake, Mr Wriothesley writes, implore our royal master to be careful who comes into his company or near his person. And you, sir, you be careful too.

Ambassador Chapuys is limping. 'You. Me. Your king,' he says. 'You would think it was a nation of cripples, Thomas. It's the climate.'

'It rains as much in Brussels.'

Eustache concedes that. 'I will not be capable of riding to Dover. I must arrange a horse litter –'

'Allow me to take care of it. And your baggage too.'

The ambassador bows. They sit down to Lenten fare. Chapuys has little appetite. England has never been a popular posting: the barbarous tongue and, as Chapuys says, the weather. But when he imagined the end of his embassy, he imagined an orderly withdrawal, and the customary present from the king. 'What do you hear of young Wriothesley?' he asks. 'I have written most earnestly – and Thomas,

I am telling you the truth here – I have said to Brussels, "Do not for God's sake mistreat this young man, who is a great favourite both with the King of England and with my lord Cremuel." I trust they will heed me and your boy will soon be on the road.'

The aim is to have Call-Me pass through the gates of Calais as the ambassador's ship docks. At some point, unseen, the two should pass each other. 'Just as long as you do not steal away by night,' he says to Chapuys. 'I do not want to have to put soldiers outside your house.'

The ambassador holds up his hands. 'I would not be sitting here, if I intended any such practice. Only I would not have chosen to leave before my successor is inducted. There is such scope for misunderstanding.'

Chapuys is to be replaced by the Dean of Cambrai: a good fellow, coarse-fibred and plain-spoken. He will probably misunderstand everything, and certainly misunderstand the king. 'I have often pitied you, Cremuel,' Chapuys says. 'Henry is a man of great endowments, lacking only consistency, reason and sense. But at least you can meet him face to face. You can see what he makes of what you are telling him. With my master at such a distance, I always fear I will be misunderstood. Or that those who have the good fortune to come into the Emperor's presence will exercise the art of interpretation against me. You lack old friends. I mean, men of great family. I do not come from a place as low as yours. But you know how it is – I am the boy who always had to send the money home. I have had a little luck, and I have striven to the utmost of my talent. But in the end I cannot help but feel that much of my career has been like yours, Thomas.' He folds his napkin. 'Accidental.'

Christophe and Mathew come in and clear dishes. Chapuys stares at Mathew. 'Boy, did I not see you at Horsley?'

'Horsley, sir?'

'The Courtenays' house, in Surrey. As I think you know well.'

'Mathew came to me from Wolf Hall,' he explains.

'I am more concerned with where he has been since. And how a waiting-boy comes to speak French, though with such a country-man's accent I can hardly understand him.'

'He is a quick learner,' he says easily. 'I am sending him to Calais soon, where he may polish himself up a little.'

Mathew is so shocked he treads on Christophe's foot. 'Oaf,' Christophe mutters. '*Bon voyage.*'

'You mean, you are sending him to Calais where he may spy on Lord Lisle.' Chapuys sighs. 'Well, I must ...' He crosses himself, murmuring a Latin grace. Painfully he levers himself to his feet, and gathers his gown as if he feels a draught.

He, Lord Cromwell, extends his hand. 'I trust that when you reach the other side you will not complain of your treatment?'

He thinks of Eustache in his garden tower at Canonbury; the thundery evening when, quibble by quibble, a hair's-breadth at a time, they edged the Lady Mary from wreckage to salvage. He remembers Christophe squatting at the base of the tower, his knife in his hand.

Richard Cromwell comes in. 'Ambassador, your people are here.'

Chapuys hesitates. '*Mon cher*, I do not know when I shall return. Should we by some mischance, never again ...'

'Oh, none of that,' he says. 'We are stout of heart, Eustache, if not sound in limb.'

They embrace. The ambassador goes out, dispensing largesse to the household. He sits down at his desk. There is a letter from Carew's widow Eliza, asking him to sort out her affairs. He owes her gratitude, he feels. Carew's death has opened up opportunities to promote his own folk. When Richard comes back he asks him, 'You would not like to go into the privy chamber, nephew? The king is sending Rafe to Scotland again, and I need people as close as I can get them.'

A clerk puts his head around the door. 'Nothing from Wriothesley.'

'We will not hear tonight.' Any messenger on the road will be storm-lashed into shelter. Call-Me is in transit, we trust. He is at an inn: tallow candles, a cold bed; strangers' faces; Imperial guards on the door.

'I feel sorry for Chapuys,' he says to Richard. 'Going out into the rain.'

He feels someone has attached a weight to his heart. Not a big weight: just a small leaden bob, so he feels the drag. He turns back to his paperwork. He is occupied in setting up a new council, the Council of the West, to govern the parts beyond Bristol. He says to Wolsey – *le cardinal pacifique* – trust me, your Grace, I keep my mind on what I shall do come the peace. I am going to secure this German alliance for the king, and a bride.

Surely that will tempt the old ghost out? But the cardinal shows no sign of listening at all. He doesn't even ask, what about Duke Wilhelm in Cleves? Is he dead of papal poison, as your man Wriothesley says?

He is not. He is alive and willing to talk.

The dukedom of Cleves-Mark-Jülich-Berg lies on both sides of the Rhine. Its ruler Wilhelm is twenty-two years old, and through his mother has a claim, which he is pressing, to the land and seacoast of Guelders: a claim which the Emperor disputes. Duke Wilhelm shows great independence of mind. He is a reformer, but not a Lutheran. His church is under his own control. He guards some of Europe's vital trade routes.

He, Cromwell, sits down with the king's council and lays before them certain facts. He introduces them to the substance called alum, without which we cannot dye cloth.

In our grandfathers' time we bought alum from the Turk, who would never take cash alone, he wanted arms – thus equipping himself for war on Christians, using their own money. Then sixty years back a deposit was found at Tolfa near Rome, a deposit so rich that they say it will never run out till the Day of Judgement. The Vatican brought in the Medici to run the trade and invented a new and grave sin: trading in alum without a licence. Later it was Agostino Chigi, that prince of bankers, who ran the monopoly: and you should see the villa he built, on Tiber's shores.

Now the Pope has us under his bale and ban. We need a source, we need a conduit, if our industries are not to collapse. We use alum in tanning, we use it in the manufacture of glass; doctors use it to heal

642

wounds. The Spanish have a small supply. It is low-grade and anyway they will not sell it to heretics. But the ruler of Cleves, who has two sisters who want husbands, also has reserves of this treasure, which at its finest takes the form of crystals, huge clear crystals like jewels for a giant.

Perhaps alum is not the foundation for a love match. But members of the king's council agree: you have reason on your side, Lord Cromwell.

So what about the young ladies themselves? They are of great line-age, descended from the royal line of France and from our own King Edward I. They are good girls, from whom their mother will be sorry to part. It is true that our visiting envoys have never been allowed to see them. They have been in their presence, but the virgins of Cleves are modest by custom; throughout the interview the sisters sit in silence under their veils.

When he arrives in the privy chamber the doctors are on their way out, the foremost carrying a flask of urine. The man wears an expres-sion of pious gratification, as if he's found the Holy Grail.

'Come in,' the king says. 'I am exhausted from my travels, my lord.'

Over his embroidered nightshirt the king wears a jerkin lined with lambskins. His cap is pinned with a vast spinel, a purple stone with a glow soft as velvet. By his elbow stands a white basin containing his blood. The king's eyes flit to the basin, then to his; he looks apolo-getic. Henry is a fastidious man and would probably not like to encounter a bowl of gore. But he, Cromwell, is as indifferent as a butcher.

'Writs have gone out for the new Parliament, sir. I intend it will be a tractable one.'

He takes papers out of his bag, and a package. Henry's eyes light on it. 'What have you brought me?'

It is a work is called *The Solace and Consolation of Princes*, written by an adviser to the princes of Saxony. Henry turns it over in his hands. 'A wife would be a consolation.'

'If she brought us good allies, sir.'

The king falls to reading the book. But he interrupts him. 'My friends at the Fuggers' bank tell me Charles is raising cash.'

'For soldiers?'

'Yes. But to send into Barbary. They say he will not leave Spain himself. The Empress is having a child and he is concerned about her. She is subject to fevers, as your Majesty knows.'

The king is silent. No doubt his mind has slid elsewhere, to those worrying days of women's confinements: to Katherine, to Anne, to Jane. At last he says, 'Did you hear the Earl of Wiltshire is dead?'

Thomas Boleyn. 'God assoil him. I hear he made a good Christian end.' He pauses. 'Will your Majesty bestow his title elsewhere?'

'Well, he leaves no son.' Henry barks with laughter and shuts the book. 'George Boleyn is forgot.'

Not by me, he thinks. I sometimes dream of him, as I saw him last in the Martin Tower: his seeping tears, and his hands shaking, naked without their rings. He says, 'Cleves agrees to send pictures of the young ladies. But their painter is sick, so there may be a delay. From what I hear, it is no wonder they keep the Lady Anna veiled. They say in beauty she excels the Duchess Christina as the golden sun excels the silver moon.'

'Steady,' the king says. He laughs.

'I think if we send new envoys, the ladies will show their faces.'

'I am sending Dr Carne. And Nicholas Wotton.'

He is surprised. He did not know the king had planned so far. Neither man could be called a friend of his. Henry is watching him. 'I am glad of it, sir. They will not be partial. We can all trust their reports.'

He stops, because the young fellow Culpeper is oozing in, Howard ears pricked. 'May it please your Majesty,' Culpeper says, 'the doctors have sent me. May I take the basin of blood?'

Outside, Jane Rochford is waiting for him. 'Any nearer to a queen?' She has a bag with her. 'This is for you. From my lord father.'

'A book?'

'Of course, a book. What does my father ever send, but a book?'

'It might have been a venison pasty. The older I get, the more I hate Lent.'

He glances at her face, as he takes out the present: her discontented mouth. She says, 'We want to know which of the sisters he will choose. Unless he means to have them both?'

She is waiting. He turns over the leaves. It is Niccolò Machiavelli's book, and inside is a note from Lord Morley, suggesting he shows it to the king; he has marked the most interesting passages, he says, by drawing a hand in the margin.

'Well?' she says.

'I read it years ago, when it was still in manuscript. I shall write and thank your lord father, of course.'

'Not "Well?" about the book,' she says. '"Well?" about the princesses. Which one will he take? They say one has brown hair and one blonde.'

'I hope I shall not be called on for the Judgement of Paris.'

'Go for the blonde, is my advice.'

He hands the book to Christophe. 'His tastes may have changed.'

She looks at him as if he is simple. 'I do not think blondes go out of style. By the way, the Howards sent a little lass called Katherine, to see if we would have her among the new queen's maids. Succulent and plump, and I doubt she has passed her fifteenth year.'

'Send her away.'

'As you wish. Though I think you could win her from Uncle Norfolk if you winked at her and gave her an apple. I never saw a simpler maid – a little rosebud mouth hanging open, like a suckling at the teat. What shall I say to the Howards?'

'Put them off. Make sure she does not show her face till I have the marriage contracts signed.'

'I hear the Duke of Cleves has asked for the Lady Mary's portrait. It is time she made herself useful. And from what I hear, the most useful thing she could do is marry a German.'

'We do not send pictures of our princesses abroad. It is not our custom.'

She tilts her head. 'You invent customs very readily.'

He bows, as if she were complimenting him. It is the only thing to do, as he cannot well give her a slap. He says, 'Duke Wilhelm's envoys know Mary's virtues and qualities. They have seen her.'

'But not when she has toothache,' Rochford says gaily.

He tucks Lord Morley's gift under his arm. The king has nothing to learn from Niccolò's book. But it may pass an hour for him, when his leg is giving him pain.

When Mary is asked whether she would like to marry into Cleves, she says she will do as her father tells her, but that given her choice, she would rather stay in the land of her birth and remain a virgin. It is a modest answer, which no one can fault.

When he gets home Richard Riche is waiting. 'Ricardo,' he says, 'I shall want your help preparing for the Parliament. We shall be working long hours.'

'When do we not?' Riche says, like a man rising to the challenge. 'I hear Wriothesley is to sit for Hampshire?'

'I think he deserves it, after his travails abroad. I look for his return every day.'

'A pity he did not have better success, and bring back a bride. And Bishop Gardiner is the king's man in Hampshire – it will offend him, to have a rival.'

He nods: that's the idea.

'And young Gregory to sit – do you think he is ready? Forgive me, but your ill-wishers are bound to raise the point.'

'The business is great. The hours are long. I do not see it as an occupation for old men.'

Riche offers papers. 'Would you cast an eye? It is the pension list for the surrender at Shaftesbury. You always said the abbess would fight till the last ditch. But we have found a sum to buy her off.'

We should not begrudge. It is a rich house. He runs a dry quill down the list. There is the name he is looking for: Dorothea Clancey. 'Do you know if the ladies have decided their future?'

'Not our business, sir.' But then Riche softens. 'I look back fondly on our ride to Shaftesbury. I always think it a pleasure to be in your company for a day, my lord – and a privilege too. I relish to see how your lordship transacts business among all sorts and conditions of people. I am the better instructed, and I profit by it.'

Pleasure and profit. What could be more fitting for Richard Riche? The door is flung open. Christophe erupts into the room. 'Look who!'

'Call-Me!' He opens his arms wide. The traveller, muddy from the Dover road, falls into them.

'We lost sight of you!' He hugs him. 'Chapuys wrote to me from Calais – I think it was to say you were on the seas, but his words were all washed by salt water.'

'As mine,' Call-Me says. With his glove of red Spanish leather, he knocks a tear from his cheek; plucks off his hat, with its sweeping ostrich plume, and throws it down on the desk. 'Sir, I cannot tell you how glad I am to see your face. Twice or thrice I made sure I was dead. I did not know what to wish for – that the king would fall in love with Chapuys and hold him till my escape, or that he would boot him into a boat, so I might start for home.'

'It was the time between that we feared.' Rafe is standing in the doorway. 'When you were dissolved – neither here, nor there, nor in Heaven nor on earth.' He crosses the room, and kisses the hero's cheek. 'Welcome home, Call-Me.'

Riche is looking at them puzzled: as if they were a tribe of Indians, at some feast of theirs.

'Oh, and the knave Phillips!' Call-Me exclaims: as if he must get it over. 'Sir, you could not reproach me more than I reproach myself.'

'Be at ease,' he says. 'A man like Phillips is an affront to God and reason. If I had been on embassy at your age, I am sure I should have been deceived, if only out of zeal for my country's good.'

Riche says peevishly, 'My lord would rather have Wyatt safe home than you. Wyatt has things to tell him.'

'Oh?' Wriothesley says.

'Schemes for how we might set Italy in a roar,' Riche says. 'In Toledo he has the envoys of all nations in and out of his lodging and he spins them like a whipping top. Venice goes out of the back door, Ferrara comes in the front, while Mantua hides under the table and a Florentine up the chimney. He hears so many intrigues he says his skull is splitting. But he will not spill the facts except in secret to my lord.'

'Oh,' Wriothesley says. Richard Cromwell comes bounding in, hallooing like a houndmaster, and pounds him with his fist. Call-Me pounds him back, till Rafe says, 'Wriothesley, go home to your wife!'

'I should.' Call-Me blushes. He glows. He picks up the ostrich-feather hat and sweeps the air, and catches a candle in its arc.

It is Richard Riche who steps forward and pinches out the damage. 'Digits of iron,' he says diffidently.

The papers from Shaftesbury lie unattended. When the boys have gone, he stands over them, moving his forefinger over the name of the cardinal's daughter. The air smells of burning plumes. He picks up his pen and signs her off.

Within a week he hears that Mr Wriothesley has bribed or frightened one of the cipher clerks, and got the key to Wyatt's letters. It is Rafe who tells him: sheepish, ashamed of what Call-Me has done. He himself is more amused than angry. Good luck to him, if he can disentangle the Italian schemes. Wyatt says, start fires in the Pope's backyard. Use your money and your expertise to fan the sparks of conflict between states, then keep Rome busy quenching the blaze. It might work, he thinks. It might just as easily blow back in our faces.

He says to Rafe, 'In the cardinal's day, when I was his man of business and Stephen Gardiner was his secretary, I would have opened Stephen's letters if I could.'

And where I could, I did. And I would still. And I do.

He calls in Hans: 'Paint the Lady Mary. I need to send her likeness to the Duke of Cleves.'

'You want this match?' Hans says.

'Certainly.'

'Listen, I do not flatter.'

'Not in my case, certainly. But you made Thomas More look congenial.'

'I do not flatter because I dare not. The king relies on me. But if I paint our little shrew faithfully, Wilhelm will take fright. Therefore I cannot see the advantage for me in this commission, or how it could end well.'

'You would not refuse to paint the king's daughter, surely? You will find a way, Hans.'

'People say, when all offers for Mary have failed, she will turn to Cromwell.'

'That is nonsense.' He thinks, she hates me: can Hans not see this? 'You speak as if she is an ancient lady. She is, what, twenty-two, twenty-three?'

'She looks more. Her prospects oppress her.' Hans laughs.

It is true it would not be easy for a stranger to guess Mary's age. Sometimes she looks like a pallid child, sometimes like an old woman. There will be a sweet moment, he thinks, half an hour on some ordinary afternoon, when she looks like herself.

At Greenwich this Easter he watches Mary; he knows the court is watching him, watching her. She has recently bought a hundred pearls, and has spent three hundred pounds on clothes for the feast. In yellow damask and purple taffeta, she plays with the little prince. She takes a hand at cards, plays the virginals, gossips with her ladies, and rides out into the fresh air as the winter relaxes its grip.

When the Courtenays and Poles were arrested, the king had his daughter's household questioned. She was asked to hand over her letters from Chapuys, and was able to supply a bundle, empty in content; the ambassador had written them specially, at a hint from him, and lent them various dates. If Mary had claimed to have received no letters, the king would have suspected she had burned them. Which he is quite sure she has.

Mary can play such a game as this, needing no explanations. But the week of the beheadings, the king had to send her Dr Butts, who found her so faint she could hardly stand.

She will miss Chapuys, no doubt. But it is spring, and at court her father makes a fuss of her. He, Lord Cromwell, escorts her to watch the tennis play. He says, looking sideways at her, 'I hear Duke Wilhelm is very handsome.'

'That does not weigh,' she says equably.

'No, but better than the other thing. By the way, do not let people tell you he is a Lutheran.'

The balls whistle across the court. 'My lord Cromwell,' she says, 'I don't let anybody tell me anything.'

The king's Easter pieties are as fervent as any papist could wish. Good Friday saw him shuffling to the crucifix on his knees. The German envoys are aghast. If this is what he does at Easter, what will he do on Ascension Day? As Christ rises bodily to Heaven, will your king have himself hoisted on a rope and pulley? Will he bask among the goddesses on his ceiling, till at Whitsuntide he descends in the form of a dove?

He, Lord Cromwell, is planning his own Ascension Day. He has devised a new order of precedence for the realm, to be enacted by Parliament. From now on, it is not your noble and ancient blood that will place you in the hierarchy. It is what job you do for the king. The king's Vicegerent – that's him – outranks the bench of bishops. The king's Secretary, once created a baron, outranks all barons. If the Lord Privy Seal was born a commoner, he can still sit higher than a duke. Christophe says, 'If all your offices were counted, you should have a ladder on a chair, and a ladder on that, and a throne perched up in the clouds, to look down on Norferk and the foes, and spit on them.'

Thomas Howard does not lose under the new scheme, but he can still grumble about the elevation of others. 'As for Gardineur,' Christophe says, 'who is only a little bishop, he will gnash his teeth right out of his head.'

Under a painted ceiling, under a hard marbled sky, he sits putting together his programme for Parliament. The last of the monasteries will go down and the king will begin to found colleges and cathedrals in their stead. There will be devices for poor relief and the defence of the realm, and a device for unity in religion: what form it will take, he hardly knows, but the king wants it.

His daughter writes at last from Antwerp. Things are difficult here, I might come to England if you will receive me? He writes to her, trust to Stephen Vaughan for help. Though our ambassadors have come home, Vaughan stays in Antwerp as head of the English merchants. He will arrange your passage.

If she comes she will be in danger, and a source of danger too. The king has made it clear that certain sectaries must avoid his realm. He can ask for her discretion. Can he ask her to dissimulate? He has asked it of others. He says to himself, if Cranmer can hide a wife, surely I can hide a daughter. He has many houses, and is always getting more. When you look at him these days you think of Jupiter, planet of increase.

One morning after Easter he wakes with a heavy, aching head, his neck stiff. He cannot eat, goes out on an empty stomach to the council meeting. The king will not preside today. Henry is at his manor house at Oatlands, which he is planning to rebuild. Then perhaps he will go on to Nonsuch, to see what progress Rafe is making.

The council is waiting. He drops his papers at his place. 'Couldn't you get on without me?'

Fitzwilliam says, 'It is more that we dare not.'

'You are out of humour, my lord Southampton. Is your guest tormenting you? Lady Salisbury cannot be easy. I promise I will take her away to the Tower.'

'I have been asking you to do that since Christmas. And you need not guess at the cause of my humour. I am not a woman. Ask me and I will tell you.'

Perhaps Fitz is jealous of his new offices? Captain of the Isle of Wight. Constable of Leeds Castle. Or perhaps someone has dropped a word of poison in his ear: Lord Cromwell doubts your commitment to the gospel.

Lord Audley says, 'Shall we get to the agenda? Letters come from my lord Norfolk –'

He lets Audley thrash through the duke's latest complaints, while he pins Fitzwilliam with his gaze. You would think Fitz is doing well enough: an earl, and Lord Admiral. Perhaps, he thinks, he is jealous because I have a son I can put into the Parliament. And Fitz has not.

Presently, under his scrutiny, Fitzwilliam grows upset and spills his papers. A little clerk has to fall to his knees and weave around their feet like a cat. Gardiner laughs out loud. He says, 'Glad to see you merry, Winchester.'

His head is pounding. As the meeting rises, Audley says, 'Now don't be late again, my lord. We are the fellowship of the Round Table, you know, and that chair of yours is the Siege Perilous. It stood empty for ten thousand years, till Lord Cromwell came to fill it.'

Next day he cannot get out of bed. He tries to say his prayers, but all he can recall is a sermon Latimer preached, on a hot July day, it would be the summer Anne Boleyn came down. *But God will come, God will come, he will not tarry long away. He will come upon such a day as we nothing look for him, and such an hour as we know not. He will come and cut us in pieces.*

By the time Dr Butts arrives, he is able to give an account of himself. He has been at the Sadlers' house, and the children have come out with measles, is it possible ...? Old women claim you only have it once.

Butts frowns. 'If it is the measles we will soon know, but you must stay away from court.'

This infection kills children but he does not think it will kill him. He has his papers brought in. By noon he is working. By next day he is ready to go out, his entourage assembled, his papers in hand. But then he sits down, and does not feel he will get up again. He is transfixed, watching his old enemy emerge from the mist. You would think he would recognise his Italian fever by now. 'Parliament will be meeting,' he says, 'and I must ...' His sentence tails off. Already weakness like tepid water is trickling through his limbs.

He hands his papers to Richard. 'Will you get a message to the king? No – go in person. Ride where he is. Tell him I will see him soon.'

The shivering begins. He has a clerk follow him to his room, and dictates letters until the trembling means he has to clench his jaw: and even then, between spasms, he is able to dictate.

Anne Boleyn used to say to him, 'You are only ill when you want to be.' How wrong she was.

In the first access of the fever, it is George Boleyn who is lurking behind the door. There is a noise, low conversation or insects, perhaps a fly banging its head and cannot get out, *buzz buzz* against the pane. He sees the door is ajar. George will slide through it: perhaps on the bolster, already soaked with sweat, he will lay his blind and weeping head.

The doctors say, 'You know the procedure, my lord. Bed rest and small beer.'

And the pungent remedies, that never do any good, but when you are lucid and can hold yourself up, you swallow them, because it cheers up the people around you.

'I want Wriothesley,' he says, 'where is he?'

'He has gone down to Hampshire, sir, to prepare for his election.'

'Norfolk will be back for the Parliament. He will make speeches. What shall I do?'

'Sir, this fever was, before parliaments were thought of.'

This fever was before the Bible was written, in English, Latin or Greek. It was before the Table was round, before Troy burned. It destroyed folk before the Flood, and afflicted the first men when they were exiled from paradise. Abel was weak from a bout, and that is how Cain slew him.

His whole body aches. His eyes swim. He hears timbers creaking about him, like the timbers of a ship under sail, and he thinks he is back at Austin Friars, and his wife is still alive. He thinks of himself flying through the hours of darkness, reassembling himself on his bed: as they say the home of the Virgin Mary flew to Italy, and rebuilt itself among people who appreciate it.

But when morning comes and they open the shutter – the light in his eyes like a knife – they say, no, you are still here at St James's. But anything you want, we can go and fetch it.

He thinks, where did I go? I was travelling all night.

He sits up. 'Today I shall work.' One day the fever rages, next it abates, next it rises. Soon he will have gone through the full cycle. He can sit up in a chair, but he has no illusions, he has not seen the worst. If I am going to die, he thinks, there are papers that ought to be destroyed. But then if I live, inconvenience will ensue. Surely death will give me notice. We have met before. He should not be churlish like a stranger.

The doctors say, 'In extremity, who would you like?'

He stares. 'Who would I like?'

'The Bishop of Worcester? The Archbishop of Canterbury?'

'Oh, I see. A confessor. Not Gardiner. If he saw me on my death-bed he would tip me out of it, so I should die on the floor.'

He goes through his work at double speed. Instructions for Mr Sadler, soon to lead a mission to Scotland. A letter to Wyatt, to say the king has named his replacement. He asks his French secretary to come in. 'Nothing from Paris today? Letters from Edmund Bonner?'

He signals for a basin and vomits neatly. He stares at what his body has produced. 'What do we hear of the Venetians?'

The fleet is manoeuvring, was the last information; they are preparing a power against the Turk. The German princes are meeting in Frankfurt: any dispatches?

Sir, they say, we will bring you every letter as soon as it comes in, but you must go back to bed now. Your malady rushes on you fast.

When he was a boy in Putney he used to pick up coins from the mud of the foreshore. They were thin and worn and bore the features of monarchs almost erased. You could not spend the money; it was not even good to clink in your hand. All you could do was put it in a box and wonder about it. If so many coins are washed up, how many does the river conceal, in its channels and deeps? A treasury of princes, squinting up at the hazy light, each with a spoiled single eye, like Francis Bryan. He lifts his head. 'How *is* Francis? Is he still alive? I forget.'

'Oh yes, my lord,' they say. 'Sir Francis is still with us, he made a recovery both from his illness and the king's displeasure. As we trust you will too.'

His displeasure! I am sure I have displeased him, he thinks. Look how he steamed and glared, that day I took a holiday. Look how he pawed the ground and rolled his eyes. This is what Henry does. He uses people up. He takes all they give him and more. When he is finished with them he is noisier and fatter and they are husks or corpses.

He is not sure if he has spoken aloud. But he knows that he is in his barge, his flag flying. He can feel the river moving beneath, and Bastings conveying him to some further shore. In his fever he thinks Becket is back in his niche above the water at Lambeth Palace. Bastings says, I told you he would return. Man and boy I have been saluting him, my father before me.

Nonsense, he says. Becket is in the cellar locked in a box. If I die, fire my bones from a cannon. I should like to see Gardiner's face!

Next day he sends courteous messages to the new Frenchman, Marillac. Ambassador Castillon is back home, but the new man has already seen the king at Greenwich. He is uneasy about what has passed while he has been in the grip of his malady; besides, he would like to hear any news from Persia or the east, which the French always get before we do.

On the day when the fever abates, you measure the hours and you live in dread; it is coming, inexorable as nightfall. Shuddering, stricken, he is helped back to bed, just as they are bringing in word that envoys have arrived from Cleves: they are here in London, they are asking for Cromwell right now. He is burning with heat like an armourer's shop; he is in the forge, he is ash. His father Walter comes in and shouts, you fool of a boy, if you don't caulk the bellows how am I to get a blaze?

You fool of a father, he shouts back. Don't you think it's hot enough?

But once you have been in Italy you can never really get warm. The English sun has half a heart, it flickers and lurks, it sinks when you least expect it: then comes the autumn, the warm and smoky rain.

Once he was at Launde Abbey, in the cardinal's service. Launde is lush pastureland, it is quiet, only the murmur of bees over the herb garden and the drone of prayer. It is summer, and he sits at ease in an arbour, talking with the brethren. Brother Urban holds a gillyflower. He speaks of the Holy Ghost. Fleecy clouds sail above.

Now he is at Launde in winter. The trees are silver, and a cold sun shines from a clear sky. He is tramping, Brother Thomas Frisby at his side, the snow crunching under his boots, his blood singing in his veins. All around, scattering from the misted eye, the tracks of small birds and animals, cut into white like some code or lost alphabet. God sees them, two black figures under enamelled blue.

Then with a yell, Frisby disappears. In a hollow on his back he thrashes, and he, the cardinal's man, plunges to the rescue. He shouts and heaves, the world sliding under his feet, and snow flies about him like feathers. Frisby's shape cuts deep into the white, his habit spread; he stretches out his arms, his feet scrabble for purchase, he grunts, flounders, curses – then he, Thomas, has him on his feet, the monk's eyes screwed up against the glare, his nose red, his laughter ringing in the air. They embrace, snow sliding from their cloaks; grace seeps through them like *aqua vitae*, as they haul each other towards the abbey and the sound of bells.

The Prior of Launde is standing over him, with the face of Dr Butts. 'By the Mass,' he says, 'I have never known a living man so chilled.' Another minute, and he will be a block of ice. He thinks, they will be able to put me in a cellar and chip from me all summer. They can stir me into crushed strawberries with elderberry wine.

He wakes: tentative at first, his hand creeping over the sheets. He is not at Launde at all. They have piled so many blankets on him that he resembles a blockhouse or fortification. I could stop the Turks, he mutters.

He sits up. He signals for a drink. They have lit candles. He thinks, I wonder what happened to Frisby? He cannot be any great age. I will have Launde, when the abbot surrenders it: Launde for myself. I shall go and live there when all this is over. I shall be Lord Cromwell at home. In summer I shall sit in the arbour. In winter I shall walk on the ice.

There is a letter from Melanchthon. There is another from the Duke of Saxony. They come in and say, 'My lord, Master Gregory is here, ridden hard from Sussex.'

Gregory comes and stands at the foot of his bed. He looks at his father. 'Christ,' he says.

He says, 'Oh, God help us Gregory, don't tell me I am wasted and wan. It will take more than a bout of this ague to part me from my life. They should not have disturbed you.'

Gregory says, 'I was coming up anyway. For the Parliament.'

He says, 'Richard Riche was right. You are too young.'

'He said that?' Gregory is amused.

He says, 'Gregory, after Jane died, you asked me, who will you let the king marry next?'

Our sweet Jane. A tear rolls from his cheek. His folk run about in a panic. 'My lord is crying!' Naturally, they have not seen it before.

He wipes the tear away. 'I have letters out of Germany. My clerks are making translations now. The princes have given their word in our favour. For a marriage into Cleves, for the king. Now bring me, will you, ink and paper?'

'You are not able,' his son says.

He says, 'Gregory, I must use my time. I have less than twenty-four hours.' Before my bargemaster rows me again, and dips me in the river Styx.

* * *

But it is some time till he returns to business: a night, a day, a night. He has gone down to Putney. For some time – now he is fourteen, fifteen – he has been hanging about at the Williamses' house in Mortlake. His sister Kat has married into these respectable folk, and they say, 'Young Thomas, he's a clean biddable lad: writes a fair hand, good with figures, steady around horses, and not too proud to chop firewood or swill out the yard. Anybody would have him apprentice, and be glad of him.'

They talk about him as if they were selling him.

'Poor little lad,' a woman says. 'Walter knocks him about. But then you know what Walter is.'

The Williamses know nothing of the imperatives of your life, as you lead it now. They know nothing of the tangle of Putney feuds, the network of obligations to fight and win that has ensnared you since you could walk: sure as any duke, you have honour, honour must be served. The Williamses are good people, and that protects them from the need that gnaws you: the need for everything you haven't got and they'll never want.

The Williamses say, 'We could get the boy a place. There's Arthur Whatyoucallit, over Esher way. He wants a lad.'

He cannot bear it, this place he will get. He cannot be Arthur's lad, over Esher way. He has to be some other lad, that would make Esher quake.

The time he spends with his sister, it gets him out of Walter's way, but then again it allows the eel boy to arm his band. Since he was seven years old the eel boy has been his enemy. He does not know how the feud began. But he remembers dipping the eel boy's head in a barrel, holding him under till the bugger nearly drowned.

Now when he goes swaggering home, the eel boy and his friends are waiting. 'Oy,' they call. 'Oy, Put-an-edge-on-it.'

They call him that because Walter grinds knives. They sing when they see him:

'I lay ten year in Newgate
Methought I lay too long:
My whoreson fetters hurt me sore,
My fetters were too strong.'

They call out, 'You Irish bastard, that go in a bald dogskin!'

Is Walter Irish? He denies it, but you wouldn't put it past him.

They shout, 'You killed your mother when you were born. She couldn't stand to look at you, out you slid and she cut her throat.'

His sister Kat says, 'Don't listen to them. That's not what occurred.'

He calls back, 'You devil's turd, eel boy, are you tired of life?'

Eel boy calls, 'I'll dint you, craphead.'

'When?' he says.

'Saturday night?'

'I'll skin and salt you, and fry you in a pan.'

So then he has to do it.

Saturday night you chased him uphill. By then you had created a deep fear in his heart, by messages transmitted through acquaintances of yours. If eel boy thinks (and he has had days to think) he will recall that he has lost every bout he has fought with you. He can't fight history, so he runs, because what else can he do? He could stand on the high road, and offer his hand: but then, Thomas Craphead would slice his fingers off.

If he runs to his uncle's warehouse, eel boy believes, he'll escape you. He'll go charging past the watchman at the gate, who will bustle up and strong-arm you, 'Crummel, what do you here?'

But there is no watchman tonight, as you well know. When you issued out, Walter and his mates were an hour into strong ale. He's a beast of a brewer, but he keeps back the best for his crew. And it's Wilkin the Watch who sticks his face out of the room: 'Drink with us, Thomas?'

He says, 'I'm going to church.'

Wilkin retreats, withdraws his slack glistening face. From behind the door, rollicking song: *By Cock, ye make me spill my ale …*

You walk, under the waning moon. Only when you sight eel boy do you break into a trot, an easy pace that will take you unwinded to your destination. When you enter the yard he is not in sight. But there is no one to stop you following him into the darkness, into the undercroft, where under deep vaulting, behind chests and boxes stamped with the devices of alien cities and their trading guilds, eel boy has burrowed in.

You think of the home you left. You wonder where Walter and his mates have got to with their song. With its refrains and variations they can draw it out an hour or more. Walter likes to take the lass's part, squealing as she is backed against the wall: *Let go I say…*

Then the men chorus: *Abide awhile! Why have ye haste?* and mime pulling their breeches down.

Luckily, when they sing this song, there is never an actual woman in the room.

Down in the cellars your eyes have adjusted to the gloom. You want to laugh. You can hear the rasp of the boy's breath. You move towards him, and you let him know that you know exactly where he is. 'You might as well wave a flag,' you call.

You halt. If you stand longer (and you have the patience) he will begin to cry. Beg.

Let go I say…

And if you stand longer still, he might die of fright: which would save a mess on the floor. You take the knife out. Can he see you? The only light is from a high barred window, and it is not so much light as an alleviation of the murk. Not much point his uncle barring the window, is there, if Wilkin rolls out and leaves the door unlocked? You remark on this. 'Go on,' you call, 'agree with me.' His breath now sounds like three cats in a sack.

Eel boy was only ever brave with his cousins and brothers about him. 'Now you shit yourself,' you tell him: his calm instructor, his guide.

When you move the crate (you are strong, as the Williamses say) you see his face, blank and white as a sheet stretched on a hedge. It must provide its own pallid light, because you look straight into his eyes. You are surprised by his expression. 'You look glad to see me,' you say. He steps forward, as if in greeting, and in one smooth unhesitating action, offering his soft belly, he impales himself on the blade.

It's the sudden heat that shocks you, the contaminating swill across the stone. You bend and pull out the knife. Something comes with it: a loop of his tripes. Your first thought is for the blade. You wipe it on your own jerkin, an efficient action, one-two. You don't look down: but you feel him at your feet, a lumpen mess. At once you offer a prayer.

You bend down stiffly, like an old man. Perhaps you accede too readily to the idea that he is dead, but you close his eyes, reaching down into the pool of darkness. You do it delicately, as a virgin might finger fruit. If the pool of gore appears modest, it is because his bulk is hiding it. But when you shift him, flopping him over, you see the neatness with which he is pierced.

You cannot guess later what makes you decide to move him. Perhaps you thought he was not dead but pretending. Though what quality of pretence does it take, to let your eyelids be pressed shut?

Later you comprehend nothing of your choices that night. Thomas Craphead was in charge, his arms and legs working independently of his soul. So you dragged eel boy, his red head bumping along, sedate. Your pace is necessarily slow: *Abide awhile, why have ye haste?* Outside, it is warmer than in the cellar. The street is empty, till you see the watchman, heading home. His walk is the purposeful sway of a man in drink, still hoping to pass as an upright citizen: ask him, and he'll say he's swaying like that just for fun. 'Straight as a ...' the old sot shouts. He has baffled himself; he can't think what is straight. 'Put-an-edge-on-it! You're out late.'

He's forgotten he saw you earlier. That he invited you to a bench at his song school.

Wilkin blinks: 'Who's yon?'

'Eel boy,' you say. No point pretending.

'By Cock, he's had a skinful! Taking him home? Good lad. Got to look out for your friends. Want a hand?'

Wilkin heaves, and vomits at his own feet. 'Clean that up,' you say. 'Go on, Wilkin, or I'll rub your head in it.'

Suddenly you are outraged: as if the only thing that matters is to keep the streets clean.

'Shog off,' Wilkin says. Glassy-eyed, he lurches away. You watch him go. He is heading in the direction, vaguely, of his place of work. You can't resist it: you shout after him, 'Don't forget to lock up.'

You could, if you had a friend to help you, put the boy in the water. If dead he will sink, if alive he will ... sink. It is a still night, there is no sound from the river, and you feel he would slip down the bank, frictionless, unresisting as if oiled, and go into the Thames with a whisper. You can see it: how the surface simply slides away from him, like a bored glance.

But you can't do that. It's not compunction. It's that strength has flowed out of you. You take out your knife from its sheaf. You give it another wipe on your sleeve. Truly, you would not know it had seen action. You put it back. You feel a powerful impulse to lie down beside eel boy and sleep.

When you get back, Walter and his boys are still bellowing. You are astonished. You thought it was three in the morning. You expected dowsed lights, shutters, padlocks. But there they are, still roaring away: *Come kiss me! Nay! By God ye shall ...*

The door opens. 'Thomas? Where been?'

You don't answer.

Walter sounds as outraged as you were, when Wilkin fouled the highway. 'Don't you turn your back on me!'

'Christ, no,' you say. 'He'd be a fool and short-lived, that did that.'

Walter raises his hand. But something – perhaps his own unsteadiness, perhaps something in your eye – makes him back off. 'I'll be right with you, lads,' he shouts.

They've reached the part where they rape the maid. Walter will be required to imitate her cries. *Now have ye laid me on the floor ...*

Walter's eyes are bulging. He points. 'Thee, Thomas, in the morning.'

'Thee anytime. Now?'

The knife is next to your heart: ready for use. Though you could lie down and slumber. You could fall at his feet: *Father, I have sinned ...*

'Walt!' some dolt roars. 'Come back in!' Out rolls the squinting knave and claps his father's shoulder, lays hold of him by the collar. The door slams. He watches the place where his father isn't. From behind the door, a flurry of shrieks, as the maiden cries for her mother.

One day soon he will be indefeasible. One day he will drag Walt into the light of day, and fell him in common view, the good folk of Putney watching: and if they care to come from Mortlake and Wimbledon, they will find it worth their while.

'Father, I am ready,' says Noah's son in the play. *Axe have I, by this crown, as sharp as any in all this town. I have a hatchet, wonder keen, To bite well, as may be seen ...*

Then Noah and his sons make a ship. And sail forth, on God's tide.

In his fever, he thinks the Archbishop of Canterbury arrives. Cranmer, not Becket: even so, it might have been a dream. When he sits up, 'John Husee is without,' they say. He groans. He has a band of negotiators working on the purchase of Lisle's property at Painswick. Lisle bleats they have neither heart nor conscience, but what does he expect? They're lawyers.

Lisle wants special treatment, from high and low. He has owed the king money for ten years, and humble men too. He owes his grocer, Blagge. The drapers Jasper and Tong supply him no longer. People in the city complain to him about Lord Lisle's debts, as if he ought to pay them.

Help me out of bed, he says. He sits in a chair, wrapped up against April. 'Give out that I am better. Is Norfolk back for the Parliament? And Suffolk? Is Mr Wriothesley come up? And is Gregory here?'

'Master Gregory has been and gone away again.'

He has missed St George's Day, the chapter of the Garter. The recent executions have opened vacancies among the knights.

They tell him William Kingston has been elected, an honour long deserved.

He says, how stands Bishop Gardiner? Has he fallen in with the king, or out with the king, these few days while I have been lying sick?

Christophe says, 'Gardineur – what does he know, sir?'

'Less than he thinks.'

'You are sharp this morning,' Christophe says. 'But in your fever you groaned and said, "Stephen Gardineur knows."'

Stephen went down to Putney. He truffled about in the mud. He said, *Cromwell, I know more of you than your mother knows. I know more about your past than you know yourself.*

'And is Thomas Boleyn truly dead?' he asks. 'Or did I dream it?'

'As dead as his daughter.'

In the access of his fever he had seen Anne the queen, walking to the scaffold, the wind pawing her. He heard her final prayer, ripped away from her lips, and he saw the veiled women who steadied her for the headsman: saw them step away, and lift the hems of their garments clear.

Gregory comes back once he hears he is awake. Gregory Cromwell, member of Parliament: grass-green velvet with a curling black feather in his cap. He says, 'Father, the new French ambassador and the new Imperial ambassador visit each other every day. They walk with their arms linked, billing like turtle doves. But what we hear is, the traitor Pole finds cold entertainment with the Emperor.'

Reginald Pole cannot understand why Charles does not place the conquest of England at the top of his list. Charles tells him wearily, I am only human. And there is only one of me. And I can only lead one army at a time. Any season, I must be ready against the Turks.

But the Turks are the enemy without, Pole pleads. And the English the enemy within. Should they not be dealt with first?

Charles says, 'Bless you, Monsieur Polo: if we wake tomorrow and the Turk is at the gates of Vienna, will you say the enemy is within, or without?'

In this Parliament we will have a bill of attainder against Pole's mother and against Gertrude Courtenay. They will be named traitors without need of further trial. He, the Lord Privy Seal, limps to the Parliament house and shows the silent assembly a figured vestment found in the possession of Margaret, Countess of Salisbury. It quarters the arms of England with a pansy for Pole and a marigold for the Lady Mary, signifying their union; between them grows a Tree of Life. It was turned out of Margaret's coffers, he asserts, by those sent to search her houses. He says, I always maintained that embroidery would get her into trouble.

Margaret Pole is moved to the Tower. The king is pleased to spare her life, for now. He thinks of all the times Margaret neglected to give him his title, making him plain Master Cromwell. She sees who is the master now.

He dreams of a disembodied self walking in deep woods. There are mirrors set among the trees.

When he drags himself to where the king is, papers in hand, he finds Gardiner there first. Gardiner says, 'You look very ill, Cromwell. There is a rumour flying around that you are dead.'

'Well,' he says modestly. 'As you see, Stephen.'

The king says, 'I am feeling better myself. Is this inconvenience over, do you suppose?'

The fever, he means: the waves of nausea, the racking aches, the raging headache. 'Majesty, I have some news from Cleves.'

He waits for the king to dismiss Stephen. But Henry only says, 'Yes?'

'I know the Bishop of Winchester has much in hand. Perhaps he would like to continue his day?'

But Henry makes no sign. Stephen seems to puff up, like a toad.

Deliberately he turns away from him, to address the king. 'Duke Wilhelm would like to be assured of the dower arrangements for his sister and,' he hesitates, 'how she would be left, if your Majesty were to pre-decease her.'

'Why does he think that likely?' Gardiner asks.

He keeps his eyes averted. 'Such arrangements are comprehended in any marriage contract. You cannot be so ignorant of the wedded state that you do not know that.'

Stephen says, 'I imagine the lady would be struck to the heart. She would care more about the loss of the king's person, than for any worldly advantage.'

He flicks a glance at Henry: he sees he is entranced by the bishop's words. 'That is why a bride's kin make the contract, and in advance. So when she is new-widowed she does not weep herself out of her rights.'

Henry says, 'I am known for generosity. Duke Wilhelm will find nothing to complain of.'

'There is another matter,' he says, reluctant. 'Our man Wotton is writing to your Majesty. A little over ten years ago, a marriage was proposed between the Lady Anna and the heir of the Duke of Lorraine. Now –'

'But that business was raised last year,' Henry says. 'When the contract was drawn the parties were but ten and twelve years old. No contract holds good until they affirm it, having reached a fit age. Therefore I see no impediment to our union. Why is the matter brought up again? I see the Emperor's hand in it. He is determined I shall not wed.'

'All the same, we had better see the paperwork,' Gardiner says.

'It seems to me,' he says, 'that Cleves would never have offered the Lady Anna if she were not completely free.'

Gardiner is stubborn. 'I would like to see articles of revocation.'

'It is my understanding that the marriage contract was written into a larger text, which was not formally revoked because it was part of a treaty of friendship and mutual aid …' He closes his eyes. 'I will ask someone to write it all down for you, Gardiner.'

'And bring it before the whole council. Or it would be unsafe to go any further.'

'Unsafe?' Henry stares at him. He seems to be disputing his choice of word.

'Unwise,' Gardiner concedes.

'In any event,' he says, 'though the king prefers Lady Anna, as being the elder and of meeter age, if there did prove to be an impediment, there is nothing against the Lady Amelia. And – here is good news – they are able to provide likenesses.'

Gardiner says, 'I wonder where they found those, all of a sudden. I thought Cranach was ill.'

'Perhaps he has powers of recovery,' he says, 'like me.'

'How old are they?'

'The princesses?'

'The portraits,' Gardiner says.

'Recent, I am assured.'

'But if our envoys have not seen either lady, how shall they swear to the likeness?'

'They have in fact seen them,' he says. 'But they were somewhat cloaked and veiled.'

'I wonder why?'

Henry says, 'You see! Would not this delight the Emperor? Division among my councillors? Contention and strife?'

He and Gardiner face each other. The bishop is not there to discuss the king's marriage. He's there on God's business, or so he would claim. The king wishes to make an act of Parliament to abolish diversity in opinion: by which he means, the expression of opinion. Gardiner has come to push him on six articles of faith laid before Convocation: to persuade the king to the Roman line, body and blood.

There is no doubt, his sickness has set back the cause of the gospel – his brothers too afraid and too disunited, without him, to present a firm front. Norfolk has placed a sycophant in the Commons as Mr Speaker. In the Lords, the duke himself crusades, bringing to the table these six articles and wrangling about them with every confidence – though he knows as much theology as a gatepost. Gardiner has whipped in the bishops who stick by ancient doctrine, and they conspire together from breakfast to supper, talking like rank papists and raising their glasses to toast old times. While the Lord Privy Seal is sweating in his sickbed, while he is writing letters all over Europe searching out allies and friends, while he is occupied in finding nearly fifteen hundred pounds a day to pay and victual the mariners who man the ships at Portsmouth – his enemies have stolen past him, and by the end of the Parliament, they will have six articles passed into law.

The king says, 'My lord Cromwell, if that is all –?'

He bows himself out. Culpeper is attending; the boy slides up to him: 'You need a seat, my lord? A cup of wine?'

He needs to hit somebody. He waves the boy back. When he gets home he is shaking with fatigue. He has forgotten how much bruising energy it takes to confront Stephen Gardiner. He throws his papers down. 'Ask the German guests to come and see me. We will plan a feast. Send Thurston up.'

He talks as if his illness is behind him, but he knows it has not run its course. He prays the fever will weaken itself through successive bouts. It is vital that this summer he is by the king's side, so he must be fit for long days of hunting. Every absent day he loses advantage. If kings do not see you they forget you. Even though nothing in the realm is done without you, kings think they do it all themselves.

Still: I am Vicegerent, he tells himself. I, not Stephen, am Chief Secretary and Lord Privy Seal. I am first in the king's council and first in his estimation, and I am well able to wimble holes in the bottom of papist boats. Every day now is Ascension Day. However much Thomas Howard mislikes the scriptures, there will soon be Bibles enough for every parish: and I standing at the king's side, handing them out. As for Gardiner, what does he truly understand, of the king's mind and temper? What does he know of the revenue? What does he know of the defence of the realm?

On a fine day in May, assembling at dawn, the armed might of London passes before the king at Whitehall. There are some sixteen thousand men in array, and of them he has furnished fully one-tenth himself. He had intended to ride at their head, but weakness confines him to St James's, where he watches from the back gate: but to bear him company the king sends John de Vere, Earl of Oxford, Lord Great Chamberlain. Gregory and Richard on their white horses ride together: faces intent, armour blazing, the Cromwell flag rippling.

In Italy, he thinks, when I was a soldier, I picked up a snake for a bet. My comrades counted slowly, one to twenty, while I tightened my grip. The snake twisted in my hand and sank its venom deep into my wrist. But I gripped the noxious beast till I pleased to let it go. I took the poison and I never died. The witnesses stuffed my pockets with their money. And God damn the man who says I didn't earn it.

When the days are fine, and the air sweet after Evensong, the king cruises up and down the river in the royal barge and shows himself to the people, his gold pilot's whistle around his neck, on his face a beaming smile; his musicians follow in a second barge, playing drums and fifes. The people line the bank and cheer. Whit Sunday is observed with great ceremony, as in papist days. Richard Riche spends the holiday drawing up a huge list of the king's debts.

News comes from Spain that the Empress is dead, with her new baby. The king orders full court mourning. St Paul's is hung with black drapes and the banners of the Holy Roman Empire. The dukes of Norfolk and Suffolk lead the ceremonies. He stands as far from Norfolk as he can, without losing sight of him, or losing precedence.

Ten bishops attend, and Stokesley leads the requiem. Stokesley looks ill, he thinks: though since he is an old crony of More's, he should have felt invigorated by those six pernicious articles in the bill. Every parish in London tolls its bells for the Empress, the unknown lady who has never set foot here. Far into the night they clang. Bats and demons whirl in the air.

Wyatt writes from Toledo that his bags are packed, and the Inquisitors, though reluctant, will part with him. But the Emperor has gone into seclusion in a monastery, to mourn his wife, so he must wait – he means to take formal leave, not scuttle away like some churl in debt. 'Though he probably is,' Rafe says. 'In debt.'

Bess Darrell writes from Allington: Cromwell, where is Wyatt? Each hour seems like a year to me.

From Italy come reports of two comets seen on one day. Suppose one comet stands for the end of the Empress: what else does He have up his sleeve, the creator of the moon and stars?

Cranmer comes to see him. 'I am clean amazed,' he says, 'I am perplexed, that Parliament could set back the cause of good religion. God's ways are very strange, to have stricken you down just at this time.'

'You can't fault Gardiner's timing,' he says. 'Or Thomas Howard's.'

'I am not sure …' Cranmer struggles. 'That is … one cannot wholly blame …'

'You're not going to blame the king, are you?'

Better blame Norfolk, and bishops Gardiner, Stokesley and Sampson, than wonder aloud whether Henry is weak or duplicitous or incapable of seeing his own interest.

'Our friends from Germany are appalled,' Cranmer says. 'I have to defend our master to them.'

'How do you do that?' he asks, interested.

'Where was Lord Audley in this? Opening and shutting his mouth like one of those wooden idols worked by strings. And Fitzwilliam – I thought he stood your friend.'

He no longer trusts Lord Chancellor Audley. He no longer trusts Lord Admiral Fitzwilliam. Count up the bishops and perhaps ten of them are sound. This is how the king has been able to put through a bill that, among other measures, requires married priests to abandon their wives, on pain of hanging. The measure is deferred a week or two, to allow farewells.

'What will you and Grete do?' he asks.

'Part. What else can we do?'

'And your daughter?'

'Grete will take her back to Germany.'

It would be thought a sin, in other circumstances, to put a family asunder. Cranmer says, 'We begged the king, put the question to the universities – we begged him to search the scriptures, and find where it is forbidden, for a man to have a life companion. I cannot

670

understand him. It is he who insists, marriage is a very high sacra-ment, in existence since the world began. Then why does he deny it to so many of us? Does he think we are not men, as he is a man? And also, once the bill is passed, none of us will preach on the Blessed Sacrament, its nature. We dare not. We would not know what it is safe to say, without being tripped by the law and cited for heresy.'

This is what the king calls concord: an enforced silence. Bishop Latimer and Bishop Shaxton have openly opposed the king; they cannot continue in office. Cranmer says, 'I have thought of resigning myself. What is the use of me? Perhaps I should pack my bags and go with Grete.'

'You told me, in a similar case, I should take heart and take the long view.'

'How long?' Cranmer is shaken into bluntness. 'Till he dies? Because for all that has been said and done these ten years, if we have lost Henry now, we have lost him for ever.'

'He is not constant in error, is he? What is written on parchment may have no effect in practice. Any ordinance, any measure, I can delay, I can –' he hesitates over the word 'frustrate' – 'I can work with it,' he says. 'There is scope to walk all around these new articles of faith, and ease them in this direction or that –'

'Except one,' Cranmer says. 'My wife and child are not subject to loose interpretation. They are either here, or in Nuremberg. They cannot hover between.'

'You may see Grete again. If I can get the king his bride, we may be able to hold our heads up in Europe.'

'I doubt the marriage will be made. We are alienating our friends.'

He shrugs. 'I am running out of ladies. And in Cleves they are not Lutherans, after all. They may find it possible to live with this new order.'

'What about your daughter?' Cranmer says. 'She cannot come here now, can she? Not and keep her religion?' He does not wait for an answer: but before the eyes of the Vicegerent, as he paces, Canterbury starts to talk himself around. He is like a man retreating from a cliff edge: in despair he thinks he will throw himself down on the rocks, but then he feels the blue air bouncing him along to perdition, he feels the wind in his lungs, he sees the gulls flying below, he is blown like a feather to the brink, and then he digs his heels in, he grabs at the sparse bent shrubs, screws up his eyes and holds tight for his life. He says, 'You will not hear me speak against the king.'

'No one asked you to.' He feels cold. He wants to put his head down on the desk.

'I cannot think he means ill, or to distress his subjects. It must be his qualms, his scruples, are genuine, and they have tormented him, perhaps, more than we know.'

'Perhaps,' he says.

'He has carried knowledge that has been a burden to him. He has looked the other way. He has spared me, for one.'

'Our rulers count up our derelictions,' he says. 'They may say nothing, but they keep a secret book.'

'We know what Christ requires of us,' Cranmer says. 'We know what charity is, and what obedience, and we know His teaching, blessed are the peacemakers. Much though I mislike it, I see that peace is what the king intends. All good subjects will follow him.'

'Naturally,' he says. 'Or suffer.'

His ill-wishers say Hugh Latimer will be hanged before Christmas. He means to prevent that. But Cranmer's wife will be on a boat before the week is out, and there is nothing he can suggest to hold her here.

Just in case there should be any mistake – in case any fool should take the king for a papist – we have a Water Triumph. A burning June day and, well wrapped up, he stands beside the new French ambassador, explaining the spectacle. Before the eyes of king and court, a galley full of Romans fights true-born English sailors. Cardinals are cast into the Thames, splashing and screaming, while drummers beat out a victory tattoo. The sun dances, the pipes blare, the papal tiara goes bobbing downstream. 'By St Jude!' Marillac exclaims. 'I trust those fellows can swim?'

'They were handpicked,' he says, 'at my request.' He sighs. 'One has to tell people every little thing.'

The king is cheering from beneath his canopy. The dukes are thundering their appreciation. Gallants are throwing money in the Thames.

'Still, it is a good show,' the Frenchman says generously. A barge is fishing up the combatants from the water. 'Their costumes I think will not be able to be used again.' He chuckles. 'But what does Henry care? You have made him rich, have you not?'

'You see our navy is building,' he says. 'I myself will be pleased to escort you on a tour of our southern ports, if you care to ride out now the weather is better.'

A diplomatic pause. He eyes the new ambassador sideways. He is not above thirty but said to be astute: shrewd enough to quit his country some years back, when there were whispers that he favoured Luther. He went east with his cousin, who was ambassador to the Turk, and was presently made ambassador in his turn; now, whether he regards his sympathy with reform as a youthful folly, or whether François has picked him as likely to get on with Cremuel ... who knows? He says, 'We English have to put on a show for you. We do not want to be overshadowed by your last posting.'

The gallants are surging away, in the king's wake. They are going to cross to Southwark to see a bear baited.

'They remember you well, in Constantinople,' Marillac says. 'You are spoken of.'

He stifles his surprise. It will be some random Englishman, another rover called Thomas.

'By the way,' Marillac says, 'officially I am not here. I have stayed away in protest.'

'I understand. I am often in two places, or no place. And I agree it is not a seemly spectacle, though you will admit it is entertaining. You know, I miss your countryman Dinteville, he was always so gloomy he made me laugh. I thought your king might send him again.' He adds hastily, 'We are glad to have you, of course, that goes without saying.'

Marillac turns to look at him, astonished. 'You have not heard? Of the great disgrace?'

He thinks back, to when the late dauphin was poisoned. 'I understood there was some slander spoken – but the family were cleared, surely?'

'Oh yes, as far as that goes. But there was a further scandal. The whole house is undone. Sodomy, I fear.'

His heart sinks. 'Where is Dinteville now?'

Marillac shrugs: who cares? 'Italy, I think.'

Murder first, then sodomy. It sounds like something Gardiner would dream up, to ruin a foe. He thinks of the ambassador, muffled in his furs, splendid as Hans painted him: the broken lute string, the skull badge he retained in his cap. He says, 'If he were here with us today, he would be shivering, and hastening home to a good fire and spiced wine.'

Marillac laughs. 'We are well able for the weather. So, shall we row across and see the bear?'

When Parliament closes and before the court disperses, the king orders a dinner. Cranmer is to give it: he is to hold it at Lambeth Palace; Norfolk is to attend, and Stephen Gardiner; Cranmer is to do his office as archbishop, and reconcile all parties, sitting them down in amity and feeding them junkets.

It is the beginning of a hot summer, much drier than in recent years – you would say almost a drought, if it did not tempt Heaven to drench you. It seems sometimes as if it has been raining ever since the cardinal came down.

They are not far into the dinner when Gardiner accuses him of murder. The talk has turned to Rome, and to the city's monuments and squares, its faded glories. 'You were there when Cardinal Bainbridge died,' Gardiner says, wiping his mouth. 'Interesting, that.' He says to the guests at large, 'It was given out that one of the cardinal's household poisoned him.'

He leans forward: 'You know different, do you?'

Along the board, knives are set down; guests stop chewing to listen. Gardiner turns to Wriothesley; he's young, he doesn't know these things. 'They arrested a priest, name of Rinaldo. They crushed his legs till the marrow seeped out – which does throw doubt on the coherence of his confession.'

He – the Lord Privy Seal – sits back and surveys Gardiner. He knows he is baiting him, and that he must not take the bait. 'It's twenty-five years, Stephen. Most of the people who know about it are dead.'

'Bainbridge took ill at the dinner table,' Gardiner says. 'A powder in his broth.'

'Yes,' Norfolk says helpfully. 'Like when Bishop Fisher was poisoned. When the cook was boiled alive.'

A murmur of distaste runs around the table. 'We are losing our appetites,' the Lord Chancellor objects.

'The powder was bought in Spoleto,' Stephen says. 'I know the shop.'

He laughs. 'And does the shop know you?'

Norfolk says, 'What would be the rate for a murder among the Romans? Because this priest, Rinaldo … I suppose somebody fee'd him?'

'Naturally,' Gardiner says. 'Bishop Gigli.'

He can see Norfolk's memory working. He's chewing the name, as if it were overcooked: Gigli, Silvestro Gigli. 'Bishop of Worcester,' Norfolk bursts out. 'Wolsey's crony.'

'Exactly,' Stephen says. 'Wolsey's chief friend in Rome. Once Bainbridge was removed, Wolsey was clear to be the next English cardinal.'

There is a silence: which he breaks, signalling to a boy for more wine. 'Half the city wanted Bainbridge dead. The French hated him. The Florentines hated him. And he was in debt.'

'You saw the books?' Gardiner says. 'Who let you in?'

The capons come in and the carvers do their office. In Rome, at the Pope's table, the carver holds the meat skewered and swipes slices from it in mid-air; it lends an air of crisis to the mildest repast. He, Lord Cromwell, puts down his cup and turns to the guests, opening his hands, smiling: 'I always assumed the Pope's master of ceremonies killed Bainbridge. He hated him because he was English and was always genuflecting out of his place, or turning up with the wrong type of crozier. The Curia thought he was a barbarian.'

Cranmer, at the head of the table, is fidgeting. 'How were you in Rome, my lord Cromwell?'

'Private business. I didn't know Wolsey then.'

Gardiner says balefully, 'You always knew Wolsey.'

It was Corpus Christi, 15 June, when Bainbridge ate the broth and was seized with colic. The doctors purged him, and he was well enough to go out to supper that night. Would he want to miss the Cretan wine, the caviar, at Cardinal Carretto's house?

Next day Bainbridge was raging about as usual and kicking the servants. It was not till 14 July he collapsed and died. They arrested the priest Rinaldo because Bainbridge was known to have struck him in public, and they saw he had a grievance.

After three days of torment in the papal dungeons, Rinaldo managed to get hold of a knife. He stabbed himself ineptly, though he did a better job than Geoffrey Pole. It took him a day or two to die, and then the Romans hanged his corpse in public. Before they quartered it, he saw it dangling – he, Cremuello the *oltramarino, giovane inglese*. Rinaldo had labels tied to his feet stating his crime. He had confessed that Gigli gave him fifteen ducats to kill his master, but that detail was not written on the labels. It would have blown a hole in the Vatican's wall of secrecy. Bishops and cardinals slay each other, and humble men suffer for their crimes.

That summer was hot even by the Roman standard. At nightfall the very stones seemed to sweat, breathing out the day's accumulation of lies. He himself moved through the heat, smooth and silent and untroubled. Since the snake bit him, something of its nature had entered his blood, and he could lie coiled till needed.

Norfolk says, 'I was never at Rome. I knew Bainbridge, of course. He was choleric.'

'Yes, and he was fifty or more,' Cranmer says. 'And he drove himself. Such men perish in the heat. Besides, I always heard the priest retracted his confession before he died.'

'So who was the murderer?' Stephen says.

Call-Me says, 'You are seriously accusing Lord Cromwell?'

'He was no lord in those days,' Norfolk says.

No more was he. He can see himself now, at twilight, lurking in the Piazza Navona. Since he got his red hat, Bainbridge took himself seriously as a future pope, and set his stall out in fine style. He took a lease on Francesco Orsini's palace, with easy access to the Vatican and the English Hospice where his countrymen lodged. The front was imposing, loggias, terraces; Bainbridge fitted it out with money from the Sauli bankers, and he owed the Grimaldi as well. Any number of people would have employed Cremuello to watch Bainbridge's back gate, and several did; he split the intelligence between them, with attention to what they wanted to hear.

While lurking there he fell into talk with a street girl, teasing her about her hair. She had bleached it, but now it was grown out by a hand's span. Your sable locks are just as good, he said, a novelty for Englishmen; we have enough of tow-heads. You're English? she said. Jesu, one would not know it. So that is why you are watching the house of the English cardinal. Are you homesick for the sounds of your countrymen carousing? Watch presently, and some of them will come out and spew in the street.

Later that night she said to him, now I'll tell you a thing. Romans, Tuscans, Frenchmen, English, Germans: all pay out for blondes. It is a shame for me and my sisters in the trade; we are born wrong. I would bleach it again, but after a certain point it falls out, and no man of any nation wants a woman who is bald.

She yawned. Well, that was nice, she said, you would like to do it again in a different position? By the way, if you want a job in the palace among your countrymen, I can get you in there. My cousin works in the kitchen.

She mistook him for a clerk fallen on hard times. After all, he dressed like one. He turned to her and negotiated the new position and its price. How had one the energy, in that heat? But you don't feel it so much when you are young.

'My lord?' Wriothesley says

'I'm sorry,' he says. 'My lord bishop, I forget what you were saying?'

'Wolsey,' Stephen says deliberately, 'had scarcely the grace to hide his hand in the murder. He and Bishop Gigli were fast friends, till they scrapped about who got Bainbridge's vestments after he was dead. Wolsey wanted them packed up and sent to London for his use. When I was his secretary, I saw the letters in the files.'

'You know what I think?' Norfolk says. 'We're better off without cardinals, and proud old prelates such as we used to have. Now the archbishop here,' he jerks his thumb at Cranmer, 'at least he conducts himself humble-wise. You can tell by his countenance he spends his time at prayer, instead of browbeating noblemen and plotting their downfall and wrangling and cheating and embezzling. All of which were daily proceedings with Thomas Wolsey.'

'My lord Norfolk,' he says.

'Yes, and promoting false knaves to positions of trust, and soliciting bribes, falsifying deeds, bullying his betters, and consorting with conjurers and generally thieving, lying and cheating –'

He rises from his place.

'– to the detriment and ruin of the commonweal and the shame of the king.'

He has the duke in his grasp. He holds him at arm's length. He could easily jerk him forward then kick his feet from under him.

Cranmer shoots to his feet. 'For shame, Thomas, he's an old man.' He takes a grip on Norfolk's coat and tries to pull him free, as if he were a pike on a gaff and he wants to put him back in the stream.

It is only when sweat starts out of the archbishop – or possibly tears – that he, Cromwell, drops the duke. Thomas Howard swears at him, a horrible oath like a gunner.

The servants come in. The meats are cleared. They sit glaring at each other over the ginger comfits.

'Well,' Stephen says, 'I don't know when I enjoyed a peace conference as much as I enjoyed this one.'

It is time for the king to quit London for the summer. He will go as soon as Parliament rises. The entourage will first lodge at Beddington, the pleasant house that belonged to Nicholas Carew. Then 7 July to Oatlands, from there to Woking.

Months, years have gone by, when Lord Cromwell has never thought of his early life; when he has pushed the past into the yard and barred the door on it. Now it is not Gardiner's questions about Italy that trouble him: Italy keeps its secrets. It is Putney that works away at him, distant but close. When he was weak from fever the past broke in, and now he has no defence against his memories, they recapitulate themselves any time they like: when he sits in the council chamber, words fall about him in a drizzling haze, and he finds himself wrapped in the climate of his childhood. He is a monk who descends the night stair, still wrapped in dreams, so that the shuffling feet of his brethren are transformed to the whisper of leaves in the forests of infancy: and like a hidden creature stirring from a leaf-bed, his mind stirs and turns, on a restless circuit. He tries to tether it (to now, this time, this place) but it will roam: scenting the staleness of soiled straw and stagnant water, the hot grease of the smithy, horse sweat, leather, grass, yeast, tallow, honey, wet dog, spilled beer, the lanes and wharves of his childhood.

He picks up his quill: the king could spend perhaps six days in Woking, where he, Lord Cromwell, could join him? Then to Guildford ...

It is the night of the waning moon. He can smell the river, and the odour of the eel boy, who has beshitten himself. Eel boy slumps at his feet, too heavy to drag further. Thomas Craphead no longer knows what to do. A great and mortal weariness has overtaken him, a lassitude that trickles through him from brain to feet. So Craphead, clueless, had crawled home.

Walter and the boys went on drinking till his father fell snoring across a trestle table and at some dark hour woke and stumbled upstairs. You would expect he would lie snorting and sweating till noon. Perhaps Thomas Craphead counted on that and thought, while good folk are still abed, I will go out to the river and see if eel boy is alive or dead. See if he lies where I left him, or if someone has picked him up with the morning's flotsam, returned him whence he came or fed him to swine.

But God knows what he thought. He woke hollow, shaking, empty of logic or plan. In the daylight he cleaned his knife again, but he left it down when he went into the brewery yard.

Never underestimate Walter, his violence and cunning. The first blow came from nowhere and stunned him. There was blood in his eyes and after that Walter could do what he liked. He did it with his feet and he did it with his fists, till he, Thomas, was a bleeding jelly on the cobblestones, and his father stood over him and roared, '*So now get up!*'

There is a stir in the air. My lord Privy Seal looks up from the king's itinerary. Call-Me-Risley is here, flitting against the light in yellow. He throws himself into a chair and shouts for small ale. He fans himself with his hat. 'Gardiner,' he says. 'Jesus! To accuse you of murder! Though if you did rid the world of a cardinal, what of it? It was in another jurisdiction, and a long time ago now.'

He says, 'I'll pull Stephen down. Just watch me.'

Call-Me eyes him. 'Yes, I believe you.'

'I'm doing these,' he says. 'Excuse me.' He turns back to the paper. After Guildford, Farnham. Every town must be certified clear of plague before the king enters the neighbourhood. At the slightest suspicion, his route must be changed, so there must be extra hosts standing by, their silverware polished, their feather beds aired. 'Farnham to Petworth? How far is that?'

'Scant twenty miles cross-country,' Call-Me says. 'But more if it rains and you go round about.'

Twenty miles is what the king can ride, at present. 'Do you know the king is planning a visit to Wolf Hall?'

Call-Me considers. 'It is small, for his train.'

'The Seymours will move out. Edward has it planned.' He thinks of the shade of Jane, walking in the young lady's garden; he thinks of her alive under the green trees, in her new carnation-coloured dress.

He frowns over the papers. 'Suppose he rides from Petworth to Cowdray, to William Fitzwilliam? Then to Essex ... Ah, here comes Mathew.'

Mathew carries in a bowl of plums and sets them down reverently. 'The fruits of success,' Wriothesley says, smiling. 'I congratulate you, sir.'

He used to think that the plums in this country weren't good enough, and so he has reformed them, grafting scion to rootstock. Now his houses have plums ripening from July to late October, fruits the size of a walnut or a baby's heart, plums mottled and streaked, stippled and flecked, marbled and rayed, their skins lemon to mustard, russet to scarlet, azure to black, some smooth and some furred like little animals with lilac or white or ash; round amber fruits dotted with the grey of his livery, thin-skinned fruits like crimson eggs in a silver net, their flesh firm or melting, honeyed or vinous; his favoured kind the perdrigon, the palest having a yellow skin dotted white, sprinkled red where the sun touches it, its perfumed flesh ripe in late August; then the perdrigon violet and its black sister, favouring east-facing walls, yielding September fruits solid in the hand, their flesh yellow-green and rich, separating easily from the stone. You can preserve them whole to last all winter, eat them as dessert, or just sit looking at them in an idle moment: globes of gold in a pewter bowl, black fruit like shadows, spheres of cardinal red.

He says to Mathew, 'You remember when we hunted at your old master's house? The day the king lost his hat?'

Mathew grins. Who could forget the hunting party riding home, their faces baked like hams?

When the wind takes off a gentleman's hat, his companions at once take off theirs. The courteous man says, put on your hats again, do not suffer for my sake. But the king, though he would not accept another man's hat, never thought to tell them to cover; so they came home blistered and striped. He says, 'You should have seen Rafe Sadler. His eyes were boiled in his head.'

Mathew says, 'My friend Rob led a search after the king's hat, but we found naught. He had St Hubert in his cap badge, and his eyes were real sapphires, so I doubt not we would have been rewarded had we found it.'

He picks up his pen. Returns to the royal summer. The king will go to Stansted, then Bishop's Waltham, presently to Thruxton; then leaving Hampshire, he will ride west. In Savernake, Hubert squints down, entangled in branches. In high summer we will ride the same paths and he will see us as we are now: girth thickened, sins multiplied.

'Mid-August,' he writes. 'Five days. Wolf Hall.'

II
Twelfth Night
Autumn 1539

In August Hans rolls up the bride, brings her home, and slaps her on a panel for the king's inspection.

'I had to be quick,' Hans says, 'make sure she was dry before I could take my leave. I brought Amelia too, the young one. But frankly, Amelia is not so much.'

'Show me Anna first,' he says. He steps back to admire her, a shining princess who is more metal than flesh. Her clothes mould her, like the armour of some goddess, and look as if they would stand up by themselves. You drag your eyes upwards from her gleaming breastplate to her face. It is a serene oval, vulnerable, bare. It is not so young and rosy as Christina's, but shows a modest charm. She has tender eyes, veiled: the Holy Virgin, brooding over her unexpected turn of fortune. 'Henry should like her,' the painter says. 'I would. You would. It is a good picture. You would not guess how I sweated over it.'

'Show me Amelia,' he says.

Should Duke Wilhelm die without heir, Anna as the elder stands to inherit more. Amelia would require extraordinary beauty, to make up for her lesser prospects.

He examines her. Darker. Face longer. Her brows defined. 'She reminds me of the other one. Boleyn.'

Hans turns her to the wall.

* * *

Henry stands before the image of his bride and his eyes, like those of his councillors, travel from her middle upwards. Time passes: the sand running through the glass, the river flowing to the sea. Henry nods. 'Very well. I shall hear more of her from our envoy Dr Wotton, shall I not?' He hesitates, with a flicker of a smile. 'Tell Master Hans, all good.'

Edward Seymour has written from Wolf Hall. He is flush with the success of the recent royal visit, reassured that his family will lose no pre-eminence with the king's remarriage. He says, the king should take the Princess of Cleves, we need the alliance, and from all I hear she is a gracious lady and will give him more children; I do not think he can do better.

The Duke of Suffolk gives his voice in council: it is right and proper that our king should marry into a royal house. The Seymours are a good enough family, no doubt, says Charles: but the marriage brought the king no credit abroad. As for the house of Cleves – do they not travel down the Rhine in boats drawn by silver swans?

He, Cromwell, smiles. 'Perhaps in former times, my lord Suffolk.'

The Emperor is reported to dislike the match very much. The French are disaffected, the Scots grizzling. Our king is hunting. Most days he keeps well. The physicians report a feverish cold and a worrying stoppage of the bowels, but next day he is back in the saddle, with Fitzwilliam and a party of ladies, and together they kill a dozen stags. His party travel from Grafton to Ampthill, to Dunstable, down through Bedfordshire, and the king is merry, easy company, as he has not been for many a year. He is Henry the Well-Beloved, with a wife in prospect and a feather in his cap.

And he, Cromwell, makes a survey of the king's game, because he is chief justice and keeper of the forests, parks and chases that lie north of Trent. His survey begins in early June, in Sherwood Forest, and by September his people have counted 2,067 red deer and 6,352 fallow deer, clerks recording their lives in a parchment book of sixty-eight pages. They have scoured the greenwood and know the secrets of its undergrowth life; but they have not found Robin Hood, or the green men who shoot and feast with him.

Within a week or two Hans has painted the bride again, from memory and from his larger portrait: so that the king can carry her with him, he has confined her in an ivory miniature. 'Look, my lord Norfolk,' Henry says. 'Is she not well and seemly?'

Norfolk grunts. His eyes travel sideways waiting for him, Cromwell, to speak.

Once they had recovered from the dinner of reconciliation, he and Norfolk had to learn to be in the same room again. He had abased himself with an apology. Norfolk had snorted. Fitzwilliam slapped their backs: 'Shake hands like Christians.'

He touches the duke's bony calloused palm: showing willing. Though he is not sure Norfolk is even a Christian. He worships his forebears. He has been as greedy for monks' lands as any man in the realm, but says he will not let Thetford Priory go down, because his folk are buried there. Or rather, he will have it reformed into a college of priests, who will pray for the souls of his ancestors. The duke explains it, as he stamps alongside him: 'They will pray for them, Cromwell, as long as this world endures.'

He says politely, 'That's a lot of prayers.'

Wotton's report is in. As the king's representative, he has seen Anna at home with her mother. The Duchess Maria – the dowager – is a sober Catholic matron who keeps her daughters close to her elbow, and has brought them up simply, narrowly, piously. It is not thought proper in Cleves for young ladies to be troubled with books or tutors. Accordingly, Anna speaks no language but her own.

'Cromwell will be able to talk to her,' Henry says. 'He knows all modern tongues.'

'I fear not,' he says. 'Master Sadler is a better man for German. I learned mine in Venice, and from the Nuremberg merchants mostly. It is not like the tongue the Lady Anna speaks. Nor am I equipped for conversation such as ladies like, knowing only the terms for buying and selling.'

'If I am truthful,' Norfolk says, 'I never know what we are meant to talk to women about. They don't like anything a man likes.'

He says, 'My wife had no languages, but she knew everybody in the wool trade. She could keep books as well as any clerk, and when I came home from a journey she would have sent to Lombard Street and she would have the morning's exchange rates jotted down in columns. She could always tell you how currency was moving.'

They make their progress past the king's guards. 'I think you like being low-born,' Norfolk says. 'I think you're boasting of it, Cromwell. Being a tradesman.'

The king's chamber servants meet them, bowing. Whatever roof shelters Henry, hunting lodge or palace, the etiquette is the same, a ring of protection sealed by familiar faces and expert hands: by a monogrammed close stool with a kidskin seat, by a stack of linen cloths for a sore royal backside; by a holy water stoup, by great blazing candles of wax at close of day, by the sanctuary of velvet bedcurtains. But now Henry smiles and blinks in the sunshine, a summer king.

The duke dives in. 'Majesty! I think you might employ my son Surrey on a mission to Cleves. An envoy of noble blood would gain us credit, surely?'

He, Cromwell, frowns. 'I don't think we need credit. We are past that stage.'

'It is true,' Henry says blithely. 'All Duke Wilhelm's councillors are in accord. We need not disturb your boy. I know he is occupied with our defences in your own part of the world. It were a pity to divert him.'

Norfolk's brow furrows. 'What about the money? What will she fetch?'

He says, 'Wilhelm will give a hundred thousand crowns with his sister. But it will remain on paper.'

'What, not pay it?' Norfolk is shocked. 'Are they paupers?'

Henry says, 'We are pleased to waive what is due. The duke is young and has great charges. You know he has entered into Guelders, which is his right. But he must be ready to defend it against the Emperor.'

He, the Lord Privy Seal, has told the Cleves delegation, 'My king prefers virtue and friendship to hard cash.' Relieved, the Germans exclaim, By God, what a very gallant gentleman he is! But we expected no less.

'The arrangement must not leak out,' Henry says. 'Wilhelm would be shamed. Soon I shall call him my brother, so I would wish to spare him embarrassment.'

'What about her journey?' Norfolk says. 'It costs, moving a princess.'

'We have ships,' Henry says.

The duke bristles. 'Any impediment? Affinity? Are they kin?'

'Anna is the king's seventh cousin.'

'Oh,' Norfolk says, 'I suppose that's all right. We need no interference from the Pope, then. By Jesus, no!'

The king says, 'I confess I was surprised we have no language in common, but our envoys say she has a good wit, and I am sure she will learn our tongue as soon as she puts her mind to it. Besides, everybody speaks a little French, even if they say not – do you not think so, my lord Cromwell?'

'Duke Wilhelm's advisers speak French,' he says. 'But the lady –'

The king interrupts him. 'When Katherine came from Spain to marry my lord brother, she spoke neither English nor French, and he had no Spanish. The king my father had thought, no matter, she is said to be a good Latinist, they will get along that way – but as it proved, they did not understand each other's Latin either.' The king chuckles. 'But they had goodwill towards each other, and were soon affectionate. And of course, we will be able to make music together. If she does not know the words to English songs, I am sure she will know them in other tongues.'

He says, 'In Germany, I understand, great ladies do not have music masters. A lady there would lose her good name by singing or dancing.'

The king's face falls. 'Then what will we do after supper?'

'Drink?' Norfolk says. 'They are great drinkers, Germans. They are known for it.'

'They say the same of the English.' He gives the duke a fierce look. 'Lady Anna takes her wine well-watered. And they do not forbid music, not at all. The Duchess Maria listens to the harp. Duke Wilhelm travels with a consort of musicians.'

All this is true. But our men in Cleves have told him the duke's court is sedate to the point of tedium. By nine at night every man has gone to his own chamber, not to issue out till daylight. You can't get so much as a glass of wine without troubling some high official for the keys.

'My wife and I will hunt,' the king says. 'We will enjoy the pleasures of the chase.'

'I believe she can ride, Majesty.'

'She must. She has to get about,' Norfolk says.

'But I am not sure if she shoots. She can learn.'

The king seems puzzled. 'They don't hunt either, the ladies? Do they sew all day?'

'And pray,' he says.

'By God,' Norfolk says, 'she'll be grateful to you, for taking her out of that place.'

'Yes.' Henry sees it in a new light. 'Yes, her life must have been a trial, bless her. And no money of her own, I suppose. She will find our ideas quite different. But I trust –' He breaks off. 'Cromwell, you are quite sure she can read?'

'And write, Majesty.'

'Well, then. When she is married and here with us, she will find honest pastimes. And when all is said, it is a wife we want, not a learned doctor to instruct us.'

Henry draws him aside. He looks over his shoulder to see that Norfolk is out of earshot. 'Well, my lord,' he says, diffident. 'It has been a long road to get here. I thought no one would have me.' He laughs, to show it is a joke. Not have the King of England? 'Only I regret the Duchess of Milan. I shall be angry if I hear she is promised to some other prince. And I am sorry I never saw her with my own eyes. I had inclined myself towards her.'

'I regret it was not to be. But this way, you owe nothing to the Emperor.'

'Kings cannot choose where to bestow their hearts,' Henry says.

'I see I must frame myself to love elsewhere. But you can tell Master Holbein I am pleased with his picture of the Duchess Christina. I think she is standing in the room, and about to speak to me. Tell Hans I shall not part with it. I shall keep it to look at.'

'Of course,' he says. 'Perhaps not in the new queen's view, sir.'

The king says, 'Give me some credit, my lord. I am not a barbarian.'

He goes to the Tower. He walks through the apartments where the queens of England sleep, the night before they are crowned; where Anne Boleyn spent her last days. Jane never lodged here, she never lived long enough to be crowned, there was always the plague or the rebels, or we were going to do it in York – but in the end we never did it at all. A tinker from Essex, drinking in the Bell not far from where he stands, has given scandal to the folk of Tower Hill by bawling in his cups that Jane was murdered by her own child. Edward will be a slaughterer, the wretch shouts, just like his father.

You know the end of this story. The watch comes, and bears the tinker away. What is such a fellow fit for, but to be whipped at the cart's arse or hanged? Lord Cromwell stands before the image of the late queen, painted on the wall by an uncertain hand. He sees a pale round face, a fall of yellow hair. He wonders, will it double for Anna? Or must I repaint? I should not like to obliterate such a good lady. Anne Boleyn is lurking within the plaster, her dark gaze burning through.

He thinks, I wish the court would call Anna by that name, not use Anne. But women are to be named and renamed, it is their nature, and they have no country of their own; they go where their husbands take them, where their father and brothers send them. A trip down the street for them can be as big as a voyage across the sea. Jane Rochford talked about it once. I was given like a hound pup, she said, though with less thought: I was handed over, my future gone. (And her father, Lord Morley, such a grave and patient scholar.)

While he is at the Tower he visits Margaret Pole. No prayer book at hand, no sewing in her lap, she is sitting idle in a shaft of sun, which lights her long Plantagenet face; she looks like one of her foremothers, set in a glass window. 'My lady?' he says. 'I trust you are comfortable. You must prepare for a long residence.'

'Better than the other thing,' she says. 'Or does the king hope this winter will kill me? I see that would be a way forward for you.'

'If you have complaints of your treatment, put them in writing.'

'I know why you keep me alive. You still believe my son Reynold will come and redeem me. You think he will hand himself over for love of me.' She considers him. 'Would you have done so much for your mother, Master Cromwell?'

He is stony. 'If you require anything, put that in writing too.'

'You will soon know better about Reynold. He would not cross the street to save a woman, though she were the woman who bore him.'

'He cares more for a plaster statue,' he suggests.

'In truth he envies me my state. He thinks I have the chance to earn a martyr's crown.'

'By being churlish to me? You can say what you like to me, madam. I have heard it all before. You can call me plain Cromwell or call me a cur. It will not alter my policy.'

'I have noticed,' she says, 'common men often love their mothers. Sometimes they even love their wives.'

In the first week of September a contract of marriage is signed in Düsseldorf. Wilhelm's envoys are on the road that same day, to carry the papers to England. Everyone is happy except Archbishop Cranmer, who says, 'I am afraid, my lord.'

He stifles the impulse to say, aren't you always?

'To lack a common language, it is not a trivial thing. Believe me, I know.'

'I thought you were happy with Grete.'

'And so I was. But I chose her for myself. We had spent time together. We could not talk except through others. But we felt that ease between us, that betokened a happy household.'

He says, mischievous, 'My lord of Norfolk says, no point talking to women, you can do your husband's part without it.'

'Norfolk?' Fitzwilliam is coming in with the other councillors. 'All he knows is to fell a maid and jump on her.'

'I believe it,' Charles Brandon says. 'No way with women.'

Cranmer says, 'Very well, you are pleased to make sport of me. But I do not believe the king should let others choose his bride. Did he not say to the French, bring your ladies to Calais, so we may talk? Did he not say, I cannot be beholden to any man's choice, the thing touches me too near?'

'He wanted to marry Christina without seeing her,' Charles Brandon says reasonably. 'He trusted her picture, and he heard Mr Wriothesley say she had dimples.'

Fitzwilliam says, 'He had his pick before. He picked Boleyn. She was his choice entirely. His unholy mistake, which we had to clear up.'

Cranmer opens his mouth to reply, but he, Cromwell, says, 'I think you should be silent on the topic of matrimony. What has it to do with bishops?'

Cranmer looks cowed. He makes a sign as if to say, peace.

All summer the council runs after the king, up-country, following the slaughter of deer. Bishop Gardiner soon arranges to have himself kicked in a ditch. Those six articles that Parliament passed have made him over-confident. When the name of Robert Barnes is raised in council, Gardiner sniffs; then he shuffles his papers, unpleasantly; then he picks up his folio and slams it down again on the table, until he, Lord Cromwell, says, 'What?' and the king says, 'Let us hear it, Winchester.'

'Heretic,' Gardiner says.

He says, 'Dr Barnes is the king's chaplain. He has been deployed for some months in winning friends for us, in Denmark and among the Germans.'

'So I am told,' Gardiner says. The bishop's nose is a beak, his hooded eyes gleam; the suffering man on his pectoral cross scowls at the company. 'I suggest we look at a man's friends, to know who he is. If Barnes is not a heretic himself, he is black with heretic pitch. Defiled.'

'But he is my accredited envoy,' Henry says. 'If I find him sound, so must you. I defy anyone to show how or where I have departed from holy and catholic doctrine, or show where in this realm heresy is entertained.'

'I'll tell you where,' the bishop says. 'In the houses of the Lord Privy Seal. At his very table.'

Audley says, 'But I have heard Cromwell say he wished Luther were dead.'

Gardiner flushes. 'But since those days, Luther has praised him.'

'I did not solicit the praise.'

Gardiner turns in the king's direction, sweeping his paw across the table as if sweeping off dice. 'I do not claim he is a Lutheran. That is not my complaint.'

'What is he, then?' Brandon says.

Gardiner turns to him. 'You mean, my lord Suffolk, what other heresies are available, to such a man? Lord Cromwell has friends in Switzerland – can he deny it? – and like Luther they write to laud him, he is their great hope. We know what they believe. The Holy Sacrament is not holy. Corpus Christi is a piece of bread and may be bought at any stall.'

'I am no sectary,' he says.

'No?'

'I am no sacramentary.'

Gardiner leans towards him. 'Perhaps you would like to say what you are? Instead of what you are not?'

Lord Audley says, 'These sectaries, Stephen – do they not hold their goods in common?' He grins. 'I should not like to be the knave who tries to hold Cromwell's goods in common. By God, he would get a buffet!'

The king leans forward. His voice shakes. 'Winchester, you may leave us.'

'Leave? Why?'

The king's beard bristles. He looks like a hog's pudding about to burst its skin. He, Cromwell, advises, 'My lord bishop, go before the guard comes in.'

Gardiner has the sense to lurch to his feet, but he cannot forbear to give his stool a kick. It is an exit from the royal presence only Stephen would dare, he tells Wriothesley later: rude, churlish, possibly final?

'But now he will be plotting out of sight,' Call-Me says. 'I'm not sure it's better.'

Call Me had stood outside the council chamber; heard the king scream his opinion of the bishop; been dashed against the wall by Gardiner, with a shove and a snarl of 'Get out of my way, Wriothesley, you damned traitor.'

Audley comes out. 'By the Mass, gentlemen, I think one of these outbursts will land Winchester in the Tower. He can't read the king, can he?'

Wriothesley re-adjusts the hang of his short cloak, resettles his cap. 'My lord, did you receive word of Bishop Stokesley? He is ill.' They turn to look at him. 'Not likely to last the night.'

'God have mercy,' he says, grave and pious.

The season looks better already. Stephen off the council, Stokesley twitching his last. Clear skies.

He rides into Kent. At Leeds Castle, standing under the great walls and down by the moat, he talks to his son Gregory, air and water encircling them, the scudding clouds reflected in the blue, the whole world fluid and flickering. 'I am expecting couriers from Cleves. Once the contract is signed here, Anna can set out. I do not like a long sea journey for her, not at this time of year. If Duke Wilhelm can get her a safe-conduct, I am going to bring her overland to Calais. The moment she touches English soil, I want you to be there, paying reverence on my behalf.'

'In Calais? Shall I cross?' Gregory's eyes widen, as if he is looking at the sea.

'And your Bess will be amongst her ladies when she arrives. I want Anna to look to us for anything she needs – for company, for advice –'

'For interpreters,' Gregory says. 'I hope my French will suffice, when I am across the sea.'

'You will thank me for your Latin too, and that I kept you to your books.'

'Oh, the books,' Gregory says. 'I was oppressed by them. I thought you meant to have every volume printed, and to force the content into my head.'

He turns his head to look at his son. The stiff breeze ruffles Gregory's hair, and whips the water into ridges. He drops his eyes to the water's edge, where a scum of stalks and dead leaves heaves against the stonework, solid as a serpent's back. 'You cannot know too much. I meant it for your comfort.'

'I was afraid of you.'

But of course, he thinks, it is usual for a son to fear his father, it is the way the world is made. 'I tried to be a tender father to you. I never once struck you.'

'You were too busy to strike me.'

'Well,' he says, 'I suppose I could have delegated it. Come in. The wind is getting up.'

To the left of him, through two tall pointed arches, willow trees and a scudding sky. They duck through a doorway, turn sharp right to climb the stairs into the great hall. From the chapel you can look down into the water, shifting blue to grey and back to blue; it is a mirror to every change in the weather. It was Henry Guildford, God rest him, who put in the upper floors here, the wide windows and great fireplaces – before Anne Boleyn rousted him out of his offices and he went home to fade and die. A few pomegranates are left from the old days – Gregory shows him – and carvings of castles which, he tells his son, represent the turrets of Castile. Six queens have lived here at Leeds, and now it shelters the blacksmith's great-grandsons: little Henry now toddling in his smocks, the baby Edward swaddled in the cradle. 'There is a Mass book here,' Bess says, 'which they say belonged to Queen Katherine.' She fetches it from its locked chest. He turns the pages in search of inscriptions.

He rides into Huntingdonshire, to see nephew Richard. After all, he will have no holidays till this time next year. All summer Lord

Lisle has been sending over from Calais a procession of evangelicals, men whom he says should be examined in London, as he cannot deal with them. Once they disembark, Gardiner sets about them with relish, bullying them into swearing to every pernicious article he has pushed into the statute book. Stephen may be off the council, but he is still a power. Where does he find his boundless malice? Servants he has planted tell him, 'What Winchester wants to force out of the Calais men is a connection to you, Lord Cromwell. He tries to goad them into naming you, into claiming your protection. If they have ever been in the same church as you, ever stood through the same sermon, Gardiner looks to make something of it.'

So what to do? It is half his work to protect the friends of the gospel from themselves, to keep them circumspect and keep them out of custody. Fevered brethren will fall foul of Parliament's new articles. Then it will be, 'Good Lord Cromwell, deliver us from prison!' What if he cannot? If he, Cromwell, speaks boldly for the Calais men, it will be worse for him, and no better for them; so he must act, if he can, secretly, dexterously, to mitigate the damage Gardiner and his friends will do.

He is happy to ride away from Westminster, where everybody is watching everyone else. Richard is building his new house at Hinchingbrooke. A little convent has been closed, that has been there time out of mind, its numbers dwindling. Workmen, breaking up an old floor, have come to him, mattocks in their hands, dismayed: 'Mr Richard, see what we have turned up …'

He goes to see. The workmen kneel and pray while the bones are lifted. At first it is hard to tell how many of God's creatures are jumbled here. Two sets of bones, as Richard thinks, but they are not two nuns, as you might expect: one of them has a huge jawbone and giant-killer's shoulders. Already the builders are making up stories about them. They are a runaway lord and lady, absconding for love of each other, whose flight has been arrested by a jealous count, or earl, or petty king. Standing hand in hand, they have been slain by their pursuers. No one can stop them mingling their persons now.

'The workmen take them to be very ancient,' Richard says. 'I suppose we will never know what their names were. But it did not seem right to put them down in the nuns' graveyard.'

He imagines the bony virgins, shrinking from the presence of a man of heroic size. 'And so?'

'So I put them back where I found them,' Richard says. 'I can live with them under my floor, they are not likely to get up and walk about at night. I was obliged to allow prayers for their souls, the workmen would have downed tools if I had done other. But I will not let them alter my building plans.'

Already the neighbourhood believes that a drowned nun wails about the place, lamenting her sins and looking for the shameful babe she bore. Drip, drip, she comes at twilight, the sodden train of her habit slapping the stone floors. He says to Richard, perhaps she did not drown herself at all, but left a note and ran off to a new life, like Robert Barnes.

When the delegation from Germany arrives – Duke Wilhelm's people, and envoys from Saxony – the king is still hunting. He sends word that he, Cromwell, should leave aside all other duties, and devote himself to them. By the third week in September the king is at Windsor and ready to receive them himself. His representatives are waiting to conclude the matter: the Duke of Suffolk, Cranmer, Audley, Fitzwilliam and Cuthbert Tunstall, Bishop of Durham. It is a selection that should satisfy all parties, except for Norfolk and the Bishop of Winchester, who think they should have the rule of all. The Duke of Saxony, who is Wilhelm's brother-in-law, is clear that he will not make a diplomatic alliance with England while the six articles are in force; he will not tolerate practices that have no warrant in scripture. 'But we are sure, Lord Cromwell,' the envoys say, 'that you will be able to ease Henry to a better way of thinking, now that you are fit and well again. After all, if you had been on your feet and in your Parliament house, those articles had not passed. Once Lady Anna is here, the bridegroom will be mellow, persuadable, and you will press your advantage.'

Melanchthon himself, they say, is writing to the king to urge him to rescind the new laws. It is no shame in a prince, to have second thoughts.

When the king's team enquires into the old contract that Cleves made with the Duke of Lorraine's son – the one where the parties were still children – they are told the documents are still not to hand. He, Lord Cromwell, thinks they have probably lost them; it happens. 'My bride can bring them when she comes,' the king says. He does not want delay. The Emperor is in France – made welcome on the soil of his old enemy. He is riding to the Low Countries on a mission of revenge: the city of Ghent has revolted against him, and he means to get its submission in person. It would be easier for him to go by sea, but he is afraid of English waters. Our ships might sail out to inter-cept him. A storm, even, could drive him onto our shores.

'That would be an ill wind,' the Imperial ambassador says. He seeks safety in proverbs because he has nothing useful to offer. As for Marillac, you get nothing from him: 'Oh, I wouldn't know about that, my lord, I must refer it upwards.' Or, 'This is beyond my remit – I say that without prejudice, of course.' If Marillac could find a way to stop the wedding, he would exert himself, but meanwhile he dines with the Spaniard and boasts, 'All Europe rejoices in the continued amity between our masters.'

'I think we had better get Wyatt back in harness,' he says to the king. 'Send him to join the Emperor on his progress through France. If anyone can seed trouble, Wyatt can.'

Wyatt has had the summer at Allington with his mistress. He should be well-rested. His Italian intrigues have come to nothing, because the king will not back any scheme that puts English boots on foreign soil. Wyatt is disappointed, but the king says, 'Your friend here, I mean Lord Cromwell, has always advised me that such ventures cost too much, and one never knows the final bill.'

On 5 October, early in the morning, the marriage articles are signed at Hampton Court. There is no need to read the banns because Cranmer has waived them. Now nothing is wanting but consummation. The king hands a ring to the Cleves delegation, though he demurs with a smile from putting it on any gentleman's finger, as would have been the practice in former times. He says, 'When my sister Mary married King Louis, God rest his soul and hers, the duc de Longueville came over as his proxy, and we were all witness in the great hall at Greenwich. They said their vows, and Longueville gave her a ring and kissed her, and they signed – then she was sent away to put on her nightgown' – the king blushes faintly – 'and they lay down on a bed together, and Longueville parted his gown – out came his hairy leg, naked, and touched her – truly, when I thought about it afterwards, there were young girls present, and I did not think it was necessary or seemly. But the French expected it.'

That is what the French are like, the Germans say. A coarse nation, always pushing for things to be done their way.

The king is sending gifts to his bride, and a letter. He looks shy, as if he's going to say, can you write it for me, Crumb? 'What language shall I use?'

'Latin or French, Majesty, it is indifferent. Duke Wilhelm will make the contents known to her.'

'Yes,' Henry says, 'but I don't know what to put. The usual compliments, I suppose. After all,' he cheers up, 'she is not a lady who is used to love letters. It is a great thing, I find, to know she has never looked at a man before. Like Jane. Jane had no fancy towards anyone, until she knew of my honourable regard. Even then, she was not easy to persuade, was she? Such immaculate ladies are not found these days. But it appears you have discovered one other.'

By 20 October the ambassadors of Cleves are back in Düsseldorf. The Emperor grants a safe-conduct for Anna to pass through his territories. Much as he mislikes the alliance, he will not harass a lady on her matrimonial journey; his aunt, his regent in the Low Countries, insists the Princess of Cleves should be shown every courtesy and even provided with an escort.

Thurston says to him, 'You know that cat that you fetched from Esher in your pocket, in the cardinal's time? Master Gregory took against him, and called him Marlinspike? Well, I think I saw him on the wall the other day, with a piece of a rabbit under his paw. But I said to myself, can any cat live that long?'

He says, 'The cardinal's cat would be a prodigy of nature, I suppose. How did he look?'

'Torn up a bit,' Thurston says. 'But aren't we all?'

This winter, the king is taking the surrender of the great abbeys, with their manorial titles and broad acres, their watercourses, fishponds, pastures, their livestock and the contents of their barns: every grain of wheat weighed, every hide counted. If some geese have flocked to market, cattle strolled to the slaughterhouse, trees felled themselves, coins jumped into passing pockets … it is regrettable, but the king's commissioners, men not easy to deceive, could not go about their work without their presence being heralded: the monks have plenty of time to spirit their assets away. Treat the king fairly, and he will be a good master. When St Bartholomew surrenders and its bells are taken to Newgate, Prior Fuller is granted lands and a pension. Officers of the Court of Augmentations move into its great buildings, and Richard Riche plans to turn the prior's lodging into his town house. In the north country, Abbot Bradley of Fountains settles for an annual pension of a hundred pounds. The Abbot of Winchcombe, always a helpful man, accepts a hundred and forty. Hailes surrenders, where they displayed the blood of Christ in a phial. The great convent at Syon is marked for closure, and he reminds himself of Launde, where Prior Lancaster has been in post for three decades, which is too long. It has not been a pious or happy house these last years. When questioned the prior would always declare, *omnia bene*, all's well, but it wasn't: the church roof leaked, and there were always women about. All that is over now. He will rebuild it, a house after his own liking, in England's calm and green heart. In dark weather he dreams of the garden arbour, of the drifting petals of the rose, pearl-white and blush-pink. He dreams of violets, hearts-ease, and the blue stars of the pervink, or periwinkle, used by our maids as lovers' knots; in Italy they weave them into garlands for condemned men.

In November he writes in his memoranda, 'The Abbot of Reading to be tried and executed.' He has seen the evidence and the indictments; there is no doubt of the verdict, so why pretend there is? The days of the great abbeys died with the north country rebellion. The king will no longer countenance subversion of his rule, or the existence of men who lie awake in their plush curtained lodgings and dream of Rome. Thousands of acres of England are now released, and the men who lived on them dispersed to the parishes, or to the universities if they are learned: if not, to whatever trade they can find. For their abbots and priors it mostly ends with an annuity, but if necessary with a noose. He has taken into custody Richard Whiting, the Abbot of Glastonbury, and after his trial he is dragged on a hurdle through the town and hanged, alongside his treasurer and his sacristan, on top of the Tor: an old man and a foolish, with a traitor's heart; an embezzler too, who has hidden his treasures in the walls. Or so the commissioners say. Such offences might be overlooked, if they were not proof of malice, a denial of the king's place as head of the church, which makes him head of all chalices, pyxs, crucifixes, chasubles and copes, of candlesticks, crystal reliquaries, painted screens and images in gilt and glass.

No ruler is exempt from death except King Arthur. Some say he is only sleeping, and will rise in an hour of peril: if, say, the Emperor sends troops. But at Glastonbury they have long claimed Arthur was as mortal as you and me, and that they have his bones. Time was, when the abbey wanted funds, the monks were on the road with their mouldy head of John the Baptist and some broken bits of the manger from Bethlehem. But when that failed to make their coffers chime, what did they arrange to find beneath the floor but the remains of Arthur, and beside him the skeleton of a queen with long golden hair?

The bones proved durable. They survived a fire that destroyed most of the abbey. Over the years they attracted so many pilgrims that Becket's shrine waxed jealous. Lead cross, crystal cross, Isle of Avalon: they wrung out the pennies from the credulous and awed. Some say Jesus Himself trod this ground, a bruit that the townsfolk encourage: at St George's Inn they have an imprint of Christ's foot, and for a fee you can trace around it and take the paper home. They claim that, after the crucifixion, Joseph of Arimathea turned up, with the Holy Grail in his baggage. He brought a relic of Mount Calvary itself, part of the hole in which the foot of the cross was placed. He planted his staff in the ground, from which a hawthorn flowered, and continues to flower in the fat years and the lean, as the Edwards and the Henrys reign and die and go down to dust. Now down to dust with them go all the Glastonbury relics, two saints called Benignus and two kings called Edmund, a queen called Bathilde, Athelstan the half-king, Brigid and Crisanta and the broken head of Bede. Farewell, Guthlac and Gertrude, Hilda and Hubertus, two abbots called Seifridus and a Pope called Urbanus. Adieu, Odilia, Aiden and Alphege, Wenta, Walburga, and Cesarius the martyr: sink from man's sight, with your muddles and your mistranscriptions, with the shaking of your flaky fingerbones and the compound jumble of your skulls. Let us bury them once and for all, the skeletons of mice that mingle with holy dust; the ragged pieces of your tunics, your hair shirts clumped with blood, your snippets and your off-cuts and the crisp charred clothing of the three men who escaped from the Burning Fiery Furnace. That lily has faded, that the Virgin held on the day the angel came. That taper is quenched, that lighted the Saviour's tomb. Glastonbury Tor is over five hundred feet high. You can see for miles. You can see a new country if you look, where everything is fresh, repainted, re-enamelled, bleached, scrubbed clean.

The king picks out jewellery for the bride. The gems repose in caskets of ivory and mother of pearl. The letters 'H' and 'A' are entwined in plaster and glass: a strange sight, after such labour to erase them. The king says, get me musicians from Venice, against the coming of the new queen. If they bring new instruments, so much the better.

The Princess of Cleves will arrive in a godly nation. Printing of his Bible speeds. Mr Wriothesley asks him, 'Sir, did the French send you the sheets they impounded? Why would they favour you?'

He doesn't answer. Mr Wriothesley looks hurt: as if he has not been trusted.

'Bonner has been helpful,' he says, 'working among the French. He is not the blunderer you take him for.'

When Edmund Bonner returns from France he will be appointed Bishop of London. It will ease conditions for our preachers. Bishop Stokesley may be worm-food, but so is Thomas More. The smell of them lurks above ground, and their brawling supporters are ever alert to pull gospellers from the pulpit.

'I know Bonner is your man,' Wriothesley says, sulking. 'But he won't last, the French don't like him.'

'They don't like me,' he says.

You gain a point and lose a point, gain and lose.

The ladies gather at court, ready for the new queen. The matrons Lady Sussex and Lady Rutland have the sway, and say who can have what place and what duties, and what they should wear. Margaret Douglas, the Princess of Scotland, is the senior lady by rank. Her friend Mary Fitzroy is brought up from the country to serve. The Lord Privy Seal's family are in place: Edward Seymour's wife Nan, Gregory's wife Bess. Lady Clinton will be on the strength, Richmond's mother; but not Lady Latimer? The boys of Austin Friars are dismayed. How will Lord Cromwell woo her, they ask, digging each other in the ribs. We know he writes her great letters: but she has been so long now from court, she will have forgot his many charms.

Jane Rochford will head Anna's privy chamber. She has a sufficient income, since Thomas Boleyn died. She could retire to Norfolk and live in her house at Blickling. But what would be the point of that? She is not much over thirty, for all she has seen. 'How do you like the new maids of honour?' she asks idly, as they pass in a chattering knot. Their short veils swish after them, and their French hoods are pushed as far back as they dare.

He smiles. 'They seem very young this year.'

'That is you, getting older. The maids are the usual age.'

'That one looks familiar.'

Jane Rochford hoots with laughter. 'I should think she does. That is Norfolk's niece. Catherine Carey, Mary Boleyn's girl. You had a passage or two with her mother.'

He is shocked: Mary's little daughter, grown up to marriageable age. 'I never had passage with Lady Carey.'

'And the moon is made of cheese,' Lady Rochford says. 'Calais, have you forgot? Harry Norris said to me, Mary Boleyn and Thomas Cromwell are out in the garden together, I do not think it's for their health, do you? I said to him, No, Harry, but for their recreation, and he laughed. Oh, dear Lord, he said, suppose he makes a little Cromwell?'

'That we were in the garden, I concede.'

Lady Rochford is laughing at him. 'All I know is, next day Mary was in a giddy humour and had bruises all over her neck. Harry Norris said to her, Cromwell worked you hard then, Mary – you see what it is to have a rough man for your lover – I hope you have fixed another meeting tonight, because no one else will want you, your flesh is so dappled you look like a fish on the turn.'

He thinks, Norris was a gentleman, he would not say such a thing. But then, of course, like all those gentlemen about the late Anne, he was capable of more than we knew.

'William Stafford was in the garden too,' he says. 'He that Mary married, afterwards. She must have liked his love-making. She had no experience of mine.'

'If you say not. But what I heard was, you pulled out a dagger and held it to his throat, drove him off and then dragged your prey indoors.'

Part of this is true. Stafford came up behind him in the dark. He took him for a murderer. He remembers the man trying to squirm away from him, the stuff of his jacket bunched in his fist.

'Well, however it may be,' Rochford says, 'that sweet creature is Mary's girl. And the little chicken she has by the hand, that is Norris's daughter, Mary.'

He glances at Mary Norris. He cannot see she is like her father. Her mother died young, he scarcely remembers her. He is uneasy. 'Uncle Norfolk's ward,' he says, 'is she not?'

'Trust Uncle Norfolk,' Rochford says, 'to put his folk in. His ward Norris, and his niece Carey – and he has another niece, one of his brother Edmund's batch.'

Edmund Howard, God rest him. He was a poor gentleman, one of Norfolk's half-brothers: five children of his own, and five stepchildren at least. He once declared to the cardinal that if he were not a lord he would go out and earn an honest living by digging and delving, a labouring man; but rank condemned him to indigence.

'Here Norfolk comes,' Rochford says. The duke struts in with a tiny girl on his arm. 'That is the one, Katherine Howard – she we sent back because she looked twelve. But they swear she is of sufficient age, and here she is again.'

He hears the girl say, 'Uncle Norfolk …' in a clear, childish voice. She is pulling at the old brute's arm, trying to attract his attention to something.

'He has a peach there,' Mr Wriothesley says. 'I could spend an hour, my lord, could not you?'

'I don't know I could,' he says. 'I think Uncle Norfolk's shade might come and lie between us.'

The child's flower face turns on its stem, her lips emit a stream of chatter. Norfolk's face wears an expression of strained tolerance – he is alert in case the king comes in. The girl forgets her uncle, drops his arm and stares around. Her glance slips absently over the men, but rakes the women head to toe. Clearly she has never seen so many great ladies before; she is studying how they stand, how they move. 'Sizing up her rivals,' he says; she has no guile.

'She has no mother, bless her. She was but an infant when she died.'

He casts a glance at Rochford. 'A soft word from you, my lady.'

'I am not a monster, my lord.'

Mary Norris and Catherine Carey are eyeing up their new companion. Rochford says, 'Would you call her blonde? Or red?'

He would not call her anything. His gaze has moved elsewhere.

'I wonder who paid for what's on her back,' Rochford says. 'That cloth did not come out of the old dowager's wardrobe. And those rubies – did they not belong to Anne Boleyn?'

'If they did, they should be back in the king's jewel house. How did they come into Norfolk's hands?'

'Ah, that got your attention!' Jane Rochford says.

On 26 November, Anna leaves her home to travel towards Calais. She will have an escort of some 250 persons, and her ladies travelling with her, so there are times when they will not make more than five miles a day. Drums and trumpeters precede her, and she travels in a gilded chariot emblazoned with the swan emblem and the arms of Cleves-Mark-Jülich-Berg.

Gregory comes to Austin Friars for final instructions. 'Now I will repeat them back to you,' he says. 'Write home the minute I see Anna. Make sure she knows who I am. Be kind. Be patient. Make sure she has the things she likes to eat. Give her a purse of ready money.'

'And do not embark for home without checking that all her train's debts are paid. It may be the weather delays you.' He thinks of the king, six years back, penned in the fortress with Anne Boleyn. 'Be aware that the longer you stay, the more the household will be tempted by French merchants. By the way, keep your own accounts.'

'You know you are talking to me as if I am Wyatt?'

'Yes,' he says. 'And you are flattered.'

Gregory smiles. There is a shout from below. 'My lord, do you want to be disturbed?'

It seems from the noise that everybody is running outside. Gregory goes down. A moment later, he storms back up the stairs: 'You have to come and see.'

In the courtyard is a wagon, guarded by four carters. On the wagon is a crate or cage, open at the front, barred. His first impression is that they are guarding an area of darkness, but then a movement betrays something within. He sees an expanse of spotted fur, and a pugged head that flinches from the light. It is a leopard. Its fur is crusted with its own shit and vomit, or so it seems from the smell.

He pulls his gown around him. His folk stop staring at the animal, and start staring at him. He has an impulse to cross himself. Such a distance it has come, perhaps from China: how can it be still alive?

'Do you think it's hungry?' Thurston says. 'I mean, do you think it's hungry this very minute?'

The bars are stout, but the household keep their distance. The creature presses itself away from them. It can't know it's arrived at its destination; it thinks this is some way station, in its procession of cramped and stinking days.

The wagoners are staring around them while they wait to be paid. They are Englishmen, and they have fetched it as bidden from Dover, fearful that it would break out and terrify the population of Kent; and so, they hint, it is worth a sum on top of the usual. It's not, one of them says, like fetching up a pile of logs.

'So who did you pick it up from, at Dover?'

One of them says, mildly belligerent, 'The usual man.'

'Have you papers?'

'No, sir.' Another says, in a burst of inspiration, 'We did have papers, but it ate them.'

Where it was before it crossed the sea, they don't know or care. 'Where would you find such a thing except among heathens?' one of them asks. 'Probably you ought to fetch a priest to it and have it blessed.'

'It looks as if it would eat a priest,' Thurston says. He chuckles appreciatively.

Well then: it appears the donor's name has been detached from it, somewhere on the journey. He pictures some turbaned potentate, waiting for thanks. What he'll do is, he'll thank everybody. Thank you for the marvel, he'll say.

Gregory says – it's the first sense anyone has spoken – 'Do you think it's meant for the king?'

That could be: in which case it is just another item that crosses his desk. Dick Purser is at his elbow. 'Dick,' he says, 'it will need a keeper, till we can get it to the Tower. It cannot go to the king in its present state. I think it can go no further.'

Credit to Dick, he does not say, no, not me, sir. He pulls off his cap and passes his hand over his stubble hair.

There is a shout. 'Look, it stirs!'

Until now the beast was torpid. Now it stands up, and in the cramped fetid space it stretches itself. It takes a pace forward, and that pace brings it to the limits of its freedom, and it stares at him, at *him*; its eyes are sunk deeply into its folds of fur, so you cannot see its expression, whether awe, or fear, or rage.

There is quiet. Dick says uneasily, 'It knows its master.'

As an arrow its target. He feels pierced by its scrutiny: thin as it is, a walking pelt. The first thing is to get it off the wagon. 'Pay these men,' he says. It will have to stay in its travelling gaol till one more capacious can be built, but the stench can be decreased by washing away its excrement. We'll need to feed it so that it fills its skin.

'What do you think?' he says to Dick Purser. 'Are you man enough?'

Dick grows taller inside his jerkin. Gregory says, 'With respect to you, my lord father, you always say that to people, when you want them to do something that can in no case be to their advantage.'

'Aye,' Thurston says. 'What he means is, Dick Purser, are you fool enough?'

Dick says, 'If I was to keep this beast, and be over the dogs as well, I'd need a boy, to train up.'

'You can have a boy.'

'It would eat a side of beef a day.'

'You can indent for it. We'll work you out a budget.'

'On one proviso.' Dick glares around him. 'I am its sole keeper. Nobody to poke it with a stick. In fact nobody to come at it unless I say so. I don't want it stirred up once I get it quiet. Nobody to walk by it with greyhounds, taunting it.'

Gregory says, 'I marvel that God could create it.'

'That He could even dream it,' he says. Think of the faith of the men who carried it! Not these carters, but those who have guarded it, every stage of its journey, and wedged food into its cage, thrust water at it. You cannot complain it is in poor condition, when you think that at any time they could have put a spear in its throat, and then sold its hide for a great sum.

The animal so far has made no sound. It does not now, but still it stares: it stares at Lord Cromwell, Lord Cromwell of Wimbledon,

Lord Keeper of the Privy Seal. It is thinking how to skin him from his furs, with one scalping flick of its paw. He must, in its starved computation, equal two sides of beef at least. Gregory says, 'Suppose it wants its prey live? Dick Purser will have to run down a stag.'

Dick moves forward, as if to make it a speech of welcome. Still the beast gazes at him. As if it saw space behind him. As if it did not see the bars.

He goes back to his desk. He is looking over the pensions list for St Albans. Before his papers flit patches of dark and light, the broken pattern of the beast's fur.

On mature consideration, he revises his picture of the turbaned potentate. Perhaps it was sent by some petty lord across the Narrow Sea, who had come by the creature and thought, this will ingratiate me with Thomas Cremuel, they say the man has an insensate yearning for what's expensive, and will keep it to show off to his peers.

When he sees William Fitzwilliam he tells him all about it, as they are going into the council chamber. Fitz groans in sympathy. 'Some fool sent me a seal. Three pails of fish every hour, and yet she had not dined. In the end I gave my wife directions, and she was made into pies.'

In Fitzwilliam's train to Calais go Thomas Seymour, brother of the late queen, along with that old Calais hand Francis Bryan, and others who are no strangers to that shore: the least of them is William Stafford, Mary Boleyn's husband. Some of the party are seasick, but not me, Gregory writes. He, Cromwell, smiles, reading out the letter to Mr Wriothesley. Inheritance is a strange thing. No one knows what traces our fathers leave. 'If I have passed on a strong stomach,' he says, 'good enough. My father must have had one too, or he would never have kept down his own ale.'

'Sometimes I think –' Call-Me breaks off.

'What?'

'I agree with Uncle Norfolk. The higher you rise in the king's service, the more you mention the low place you come from.'

'The more others mention it, you mean. I am not ashamed of it, Call-Me. I never say my father taught me nothing. He taught me to bend metal.'

He is a busy man. He has not time to read every curt note life sends him. But he reads this one: 'You do right to draw it to my attention. I will amend.'

While the welcome party are on the sea, the Abbot of Colchester is in the air. Colchester had signed up to the king's supremacy, he had taken the oath. Then he gave backword, in whispers behind the hand: More and Fisher were martyrs, how he pitied them! When he was called upon to surrender his abbey, he said the king had no right to it – which is to say, his will and laws are null. He is head neither of the spiritual realm nor the temporal; in effect he is no king, and Parliament can make no law. According to the abbot.

It is the last of the hangings, he is sure. They were infecting each other, Colchester, Glastonbury and Reading. But now resistance to the king's will is broken. All other houses can be closed by negotiation: no more blood, no more ropes and chains. No more examples are needed; the traitors' banner is trampled, that portrayed the Five Wounds. Superstitious men in the north claim that in addition to his principal wounds, Christ suffered 5,470 more. They say that every day fresh ones are incised, as he is cut and flayed by Cromwell.

It is not written that great men shall be happy men. It is nowhere recorded that the rewards of public office include a quiet mind. He sits in Whitehall, the year folding around him, aware of the shadow of his hand as it moves across the paper, his own inconcealable fist; and in the quiet of the house, he can hear the soft whispering of his quill, as if his writing is talking back to him.

Can you make a new England? You can write a new story. You can write new texts and destroy the old ones, set the torn leaves of Duns Scotus sailing about the quadrangles, and place the gospels in every church. You can write on England, but what was written before keeps showing through, inscribed on the rocks and carried on floodwater, surfacing from deep cold wells. It's not just the saints and martyrs who claim the country, it's those who came before them: the dwarves dug into ditches, the sprites who sing in the breeze, the demons bricked into culverts and buried under bridges; the bones under your floor. You cannot tax them or count them. They have lasted ten thousand years and ten thousand before that. They are not easily dispossessed by farmers with fresh leases and law clerks who adduce proof of title. They bubble out of the ground, wear away the shoreline, sow weeds among the crops and erode the workings of mines.

On 11 December Anna arrives in Antwerp. The English merchants, led by Stephen Vaughan as their governor, meet her four miles outside the town with eight score of great torches held aloft, the flames licking and kissing the twilight. The whole city has turned out, Vaughan writes, more than would come out to see the Emperor. Anna is gentle in manner, he says: a smiling, sedate princess, encased in her strange glittering gowns. She brings a troop of ladies dressed in the same fashion, but not one of them fairer than she.

Vaughan does not mention Jenneke. Whether he has seen her. But then, the posts are not always secure.

Next day Anna is en route to Bruges. From Bruges she goes to Calais, where Fitzwilliam and his train ride outside the walls to meet her.

It is barely light. Her escort, their horses trapped in black velvet, seem to materialise from nowhere. As they approach the walls, guns are fired in salute, so the party proceeds, through smoke that obliterates their vision, to the Lantern Gate.

Once Henry has settled his own marriage, he turns his mind to Lady Mary. The Duke of Bavaria has come into the realm, with a modest entourage as the king advised: unmarried, a very proper man. He assures the king he will make no demands. He will take Mary purely for friendship's sake, to strengthen the German league against Emperor and Rome.

He sends Mr Wriothesley up-country to prepare the lady for a meeting. Call-Me is his usual messenger now. Mary has warmed to him, and made him a satin cushion with his family coat of arms.

710

He, the Lord Privy Seal, is working with the Household officers on the final plans for the queen's grand reception. He has included Lady Mary in a place of honour, but the king says, perhaps not, Crumb. They might take it ill in Cleves. That sort of thing, parading one's bastards, we leave to the Scots.

He bows. Agrees it might be better if the two ladies meet privately: stepmother and stepdaughter, just a year apart in age. Let them sit down and get to know each other. Perhaps they will walk hand in hand together, as Mary did with Queen Jane.

He says to Call-Me, put the new offer to Mary, but expect her usual reply: would rather stay a maid, but will obey her father. Take it as it is given, and leave; state Bavaria's merits, but do not over-persuade her. Because when you have gone she will rage about, saying she would rather be eaten by wild beasts than marry a Lutheran.

The king is pleased with Duke Philip. He brings him into his chambers at Whitehall, to show him the Henry on the wall. If the king sees any gap between the monarch that Hans painted and the man who exhibits him, it does not trouble him. 'Behold my last queen,' he says. 'Most excellent among women.'

They are speaking Latin. Philip bows to the image.

'Behold my father.' Now the king reverts to English. 'Do you know, he had only seven ships, and two of them not fit to put to sea? Whereas I have been able to send fifty ships to Calais, merely for the escort of your cousin of Cleves.'

Behind his son, the figure of the old king shrinks a little.

'I felicitate you,' Philip says. He may not speak English but he gets the gist. 'Most valiant of princes,' he adds.

The king draws him aside. Philip served against the Turk, when they laid siege to Vienna. The king wants to hear his war stories. They are closeted all afternoon.

A day or so later he is on his way up to Enfield, Rafe with him, to see Mary himself. 'Your presence alone will have an effect,' Rafe says. 'She will know the king is in earnest.'

Henry has already begun talking terms. He has asked for a draft contract.

711

Mary keeps him waiting, but he sees she has dressed up: a sweep of black velvet gown, a bodice of rosy satin. 'How was the road, my lord?'

'Miserable,' he says. 'But not impassable. We shall be able to get you to Greenwich, if it pleases your father to order you there. And your new apartments in Whitehall are building. I am just drying the plaster out. I have seen the glaziers this last week.'

'HA-HAs?' she says.

'Yes. And the emblems of the queen's grace.'

'It seems odd to me,' Mary says. 'To call her the queen. When we have never seen her. Still. I congratulate my lord father. Naturally.'

'Duke Philip is a well-made man,' he says. 'Fair. Blue eyes. Not unlike your lady mother, in colouring.'

She looks out of the window.

'I thought Mr Wriothesley might not have told you that.'

She smooths her hands down her skirt, and hums a little. *When sparrows build churches upon a green hill …*

'What we don't want from you,' he says, 'is any late retraction. You say yes, yes, yes, and then at the last minute you say no. Because that would leave the king embarrassed.'

'Yes,' she says. 'No.' He waits. 'Yes, it would leave him embarrassed. No, I would not do it. I have said I will obey.'

'The king is a tender father, he would not force you into a marriage with a man you cannot love.'

Mary raises her eyebrows. 'Yet he forced Meg Douglas out of marriage, to a man she swore she would die for.'

'Oh, Tom Truth,' he says. 'He wasn't worth a princess's funeral.'

'Love is blind,' Mary says.

'Not invariably. You should meet him. Philip.'

Rafe says, 'You would like to come to court, wouldn't you? I am sure you would.'

'Master Sadler,' she says, 'why are you talking to me as if I were a nursing infant?'

Rafe snatches off his cap in exasperation. He, the Lord Privy Seal, says, 'Because you enforce us.' He crosses the room. He takes her hand. 'I implore you, my lady. Act as a woman, not a child. Let fate lead you before it drags you.'

Outside, Rafe says, 'She will meet him. She is curious, I can tell. And what would Chapuys advise her, if he were here? He would say, do not anger the king.'

He nods. He forgot to play his Chapuys card. But then, he has a great deal on his mind.

Back in London he sits down as bidden with Bishop Tunstall, and they work out terms. Philip can take Mary back with him, at his own expense. 'Well,' the bishop says, 'you have wrestled her signature onto paper before now, my lord. God knows how you brought her to conformity before this, but you did.'

He throws down his pen. 'But if she has to be carried to the priest for the blessing, I will not do it. The king must do it himself.'

'He would not ask me,' Tunstall says dryly. 'I am in my sixty-sixth year. Age has some advantages. As you will learn, my lord, if as I pray God grants you long life.'

After his summer of recreation, his vivid autumn in forest and field, the king seems jaundiced: pinch-faced, pale as pastry. They sit over letters from abroad, in a room drained of light: the air is black-grey, water mixed with ink. Beyond is an imagined country, drowned pastures and sodden copses, drenched fields and woodland, cob walls and thatch, churches and farmsteads.

Wyatt, riding to Paris, has caught up with King François. An empty exchange of compliments has ensued: Wyatt congratulates François on his continuing friendship with the Emperor, and François, putting his hand on his heart, swears continuing devotion to his English brother, Henri.

Then Wyatt rides to overtake the Emperor on his progress. The same pointless swapping of pleasantries; but then someone raises the subject of Guelders, the territory the young Duke of Cleves claims as his own. Charles becomes impassioned. Henry should advise his new brother-in-law to obey his overlord and Emperor, and give way to his sovereign claim. Otherwise he will suffer, as the young and rash do suffer. Let him be warned.

Wyatt is shocked. Charles is a laconic, self-contained man. Almost never does he open his heart; he speaks behind the hand, works his will in crooked ways. So what does this vehemence mean? Will he turn his army on Henry's new ally?

The Emperor and François have met face to face. It is said they will celebrate Christmas together and be in Paris for New Year. Even the Pope is afraid of the secret practices they will work between them. Wyatt detects Rome's agents, lurking in corners. He says, I can find out what passes between these princes; but you in London must give me pretexts, for coming into their company every day.

'This pretended alliance,' Henry says. 'Neither ruler dare turn his back on the other. That is what keeps them in the same town. It is not friendship but its opposite.'

'All the same,' he says, 'their league has endured longer than we could imagine.'

'Wolsey would have broken it up.'

He gives Henry a long look. 'No doubt.'

'We have people in France we retain,' the king says. 'But they are not loyal, they will turn for a halfpenny. We have few friends in either court.' He sucks his lip. 'Especially you, you have few friends, Cromwell.'

'If I have incurred their malice, I count it well done. As it is for your Majesty's sake.'

'But are you sure about that?' Henry sounds curious. 'I think it is because of what you are. They don't know how to deal with you.'

'Likely not. Majesty,' he says, 'you must realise, they want me displaced, so that you might be the worse advised. That is why they try to poison your mind against me. Any fantastical story will serve.'

'So you would recommend, if I hear you have exceeded your office, or that you have slacked my instructions or reversed them, I should ignore the bruit?'

'You should speak to me before you believe anything.'

'I will,' Henry says.

He gets up. He is too restless to sit still. It is not like him. He can usually find some semblance of ease even when, as today, the king is fretful and morose.

Henry says, 'You know, I think you have never forgiven me. For parting with Wolsey.'

Parting with him? Christ in Heaven.

'I think you blame me for his death.'

He goes to the window. In the park the trees are marrying the darkness. You can't see where the rain ends and the shadows begin.

'We are making up the preliminary accounts for Westminster Abbey,' he says. 'They will surrender in the new year. Riche has too much paper on his desk to take the surrender now, or they would not keep your Majesty waiting.'

Henry says, 'You remember John Islip? Westminster was much decayed when he came in as abbot.'

'Near bankrupt, sir. Though that must be forty years ago.'

Islip went through the books and put the abbey's rents up. Once he had rebuilt the shrine of Edward the Confessor, it brought plenty of trade in. 'Islip was a clever man,' Henry says. 'My father used to take me to see him when I was a child, at his house over Tothill Fields. The road was a disgrace – the ways so foul, the cattle churning up mud by the ponds – you'd see dead dogs, and pigs rooting, and all manner of carrion.'

'It got worse, sir, when the sewer burst. But I've drained it now.'

Who but Cromwell? Your man for watercourses and sewers, charnel houses and spoilheaps.

'But when he died,' Henry says, 'do you remember the funeral? It was a wonder to behold, it was more like a victory parade than a burial. Down Willow Walk with the banners flying. The monks chanting in procession. I have never seen such an incense cloud, the abbey walls seemed to be melting. And the feast afterwards, in his honour. You know it's only six years? It seems a lifetime.'

When Bishop Stokesley died last September we hung the churches in black, no reverence was wanting. But Islip died in the Roman world. Henry says, 'My father wanted King Harry VI to be made a

715

saint, and that would have enriched the abbey too. But when he heard Rome's price, it made him curse.'

'The insensate greed of the Vatican, it beggars belief,' he says. He would rather say something original, but he gives the king what he wants.

'My father would send Islip wine,' Henry says. 'And the monks would send him back a marrowbone pudding. He used to eat them when he was young, I think, when he was a poor exile. It was a dish he liked above anything.'

'My father too,' he says: surprised to remember it.

'You can get those puddings for a penny,' Henry says. He smiles. 'They must have been easy to please, our fathers.'

'If God glanced down now, what would He see? Two ageing men in failing light, talking about their past because they have so much of it.' He hardly likes to break the moment. But the candles will be coming in.

Henry says, 'Tom, it is a long time now since I first saw you.'

'It is more than a decade,' he says. 'Since then I have had the privilege to come into your presence –'

'Almost daily, isn't it?' Henry says. 'Yes, almost every day. I remember – I knew you by sight, but I remember our first interview. Suffolk, he did not know what to make of you. I knew, though. I saw your sharp little eyes. You told me not to go to war. Never fight, you said, you can't afford it. Skulk indoors like a sick child – it will be good for the treasury. And I thought … by St Loy, the man has some stomach. He has some gall.'

'I trust I did not offend.'

'You did. I overlooked it.'

The king's voice seems to be fading, like the light. 'Islip was Wolsey's friend,' he says. 'So I made him my councillor, but I never took to him myself. He had a nose for heresy though. Wolsey used to send him among your friends, the Hanse merchants. Down at the Steelyard.'

The king passes a hand over his face, as if wiping away Islip, the abbey, the heretics, their house. 'You offended, and I forgave. A ruler must do it. I am greatly altered these ten years. You, not so much. You do not surprise me as once you did. I do not think you will surprise me again, considering all that you have said and done – some of it miraculous, Tom, I will not deny. You work beyond the capacities of ten ordinary men. But still I miss the Cardinal of York.'

When he goes out he can feel the pulse in his neck jumping. Wriothesley is there. 'He is tired of me,' he says cheerfully. 'He told me so. I am bested by the cardinal's ghost.'

Call-Me says, 'I wondered what was happening, in there in the dark. Was he giving the cardinal a chance to appear?'

In his graveclothes. His shroud muffling his skull. The dead are more faithful than the living. For better or worse, they do not leave you. They last out the longest night.

While the bridal party is held up in Calais by bad weather, they pass the time in jousting and visiting from house to house, devising masques and plays. A merchantman is reported wrecked off Boulogne, casting onshore a cargo of wool and Castile soap. He imagines the ocean foaming, bubbles on the crest of each wave. Please God fetch Anna soon: the king is anxious. Fitzwilliam sends him the tide tables. If the cardinal were here, he says sardonically, no doubt he could whistle the wind into the right quarter.

Everyone who has seen her seems delighted with the new queen. Lady Lisle writes to her daughter Anne Bassett, one of the new maids of honour, and Anne takes the letter to the king, handing it with her deepest curtsey.

The king reads out the letter. '*Good and gentle to serve and please.* So there you are,' he says to the girl. 'What news could be better? You will have a loving mistress, and I a loving mate.'

Anne blushes. 'Mate' seems blunt. Possibly she doesn't like to think of the king in bed. How times change. Ten years back she would have been in bed with him.

* * *

In Calais Anna is lodged in the queen's apartments at the Exchequer. Fitzwilliam writes that she has invited the English lords to supper. She is used to dining in public, and does not know it is no longer the custom of English kings. But she means well; she wants to see her new countrymen at table and learn their customs. Her manner was regal, Fitzwilliam reports. He and Gregory spend an hour with her teaching her card games that the king likes. It is her own idea, and a clever one.

The wind changes. 27 December, Anna lands at Deal, in the rain and after dark. They row her ashore, a princess coming out of the sea. She will go from Deal to Dover, from Canterbury to Rochester, and by the first week of the new year she will be approaching London from the east. The king will meet her at Blackheath, conduct her to Greenwich palace, and marry her by Twelfth Night.

III

Magnificence

January–June 1540

The king's new castle at Deal is a way station for Anna to wash her hands, take a fortifying glass of wine, and then pass on to Dover. She is escorted by Charles Brandon and by Richard Sampson, the Bishop of Chichester, that tight-lipped prelate so experienced in the making and breaking of the king's unions.

Brandon has his young wife with him. She is of a quick, warm nature; what could be better for an uncertain bride, than to be welcomed by a smiling young duchess who will divine what she needs? You can't expect Charles to know, Bishop Sampson still less. But Charles cuts an impressive martial figure. And Sampson will take himself off to a corner and busy himself with paperwork.

In Dover, God willing, Anna's baggage will catch up with her. Next day she will set out – with her chaplains and her secretaries and her musicians and maids – to Canterbury, where she will meet the archbishop. She will want ready money, and so he, Cromwell, has arranged for a gold chalice to be presented, fifty sovereigns inside. As she passes through to Rochester, Norfolk will escort her with a large party of gentlemen. There are no plans for her to meet the Bishop of Winchester. That treat can be saved up. After all, Lord Cromwell's boys say, we don't want her to turn tail and start wading out to sea again.

The weather en route is foul. But the bride was not seasick, and thinks nothing of travelling with the rain and hail in her face. The masters of ceremony are relieved, because they have planned a huge reception at Blackheath outside Greenwich palace, and if she does not keep on schedule they will incur heavy costs. He, Lord Cromwell, expects the countryside to turn out. He has had the streets at Greenwich cleaned and gravelled, and barriers erected so the crowds don't push each other into the Thames.

All winter at Austin Friars he has been laying in muscatel and malmsey with a view to celebration. In the bakehouse they are making *Striezel* to take to Anna and her ladies, and the smell of cloves and cinnamon and orange peel has crept through the house. When Lizzie was alive, Twelfth Night was their occasion to feast their neighbours. They would enact the Three Kings, their costumes patched with every gilded offcut, scraps too small for the greediest tailor. Every hand that could hold a needle would go to work, and Lizzie would make them cheer while they sewed. One year they made Anne Cromwell into a cat with a coney-skin tail, and Gregory into a fish with shining silver scales; the low winter light slid over him, and he glimmered in the dusk.

He wonders how his daughter Jenneke is faring, and when he will see her again. He does not say to himself 'if', because he is always inclined to think the world will turn our way. It seems strange to him that Lizzie never saw her. She would have accepted the stranger; she knew when they married he was a man with a past.

It is a long time now since the women of the house put his little daughters in their graveclothes. He has got used to a certain feeling of tightness that settles behind the breastbone, that comes around by the calendar: Easter, St John's Day, Lammas, Michaelmas, All Souls and All Saints.

The year 1539 is drawing to its close, and when he enters the king's presence at Greenwich with a file of business in his hand, he is prepared to find the king playing the harp, or listing the New Year presents he hopes to receive, or merely making paper darts, but in any event unprepared for work. But there is a stir in the privy chamber, and young Culpeper comes out: 'You will never guess, sir! He is going himself to Rochester, to meet the queen.'

He pushes his files at Culpeper. 'Wriothesley, come in with me.'

Henry is bending down, peering into a trunk the Wardrobe has sent. He stands up, cheerful: 'My lord, I have decided to make speed and meet the bride in my own person.'

'Why, sir? It will only be a day or two before she arrives.'

Henry says, 'I want to nourish love.'

'Majesty,' Mr Wriothesley says, 'with all respect, was this not aired in council? It was your councillors' earnest prayer that your Majesty spare himself the journey, and greet the queen at Blackheath. And you were pleased to accede.'

'Can I not change my mind, Wriothesley? At Blackheath there will be music and ordnance and processions and crowds and we shall not speak a dozen private words before we must ride back here to the palace, and then it will be hours before we have a chance to be alone. And I want to surprise her, and gladden her heart, and bid her a proper welcome.'

'Sir, if you will be advised by me ...' he says.

'But I will not. Admit it, Cromwell, you are no adept in courtship.'

True. He's only been married once. 'She is hardly off the ship, sir. Think how shamed she will be, if she cannot appear at her best.'

Mr Wriothesley adds, 'And she may, of course, be overwhelmed by your Majesty's presence.'

'But that is why I must go! I will spare her anxiety. She will be working herself up towards great ceremonies.' Henry smiles. 'I shall go in disguise.'

He closes his eyes.

'It is what a king does,' Henry tells him. 'You cannot know, Cromwell, you are not a courtier born. When my sister Margaret went into Scotland, King James and his hunting party surprised her at the castle of Dalkeith, he in a jacket of crimson velvet, his lyre slung over his shoulder.'

One has heard. The dashing youth with burning eyes, swift to bend the knee; the bride in the pretty confusion of thirteen summers, her cheek blushing, her body trembling.

Mr Wriothesley says, 'May I ask, what disguise does your Majesty mean to adopt?'

They exchange a glance. When Katherine was queen she was repeatedly ambushed by Robin Hood, or Arcadian shepherds. When they threw off their disguise, lo and behold! It was the king and Charles Brandon; it was Charles Brandon and the king.

'I have sables for her,' Henry says. 'Perhaps I should arrive as a Russian nobleman, in great fur boots?'

Mr Wriothesley says, 'Unless we send word ahead, I am afraid that your Majesty might alarm his own guard. It could lead to –'

'A shepherd, then. Or one of the Magi. We can quickly get disguisings for the other two kings. Send to Charles –'

'Or perhaps, sir,' he says, 'just go as a gentleman?'

'A gentleman of England.' Henry is thoughtful. 'A gentleman with no name. Yes,' he looks downcast, 'very well, I shall be ruled by Lord Cromwell, as all the foreigners claim I am. I shall astonish her anyway.' He pauses and says kindly, 'My lord, I know it is not what we agreed. But a bridegroom must have his caprices, and disguising always gives pleasure. The dowager Katherine,' he says to Wriothesley, 'she would pretend not to know me. Of course, she did but play with me. Everybody knows the king.'

Thomas Culpeper follows them out. 'Your papers, gentlemen?'

Wriothesley snatches them. He, Lord Cromwell, walks away. 'Christ,' he says.

Culpeper says, 'You did what you could.'

He thinks, I spoke to him as a subject to a prince. What if I had taken courage and said: Henry, I am advising you, man to man, not to do it?

Culpeper says, 'Why are you apprehensive? Everybody praises her, don't they? Are you afraid he will find her not as reported?'

'Cease to hang on my sleeve, Culpeper.'

Culpeper smiles. 'I know she will find him not as reported. We appreciate you bend the facts, Lord Cromwell, to please foreigners – but you have not described him as a god, I hope? Is she expecting Apollo?'

'She is expecting a proper court reception. It is what her people have prepared her for.' He turns to Wriothesley. 'I need someone to make speed to Rochester and warn her. The king will come on the river with a small train and Anna should be ready for him. No heralds, no ceremony – he will enter her chamber and she should be astonished.'

'So you are going to spoil his surprise,' Culpeper says. 'She must not know him, then she must? She will be lucky to time it right.'

'I wonder,' he says to Wriothesley, 'should I have insisted I go with him?'

Call-Me says, 'It could be worse, sir. At least he's not going to wear his Turkish costume.'

The king intends to join the queen in Rochester on New Year's Day, and stay overnight; even if he sends a messenger back to say how he likes her, it will be hours before word arrives at Greenwich.

So, he thinks, the news can come to Austin Friars almost as fast. He journeys home, to start 1540 under his own roof.

He goes early to his desk. It is a day found, he tells himself. But he pushes away a bundle of letters from Carlisle, picks up a book. It is Rolewinck's history, where all the dates before Christ are printed upside down. Jane Rochford's father sent it, and he can never just leave you to read; he writes *Mirabilia!* beside events he particularly enjoys.

He turns the pages to look at the pictures: Antioch, Jerusalem, Temple of Solomon and Tower of Babel. Rolewinck starts his story in the year 6615 (upside down). He is reading about the coronation of Pope Innocent – which occurred, more or less, the year that he himself was born – when his spaniel Bella runs yapping to the door. From below he can hear, 'Happy New Year, Mr Gregory!'

Bella runs in excited circles. He calls down: 'Gregory? Why are you here?'

Gregory bangs in. He does not pause for a greeting. 'Why did you let this happen? Why did you not stop him?'

'Stop him?' he says. 'How? He said it was to nourish love.'

'You should have prevented it, sir. You are his councillor.'

'Gregory, drink off a cup of this, and get warm. I thought you were staying with the queen?'

'I came to warn you. Henry passed the night, but now he is on his way back.'

One of Thurston's boys comes in with a platter of pastries, and whisks off the cloth. 'Venison and currant jelly. Pike and horseradish. Plum and raisin.'

'You see,' he says, 'this is why I've come home. At court your food has to walk half a mile, you get it cold.'

Another boy brings a bowl of hot water and a napkin, and Gregory is forced to silence till they are alone. Bella capers on her hind legs as if to divert them. He thinks of the scenes he used to stage with George Cavendish, the cardinal's man. He would say, 'Show me how it was, George – who sat where, who spoke first.' And Cavendish would jump up and play the king.

He can lay out this stage in his mind, where bride and groom meet: the old hall at Rochester, the great fireplace with its carved emblems: a fern, a heart, a Welsh dragon holding an orb. He can follow the king with his train of merry men; they hold their masks loosely, playfully, because they expect to be recognised in seconds. And indeed, as they pass, the new queen's servants kneel.

'Anna was warned?' he asks. 'She was ready?'

'She was warned, but she was not ready. The king billowed in, but she was looking out of the window – they were baiting a bull in the courtyard. She cast a glance over her shoulder, then she turned away to the sport.'

He can see what Gregory saw: the bulky shape of the king blacking out the light. And the foggy outline of the queen, with the window behind her: the blank oval of her face, a swift glance from her dark eyes, and then the back of her head.

'I suppose she did not believe a prince would come in secret. Maybe Duke Wilhelm goes everywhere with trumpeters and drums.'

Even to nourish love, he thinks. There is talk that the Emperor has offered Anna's brother the Duchess Christina as his bride, if he will hand back Guelders without a fight. He thinks, if I were the Duke of Cleves, I would not give my sea coast for her dimples.

'The king bowed low.' Gregory takes a gulp of his wine. 'And addressed her, but she did not turn. I think she took him for – I do not know what – some Jolly Jankin dressed up for the festival. And so he stood, his hat in his hand – then her people swarmed in, and someone called out, "Madam," and a phrase to alert her ...' Gregory falters. 'And then she turned. And she knew who he was. And as Christ is my Saviour, Father, the look in her eye! I will never forget it.' Gregory sits down, as if at the end of his strength. 'Nor will the king.'

He picks Bella up, and begins to feed her a pastry, crumb by crumb. 'Why should she be astonished? I made no false representation.'

'You did not tell her he was old.'

'Am I old? Is that what you would first think of, if you described Cromwell? *Oh, he is old*?'

'No,' Gregory says unwillingly.

'She knew his date of birth. She knew he was stout. Surely, enough gentlemen from her court have passed to and fro? And Hans – Hans could have described him. Who better?'

'But Hans will never get himself in trouble.'

That much is true. 'What did the king do?'

'He fell back. Any man would have been stricken. She flinched from him. He could not miss it.'

'And?'

'Then she recovered herself. She dissimulated marvellous well. And so did he. She said in English, "My lord and my king, welcome."'

It was for him to say, welcome. 'Go on.'

'She made a smooth curtsey, very low, as if nothing had occurred. And the king smiled and uplifted her. He said, "Welcome, sweetheart."' What it is to be royal, he thinks. Gregory adds, 'His hand was trembling.'

In his imagined hall at Rochester, the light is failing. Below the queen's window, soundless, the bull-baiters roar. The dogs hang from the bull's flesh. Slow gouts of blood patter onto the paving. 'And the king's gentlemen? What did they do?'

What he means is, did they see it all?

'Anthony Browne was behind him, carrying the sables for her. But Henry waved him back. He was looking in the lady's face and all the time talking.'

'Gregory,' he says, 'did Hans paint her truly?'

'He would not dare do other, would he?'

'And she is beautiful?'

'Not sideways. She has a long nose. But you know he had no time to draw her from all angles. She is pleasant-looking. She is a little marked with smallpox, but I only saw that when the sun chanced to come out. The king cannot have seen it, he had turned his back.'

She is lovely in the shadows, then. And when facing front. He could almost laugh. 'Is he disappointed?'

'If he is, he did not show it. He led her by the hand. They went aside and sat down with the interpreters. He asked how she liked England and she said, very well. He asked, how was she entertained in Calais, and she said, very well. He congratulated her on making the voyage so bravely, and asked had she been on the sea before? When they translated this, she looked startled.'

He pictures the king, sweating with the effort. His eyes roaming around, looking for a diversion.

'The king called for music. A consort came in and they played "O fair white hand that heals me". She attended to it very sweetly. She said, through the interpreter, she would like to learn to play some instrument. The king said, easier when young. She said, I am not so old, and my fingers are kept supple by plying my needle. The king asked, could she sing, and she said, in praise of Mary and the saints. He said, would she sing, and she said, not before all these lords, but I will sing when we are alone. And she blushed.'

'That is a very proper modesty.' Think of Anne Boleyn; she would have sung in the street, if she thought it might get her some attention.

'We say we like modesty,' Gregory picks up one of the pastries, and Bella, at his feet, touches him with her paw. 'But really we prefer it when maids show their favour plain. We like to know we are well-accepted, before we begin to court them. I should never have dared speak to Bess, if you and Edward Seymour had not helped me. If a woman might despise us, we would rather avoid her.'

And when we find the courage to present ourselves, he thinks, we do not want to see shock on her face. 'So you think damage is done?'

'I don't see how she will undo that first moment, even if she were the Queen of Sheba.' Gregory takes a bite of his pastry; Bella leans against his shin and adores him. 'They went into supper. She was very attentive, turning her eyes to everything he said. It is a poor beginning, but considering one cannot talk to her, I like her very much, and so do we all. Fitzwilliam himself says, she is as good a woman as he will find if he scours Europe.'

'I think he has scoured it,' he says. 'I have, at least. Well … he will understand, when he thinks about it, that she was startled. And you say yourself, he was happy enough afterwards.' He considers. His eye falls on Lord Morley's history. 'We must roll back time. It will be as if the king blinked, and then lived that first moment again.'

Gregory says, 'But is that how time works?' As the pastries disappear, the plate's pattern emerges. *Fatto in Venezia*, it depicts the Fall of Troy: the wooden horse, the screaming women, the rolling heads, and the towers in bursts of flame.

Wonderful, how they get it all in.

He arrives at Greenwich not long after the king. 'My lord, his Majesty is in his library.'

Henry sits amid boxes of books. 'These are from Tewkesbury Abbey.' He rises heavily from his chair. 'Cromwell, we have not had the papers from Cleves about the Lorraine marriage, the pre-contract. It was stated emphatically the lady would bring them with her, but it appears she did not. Even the least suspicious man would ask himself why they have still not shown them, after all these months.'

He begins to speak, but the king holds up his hand. 'I cannot proceed. I cannot marry her till I am sure she is clear of all past promises.'

The king closes one fist in the other. 'I find the lady nothing so well as she is spoken of. Fitzwilliam wrote from Calais and praised her outright. Lisle too. What made them do so?'

'I have not seen her, sir.'

'No, you have not seen her,' the king says. 'You have been at the mercy of reports, as have I, so you cannot be blamed. But when I encountered her yesterday, I tell you, I had much ado to master myself. A great outlandish bonnet with wings sticking out either side of her head – and with her height, and stiff as she is – I thought to myself, she looks like the Cornhill Maypole. I believe she had painted her mouth, which if true is a filthy thing.'

'Her attire can be changed, sir.'

'Her complexion is sallow. When I think of Jane, so white and clear, a pearl.'

Golden lights waver on the ceiling. They play on the crimson plaster roses, the green leaves between, the blood-washed thorns. 'It is the journey,' he says. 'All those tedious miles with a baggage train, then the delays, and the voyage.' He thinks of the hail in her face on the Dover road. 'As for the papers, I cannot guess why the ambassadors have not brought them. But we are assured the lady is completely free. We know there was no pre-contract. We know the parties were not of age. You said yourself, sir, it is no great matter.'

'It is a great matter, if I think I am married, and find I am not.'

'Tomorrow,' he promises, 'I will talk with the queen's people.'

'Tomorrow I meet her at Blackheath,' the king says. 'We start at eight o'clock.'

It is forty years since a bride came here from a far country: the Infanta Catalina, who brought Moorish slaves in her entourage when she left Spain to marry Arthur. That wedding was public and splendid. This time the marriage celebrations must give way to the church's rites for Epiphany. All hangs, therefore, on the public welcome he has devised for Anna.

At Greenwich he lies in bed, listening to the wind.

728

What means this when I lie alone?
I toss, I turn, I sigh, I groan.
My bed to me seems hard as stone
What means this?

He wonders, where does Wyatt lie tonight? With whom? I dare swear he is not alone.

I sigh, I plain continually.
The clothes that on my bed do lie
Always methinks they lie awry
What means this?

Only a raging storm will stop tomorrow's reception. The king may decide to delay the marriage, but he cannot leave his bride out on the heath. He cannot undo the anticipation of the countryside, when it has been stirred up by heralds, and the welcome proclaimed through London.

Three times he rises and opens the shutter. There is nothing to see but a muffled, starless black. But the drumbeat of rain falters, dawn stripes the sky in shades of ochre, and the sun feels its way out of banks of cloud. By nine o'clock, when he is at Blackheath on horseback, there is a white haze over the fields: in that haze, the freefolk of England. A steady roar comes from the river, where hundreds have turned out in any craft they can command, their home-made flags and banners hanging limp in the still morning. They are bashing drums and tootling fifes, bawling out songs and sporting on their persons knitted roses. Some are toddling along the banks inside pasteboard castles, their heads sticking out from the crenellations, and others have fabricated a canvas swan of monstrous size, which turns its neck from side to side and waddles along, a dozen pair of feet in workmen's boots emerging beneath its feathers. Harness bells jingle. Men and horses breathe vapour into the air. He finds he is sweating inside his velvet. He is irritating even himself, trotting up and down, on and off his horse, his eyes everywhere, mouthing pointless exhortations: stand here, move along, attend, follow, kneel!

Charles Brandon tips his hat to him. 'Weather a credit to you, Lord Cromwell!' He laughs, and spurs off to join the other dukes.

The chaplains, the councillors, the great officers of the royal household, file in their ranks: the gentlemen of the privy chamber, and the bishops in black satin; the peers, the Lord Mayor, the heralds, the Duke of Bavaria wearing the collar of the Golden Fleece; the king himself, in a wide expanse of light, mounted on a great courser, in purple and cloth of gold, his garments slashed and puffed, sashed and swagged, so studded and slung with belts of gemstones that he seems to be wearing a suit of armour forged and welded for Zeus.

The queen waits for the royal party in a silken pavilion. He prays the wind will not get up and toss it in the river. Anna is dressed in the best fashion of her country, her caul topped by a bonnet stiff with pearls, her gown cut full and round, without a train. She glitters as they enthrone her on her mount, side-saddle and facing left in the English fashion. No one knew what to expect from a German: Spanish ladies ride to the right; he hears the Lord Chancellor say, thank God for that, we do not want him to think of Spaniards. He says stiffly, 'Nothing has been left to chance, my lord. I have spoken with her Master of Horse.'

By afternoon – drums, artillery, several changes of clothes – the glow has gone from the sky and the air is dank and greenish. Gardiner rides up: 'How did you hold the rain off?'

'I sold my soul,' he says calmly.

'I hear there was an upset at Rochester.'

'You know more than I do.'

'So I do. High time you admitted it.' Gardiner smirks and rides away.

The French ambassador reins in beside him: 'Cremuel, I have simply never seen so many fat gold chains assembled in one place. I commend you, it is no small matter to keep five thousand people on time and in their ranks. Though frankly,' he sniffs, 'the whole of it does not equal even one of the ceremonial entries my king makes in the course of a year. And they would be, I believe, twenty or so in number.'

'Truly?' he says. 'Twenty occasions like this? No wonder he has no time to govern.'

Marillac's horse shifts under him, sidestepping. 'What do you think of the lady? She is not as young as one expected.'

'I do not like to contradict you, but she is exactly the age one expected.'

'She is very tall.'

'So is the king.'

'True. On that account he wanted to marry Madame de Longueville, did he not? A pity he did not work harder at it. I hear she will give King James a child this spring.'

He says, 'The king has good expectation of children with this lady.'

'Of course. If she can rouse him to action. Be honest, she is no great beauty.'

He admits, 'I have hardly seen her as yet.' It is as if they are conspiring to keep him away from her. He can see only a stiff, bright-coloured figure, like a painted queen on an inn sign. She has ridden the last half-mile to meet the king, both of them on horses so splendidly trapped that you can hardly see their hooves as they tread the ground. Meg Douglas follows in first place, and after her Mary Fitzroy. The ladies of the court travel behind in a line of chariots. Gregory's wife wears the revenue of two manors on her back, but it is his pleasure; it is a long time since he had a woman to dress, and he says to Marillac, 'Look, my son's wife, is she not handsome?'

'A credit to you,' Marillac says, and indicates with his whip: is that the Scottish princess? And is that Norfolk's daughter, my lady Richmond? 'No new husband for her yet?'

There was talk last year of marrying the girl to Tom Seymour, but nothing came of it, no doubt because her brother knocked it back; Wolf Hall is a hovel, as far as Surrey is concerned, and the Seymours are peasants who live by trapping rabbits.

He wonders, why does Marillac care about Norfolk's daughter? Has he got a French husband in mind for her? The French give

Norfolk a yearly pension but perhaps they are looking for closer ties?

Bess glances in his direction; he raises a hand, but in a stealthy way, in case he appears to be giving a signal for some démarche. In the next chariot come the maids of honour: Lady Lisle's daughter Anne Bassett, and Mary Norris looking chilled, and Norfolk's plump little niece Katherine, gawping about her as if she were in church.

The ground has been cleared to make a path for the king and queen right to the palace gates. They ride together into the inner court. There they dismount and the king, taking her arm, leads his bride into the palace, sweeping his great plumed hat about him to show her, all this is yours, madam, all that you see. The music from the river follows them: fading only as he, Lord Cromwell, follows them indoors, where the torches are already lit in welcome.

It is now that he sees her close for the first time. He has braced himself, his face fitted with a carefully neutral expression. But there is nothing to offend. Quite the opposite; he feels he knows her. It is true her complexion is dull, but it is as Gregory says, she is a pleasant-looking woman, who might be married to one of your friends; the city wife of a city merchant. You can imagine her rocking a cradle with one foot, while talking about the price of pork.

Anna looks him over. 'Oh, you are Lord Cromwell. Thank you for the fifty sovereigns.' One of her entourage speaks in her ear. 'Thank you for everything,' she says.

Sunday morning: he breaks it to the delegation from Cleves that the bridegroom wants a delay. They are taken aback. 'We thought we had been through all this, Lord Cromwell. We have furnished copies of everything relevant.'

He maintains a civil stiffness; he does not want them to see he is as exasperated as they are. 'The king is enquiring for the originals.'

We have explained again and again, they say, that we do not know what those would be: since the promises of a marriage, such as they were, were rolled up within a larger treaty, which was several times amended, and so …

'I advise you to produce them,' he says. He sits down, and, though it is early, indicates a jug of wine should come in. 'Gentlemen, this should not be beyond our wit to solve.'

Not all the Cleves gentlemen are fluent in French. One nudges another: what did he say? 'May I refer you to precedent? When Queen Katherine – I mean, the dowager Katherine, the late Princess of Wales –'

Oh yes, they say, Henry's first wife ...

'– when her mother Isabella married her father Ferdinand, they needed a dispensation from the Pope, but it was delayed –'

Ah, we understand, they say. Rome angling for more money, was it not?

'But everything else was ready, and so Ferdinand's people stepped aside and created what was required ... papal seals and all.'

So what are you advising? they say.

'I would not presume to advise. But do what you must, to satisfy the king. Search your baggage. Look between the pages of your Bibles.'

We need time to confer, they say.

'Be quick,' William Fitzwilliam says, coming in.

Oh, we will, they say. We cannot brook delay. The rumours would be running everywhere, imagine what the French would say, imagine the lies the Emperor's people would spread. They would be saying he does not like her. Or that she finds him too old and stout and is protesting she will not do it.

'You gentlemen must come to the council after dinner,' he says, 'and spell out to them the danger of such rumours. The king will join us when he and the queen come from Mass.'

He walks to the council chamber with Fitz. Fitz tugs his arm. 'Is there no help for it? Henry is seething inside, I know him.'

True, he thinks, you know him. He threw you out of the council, stripped of your chain of office: till he changed his mind, or I changed it for him.

'The papers are an excuse,' Fitzwilliam says. 'He dislikes her or he is frightened of her, I know not what it is. But mark this, Cromwell

– I will not be stuck with the blame, just because it was I who met her in Calais.'

'No one seeks to blame you. It is his own fault, if fault there is. For rushing about the countryside like a love-lorn youth.'

The councillors are already assembled. Cranmer is seated, as if his strength has given out; he makes to rise, then sinks down again. The Bishop of Durham inclines his head: 'My lord Privy Seal.' His tone suggests he is consecrating something; or handling fragile remains, ready to disintegrate.

He nods. 'Your Grace.' Tunstall knows the Lord Privy Seal has been examining his affairs for months: enquiring what he does up in Durham, and what he truly believes. So these days he takes his seat charily, like a man who thinks he might have it kicked from under him.

Thomas Howard bustles in. He looks bright-eyed, as if there were something to celebrate. 'So, Cromwell. He wants to get out of it, I hear.'

He sits down, not waiting for the duke to sit. 'The King of France and the Emperor are seeing in the new year together. They have not been so close in our lifetime. They are like planets, gentlemen, and their conjunction draws sea and land after them, and makes our fates. They have a fleet and funds to come against us. Our forts are still building. Ireland is against us. Scotland is against us. If we are not to be overrun this spring we need the princes of Germany on our side, either to send men to our aid or to engage our enemy till we can defeat him or force a truce. The king needs to make this marriage. England needs it.'

Charles Brandon looks mournful. 'He agreed to it. He signed up. He cannot jib now.'

Norfolk says, 'What happened at Rochester?'

'I can't say. I wasn't there.'

Norfolk's nose is twitching. 'Something passed between them. Something mislikes him.'

Lord Audley says, 'I agree with my lord Suffolk. The king has gone too far in the matter, he would need a very sound reason to withdraw now. He was convinced before that she was free to marry. And she seems a good enough woman to me.'

'Perhaps you do not understand a prince's requirements,' Norfolk says.

'No?' Audley gives him a glance that would peel an egg. 'If she does not come up to them, your Grace, I for one am not to blame.'

'Cromwell thinks the king should blame himself,' Fitz says. 'For going with haste to Rochester.'

'Blame himself?' Tunstall says. 'The king? When has that happened? You would think Cromwell had never met him.'

He says heavily, 'I suppose I might institute a delay.'

'What good would that do?' Fitz asks.

He thinks, time might soften the memory of the moment they met. Henry might forget the look in her eye. But he does not know if Fitz witnessed it. So he says nothing.

Cranmer, good Christian that he is, refrains from saying, I told you so. Instead he says, 'I accede to all your reasoning, my lords. And yet I am afraid the king's conscience will be troubled, till he sees papers that will satisfy him. He has been deceived before. He should not enter into matrimony unless he gives his hearty consent, body and soul.'

Cranmer is too good to live. He forgets his own troubles and considers only Henry's. He speaks across Norfolk to the archbishop: 'The Cleves ambassadors have come to me just now with an offer. Two of them will stay here as sureties, till the papers are sent.'

Norfolk says, 'Stable them till Easter? By the Mass, no!'

'It seems unnecessary,' Cranmer says. 'We do not doubt the people in Cleves have made diligent search. I do not even doubt the lady is free. But it is the king's doubts we have to reckon with.'

The door opens. They kneel. 'Well,' Henry says, 'what have you devised for my relief?'

'Nothing, sir,' Cranmer says.

'That is honest, at least. I begin to suspect there is less honesty in my councillors than a king should look for, and no good faith in those who offer themselves as allies and friends.' Henry looks around, addresses Suffolk: 'Charles, you were there in Windsor last September, were you not? When Duke Wilhelm's people swore they would bring the documents full and entire?'

'Aye, that they did,' Brandon says. 'Otherwise we would not have put our hands to the marriage treaty, would we? But,' he says gently, 'I think it is done now, you know.'

'We can hold off a day,' Fitz says. 'Cromwell thinks so. Though I do not see the point.'

'I am not well-handled,' Henry says. 'You may as well rise, gentlemen, I see no point in sitting here with you. Cromwell, walk with me.'

'Well, you have seen her now,' Henry says. 'Is it not as I have told you?'

He says, 'She is a very gentle lady, all agree. And it seems to me her manner is queenly.'

The king snorts. 'It is for me to know what is queenly.' He checks himself. 'I was wrong about her mouth, perhaps.'

Sweet as a berry. Naturally red. He decides not to say so. It is a hopeful sign, if Henry will admit he has misjudged her in the smallest particular.

The other councillors have fallen behind, but the king's guard keeps pace, obliged to close their ears. He says, cautiously, 'You do not think she is like her picture, sir?'

'I do not fault Hans. He drew her as well as he could considering all the –' the king dashes a hand against his jacket '– the armour. She is so tall and stiff.'

'Her height lends her distinction.'

'Have you inspected her shoes?' the king demands. 'I think she must wear raised soles. Tell her women, there is no ordure on the floor of our houses. I don't know what she is used to.'

It can all be altered, he says, clothes, shoes, and the king says, 'So you keep telling me. But if I had known before what I know now, she would not have come a foot into the realm. It is a matter of ...' The king shakes his head. He pats his garments, as if he is feeling for his heart.

Monday, 5 January: two of Anne's people, Olisleger and Hochsteden, come to his own chamber on the north side of the palace, where they take a solemn oath that Anne is free to marry, and commit to search out all relevant documents within three months. Their offer to remain in England, Henry has waved away, adding that Anne's entourage is bloated and that they should feel free to take some of their country-men with them when they go. Each principal gentleman in her train is to have a reward of a hundred pounds to speed him on his journey.

An agreement is drawn up and they sign for England: Cranmer, Audley, himself, Fitzwilliam, Bishop Tunstall.

Cranmer, his face harrowed, heads to the queen's room, a great Bible following him in the hands of an interpreter. Inside the Bible, if you looked, you would see a picture of the king handing the scriptures to the people, who mill at the bottom of the page, where they cry 'Vivat Rex!' or 'God Save the King!' – the lower orders preferring English.

The king glowers at his councillors, and retires into his inner rooms. Musicians come and set up their instruments and play.

In a short time Cranmer returns. Anna has taken an oath without hesitation, he says, to state that she is perfectly free from any marital tie. 'She said she was glad to do it. She was by God's grace most prompt and certain. She almost had the book out of my hands, so eager is she to please your Majesty. She wishes to be married without delay.'

He thinks, she is afraid of her family. What they will say, if she is sent back.

Henry groans. 'Is there no help for it? Must I must put my neck into the yoke?'

He was right to think that when she came from the sea the bride would be rebaptised. She left the ship as Anna. Now she is land-locked as plain Anne, as if the king and all his treasury has not a syllable to spare.

* * *

Tuesday morning, raining, the councillors convene at seven. Usually he begins his working day by six, but he has put off all other petitioners, asking only for any dispatches from abroad to be treated as urgent.

Mr Wriothesley is perched on a table, watching him get into his wedding outfit. 'What dispatches are you expecting, sir?'

Christophe drops his shirt over his head. 'I bear in mind that the Emperor is a widower.' His head emerges from the linen. 'I would not put it past him to choose this week to announce his marriage to a Frenchwoman.'

If he did, he thinks, that would sharpen Henry's appetite for his own bride.

'God forbid!' Call-Me says. 'Wyatt is with the Emperor, he would have to prevent it.'

'He would abduct the lady,' Christophe offers. 'Declaim a sonnet. Biff-boff with her in some roadside inn. Return to Emperor in used condition.'

In the king's apartments, the councillors are talking in low voices, as if in the presence of someone dying. William Kingston: 'My lord, this cannot be true? That the king has taken against the lady?'

He puts a finger to his lips. He has just endowed Anna with the first of many grants that will guarantee her income as queen. Her household is set up, a mirror of the king's. The Earl of Rutland is her chamberlain. She has priests and pages, washerwomen and pastry cooks, cupbearers and ushers, footmen and grooms, auditors, receivers and surveyors. When the Cleves delegation arrives, he means to dwell on these details to reassure them – because yesterday's ill-will, the tension in every look and gesture of the English, has escaped no one. His hope is that he can prevent them translating the tension into any sort of insult, which they will relay back to our allies.

Fitz comes in. He says abruptly, 'I suppose we still need, what was it, alum?'

'Yes,' he says. 'And friends, we need friends as we never have before.'

Back in autumn he told the councillors, alum is very hard to extract. You must cut to the marrow of the mountains and prop your workings as you go. Now he enlarges on it to Fitz: you need heavy hammers and steel pikes and wedges. It is quickest to employ explosive devices. 'The miners call them *Pater Nosters* – because when they go off, you jump out of your skin and shout, God Our Father Almighty!'

But Fitz is not listening. His head is cocked to sounds of dissatisfaction coming from the inner room. When the king himself comes out he is already dressed in his gown of cloth of gold strewn with silver flowers. 'Where is my lord Essex? He is supposed to escort the bride. He is late, what will she think?'

'May I offer?' Fitz says, unwilling.

The king says, 'It has to be an unmarried man, some custom they have in her native land – pointless, but she will want it to be observed.' Henry's eye falls on him. 'You fetch her, my lord Privy Seal.'

'I am not worthy,' he says.

Henry says, 'You are, my lord, if I say you are.'

The door is flung open. Henry Bouchier – old Essex – limps in. 'What?' he says, looking around.

'LATE!' the courtiers roar.

'Ah, well, dark mornings,' Essex says. 'Fires low, boys half-asleep. Ice on the path, what would you? Needless to imperil oneself. What's the hurry?'

'We want her before she is beyond the age of childbearing,' Mr Wriothesley breathes. 'Ideally, in the next decade.'

Essex looks around. 'Is Cromwell going for her? Won't she be insulted, Majesty? She must know he was once a common shearsman, does she not?'

'Barely that,' he says. 'I drove geese to market, my lord, and plucked them for the warm feather beds of earls.'

'Oh, get on,' Henry says. 'Get on, Cromwell, make haste, what matter who does it?'

The gentlemen of the privy chamber look at him, shocked.

'Sir,' William Kingston says, 'everything matters. Of this sort.'

Someone with presence of mind holds the door open, and Essex limps through. The king turns to him, his voice low and vehement: 'I tell you, my lord, if it were not for fear of making a ruffle in the world, and driving her brother into the arms of the Emperor, I would not do what I must do this day, for none earthly thing.' He lifts his head. 'Gentlemen, let's go.'

They keep a stately pace to the queen's side, to allow the bride to arrive first: that is how royal people do it, a king waits for no one. In the queen's closet Cranmer stands ready, his book in his hands, his stole about his neck. 'Where is she?'

A rumbled jest from Brandon: 'Perchance Essex died on the way?'

The king pretends not to have heard. He is dignified as a bride-groom must be; they never hear the sly asides of their companions, who hint that they will be happy when it is dark. Over his glittering gown the king wears a coat of indigo satin, furred. Light glints and slides from his many surfaces. His lips move, as if in prayer.

When Anne appears, she wears a gown strewn with flowers, like the king: hers are not silver, but pearl. Her blonde hair is loose, falling to her waist, and entwined around her coronet a garland of rosemary. She no longer looks like a grocer's wife, but like what she is: a prin-cess whose childhood was spent in a high castle on a crag, from where you can see for miles.

It is a short and simple ceremony. Nothing is required of her but to stand still and look cheerful. The archbishop glances around him, when he asks if any impediment is known: as if he offers chances to all comers. No one speaks. Cranmer bobs his head as if taking cover. The king makes his vows. Then at his archbishop's signal, he turns, takes the queen by the elbows, and plants a kiss on her cheek. Stiffly, she turns her head; ducking around her winged head-dress, the king kisses the other cheek. The red lips are pursed, ready for him: but nothing doing.

Cranmer says, *Deo Gratias.* The king and queen leave the closet hand in hand. Fanfares sound. Courtiers cry, *Gaudete!* The council-lors follow to the feast.

* * *

For once he hardly notices what he eats. Usually, after a dinner like this, the king's councillors knot together in a corner and talk about hunting. But when the pipers come in Norfolk is prevailed upon to dance with his niece Katherine. Fitz watches him, gloomy. 'I suppose this was worth getting out of bed to see?'

'You will not dance, Lord Cromwell?' Culpeper says. 'If my lord Norfolk can, you can.'

Mr Wriothesley says, 'If only Lady Latimer would come in. Then my lord would caper.'

'You will not let that joke go,' he says amiably. 'Lord Latimer is younger than the king. And in health, as far as I know.'

Health and prosperity. Lady Latimer's brother William became Baron Parr last year. And her sister, who served Jane the queen, is now a gentlewoman in the new queen's privy chamber.

Norfolk's niece giggles at her uncle's show of high spirits. She is soon on her feet with the other maids: a lively dancer, her cheeks flushed. Into the fray go the young gentlemen, kicking up their heels. The king watches them with a tolerant smile. When they rise from the table, Henry holds out a hand to the queen, and leads her to the portrait that Hans has given him for a New Year gift. The councillors follow, like goslings in a line. A curtain is drawn back, revealing Edward the prince in red and gilt. Below his broad infantine forehead, under his feathered cap, his eyes glow. One open palm is held out; in the other he clutches his jewelled rattle, wielding it like a sceptre.

'Master Holbein painted it,' the king says; she understands that.

'What a darling prince,' she says. 'When shall I meet him?'

'Soon,' the king promises.

'And your lady daughters?'

'Presently.'

'And Lady Mary is to be wed?'

There is a hasty conference among the translators. An emphatic shake of the head makes Anna look sorry she spoke. The king turns to speak in French to the Cleves envoys. 'We take pleasure in the company of the Duke of Bavaria. So there is no haste in the matter, and much to be discussed.'

He, Lord Cromwell, employs Italian, which Olisleger understands a little. His gesture cuts the air: drop it.

The king continues, showing off his son. 'Edward is my heir. My daughters are not my heirs. Does she understand that?' He turns back to the picture, his face softened. 'That little chin of his, that is Jane's.'

The king and queen part, bowing to each other, the queen turning towards her own rooms. The interpreters and the Cleves delegation set into each other, buzzing and elbowing. He leaves them to it and walks away. A message comes: the queen will speak with Lord Cromwell.

When he arrives Anna is still in her wedding dress. Norfolk's niece is sitting on the floor, holding a needle and thread, an inch of the queen's hem beneath her fingers. In her lap is Anne's garland of rosemary. A knot of Cleves ladies are laughing in a corner. Jane Rochford gives him a nod. The queen takes off her wedding ring and shows it to him. Her chosen motto is written around it: *God send me well to keep.* What goose suggested that to her? It should have said, God send *him* well to keep.

'Thank you for the cakes,' the queen says. 'We enjoyed them. A taste of home. You have visited my home?'

He is sorry to say he has not.

'I hoped for letters at Calais. But there was nothing for me.'

Poor lady, she is homesick. 'The posts are bad at this time of year,' he says. 'I myself am awaiting news from our ambassadors in France.'

'Yes,' she says, 'so are we all. To know whether the amity continues. It seems harsh to wish for discord, when we have grown up praying for peace. But I know my brother Wilhelm would be relieved if the Emperor and the French king were to set about each other with their fists and teeth.' She laughs.

'War for them is peace for us,' he says, 'their discord our harmony.' He realises she is not uninformed, or lacking in eloquence, and also that he can partly understand her. But he would not speak to her without an intermediary. He cannot afford to create a misunderstanding. It is risky enough even when the translators are doing their best.

'Where is the young Gregory?' she asks in English. 'So well he entertained me in Calais. What a good boy.'

There is a murmur of pleasure and surprise from the ladies. 'Well spoken, madam!'

Katherine Howard looks up from her work on the floor. 'Can't get the needle through. This stuff is as tough as hide. It needs some great bodkin.'

There is a little laughter, edgy. Mary Norris blushes, guessing at something unfit for maiden ears. Jane Rochford says, 'Get the whole thing off her. She will not be wearing it again till it has been made over in our English fashion.' She reaches down – a comradely gesture – and pulls the young Howard to her feet.

He is making his farewells, but Anna calls him back. She seems preoccupied with the fifty sovereigns he sent her, as if he might expect to be paid back. She explains she has broken the coins into those of lesser value and given some in largesse. Women came out of their houses, she explains, at –

'At Sittingbourne,' Jane Rochford says.

'– offering me delicacies to eat.'

He says to the interpreters, 'Tell her whenever she issues out, she should carry suitable coins – or have them carried, in her case. She need not wait for gifts to be made her, but should hand them freely to bystanders. Be generous especially to children, as it stores up goodwill for the future.'

Jane Rochford is studying Anna's lips as they move, as if to pick out the words. She is a woman with a good wit, he thinks, but she has never found a use for it; perhaps this is her time to shine. Soon the great ladies, Bess Cromwell included, will go home to their households and children, and Rochford will assist Lady Rutland with the queen's daily round, keeping a hand on the young maids and ensuring order and piety.

One of the interpreters asks him, 'My lord, what comes next?'

'Evensong,' he says. 'Then the French ambassador will be joining us for Caesar's invasion of Britain, with more bagpipes and drums; then it will be tumblers or magicians, then supper and bed.'

At twilight they play Britannia unconquered. The queen sits up straight and looks alert, while one of the interpreters rehearses to her what will unfold: the repulse of the Romans, how the island stood firm and resisted tribute. He recognises the King of Britain as one of George Boleyn's men.

Henry will like the queen to see what manner of countrymen she has now: they refuse all slavery, detect all knavery. The monarch that was then, in Caesar's time, armed the Thames itself, planting iron-tipped staves below the waterline to rip out the belly of the Roman ships. When the survivors hauled themselves to shore, the Britons butchered them.

There were ninety-nine kings, the chroniclers tell us, before we came to our present monarch. He suspects them of snipping sections out of history, so Henry makes one hundred.

'I don't suppose you have anything like this at home,' the king says to Anna.

The remark is laboriously relayed to her.

No, she says. More is the pity. She looks bewildered.

The players take up their stance and menace each other with drawn blades. Solemnly, they perform the actions of fighting men, till those who are Romans fall to their knees and then judiciously, thoughtfully, checking the floor is clear, topple forward on their faces. The maids of honour nudge each other, laughing. The king glances over at them, and smiles, like a man reminiscing. He says to his wife, 'Kings of Britain have conquered Rome.'

He, Lord Cromwell, keeps finding reasons to get up and walk about, to speak to one and then another. He views the queen from different angles and in different lights. Some expressions need no translator; he sees she is resolute, whatever the evening may bring. Behind the rampaging battle there is a pavilion made in twenty-six sections, with windows like a house. It was sewn over with 'H&K' but that has been unpicked. The walls are purple and gold, and the lining is of green sarcenet – which lends a spring-like air. 'Anybody could issue forth from that tent,' he says. 'King Arthur himself would be proud.'

'Is there much more of this?' the French ambassador enquires.

The interlude comes, and everybody sits up. First a masque of lovers is played. Two gentlemen hold lyres, their expressions bereft, their garb sewn over with scallop shells: they are the heart's pilgrims, they declare.

'There are no other sorts of pilgrims now,' Norfolk says. 'Even Walsingham is down.' He grimaces. 'It seems to me this conceit is stale. The master of revels thinks to save a little money.'

'I am all for that,' he says.

Presently two maidens come out of the tent, and are kind to the swains. They dance a little jig together. 'That's my niece, Katherine,' Norfolk says. 'Edmund's girl.'

'I know.'

'How do you like her?'

He has no opinion. The lovers hop away, arm in arm, and in come Friar Flip-Flap and Friar Snip-Snap, trying to pickpocket the spectators, till one races in with a dog and chases them. The dog's name is Grime. He yearns towards dainties held out to him, and his keeper hauls him back. Beneath the keeper's hood, a familiar face. 'Is that Sexton? I thought I had banished that churl for good and all.'

The boy Culpeper says, 'He must find some employment, I suppose. Nicholas Carew took him in but Carew is dead.'

Sexton leaves Grime to tussle with the friars, ambles off and comes back in another guise, his belly thrust out, wearing purple and with great sleeves like a ship's sails. He is Privy Seal, he says, a man low born, whose dam and sire he hides in his sleeves for shame.

Anger washes through him like a wave, and out again. He says to Marillac, his neighbour, 'It is an outworn jest, once made against the cardinal.'

'Ah yes, your old master,' Marillac says. 'I was warned never to refer to him, but you use his name freely. Strange that people are still arguing over him. What is it, ten years?'

He points to Sexton. 'You should have seen that fellow, how he screamed when he was parted from the cardinal and conveyed into the king's service – I say "conveyed", because we had to bind him and throw him in a cart.'

Sexton loops nooses around the necks of Snip-Snap and Flip-Flap. They stagger and protrude their tongues. He calls out, 'Sexton! Beware! Perhaps I have a rope for you in my great sleeve.'

Sexton looks straight at him. 'Tyburn is no jest, Tom. For him it is a jest,' he points to the king, 'and for her, and for me, but not for thee, Tom, not for thee.'

Grime is circling and about to crap. The king's lips tighten. He makes a gesture: get dog and keeper out, remove friars too. Sexton runs, raising his knees high as if leaping over puddles.

The Britons come in again, to a spatter of applause, carrying the river Thames looped over their arms. Lord Morley sits forward on his stool: 'Shall we have the war machines of the Emperor Claudius? Vespasian, and the Siege of Exeter?'

'By my faith,' Norfolk says, 'it's been a long day for us councillors, my lord. And the king will want to have the queen apart, will he not?'

'There ought to be giants,' Gregory says. 'Gogmagog was twelve feet tall. He could rip up oak trees, no effort at all, it was like picking flowers. There was another giant, Retho by name, who made himself a great beard with the beards of men he had slain.'

'Like Brandon, what?' Norfolk says. He laughs with pure delight. It is once a decade he makes a joke.

The Thames unrolls, a length of patchy blue. To aid the players, the maids seize the ends and ripple it. Lord Morley says, 'I am afraid a great part of the story is missed. Britain had kings before Christ was incarnate. You will find it all in Geoffrey of Monmouth, his book.'

He says, 'My lord, I have read that not all those princes were lucky, and few of them were wise.' There was the prince who drowned in the river Humber, which they named after him. There was Bladus, who flew over London on home-made wings: they had to scrape him off the pavements. Rivallo was a good king, or well-intentioned at least: but during his time it rained blood, and swarms of flies ate

746

Englishmen alive. And if you go further back, the nation was founded on a murder: Trojan Brutus, father of us all, killed his own father. A hunting accident, they claimed, but perhaps there are no accidents. Those mis-aimed arrows, and the ones that bend in flight: they know their target.

Gregory says, 'Geoffrey of Monmouth, he was such a liar. I wager he wasn't even born in Monmouth. I wager he was never there in his life.'

The queen stands up, at some invisible signal or perhaps some inner prompting. Her ladies rise and flock about her. The Howard child has to be nudged; she is gaping at a lutenist with a well-turned leg. The evening is winding to its conclusion. The musicians will play the king to his own chamber and then put away their timpani and viols. Henry's face shows nothing, except traces of fatigue. Mr Wriothesley bends and speaks into his ear: 'Do you wish you could read his thoughts, sir?'

'No.'

The privy chamber gentlemen rise and follow the king. The clergy are assembling to go in procession and bless the bed. Every night the king's sheets are sprinkled with holy water, but tonight he needs Heaven's special regard: the attention of the angels and saints, fixed on his privy member. Culpeper says, in passing, 'Now all he has to do is climb aboard and make a Duke of York.'

The king has had a new bed made, very wonderfully carved. He, Lord Cromwell, cannot lie still in his old one, but must walk about. The palace is quiet. Fires are damped. He encounters no one but guards who salute him, and two giddy young lords, wearing red and yellow masquing bonnets, one dancing while the other claps. At the sight of him the dancer skids to a halt. The beat is missed, trapped between his friend's palms.

'Go to your cribs,' he tells them. 'If you are lucky, in the morning I shall have forgotten your names.'

Abashed, they pass him their bonnets, as if they do not know what else to do with them. 'They are hats for Tartars, my lord.'

They ought to have strings or ribbons, he remarks. You would think the wind would pluck them off, as they gallop the snowy wastes.

The boys ramble away, arms linked. He calls after them, 'Pray for me.' He hears their laughter as they sway downstairs.

He walks back to his rooms, closes his door. Give a man a Tartar hat and he will try it on, whether he has a mirror or no. But he is out of heart. He leaves the hat on Christophe's pallet, so when he wakes he will think he is still dreaming. All night, in his broken sleep, his countrymen fight Caesar's legions: slow, dogged, their movements enmired.

He is up at dawn, sitting down in his chambers with Richard Riche to talk about the surrender of the abbey at Malvern. Riche is yawning. 'I wonder …' he says, and breaks off.

'Shall we just keep our mind on the figures?' Christophe comes in with pots of small beer. He is wearing the Tartar hat and Riche says, 'Why is he …' His sentences keep failing him, as if they are lost in mist.

A messenger comes in, sent straight up in his boots, blue-nosed and splashed from the road. 'Urgent, my lord. From York, for your hand.'

'Jesus spare us,' Riche says. 'Don't tell me the countryside is up again?'

'Too early in the year, I think.' The seal is already broken; he wonders why. He reads: York's treasurer says he will have to shut down his office if he does not get two thousand pounds by the week's end and as much again to follow: the bills have come in for the harbour at Bridlington, and the northern lords are clamouring for the pay-out of their yearly grants and pensions.

Norfolk stamps in. 'Cromwell? You see that from Tristram Teshe?'

He glares at Norfolk; then at the messenger, who avoids his eye. 'By Our Lady,' Norfolk says, 'Teshe should take those barons by their napes and shake the living Jesus out of them. If it were me, I would make them wait for their money till Lady Day.'

Fitzwilliam is on Norfolk's heels, sour and not yet shaven. 'If he tries to hold them off, my lord, some of them may ride over to the Scots. Or exact payment by plundering it.'

Mr Wriothesley comes in. 'From Wyatt, sir.' He has opened the letter already. François and Charles are still together, prolonging the season of goodwill. 'Wyatt says the Emperor looks like thunder whenever our realm is mentioned.'

'Not surprising,' he says. 'Our king well-married, and no thanks to him.'

He strides out towards the king's presence chamber and his arms fill with petitions from courtiers, with letters and bills. He hands them back to Wriothesley, to Rafe. A pity that neither Rafe nor Richard Cromwell was on the privy chamber rota last night; then he would have been sure of good information. Perhaps he should have arranged that? He says to himself, I cannot think of everything. He hears the king's voice saying, why not?

The Cleves delegation is there before him. They are spry and hopeful, and declare they have heard Mass already. 'And,' they say, 'we have a present for you, Lord Cromwell, to mark this auspicious day.'

The Duke of Saxony, Wilhelm's brother-in-law, has sent him a clock. Taking it, he murmurs his appreciation. It is the neatest he has seen, perhaps the smallest – a drum-shaped object you can hold in your palm. The English gentlemen are playing with it, passing it from hand to hand, when the king comes in. 'Sir, present it to him,' Rafe whispers.

The Germans nod regretfully; they understand this sort of sacrifice. Henry takes the clock from his hand without looking at it. He goes on talking to one of his privy chamber gentlemen: '… fetch back Edmund Bonner, as I have promised, and send my brother of France an envoy more agreeable and modest.' He breaks off. Turns to the Cleves ambassadors: 'Gentlemen, you will be pleased to know …'

'Yes, Majesty?' They are eager.

'… I have sent the queen her *morgengabe*, as I think you call it, a gift in accordance with the custom of your country. We will let you have written details of the value.'

749

They are hoping to hear more. But the king has closed his lips. He does not even mention the clock. Normally he would be delighted by such a novelty – would examine its workings and ask for another one, this time with his portrait in the lid. But instead he looks down at it with a sigh, a mechanical smile, and hands it on to one of his suite. 'Thank you, my lord Cromwell, you always have something new. Though sometimes not as new as one would wish.'

There is a heartbeat's pause. Henry nods to him: 'Come apart.'

He stares at the king. Disassemble? Disperse? Then he recovers himself. 'Yes. Of course.' He follows.

Sometimes with the king it is best to be brisk and show yourself a good fellow. As if you were elbow to elbow at the Well with Two Buckets, sharing a pint of Spanish wine. He thinks, I'd knock it back if I had some. Or Rhenish. Aqua Vitae. Walter's beer. 'How liked you the queen?'

The king says, 'I liked her not well before, but now I like her much worse.'

Henry glances back over his shoulder. No one has approached them. They are alone, as in a wasteland.

Henry says, 'Her breasts are slack and she has loose skin on her belly. When I felt it, it struck me to the heart. I had no appetite for the rest. I do not believe she is a maid.'

What the king is saying is preposterous. 'Majesty, she has never strayed from her mother's side …'

He steps back. He wants to walk away: for his own protection. He sees from the corner of his eye that Dr Chambers and Dr Butts have come in, with their modest caps, their long gowns. The king says, 'I will speak with those gentlemen. No word of this should escape.'

No words escape from him, as he draws back from the king's path. And no one addresses him, but clears his way, as he walks the length of the presence chamber and through the guard chamber and passes from view.

* * *

The two physicians are the first to seek him out. He is reading Wyatt's letter, and lays it aside with the scenes it conjures, distant but clear. Wyatt is a presence even when he is absent, especially when he is absent. His letters are close narratives of diplomatic encounters. Yet, however tight you pin your attention to the page, you feel that something is escaping you, slipping into the air; then some other reader comes along, and reads it different.

Butts clears his throat. 'My lord Cromwell, like you we are forbidden by the king to speak.'

'What is there to say? We would speculate about the queen's maidenhead. Such talk belongs to chaplains in confession, if it belongs anywhere at all.'

'Very well,' Butts says. 'Now you know, and I know, and the king knows, that in such unmentionable matters he has been wrong before. He took the dowager Katherine to be untouched, though she had been wed to his brother. Later, he thought the contrary.'

Chambers says, 'He thought Boleyn was a virgin, then he found she was unchaste since her French days.'

Butts says, 'He knows the breasts and belly are evidence of naught. But just this morning he is ashamed and out of heart. When next he tries her it may be a different result.'

Chambers frowns: 'You think so, brother?'

'All men do sometimes fail,' Butts says. 'You need not look as though that is news to you, Lord Cromwell.'

'My concern,' he says, 'is that he does not make this accusation again, that she is no maid. Because if he does I have to act upon it. However, if he says he mislikes her, has a distaste for her person –'

'He does.'

'– if he admits he has failed with her –'

'– then perhaps you have a different sort of problem,' Butts says.

'I do not believe he has spoken to anyone,' Chambers says, 'except us. One or two of the privy chamber, possibly. His chaplain.'

'But we fear the news will soon spread,' Butts says. 'Look at his face. Would anyone take him for a happy bridegroom?'

Also, he wonders, has Anna confided in anyone? He says, 'I had better try and cheer him.' Nagging at his attention is the treasure he needs to dispatch to York. He thinks, I do not want to be with Henry but I cannot risk his being with anyone else. I will have to dog his footsteps like the devil. He says, 'What shall I tell the ambassadors of Cleves?'

'Need you tell them anything? Let the queen speak for herself.'

Chambers says, 'I do not think she will make any complaint. She is too well-bred. And innocent, perhaps.'

'Or,' Butts says, 'perhaps of sufficient sense to see that that a bad beginning may be recouped. I have advised the king to keep to his own chamber tonight. By abstinence, appetite may increase.'

'Time was when they used to display the bedsheets,' Chambers says. 'It is lucky those days have passed.'

But the king's looks tell the tale. Thinks of all the people who crowded into the room at Rochester, to see him nourish love. At the first moment he saw Anna, he saw himself in the mirror of her eyes. From that instant it was written that there would never be love or affection between them. From that time he had no curiosity as to what he would find under her clothes: just teats and her slot, pouches of skin and hair.

He seeks out Jane Rochford. 'Our opinion is, nothing happened,' she says.

'What does Anna say?'

'Anna says nothing. Did you think we would fetch the men in this morning, to interpret?'

'There are women who can do it.' There are: because he has found some.

Jane says, 'I think it is better if she keeps her own counsel and we keep ours, yes? If he has failed, no one wants to know that, surely? What can you do with the information?'

'You are right,' he says. 'It is of no value. Therefore, take heed, it should have no currency.'

Rochford turns back to him, as if relenting. She says, 'He lay on her, is our view. I think he put his fingers in her. *C'est tout.*'

The council meets. No messages have come from the queen. Her own people, both ladies and gentlemen, have visited her and come away looking unperturbed. It is clear that we are living in a dual reality, such as experienced courtiers can maintain. For many years now, more years than we can count, the King of England has been a fair youth. So often, he has been married, and then unmarried; and the dead have been in Purgatory, and plaster saints have moved their eyes. Now the councillors shoulder their double burden: their knowledge of the king's failure, and their pretence that he has never in all his days met with anything but success.

'We should not be discouraged,' the Bishop of Durham suggests. 'Allow a little time. Nature will take its course.'

Norfolk looks puzzled; surely Tunstall is no friend to Germans? Tunstall says, 'I find no fault with the lady. Whatever her brother may be, she is not herself a Lutheran. And perhaps it is time, for England's sake, to reconcile our differences, through her person.'

Norfolk says, 'If Henry could take some air in the day it might go better at night. Skulking by the fire with a book will not help him.'

Fitzwilliam says, 'Unless a book of bawdy. That might.'

Edward Seymour says, 'He never had trouble in my sister's day.'

'Not that you know of,' Norfolk says.

'But he loved her,' Cranmer says, his voice low.

Norfolk snorts. Seymour says, 'True. That match was for love, this for policy. But I agree with Bishop Tunstall. I see nothing wrong with her.'

Riche says, 'There is nothing. Except his dislike.'

Bishop Sampson says, 'The king being as he is, you took a gamble, Lord Cromwell.'

He says coldly, 'I acted for good and sufficient reason. If I promoted the match, it was with his full permission and encouragement.'

Cranmer says, 'It may be … and it is only my own opinion …'

'Do not make us drag it from you,' Fitzwilliam says.

'... there are those who believe every act of copulation a sin –'

'I did not think the king was among them,' Tunstall says pleasantly.

'– though a sin that, of necessity, God will forgive – yet one must come to the act, not only with intent to engender –'

'Which the king surely does,' Lord Audley says.

'– but also with the object of a pure merging of heart and soul, arising from a free consent –'

'You've lost me,' Suffolk says.

'So if he, or she, were to have any reservation, in mind or in heart – then to the scrupulous, an impediment might appear –'

Audley cuts him off. 'What impediment? You mean the pre-contract?'

Cranmer whispers, 'The king has read a great deal in the Church Fathers.'

'And later commentators,' Bishop Sampson says. 'Who are not always helpful, tending to dispute how men sin and in which way, when they are abed. But sin they do.'

'Even with their wives?' Suffolk looks stricken.

Sampson says, with dry malice, 'That is possible.'

'Bollocks,' Norfolk says. 'Cromwell, is that in the scriptures?'

'Why doesn't your lordship try reading them?'

Audley clears his throat. All the councillors turn in his direction. 'Just be clear. His incapacity –'

'Or unwillingness –' Cranmer adds.

'– or unwillingness – is it anything to do with the papers from Cleves, or not?'

Cranmer will not commit. 'Scruples are of various sorts.'

'So will it be helped by getting the papers?' Riche asks.

'It couldn't hurt, could it?' Bishop Sampson says. 'Of course by then it will be Lent. And he will not sleep with her in Lent.'

'We shouldn't be talking like this.' Suffolk looks stern. 'We are men, not gossiping housewives. We lack respect for our sovereign lord.'

Fitzwilliam slaps the table. 'You know it is me he blames? He says I should have stopped her at Calais. I wrote to him she was like a princess, and she is. Nothing else was in question. Is it for me to feel her duckies and write home my opinion, and send it by post horse and boat?'

The door opens. It is Call-Me. He looks as if he is walking on hot pebbles. 'Get out!' Norfolk bellows. 'Interrupting the council!'

Call-Me says, 'The king. He is coming this way.'

They stand, with a scraping of stools. Henry's eyes pass over them. 'Squabbling?'

'Yes,' Brandon says sadly.

He cuts in: 'Your Majesty values concord, and rightly. But I cannot and never will come into concord with those who give wrong advice.'

Charles Brandon says, 'But it is very good of you to join us, sir. We did not look for you. We hardly expected you. We rejoice to see you. We –'

'Yes, enough, Charles,' Henry says. 'It is time we talked about the Duke of Bavaria, his suit to my lady daughter.'

'Bless him,' Charles Brandon says: as if the young duke were sick.

'My lord Privy Seal,' the king says, 'you and Bavaria went up to see the Lady Mary, did you not? And then of course, she was fetched to Baynard's Castle, and she and the duke were permitted some discourse. That would have been about Christmas Eve?'

The king talks as if there is some mystery, and he is trying to penetrate it. He bows his assent: yes, all that is true. Philip had wished to present Mary with a great cross of diamonds, but the councillors had deterred him. If the match were not to go ahead, would a present of such value need to be returned? It is a sticky point of protocol. Word went out to the goldsmiths, and a cross of lesser value was found.

The Lady Mary had walked with Duke Philip in a bare winter garden at Westminster, where life was shrunk to its roots. They had spoken: partly through an interpreter, partly in Latin.

When the cross was presented, Mary had kissed it. And kissed Philip. On the cheek. 'Which is a good sign, by God,' Brandon says. 'For she never kissed any of us.'

'You have not the rank,' the king says. 'That traitor Exeter was the last who did. Being her cousin.'

Bishop Sampson leans forward, frowning. 'Philip is not her cousin, is he? Or if he is, in what degree?' He jots a note to himself.

Henry says, 'It appears to me our friendship with the German states would be greatly strengthened if we made this match.'

There is silence. The king half-smiles. He has always prided himself on the surprises he gives his councillors. 'If I can sacrifice myself for England, why not my daughter? If I must breed for my nation, why cannot she? I am assured by Cromwell she will be conformable. He always gives me that assurance, and yet nothing ever comes of it. Bishop Sampson, perhaps you would go to her, and prepare her for marriage?'

Sampson compresses his lips. He can barely force a nod.

He, Thomas Cromwell, says, 'In Europe they are claiming the marriage is already made, and against the lady's will. Vaughan says Antwerp is talking about it. Marillac believes it, or pretends to. The word has gone out to François.'

Henry says, 'They think I would enforce her?'

'Yes.'

Henry stares at him. 'And?'

'And so I think, your Majesty not offended, you had better reverse your intentions, disappoint the duke, and bid him a swift journey home. Otherwise you will be doing exactly what your foes expect. Which is never good policy.'

Edward Seymour covers his mouth. Mirth escapes.

Henry is silent, mouth pursed. Then he says, 'Very well. I shall do something else for Philip. The Garter, perhaps.' He rubs the bridge of his nose. 'You had better not close off his hopes. Tell him he may return. Tell him I shall always be glad to see him, at some date not yet decided.'

'Majesty, your daughter will never marry,' Norfolk says. 'Cromwell breaks every match proposed for her.'

The king gets up. He rubs his chest with one hand, steadies himself with the other. They are all on their feet, ready to kneel:

sometimes he exacts it, sometimes not. Norfolk offers, 'My arm, Majesty?'

'What use is that?' Henry says. 'I could better hold you up, Thomas Howard, than you me.'

The door is flung wide for the king's exit. Call-Me falters in, and hovers. Only then do they notice that the Duke of Suffolk is still seated at the council board. He rocks to and fro on his stool. 'Poor Harry, poor Harry,' he moans. Tears course down his cheeks.

On 7 January the king sleeps alone, as his doctors have advised. For the next two nights, his gentlemen escort him to the queen's rooms.

Dr Butts comes to him. 'Lord Cromwell, it is all naught. I have told his Majesty not to enforce himself.'

'In case injury comes to his royal person,' Chambers says.

'He says he will still go to her suite every other night,' Dr Butts says. 'So it will give rise to no talk.'

Chambers says, 'He claims she has displeasant airs about her. You might talk to her chamberwomen. See if they are washing her well enough.'

He says, 'You go to them if you like.' He pictures them sousing and soaping Anna, scrubbing her in the Thames and beating her on stones; hauling her up and wringing her. 'I would stake my life she is a virgin.'

'He seems to have dropped that line of talk,' Chambers says. 'Now he only says she disgusts him. But he claims he is capable of the act itself. Or capable of emission, at least. Which will be a relief to you to know, if you have to take him to market again.'

Dr Butts whispers: 'He has experienced … you understand us … *duas pollutiones nocturnas in somne.*'

'So he thinks he could do it with another woman,' Chambers says.

'Has he anyone in mind?' He thinks, I am like Charles Brandon: I am ashamed to hold such conversation.

* * *

At the next council meeting the Lord Chancellor says, 'If the king and queen are civil to each other by day, it will help counter the rumours. And I think we can rely on them for that.'

'When he was with the other one,' Fitz says, 'and he couldn't tup her, he blamed witches.'

'Superstition,' Cranmer says. 'He knows better now.'

Norfolk says, 'Well, Cromwell? What to do?'

He says, 'I have done nothing, but for his safety and happiness.'

He overhears a young courtier – it is a Howard of course, the young Culpeper: 'If the king cannot manage it with the new queen, Cromwell will do it for him. Why not? He does everything else.'

His friend laughs. What alarms him is not their mockery. It is that they take no care to keep their voices low.

When the council meets they should, he feels, put down sand to soak up the blood. It is like the *champ clos* for a tournament, sturdily fenced to stop the spectators getting in or the combatants getting out. The king stands in a watchtower, judging every move.

That night he writes to Stephen Vaughan. He tells him what he tells everyone abroad: the king and queen are merry, and all here believe the marriage a great success.

I am lying even to Vaughan, he thinks.

Richard Riche asks him, 'What do you hear from your daughter in Antwerp?'

'Nothing,' he says.

Riche says, 'It may be as well. The king has a sharp nose for heresy. Of course, my lord, since you have been such a traveller in this world, you may have other offspring, unknown to you. Do you ever think of that?'

'Yes, Wolsey mentioned it a time or two.' He thinks, if Jenneke made a claim on me now, I don't know if I could meet it. He ushers Riche out as Wriothesley comes in. Clearly he has been eavesdropping on Riche, because his face is flushed. He says, 'That man has no feeling at all. He is a tissue of ambition.'

He thinks, but that is what Riche tells me about you. But while I rule, you do your best for me, and your best is very good. I must place my trust, even if I have misgivings. I cannot work alone. The Seymour boys have their own interests at heart, why would they not? In these strange times Suffolk is my well-wisher, but Suffolk is stupid. I cannot count on Fitzwilliam for support, he is busy defending his own position, and blames me because he is blamed. Cranmer is frightened, he is always frightened. Latimer is disgraced. Robert Barnes I would not trust with his own life, let alone mine. Manuals of advice tell us you should fear weak men more than strong men. But we are all weak, in the presence of the king. Even Thomas Wyatt, who can face down a lion.

A realm's chief councillor should have a grand plan. But now he's pushing through, hour to hour, not raising his head from his business. The city is full of Germans – official, unofficial – who believe that he will make the king a fit ally for Luther. Lord Cromwell, they coax, we know that it is you who day by day softens the force of last summer's laws. 'We know in your heart you wish a more perfect reformation. You believe what we believe.'

He indicates the king, standing at a distance: 'I believe what he believes.'

At Austin Friars he goes out to see his leopard. Dick Purser knows the beast's habits, her sullen whims, her episodes of dangerous friskiness. 'Dick,' he says, 'you mustn't think you can get friendly with her. You mustn't think you can let her out.'

He looks at the brute and she looks back at him. Her golden eyes blink. She yawns, but all the time she is thinking of murder. She gives herself away by the twitching of her tail.

Dick says, 'What would she say if she could speak?'

'Nothing we would understand.'

'I never thought I would be keeper of such a beast, that day you came to get me from More's house.'

He puts his arm around the boy's shoulders. Dick Purser is an orphan; it was More and Bishop Stokesley who hunted and hounded his father, setting him in the pillory and shaming him as a heretic, and it was their ill-treatment, he is sure, that killed him. More wanted credit for taking in the boy; and credit again, for whipping heresy out of him. Sir Thomas bragged he had never struck his own children, not even with a feather. But he did not extend the courtesy to the children of others.

He himself had turned up, dry-mouthed with rage, on More's doorstep. He would not send a servant to do it, nor would he wait in the outer hall for More to be at leisure. 'I've come for Purser's son. Give him to me, or I'll lay a complaint against you for assault.'

'What?' More said. 'For correcting a child of the house? People will laugh at you, Master Cromwell. Anyway, the rascal has vanished. Fortunately he took only what he stood up in. Or charges would lie.'

'I hear he took your blessing. You could see the marks.'

'He's probably run to your house,' More said. 'Where would he seek shelter, but a heretic roof?'

'Beware an action for slander,' he said: one lawyer to another.

'Bring one,' More said. 'The facts would be aired. Your book trade connections. Your dubious associates. Antwerp, all that. No ... you go home, you'll find the wretch at your gate. Where else would he go?'

To the wharves, he thinks, to the docks. To take ship. To do what I did. He could do worse. Or then again perhaps he couldn't.

Now he pays Dick Purser twelve pounds a year. He gets fourpence daily for the leopard's keep.

He goes to see Lord Rutland, Chamberlain of the Queen's Household. Their conversation is circumlocutory, but Lord Rutland is clear that he does not meddle in bedroom matters.

He will speak to his wife, he offers. Lady Rutland speaks to the senior lady among the Germans. Next day Anna leaves off her bonnet and appears in a French hood, the oval framing her face and showing off her pretty fair hair.

He says to Jane Rochford, 'Is there a colour that would make her skin look fresher? The king keeps mentioning Jane.'

'Jane was not fresh,' Rochford says, 'she was pallid. She looked as if she lived under an altar cloth. Not that she was so holy. She spent her time frightening Anne Boleyn.'

Mary Fitzroy says, 'You cannot expect the queen to glow, my lord. She hears the king is unhappy, and the more English she learns, the more explanation she will require.'

'Oh, I don't think she will,' the child Katherine Howard says. 'She has heard that the king's first wife was divorced because she kept asking God to pardon him, using a loud voice in Latin. And that he killed Anne Boleyn because she gossiped and shrieked. And that his third wife was beloved because she hardly talked at all. Therefore she aims to imitate Jane. Only not die.'

Rochford says, 'Perhaps you'd like to come in yourself, my lord, and wash and dress her? We'll stand her naked before you, and you can do the rest.'

He says, 'If she confides in you, come to me.'

Through the interpreters he learns what Anna expects of marriage. Her parents did not marry for love, but love followed. They wrote poems for each other. She understands the king has written verses in his time, and wonders when he will write one for her.

The ambassadors of Cleves ask, 'This long while past, when your king was without a wife, did he take mistresses?'

'Our king is virtuous,' he says.

'We do not doubt it,' the ambassadors say. 'Though there could be other reasons.'

He says to Fitzwilliam, 'Advise the king to make some public demonstration of his affection.'

'You do it,' Fitz says.

'No, you.'

Fitz groans.

Later that day, before his assembled court and the Germans, Henry calls for the queen, takes her by the hand. 'Come, dear madam.' He looks around his councillors – their faces, willing him on.

He grapples her to him. Anna's forehead rests against his gem-studded breast. As if she might struggle, the king holds her fast. As if she might escape, he tightens his grip.

Anna's body is rigid, flattened. Her mouth is buried in his furs. She attempts to twist sideways, so she can breathe. Her hand, bunching up her skirts, contracts into a fist. Her head strains backwards. She emits a gasp. Then, her back to the witnesses, she is silent.

Gregory whispers, 'Perhaps he has killed her?'

Wriothesley says, 'Majesty … would it be best if …?'

'What?' Henry releases the queen. He steps back as if to say, there now – you all saw I tried.

Anna peels away from him. She seems unsteady. Her gaze flutters to Fitzwilliam, to Gregory, to the men she knows, and she moves stiffly towards them, a hand extended, limp as if the fingers were broken. Branded in her cheek is the imprint of the king's gold chain.

By the end of January Wyatt has obeyed the orders that come from London by every messenger, carried on every tide. He has put in the tip of his knife to prise open a gap between the Emperor and François.

Wyatt has appeared before Charles, the occasion public and grand. Why, he asks the Emperor, do you not keep your promises? We have extradition treaties, and yet you allow English traitors free passage to join that monster, Pole. Are you so ungrateful for all my king has done for you?

'Ungrateful? I?' The first gentleman of Christendom flashes into rage. His councillors, in shock, pull back into a huddle and confer. One of them steps forward: 'Perhaps we have misunderstood you, Monsieur Guiett? Or perhaps you misspoke? After all, French is not your first language.'

'There's nothing wrong with my French,' Wyatt says. 'But I can repeat it in Latin if you like.'

Charles leans forward. How dare your master use that word, *ungrateful*? How can a charge of ingratitude be levelled against an Emperor, by the envoy of some poor little island full of heretics and sheep? An inferior person, a king, cannot expect gratitude. The Holy Roman Emperor is set above mere kings. Their natural position is at his feet.

Wyatt draws back. 'All is said, sir.' In seeking to insult Henry, the Emperor has insulted all princes, his French ally included.

When Wyatt's letter arrives Mr Wriothesley reads it out. 'It is like a play!' William Kingston says. A tentative smile spreads over the faces of the councillors. There are matters that lie between François and Charles – old quarrels – always ready to spark. Once the fire takes hold and burns their treaties, Englishmen can sleep safe.

'Then, Cromwell,' Norfolk says to him, 'we will not need your German friends, will we? Your friend Wyatt works contrary to your purpose.' The duke enjoys the thought. 'Should he succeed, what a fool you will look.'

At Valenciennes on the river Scheldt, Charles and François part company. The Emperor takes a power and moves east. 'And Wyatt with him,' he says to Henry. At his elbow to needle him.

For a day or two they are without news. Then it becomes clear that Charles is heading towards his rebel city of Ghent. The citizens know what to expect. Charles has already executed one of their leaders, a man of seventy-five, by putting him on a rack and pulling his body apart: having shaved him first, trunk and poll, so that he was bald as a new-born babe.

Henry says, 'The Emperor loves warfare. When he leaves Ghent he will march on Guelders. And Duke Wilhelm will call on my aid, which I cannot well deny him. And if I were to be drawn into war, it would not be by my desire, my lord Cromwell, but – strangely – by yours.'

Richard Riche comes to consult him about the pensions list for Westminster Abbey. The abbot says he is dying, but perhaps this is a ploy to get a better pension? The abbey is to be a cathedral now, and (if he lives) the abbot will be its dean. Henry will not demolish the sacred place where kings are crowned. Nor will he disturb his mother and father, who lie in bronze above ground, and below ground in lead; all day candles stout as pillars flicker around them, bathing them in a greenish perpetual light. The abbey's relics will be moved, but images and statues survive. Doubting Thomas kneels to put his fingers into the bloody gash in his Saviour's breast. St Christopher carries his God, who crouches on his shoulders like a favourite cat. On the walls of the chapter house, St John sails to Patmos, a forlorn exile blotting his eyes. The useful camel and the dromedary pace the desert sands, while the roebuck tramples verdure beneath delicate hooves, and the patriarchs and virgins stand shoulder to shoulder with the confessors and martyrs, their beady eyes alert. The monuments of dead monarchs draw together, as if their bones were counselling each other; and the prophetic pavements beneath them, those stones of onyx, porphyry, green serpentine and glass, advise us through their inscriptions how many years the world will last.

'Why do they need to know?' he asks Richard Riche. 'It's a wonder to me any of the monks could live past thirty.' As their rule forbids them to consume flesh in their refectory, they keep a second dining room, where they can satisfy their appetites for roast and boiled meats. At the solemn feasts of the church, they make a dish they call Principal Pudding. They use six pounds of currants, three hundred eggs, and great bricks of suet. They showed it him once as it was getting ready, as if they were giving him a treat: a fatty, oozing mass, a welling bolster speckled black as if with flies. 'It is worth suppressing the abbey,' he says, 'to suppress the pudding.'

He, Thomas Cromwell, stands looking up at the fan vaulting of the new chapel. 'I swear the pendants are shifting. When I was first here they looked true.'

'It is only the building settling,' the monks say. 'It happens, my lord.'

There is an indulgence granted to those who attend a Mass here, which all of us will need one day: it is called the Stairway to Heaven. St Bernard in a vision saw souls ascending, rung by rung into eternity; angels give them a hand to balance, as they hop off the last rung into bliss. It is easy to climb. Harder to know what to do when you get to the top. As we labour upwards, the Fiend shakes the foot; and treads can snap, or the whole structure sink in boggy ground. He says to Riche, 'Ricardo, do you think there is a flaw in the nature of ladders, or a flaw in the nature of climbers?' But it is not the sort of question to which the Master of Augmentations likes to apply his mind.

At the end of the month Edward Seymour goes to Calais, Rafe Sadler to Scotland. If King James wants a favour, he tells Rafe, he should cultivate his uncle Henry, rather than embroil himself with François, who will use Scotland as a vassal state. And if Rafe can detect any rift between James and the Pope, he should widen it. The King of Scots should be shown the advantages of taking control of his own church, and alerted to the resources of his monasteries: every ruler wants money, and here it is for the taking.

Rafe's journey is slowed because he has to take a string of geldings, which the king wishes to present to his nephew.

'Write to me,' he says, 'at every opportunity.'

The loss of the boy is like a cold wind on his neck.

When the court moves to Westminster, they go by river, accompanied by merchant ships, musicians aboard. A salute is fired from the Tower. The citizens line the trembling banks and cheer.

At Westminster the king continues to visit the queen every second night. The Germans ask, 'Majesty, when will the coronation be?' He, Cromwell, reminds the council it was planned for Candlemas; but Candlemas is past. Norfolk says, 'We know why you want her crowned. You think once the king's laid out the money, he won't send her back.'

'Send her back?' He has to simulate outrage.

From the queen's side of the palace, silence. The women brush by him frowning: there is always somewhere they have to be. There's a question he ought to be asking Anna, but he doesn't know what it is; or perhaps an answer that she needs from him. In stories, when you are in the forest you meet a lady, veiled and shrouded, and she asks you a riddle. If you get it right her clothes fall off at a glance. Her body glides into your arms, and her light merges with yours. But if you get it wrong she withers into a hag. She puts her hand on your member and it shrinks to the size of a bean.

He brings Charles Brandon to Austin Friars. He shows him the leopard, with which Charles is well pleased, and then takes him into his confidence: the king now affirms that as he will never love the queen he cannot do the act. 'Cannot, will not – to the state, it is all one.'

Suffolk looks grave. 'Given up completely, has he? I didn't know that. Does Thomas Howard know? Do the bishops know? Any other man, you could suggest ...'

He cannot imagine what Charles is going to say.

'You could suggest, try thinking about another woman. But if Harry thought of another woman, he'd want to marry her. Then where would you be?'

At court he studies Norfolk's niece. When a man's eyes rest on her, which is very often, she ruffles her feathers like a plump little hen.

Thomas Howard is to go to France, the king says. He wants to penetrate the mind of François and thinks a great nobleman might succeed. 'It needs someone of my lord Norfolk's stature,' he says.

Young Surrey says to his hangers-on, 'It is only by Heaven's providence that the king has a nobleman left to send. Cromwell would extinguish us all, if he had his way.'

Wriothesley pursues him: 'Sir, you see Norfolk is eager to begin his mission? When before, sent abroad, he always dragged his feet? And I fear his French is not adequate.'

'Perhaps he will stay quiet and get a name for wisdom.'

Richard Riche says, 'You might try that sometime, Call-Me.'

Norfolk will have the support of Sir John Wallop, now appointed resident ambassador. *Valloppe*, the French call him. He is an experienced diplomat, but he would not have been the Cromwell choice: too friendly with Lisle, for one thing. He has his boy Mathew in Calais now, so he knows what goes on in the Lord Deputy's house. He is waiting for one incriminating letter to turn up on his lordship's desk, or perhaps in her ladyship's sewing box – a letter to, or from, Reginald Pole.

In the days before he embarks, Norfolk is seen at Gardiner's house in Southwark. 'It is natural my lord should take advice,' he says equably, when reports are brought to him. 'Because Gardiner was our ambassador in France for so long.'

'It is not that,' Wriothesley says. 'They are working something together.'

'Yes. Well. I am working something myself.'

When Norfolk sees the surprise I have for him, he will never stir from his hearth again.

The Lenten fast of 1540 is kept in the strict old manner, under the eye of Gardiner and his friends. It is as well to let them have their way in small things, where they are vigilant. Thurston gets them through on saffron bread, onion tarts with raisins, baked rice with almond milk, and a new sauce for salt fish made with garlic and walnuts.

On Valentine's Day, preaching wars break out. Gardiner against Barnes, Barnes against Gardiner. They are both bitter men, but Gardiner has nothing to lose, while Barnes stands in peril of his life. Barnes will break, as he once did before Wolsey. It's not his faith, but his temperament that will fail. He is not Luther. Here he stands: till Gardiner knocks him across the room.

The Londoners, crouching under makeshift shelters, jostling beneath oiled canvases, listen to their sermons with their eyes screwed up against the rain, their hair plastered and their ears a-swill. Yet old wives say we shall have a hot summer. For now, as the poet says, no fresh green leaves, no apple trees, but thorns. Iron winter has a grip, the day he goes to Henry to ask for mercy.

'Is this about Robert Barnes?' Henry says. 'It appears I was much deceived in him. Gardiner says he is a rank heretic. And to think I entrusted him with England's business abroad! You are close enough to the man, you were derelict in not knowing his opinions and laying them bare. I suppose you did not know them?'

'I am not here to speak for Barnes.' In his mind he goes out of the room and comes in again. 'I am here about Gertrude Courtenay, sir. We might release her. Keep the evidence on file. Her fault is credulity, which women cannot help; and loyalty to those passed away, a thing your Majesty understands.'

'Katherine is never truly dead, is she?' Henry sounds exhausted. 'And there are some who will never accept she was not my wife.'

'Lady Exeter will need means to live, so if your mercy further permits, I will arrange an annuity out of her husband's lands.'

'God curse him,' Henry says. 'Very well, release the woman, keep Exeter's child in ward; I want no traitor whelp running free through the realm.'

He makes a note. Henry says, 'Cromwell, could you have a child?'

He is startled. 'I think you could,' Henry says. 'You are of common stock. Common men have vigour.'

The king does not know they wear out. At forty a labourer is broken and gnarled. His wife is worn to the bone at thirty-five.

'I thought I would get another son from this marriage,' the king says, 'but there is no sign God intends it.' He sinks into his chair, turns over a few leaves of paper. 'We might write to Cleves this moment. You could write at my dictation, as we used to.'

He says, 'My eyes are not what they were.'

So much for common stock. 'But you still write letters,' Henry says, 'I am familiar with your hand. I want you to ask Wilhelm himself where those papers are, that show if his sister was married, because –' He leans his elbows on the table, his head in his hands. 'Cromwell, can we not pay her off?'

'We could offer her a settlement, yes. I do not know how much we would have to find to placate her brother. And I do not know how to salvage your Majesty's reputation, if you renounce a lawful match. It would be hard to hold up your head before your fellow princes. Or come by another wife.'

'I could come by one tomorrow,' Henry says harshly.

The door opens, cautiously. It is the boys with lights. 'Bring candles here,' he says. But the king seems to have forgotten the letter. Henry waits till they are alone again, but even then he does not speak; till the warm light diffuses through the room and he says, 'You remember, my lord, the day we rode down to the Weald? To see the ironmasters, and find out new ways of casting cannon?'

An icy vapour breathes on the windowpanes. Henry's diamonds, as he moves, look like steel beads, or those seeds that fall on stony ground. He waits, the quill beneath his fingertips. 'Those were brighter days,' the king says. 'Jane could not travel, being great with my heir. She did not like me to leave her, but she knew we had long planned the excursion, and your lordship's press of business being what it is, and the duties of a king being what they are, she would not ask me to forbear. I remember rising early and, it being about St John's Day, it was light before the permitted hour for Mass; Jane said, will you tarry till your chaplain comes? And I tarried, because the fears of a woman in that condition, they must be heeded. It will be only two nights or three, I said, though we shall take it at an easy pace. We shall listen to the birdsong and ride, like knights of Camelot, through the woods. We shall enjoy the sunshine.' Henry pauses: 'The sunshine, where did that go?'

'God made February, sir, as well as June.'

'Spoken like a bishop.' Henry looks up. 'I want you and Gardiner to be reconciled.'

We tried that, he thinks.

'At Easter, sit down together.'

'On my honour, I will attempt it.'

Silence. He thinks, perhaps what I said was not good enough? 'I will make peace if I can.'

The boys have not closed the shutters. He rises to do it. Henry says, 'Leave those, I want what light there is.' Beyond the glass gulls swing by, as if they have mistaken the towers of Westminster for a sea cliff.

Henry is watching him. His vast hands have fallen onto his gown, limp and empty. He says, 'But when I think about it, Cromwell ... I recall we never made that journey.'

'Into Kent? No, but it was projected –'

'Projected, yes. But always some reason we could not go.'

He sits down again, facing the king. 'Let us say we did, sir. It is no harm to imagine it.' England's green heart: distant church bells, the shade of the trees from the heat. 'Let us say the ironmasters gave us

769

their best welcome, and opened their minds to us, and showed us all their secrets.'

'They must,' Henry says. 'No one could keep secrets from me. It is no use to try.'

He goes out: one hand against the wall, he utters a prayer. The Book Called Henry has no advice for him.

The king has moved from his native ground: as if he has entered another realm where cause does not link to effect; nor does he care how he opens his heart. Think of the days when the Boleyns came down. The king had written a play, about Boleyn's monstrous adulteries. He kept it in a little book in his bosom, and tried to show it to people.

In January he said, Cromwell, you are not to blame. Now you can hear him thinking: one thing, one thing I wanted him to do for me, and he would not.

He thinks, it would be hard to free him but not impossible. It would be a victory to Norfolk and his ilk, it would be encouragement to the papists and an end to the new Europe. How often do you get the chance to reconfigure the map? Perhaps once in two or three generations: and now the chance is slipping away. Wyatt and the operation of time will break France and the Emperor apart, and we will be back to the old, worn-out games that have lasted my lifetime.

Then Harry will want a new wife, and God knows who. A song drifts into his head, it must be one Walter sang:

> I kissed her sweet, and she kissed me;
> I danced the darling on my knee.

Next he will choose some papist, and I will wish I were far away. If I had stayed in Italy I could have had a house in the hills, with white walls and a red-tiled roof. A colonnade shading its entrance, shuttered balconies against the heat; orchards, flowery walks, fountains and a vineyard; a library with frescoes depicting animals and birds, like the paintings in the chapter house at the abbey.

At the Frescobaldi villa the girl came every morning with her basket of herbs. You struck the jars of oil as you passed, and the note told you how full they were. After the kitchen boys stopped picking fights with him, he taught them English catches and rhymes. Under blue Italian skies, they sang of misty mornings, of ash and oak, of sudden loss of maidenheads in the month of May.

Then one day the master whistled him to the counting house, and he left his apron on the peg. After that, among the Frescobaldis he became a confidential aide. Visiting the Portinari family, he was a friend of the young men of the house. No one said, here's the blacksmith's boy, don't let him in. When he left the Frescobaldi bank he went to Venice. There at his workplace they had a long chest with carved panels, showing St Sebastian stuck with arrows. Every night he used to pack the ledgers away, dropping the key into his pocket; he had never given the martyr a glance. So how is it he can see him now? There are longbowmen on one side. Crossbowmen on the other. He is pierced from every angle.

He walks away from the king's rooms. *I kissed her sweet, and she kissed me …*

In the next days he finds his benevolence is tested and his patience is running short. When a spy is taken and proves resistant, he does not go along to the Tower to bribe or cajole or trick him; he values speed. Rack him, he says: and appoints three men to take down the result. Come to me first thing in the morning, he says, and tell me of your success.

Before Norfolk arrives home from France, he has invaded the duke's own country. He has closed Thetford Priory, where the duke's fore-bears lie. They have been witnessing miracles at Thetford for three hundred years, ever since they turned up a cache of relics, neatly labelled, that included rocks from Mount Calvary, part of Our Lady's sepulchre, and fragments of the manger in which the child Jesus was laid. Now comes the greatest miracle of all, Thomas Cromwell, the Putney boy: who holds that the passage of time does not add lustre to fakes, and that there is no need to reverence a lie because of its antiquity.

What is to happen to the honoured dead? John Howard is buried here, shot out of his saddle at Bosworth and dead before he hit the ground. So is the duke's father, that same Thomas Howard who pulped the Scots at Flodden, and spread their broken limbs over the fields. And this is where, more recently, young Richmond was deposited, the king's bastard and the duke's son-in-law.

Will the family have to build new tombs? It is an insult to the Howard name, Norfolk shouts, and a crippling expense as well. He comes to him with a question: 'Cromwell, do you hold me in contempt? Mind yourself. I shall have your guts.'

'Fighting talk,' he says. 'We haven't had such talk since the cardinal's day.'

'My father must be prayed for,' the duke roars. 'If not at Thetford, then somewhere else.'

Riche says, 'What, you mean at Lord Cromwell's expense?'

He thinks, why don't you just give up on him, your old dad? Let him take his chances?

'"Flodden Norfolk", they called him,' the duke says. 'A father named after a battle. How do you like that, Cromwell?'

Howard takes himself off, cursing. He has been cursing since he returned from France; once there, he had been advised to cultivate François's mistress, as the way to the king's confidence, and he is still peppered with shame at having to beg favour from a woman.

Wriothesley says, 'He takes such pride in his ancestors, I do not think he will forgive you for turning them out. And I do not think he has disclosed all the dealings he had with the French, not by a long way.'

Richard Riche says, 'The French hate you. And Norfolk encourages them.'

Wriothesley says, 'Did I not advise you, sir, when the Boleyns came down? Break Norfolk, I said, while you have the chance.'

* * *

Robert Barnes comes to Austin Friars: once again the drowned man, washed up his stairs. If he had known Barnes was coming, he would have had them stop him at the gate.

Barnes says, 'Winchester thinks, if he pulls me down, you go down with me.'

He nods: that seems a fair summary. 'You could run,' he suggests.

'Not this time,' Barnes says. 'I am too tired. You always say, prudence. Circumspection. How long must God wait, for England to embrace true religion?'

'Another decade,' he says. 'Not long, by His standards.'

Barnes stares at him. 'You mean till Henry is dead? But what if the prince never reigns? What if Mary comes in?'

'Then we're all dead,' he says.

On 12 March, the Earl of Essex, Henry Bouchier, falls from his horse, breaks his neck, and dies on the spot. 'God forgive me,' Charles Brandon says. 'On the king's wedding day I made a jest about him, that he was not long for this world.'

'My lord,' he says, 'it is nowise your doing.'

Where will old Essex go? Straight to Judgement? Or will he lie quiet in his grave till the Last Day? Will he work off his sins in Purgatory for half a million years, or is he already at his destination – at the top of the Stairway to Heaven, or in a pit of the Inferno reserved for earls?

The most part of the court does not care. Except on Sundays or if they are taken sick, they do not give a fig for the disputes of Gardiner or Barnes. They only want to know what will happen to Essex's title. The earl had no heir. His son-in-law expects to get the nod, but no one knows where to lay their bets.

Palm Sunday, news comes of the death of John de Vere, fifteenth Earl of Oxford. This death is not a shock; Vere has been unwell for months. His heir is of full age and will succeed as sixteenth earl; and it is assumed he will also be appointed to his father's office of Lord Great Chamberlain, the head of the king's household.

'Not necessarily,' Mr Wriothesley says. His family being heralds, he has these matters at his fingertips. 'Vere was named to that office in the year 1133, in the reign of the first Henry. And there have been very few chamberlains since who were not of that blood. But it is not theirs of right. The king can appoint whom he pleases.'

He has no time to discuss it. There is a new ambassador he must receive. Cleves has sent us a resident at last. His name is Dr Carl Harst and he has previously represented Duke Wilhelm in Spain. He has no English, and no documents: also no lodging, a meagre allowance and very little style about his clothes or his person. He says to Wriothesley, 'I wish they had sent a better sort of man – I am afraid the court will laugh at him.'

'At his expectations,' Wriothesley says, 'certainly – for they are all wrong.'

By now, Duke Wilhelm will have had a letter from his sister. Writing herself in her native tongue, Anna has told her brother she could wish for no better husband: she thanks her family for promoting her happiness.

Lady Rochford has spoken to him. 'She does not know what to do. She pretends all is well but she is like a jackdaw waiting for figs to ripen, living on hope.' Rochford laughs. 'Lent is over, and no man however pious can refuse his wife. We say to her, "Madam, what does he do? Once the candle is out?" She says, he kisses me and says, "Good night, darling." Then in the morning, he rises and says, "Farewell, sweetheart." We said to her, madam, if this is all that occurs, it will be a long time before we have a Duke of York.'

'Hush, Jane,' he says.

'Everybody is talking. How long do you suppose you can keep it from the Germans?'

Footsteps behind them: one of the maids. 'You seem to be everywhere, Mistress Howard.'

Katherine gazes up at him. 'Yes.'

He prices her up. 'New dress?'

'Uncle Norfolk.'

'Do you bear a message, or have you come here to dazzle my senses?'

She dips her head. 'The queen and Lady Mary will walk in the gallery with you. My lord.'

Outside the rain runs down the windows: lead men on rooftops spout it from their maws.

The ladies of Anna's privy chamber have already told him that her meeting with the Lady Mary has not been a success. Against all the evidence, Mary takes Anna to be a Lutheran; while Anna has been made wary by her own people, who have long assumed Mary spies for the Emperor.

In the gallery he walks with a lady on either hand: Anna spring-like in yellow, Mary in her favoured crimson. 'Rain again,' Anna says, showing off her English.

'I fear so,' he says.

Henry has said to him, talk to her, Cromwell: can't you talk to her? I dare not, he said, and Henry said, why not, if I give you leave? He had thought, because I do not know what you want me to fetch away from the conversation. Do you want her to turn herself into a woman you can love, or a woman you can repudiate?

Mary says, 'I understand your friend Dr Barnes will soon be in ward. And other preacher friends of yours.'

She leaves a pause for him to say, Barnes is not my friend. He does not fill it. Anna walks beside him, blithe, unheeding, her fingertips on his coat. He feels as if the Lutheran clock is still in his palm, the fidget of its workings disturbing his pulse. Its case was made by an artist; its machinery, by a gunsmith.

'What does Barnes expect?' Mary says. 'First he says he recants. Then he repeats his errors. Were you there?'

'Yes, madam. Days and days of sermons.'

'Let me have notes on them,' she says. As if he were her clerk. He bows. She says, 'I believe all is awry in Calais.'

'Lord Lisle is expected here for the Garter feast. No doubt some reckoning will be made.'

'Strange times, my lord. Two great lords dead.'

The gallery is hung with the king's new tapestries, depicting the life of St Paul. A queen, a king's daughter and a brewer's son, they have walked the road to Damascus, blinded by the light; they have sailed the Middle Sea. Now they pause before the Sorcerers of Ephesus who, converted by the saint, are burning their books. He feels he would like to reach into the weave and pull them out of the fire.

At Gardiner's house they have capons with figs, Crustade Lombarde and chopped chicken livers with hard-boiled eggs; they have spiced wine custards and jellied veal. He, Cromwell, is there at the king's command, and he looks at his dinner because he does not want to look at the Bishop of Winchester. He does not want to look at Thomas Howard either. He did not even know he was going to be there, until he saw his barge moored.

Coming in, he says, 'Why are you here, my lord duke? I thought there was plague in your household. You should not be near the king.'

'I'm not,' Norfolk says. 'I'm near you.'

Gardiner seems inclined to emollience, like a good host. 'I understand a servant died, but my lord had not been within fourteen miles of him.'

'He didn't die, and it wasn't the plague,' Norfolk says. 'Nobody else in the house took sick. Nothing ails me, I assure you. At this time of year I eat a tansy pudding to purify my blood.'

'You are always very tender of your person,' he says. 'You too, my lord bishop.' They sit down. Wine is poured. He turns to Norfolk. 'I remember when Stephen was secretary to my lord cardinal, and we both went to Ipswich, to prepare for the opening of my lord's college. I put up the hangings myself because they were so slow, and I carried in benches and trestles – and this good companion of mine, he stood by and directed me, and advised me out of his charity not to strain my back.'

Gardiner says, smiling, 'I only exert myself in a good cause.'

Norfolk bangs his goblet on the board. 'Ipswich?' Never was the word spat out, as the duke spits it. 'To get funds for his wretched school at Ipswich, Wolsey pulled down the priory at Felixstowe – and that was *my* priory. I rejoiced when his college was closed. I hope it falls in ruins. By God, how is it this realm is so unjust? If it is not Wolsey cheating me, it is his worshipper here. Wolsey was your God, Cromwell. Your butcher God.'

'I must agree.' Gardiner puts down his knife. 'It amazes me, Cromwell, that you still do not see Wolsey for what he was. He was corrupt and he was grandiose. You know yourself that when he lost the king's favour he wrote to foreign princes, asking their aid. Without the king's knowledge, over the king's head, he set up his dealings as if he were a prince himself. What do we call such a man? We call him a traitor. If someone had given you the brief, you yourself would have convicted him.'

'Aye,' Norfolk says. 'You would not have broken sweat. Still, I suppose it is something, that a man like you feels gratitude. What had you, when you came to court? Wolsey owned the shirt on your back. Now stir yourself, and show your gratitude to the king, who has done so much more for you. Take your Germans and kick them out of door.'

A boy approaches with a jug. Stephen frowns at him: the boy drops back to the wall. It is not like Thomas Howard to be the worse for drink, but he must have had a skinful before he left his house. It is to give him courage, he thinks: and by God he will need it.

He bunches his fist. He bangs it on the table. The dishes leap. 'The whole council approved the match. You signed, Thomas Howard, as I did. As for the lady, the king could not get her here fast enough.'

'No, by the saints,' Norfolk says, 'it is you who burdened and chained him. And I tell you, he wants to be free. Have you not seen him looking at my niece? He cast a fantasy to Katherine the first time ever he did see her.'

'If you want power,' he says, 'get it like a man. It does not become your grey hairs, to play Pandar.'

'God rot you!' The duke stamps his feet, pushes back his chair, hauls his napkin loose from his person. Gardiner has opulent linen and it looks as if he is fighting his way out of a tent. 'I'll not sit here to be called a bawd!'

As the duke stands up, he stands up too. The servants flatten themselves against the wall. There is a red blink in the corner of his eye. There is the knife at his heart: cold under his coat, ready in its sheath, and his hand moves to it, as if it acts by its own will.

But Gardiner steps between them. 'No fists today, my lords.'

Fists? he thinks. You don't know me. I could carve him like a goose, before you were out of your seat.

Smiling as if it were a ladies' bowling match, Gardiner flings his hands in the air. 'Well, my lord Norfolk, if you must leave us, you are a busy man.' He smiles. 'We will give your dinner to the poor.'

When the duke has made his noisy exit, shouting for his guard and his bargemen, they sit down again, and Stephen reaches across the table and pats his arm.

'Say it, Stephen.' He is glum. '"Cromwell, you forget yourself, we're not in Putney now."'

Stephen signals for the wine jug. 'Insult is a fine art. I wondered for a moment if he knew who Pandar was. I thought you might have been too subtle.'

'No, not today,' he says. 'I'm not feeling subtle at all. Forgive me. I see we must make efforts towards each other, and I can do better, and will. I am sure I have things you want, where I could oblige you, and there are things I want –'

'You want Barnes let out,' Gardiner says. 'Is he reformable, do you think? I am always sorry to see a Cambridge man go into the fire. I spoke for him, you remember, years back, when he came before Wolsey.'

'If you say so.'

'Otherwise he would have gone straight to the Tower. Which would have saved time, I suppose. I see no good he has brought to

England, for all his traffic as ambassador. The king repents him that Barnes was ever employed.'

They bring in pickled greens, and pears in an aromatic syrup, and quince marmalade. Stephen says, 'Norfolk is precipitate, but he is right. Don't you feel the wind changing? You told the king that without the Germans he was destitute of friends. And that was true. But once the alliance melts away, Henry will be courted again, by France and Emperor both.'

'I do not understand how Norfolk thinks he can see the future. When usually he cannot see the end of his nose.'

'You forget, it is only weeks since he was in France himself. I believe that François made overtures of friendship that were – I will not say hidden – but they were private. Entrusted to the duke, but not to you.'

So, he says.

'I know you have people of yours in every man's service, at home and abroad. I know they are spying and prying and copying and purloining from chests and thieving keys. I have suffered from them in my own house.'

'As I have suffered, Stephen. From *your* men.'

'But you are not omniscient. Nor are you omnipresent. Have you been thinking you were? Did you think you were God?'

'No,' he says. 'God's spy.'

'Then spy out the facts,' Stephen says. 'If the king believes he does not need the friendship of Cleves, then considering his intractable dislike of the lady, there is only one course, which is to work out how to free him.'

He pushes his glass away. Like Norfolk, but less hastily, he extracts himself from the table linen. Gardiner is no fool. A demon, but no fool. 'Good marmalade,' he says. 'I think it is Lady Lisle's recipe? The king often praises it.'

'She sends it to us all,' Gardiner says, as if excusing himself.

'To all those she wishes to please. Does she wrap letters around it?'

Gardiner looks at him with appreciation. 'By God, nothing gets by you, does it? Not even the preserves.' He sighs. 'Thomas, we both know what it is to serve this king. We know it is impossible. The question is, who can best endure impossibility? You have never lost his favour. I have lost it many times. And yet –'

'And yet here you are. Looking to be back on the council.'

Stephen ushers him out: the open air. 'You know what the king wants. That we should sink our differences in service to him. That we should declare ourselves entire perfect friends.'

They touch palms, coldly. As he runs down the steps to the wharf, Stephen calls, 'Cromwell? Mind your back.'

It is a raw day of splintering sunlight, the first sign of the season changing. His barge takes him back across the river. On his flag, little black birds flutter: the cardinal's choughs, dancing about their pole.

His bargemaster says, 'We saw the duke's barge, and we said, by the Mass, pity my lord – Norfolk and Gardiner, both?'

He says, 'I feel to my master the king as I do to Christ, hanging between two thieves.'

He takes off his glove, slides a hand inside his garments. When his hand appears again, his knife is in it. 'Christophe?' he says. 'This is yours now. Try not to use it.'

Christophe turns the knife over in his hands. 'I shall stand taller for owning it. Why do you part with it now?'

'Because I almost stuck it in Norfolk.' From his crew, a subdued cheer. 'You can tell Mr Sadler I have surrendered it.' Rafe wanted me to grow up, he thinks, before I grow old.

Bastings asks, 'Did you make it yourself, sir? When you did that sort of work?'

'No. That one I made … I lost it. This was given me by a young lady in Rome. I have had it for some years.'

'And put it to some use, I warrant,' Bastings says admiringly. 'Sir, a thing you should know. That little lass of the duke's, I hear she is spoiled. There is one in the old duchess's household boasts he has had his fingers in her cunt. He says he has felt it in the dark and he would know it among a hundred.'

'Where did you hear that, from the watermen?' He wraps his cloak around himself. Even if it is true, he thinks, what can I do with it? If the king is in love he will trample anyone who gets between him and his sport. He says, 'Bastings – consort with men with cleaner minds.'

I shall forget I ever heard it, he thinks. He is rowed across the Thames, furiously forgetting it. One among a hundred?

> I kissed her sweet, and she kissed me;
> I danced the darling on my knee.
> My fancy fairly on her I set:
> So merrily singeth the nightingale.

Mr Wriothesley is waiting for him. He tells him, 'You can write to the ambassadors that Winchester and I have dined. That we now understand each other perfectly.'

Wriothesley says, 'Shall I add some such phrase as "all past displeasures be now forgot"?'

'At your discretion, Mr Wriothesley.'

Sometimes it seems to him we have not made any advance since Epiphany. The Romans and Britons are still fighting through his dreams. They advance, retreat, press forward again. They slash, they stab, they feint, they duck; they raise their armoured limbs slowly and chop, chop, chop.

In Calais, a new commission is sitting to find out heretics. Norfolk started it, when he passed through: setting a fire there, then stepping on a boat and sailing away. He says to the king, 'Why don't we find out traitors instead? Forty Frenchmen under arms could take Calais in an hour. The rot is within, and I do not mean the townsfolk, I mean those who have charge of all.'

The king says, pained, 'Lord Lisle is very dear to me.'

'I won't trouble Lord Lisle,' he says. Not yet: I will start with his friends. 'I want certain papers. Wyatt has told me what to look for. He knows all about Calais.'

'Oh, Wyatt,' the king says. 'What he says he does not mean, and what he means he does not say.'

It is Bishop Sampson who is his immediate target. Putting him under house arrest, he impounds his papers and scours them for any hint of dealings with Pole; any hints that others, among his friends, might have dealt with Pole. When the king says, well, Cromwell, what proof, he says, sir, it is intricate work. It is like putting together one of the pavements at the abbey. You have triangles and circles, rectangles and squares. You have limestone and porphyry, serpentine and glass. You must work with the eye of faith: the onlookers will not see the pattern, till suddenly they do.

Now the season changes. Each brightening day is made up of other days he has known. He sees a flock of chaffinches rise like flying roses from a still pool. His hawks watch dust motes as they flitter against a wall, as if the sunlight is a living thing, their prey.

Henry calls him in. 'I must put a matter to you. It is a matter of some gravity. Come with me here into my closet and close the door.'

A window is open. Someone is singing outside. He thinks, is this where all my broken nights have led me, my unquiet dreams?

> In slumbers oft for fear I quake.
> For heat and cold I burn and shake.
> For lack of sleep my head doth ache
> What means this?

He follows the king. What can you do but, as Cicero says, live hopefully, die bravely?

He goes home to a disturbed household. Call-Me meets him, a document in his hand. 'Sir, you had better see this at once.'

It is a transcript – a copy, let's be blunt – of a letter from Ambassador Marillac to François. 'Marillac says the king is about to arrest Cranmer. He is to go to the Tower, with Barnes.'

Call-Me has put a man in the ambassador's train. 'Well done for this,' he says. The paper feels hot.

'There is worse, sir. Marillac says the king means to take the Privy Seal from us and give it to Fitzwilliam. And that he will cast you down from your office as Vicegerent, and raise up Bishop Tunstall.'

He says, 'I have just been with the king. I know he is swift to reverse his policies, but he has not had time to do this in half an hour. I have come straight from him and I bring news. It is good news for you, and I hope you will think so.'

He is about to say, go and get Rafe, but Rafe is already coming in, his eyes on Marillac's letter. 'Can I see the text, sir? Call-Me will not part with it.'

'Ignore it,' he says. 'The ambassador sits in his lodgings concocting these fantastical tales – they only need Sexton in an ass's head and Will Somer as a Spanish harlot.'

Rafe and Call-Me look at each other. Rafe says, 'The original letter will be on the Dover road by now. Do you want the rider to have an accident?'

'He could lose his missive in a puddle,' Wriothesley suggests.

The suggestion is so mild it makes him laugh. 'Let it go,' he says. 'If France gets his hopes up, so much the sweeter. He would like to see me dismissed, and the king served by boys and fools.'

'Which are we?' Wriothesley says.

'Neither, you are the chosen ones. Be quiet and hear my news, you will be better for it. You know ever since I have been Master Secretary I have tried to be with the king's person – but I am always wanted at Westminster – so you know what my life has been.'

Those days that roll from dawn to dawn. *For lack of sleep my head doth ache ...* 'With the king's permission, I am going to divide my duties. I have broached it with him before, but the time is now.'

Mr Wriothesley offers to interrupt, but he continues. 'You will divide the task. Each of you will be Master Secretary. You will split your time so that one of you is in Westminster, the other with the king. I will make machinery, so that your work passes perfectly from hand to hand.'

'A prodigy of nature,' Rafe says. He is astonished. 'Two bodies with one head.'

'One awake and one asleep,' Wriothesley says.

'You will both be knights. You will both be raised to the council. When Parliament meets, you will sit in the Commons, and I in the Lords.' He slaps his hands on their shoulders. 'You know what I have made this office, by God's grace and the king's. Nothing eludes it. Nothing lies beyond it. Everything starts with you. And with you, everything stops.'

He sits down. 'Now, also –'

'There is more?'

He holds up a hand. Sudden pleasure afflicts like sudden pain, and leaves you dizzy, numb. At such times in your life, if ever you see such times – if fortune favours you, as fortune favours the brave – you lose for a moment a sense of the firm boundaries of yourself, and become light as air. 'I am to have Oxford's post, Chief of the Household, Lord Great Chamberlain. His son keeps his peerage, as is natural, but as poor Essex had no heir direct, I am to have his title.'

He had thought the sands of time were running out: running through the cracks in the shining bowl of possibility he holds in his hands. 'Now all is mended,' he says.

Call-Me flushes. 'I congratulate you, sir, from the bottom of my heart.'

He says, 'The king explained to me how I was an aspect of his glory. He said, "It is not given to every ruler to look past a man's provenance to his capacities. God gave you talents, Cromwell. And he caused you to be born at such a time and place that you could use them in my service."'

'And you kept your countenance?' Rafe says.

'I did, so please keep yours. He is right to congratulate himself. He thinks of the laws passed and the money made. If I were a prince and I had Cromwell, I would think myself Heaven's elect.'

'I wonder why now,' Call-Me says. 'In justice he might have done it long ago. But he knows it will give much offence.'

'Not as much offence, as it gives delight,' Rafe says. 'Tell the household. Send to Mr Richard. Get Gregory. By God! Will Gregory be called Lord Gregory now? Will he have the title?'

Below, a roar goes up. Thomas Avery shoots in, embraces him. 'Sir, they will all expect some increase in their wages.'

'That is fitting, as they will be serving an earl.'

The room fills up with his people, faces shining. He draws Avery aside. 'You remember what I told you? About my money abroad?'

Avery is surprised. 'I do, sir.'

'So you know what to do?'

The boy frowns. 'Forgive me, but your lordship is talking as if your fortunes were reversed. As if you had suffered a blow of fate, instead of great promotion and honour.'

'Find my daughter,' he says. 'Open a channel to her, so she can have funds.'

She can use my money, he thinks, though not my love.

'When I left the king –' he says. He breaks off. Truth is, he had stood on the threshold and thought, those I want to tell are dead. I want to tell my good master Frescobaldi, and my friends in his kitchen. I want to tell the boy who, as I walked upstairs to the counting house, was scrubbing the stairs. I want to tell Anselma, and my wife and children, and the girl in Rome who gave me my knife. I want to sing Scaramella: *Scaramella to the war is gone, bomboretta, bomboro.* I want to tell Wolsey, and get his blessing. I want to tell Walter, and see his face. News will travel to Putney: Put-an-edge-on-it has been made an earl! He wants to tell the eel boy; he wishes he were alive, so he could go down there, dig him out of his drinking den, and pound it into his skull.

At Austin Friars, the watchdogs get an extra bone. The leopard an extra carcass. Anthony the jester goes about the house, his face solemn, ringing his silver bells.

On a fine spring day, his new style is proclaimed. The new secretaries are at work. Sir Call-Me-Risley reads the patents of creation that make him an earl. Sir Rafe Sadler proclaims him Lord Chamberlain.

When Marillac next comes to court, the ambassador sees him, starts, and goes the other way. He feels some sympathy: the ambassador tells his king what he wants to hear, and though he is across the sea he must guess at the irritable requirements of a sick man. They say François cannot ride half a mile these days. They say he is dying. But he has died so many times, in popular report. Like our king, he rises again.

Henry says, 'Ambassador Marillac declares he can no longer transact business with Cremuel present. He believes you are a spy for the Emperor.'

'That puts us in a difficulty,' he says.

'Not necessarily. I can see him alone.'

He bows. It has always been the king's belief that prince speaks to prince, and common men crouch just within earshot, ready to scurry at command. Henry says, 'We must mollify François. If he lives, he may make a new treaty with me. And the Emperor, too, I see we must begin to conciliate him.'

He hears the message. Work both sides of the bank, Cromwell. As we always have.

Sometimes, he says to Wriothesley, the best thing you can do is to pick up your papers and get yourself out.

From the French court, no reaction to his promotion: or none polite enough for the record. From the Imperial court, an equal silence. But congratulations from Eustache Chapuys, who waits in Flanders for Charles to send him back as ambassador: which he will do, Chapuys says, as soon as the rift with England is mended.

A rumour has taken hold in the city that Anna will be crowned at Whit. He does not counter it. It will spread abroad, and tend to calm. Dr Harst visits the queen, but what he draws from her is a mystery. Harst is useless, always pestering him with incomprehensible requests about protocol. He, the Earl of Essex, is busy, because Parliament will open and he has packed the schedule with legislation. The king expects him to raise taxes. The money from abbey lands is slow to come in; as he once had to explain to the cardinal, it is delicate work, to turn real property into hard cash.

He speaks in the Lords, not about taxes, but about God: setting forth the king's intent, which is harmony. He feels he has never spoken so well, nor said so little.

After the first session, Master Secretary Rafe comes to him: 'Richard Riche is not content. He thinks, with so many changes, he should have been promoted.'

To what? What better thing could a man be, than Master of Augmentations? Riche has his estate in Essex. He has received Bartholomew, one of the greatest of London priories. But Rafe says, 'He has conceived a grudge, sir. Because you do not love him as you love Thomas Wyatt.'

'Wyatt will soon be home,' he says. It is perverse of Riche to raise a comparison. 'It just shows …' he says to Rafe; but he lets his sentence trail. It shows how unaccountable men are, what they harbour in their souls: which by no means shows on their faces.

Rafe says, 'You remember your neighbour Stow? When he came with a complaint, saying you had stolen part of his garden?'

'There was no trespass. Stow had his fence in the wrong place.'

'We know that at Austin Friars. You said, I know where my boundaries are. But Stow went through the town bad-mouthing you. His family complains and everybody believes them.'

He reads the lesson that Rafe intends. He has stolen nothing from the Earl of Oxford's family. But the Veres think they own the chamberlain's post by long continuance in it, and they intended to hold it while the world endures.

When he meets Gardiner, the bishop says, 'My congratulations, Cromwell.'

'Essex,' he says. 'I am Thomas Essex now.'

'You confounded the French,' Gardiner says. 'They were sure the Cleves debacle had finished you. And if not Cleves, then the heretics in Calais, claiming you for their own. Do you know there was a soothsayer called Calchas, who survived his predicted hour of death, and died of laughing?'

'But then there was the poet Petrarch. He lay as one dead for the best part of a day. His people were praying for his soul. But just before the burial party was due, he sat up – and then he lived another thirty years. *Thirty years*, Stephen.'

* * *

Parliament assembles and the court is filling up, the biggest court in years. He sees Jane Rochford in conversation with Norfolk. They look earnest; her kinsman is showing her some deference, by God.

He traps her later, his tone teasing. 'What was Uncle Norfolk telling you?'

'Things convenient for me to know.'

She swings away from him, haughty, angry: useless. He thinks, I've lost her. When did that happen?

His son's wife comes to him; 'I bring news of needlework. I know your lordship is interested.'

He tilts his head: I'm listening.

'I was bidden to do a piece of work. One of the maids could have done it, but it was handed to me out of malice. It was something of Jane's. Jane the queen, my sister, it was her girdle book, her little prayers. I was told, take this and pick the initials out. I said, I will not do it. I am Mistress Cromwell, not some servant.'

'Lady Cromwell,' he reminds her.

'I should have said so, should I not? I forgot. My title is too new.'

She is on the brink of angry tears, and he would like to put his arms around her, but better not. Bess should not be stitching, unstitching; she could run a field camp, or direct a siege.

'The next thing I see, Katherine Howard is wearing it at her waist. It is not the first gift she has had, that belonged to some lady better than she will ever be. The king wants to have her in his bed, to maul her about and see if he can do aught. And her people will say to her, do not gratify him, do not give way, do not so much as glance in his direction. I know.' Her face is set. 'We Seymours did it ourselves. We cannot complain – though we do. The Howards believe he might marry her. And who is to say he will not?'

He feels weary. 'What does Anna say? She must know.' He has seen her demeanour: sullen, listless. 'She should give the king no cause to complain. If I were to advise her –'

'But you do not. You don't go near her.'

If he were to counsel Anna, it would be to patience. The dowager

Katherine won the admiration of all, when she sat smiling by the king she supposed her husband, through hours of court ceremonies, hours which stretched into years. Never was she seen with tears on her cheeks, or an angry frown.

'Yes,' Bess says, 'Katherine was a great pattern for womanhood. She died alone and friendless, did she not?'

On May Day, Richard Cromwell is to fight in the tournament at Greenwich, scheduled to fill five days with combat, spectacle and public rejoicing. He rides for the challengers, called the Gentlemen of England: among his team-mates, the gallant and handsome Thomas Seymour, and among his foes, the young Earl of Surrey, making his public debut in the lists.

Gregory no doubt will fight next year. For now he is a practice opponent. He has not Richard's weight, but he has style and no fear, the best armour, the best horseflesh.

'Tom Culpeper,' Gregory explains. 'We are studying what he will do. He is the king's favourite, he has money laid on him. Richard is drawn against him in the foot combat. He does not come against him in the joust.'

The foot combat is the most ruthless of all the tournament games. It is *ad hominem*. There is no place to hide.

'A likely young man,' he says. 'He is handsome.'

'Not when I've finished with him,' Richard says.

Both Suffolk and Norfolk are present when the contests open, and they greet each other with their usual empty civility. Suffolk would rise from the dead, he declares, to be at such an occasion, because in his day he held the palm: myself and the king, he says, always Harry and me. Gods, we were, in our time.

If you sit close to the king, under the canopy with the arms of England and France, you feel his body rigid with tension, his muscles jumping as if he were himself in the saddle. Henry sees, notes, scores every move, and at the end of a bout he drops back in his chair, releasing his breath as the winner and loser are led away, their lathered horses sidestepping and curvetting, their helmets off to acknowledge the crowd.

Young Surrey rides seven times: he has no special success, but he is not unhorsed either. Norfolk, he suspects, prefers proper fighting. The Howard entourage make a good deal of noise, but provided a show is made, and the family honour is upheld, the duke seems little interested in the finer points. He is not one to pine for old times, when it comes to a contest of arms; given his choice, he would haul up a cannon, and blast the foe to Jerusalem.

Between the contests musicians play. They sing 'England be Glad', their voices lost in the open air. Then they play the Bear Dance, and Montard Brawle, which makes the ladies jump in their seats and beat time, and all those who are not in armour clap their hands. The queen is sedate, her hands folded, but she watches all that passes with a wide and interested gaze; she looks to the king for a signal for when to applaud and when to despond.

He, Essex, goes in and out, as messengers call on him. 'News from Ireland,' he says briefly to the king. While the silk pennants flutter and the trumpets call, he is crawling through bog and brush, after the O'Connors, the O'Neills, the Kavanaghs and the Breens: the wreckers, burners and despoilers, ready to open their ports to Pole's ships.

When Richard makes his first run, his lance lifts his opponent clean out of the saddle. It is the cleanest strike seen in years. You have seen a vulgar boy plunge his knife into a loaf, and wave it around on the point? That is how the enemy is hoisted, flying into the air while his horse carries on without him. You hardly hear him hit the ground because the courtiers are yelling like drunks at a bear-baiting.

Richard collects his horse and turns him. His grooms rush to the end of the barrier to make sure he wheels wide of the tilt. Richard shows the crowd his mailed glove, empty, as if they did not know his lance was splintered. Henry is on his feet, a blaze of gold. He is beside himself, laughing and crying. They are waving Richard back to the king, but through the narrow slit in his helmet most probably he cannot see the signal; now a squire takes his bridle, and his mount flecked with lather steps up, snorting, harness ringing. The king takes a diamond from his finger: he is mouthing something; Richard's mailed arm reaches out.

Next day is Sunday. Richard Cromwell kneels, and rises Sir Richard. Henry kisses him. He says, 'Richard, you are my diamond.'

On 3 May the challengers and the answerers fight on horseback, with rebated swords. Fitzwilliam, Lord Admiral, sits beside him and talks below the clatter. 'The word from the border is that the Scots are gathering a fleet. Their ambassador says James plans to sail to France to visit his kin. But our agents say he is bound for Ireland.'

He glances across at Norfolk. 'A pity the Scot does not come by land. My lord is always looking to fight his father's battles over again. He is short of glory these days.'

Fitzwilliam says, 'I want twenty ships. I must be at the Irish coast before James, to chase him back to the open sea.'

He nods. 'I will see you supplied.'

A great roar rises from the crowd: another knight spilled from his saddle to the green and springy ground, crunching in his weight of mail and tumbling arse-over-pate. The winner removes his helmet: the spectators applaud: *Cromwell!* they shout. Fitzwilliam says abruptly, 'You are popular in this arena.'

'It's my nephew they are shouting for. I should send Richard to the council in my stead, to explain what I have spent.'

The bills are coming in for the conveyance of the queen by land and sea. Her thirteen trumpeters alone have cost us near a hundred pounds. Just this morning he had a chit for more than a hundred and forty pounds for work on the king's tomb – which is unfair, considering that Henry is never going to die. He complains, 'It has cost us two thousand marks to honour the Duke of Bavaria as we waved him goodbye.'

The Lord Admiral says, 'Surely that would be a sound investment for you? Even if you found it from your own purse.'

He does not ask Fitz to enlarge on what he means. He is thinking about the tomb: one hundred and forty-two pounds, eleven shillings and tenpence. Have you ever seen the Wound Man, in a surgeons' manual? There is a caltrop beneath his foot, a spear through his calf, and between his ribs an arrow, the shaft snapped. There is a cleaver in his shoulder, a sword in his gut, a dagger through his eye. He is bleeding money. Just as well he has persuaded Parliament into a two-year subsidy for the king. It will not be popular in the country. But there are forts to build, as well as ships to fit. He never believed in the amity between François and the Emperor, but he does believe they would put aside their quarrels for an immediate object: the invasion of England. He says to Fitz, 'They will come in by Ireland if they can, either one of them. Conciliate them, the king says; but he is a fool if he believes anything they say.'

'I'll tell him you said so, shall I?'

Down below, the arms of Cromwell snap in the breeze. For Richard, these are the greatest days of his life. More than his marriage, the birth of his sons, his grants of lands, his commissions under the king; more than his prosperity, his security, are these moments when muscles and bone and the conqueror's eye are indefeasible; when the heart leaps and the sight dazzles and time seems to stretch on all sides and cushion you like a snowfield, like a feather bed. He thinks of Brother Frisby, tumbled in the snow at Launde, shining like a seraph.

Richard is a hard-headed man. He knows this way of knocking a man over is arcane, expensive, obsolete. But he wants to rise in this world, as Cromwells do. His grandsire was a Tudor archer. His father plied the law. Now he is a knight of the realm. Surrey's expression, beneath his helm, can only be inferred.

Fitz says, 'Did you ever don helm and harness, my lord?'

By Christ no, he thinks. We pikemen were too poor for mail. We went in boiled leather which we hardened by prayer. We wore other men's boots.

Blowing in from the coast, Wyatt does not even sit down before he says, 'Bonner is Bishop of London? You think that serves you?'

'He is. I did. I doubt him now.'

Bonner is a plump pink man; he looks foolish, but his brain is as sharp as a sharpened nail. He is back from France, installed in his see, and already it seems he may be an ingrate, or double. He, Essex, is not easy to mislead, but these days men are friends at the gate and foes at the door. 'I thought he was one of us. Perhaps he's every-body's. But still,' he says, 'Bonner knows things. About Gardiner, his practices in France.'

'You should not promote a man because he hates Gardiner. That is no safe way.' Wyatt walks about. 'I hear you dined.'

'I dined. Stephen looked as if he were swallowing tadpoles.'

'You have had Suffolk here, your people say. Be warned. He will not stand with you if you need a friend.'

'You and Brandon have been at odds for ten years. And I have forgotten why.'

'So have I. So has he. It does not mean we can make peace.'

'Go home to Bess Darrell,' he says. 'Go down to Allington and enjoy the summer. Bess has helped me. And I am now able to help you in your turn.'

'You owe me nothing,' Wyatt says. 'The obligation is all the other way. I have been in agony, as to what you would think of me. I obeyed my instructions. Make a breach, you said, tear François and the Emperor apart. I have done it, but I fear I have not helped you.'

'Their enmities were so old, so ingrained,' he says, 'that you should not give yourself all the credit. They only reverted to the pattern they knew. Anyway, you followed your instructions, what else could you do? Be assured, it is no detriment to me.'

'Except you stand to lose your queen.'

So Wyatt knows everything. The waves of the Narrow Sea rustle like sheets, whispering through Europe the news of Henry's incapac-ity. 'It will be a poor game without her, it's true.'

Wriothesley comes in. 'Wyatt? I thought it was you.' They embrace, comrades-in-arms. 'You can explain to us what is happen-ing here.'

'But I have been out of the realm,' Wyatt says.

'That does not weigh. In it, out of it, we neither walk on the earth nor swim nor fly, we do not know which element we dwell in. Summer is coming, but the king rains and shines like April. Men change their religion as they change their coats. The council makes a resolution and next minute forgets it. We write letters and the words expunge. We are playing chess in the dark.'

'On a board made of jelly,' he says.

'With chessmen of butter.'

Wyatt says, 'Your images upheave me.'

'Then make us better ones, dear heart,' Wriothesley says.

When they embraced, he saw Call-Me's eyes over Wyatt's shoulder. They were like Walter's eyes, one day when he had burned himself in the forge. He had walked away, silent, to plunge his arm in water: he uttered nothing, neither oath nor self-reproof, but sweat started out on his forehead, and his legs buckled.

This year, business tears him away from the feast. The Lord Deputy of Ireland must be replaced, and the need is urgent. It is four or five years since he backed Leonard Grey for the post: well, there again he was mistaken. There are councillors who say the only way forward is to depopulate the island and resettle it with Englishmen. But, he thinks, the Irish would shrink into the interior, and hide in holes where rats could not live.

He says to Audley, 'There are rumours that Pole's army has landed in Galway. Or else in Limerick. I doubt Reynold could tell them apart, or say if he was in Ireland or the Land of Nod. If his past wanderings are any guide, he will try to invade us by way of Madrid.'

Audley looks at him: how can you make a joke? He is solemnity personified, now he has been elected to the Garter, and has a chain and a new George shining on his breast.

When Lord Lisle got a permit to leave Calais for the Garter feast, he thought it a mark of favour. He is surprised to be ordered before the council, and questioned. It is an open secret that members of his household have quit their posts and made their way to Rome. The boy Mathew, among others, has brought home fat files of evidence. But the Lord Privy Seal has not got what he wants – one damning document, to link the Lord Deputy to Pole.

Rafe says, 'At this point we usually arrest Francis Bryan, do we not? When we cannot make the answers fit the questions?'

He smiles. Bryan knows all about Calais, it is true. He could help bring Lisle down, maybe also the ambassador Valloppe. But who will believe Francis? The Vicar of Hell has drained too many cups. He has played too many hands, he has given too much offence: if you think *in vino veritas*, look at Francis. Yet he knows everybody's secrets, and appears to be everybody's cousin. He has friends in every treasury, watchmen at every port.

Rafe shrugs, as if trying to shift an ill-balanced load. We servants of the king must get used to games we cannot win but fight to an exhausted draw, their rules unexplained. Our instructions are full of snares and traps, which mean as we gain we lose. We do not know how to proceed from minute to minute, yet somehow we do, and another night falls on us in Greenwich, at Hampton Court, at Whitehall.

The king wonders aloud, what shall we do when knights of the Garter are found to be traitors – men like Nicholas Carew? Certainly their names should be stricken from the volumes that contain the history of the order. But will that not mar the beauty of the pages?

The decision is that the disgraced name should remain. But the words 'VAH! PRODITUR' should be written in the margin, so the man is branded for ever.

Vah! He thinks of Gardiner, trying to cough up his tadpoles: by now his evil mind has swollen them, he will have to spew them as frogs. 'The man he needs is St Aelred,' Gregory says. 'When the saint met with a swollen man clutching his belly, Aelred at once stuffed his fingers down the patient's throat; he vomited, with his frogs, seven pints of bile.'

He says to his son, 'I have some news for you. It is a blow, I must confess.'

In making him earl, the king has granted twenty-four manors in Essex, besides holdings in other counties. But in return he wants the manor of Wimbledon, and the house at Mortlake.

Gregory blinks. 'Why?'

'You know he cannot ride so far now. He wants to join one great park to another, so he can move west of London and still be on his own ground. I will show you the map. You will see the sense in it.'

He does not open his account books to work out how much money he has spent on his Mortlake house. He thought it would be his for life.

Gregory says, 'You won't miss your old haunts, surely?'

Since he was a child Gregory has moved in the orbit of princes. Putney's nothing to him, those fields that Walter scrabbled for, the sheep-runs for which he fought his neighbours.

Gregory says, 'Take heart, my lord father. Not only was Aelred good for stomach pains, he was sovereign for broken bones. He made the dumb to speak.'

He asks, 'What did they say?'

When he judges the time is right, he sends men for Lisle: ten at night, to rouse him from his bed and take him to the Tower. He will order Bishop Sampson moved there too. It will be convenient to get their confessions together, as the facts are so enmeshed. He does not need the bishop arraigned, just in ward, out of the council and out of the pulpit. Cranmer will take the vacant place in the rota at Paul's: it is time the lovers of scripture had their say. The other bishops should take warning by Sampson's arrest. He has five names on his list. He lets that fact be known. Which names they are, he holds back.

Lisle, too, can be held till the evidence fits. In Calais he can be replaced with a man more active and competent. He thinks about Wyatt: why not? The French are frightened of Monsieur Hoyet. Though, as someone says, they hardly fear him as much as the English do.

The day after Lisle's arrest, the man John Husee waits for him at dawn, to implore. He says to him, 'Keep yourself out of this, Husee. You have been a good servant and deserve a better master.'

Honor Lisle is still in Calais. Mr Wriothesley says, 'On consideration, sir, we should have secured her with her husband; of the two, she is the more papistical.'

'She can be held at home,' he says. 'Arrange it, would you?' He sees, in an instant and for the first time: I am not ruthless enough for Sir Thomas Wriothesley.

Now he tells Husee, 'Lady Lisle were better, if she has letters, to surrender them rather than burn them. I am adept at construing the ashes.'

After the king gives permission for his uncle's arrest, he retires to prayer. But he will not see Lord Lisle, for all his begging. The news has come from Scotland that his new wife has given King James a son. 'I could have married that lady,' the king says. 'But my councillors were too slow to act, and unwilling.'

In the noble city of Ghent, the Emperor sits in a hall draped in black, dealing out fates. He strips the guilds of their privileges, levies a fine, impounds weapons and knocks down part of the walls as well as the principal abbey, announcing that he will build a fortress garrisoned with Spanish troops. He parades the chief citizens barefoot, in the smocks of penitents, nooses around their necks. The executions have gone on for a month.

In times past you have thought, if you have to get into bed with Charles or François, Charles is the less diseased. But now who can choose: two loathly partners, sweating and seeping? 'They call our king a killer,' he tells Brandon, 'but when I compare –'

'By God, they have gall!' says the duke. 'With all of his troubles with men and women both, with traitors and rebels and councillors false, I call him an anointed saint.'

Norfolk and Gardiner visit each other as they did before the duke went to France. His informants say, 'Norfolk has the girl Katherine with him. At Gardiner's house they played a masque. It was *Magnificence*. Sir, they played it against you.'

It is an old thing of Skelton's, written against Wolsey in his time. When carters become courtiers, is the burden of it: how the upstart vaunts, how he sins, how the commonwealth is abused. The players are Collusion and Abusion, Folly and Mischief, and Magnificence himself, who proclaims:

'I reign in my robes, I rule as me list,
I drive down these dastards with a dint of
my fist.'

But at length Magnificence is brought low, he is beaten and shamed, spoiled of all he has and plunged into poverty. Enter Despair, tempting him to make an end by stabbing or hanging himself, the sorriest knave that ever was damned.

Just in time comes Good Hope, and saves him.

But if you think your audience would prefer it, there is always the choice to end the play early, leaving Magnificence in the dust.

Rafe says, 'Call-Me was there. At Gardiner's masque.'

'Was he?' He is disturbed. 'Looking after our interests, I am sure.'

Whispers have come from Gardiner's private office. The bishop has set his people to look into Call-Me's finances. They share territory in Hampshire; their business cannot help but be entangled, and if there is sharp practice, it could not long be hidden from the bishop. He says, 'I wish Call-Me would come to me, and let us look at the figures together.'

Sometimes transactions have holes in them. Sometimes columns fail to tally. To mend the matter, it is possible to be ingenious, without being dishonest.

He says, 'If Gardiner sends for Call-Me, he has no choice but to answer. If something is alleged against him he must hear what it is.'

He thinks, Wriothesley will accuse me of teaching him covetousness. I would have taught him accountancy, if he had ever sat still to listen. He says to Rafe, 'Perhaps there is a deal to be done. Gardiner has much to hide himself, if someone cared to spy it out.'

After the evening of the masque, Katherine Howard does not return to her duties at court. The queen's people report that Anna is relieved to see her go. But Anna does not know our history, or she would realise this bodes her no good. The maid has been re-installed at Lambeth, in her family's house, but now she has maids of her own and is served with deference by those who hope she will carry them to high fortune. In the evenings, the king's barge crosses the water.

His minstrels play 'The Jester's Dance', and 'La Manfredina' and 'My Lord and Lady Depart'. Henry stays with her till late, rowing back after sunset, the drums and flutes silent.

He thinks of the surgeons, their bloody book. Carved and pierced and sliced, Wound Man stands upright on the page. He holds out his arms, one half-severed at the wrist: 'Come on, come on, what else have you got?'

He has kept his word to the king: a tractable Parliament has given the treasury what it needs. Before summer it will disperse, without a day appointed to meet again. Though he, Essex, has shed his duties as Secretary, he seems more pressed than ever, preparing for invisible dangers. If Pole is really heading to Ireland, his sails are not seen. Lord Admiral Fitzwilliam leaves his captains on watch, and returns to take his place in council.

The fact that Lord Lisle is in the Tower does not prevent him hurling accusations. The only way to stop him would be to stop asking questions. He insists that Lord Cromwell has acted as patron of all heretics in Calais these seven years past, circumventing justice and holding in contempt the king's commands.

Lisle will not be specific, when and where and who. In his position, you would fling mud and hope it would stick. His wife is now under house arrest. He, Essex, is unsurprised to hear that the Lisles have not paid their household servants for two and a half years.

6 June, the king calls him in. 'My lord, I hear you have been assailed.'

Assailed? 'I am used to that.'

'Insulted openly,' the king says, 'at the performance of a masque. But I have let it be known, that those who denigrate Cromwell, denigrate their king. It is for me, no one else, to reprove or reward my servants.'

They have not spoken – the king and his chief councillor – about the Duke of Norfolk's niece. Now the king allows himself one angry outburst. 'I pay a compliment to some sweet little fool, and the world says I am going to wed her. What have you done to counter this?'

He says, 'It is Norfolk's part to counter it. Besides, the world is answered, surely. Your Majesty cannot marry. He has a wife.'

Henry says, 'Wilhelm was in Ghent. He saw the Emperor. They have reached some accommodation. Or else – I know not which – they have reached some impasse.'

Something is needling Henry, beyond the matter at hand, making him querulous, edgy. I will know by and by, he thinks, I shall not avoid knowing. He says, 'We are not yet informed what has passed in Ghent. And I would not trust the first information. I never do.'

'Well, it is you who gets it,' Henry snaps. 'I know letters come to you, that should come to me. I am obliged to send to your house, and be a suitor for knowledge of my own affairs. Surely someone can tell us whether Cleves and the Emperor have parted friends? For if they have not, then it signals war. It is no good to go to Parliament and get me the subsidy, my lord, if it is spent at once, on a war I do not want, for a man who uses me ill –'

'I do not believe Wilhelm will go to war.'

'Oh? Then you think he is making terms with the Emperor? Behind my back? I have long suspected Cleves is not honest. He wants to play me and the Emperor both. He wants the surety of my troops behind him, so he can stand up and make demands of Charles. He wants Charles to give him the Duchess Christina, and he will try to keep Guelders too.'

'A bold scheme,' he says, 'but he might contrive it. Would you not do the same?'

'Perhaps if I had no conscience,' Henry says, 'and no fear. No sense of duty owed. Perhaps if this were twenty years back. Your man Machiavelli claims that fortune favours the young.'

'He isn't my man.'

'No? Then who is?'

'You were seen in the mirror of princes, before I ever showed my face. You lack no art or craft to rule.'

'And yet,' Henry says, 'you break my heart. You claim, all I think and do is for you, sir. But you refuse to extricate me from this unholy, unsanctified misalliance. You would leave me cursed – without hope of further offspring, allied to heresy, and exposed to the peril and expense of war.'

'Excuse me,' he says. He walks across the gallery, to where the sunlight floods in, and hides from him the sight of a knot of courtiers, staring at him from a distance. He thinks, I am walking above the clouds.

He turns. 'Your Majesty keeps Christina's portrait behind a curtain.'

'I could have had her,' Henry says, 'if you had pleased. Nothing would satisfy Cromwell, but I must wed a Lutheran's sister.'

'Your Majesty knows, I think, that Duke Wilhelm is not a Lutheran. Like your Majesty, he walks his own path, a guiding light to his people.'

The king begins to speak – then hesitates, abdicating from his own thoughts. When he continues, it is lightly, as if he is trying out a joke. 'Norfolk has asked me, how much was Cromwell paid, to arrange the Cleves match?'

'He knows where I get my income, I have no doubt. As you do, sir.'

Still that buoyancy in Henry's voice: 'I told you, nothing is secret from me. Norfolk says, "And besides what he received to make the match, what is he paid to arrange the continuance?" It must be a huge sum, Norfolk thinks, for you to run against my displeasure, ever since the turn of the year.'

He must pick his words carefully: make no promises he cannot keep. 'I will do what I can, but if you repudiate the queen, I cannot avert evil consequences.'

'Are you threatening me?' Henry asks.

'God forbid.'

'He does.'

The king turns away and stares at the wall. As if he has become entranced by the panelling, absorbed into the linenfold.

* * *

Next day he is not due to see the king. But he half-expects some message. Henry loves to run you about the countryside, cries of 'Urgent, Urgent,' sounding in your ears, like the cries of hounds on the scent.

A letter comes. He reads and digests it: the king's orders. He files it. He waits to be summoned: nothing. He pulls the letter out of his files, and gives it to Wriothesley: he thinks, Call-Me will pull it out anyway, his curiosity will get the better of him, and if he is reporting to Gardiner – well, let him. These next few days, we must try conclusions.

Wriothesley says, the letter in his hand, 'The king would not elevate you, sir, only to destroy you. And he would not make these requests, if he did not mean you to see them through.'

The Book Called Henry: *never say what he will not do.* He sits down. 'I understand he wishes a resolution with the queen's grace. But my difficulty is, I must break it to the council as news, that the marriage is not consummated. I can tell Fitzwilliam, the king says. And one or two others if I must. Whereas everybody knows already. They know the thing failed at the outset.'

He passes a hand across his face. His Irish files lie untouched. It is supper time, and he does not want his supper, and Secretary Wriothesley looks as if he has no appetite either. Which is a pity, as Wyatt has sent early strawberries from Kent.

Call-Me says, 'You can work with the pre-contract, sir. You have done more difficult things. We would have to find a pension for the lady. And whatever the brother demands, by way of recompense. Though as she is still a maid, Cleves may find her another husband, and that would be a relief to our exchequer.'

He thinks, Anna may feel she has had enough of men. His fingers inside her. *C'est tout.*

'To save the king's face,' Call-Me says, 'we will mention his scruples. The fear that the lady might be unfree, and contracted to Lorraine, weighed so heavy on the king's mind, that he determined to leave her intact, till the matter should be resolved. Which it has not –'

'But why should I attempt –?' he says

'– and by now the king believes, as any man would, that the councillors of Cleves deliberately delay –'

'– why should I? If Anna goes, in comes Norfolk with his little drab on his arm. He thought he could rule through his other niece, but Anne knocked him back. This one will be tractable, you can tell by looking at her. Norfolk believes he can put me out of the council, and he and his new friend Gardiner will lead us back to Rome. But I won't go, Call-Me. I'll fight. And when you see Stephen again, you can tell him so from me.'

He sees Wriothesley shrink, like a dog under the whip. He is whimpering beneath his burden of knowledge, as all the king's creatures do.

That night he dreams he is at Whitehall, on the spiral stair that leads to the cockpit. Here below ground the gamecocks circle, red birds and white, their feathers raised into ruffs. Here they sport, rising with a flurry of wings into the air, talons locked: flailing with steel spurs, pecking at eyes, gouging breasts and ripping wings. Here one dies, while the spectators roar and stamp; spattered with blood, they slap palms and pay their debts. The dead cock is raked from the sand and thrown to a cur.

In the morning he is at Westminster, where he attends the sitting of the Lords. He dines. At three in the afternoon he is making his way to the council chamber, Audley at his side, Fitzwilliam behind him. Norfolk flitters through the sunlight, either before or behind, conversing with minions who have their swords at their sides.

It is a boisterous day, and as they cross the court the wind takes his hat off. He grabs at it, but it is gone, bowling in the direction of the river.

He looks around the party, and the nape of his neck bristles. The councillors make no move to uncover. They continue walking. He strides out as if to shake them off, but they bunch around him, matching their pace to his.

'An ill wind,' he says, 'to take off my hat, and leave yours.' He remembers Wolf Hall, the still evening, Henry's arm around his shoulders. The interior of the house opened before them; musicians played the king's song, 'If love now reigned', and together they strolled in for their supper.

Now the sunlight picks out a silver thread in the stuff of Lord Audley's jacket. It dapples the Lord Admiral's coat of blue brocade. It makes a red flicker at the corner of his eye and he puts his hand to his chest, over his heart, but his knife is not there: only silk, linen, skin. Rafe was right, of course. When you need it you can't use it.

From below, a tug at his sleeve. 'You lost this, my lord Essex?'

The little lad is puffed with pride: at the hat retrieval, and at knowing which lord is which. He reaches for a coin, looks into the upturned face. 'Don't I know you? You used to bring rushes to York Place.'

'Bless you,' the boy says, 'that would be my brother Charles. I am George, I am as like to him as my mother could form me. It's easy to mistake us and many do it. But Charles –' He reaches up, to show the size his brother is now.

'He must be,' he says. When Charles carried rushes, Anne Boleyn was a mere marquise: and because he was on his way to her lair, Charles had asked him, 'Have you a holy medal, to protect you?'

He says, 'Commend me to your brother. I hope he thrives? And you too, master. Thank you for my hat.'

He thinks he sees Stephen Gardiner, a black shape against rosy brick. Where are the secretaries, he thinks, one or both should attend … His throat is dry. His heart is shaking. His body knows, and his head is catching up; meanwhile, we are bound for a council meeting.

They have passed undercover. The summer day recedes. He thinks, I have parted with my last supporter there: George whooping across the close, spinning his reward in the air. He cannot see Riche. He thinks, Wyatt told me Charles Brandon would not help me, and he cannot if he would, he is not here. But Norfolk has stolen in behind him. Flodden Norfolk, a father named after a battle: how do you like that, Cromwell?

He thinks, my father Walter would not have left his knife at home. If my father were here, I would not be afraid. But the enemy would. If Walter were here, they would be crouching under the council board, pissing themselves.

He looks around. 'Is my lord archbishop on his way?'

Fitzwilliam says, 'We do not expect him.'

Gardiner has followed them in. He is blocking the door. 'What's this, Winchester?' he says. 'Are you back on the council?'

'Imminently,' Gardiner says.

'We'll see how long that lasts, shall we? Anyone take a bet?' He sits. 'Our numbers are down. But shall we begin?'

Fitzwilliam says, 'We do not sit down with traitors.'

He is ready for them – on his feet, his jaw set, his eyes narrowed, his breath short. Norfolk says, 'I will tear out your heart and stuff it in your mouth.' The clerks, their folios held across their chests, have stepped back to let the king's halberdiers fill the room. The councillors fall on him. Like pack animals they yelp and snarl, they grunt and flail. Fitzwilliam is trying to pull his Garter badge from his coat. He bats him away, gives Norfolk a shove that knocks him into the table. But Fitzwilliam comes back. They tug, kick, haul. He is barged and buffeted, his gold chain is off, and he puts his head down, he puts his fists up, he lands a blow, and he is roaring, he is convulsed with rage, he does not know what he says, nor cares: and then it is over. They have taken the chain and the George. Someone has swept his papers from the board.

William Kingston is a big man and the councillors fall back for him. 'My lord? You must come with these guards.' He speaks like a man with perfect faith. 'You will walk with me advisedly. I will hold fast by your side and lead you through the crowd.'

There is only one place Kingston leads you. At the sight of Kingston with a warrant, the lord cardinal's great heart failed him. His legs would not hold him up, and he sat down on a chest; he made his lament and said his prayers.

In the doorway, Gardiner says, 'Adieu, Cromwell.'

He stops. 'Give me my title.'

805

'You have no title. It's gone, Cromwell. You are no more than God made you. May He take you to His mercy.'

The sunlight whites out the spectators. The councillors surge out after him. Evidently they will do no business; or they regard it as done.

He thinks, the only man who could help me now is the man who shot Packington. He might not succeed with so many targets. Where would I direct his aim?

There is a boat waiting for him. It has been organised so neatly you would think he had done it himself. A two-minute brawl, he thinks, but they must have reckoned on that. Perhaps somebody gets a fist in his face – but there are so many against one. They know the end of it all. They dust themselves off, they bundle me out.

Today is 10 June. It was three in the afternoon when he crossed the court and lost his hat. It is not yet four. There are hours of daylight left. He says to Kingston, 'My lord archbishop is not arrested?'

'I have had no such order,' Kingston says brusquely; then adds, 'Be easy in your mind about that.'

'Gregory?'

'I saw your son in the Commons, an hour ago. I have no orders there.'

'And Sir Rafe?' He is careful about titles today.

'It is possible he was waylaid, to keep him from the meeting. But again, I have no orders about Master Secretary.'

He does not ask, what about Wriothesley? He says, 'Will you send for someone from my household, to wait on me till I am released?'

Kingston says, 'It is not our custom to leave a gentleman without a servant. Give us a name and he will be fetched.'

'Send to Austin Friars, and ask for Christophe.'

He thinks, they have bruised me, but it will not hurt until tomorrow. The water rocks beneath them, cerulean blue. The Tower is in sight. The flint sparkles like sunlight on the sea.

PART SIX

I

Mirror

June–July 1540

Sunset, Christophe stands on the threshold. His clothes are torn and his eye is blacked. 'They made me swear an oath,' he says, 'that if I stayed with you I would report any treason you spoke. I swore it, and then I went outside and spat.' He paces the room. 'The river lies beyond. Escape can be committed.'

'Turniphead,' he says. 'How can escape be committed? And if it could, how would that leave my family? Do you think you are all coming with me, to Utopia in one big boat?'

He thinks, at least Christophe has not stuck my knife in anybody; or if he has, they haven't found the corpse.

'They came trampling,' the boy says. 'They demanded keys and I said, give them nothing. But Thomas Avery and those people, they obeyed.'

'They had no choice.'

'They came like an army. "Everything here belongs to the king." They carried our money away from our strongroom. They broke the lock on our closet, where you alone have the key. I said to one, "Watch your feet, you beast of the field, if you walk mud on that carpet of silk flowers, the Lord Cromwell will personally shred the flesh from your bones." But no, he walked on it. They went down in the cellars with torches. They came up and said, "Bones!"'

Bones and relics, some nameless, some marked with their origin. He thinks, I will send a message: go down to the cellar and find Becket, then pull his label off. That will finish him.

He asks, 'Who led them?'

'Who would it be, but Call-Me?'

He looks up. 'You were not surprised?'

'No one was surprised. But we were all disgusted.'

He thinks, when Gardiner approached Wriothesley, he did not put a reasonable proposition: which do you choose, Cromwell or me? His offer was: choose me or death.

Christophe says, 'They threw your papers in boxes to carry away. Call-Me directed where to go – look in this chest, open that. But he did not find all he expected, so then he shouted. Thomas Avery said, "I have suspected Call-Me for months – why did my master entertain him?"'

'Christ entertained Judas. Not that I force the comparison.'

'Then Richard Riche came. He also shouted. "Look in the yellow chest in the window."' Christophe grins. 'The yellow chest is gone.'

Gone with it are his letters from the Swiss divines: which would injure him. They may choose to say he is a heretic who denies that God is in the host. But they will have no evidence. And he has no difficulty in saying that God is everywhere.

'All look for your restoration,' Christophe says. 'You will walk back in and all will be as it was. Meanwhile, I am here to serve you.' He gazes up at the gilded ceiling. 'I feared to find you in a dungeon.'

'Have you not been here before?'

He rebuilt these rooms himself, seven years back, for Anne Boleyn to lodge before her coronation. It was he who reglazed them, and ordered the goddesses on the walls; who had their eyes changed from brown to blue, when Jane Seymour came in. You enter through a great guard chamber. There is a presence chamber, where he now sits in a large light space; there is a dining room, a bedroom, and a small oratory. 'It is not for my comfort,' he says, 'so much as for those who will come to put questions to me. I expect them soon.'

For the king's councillors were prepared for my arrest, if I was not. How did they work it? What backhand whispers, what lifts of the eyebrow, what nods, winks? And what conferences with the king, their informants greasing in as I went out? No wonder Henry turned his back on me when last we spoke. No wonder he addressed himself to the wall. He says, 'Tell Thurston not to hang up his apron. I want him to send in my meals.'

'When you get out,' Christophe says, 'we nail down Norferk, pull his head off and toss it to the dogs. Riche, I'm spiking him to the floor and rats can nibble him, he can die slow as he likes, I am cheering. Call-Me, I am cutting his legs off and watch him crawl around the courtyard till he bleeds to death.'

He puts his head in his hands. He feels weakened by Christophe's agenda.

'It is to me entirely enjoyable,' Christophe says. 'I look forward. As for Henri, I shall kick him down Whitehall like a pig's bladder. Once he is exploded, we shall see who is king. When he is a smear on the cobbles, we shall see who is the last man standing.'

That first night, left alone, he tries to pray. Chapuys had asked him once, what will you do when one day Henry turns on you? He had said, arm myself with patience and leave the rest to God.

There are books which say, contemplate your final hour: live every day as if, that night, you go not to your bed but to your bier. The divines recommend this not just for the prisoner or invalid, but for the man in his pride and pomp, prosperity and health: for the merchant on the Rialto, for the governor in the senate.

But I am not ready, he thinks. Let me see the foe. And the king is mutable. Everybody knows that. We complain of it all the time.

Yet is there an instance – he cannot think of one – where, having turned his face away, Henry turns it back? He left Katherine at Windsor and he never saw her again. He rode away from Anne Boleyn, gave directions to kill her, and left her to strangers.

He has read a library of those volumes called Mirrors for Princes, which state the wise councillor must always prepare for his fall. He should embrace death as a privilege; does not St Paul say, I covet to be dissolved with Christ? But he covets nothing more than to be in his garden on this soft evening, now fading unused beyond the window: where a strong guard stands, in case Cromwell decides on a breath of air.

He puts his hand to his heart. He feels something alien inside his chest – as if the organ has been forced out of shape, stretched at one point and squeezed at another. How many days left? My enemies will try to rush Henry. In case they cannot keep him in this destructive frame of mind, they will want me killed this week. But if the king wants to be free of Anna, he should keep me alive to help him, and perhaps it will not be a simple matter or short. If I can survive two months, by then Henry will have quarrelled with Gardiner, and when he turns to Norfolk what will he find, but obstinacy and incapacity and spleen? So who will govern for him? Fitzwilliam? Tunstall? Audley? They are good enough men – good enough to be a chief minister's assistant. Three months, and his affairs will be in such disarray that he will be beseeching me to come back.

And I shall say, 'Not me, sir: I've had enough of you, I'm going to Launde.'

But next moment, within a heartbeat, I would snatch the seals from his hands: now, Majesty, where shall I begin?

He thinks of Thomas More, in ward for fifteen months. Continually he scribbled, till his pen and paper were taken away. Although, More could have freed himself at any moment. All he had to do was say some magic words.

When the Giant kills Jack, the Giant himself begins to fail. He is worn down and diminished with loneliness and regret. But it takes the Giant seven years to die.

Next morning Kingston comes in at eight o'clock. 'How do you?'

'I do very ill,' he says.

There are mirrors in the queen's lodging, as you would expect. He has seen himself, paper-faced, unshaven, unsteady.

'I have seen this before,' Kingston says. 'It afflicts not a few prisoners, in their early days. Especially if their downfall is sudden.'

'What remedy?'

Perhaps no one has ever asked Kingston this before. But he is not a man to hesitate. 'Accept it. Settle your mind. Make your reckoning with yourself, my lord.'

'I am still "my lord"?'

Kingston says, 'You came in here as Earl of Essex, and you are Essex unless I am told otherwise.'

So Gardiner was wrong: wrong on big things and wrong on little things. He is not sure if his earldom is a little thing. In the sight of God, perhaps it is. But he had felt it, this last two months, as protection, a wall the king had built around him.

'Also,' Kingston says, 'the king has sent money for your support while you are here. He wishes you to be kept as befits your rank.'

He wants to say, my support for how long? Kingston answers without being asked: 'The king will fund what is needed. No term is set.'

Till yesterday, he had money of his own. Now he is the king's beggar. Kingston says, as if it were a matter of indifference, 'Your boy is here.'

An uprush of anguish: 'Gregory?'

'I mean young Sadler. Or rather, Master Secretary, Sir Rafe, one forgets these recent promotions. No, bless you, he is not in ward, I mean he is without, he is waiting for you. Call for anything you need.'

In his black clothes Rafe looks overheated. 'Morning, sir. That wind has dropped. It's as warm as August out there. They say this will go on all summer. We can't be suited, can we? Warm, cold, we're always complaining.' His glance flits up and down the room, because he cannot look at his master. He takes off his cap and crushes it, his fingers bruising the velvet.

'Rafe,' he says, 'come here.' He embraces him. 'Kingston frightened me, I thought they had arrested you.'

Tentatively, Rafe touches his sleeve, as if to test if he is still solid. 'I think they would have, except the king does not want the disruption to his business. I hardly know where I am. Early this morning I sent Helen and the little ones out of London.'

'They will be watching you.' He sits down again. 'I am ill, Rafe. My breath comes short. I feel crushed, here. Kingston tells me I have to get used to it.'

'It is shock, sir. I did not know myself what was happening, or I would have got a warning to you somehow. As we were going into council, they had someone call me back for some footling piece of business – and next thing, as I was hastening in your direction, I saw a crowd streaming away. Audley said to me, "Your master is arrested, and I am going to the Parliament house to announce it." He was prepared. He had the paper in his pocket. He was just waiting for word from the guard.'

He thinks, I had scarcely a foot in the boat, and they were rowing me across the Styx. 'And how did Parliament take it?'

'In silence, sir.'

He nods. Both Lords and Commons might have been astonished, that a man made an earl in April is by June kicked out like a dog who's stolen the beef. But then, Parliament men do not expect to understand the king's mind. He does not answer for himself downwards, to his subjects – only upwards, to the Almighty; and perhaps, these days, not even that. To hear Henry talk, you would think God ought to be grateful, for all Henry has done for him in England these last ten years: the way he's set him up, got his big book translated, made him the common talk.

Rafe says, 'Edward Seymour went at once to the king, to speak for Gregory.'

'Did he speak for me?'

'No, sir.'

'Did anyone speak for me?'

'Yes. But I was not heard.'

'Not Cranmer?'

'Cranmer is writing the king a letter.'

'Try and get me its content.' He lowers his head. 'When I think of Call-Me … I wonder what inducement … I suppose I expected it of Riche. Though I have been good to them both.'

Rafe would be justified in saying, I told you at the first not to trust

Call-Me. Instead he says, 'All the years we have known him, I think he has been trying to show us his own unhappy nature. How fretful he is, how ill-at-ease, how envy eats away at him. He was trying to warn us about himself.'

'It is my vanity, really. I did not suppose anyone would prefer Gardiner's service to mine.'

'Gardiner has threatened him. But you know that. As for Purse, he runs to the day's winner.'

'Tell Gregory,' he says, 'to be as humble as he finds it necessary. He will be questioned, and he should say what they want to hear. Richard too.'

'Richard is enraged. He wanted to go straight to the king and break in on him.'

'Tell him to do no such thing. He should rest quiet, and keep away from Gregory, and both should keep away from you. Do nothing that could be called conspiracy. I know how Henry's mind works.'

Even as he says it, he thinks, that can't be true, or I wouldn't be here. Separation from his friends will not save my son. Money abroad will not save him. All he can do is to comply with Henry exactly, till his killing fit passes. 'How did he take it, Gregory?' He pictures his boy inconsolable, crying like a child.

'He is pensive, sir.'

Pensive? But then, if they had come to him when he was a boy to say, 'They're hanging your old dad tomorrow,' he wouldn't have been pensive. He'd have said, 'I'll be there early! Are they selling pies?'

He asks, 'Has the king let fall a word about what charges to expect? Or Audley has, perhaps?'

Rafe looks away. 'It appears to be about Mary as much as anything. The stories of how you meant to marry her. The king has decided to hear them at last. He has written to François about it – in his own hand, I am told. He has sent for Marillac, to explain your arrest to him. Though I think it is Marillac who will explain it to the king, because the French were active in those rumours.'

'Chapuys started them.'

'Perhaps. Who knows where it began? Perhaps in Mary's head. I would not be surprised. She is a very strange woman.'

'No,' he says, 'she is innocent in this, I swear.'

'You have always thought better of her than she deserves. I doubt she will stir for you, sir, though we all know you saved her life. Henry believes – but I do not know how he can believe it – that you meant to wed her and then thrust him aside and become king yourself.'

'That is ludicrous. How could he think that? How could I? How could I even imagine it? Where is my army?'

Rafe shrugs. 'He is frightened of you, sir. You have outgrown him. You have gone beyond what any servant or subject should be.'

It is the cardinal over again, he thinks. Wolsey was broken not for his failures, but for his successes; not for any error, but for grievances stored up, about how great he had become.

He asks, 'Did they take my books?'

'Tell me what you want and I will get it.'

'Will you find my Hebrew grammar? Nicolas Clendardus of Leuven. I have it at Stepney. I have wanted to study it. I lacked leisure.'

Clendardus advises, grasp the basic rules before you advance to detail. They say with his help you can learn the rudiments in three months. I might not live that long, he thinks, but I can make a start.

12 June, first interrogation: 'We might begin with the purple satin doublet,' Richard Riche says.

Riche sits at one end of the long table, with Gardiner and Norfolk established in the places of honour; and Master Secretary Wriothesley, restless and unhappy, at the other end. 'You know,' he says, as Norfolk and Gardiner take their seats, 'I never knew you as such great comrades, till lately. More likely to abuse each other roundly, than sit together as friends.'

'We have not always seen eye to eye,' Norfolk says. 'But one thing we have in common, Winchester and I – when we scent the truth, we stick on the trail. So beware, Cromwell. Whatever we suspect, we will have out of you, one way or the other.'

It is as crude a threat as ever made. He says, 'I will tell you the truth, as I know and believe it. There is nothing for you beyond that.'

Gardiner sharpens his pen. 'They say Truth is the daughter of time. I wish time bred like rabbits. We would arrive at a reckoning sooner.'

A clerk comes in. He greets him in Welsh. 'Give you good morning, Gwyn. Nice sunny weather.'

'None of that,' Norfolk growls. 'Get this fellow out and send another scribe.'

Gwyn gathers his gear and exits. It takes time to locate a clerk that suits Thomas Howard, and one Thomas Cromwell does not know. At length they are settled. Wriothesley says, 'Will you go on, Riche? The doublet?'

Riche lays a hand on his papers, like one putting it on the gospels. 'You understand, sir, that it is my duty to put these questions to you, and that I bear you no ill-will in the doing of it.'

He recognises a disclaimer. Riche thinks Henry might recall him. He says, 'Can I see the king?'

'No, by God,' Norfolk says.

Wriothesley says, 'That is the last thing –'

Riche says, 'Whatever gave your lordship that idea?'

He takes his ruby ring from his finger. 'The King of France gave me this.'

'Did he?' Norfolk cries out to the clerk. 'Make a note, you!'

'And when he did so, I took it to our king. Who in time was pleased to return it to me, saying it would be a token between us, and that if I were to send it him, even if I did not have my seal, even if I were not able to write, he would know it came from me. So I send it him now.'

'But what is the point?' Gardiner says.

'A good question,' Riche says. 'The king knows where you are. He knows who and what you are.'

'It will remind him how I have served him, to the best of my capacities and to the utmost of my strength. As I hope to do for many years yet.'

'That is what we are here to determine,' Riche says. 'Whether you have served him or no. Whether you have abused his confidence, as he believes, and whether you plotted against his throne.'

Riche must somehow be assured, he thinks, and Wriothesley too, that if Henry frees me I will not revenge: or they will kill me in a panic. 'How, plotted?' He asks civilly, as if it were a matter of passing interest.

'Letters have been discovered at Austin Friars,' Gardiner says. 'Highly prejudicial to your claims to be a loyal and quiet subject.'

'Clear proof of treason,' Norfolk says.

'I am waiting for you to tell me what they are. I cannot guess what you might forge, can I?'

'They are Lutheran letters,' Riche says. 'Letters from Martin himself and his heretic brethren.'

'Melanchthon?' he asks. 'The king writes to him.'

Gardiner glares. 'And also from German princes, urging on you a course most injurious to king and commonwealth.'

'There are no such letters,' he says, 'they never existed, and even if they did –'

'Lawyer's logic,' Norfolk says.

'– and even if they did, and if they contained seditious matter, would I keep them in my house for you to find? Ask Wriothesley what he thinks.'

Gardiner looks at Call-Me. 'What I think ...' he hesitates, 'what I truly ...' He stops.

'Pass on,' he says. 'Or are you waiting for me to set the agenda and run the meeting? I think you wanted to know about my wardrobe.'

'Yes, the doublet,' Riche says. 'We will begin there, and return to the treasonous correspondence when Mr Wriothesley is more himself. In the cardinal's day you owned, and were seen to wear, a doublet of purple satin.'

He does not laugh, because he sees where this is tending.

Norfolk demands, 'What gave you the right to wear such a colour? It is the preserve of royal persons and high dignitaries of the church.'

Riche says, 'Was it perhaps violet? If violet, it can be excused.'

Wriothesley says, 'I saw it myself. It was purple. And moreover, you had sables.'

He thinks, not like the beautiful sables I have bought since. 'I feel the cold. Besides, they were a gift. From a foreign client who did not know our rules.'

Riche's brow furrows. This answer takes him in so many promising directions he hardly knows which to follow. 'When you say a client, you mean a foreign prince?'

'Princes did not send me gifts. Not at that date.'

'Still,' Gardiner says, 'if your client did not know the rules, you knew them.'

Norfolk sticks to his point: 'It was above your rank and station, to dress as if you were an earl already.'

'True,' he says, 'but why would your lordship object, if the king did not? He would not like to see his ministers go in homespun.'

Norfolk says, 'The doublet is only a single example, of your insensate ungodly pride. It's not just your attire that offends. It's the way you talk. The way you put yourself forward. Interrupt the king's discourse. Interrupt me. Scorn ambassadors, the envoys of great princes. They come to your house, and you give out you're not in, when you are in. Then they hear you in the garden playing bowls! They know when they are held in contempt.'

'Speaking of ambassadors ...' Riche says.

Gardiner snaps, 'Not yet.'

Norfolk says, 'The king has entrusted you with high office. And you scant the procedures that are laid down. You reach across and put your signature to some scrap of paper, and thousands are paid out without a warrant. There is no part of the king's business you do not meddle in. You override the council. You pull state policy out of your pocket. You read other men's letters. You corrupt their households to your own service. You take their duties out of their hands.'

'I act when they should act,' he says. 'Sometimes government must accelerate.' He thinks, I cannot wait for the slow grindings of your brain. 'We must move in anticipation of events.'

'I do not see how,' Riche says. 'Unless you consult sorcerers.'

The gentlemen glance at each other. He says, 'Are you done about the doublet?'

Messengers come in and whisper in Gardiner's ear. A paper is given him, and shuffled surreptitiously to the duke, but not before he, Thomas Essex, catches a glimpse of the seal of the King of France. Norfolk seems pleased by what he reads – so pleased he cannot keep it to himself. 'François congratulates our king on his initiative.'

'Your putting down,' Gardiner clarifies. 'The French have much to tell us, regarding your ambitions. Not to mention your methods of discharging our sovereign's trust.'

It is then he grasps what has eluded him: the timing, the personnel. It must have been in early spring, when Norfolk was so keen to cross the sea, that François first hinted at an alliance and named his price. The price was me, and the king baulked at it: until now.

He says, 'The French like to deal with you, my lord Norfolk.'

Norfolk looks as if he has been congratulated. By the living God, he thinks, I do not know which is greater: Norfolk's vanity, or his stupidity. Of course the French prefer a minister who they can bewilder and trick and – if it comes to it – purchase.

'I want to take us back …' Riche says.

'I am sure you do,' he says. 'You had better change the subject, because you are in danger of proving how bad a minister I have been for François.'

Riche is leafing through an old letter-book. 'You made a great deal of money in the cardinal's day.'

'Not so much from Wolsey. From my legal practice, yes.'

'How did you do that?'

'Long hours.'

'Wolsey commonly enriched his servants,' Wriothesley says.

'He did – as Stephen here can testify. But one had expenses. The cardinal fell from grace before his debts could be paid. His enemies fell on his assets. He cost me money, in the end.'

'When you say his enemies, you mean the king?'

'Oh, give me some credit, Gardiner. Am I likely to gratify you by calling the king a thief?'

'You adhered to Wolsey,' Riche says, 'even when he was a proven traitor.'

'What you call "adherence" is what the king called loyalty.'

'He does,' Wriothesley says. He sounds almost tearful. 'I have heard him.'

He looks up at Call-Me. I don't care how you cry. You've picked your side. He says, 'The king regrets the cardinal. He misses him to this day.'

Gardiner says, 'Can we leave the cardinal out of this? It is a living traitor we seek.'

Riche says testily, 'I want to get on, I want to get on to Lady Mary, but I cannot do that without mentioning …'

Gardiner sighs. 'If you must.'

Riche says, 'You wore a ring, which Wolsey gave you. It was said to possess certain properties …'

'You covet it, Ricardo? I can have it sent to you. It will save you from drowning.'

'You see!' Norfolk says. 'It is a sorcerer's ring. He admits it.'

He smiles. 'It preserves the wearer from wild beasts. It also secures the favour of princes. It doesn't seem to be working, does it?'

'It also …' Riche is embarrassed. He rubs his upper lip. 'It also, allegedly, makes princesses fall in love with you.'

'I'm turning them away daily.'

Wriothesley says, 'You didn't turn the Lady Mary away.'

Riche says, 'You presumed, and the king knows it, you presumed to practise upon her, to insinuate yourself with her, to ingratiate yourself, so that she referred to you as,' he consults his notes, *'my only friend.'*

'If we are speaking of the days after the death of Anne Boleyn, then I think it is true, I was her only friend. Mary would be dead now, if I had not persuaded her to obey her father.'

'And why were you so interested in saving her life?' Gardiner asks.

'Perhaps because I am a Christian man.'

'Perhaps because you hoped she would reward you.'

'She was a powerless girl. How could she reward me?'

Norfolk says, 'It was your dreadful presumption, offensive to Almighty God, to attempt to marry her.'

'For instance,' Riche says, 'upon a certain occasion, you were her Valentine and made her a gift.'

He is impatient. 'You know how that works. We draw lots.'

'Yes,' Wriothesley says, 'but you rigged the ballot. You have boasted of your ways to manipulate elections of any sort. Even the draw at a tournament – I offer this, and my recollection is perfectly clear – the day your son made his debut in the field, you told him, never fear, I can get you on the king's team, then you will not have to run against his Majesty.'

'Gregory told you that?'

'He told me that very day. You hurt his pride.'

'He spoke in innocence. And to you, Call-Me, because he took you for his friend. But I suppose you must use what you have. Valentines? Sorcerers? Any jury would laugh you out of court.'

But, he thinks, there will be no jury. There will be no trial. They will pass a bill to put an end to me. I cannot complain of the process. I have used it myself.

Riche is frowning. 'There was a ring,' he says. 'I think you offered Mary a ring, summer of 1536.'

'It was not a lover's ring. And in the end it was not a ring at all, it was a piece to wear at her girdle.' He closes his eyes. 'Because it was too heavy. There were too many words.'

'What words?' Norfolk says.

'Words enjoining obedience.'

Gardiner affects to be startled. 'You thought she should obey you?'

'I thought she should obey her father. And I showed the object to his Majesty. I thought it a wise precaution, against the kind of insinuation you make now. He liked it so well that he took it for himself, to give to her.'

Wriothesley drops his eyes. 'That's true, my lord. I was there.'

Riche gives his colleague a poisonous glance. 'All the same, the volume of your correspondence with the lady, your manifest influence with her, the nature of the information she confides to you, information that concerns her bodily –'

'You mean she told me she had toothache?'

'She confided things proper for a physician to know. Not a stranger.'

'I was hardly a stranger.'

'Perhaps not,' Riche says. 'In fact, she sent you presents. She sent you a pair of gloves. That signifies, "hand-in-glove". It signifies alliance. It signifies, matrimony.'

'The King of France once sent me a pair of gloves. He didn't want to marry me.'

'It disgusts me,' Norfolk says. 'That a woman of noble blood should lower herself.'

'Do not blame the lady,' Gardiner says sharply. 'Cromwell made her believe only his own person stood between herself and death.'

'There you have it,' he says. 'My person. It was my purple doublet she could not resist.'

'I remember well,' Norfolk says, 'though by the Mass I cannot swear to the date –'

He, Thomas Essex, rolls his eyes. 'Let no scruple impede you, my lord ...'

'– but there were others standing by,' Norfolk says, 'so I dare say –'

'Out with it,' Gardiner says.

'– I remember a certain conversation – could a woman rule, was the topic, could Mary rule – and you, bursting in, as is your habit, on the discourse of gentlemen, said, "It depends who she marries."'

Gardiner smiles. 'It was the autumn of 1530. I was present.'

'And since that time,' Riche says, 'you have ensured that Lady Mary never makes a marriage. All her suitors are sent away.'

'And I remember,' Norfolk says, 'when the king took his fall at the joust –'

'24 January, 1536,' Gardiner says.

'– when the king was carried to a tent and lay on a bier either dead or dying, all your concern was, "Where is Mary?"'

'I thought to secure her person. To protect her.'

'From?'

'From you, my lord Norfolk. And your niece, Anne the queen.'

'And if you had laid hands on her,' Gardiner says, 'what would you have done?'

'You tell me,' he says. 'What makes the best story? Do I seduce her, or enforce her?' He throws out his hands. 'Oh, come on, Stephen – I no more meant to marry her than you did.'

Gardiner is cold. 'Kindly address me as what I am.'

He grins. 'It never seemed likely to me you should be a bishop. But I beg your pardon.'

'Leave aside marriage,' Gardiner says. 'There are other means of control. The king believes you meant to place Mary on the throne and rule through her. And to this end you cultivated your friendship with Chapuys, the Emperor's man.'

'He dined with you twice in the week,' Call-Me says.

'You would know. You were at the table.'

'He was your friend. Your confidant.'

'I have no confidants, and few friends. Though till yesterday, I put you among them.'

'I was present at your house at Canonbury,' Wriothesley says, 'when you conferred with Chapuys in the garden tower. You made him certain promises. About Mary, her future estate.'

'I made no promises.'

'She thought you did. And Chapuys thought you did.'

He remembers the ambassador's folio, on the grass among the daisies. The marble table, the envoy's suspicion of the strawberries. The gradual clouding of the day, so that Christophe said that in Islington they feared thunder. Then Call-Me, at the foot of the tower in the twilight, a sheaf of peonies in his hand.

Gardiner promises, 'Another day we will come to the bribes the Emperor gave you. For now let us pursue the matter of your marriage. The Lady Mary was not your only prospect. You took care that Lady Margaret Douglas was preserved, though guilty of wilful disobedience to the king.'

Wriothesley bursts out, 'I uncovered that whole affair! And you talked it away, as if it were nothing.'

'Not nothing,' he says. 'Her sweetheart died.' He says to Norfolk, 'I am sorry I could not save them both.'

Norfolk makes a sound of disgust. He has many brothers, he hardly misses Tom Truth. 'You put her under a debt of gratitude,' he says. 'The king's niece. What was she to you, but another path to the throne? "If I were king" is a phrase often in your mouth.'

Gardiner leans forward. 'We have all heard you say it.'

He nods. It is a habit he should have checked. Once he said, 'If I were the king, I'd spend more time in Woking. In Woking it never snows.'

'You smile?' Gardiner is shocked. 'You, a manifest traitor, who offered to meet the king in battle?'

'What?' He is blank: still thinking of Woking.

'Let me remind you,' Riche says. 'At the church of St Peter le Poor, near your own gate at Austin Friars, on or around ...' Riche has lost the date, but no matter, '... you were heard to pronounce certain treasonable words: that you would maintain your own opinion in religion, that you would never allow the king to return to Rome, and – these are the words alleged – *if he would turn, yet I would not turn; and I would take the field against him, my sword in my hand.* And you accompanied these words with certain belligerent gestures –'

'Is this likely?' he says. 'Even if I had such thoughts, is it likely I would speak them out? In a public place? Surrounded by witnesses?'

'One utters in a rage sometimes,' Norfolk says.

'Speak for yourself, my lord.'

'You also stated,' Riche says, 'that you would bring new doctrine into England, and that – and here I quote your own words – *If I live one year or two, it shall not lie in the king's power to resist.*'

'What though you are a cautious man?' Gardiner says. 'I have seen you moved to mockery, and to wrath.'

'I have seen you moved to tears,' Riche says.

'I could weep now,' he says. He is thinking, *yet I would not turn.* Perhaps I may have spoken those words. Not in public. But in

825

private. To Bess Darrell. *I am not too old to take my sword in my hand.* I will fight for Henry, I meant to say. But the god of contraries made me say the opposite. And I could have bitten out my tongue.

Riche has recovered a date. 'Peter le Poor – last day of January –'

'This year?'

'Last.'

'Last year? Where have the witnesses been since? Were they not culpable, in concealing treason? I look forward to seeing them in chains.'

He can see Riche thinking, look, now he is wrathful, now he is provoked. He might say anything.

'You admit it is treason?' Norfolk says.

'Yes, my lord,' he says patiently, 'but I do not admit to saying it. How would I make good such threats? How could I overthrow the king?'

'Perhaps with the help of your Imperial friends,' Norfolk says. 'Chapuys is not in the realm, but you have contact with him, do you not? He congratulated you, on your earldom. I hear he plans to return.'

'He'll have to go somewhere else for his dinner,' he says.

'Why do we trouble ourselves over Chapuys?' Riche says. 'It is much worse than that, as all will attest, who were in Sadler's garden at Hackney, the night the king met his daughter.'

The apostle cups, he thinks. The great bowl buried in the earth to keep our wine cool. Riche says, 'You had secret dealings with Katherine. And that night you confessed as much.'

'You have known a long while, Riche. What kept you from speaking out?'

No answer. 'I will tell you,' he says. 'Your own advantage kept you mute. Till advantage was greater on the other side. What promise have I made to you, that I have not kept? And what promises have you made to me?'

'You should not speak of promises,' Norfolk says. 'The king hates a man who breaks his word. You said you would kill Reginald Pole.'

'Not a drop of his blood is shed,' Gardiner observes.

He thinks, now we come to it. This is why Henry faults me. And so he should. This is where I have failed.

Riche says, 'There was much big talk in your household, how you would trap Reginald. One week, you would set on him murderers you knew in Italy. Another week, it was your nephew Richard who would kill him. Then it was Francis Byran, then it was Thomas Wyatt.'

Wriothesley says, 'And on that subject – one wonders, when Wyatt was ambassador lately, for what reason he held back certain letters from the Lady Mary, that the Emperor was meant to see. Was he not acting for you, as your agent?'

'My agent? For what purpose?'

'Some dishonesty,' Riche says. 'We have not yet penetrated it.'

'But no doubt we shall,' Gardiner says. 'Mr Wriothesley has overheard so much loose and treasonous talk, merely in the course of daily business. He heard you say recently that you would do the King of France a favour, if he would do one for you. One wonders what ensued.'

'Nothing ensued,' he said. 'He has not done me any favours, has he? It is my lord Norfolk who is in his graces.'

'Then why say it?' Riche presses.

'Big talk. You said it yourself. My household's full of it.'

Gardiner puts his fingertips together. 'Add the braggarts in with the rest, and your household falls little short of three thousand persons. It is the household of a prince. Your livery is seen not only through London, but through England.'

'Three thousand? With that number I would be bankrupt. Look, every man in England has applied to me these seven years, to take his son into my service. I take who I can, and bring them up in learning and good manners. For the most part their fathers pay their keep, so you cannot say I employ them.'

'You speak as if they were all meek scribblers,' Gardiner says. 'But it is well-known that you take in runaway apprentices, roisterers, ruffians ...'

'Yes,' he says, 'roaring boys such as Richard Riche was once, in days he would rather forget. I do not deny I give a second life to those who have the enterprise to knock at my gates.' He looks at Riche. 'Any chancer has his chance with me.'

'You feed the poor at your gates every day,' Norfolk says.

'It is what great men do.'

'You think they will rise in your support, a pauper army. Well, they will not, sir. They will not favour a shearsman, such as you once were.' The duke affects to shiver. 'Great man, you call yourself! St Jude protect me!'

Riche selects a paper from his file. 'I have here the inventories from Austin Friars. You owned some three hundred handguns, four hundred pikes, near eight hundred bows, and halberds and harness for, as my lord Norfolk says, an army. I have heard you say, and Wriothesley will bear me out, that you had a bodyguard of three hundred that would come to your whistle, day or night.'

'When the northern rebels were up,' he says, 'I was ashamed I could not turn out enough men of my own. So I did what any loyal subject would do, if he had means. I augmented my resources.'

'Oh, you prate of your loyalty,' Norfolk says. 'When you would have sold the king to heretics! When you would have sold Calais to foul sacramentaries –'

'I?' he says. 'Sold Calais? Look to the Lisles for that. It is to them and the Poles you should look for treason. Not to me, who owes everything to the king – but to those who think it their natural right to sweep him aside. To those who think his family's rule a mere interruption to their own.'

Gardiner says, 'My lord Norfolk, shall we come to Calais another day?'

He can see the bishop's feet under the board, barely restraining themselves from kicking the duke's shins. Presumably they are still taking testimony from Lord Lisle, and have not decided into what form of lie they will bend it.

Richard Riche taps his papers. 'My lord bishop, I have such matter here ...'

Gardiner stands up. 'Save it.'

He, Cromwell, wants to hold Gardiner back, reason with him. Winchester knows this is silly stuff – rings, sorcerers, Valentines – and he is ashamed, no doubt, of what has come out of his own mouth. But Gardiner sweeps out, Norfolk bustling after: Riche beckons the clerk to help him with his files. 'I wish you a pleasant evening, my lord,' he says: as if they were at home at Austin Friars.

Mr Wriothesley looks after them. He stands up; he seems to need support, and clings to the trestle top. 'Sir –'

'Save your breath.'

'When I was in Brussels, a hostage, I hear you did not lift a finger for me.'

'That is not true.'

'You said that if they held me in prison in Vilvoorde, you could not get me out.'

'No more could I.'

'That scoundrel Harry Phillips – you set me and others to entrap him, when you yourself were using him as your agent and spy.'

'Who told you that?'

'Bishop Gardiner. You let me suffer because of Phillips. I took him in good faith to my lodging, and he robbed me, and made me look a fool.'

'I never made use of Phillips,' he says. 'Truly. He has always been too slippery for me.'

'Sir, Norfolk wants them to hang you at Tyburn, like a common thief. And because you are a traitor he wants them to pull your bowels out. He wants you to suffer the most painful death the law affords. He is set on it.'

'You seem set on it yourself.'

'No, sir. You understand how it is with me. I can do no other than I do, I assure you. But I want to see you treated with honour. If need be I shall petition the king.'

'Christ, Call-Me,' he says, 'stand up straight. How do you think you will fare with Henry these next few years, if you are cringing and whining in the presence of a man who, you say yourself, is doomed?'

'I trust not, sir.' His voice is unsteady. 'The king gives you permission to write to him. Do it tonight.'

Gardiner stands in the doorway. 'Wriothesley?'

Call-Me tries to pick up his papers, but a letter drops out and he has to kneel on the floor to fish it from under the table. It has the Courtenay seal, and he – Essex– wants to trap it with his foot and make Call-Me scrap for it. But he thinks, what's the point? He puts out a hand to help the young man to his feet. 'Take him,' he says to Gardiner. 'He's all yours.'

Late afternoon, Rafe comes. He hears his voice and his heart leaps. He thinks, if Henry changes his mind, it is Rafe he will send.

But he knows from the boy's face there is no good news. 'And yet he permits you to visit me,' he says. 'Is that not a hopeful sign?'

'He is afraid you might get out,' Rafe says. 'He has set a strong guard. But he does not think I have a martial character.'

'What does he think I might do to him, if I did get out?'

'Here is Cranmer's letter,' Rafe says. 'I will wait.'

He walks to the window with it; he has not his spectacles, he needs some brought in. The paper seems to shake as he unfolds it. Cranmer, having heard of his treason, expresses himself both sorrowful and amazed: *he that was so advanced by your Majesty: he whose surety was only by your Majesty: he who loved your Majesty, as I ever thought, no less than God ... he that cared for no man's displeasure to serve your Majesty: he that was such a servant, in my judgement, in wisdom, diligence, faithfulness and experience, as no prince in this realm ever had ... I loved him as my friend, for so I took him to be; but I chiefly loved him for the love which I thought I saw him bear ever towards your grace ...*

... but now ...

He looks up. 'Now it comes ... on the one hand, on the other ...'

... but now, if he be a traitor, I am sorry that I ever loved or trusted him ... but yet again I am very sorrowful ...

He folds the paper. Fear seeps from the fold. He says, 'You must understand, Rafe, Cranmer and I agreed long ago, that if one of us looked set to go down, the other would save himself.'

'That may be, sir. But I think he should have got himself to the king's presence. If the archbishop had been in peril of his life, would you have stood by? I don't think you would.'

'Don't make me answer questions. It's been questions all day. Cranmer does what is in him. It is all any man can do. Rafe, what happened to my picture? That Hans made?'

'Helen took it, sir. She has it safe.'

'Where is The Book Called Henry?'

'We burned it, sir. I took my people to your house before Wriothesley came there. We burned a great many things, and raked the ashes into the garden.'

'Absence speaks.'

'But not clearly,' Rafe says. 'I do not believe they can bring a single substantial charge against you. John Wallop has written from France, with what he can dredge up. They say it was the common talk there that you meant to make yourself king.' Rafe bows his head. 'François sent a letter, and the king had me English it and read it out to the council. I myself.'

'It was a test. I hope you passed.'

'François says, now Cromwell is gone we can be friends again. I am clear in my own mind that this was what he broached with Norfolk in February. And therefore it is no wonder he and Winchester have been so bold. All their conferences behind the hand, their dinners and their masques … and of course they have the girl, parading her where the king cannot help but see her.'

'Rafe,' he says, 'would you bring me some more books? Petrarch, his *Remedies for Fortune*. Thomas Lupset, *The Way of Dying Well*.'

Lupset was tutor to the cardinal's son. He wrote not a moment too soon, for he was dead at thirty-five.

Rafe says, 'Do not yield. Do not resign yourself, I beg you. You know the king is impulsive …'

'Is he? We always say so.' But perhaps his caprices are designed to keep us working and keep us hoping. Anne Boleyn thought till her last moment that he would change his mind. She died incredulous.

When Rafe goes out he turns back to Cranmer's letter. He sees the question that his archbishop leaves for Henry: *Who will your Grace trust thereafter, if you cannot trust him?*

That evening he sits down to write to the king. The late afternoon had brought Fitzwilliam, with a fresh file which he ran through briskly: moving on to new ground, with conversations alleged, confederacies, conspiracies and – a strange one this – breaching the king's confidence by talking about his futile nights with the queen. 'But everybody knew,' he had said, baffled. 'And he gave his permission for me to talk to you, and to people in Anna's household.'

'He doesn't recall that now,' Fitzwilliam said. 'He thinks you have made him a laughing stock.'

Fitzwilliam and his hangers-on had pestered him for half an hour. Not once did his fellow councillor look him in the face till at last they took themselves out for their supper.

Christophe sets out ink and paper. He can write by nature's light; it is dusk, but a window gives onto the garden. What can he say? Once Henry had told him, 'You were born to understand me.' That understanding has broken down. He has sorely offended, and all he can do is argue that whatever his offence, he has not committed it wilfully, or out of malice: that he trusts God will reveal the truth. He begins with the usual phrases expressing his lowliness: one cannot do too much for Henry in this way, or at least, a prisoner cannot. *Prostrate at the feet of your most excellent Majesty, I have heard your pleasure ... that I should write such things as I thought meet concerning my miserable state ...*

He thinks, I have never limited my desires. Just as I have never slacked my labours, so I have never said, 'Enough, I am now rewarded.'

Mine accusers your Grace knoweth, God forgive them. For as I ever had love to your honour, person, life, prosperity, health, wealth, joy and comfort, and also your most dear and most entirely beloved son, the Prince his Grace, and your proceedings, God so help me in this mine adversity, and confound me if ever I thought the contrary.

They are rewriting my life, he thinks. They represent that all my obedience has been outward obedience, and all these years in secret I have been creeping closer to Henry's enemies – such as his daughter, my supposed bride. Perhaps I should have told him the truth about Mary. But I will spare her now. I cannot help my own daughter, I can only help the king's.

What labours, pains and travails I have taken according to my most bounden duty God also knoweth. For if it were in my power, as it is in God's, to make your Majesty to live ever young and prosperous, God knoweth I would. If it had been or were in my power to make you so rich as ye might enrich all men, God help me, I would do it. If it had been or were in my power to make your Majesty so puissant as all the world should be compelled to obey you, Christ he knoweth, I would.

He thinks, ten years I have had my soul flattened and pressed till it's not the thickness of paper. Henry has ground and ground me in the mill of his desires, and now I am fined down to dust I am no more use to him, I am powder in the wind. Princes hate those to whom they have incurred debts.

For your Majesty has been most bountiful to me, and more like a dear father (your Majesty not offended) than a master.

Certain threats his father used to make ring in his ears. I'll pound you to paste, boy, I'll flatten you, I'll knock you into the middle of next week.

I have committed my soul my body and goods at your Majesty's pleasure …

Well, Henry knows that. I have nothing, that does not come from him. And no hope, but in his mercy and God's.

Sir, as to your common wealth I have, after my wit, power and knowledge, travailed therein, having had no respect to persons (your Majesty only excepted) … but that I have done any injustice or wrong wilfully, I trust God shall bear me witness, and the world not able justly to accuse me …

It is not only kings who cannot be grateful. The fortunes he has made, the patronage he has dispensed: these count against him now, because favours that cannot be repaid eat away at the soul. Men scorn to live under an obligation. They would rather be perjurers, and sell their friends.

Brother Martin says, when you think of death, cast out fear. But perhaps that advice is easier to take if you expect to die in your bed, with a priest buzzing in your ear. Gardiner will press for heresy charges and burn him if he can. He knows about that: the green wood, the vagrant wind, and the dogs of London whimpering at the smell.

The king might grant the axe. That is the best he can hope for, unless. There is always *unless*. Erasmus says, 'No man is to be despaired of, so long as the breath is in him.'

He signs off: *Written with the quaking hand and most sorrowful heart of your most sorrowful subject and most humble servant and prisoner, this Saturday at your Tower of London.*

He dries the ink. One cannot help but lie. His hand is not notably quaking. But it is true his heart is sorrowful. He sits with his hand to his chest, rubbing it a little. 'Christophe,' he says, 'fetch in my supper. What am I having?'

'Thank Christ! I thought you had lost your appetite. We have strawberries and cream. And the Italian merchants have sent you their sympathy and a cheese.'

The merchant Antonio Bonvisi used to send food to Thomas More, dishes fragrant with spice. But More would push them aside, and say to his servant, 'John, can you find me a milk pudding?'

The Duke of Urbino, Federigo di Montefeltro, was asked what it took to rule a state. '*Essere umano,*' he said: to be human. He wonders if Henry will reach the standard.

There is no reply to his letter. No direct reply, at least. Beginning early, in tender summer dawns, the interrogations proceed into the hot afternoons, when the broad light in the chamber grows dusty. Sometimes the sessions are quiet and industrious, sometimes they are more like exchanges of insults than any proceeding of state. Like Fitzwilliam, Call-Me cannot look at him. He says, '*He* did this,' and '*He* did that,' as if Thomas Essex were not in the room. When Gardiner graces them with his presence he is grave, dry, judicious, careful to suppress the bubbling anticipation he must feel.

The clerk Gwyn sneaks back a time or two. Norfolk does not notice him because a clerk is beneath his notice, unless he offends. The clerk entertains him – the prisoner – by sometimes casting up a glance to Heaven, or turning down his mouth in disbelief at what he must record. Till Riche bursts out, 'I am not content with this clerk. He keeps looking at the prisoner.'

'So do you keep looking at me,' he says. 'I am not content with you, Richard Riche. You speak as if I have been a traitor all the years you have known me. Where has your evidence been till now? Did it fall out through a hole in your pocket?'

Riche says, 'It is no small thing, to indict a man so close to the king. I sought guidance. I prayed about it.'

'And your prayers were answered?'

Riche says coldly, 'Oh, yes.'

Once again Gwyn packs up his penknives and quills without demur, though not without a backward glance. Another clerk comes in and ahems over how to continue, until Norfolk snarls at him to start anywhere. In this way the hours pass, marked off by the bells from St Peter ad Vincula and from the city outside the walls. The questions never make more sense than they did on the first day, nor does the picture of his life ever reflect the reality as he sees it. The mirror presents an alien face, eyes askew, mouth gaping. Lord Montague, and Exeter, and Nicholas Carew suffered this estrangement from self; and Norris and George Boleyn before them. Montague had said, 'The king never made a man but he destroyed him again.' Why should Cromwell be an exception?

Florence made me, he thinks. London unmade me. In Florence the bell called Leone announces the dawn even to the blind. Then rings Podestà, then Popolo. At Terce, when the law courts open, Leone and Montarina summon litigants and advocates to their business.

When he was an infant, his sister Kat used to tell him the bells made the time. When the hour strikes, and the music shivers in the air, you have the best of it; and what's left is like a sucked plumstone on the side of a plate.

Lord Audley shows his face: shifty, ashamed. I created you, Audley, he thinks. I promoted you above your deserts, to have a compliant chancellor: and you have grown rich. 'I thought you were with me, my lord. You always posed as valiant for the gospel, but I think you were only valiant for my favour. You swore to be my friend for life.' He adds, 'I have it in writing.'

Fitzwilliam absents himself. Perhaps he has said to the king, I know Crumb is no traitor, I cannot do it?

'He is busy,' Wriothesley says.

Riche says, 'He is appointed Lord Privy Seal in your place.'

Norfolk says, 'There is more matter than your arrest, for trusted men to deal with. There are more men in this realm, than Cromwell.'

'But none so necessary to the commonweal,' he says. 'I am surprised your son Surrey is not here to gloat.'

He thinks, if they let that spider in, I shall put my boot heel on him.

He is suspicious of Gardiner's absence: what is he working at? Charles Brandon comes in, and confirms that Cromwell said that if he were king he would spend more time in Woking. He remembers another occasion: 'The king gave Crumb a ring from his own finger. And Crumb said, "It fits me exactly, it needs no adjustment."'

'And what do you draw from that?' he asks. 'That I am the right size for king? What is the right size, my lord Suffolk? Are you not nearer it than me?'

He is saddened by Brandon. To Norfolk, a Cromwell is just a blot to be erased, like a discrepancy in book-keeping. But Brandon's family made their name by audacity. He hoped there might be some fellow-feeling. Charles cannot settle to his questions, but walks about, and in time walks out of the room, calling sharply to his folk to accompany him, as one whistles to a dog.

Wriothesley says, 'You are aware that Lord Hungerford is arrested?'

'Hungerford?' He thinks that, in dwelling on Brandon, he has missed something. 'What has Hungerford to do with me?'

'That is something we mean to find out,' Riche says. 'He has written you many letters, and you have written him many replies, copies of which Master Secretary Wriothesley has extracted from your files.'

Hungerford is a West Country gentleman: a good enough lieutenant, active in his district's affairs. He is a wife-beater too, and his lady wants to be free of him; only a few days before his arrest, he, Thomas Essex, had set in train a process of official separation. He says, 'One must use such people. The king cannot be served only by saints.'

'An old woman has laid grave accusations against him,' Wriothesley says. 'She is called Mother Huntley.'

Christ help him, he thinks. We all have a Mother Huntley in our lives. Mine is called Richard Riche.

'The charges involve sorcery,' Norfolk says. 'Well, Cromwell here, he knows all about that! Conjurers' books in his cellar, were there not? When the wax doll was found, of our little prince, Cromwell could not wait to lay his hands on the culprits and their villain texts. And yet he told young Richmond, God rest him, that there were no such things as witches! When we all know that witches have done the king harm.'

'I remember that day,' Riche said. 'It was at St James's, at the time Fitzroy fell ill. Cromwell sent me out of the room, and I often wondered what passed. That is how it has always been – Wriothesley, you will bear me out? He seems to confide in you, then suddenly excludes you from his councils.'

'Now we see why,' Wriothesley says.

'However, to the matter in hand,' Riche says. 'Lord Hungerford has employed a conjurer to find out the date of the king's death.'

He thinks, Henry does not fear a false horoscope. He fears a true one: a fate that he must walk towards. He says, 'A man like Hungerford makes enemies among his neighbours. It is an easy thing to allege.'

'Do not take it lightly,' Lord Audley says. 'I assure you, the king does not.'

Hungerford may be a brute, but he is hardly a danger to the commonweal. Two weeks ago he would have been sweeping such charges off his desk and onto some lesser desk.

Riche says, 'He is also charged with violating a member of his household. *Per anum.*'

'God save us – not Lady Hungerford?'

'A servant,' Norfolk says. 'Luckily his own, not some other gentleman's. He will die for it.'

'But more to the point,' Wriothesley says, 'he is detected as a papist. A chaplain in his household had contact with the rebels in the north. We have it documented.'

'Why did you not know?' Riche says.

'Because he lied to me?' he says. 'If I could detect every lie, I could set up in a temple as an oracle.' He pictures himself in an olive grove. 'Far away from you.'

It is past dinner time and he is hungry. The duke is hungry too, but those days are gone when they might have shared a table. Christophe comes in with a chicken. A half-hour passes, in which he eats heartily enough. When his guests return, Riche follows the others with an affected dawdle that means he has something to say. He takes time in setting his papers down, squaring them up. 'Wyatt is much enriched.'

'Yes?'

'He is granted land from Reading Abbey. From Boxley and Malling. And here in London, St Mary Overy, and the Crossed Friars, and St Saviour in Bermondsey.'

'He has long coveted those properties.'

Riche smiles. 'I believe he has more than he thought he would get.'

'He will take it as a challenge. He will soon run through the income, believe me.'

Wriothesley leans forward. His face is flushed. 'My lord, do you not ask yourself, why now? It is done by his Majesty's direct command. He finds Wyatt deserves well.'

As he did at Anne Boleyn's fall. 'Well,' he says, 'what is unlucky for others is lucky for Thomas Wyatt. God smiles on him.'

Wriothesley mutters, 'Again, ask yourself why.'

'Is that a question?'

Wriothesley is mute.

He, Lord Cromwell, turns to Riche. 'No man knows better than you that grants like these are not made by snapping the fingers. Wyatt's grants were set in train months ago, when I recalled him from his embassy. They needed only the king's signature.'

'He could have withheld it,' Wriothesley says, 'if Wyatt did not please him. Clearly he did.'

Of course Wyatt would be questioned: how not? It seems he has given answers, helpful or at least not disagreeable to the king. But under what constraint, under what pressure? Perhaps Bess is having another phantom child?

'Wyatt knows your secret dealings,' Wriothesley says. 'And, as he has often boasted, the thoughts of your heart.'

'Not that they are anything to boast about,' he says. 'You strain my charity, Wriothesley. Still, when I am set at large, I will try not to hold these things against you.'

Once again that fluttering, behind his ribs, of the organ whose workings have cost Wyatt himself so much pain. *Love slayeth my heart. Fortune is depriver of all my comfort … My pleasant days, they fleet away and pass, But daily yet the ill doth change into the worse.*

He says – the words emerge suddenly, unguarded – 'What will you do without me? When a man such as Wyatt goes to work, he works for those who appreciate him. Without me you will read the lines as written, but you will never read between them. Marillac will make fools of you, and Chapuys too, if he returns. Charles and François will scramble your brains like a basin of eggs. Within a year the king will be fighting the Scots, or the French, or likely both, and he will bankrupt us. None of you can manage matters as I can. And the king will quarrel with you all, and you with each other. A year from now, if you sacrifice me, you will have neither honest coin nor honest minister.'

The clerk says, 'Lord Cromwell is ill. We should perhaps pause?'

He turns his eyes on the boy. 'Bless you for your courage.'

He is sweating. Norfolk says, 'Oh, I think he is fit enough. It is not as if he has endured any pains – which are spared him, at the king's direction, even though he is not nobly born.'

So the day passes, and another. Treason can be construed from any scrap of paper, if the will is there. A syllable will do it. The power is in the hands of the reader, not the writer. The duke continues with his outbursts, and Riche with insinuations that seldom connect one line of questioning with another. Mostly he can answer them; sometimes he has to refer them to the papers they have impounded, or lost. The truth is, as he confesses, he has meddled in so much of the king's business, that it is impossible even for a man of his capacity to recollect everything said and done. 'It is hard to live under the law,' he says. 'A minister must, unwittingly, transgress at divers points. But if I am a traitor,' he wipes his face, 'then all the devils in Hell confound me and the vengeance of God light upon me.'

Left alone at the end of the afternoon, he sits unpicking the fabric of the recent past, and always the thread leads him back to May Day. Thomas Essex at Greenwich, coming and going from the tournament ground, clerks following him with the king's business; the earl – that is, myself – throwing out a command here and there. Richard Cromwell in the arena, knocking down all comers. Our feasting of our friends and enemies, our style and courtesy, our *sprezzatura*, our lavish display: May Day undid us, for the envy and rancour it bred could no longer be suppressed. Richard has compounded with some Italians to paint a mural of his triumph in his house at Hinchingbrooke; they mean to decorate the whole room. The time may come when the scene is bitter in his eyes, but he should paint it anyway. He should not give backword to the Italians – it is how they get their living.

Within nine days of his arrest, they have put together enough matter against him to bring a bill of attainder into Parliament. They question him about religion, in order to add further charges. They ask about what he did in Calais, who he protected there. They delve further into their cache of forgeries, out of which they can adduce what they like. Norfolk says to him, 'When Mr Wriothesley went through

Antwerp on the king's business, you gave him messages for heretics.'

'I gave him a message for my daughter. My own blood.'

Norfolk says, 'You think that makes it better?'

He says, once again, 'Let me see the king.'

Norfolk says, 'Never.'

He supposes that Henry, for an hour or two together, believes firmly in both his heresy and his treason. But surely he cannot sustain the delusion? For the rest of his hours, he does not care what is true. He cultivates his grudge and grievance. No councillor can ever placate him, assuage this sense of grievance, slake his thirst or satisfy his hunger.

Before he has been a week in prison, Rafe brings him word of how the Emperor received the news. Charles seemed dumbfounded, dispatches say. 'What?' he asked. 'Cremuel? Are you sure? In the Tower? And by the king's command?'

One day the door opens; he expects Gardiner but it is Brandon again. Charles sits down, sighing heavy, on a little upholstered stool, so his knees rise absurdly under his chin. 'Why doesn't your lordship take this chair?'

But Charles sits like a penitent, puffing and sighing and looking around the room. His eyes search the painted walls, those scenes of paradises, verdant hills and brooks: 'Is *she* behind there? The other one?'

'Not in her own person, my lord. She lies in the chapel, at rest. As for the picture, I painted her out.'

'What? Personally?'

'No, my lord. I had a professional do it.'

He pictures himself, sneaking by night with a huge obliterating brush. 'You're a good fellow, Charles,' he says. 'I'd rob a house with you, if I had to.'

Brandon grins behind his big beard. 'Have you robbed many houses?'

'In my wild days, you know.'

841

'We all had those,' Charles says.

'I wouldn't rob a house with the king. You'd say to him, "Stand there and whistle if the watch comes," and at the first footfall he'd scramble off and leave you to it, your leg over the sill.'

'I don't think he'd go robbing, in all conscience,' Charles says. 'He'd be breaching his own peace, wouldn't he? And who would he rob? He can distrain our goods if he likes, and pauperise us all.' He rubs his forehead. 'I'm glad to hear you make a jest, Crumb. Look here ...' He levers himself to the vertical. 'Look here, and this is my advice. Confess you are a heretic. Claim you have been misled. Ask Harry to see you face to face and reason with you, to bring you back to true religion. He'd like that, wouldn't he? You remember how he enjoyed himself, at the trial of that fellow Lambert? Sitting above the court, all arrayed in white?'

'Lambert was burned,' he says.

Charles is deflated. 'Well, that was my idea, and now I've delivered it, so I ...' He heads for the door, plunges back. 'Your hand?'

He gives it. Charles pummels his shoulder, as if they were watching a dog fight.

When Brandon has gone he thinks, he is right, Henry would take pleasure in converting me. But there is a reason why Charles's solution will not answer. His enemies will show (to their own satisfaction) that he denies the Eucharist, and no heretic of that sort can save himself, even by recantation. What condemns him is the first of those pernicious articles they passed through Parliament last year when he was sick. His Italian fever is killing him after all.

The bill of attainder has its second reading on 29 June. Between the first reading of the bill and its second, between the second and the third, he is a dying man. When the bill passes, then by law he is dead. The only thing uncertain is by what process they will make him a corpse. If the king prefers to punish him for heresy, he will die by fire, perhaps beside Robert Barnes and his friends; if for treason, then likely enough he will go to Tyburn, to be cut up alive. Even the bugger Hungerford will get such grace as the headsman offers, but he, God knows. He dreams he is facing a door painted scarlet, or not painted but bathed in scarlet, and the wall is the same hue; the surface is wet, the floor, the wall, and the room behind the door is wet and scarlet too.

It has stopped raining. Looking out from his windows in the queen's lodging, he can see the summer dying back. He remembers the whole world a-swill, in those years before the cardinal came down. He remembers fetching Rafe to the house at Fenchurch Street, and how he dripped on the floor, and Lizzie unwrapped him from his layers. He thinks, she died before I had anything. I had Austin Friars, but it was a lawyer's house. When I was the cardinal's man she never saw me for weeks on end. I might as well have been a sailor on the sea. She stood at the head of the stairs, wearing her white cap. She said, 'Let me know when you are coming home.' I wrote my will, after she was dead, and what I had to leave to my son, in those days, was six hundred pounds and twelve silver spoons.

On the day the bill of attainder passes, Stephen Gardiner comes back. He wraps his coat around himself as if he is chilly. 'I have come to ask you about the king's so-called marriage.'

The turn of phrase is enough to make him understand what is required. 'I will write it all down for you. From the beginning.'

'Omit nothing,' Gardiner says. 'From your first negotiations with Cleves to the night of the supposed marriage. You must set forth all you heard of the lady's pre-contract with Lorraine, and record faithfully what you know of the king's dislike of and unwillingness to the marriage.'

He raises an eyebrow. Gardiner says, 'Lady Rochford and others will testify that there was no consummation. The doctors will confirm it. If she came here a maid, she leaves as one, as the king – entertaining doubts that the match was valid – refrained himself from carnal copulation.'

He thinks, I could be like George Boleyn: I could set down such matter as would raise blisters on Henry's face. But I have a son, and two grandsons, and a nephew, and my nephew has heirs. George had no children. He says, 'Getting a new wife was always my task. It falls to you now, does it? I suppose it will be Norfolk's niece? What has happened to the queen?'

'The lady of Cleves has already left the court. The king has sent her to Richmond. He has promised to join her there. But of course, he will not. It was necessary to stop her womanish lamentation – or at least, to allow it to go on at a distance.'

He thinks, she must have been frightened, poor soul. And no one to look to her welfare. 'I suppose money will salve the smart.'

'There will be a settlement. I will come to that. The annulment comes first. The king says, Cromwell knows more of the matter than any man, except my own self. You must write the truth on the damnation of your soul. You will be required to take an oath.'

'Why would I refuse?' he says. 'I would also take an oath I am a true servant and that my faith is the catholic and universal faith, not varying from that professed by the king. It were strange if my word should hold good in the one matter, but not the other.'

'You are a dying man,' Gardiner says. 'They are known not to lie. Do you want me to send Sadler, to help you write?'

He does not want Rafe to see him do this last act. He thinks, the annulment will annul me. 'I know what is required,' he says coldly. 'Leave it with me, my lord bishop. Now kick yourself out.'

He sits down. The facts marshal themselves in his mind, the phrases form themselves in order, but before he can write, he sheds a tear and thinks, I am in mourning for myself: with these papers, my usefulness gone. I could not do it again: the years of sleepless toil, the brute moral deformation, the axe-work. When Henry dies and goes to judgement, he must answer for me, as for all his servants: he must account for what he did to Cromwell. I never strove to replace him. All over England there are standing stones, petrified forms of men who hoped to rule: *Stick stock stone, As King of England I be known.* For their presumption they are condemned to stand for a thousand years, two thousand, in wind and rain; around them are smaller stones, the forms of the wretches who were their knights. Count them and – by a peculiar enchantment – you never get the same number twice. The destruction goes beyond counting. It goes beyond what the pen can record.

His narrative is the work of many hours. Sometimes Christophe comes in and peers at him, and offers a dish of raspberries, or wafers, or comfits. But he is absorbed in his story: Rochester, the bull-baiting, the lady from Cleves at the casement; the king blustering and hot in his disguise as English gentleman. The play at Greenwich, where the Romans tottered and fell; the king abed, kneading his bride's belly and breasts.

Sometimes his mind drifts away, as it must: far from this room, beyond the city walls, across the fields and into the forest. The cover is dense, as in the years before trees were cut down for houses and ships, and all the creatures now extinct are alive again, for good or ill: the beaver in the stream, the wolf gaining on you with his long stride. When a man does not know which path to take he scatters crumbs from the loaf he carries in his hand, but the birds swoop behind him and eat them. He takes off his shirt and tears it into strips, and ties a strip to a branch at each fork in the road, but the ogres who live deep in the wood tread after him and steal the linen to bind their wounds: for ogres are always fighting. He labours on, and talking trees snigger about him, hiding their expressions of contempt behind their leaves.

When his tale is done he writes the superscription: *To the king, my most gracious sovereign lord his royal Majesty.*

But he cannot think how to end it. It may be the last letter they will allow. So he writes *I cry for mercy*. He writes it again, in case Henry should be distracted: *mercy*. And once again, *mercy*, to get it into the royal skull, to pierce the royal heart.

He has dated it: *Wednesday, the last day of June. With heavy heart and trembling hand.*

This time it is true. It is trembling. He looks at it as if it is some other man's hand. Of all the words he has written, will this plea endure? Rats have eaten the laws of ancient times. They relish fish-glue and vellum; anything that was once alive, they will eat it, and then out of habit, they will eat what is dead; from the margins they chew their way in, to the secret history of England. It is the glory of the men who have worked with Cromwell that instead of merely cursing the vermin they have patched, they have mended, they have stretched a point to replace a gnawed vowel; they have been ready to substitute a digested phrase with a clause that will help the crown. But what has it availed? He has lived by the laws he has made and must be content to die by them. But the law is not an instrument to find out truth. It is there to create a fiction that will help us move past atrocious acts and face our future. It seems there is no mercy in this world, but a kind of haphazard justice: men pay for crimes, but not necessarily their own.

Rafe comes to take the letter. He has no seal, so he folds it, and before he gives it over he hesitates, trapping it under his palm. 'I always told Henry, frightening people is cheap but it doesn't get the best results. If you want a prisoner to yield you everything, offer him hope.'

Rafe says, 'I have read how the philosopher Canius, when Caligula's hangmen came for him, they found him playing chess. He said to them, "Mark this, I am winning – count my pieces on the board."'

'I make no such bold reply,' he says sadly. 'Canius still had his queen.' He pushes the letter across the table. 'Here. Everything he wants is in that package. Will Cleves make war on us now?'

Rafe says, 'It appears the duke is content to leave his sister here in England. And if she does not oppose him in anything, the king will make her fair and honourable terms.'

'Why would she oppose him? Poor lady.' To make a winter journey, he thinks, and find herself unwanted at the end of it.

Rafe says, 'Duke Wilhelm is talking to the French. Word is they have offered him a princess, and an alliance.'

'Ah, so he is not marrying Christina?'

'No, he cannot make terms with the Emperor, or not at this time. They say the French princess is unwilling.'

Unwilling. That will leave room for an annulment, when the Emperor offers something better. 'Wilhelm has not done badly out of us,' he says. 'Better than Anna.' He thinks, I doubt she will want to marry any other man, now Henry has mauled her.

Rafe says, 'The French swear they will carry their princess to the altar, if need be. She is only twelve years old, so she cannot weigh heavy.' He sighs. 'Helen, sir, begs to be commended to you. She prays night and morning for you. As do our little children, and all your friends.'

Not a great number of prayers, then, to bowl at Heaven's door. Though he can count on some from the Archbishop of Canterbury, and surely his requests roll in like thunder. And Robert Barnes is praying for me, and I for Robert Barnes. Neither of us has much to ask for now, but courage. As Wyatt writes, *Lauda finem*: praise the end.

Edmund Walsingham, the Lieutenant of the Tower, comes next day. 'Do not be alarmed, my lord. I bring no bad news. Only that you must move house.'

So his interrogators are done with him. 'Where am I going?'

'The Bell Tower, sir, next my lodging.'

'I am familiar with it,' he says dryly. 'Can I not go to the Beauchamp Tower?'

'Occupied, my lord.'

'Christophe,' he says, 'pack my books. Send to Austin Friars for warmer clothes for me, the walls are thick there.' He says to the lieutenant, 'When Thomas More was held in the Bell Tower, he was allowed to walk in your garden. Shall I have that liberty?'

'No, my lord.'

Walsingham is a tight-lipped Flodden veteran. He has been in his post fifteen years, and has no intention of making a slip-up now.

'More was not locked in. Shall I be locked in?'

'Yes, my lord.'

He puts his coat on. '*Allons.*' He says his goodbyes to the goddesses; a last flitting glance over his shoulder. No trace of Anne Boleyn. He remembers her saying – was it in this very room? – 'Be good to me.' He thinks, if I see her again, perhaps this time I will.

Out into the open air. He looks about him. All he can see is armed men. The lieutenant says, 'I trust the guard will not disturb you.'

A breath of the river air. A dance of green leaves. He feels the sun on his shoulder. A workman sitting on scaffolding, whistling, his shirt off; 'The Jolly Forester' … He feels netted by the past, suspended in some high blue instant, strung up in air. By noon the forester will be scorched.

> I have been a foster long and many day,
> My locks ben hore.
> I shall hang up my horn by the
>   greenwood spray:
> Foster will I be no more.

The walk is too brief. 'Shall I go to the lower chamber or the upper?'

When he had arrived at the Tower, they had fired the cannon: it is the custom, when a personage is brought in. The ground quakes, the river boils, and inside the accused, as he steps onto the wharf, his marrow wobbles, his spleen protests, the chambers of his skull rattle. On the threshold of the Bell Tower, on the ascending stair, he feels again this deep agitation. It is a weakness, but he will not show it to the lieutenant: just steadies himself with a brush of his fingertips against the wall.

> All the while that my bow I bend,
> Shall I wed no wife:
> I shall build me a bower at the
>   greenwood's end
> Thereto lead my life.

The doors are opened into the lower room. It is a stony, vaulted and spacious chamber. The fireplace is empty and swept clean. The walls here are twelve feet thick, and light falls from windows set high above the head. There is a figure sitting at the table. Silently he asks, 'Is it you?' Thomas More rises from his place, crosses the room and melts into the wall.

* * *

'Martin, is it you? You look well. How's my god-daughter?'

The turnkey takes off his cap. He'd been about to say, sorry to see you here, sir: the usual empty formula; best pre-empt that. 'Five now, sir, and a good little soul, bless you for asking. No harm in her.'

No harm? What strange things people say. 'Is she learning her letters?'

'A girl, sir? Only gets them into trouble.'

'You don't want her to read the gospel?'

'She can marry a man who will read it for her. Can I fetch you anything?'

'Is Lord Lisle still here?'

'I couldn't say.'

'The old lady? Margaret Pole?'

It has occurred to him that Henry might execute Margaret, now he is not standing by to stay his hand. 'Very well,' he says to Martin. 'You have orders not to talk, I understand that. Do you think I could have a fire lit?'

'I'll see to it,' Martin says. 'You always did feel the cold. I remember when you used to come in and sit with Thomas More. You'd say to him, "We should have a fire." He'd say, "I can't afford it, Thomas." You'd say, "Christ save us, I'll pay for the fire – will you stop trying to wring my bloody heart? You may be a papist but you're not a pauper."'

'Did I?' He is amazed. 'Did I say that? My bloody heart?'

'More, he would get you all of a wamble,' Martin says. 'When they rang the curfew, he'd come in from the garden and he'd sit down and write all night. He'd sit at that very table, wrapped in a sheet. It was like a winding sheet – the sight would turn me cold. Myself, I never saw hair of him, not since that day he was led away. But some claim they have. And as I am alive and a Christian man, you will hear the old fellow overhead, Fisher. You hear him dragging himself across the floor.'

'You shouldn't believe in ghosts,' he says uncertainly.

'I don't,' Martin says. 'But who are they to care, if I believe in them or not? You listen out tonight. You can hear old Fisher shuffle across, and then the chair scrape, where he rests his weight on the back of it.'

'There was no weight to rest,' he says. The bishop was so thin that you couldn't use him to stop a draught. What can you do with a man who, when he sat down to dine, would set a skull on the table, where other people would have the salt pot?

'Your boy can sleep in here on a pallet,' Martin says, 'if you don't like to sit up on your own.'

'Sit up? I'll sleep. I always sleep. Martin, if my son Gregory were brought here as prisoner, or Sir Richard Cromwell, you would tell me?'

Martin scrapes his foot along the floor. 'Aye, I would. I would try to get you word.'

There are old rush mats underfoot. He thinks, I will get something better sent from home: if anything is left.

It is a chamber for a favoured prisoner, but there is no mistaking it for an ordinary room. Still, the night passes without incident. He listens out for Fisher but the old bishop is nodding. He wakes once and thinks, kings may repent, there are examples. For a while his mind goes round and round, seeking one. The chroniclers tell us that in the reign of the third Henry, the king punished his servant Hubert de Burgh, Earl of Kent, starving him out of sanctuary and throwing him into a deep dungeon. Hubert lived two years in irons, before he escaped and got his earldom back.

With the morning Rafe comes. 'So, my letter, how did he receive it?'

Rafe's movements are slow; he looks as though he has been at work through the night. He wants to call for a cup of ale for him, but Rafe says, no, no, I must tell you what passed. 'The king turned out his councillors. And then he caused me to read your letter out loud.'

'That must have taken you some time.'

'When I had done he said, "Read it again, Sadler." I said, "The whole, sir?" He hesitated and said, "No, you may omit the story of the marriage. Read where he makes his pleas."

'The second time I read it, he seemed much moved. I did not want to break his train of thought, but then I dared to say, "It takes but one word, sir." He looked at me: "One word to do what?" He took my meaning, of course and I dared not venture further. Then he said, "Yes, I could free Cromwell, could I not? I could restore him tomorrow."

'I said, "The French would be amazed, sir" – thinking to prompt him, because you always counselled him, do what your enemy likes least.'

'But I think the French are not the enemy,' he says. 'Since about last week.'

'But then the king said, "You know, he has never forgiven me for Wolsey, and I have long wondered, to what extremity will sorrow lead him? Even when my son Richmond lay dying, he was pestering the physicians with his enquiries. Bishop Gardiner says, the cardinal himself might forgive, but the cardinal's man never will."

'I said, "Sir, I swear it, the earl is reconciled. He has let the cardinal go." But he cut me off. He said, "Here in my writing box I have his earlier letter." He turned the key and took it out and gave it to me in my hand. He said, "Read this one. Read where it says he would make me live ever young." I did so. The king said, "He cannot, can he?" I would swear, sir, that tears stood in his eyes. My heart beat fast, I thought, he will utter now: "Let Essex go." But he got up and walked to the window. He said, "Thank you for your patience, Master Secretary." I said, "I was well-trained, sir, by a patient man." He said, "Now you can leave me."'

'You did well, Rafe. You did more than I had any right to expect.'

Rafe says, 'When I was a little child you brought me on a journey. You set me by the fire and said, this is where you live now, we will be good to you, never fear. I had left my mother that day and I did not know where I was, and I had never seen London, still less your house, but I never cried, did I?'

He cries now, like an angry baby, in the ungraceful way that red-haired people do: his skin flushing, his body trembling. 'Where in the name of God is Cranmer?' he says. 'Where is Wyatt? Where is Edward Seymour? They will be ashamed for the term of their lives.'

'Cranmer will live past this,' he says. 'I do not say he will sleep well at night, but he will survive. And Wyatt will write a verse about me. And Seymour must live to guide the little prince, when he, when Henry –' He will not say it. The thought has entered his mind before now: what if a fever rises this very night, what if he coughs and strains to breathe, what if his lungs fill with water again and the poison from his leg kills him? Then the state will hold its breath. The executive arm will suspend its action, even though the knife is raised. The prince will need me. The council will need me. Edward Seymour will turn the key and let me go.

When Rafe goes out, he tells Christophe, 'Get a pack of cards.' He shows him the painted queen, shuffles and lays out three. 'Now, where is she?'

Christophe's stubby finger descends.

'No.' He turns the card up. 'Now, watch me, I am teaching you this trick. So if you are ever without money or food, the lady will provide.' He says softly, 'It is only if the worst should befall. You will go to Gregory. Or Master Richard will take you in. Tell them I say to get you a wife, to save you from sin.'

He is working on how to save his household staff. Some will go to Gregory, others to Richard – presuming the king does not strip the Cromwells of all they have. Wyatt will take his pick, now he is moneyed and has several properties to staff. He thinks, Brandon will want my huntsmen, my dog-keepers. Some merchant in the city, who knew his father, will take Dick Purser. The Italian merchants will covet my cooks. Young Mathew can go back to Wolf Hall, though his French will be wasted in Wiltshire. Back in April, when he had thought he would fall any moment, he had called together the singing children from his chapel; he had thanked them for their services, wished them good luck in their lives, and sent them home to their parents, each with a present of twenty pounds. Once he was made earl he thought, shall I recall them? Now he is glad he did not.

In Italy, when he was working for the bankers, he learned the art of memory, and has practised it through his life since. You make an image for each memory and leave them in the churches you frequent, in the streets you walk, on the banks of the river you sail. You leave them in ditches, between the furrows of a field, and hanging from trees: crossbows and skillets, dragons and stars. When you run out of real places you dream up more; you design islands, like Utopia.

Now, sensing he has less than a week to live, he must pick up his images from where he has left them, walking his own inner terrain. He must traverse his whole life, waking and sleeping: you cannot leave your memories alone in this world, for other men to own.

In the dusk the cardinal returns, as a disturbance in his vision. 'Where have you been?' he asks him.

'I don't know, Thomas.' The old man sounds forlorn. 'I'd tell you if I could.'

Offered a chair, he looks at it, averse. 'I won't sit where Thomas More sat. For what that ingrate did to me, I will never pass the time of day with him. If I smell him these days, I go the other way.'

He says, 'Sir, you know I did not betray you? Despite what your daughter thinks?'

Wolsey paces, dragging his scarlet. At last he says, 'Well, Thomas … I dare say … women get things wrong.'

His great fatigue, which had lifted when he was facing Gardiner or Norfolk every day, now returns. The feeling around his heart – that it is crushed, forced out of shape – he now understands as a deformity caused by grief. He feels he is dragging corpses, shovelling them up: Robert Aske, Tom Truth, Harry Norris and Will Brereton, little Francis Weston and Mark Smeaton with his lute. And even those in whose death no one can say he took a hand: Jane the queen, Harry Percy, Thomas Boleyn.

His mind turns over the questions that have been put to him, as if the interrogations were still going on. He thinks about Richard Riche: 'In June 1535, the prisoner said to me, "Richard, when the reign of King Cromwell dawns, you shall be a duke."'

And Audley saying, faintly, 'Riche, we cannot put that in the record. I think my lord was making a joke.'

He recalls Wriothesley, his outburst one afternoon: 'He thought he was king already. He acted like a king. I remember when French merchants came to Greenwich, the year of the ice. They had goods they pressed on his Majesty, and his Majesty put them off, saying he had spent all his money fighting the Pilgrims. But then, seeing their distress and their journey wasted, he graciously agreed to purchases. But my lord Privy Seal forced them out of the king's chambers and compounded a bargain with them, making them sell him at a lower price those goods that were intended for the king.'

He recalls that day: the ice-light in the chamber, the enticements laid before Henry: a velvet dog collar, a pair of strawberry sleeves and, for him, Lord Cromwell, the murrey-colour silk. Call-Me said, 'Be careful sir.' He remembers the strain on Call-Me's face. He didn't think he meant, be careful of me.

Edmund Walsingham comes in every day or so, and stays only long enough to witness his prisoner is still sound in mind and limb: it is as if he fears conversation will contaminate him. Kingston has his duties as councillor, and is at the Tower only on days of portent. So he has no one to talk to, except Christophe and his turnkey and the dead; and with daylight the ghosts melt away. You can hear a sigh, a souf-flation, as they disperse themselves. They become a whistling draught, a hinge that wants oil; they subside into natural things, a vagrant mist, a coil of smoke from a dying fire.

He lives in dread that the king will stop Rafe's visits. But it appears that the king still wishes him to have some news. Lord Hungerford is under sentence of death, Rafe says. 'The French ambassador is spreading the rumour he has raped his daughter. But no such charge has been brought. There is enough with the sorcery and the sodomy.'

'Marillac is emboldened,' he says, 'after all the rumours he has spread about me. There seem to be no consequences.'

He cannot find it in his heart to be sorry for Hungerford: except he is sorry for any confined creature, who knows his next outing will be his death. He would like Wolsey to come in so they could have a game of chess: though you should never play chess with a prelate, they always have a pawn in their sleeves. He craves the sight of

Thomas More, with his grey stubble of beard and his tired eyes, sitting at the table as he used to do: that table which had taken on the aspect of an altar, the candle flame tugged by a draught. In the wet spring of 1535, More had a trick of absenting himself from the scene, so that what sat before you appeared already dead, a carcass, like the silvery corpse that you find in a spider's web when the spider has died at home.

They speak of More as a martyr now, instead of a man who miscalculated the odds. He had said to Chapuys, More thought he could manipulate Henry, and perhaps he was right; but then he met what he had not reckoned on, he met Anne Boleyn. We councillors think we are men of vision and learning, we gravely delineate our position, set forth our plans and argue our case far into the night. Then some little girl sweeps through and upsets the candle and sets fire to our sleeve; leaves us slapping ourselves like madmen, trying to save our skin. It rankles with me, that some sneak thief like Riche should best me; that a fool like Polo should hole my boat, and a dolt like Lisle should drown me. Perhaps some people will say I have died for the gospel, as More died for the Pope. But most will not think me a martyr for anything, except the great cause of getting on in life.

By mid-month, the king is a single man again. Convocation first, then Parliament has acted to free him. Anna has agreed to everything proposed to her, and given back her wedding ring. Rafe says, 'Parliament will petition the king to marry again. For the safety and comfort of the realm. However disinclined he feels, personally.' He sighs. Master Secretary's chain weighs heavy.

No rain falls. The heat does not falter. It seems Henry means to kill his slave through sheer disuse. The Visconti in Milan devised a torture regime that lasted for forty days, and on the fortieth day, though not before, the prisoner died. On the first day, you might cut off the man's ear. Next day he rests. On the third day, gouge out an eye. He rests; he has another eye, but he does not know when you will choose to blind him. On day five, you will begin to tear off his skin in strips. This is not for any information he might give you. This is merely to make a spectacle, to overawe the city.

855

The third week in July his interrogators return, bringing fresh charges of corruption. There is a case that has been dragging on two years now, about a ship belonging to the brother of the Constable of France. He has the facts in his head, and he is sure he is clear in the matter, but he sees there is no defence against the version the French present. François is intent on hurrying him to the scaffold. 'I don't die quick enough for his liking,' he says to Gardiner.

'I doubt it will be long now,' the bishop says. 'Any day now the king will sign your attainder into law. Parliament will be rising. His Majesty will want to leave London for the summer.'

'How is Norfolk's niece?'

Gardiner looks gloomy. 'Very pleased with her great fortune. A giddy little creature. Still, not for me to question the king's choice.'

'Bear that in mind,' he says, 'and you'll go far, boy.' He smiles. 'Of course she is giddy. What else, at that age? You would not want her to think too much. History is against her.'

Gardiner looks pensive: 'I fear it's against us all.'

It is a busy day at the Bell Tower; Norfolk comes after, with more papers about the French ship. 'You are to write to the council about it.'

'Not to the king himself?'

'Write by all means. I do suppose, though, he will be too occupied with my niece to read it.'

'Has he said how I am to die, my lord?'

Norfolk does not answer. 'My son Surrey says, if you had been left to run your course, you would have left no nobleman alive. He says, now is Cromwell stricken by his own staff. Now it is with him as it has been with many a man who has crossed him, both simple and grand.'

'I do not dispute it,' he says. 'But it might give my lord Surrey pause, to imagine how he would order himself were he to find himself a prisoner here. Fortune and the king have raised him high, but he should not trust to that, the ground beneath our feet is slippery.'

'I'll tell him,' Norfolk says. 'By God, you wax sententious! Wise men have no need of such warnings. They wash their eyes clean every day. You think the king ever loved you? No. To him you were an instrument. As I am. A device. You and me, my son Surrey, we are no more to him than a trebuchet, a catapult, or any other engine of war. Or a dog. A dog who has served him through the hunting season. What do you do with a dog, when the season ends? You hang it.'

Norfolk ambles out. He can hear him talking to Martin outside the door, but he cannot make out what he says. 'Christophe,' he calls. 'Paper and ink.'

Christophe is surprised. 'Once again?'

He writes to the council. He denies he profited from the misfortune of the constable's brother or his ship. Norfolk knows, he writes, he was present when the matter was aired; Fitzwilliam knows about it, and Bishop Bonner, he was envoy in France, he will remember the whole affair. For an hour, thinking and writing, he is taken out of himself, as if he were back at the council board. Straight away, he begins a letter to Henry. He has a good deal to say, but he knows that if the letter strays outside the conventions of supplication, Henry will not be able to hear it – not three times, not even once. Is it possible for a man to abase himself more than he has already? By mid-afternoon, he is weary. He gives it up. He puts down the pen and allows his mind to range. Chapuys is back in London, reappointed ambassador. Back at the old game, he thinks. Henry makes a bow to the French, then a genuflection to the Emperor. The cardinal would recognise it all.

That night when Wolsey comes blinking in, he says to him, 'Be my good father. Stay with me till this is over.'

'I'd like to stay,' the old man says, 'but I don't know if I have the strength.' He seems, muttering in the corner, to be preoccupied with his own end. He talks about the candles around his deathbed, George Cavendish gripping his hand. He describes the drawn faces of the monks at Leicester Abbey, peering down at him. He talks of his hasty burial, which he seems to know all about. 'Why do I not have my right tomb,' he says, 'when I paid so much to that Italian of yours? Where are my great candlesticks? My dancing angels, where did they go?'

Martin, out of his charity, comes to sit with him. In More's last days, the gaoler says, he talked a lot – he always did talk, just not when you wanted him to. He would talk of when he was a little boy, a scholar at St Anthony's school. He would bear his satchel down West Cheap towards Threadneedle Street. On a winter's morning at six o'clock, the streets were lit only by the frost on the cobblestones. St Anthony's pigs, they called them, those little schoolfellows; by lantern light they assembled to chant their Latin.

'Did he ever talk about Lambeth, about the palace?'

'What, Archbishop Cranmer? He hated him.'

'I mean, Lambeth in Morton's day, when we were young. Thomas More was there as a boy, getting ready for Oxford, day after day at his books. Did he mention me?'

'You? What had you to do with it, sir?'

He smiles. 'I was there too.'

Uncle John says, 'See the trays? That's the young gentlemen's suppers. They're all studying hard, so if they wake up in the night, they're turning over in their head a hard problem about Pythagoras, or St Jerome. And it makes them peckish. So they need a little bite of bread in their cupboards, and a measure of small beer. Now, boy, you know the third staircase? Up the top there's Master Thomas More. He don't like disturbing, so you creep in like a mouse. If he looks up you make your reverence. If he don't you just creep out again, and not so much as a "Bless you." Have you got that?'

He's got it. He's got the tray in his grasp, and he sets off on the sturdy legs that would make you think he was well-fed. What if he sat down on the bottom step, and ate the bread and drank the beer himself? Would he hear in the night Master More crying out with pangs in his belly? 'Oh, feed me, feed me,' he whimpers in a pitiful voice, as he mounts. 'Oh, St Jerome, feed me!'

On the top step, the devil enters into him. He kicks open the door and bawls, 'Master Thomas More!'

The young scholar looks up. His expression is mild and curious but he circles his book with his arm as if to protect it.

'Master Thomas More, his supper!'

He rams it in the corner cupboard. 'Hinge wants oiling,' he says. 'I'll be back tomorrow and see to that.' He creaks it to and fro, so it makes a double squeak. He wants to ask, what's Pythagoras, is it an animal, is it a disease, is it a shape you can draw?

'Master Thomas More, God bless him!' he shouts. 'Good night!'

He is about to slam the door when Master More calls, 'Child?' He intrudes himself back into the room. Master More sits blinking at him. He is fourteen, fifteen, skinny. Walter would laugh him out of the yard. Master More says softly, 'If I gave you a penny, would you not do that, another night?'

He bounces down the stair richer. He bounces on every tread, and whistles. Fair's fair. He was only paid to be quiet in the room, not quiet outside it. Master More will have to dig deeper into his pocket if he wants to live in the silence of the tomb. He runs away, towards his football game.

After that, every night he would lurk on the stair like a demon, till More thought the danger was passed. Then he'd burst in, bellowing 'How do you, sir?' slapping his tray down so that More splashed his ink. When More reminded him about the penny he'd paid, he opened his eyes wide: 'I thought that was one time only?'

With a sigh and a half-smile, Master More disbursed.

He thought Thomas More would complain about him to the kitchen steward, who would call him in and hit him. Or perhaps the archbishop himself would call him in and hit him; or being a man of God, only harangue him. If that happened, he was planning to harangue him back. There were things old Morton should know, about how his kitchen was run: pewter that jumped off the table into some blackguard's sack, fingers that dipped straight from a laundry-maid's quim and into the fricassee.

But no one called him in. No one hit him: except the usual people, his father Walter, his sisters, his uncles, his aunts, the priest if he could catch him, Sion Madoc's dad, different members of the Williams family, the Wycks family … but it seemed Thomas More had not hit him, even by proxy. The blow was held in suspension; he felt it hovering in the air, in those years when More used to hunt out heresy, and raid the homes and shops of his friends in the city. And when the blow fell, it was from another direction entirely; it was More who suffered, bundled to the scaffold on a wet July day, one of those days when the wind seems to come at you from all directions at once: the flutter of his shirt as he stood with neck bared, rivulets like tears running down his face, and a fine mist lying over the walls of the Tower, seeming to melt them into the grey, swollen river. It was an easy death, as these things go: a single stroke.

When they met as grown men, More had not remembered him at all.

Eustache Chapuys has returned to a London that is much changed: air sullen with suspicion, a queen come and gone. The king is sweeping up not only those he deems heretics, but also remnants of papistry, so the gaols are full. The ambassador looks fatigued and frail, they say, and expresses no joy at being back in his old post. He, Cromwell, knows there is no point in asking for a visit – being a man of sense Chapuys would not come near him – but he wonders, will he be there when I suffer? He does not want his son to be there, even if it is a simple beheading; he remembers how Gregory suffered at the death of Anne Boleyn, who was a stranger to him. He says to Rafe, 'It is time for Gregory to write a letter repudiating me. He should speak ill of me. Say he does not know how he comes to be related to such a traitor. He should plead for the chance to redeem my errors and crimes, by serving his Majesty in the years to come.'

'Yes,' Rafe says, 'but you know Gregory's letters. *And now no more for lack of time.*' He pauses. 'I have had his wife Bess do it. Being the sister of the late Queen Jane, she was best placed, I thought, to touch the king's heart.'

He thinks, I was always quick in everything; but Rafe Sadler, he is quick when it matters. 'Even in the midst of his new happiness, I do not doubt he will remember Jane.'

Rafe says, 'It is forbidden to wear mourning for the death of a traitor. But Richard Cromwell says he will do it.'

'He should not,' he says mildly. 'Tell him it is not what I advise.'

All the same, he smiles. Rafe looks around. 'Shall I ask Edmund Walsingham to move you elsewhere? It makes me uneasy, this place.'

'You get used to it. If you stand on that stool, you can get a view of the Byward Tower. Try it.'

Rafe cannot see out, because he is too short. But the attempt allows him to keep his face to the wall till he is composed, and then embrace his master a last time, and go out into the hot afternoon.

When the door has closed, and Rafe's footsteps and voice have faded away, he opens his books. Volumes of legends, compendiums of saints: legends of consolation. Thank God they did not take them away; but he thinks, I must make sure they do not go astray, after. I must leave a letter about those few possessions I retain, and hope it will be honoured.

He reads the book of Erasmus, *Preparation unto Death*: written only five, six years back, under the patronage of Thomas Boleyn. It tires his eyes; he would rather look at pictures. He lays the book aside and turns the pages of his engravings. He sees Icarus, his wings melting, plummeting into the waves. It was Daedalus who invented the wings and made the first flight, he more circumspect than his son: scraping above the labyrinth, bobbing over walls, skimming the ocean so low his feet were wet. But then as he rose on the breeze, peasants gaped upwards, supposing they were seeing gods or giant moths; and as he gained height there must have been an instant when the artificer knew, in his pulse and his bones, *This is going to work*. And that instant was worth the rest of his life.

On the afternoon of 27 July, both the constable and the lieutenant come in. Kingston says, 'Sir, the king grants you mercy as to the manner of your death. It is to be the axe, and may I say that I rejoice to hear it –' Kingston breaks off. 'I beg your lordship's pardon – I mean to say, your lordship has often sought such mercy for others, and seldom failed.'

So I won't see August, he thinks. The hares that flee the harvester, the cold morning dews after St Bartholomew's Day. Or the leaf fall, the dark blue nights.

'Will it be tomorrow?'

Kingston is not supposed to tell him. But Walsingham says smoothly, 'If your lordship said your prayers tonight, you would do well.'

Kingston gives up the pretence. 'I shall come about the accustomed hour of nine, and with you will go Lord Hungerford.'

So I am to die with a monster, he thinks. Or a man who has made monstrous enemies, who have great imaginative powers to shape the condemned to their desires.

Walsingham says, 'Will you have a confessor?'

'I will if I can have Robert Barnes.'

The two officers look at each other. 'You should know he is condemned,' the lieutenant says. 'He will go to Smithfield in a day or so.'

'Alone?'

'With the priest Garrett, and Father William Jerome. We are waiting for our orders. And certain papists are expected to hang in a day or two: Thomas Abel, that was chaplain to the Princess of Aragon.'

Garrett, Jerome: friends of his and of the gospel. Abel, a veteran opponent. A crowded week, he thinks. 'I hope there are enough competent people.'

Kingston says testily, 'We do our best.'

He stands up. He wishes to be left alone. 'It is not long since I confessed, and I have had scant opportunity of sin since I came here.'

'That is not it.' Kingston is disconcerted. 'You are meant to pass your whole life in review, and discover new sins each time.'

'I know that,' he says. 'I know how to do it. I live here with Thomas More. I have read the books. We are all dying, just at different speeds.'

Walsingham says, 'The Duke of Norfolk has asked that your lordship be informed – the king marries Katherine Howard tomorrow.'

Christophe says, 'I will bring my pallet. I will stay beside you tonight.'

'You need not fear,' he says. 'I shall not put an end to myself. I shall trust the headsman to do it quicker than I could.'

'You will write letters?'

He thinks about it. 'No. I am done.'

He sends Christophe out to bask in the sunshine: to drink his health, and sit, drowsy, on a wall, among other servants, talking no doubt of the uncertainty of their fortune, with such masters.

He thinks of how tomorrow will be. By rank he is above Hungerford, so he will die first. The king's decision has spared him much agony and shame. He will pray for a clean stroke. He thinks of Anne Boleyn, ordering up her coronation clothes: '*Thomas must go into crimson.*'

On the scaffold he will praise the king: his mercy, his grace, his care for all his people. It is expected of him, and he has a duty to those left behind. He will say, I am not a heretic, I die a member of the universal church; and let the crowd make what they will of it. Though every man dreads to know the hour of his death, the Christian dreads more a sudden end, such as his father met: *mors improvisa* with no time to repent. Neighbours in Putney believed Walter Cromwell had mended his ways, given up the drinking, rowing and fighting. But one night he quarrelled with a fellow churchwarden – and it was no godly dispute, it was a row over cockfighting. Coming away, leaving the other fellow with a black eye, Walter kicked his way into the house and shouted for victuals. He was pale and sweating, the witnesses said, but still he fell on a dish of cold meat, all the time vituperating. Next he complained about his dinner, rubbing his chest and saying it had given him a pain; five minutes later he fell face-down on the table. They laid him flat, and, 'God damn you, I'm choking,' he said, 'get me up, get me up –' and that was the last word he spoke.

There was a good crowd at his burying. He, Thomas, had paid for Masses for his soul. 'Do you think it does any good?' he had said to the priest.

'Don't despair of him,' the fellow said. 'He was rough, but he wasn't all bad.'

'No,' he said, 'I don't mean, will prayers do Walter any good. I mean, do they do good for any dead person? God is watching us all our lives. Surely, if you live as long as Walter, God has formed a view. Unless He always knows.'

'That sounds like heresy to me,' the priest said.

'Of course it does. It hits your pocket. If God knows His mind, what becomes of your chantries and your rosaries and your fees for a thousand years of Masses?'

He remembers himself lying smashed and broken in the inn yard in Putney, fifteen years old: his father standing over him, his blood on the cobbles, the twine of his father's boot sprung free from the leather. Walter shouting down at him and he shouting back, *je voudrais mourir autrement* – not here, not now, and not like this.

But, no, he thinks, I was not shouting. I did not speak French. Torn and contused, I got myself off the ground and across the Narrow Sea. I fought other men's wars, for money, till at last I had the sense to earn it in easier ways: Cremuello at your service, your shadow in a glass.

One night long ago in Venice he had glimpsed a woman, a wraith in the watery mist. A courtesan, she let her lazy laughter float after her on the air; the streak of her yellow scarf was the only colour, the click of her shoes on cobbles the only sound. Then a door opened in the wall, and darkness swallowed her up. She was gone so swiftly and completely that he wondered if he had dreamed her. He had thought, if ever I need to disappear, Venice is where I will come.

Sometimes in those days he woke from dreams that threatened to drown him, his eyelashes wet; he woke between languages, not knowing where he was but filled with an inchoate longing to be somewhere else. He thinks back to his childhood, his days on the river, days in the fields. His life has been filled with fugitive women. He remembers the stepmothers Walter would bring home: scarcely had you made your duties to one of them, before Walter fell out with her, or she flounced off with her clothes tied up in a bundle. He thinks of his daughters Anne and Grace; perhaps he will meet them as women grown? He thinks of Anselma's daughter, moving slowly in his house with soft and curious eyes, picking up those things that belonged to him, his seal, his books, examining his globe of the world and asking, 'This island, where is this? Is this the New World?'

Mr Wriothesley has moved into Austin Friars, they tell him. The king has ordered him to dissolve the Cromwell household. By day, Call-Me strides through the rooms, expansive, breathing in the smell of paper and ink, rosewater and resin. But by night the leopard pads the floor, smelling the fur of long-dead animals, spaniels and marmosets, gazing upward at the nightingale mute in her cage. She sniffs out the boiled meats of a decade of dinners, and the bones of mice behind the panelling; her opaque, unmoved glance follows the flight of a bird outside the window. He thinks, I have spent hundreds of pounds on glass. Wriothesley cannot dissolve my household. He can only walk through the glass and shatter it, bleeding from a thousand cuts.

Christophe comes back. He looks unsteady: drink, or sun, or something else. He says, 'You could have stayed out longer. I did not lack for company.'

July, and the nights are short. When the light begins to fade, he sends the boy out again to find his supper, while he thinks of Heaven and Hell. When he pictures Hell he can only think of a cold place, a wasteland, a wharf, a marsh, a landing stage; Walter distantly bawling, then the bawling coming nearer. That is how it will be – not pain itself, but the constant apprehension of pain; the constant apprehension of fault, the knowledge that you are going to be punished for something you couldn't help and didn't even know was wrong; and the discord in Hell will be constant, repeating for ever and ever, a violent argument being carried on in the next room. When he thinks of Heaven he imagines it as a vast party arranged by the cardinal; like that field in Picardy, the Field of the Cloth of Gold, with palaces built on unlikely and marginal ground, acres of clear glass catching the sun. But his master should have built in a softer climate. Perhaps, he thinks, this time tomorrow I will inhabit some kinder city: the blue shadows lengthening, the sun's final rays softening the lines of bell towers and domes; ladies in niches at their prayers, a small dog with a plumed tail strolling the streets; indifferent doves alighting on gilded spires.

After supper he packs up his books. He will ask Kingston to give them to Rafe. He puts away Clendardus, his grammar. He has not made much progress with Hebrew, in part because he has been occupied with the king's business; there was never a prisoner more hard-pressed, or who called for so much ink. He wishes he had ever met the scholar – Nicolas Cleynaerts, as he is properly; his Antwerp friends say he is a very great linguist, who has spent many hours by lamplight, through the northern winters, learning to copy the loops and curls of Arabic script. In pursuit of books in that tongue he went some years ago to Salamanca, and from there to Granada, but only to be disappointed; the Inquisition is diligent these days in locking away the writings of the Arabs. Some say Clendardus will go into Africa next, and learn to read the holy book of the Mohammedans. He pictures this scholar, strolling through the markets. His diet will be dates and olives, and honeyed pears with orange-blossom water, and lamb baked with saffron and apricots.

All your life you tramp the empty road with the wind at your back. You are hungry and your spirit is perturbed as you journey on into the gloom. But when you get to your destination the doorkeeper knows you. A torch goes before you as you cross the court. Inside there is a fire and a flask of wine, there is a candle and beside the candle your book. You pick it up and find your place is marked. You sit down by the fire, open it, and begin your story. You read on, into the night.

At nine o'clock, 27 July, he kneels down and makes his prayer. He had wondered how you would recognise your dead, when you yourself go to Judgement. But as he waits out this last night, he sees how they are visible, and how they shine. They are distilled into a spark, into an instant. There is air between their ribs, their flesh is honeycombed with light, and the marrow of their bones is molten with God's grace.

He thinks he sees the eel boy looking at him from the corner of the room. Shog off, you streak of piss, he says.

He does not sleep, then perhaps he does. He dreams of four women, veiled, standing by his bed. He wakes and looks for them in the dark, but there is only Christophe, snoring on his pallet. He pictures Christophe in Calais, at Calkwell Street: his ropes of hair, his unspeakable apron. Who could guess the boy would be the companion of his last night? He thinks of the memory engine, its ledges and recesses, its vaults.

It must be that he sleeps again, because he sees himself as a child. All about him are the airy forms of playmates, other sons that Walter had, sons born before him who had died. He sees these elders, some three or four of them kneeling in profile, carved on a bench end or painted on a wall: their sizes running down from the tallest and the longest dead, to himself, the littlest and the least.

He half-wakes and asks himself, did Walter speak of such sons? Never: yet each time his father had expressed dissatisfaction with him – with, say, a boot or a fist – he had felt their frail dead presence, their silent commiseration, as a faint stir in the air.

The first bells make him sit up. He puts a foot on the floor. He hears Christophe muttering something: prayers, he hopes. He sees himself, crawling across the cobbles in Florence, damaged beyond repair: to the Frescobaldi gate.

II
Light
28 July 1540

A prisoner thinks of nothing but meals. 'Christophe, where's my breakfast? And my water to wash – I cannot meet God in this state.'

Cold sweat. He rubs his hand across his chin. They have been wary of sending him a razor: as you would be.

The boy creeps in with bread and ale. 'Martin brings cold fowl.'

'Good. See if you can get anything out of him. About what time I shall go.' He doesn't trust Kingston's schedules. He kept Anne waiting a whole day.

But Martin will not spend many words on this prisoner now; he represents a task near-done. He thinks, I did not know that, when you are dying, no one will look at you. Nor do you want to look at them. You see a pattern you cannot imitate.

He yawns. But speaks to himself: you must not be tired. If a man should live as if every day is his last, he should also die as if there is a day to come, and another after that.

Martin says – to Christophe, rather than to the prisoner – 'Lord Hungerford, they don't know how to convey him. He saw the devil in the night. He's lying on the floor bawling like a drunk.'

The sheriffs, William Laxton and Martin Bowes, come in with Kingston. They make him a civil good morning: 'Are you ready, Lord Cromwell? We are ready for you.'

They give him coins, which he will pass to the executioner, payment for his services. His coat, too, will be the headsman's perquisite. He thinks, I should have looked out the purple one. Or that violent orange coat, that upset Mr Wriothesley once. It occurs to him that when he is dead, other people will be getting on with their day; it will be dinner time or nearly, there will be a bubbling of pottages, the clatter of ladles, the swift scoop of meats from spit to platter; a thousand dogs will stir from sleep and wag their tails; napkins will be unfurled and twitched over the shoulder, fingers dipped in rosewater, bread broken. And when the crumbs are swept away, the pewter piled for scouring, his body will be broken meat, and the executioner will clean the blade.

'Messages?' Martin says. He is willing to bear them, for payment from the dead man's kin.

'Tell my son –' He breaks off. 'Tell Master Secretary Sadler … no, never mind. Send to Austin Friars and tell Thomas Avery –' No. Avery doesn't need telling twice.

He says to the sheriffs, 'There is a Plymouth man, William Hawkins, has fitted a ship for Brazil. He is taking lead and copper, woollen cloth, combs and knives and nineteen dozen nightcaps. I would have liked to know how that works out.'

The sheriffs make commiserating noises. No doubt they wish they had invested.

He looks back over his shoulder. 'Christophe, get a broom and sweep this floor.'

The boy's face crumples. 'Sir, I must accompany you. Some menial may sweep. Here,' he fumbles inside his shirt, 'I have a medal, it is a holy medal, my mother gave it to me, take it for the love of Christ.'

He says, 'I do not need an image, because I shall see God's face.'

Christophe holds it out on his palm. 'Sir, take it back to her. She is waiting for it.'

He suffers it to be hung about him. He remembers the medal his sister gave him; it lies beneath the sea. 'Now Christophe, obey me this last time. When you have cleaned the floor you may follow on behind, but no fighting. I must pray, you understand, so do not interrupt my prayer. Martin, do you pray for me too, while I am dying. And after, if I may, I will pray for you.'

He remembers what George Boleyn had said: we have a man plays Robin Goodfellow. When kings and queens have quit the scene, he comes with broom and candle, to show the play is done.

The light is early and tender, the sky eggshell blue. He can feel already it will be another hot day. He must walk out of the fortress as far as Tower Hill, where they have set up a public scaffold.

He stares, incredulous, at the bristling ranks of the guard. 'All these?' he says to Kingston.

'Wait, wait, wait!' yells the captain of the guard. 'Halt, halt, halt!'

It is only Hungerford. He is propped up between two officers, his mouth gaping, his feet dragging. The intention is for the processions to merge. Hungerford's glazed eyes pass over him as if he is a stranger. 'My lord?' he says. 'We have very little time now and I trust our pain will be sharp but will not endure. Are you man enough to bear yourself in hope? If you are truly sorry for what you have done, there is mercy enough with God.'

He has been in prison forty-eight days, during which time he has hardly stepped out of doors. Even this light seems to dazzle, so he thinks of Tyndale, walking in the bleach fields. Rafe is right, he thinks, we always complain of the weather, and today is not what it should be. An Englishman dies drenched, in the rain that has enwrapped him all his life. Then he lurks about his old haunts in the drizzle and mist, so you cannot be sure whether he is quick or dead. The climate protects him, as a cupped hand protects a candle.

They are outside the fortress, on Tower Hill. The crowd surging towards the execution ground are walking on their own dead, their foremothers and fathers. They say the bones of thousands lie underground, the men and women of London killed by plague. They fell in the streets and died where they fell, they were carried off in such haste that they were buried in their good boots, and not even their purses cut; so if any man dared dig for it, there's a fortune beneath our feet.

It is not clear, from the roaring, whether the Londoners are there to regret or revile. But the king has turned out some six hundred soldiers so it hardly matters. And perhaps they don't know themselves. After the silence of the Bell Tower, he feels he is on a battlefield, moving to the beat of the drum: *boro borombetta …*

Scaramella to the war is gone …

Now the pages of the book of his life are turning faster and faster. The book of his heart is unscrolling, the lines erasing themselves. Between his prayers run the lines of a verse:

> I am as I am and so will I be
> But how that I am, none knoweth truly
> Be it evil, be it well, be I bound, be I free,
> I am as I am and so will I be …
>
> … But how that is I leave to you.
> Judge as ye list, false or true
> Ye know no more than afore ye knew
> Yet I am as I am, whatever ensue.

His heart thuds as if it will break out of his chest. Behind him, another drumbeat, *rat-tat-tat*. It trips the rhythm of his own heart – *pit-pat, rat-tat*. He feels the surge of his blood check and stand, like a tide about to turn. He swivels his head, distressed, to the source of the racket, a drum in the crowd. The guard close in, as if to block his view. Why? Do they think it is a signal? *Rat-tat-tat*: do they think he hopes to be rescued?

Scaramella fa la gala …

'Look where you are going, my lord,' one of the guard says; and he does, and finds he is at the foot of the scaffold. 'So one arrives,' he says. Thomas Wyatt stands before him. It was Wyatt who wrote the verse: who but he? *Judge as ye list, false or true …* Wyatt holds out his hands. They have not bound him, so he is able to grasp them. 'Do not weep,' he says. 'If there is anything to forgive, I forgive it. Mind, that does not go for Stephen Gardiner. But I forgive the king. Be quiet now and you will hear me do it.'

He thinks, there is death in Wyatt's eyes. Who can better recognise it, than I? Your enemies will flourish. You will follow after.

'Go up,' one of the guard says.

He tries to shake off their hands. 'I can do this.' His heart is still tripping, racing. But they will help you whether you need it or no. Men have been known to fall. Men have been known to plummet. Men have been known to do anything and everything. Lords have stood up to death; indeed, they have stood up after death. In the days of our ancestors Thomas Fitzalan, who was Earl of Arundel, was axed down on this spot and his corpse leapt upright to say a Pater Noster. All headsmen, when they meet in their conclaves, talk of it as a fact.

His foot is now on the step of the scaffold. His mind is quiet but the body has its own business, and that business includes trembling. His head turns again. He is not looking for pardon. He knows the king is busy getting married. All he is looking for is the source of the noise, to quell it, because he wants to die listening to his own heart, till verse and prayer fade and heart says hush.

Then in the depths of the packed crowd he sees Christophe. He is pushing forward, flailing his arms. Please God he has not a weapon. His whole body braces, ready for a mêlée. 'My lord, my lord,' Christophe calls. The guard make a wall, but Christophe's arm snakes between them as if to touch him. One of the men raises his armoured fist. He hears a crack. He sees the boy's face twist in shock and pain. Holding out his arm like a broken wing, his voice hoarse, his body convulsing, he speaks his curse: 'Henry King of England! I, Christophe Cremuel, curse you. The Holy Ghost curses you. Your own mother curses you. I hope a leper spits on you. I hope your whore has the pox. I hope you go to sea in a boat with a hole in it. I hope the waters of your heart rise up and spout down your nose. May you fall under a cart. May rot rise up from your heels to your head, going slowly, so you take seven years to die. May God squash you. May Hell gape.'

Christophe is hauled away. The crowd is so thick he can hardly distinguish one man from another. There are places kept for courtiers at a spectacle like this, but he will not afford them a glance. All the bloodied waters have run under the bridges. *And now no more for lack of time.*

He is face to face with the executioner. He sees the spectators spiralling away from him, growing very small. He can smell drink on the man's breath. Not a good start. He can imagine Walter beside him, 'Christ alive, who sold you this axe? They saw you coming! Here, give it to my boy Tom. He'll put an edge on it.'

He thinks of picking up the axe and felling the headsman, but this is what life does for you in the end; it arranges a fight you can't win. In his time he has encouraged many who lack practice and capacity. In other circumstances he would take the axe from the man's fumbling grip: say patiently, 'This is how.'

The man holds out his palm. He drops his fee into it. 'Do not be afraid to strike. You will not help me, or yourself, by hesitating.'

The man kneels. He has remembered what he ought to say. 'Forgive me what I must do. It is my office and my duty. I have this cloth here, sir. Will I cover your face?'

'For what possible purpose?' Only to spare you.

'My lord, you must kneel. When you are ready, repose your head upon this block.'

After Anne's swift end he had spoken with the headsman; he read the words engraved on the blade. *Speculum justitiae, ora pro nobis.* They don't write words on the head of the axe.

He kneels. He makes his prayer. Drumbeats. *La zombero boro borombeta* ... Blink of red. He thinks, this is all I have to do: follow my master, this and no more. Reach out your hand to find the train of his robe. Look for the spill of scarlet, follow.

He eases himself down to die. He thinks, others can do it and so can I. He inhales something: sweet raw smell of sawdust; from somewhere, the scent of the Frescobaldi kitchen, wild garlic and cloves. He sees the movement from the corner of his eye as the spectators kneel and avert their faces. His mouth is dry, but he thinks, while I breathe I pray. '*All my confidence hope and trust, is in thy most merci-ful goodness ...*' In the sky he senses movement. A shadow falls across his view. His father Walter is here, voice in the air. 'So now get up.' He lies broken on the cobbles of the yard of the house where he was born. His whole body is shuddering. 'So now get up. So now get up.'

The pain is acute, a raw stinging, a ripping, a throb. He can taste his death: slow, metallic, not come yet. In his terror he tries to obey his father, but his hands cannot get a purchase, nor can he crawl. He is an eel, he is a worm on a hook, his strength has ebbed and leaked away beneath him and it seems a long time ago now since he gave his permission to be dead; no one has told his heart, and he feels it writhe in his chest, trying to beat. His cheek rests on nothing, it rests on red. He thinks, *follow*. Walter says, 'That's right, boy, spew everywhere, spew everywhere on my good cobbles. Come on, boy, get up. By the blood of creeping Christ, stand on your feet.'

He is very cold. People imagine the cold comes after but it is now. He thinks, winter is here. I am at Launde. I have stumbled deep into the crisp white snow. I flail my arms in angel shape, but now I am crystal, I am ice and sinking deep: now I am water. Beneath him the ground upheaves. The river tugs him; he looks for the quick-moving pattern, for the flitting, liquid scarlet. Between a pulse-beat and the next he shifts, going out on crimson with the tide of his inner sea. He is far from England now, far from these islands, from the waters salt and fresh. He has vanished; he is the slippery stones underfoot, he is the last faint ripple in the wake of himself. He feels for an opening, blinded, looking for a door: tracking the light along the wall.

For you perhaps, if as I hope and wish you will live long after me, there will follow a better age. When the darkness is dispelled, our descendants will be able to walk back, into the pure radiance of the past.

PETRARCH: AFRICA IX

AUTHOR'S NOTE

Eighteen months after Henry married Katherine Howard, she was accused of adultery with the courtier Thomas Culpeper. It was claimed that she had already taken lovers before her marriage to the king. She was beheaded, along with Jane Rochford, who had facilitated her affair.

Henry had no more children. His sixth and final wife was Katherine Parr, formerly Lady Latimer. The astute and scholarly Katherine, who survived him, then married Thomas Seymour – her fourth husband – and died after giving birth to Seymour's daughter.

After his divorce from Anne of Cleves, his fourth wife, Henry enjoyed a warm relationship with her. Enriched by estates that included confiscations from Thomas Cromwell, she lived in style, showed no desire to return to her native country, and survived Henry by ten years.

Henry lived for seven years after Cromwell; he was ill, disabled and dangerous. He went to war with France and devalued the currency. His son Edward was nine when he came to the throne, with Edward Seymour as Lord Protector. During Edward's reign, England became a firmly Protestant country. But Edward died at fifteen, probably of tuberculosis. When his sister Mary came to the throne she attempted to re-establish the Roman Catholic church. She appointed Stephen Gardiner her Lord Chancellor, and Reginald Pole, back from his long exile, became her Archbishop of Canterbury.

Thomas Cranmer, Hugh Latimer and many others were burned as heretics.

Reginald's Pole's mother, Margaret Countess of Salisbury, remained in the Tower after Cromwell's death and was executed in 1541. Geoffrey Pole was pardoned and released, but fled to Rome, only returning to England when Mary came to the throne. He died in 1558, leaving eleven children.

Once Henry had had time to regret Cromwell's death, he re-granted Gregory a baron's title. Gregory sometimes appeared at court, but lived quietly at Launde Abbey. He died young, and his wife Elizabeth put up a fine monument which can still be seen in the chapel. Richard Cromwell also survived his uncle's disgrace. He was appointed to the king's privy chamber, and served in the French war. He died in 1545, a wealthy man. His great-grandson, Oliver Cromwell, was Lord Protector of the first English republic.

Anselma and Jenneke are fictional. It is thought that Thomas Cromwell had an illegitimate daughter called Jane, who was probably born not long after after his wife's death. But we do not know who her mother was and can make no useful guesses.

After surviving harsh times in the years after Cromwell's death, Rafe Sadler stayed in royal service almost to his death, at which point he was around eighty years of age. When he died in 1587, he was said to be the richest commoner in England. His house in Hackney, Bricke Place, is now known as Sutton House, and is in the care of the National Trust. The adjacent King's Place, once Harry Percy's house, no longer stands.

Like Sadler, Thomas Wyatt suffered imprisonment in 1541. He was released back into the king's service, but forced to return to the wife from whom he had separated many years before, and leave Bess Darrell, with whom he had at least one son. In the autumn of 1543 he was sent to Cornwall to welcome an envoy from the Emperor who had arrived unexpectedly in Falmouth. He developed a fever, broke his journey at Sherbourne, and died there.

William Fitzwilliam succeeded Cromwell as Lord Privy Seal. In 1542 he led a fighting force to Scotland, but took ill and died before reaching the border; he left no heirs. Both Thomas Wriothesley and Richard Riche became Lord Chancellor. Wriothesley had a rocky career during what remained of Henry's reign. Under Edward he became Earl of Southampton and one of the Council of Regency, but lost out in ferocious faction fighting and died in 1550. Richard Riche, who succeeded him in office, founded a dynasty and a school, Felsted School; he left fifteen children and a fortune.

Arthur Lord Lisle remained in the Tower after Cromwell's execution. Eighteen months later the king issued his pardon, but next day, before he could be released, he died of 'rejoicing'. Honor Lisle returned to England, and lived till 1566. Her daughter Anne Bassett married Walter Hungerford, son of the man who was executed with Thomas Cromwell. John Husee remained a faithful member of the Calais garrison and worked to supply Henry's French campaign. He died two years later, but the letters he exchanged with his employers, together with letters written by Lord and Lady Lisle and their family, form a unique chronicle of the era. Like George Cavendish, Wolsey's gentleman servant, John Husee is one of history's great witnesses.

Charles Brandon, Duke of Suffolk, died in 1545, lamented by his friend the king. His granddaughter was Lady Jane Grey, who laid claim to the throne after the death of Edward, and reigned as 'the nine days queen' before being displaced by Mary, and subsequently executed.

Henry Howard, Earl of Surrey, was beheaded for treason on 19 January 1547. His father Norfolk was due to follow him on 28 January, but was reprieved by the death of the king himself some hours before. So Norfolk died in his bed, at the age of eighty.

Eustache Chapuys remained strenuously employed in Imperial service till 1545, and after his retirement the Emperor turned to him as a source of advice on English affairs. He lived in Leuven, where he founded a college for students from his native Savoy. He had an illegitimate son, who predeceased him, and having no heir he devoted some of his accrued wealth to setting up scholarships for students from England.

Marie de Guise, Madame de Longueville, who married the King of Scots despite being coveted by Henry, had only one surviving child, a daughter usually known as Mary, Queen of Scots. Mary's second husband, Lord Darnley, was the son of Lady Margaret Douglas and the Earl of Lennox.

Christina of Denmark, Duchess of Milan, was one of the most fascinating people of her era. Her long career included a happy marriage. In 1555, during the reign of Mary, she paid her first visit to England, making an excursion to the Tower of London; no doubt she was aware that if she had married Henry, she could have visited it earlier.

Mary Tudor did eventually marry – her husband was Philip of Spain, the Emperor's son. Philip spent as little time as possible in England, and Mary died, unhappy, childless and largely unlamented, in 1558. She was succeeded by Elizabeth, the daughter of Anne Boleyn. The dynasty which began its rule on the battlefield at Bosworth in 1485 ended in 1603; Elizabeth was the last of the Tudor line.

ACKNOWLEDGEMENTS

When I sat down to express my gratitude to the historians, curators, actors and academics who have given me time, encouragement and inspiration in the course of ten years, I found that the list was so long and included such distinguished names that it sounded like a vulgar exercise in name-dropping. So I would like to say simply that I am grateful to them all and forget none. I am also grateful to my publishers worldwide, and to the unseen army who dust the artefacts and guard the treasures, and ensure, as Tyndale puts it, that neither moths nor rust corrupt, and the passage of time does not destroy, what is left of the world of Thomas Cromwell.